TOTAL IMMERSION

THE COMPREHENSIVE UNAUTHORIZED RED DWARF ENCYCLOPEDIA

VOLUME 1
(A-K)

By Paul C. Giachetti

Edited by Rich Handley

Foreword by Jonathan Capps

Illustrations by Pat Carbajal

HASSLEIN • BOOKS

Total Immersion: The Comprehensive Unauthorized Red Dwarf Encyclopedia—Volume 1

Writer and designer: Paul C. Giachetti
Editor: Rich Handley
Proofreader: Joseph Brandt Dilworth
Foreword: Jonathan Capps
Illustrations: Pat Carbajal

ISBN-13: 978-0-578-15057-4
Library of Congress Cataloging-in-Publication Data
First Edition: November 2014
10 9 8 7 6 5 4 3 2 1

CONTENTS

"When it comes to weirdy, paradoxy space stuff, I've bought the t-shirt."

—Lister, "Cassandra"

Acknowledgments v

Foreword by Jonathan Capps vii

Introduction by Paul C. Giachetti ix

Abbreviation Key: A Guide to the Guide xiv

The Encyclopedia

0-9 2
A 22
B 52
C 91
D 132
E 162
F 180
G 199
H 223
I 257
J 267
K 282
L to Z . . . . . See Volume 2

"That's why I had my appendix out... twice."

—Rimmer, "Thanks for the Memory"

Appendix I: The *Red Dwarf* Episode Guide 301

Appendix II: The Universes of *Red Dwarf* 321

Appendix III: Other *Red Dwarf*-related Books 325

Appendix IV: Categorical Index . . . . . See Volume 2

About the Author 327

ACKNOWLEDGMENTS

"I have come to regard you ... as people ... I met."

—Arnold Rimmer, "Holoship"

In March 2011, I decided to try my hand at writing a reference book for Hasslein Books, the independent publishing company that I and my long-time friend **Rich Handley** started back in 2008. At that point, we had already put out two books—a *Planet of the Apes* timeline and a companion lexicon—that Rich wrote and I designed, and were in the process of putting together two more books, this time focused on the *Back to the Future* franchise. Having witnessed Rich go through this process several times, I asked myself two questions:

1) Why would anyone voluntarily put himself through that kind of laborious task, seeking out and hunting down every last morsel of material and devoting years of his life to the documentation of a single franchise?

2) Which universe, if any, would I ever be able (and willing) to dedicate that much effort and energy to without completely burning myself out?

The answer to number two was obvious: There was simply no other series of movies or television shows that I repeatedly watched on a regular basis as much as *Red Dwarf*. The first question's answer, however, I would learn over the course of the next few years, after deciding to pen a *Red Dwarf* encyclopedia.

I won't lie... it was incredibly difficult for me. Rich had made it look so easy, but I struggled with some of the elements necessary to produce a book of this nature. I sent dozens upon dozens of e-mails Rich's way, asking advice on everything from mundane grammar questions to which appendices he thought I should include. Every get-together turned into a veritable bitch-session, as I talked the poor man's ear off discussing the validity of the *Smegazines*, or dreading the amount of material in *Red Dwarf—The Roleplaying Game*, or complaining about the inconsistencies between the show and the novels (why the HELL did they change the captain from a man named Hollister to a woman named Kirk??).

To Rich's credit, not only did he answer all my questions and suffer through all my complaints, but every conversation ended with his assurance that I was the right man for the job. It didn't hurt that he is as big a fan as I, and enjoyed hearing about some of the more ridiculous entries I had to write just as much as I enjoyed talking about them. He even went so far as to rewatch the entire series, compiling lists of everything he thought should be included. On top of that, Rich graciously agreed to help write the episode synopses and categorical indexes, drastically reducing my workload so that I could focus on everything else. Add to that his role as the publication's editor (no small task, I can assure you) and I think it goes without saying that without Rich's input, both in the creation of Hasslein Books and throughout the production of *Total Immersion*, this book would simply not exist. So thank you, Rich—I simply could not have done it without you.

Several other people deserve thanks as well, and I sincerely hope I don't overlook anyone who has helped out over the past few years. My humblest apologies if I have inadvertently left anyone off this list; if I have, I'm a total smeeeeee heeeeeeee.

• **Jonathan Capps** (ganymede.tv), a founding member of the premier *Red Dwarf* fan site *Ganymede & Titan* and the website coordinator of the Official *Red Dwarf* Fan Club. Jonathan (or Cappsy, as he's affectionately known on the forums) generously donated his time and agreed to write this book's foreword, despite knowing of me only through my occasional *G&T* posts.

• **Joseph Brandt Dilworth** (popculturezoo.com), our resident proofreader and fact-checker, for not only making sure my commas and periods were well in order, but for ensuring I didn't mistakenly claim Lister had three appendixes (because *that* would just be silly).

• **Pat Carbajal** (patart-pat.blogspot.com), who created the amazing interior illustrations in this book. We first discovered Pat's work through *Timeline of the Planet of the Apes* and promptly explored his blog, constantly stunned by his sketches. Unlike on the *Apes* and *Back to the Future* books, for which he relied on his knowledge and media collection, Pat had no frame of reference for *Total Immersion*, having never seen an episode of *Red Dwarf*. This was remedied after a quick visit to eBay, and a few weeks later, any trepidation I might have had regarding his delving into unknown territory quickly melted away as the first of the sketches started coming in. In addition, Pat deserves extra thanks for "Carbajalizing" the headshots of the entire Hasslein team, which can be viewed at hassleinbooks.com's About page.

• **Sean Kennedy** (seansgallery.com), for his beautiful hull texture that was used in the design of this book's cover.

• **Steve Cafarelli** (monkeygripmusic.com), a long-time friend who offered his services as Web designer for Hasslein Books during our growing period—an offer he has likely since regretted, given our frequent requests for tweaks and changes as each book is published. Steve has taken an amateurish site designed for a single *Planet of the Apes* book and turned it into an expertly designed portal to promote all of Hasslein's current and future publications.

Other individuals who deserve my sincere appreciation for their contribution and/or assistance include (in alphabetical order): **Chris Ballard, Patty Beauregard** (ladyofthecake.com), **Leska Beikircher** (subreatropolis.com), **Simon Bromley** (bromley001.wordpress.com), **Shaun Deeley, Todd Downing** (deep7.com), **Mike Durham, David Flett** (twitter.com/David_Flett), **Sabrina Fried, Darren Gill, Antony James** (reddwarfforum.com), **Kevin Karstens** (karcreat.com), **Andrew Kenrick, Jane Killick** (janekillick.com), **Alex Newsome** (gazpacho-soup.com), **Jerry Parsons, Joanna Sharples** (reddwarffanclub.com, dimensionjump.info), **Stephen Simpson** (facebook.com/stretfordendling), **Eddy Webb** (eddyfate.com) and **Cole Maria Welch.**

In addition, I'd also like to send out a general thanks to my friends and family for putting up with me as I spent months upon months sequestered in my apartment trying to get this book out within this decade, as well as lending an ear as I vented throughout the entire process. The support you've all shown me has given me the strength to see this project out to the end.

Finally, *Red Dwarf* would obviously not exist without the brilliance of **Rob Grant** and **Doug Naylor**, as well as the many talented people both in front of and behind the camera. A special heartfelt thanks goes out to them and to the **GNP** staff for keeping the franchise going, through new shows and the **official *Red Dwarf* website** (reddwarf.co.uk), as well as to the fans who keep the universe alive with publications and websites, not the least of which are the **Official *Red Dwarf* Fan Club** (reddwarffanclub.com); **Ganymede and Titan** (ganymede.tv); the ***Red Dwarf* Forum—Home of the ScutterCast** (reddwarfforum.com); **Gazpacho Soup** (gazpacho-soup.com), which supplied material regarding Bill Pearson's Christmas script; and **Tongue Tied—The *Red Dwarf* Wikia** (reddwarf.wikia.com). Members of the various fan forums are also graciously thanked for answering any spontaneous questions I may have posted in the past.

As far as I'm concerned, you are all Aces in my book.

FOREWORD

by Jonathan Capps

"To Ganymede and Titan, yes sir, I've been around..."

–Lister, "The End"

I know it's bad form to start a foreword by talking about the act of writing a foreword, but I'm afraid I'm going to do it anyway. I was honoured to be asked to contribute to the encyclopedia, and apparently I wasn't even too far down the wish list—somewhere in-between Ainsley Harriot and the cat who played Frankenstein (deceased)—so I felt a certain amount of pressure to do justice to such an enormous and detailed book. What do you write about a *Red Dwarf* book that's already about everything? I decided to speak to what I know: fandom. *Red Dwarf* is blessed with a hugely dedicated base of fans across the world, and this book is a direct product of that.

The greatest gift that can be given to any TV show is a passionate and talented fan base. In the early days of making *Red Dwarf*, creators and writers Rob Grant and Doug Naylor were battling tooth and nail to get their show made. Even their producer, Paul Jackson, was initially skeptical that the concept of a sci-fi comedy could gain any popularity, and even though they'd snuck past BBC London's apathy by taking Jackson's spare production block in Manchester, an electricians strike threatened to further scupper the show. But it happened. It was a weird, low-budget sci-fi sitcom, shot in studios unsuitable for its scope, but people watched it. By some miracle a second series was commissioned, and from that point on the momentum was there, because the fan base was building, watching the show, demanding more and making themselves known.

In Britain especially, there's a history of comedy shows that attract dedicated fan bases, especially breakout alternative sitcoms such as *The Young Ones* and *Blackadder*, but with *Red Dwarf*'s distinctive sci-fi flavour, it also appealed to people on another level. The first two series of *Red Dwarf* were steeped in character comedy, exploring loneliness and the oft-mentioned *Odd Couple* themes defining Lister's relationship with Rimmer—but even then, the sci-fi lore was building: the Jupiter Mining Corporation, suggesting a world filled with private companies exploring and exploiting the resources of space, and later an entire history of Cat People evolving in the cargo hold of the stricken mining ship. Not only was the show making people laugh, but it was appealing to that part of any geek's brain that wants to explore, understand and take part in an interesting and new universe.

In 1989, *Red Dwarf*'s third series aired, with its new *Alien*-inspired look and feel, a new robotic main character and a more sharply focused sci-fi feeling (all while keeping a firm grasp on what makes the show funny). A year later, in 1990, a group of fans already steeped in sci-fi fandom circles at a pub in London decided to set up a club. The Official *Red Dwarf* Fan Club (TORDFC for short), of which I've been a proud team member since 2008, is still going strong, and it represents the sort of person a truly special show attracts: people who not only are willing to dedicate their time to sit down in front of the TV and enjoy the latest episode, but are willing and driven to use their talents and time to dedicate themselves to the show every day of their lives. The original Fan Club team, and those that followed them, produced a quarterly magazine and organised the convention Dimension Jump to gather like-minded fans and the show's own cast and crew together to talk endlessly about the show and, er, quite possibly drink a little bit of alcohol.

Eventually, with the increasing ubiquitousness of the Internet communities (not to mention the year-on-year increasing popularity of *Red Dwarf* worldwide), fan sites were cropping up all over the place. I started my own with a view to writing about and analysing the show I'd loved since I was a kid, all the while mixing with the official communities that had sprung up around the Fan Club and Grant Naylor Productions' own website, as well as eventually meeting lifelong friends and joining them in the joint endeavour that prominent fansite Ganymede & Titan had become. Your esteemed author of this very lexicon has been part of G&T's lively community for a good while, and it's the reason he knows me well enough to allow me to spout nonsense at the beginning of his book.

If *Red Dwarf* has a dedicated and unique fanbase to thank for its success and recent triumphant return, then I think it would be also fair to mention that I owe a huge chunk of my current life to the existence of this show. I've met a great deal of my closest friends through the communities that an obsession for this show had borne, some of whom are married and have kids through people they've met in the same communities. And maybe the point is this: When a show gives so much enjoyment and produces a world that gives people comfort growing up, inspires their imaginations and gives them the opportunity to meet people who will define their adult lives, then it's not surprising when those same people take so much enjoyment in contributing to the community the show has created, producing analysis, artwork, their own fiction and books.

Which brings us to the tome you are holding in your hands right now. The level of time, effort and skill spent detailing every aspect of the show and the universe in this encyclopedia is more than appropriate to the same qualities on display in the making of the show itself. It's honestly a remarkable achievement, and I hope you enjoy immersing yourself in every last detail of this world that Paul has so lovingly laid down for you here.

Jonathan Capps has been an active part of the Red Dwarf *online community since 2001, resulting from the creation of his own fansite, The White Hole, which mainly made its name by providing illicit downloads of obscure '80s Grant Naylor radio sitcoms. He later joined a group of insanely talented and opinionated individuals creating news pieces, analysis and podcasts as part of the fansite Ganymede & Titan, where he remains to this day. In a more official capacity, Jonathan has been a proud team member of The Official* Red Dwarf *Fan Club, acting as website designer and developer while also creating articles for the quarterly magazine and helping to organise the almost annual convention, Dimension Jump. Basically, he loves* Red Dwarf.

INTRODUCTION

by Paul C. Giachetti

"Oh smeg! What the smeggin' smeg's he smeggin' done?"

—Dave Lister, "Bodyswap"

It's a funny thing, fate. That combination of decisions, occurrences and circumstances that leads a person down one path and away from another—which, at any given moment, can put one in the right (or wrong) place at the right (or wrong) time. Science fiction is rife with stories set in alternate timelines and infinite dimensions created by fate; *Red Dwarf*'s Ace Rimmer shows us that a single decision has the power to drastically alter a person's life forever.

Well, that's all well and good for the bigger decisions, but what about the minor ones? The small, seemingly insignificant choices or events that shape everyday living? The ones that form the so-called "butterfly effect?" And why am I even bringing this up?

Because you, dear reader, are fortunate enough to exist in THIS particular dimension... one in which fate allowed the book you now hold to have been created; one in which decisions, occurrences and circumstances lined up just right from the beginning of time, to culminate in this encyclopedia of everything *Red Dwarf*. An infinite number of alternate realities spawned throughout *Total Immersion*'s gestation, timelines in which the project was erased from history, either by choices made or by the ripples of past events. Universes sprang into existence thanks to a single decision to flip a TV channel or take a bathroom break, resulting in countless dimensions sadly devoid of this publication.

To be frank, it's a smeggin' miracle this book exists at all.

I'll forgo theatrics about the creation of the universe, the solar system's formation, the miracle of life on Earth, and all the chance events leading up to my parents' meeting and eventually creating me, and instead jump straight to my early twenties, when I often watched television in the living room of my childhood residence on Long Island, New York.

At the time, *Red Dwarf* was being broadcast in the United States on Public Broadcasting Service (PBS) Channel 21. Now, it's important to note that at this point in television's history, between the dark ages during which you physically needed to get up to change the channel, and the modern age of wireless remotes allowing one to scroll through hundreds of channels a minute, we had wired, pushbutton cable boxes—big, bulky controllers lined with a dozen buttons and side switches, and covered in an ugly faux-wood casing. This monstrosity, it turned out, would be the "Goldilocks Zone" of channel-flipping technology, as far as my discovery of *Red Dwarf* was concerned. Five years earlier, and I probably would never have made it to Channel 21 while channel-surfing on that fateful day; five years later, meanwhile, and I might have seen the English fellow with the "H" stuck to his forehead and associated it with *The Young Ones* (a show that, despite several attempts, I could never really get into), and quickly flicked the channel forward.

But it was that brief pause—standard fare when using such a cumbersome controller—that allowed me to realize what I had just stumbled upon: a British sci-fi comedy, the perfect trifecta of entertainment. Dubious that I had, in fact, just discovered the Holy Grail of television programming, I watched a few minutes to get my bearings, quickly growing disappointed as the dialog steered more and more toward a ripoff of *Star Trek*. Then, as I reached for the bulky pushbutton controller to continue on to Channel 22, a line of dialog diverted the timeline and created the universe in which you now exist.

The line in question? *"Don't give me the* Star Trek *crap. It's too early in the morning..."*

...which is exactly what I was thinking at that very moment. I was hooked—smart, witty, self-effacing... this was my kind of show. I continued watching and never looked back. Years later, I would learn that Sir Patrick Stewart, Captain Picard himself, reportedly had a similar reaction to the show, nearly calling his lawyer before becoming entranced by its sheer genius. To this day, my favorite episodes stem from my earliest memories of the show: Kryten frantically attempting to remove Lister's underpants in "Polymorph," the discovery of a missing page of The Bible in "Better Than Life" (which, incidentally, mirrored my own humorous take on organized religion), and even Lister's reaction to witnessing the execution of Winnie-the-Pooh in "Meltdown."[1] Like a dog at the dinner bell, I came back to groovy, funky Channel 21 time and again, until the series' final episode aired.[2] By that point, the show's hold on me had become permanent.

[1] *Yes, I did, in fact, just admit that "Meltdown" is one of my favorite episodes; I'd like to take this moment to point out that refunds on this book are not available.*
[2] *Or, at least the final episode up to that point.*

Had this not all happened, it's certainly possible that someone, somewhere might have eventually mentioned *Red Dwarf* to me, or that the show might have otherwise grabbed my attention down the line. If so, I'd probably have bought the DVDs, watched them once or twice and put them on my shelf along with the other shows I've added to my collection. But I wouldn't have had that nostalgic feeling for the show—and I wouldn't have had the experience of buying the entire series on VHS, only to have Region 2 DVDs come out months later… then buying half the series on Region 2 DVDs and hacking my player to be able to watch them, only to THEN find out that Region 1 DVDs were being released soon thereafter.

Sure, one might say I would have saved a lot of hassle (and money) that way, but to me, the years spent searching for increasingly superior ways to enjoy my one not-so-guilty pleasure just affirmed my love for the show. Of all the franchises to which I profess fandom, none other—past, present or probable future—have earned that level of blind dedication from me.

So when I decided to try my hand at writing a lexicon of my own, choosing a universe to tackle required no thought whatsoever. There was only one choice: *Red Dwarf*. It seemed a relatively small enough franchise. Aside from nine (at the time) seasons of television episodes, at only six to eight episodes apiece (or three, in the case of *Back to Earth*), plus a handful of novels and a few other books, I wasn't aware of much else that would need to be covered. Clearly, I hadn't thought it through, as a few Google searches later left me curled up in the fetal position and whimpering silently, once I learned about *Red Dwarf—The Roleplaying Game*, the *Smegazines*, the remastered episodes, the *Geek Chase* alternate reality game (ARG) and dozens of other potential sources.

And unlike Kryten, I had absolutely NO problem mastering the emotion of ambivalence when Series X was announced a mere *two weeks* after I dedicated myself to writing the encyclopedia. More *Red Dwarf* is, of course, always a good thing—but now there was even *more* to work into the book! Still, perseverance endured and, three years later, through chance and happenstance, I finally completed my first draft. Sometime later, an unconnected series of events and decisions guided this book into your hands, completing the process. And for your contribution to the creation of this unique, one-of-a-kind universe, I wholeheartedly thank you.

A Note Regarding Style

Since *Red Dwarf* is a British comedy, many of the official and third-party books, websites, etc., that have explored the show have attempted to mirror the style of humor often associated with that genre—and with *Red Dwarf*, in particular—to varying degrees of success. I specifically chose not to do the same, however, for several reasons. First and foremost, *Total Immersion* is meant to be a scholarly reference guide to the universe; it's not necessarily meant to be IN-universe. I also felt the material, presented even in its most basic form, is humorous enough without my meddling; in my opinion, any attempt to infuse my own *Red Dwarf*-style jokes would only serve to detract from the material, and would certainly not ring true authentically. My goal is not to write comedy—it's to write *about* comedy.

Non-essential Electrics All Down, Including Spell-checker

In general, I have adhered to the spellings supplied onscreen or in print. This may cause confusion with entries pertaining to, say, hologram technology, since the terms "hologram," "hologramic," "hologrammic," "hologramatic" and "hologrammatic" have all been used interchangeably throughout the mythos. What's more, the DVD captions proved to be notoriously bad at spellings; in the event that a particular person, place or thing had several different spellings within different mediums, I went with the more official or commonly used spelling, usually deferring to the official website.

In addition, many terms had alternate punctuation, hyphenation and capitalization; the word "GELF," for example, is just as often spelled with all capitals as it is without ("Gelf")—and occasionally even with periods ("G.E.L.F."), though usually not. To simplify matters, I adhered to proper grammar, punctuation and capitalization. In the case of genetically engineered life forms, I settled on the capitalized "GELF" in this lexicon, which the official website uses throughout.

It's a (Wo)man, Baby!

Entries pertaining to *Red Dwarf*'s resident artificial intelligence, Holly, proved somewhat challenging to write, thanks to the computer's multiple iterations, with gender-specific pronouns bouncing back and forth between "he/him" and "she/her" throughout the book. Rather than settling on an impersonal gender-neutral "it," I left the pronouns relative to the computer's sex at the time of the event being documented. Anyone reading this book, I reasoned, would undoubtedly have at least a rudimentary knowledge of the show, including Holly's head sex-change, and gender-specific labeling would help readers visualize which version was being discussed at any particular moment.

> **The Crew of the Jupiter Mining Vessel *Red Dwarf*...**
>
> At various times during the television series, different characters comprised the surviving *Red Dwarf* crew—with Kryten permanently joining the lineup in Series III, Kochanski temporarily added in Series VII and VIII, and Rimmer leaving and coming back in Series VII and VIII, respectively. Because it would become ridiculously redundant to repeatedly list the specific crewmembers, one entry after another, I chose instead to use the generic term "the crew" to describe whoever was in a given scene being discussed. I surmised that anyone reading a book of this nature would have a fairly solid knowledge of the show, and would thus be able to deduce who was involved without my having to spell it out every time. This pertains to entries set on other ships as well, including the *Starbug* and *Blue Midget* shuttlecraft.

As may be quite apparent by now, I am, in fact, American.[3] This book was written and edited in the United States, and follows American grammatical and spelling conventions, with the exception of proper nouns or terms spelled out onscreen. However, because *Red Dwarf* has a legion of fans around the globe, I decided to include many regional, historical and cultural real-world references from all parts of the world, to ensure that readers would all be on the same page, so to speak. What may be well-known trivia to one fan may be the key to understanding a particular joke for another.

What Is Included

Total Immersion provides an encyclopedic reference guide to every who, what and where throughout all officially sanctioned *Red Dwarf* stories. In addition, any official source in which characters or concepts appear "in-universe" has also been mined. Because of the wide spectrum of material falling into this category, it was only natural that conflicts and inconsistencies would arise between the various media. I dealt with these on a case-by-case basis, as discussed below.

***Television Episodes*:** The be-all and end-all of *Red Dwarf*. This book covers Series I to X, as well as the remastered episodes available in *The Bodysnatcher Collection*. The majority of adventures depicted in the television series are considered to have occurred in what I call the "prime" universe, unless specifically stated otherwise in a particular episode. For the purposes of *Total Immersion*, the prime universe is labeled as such for clarity when other realities are discussed within an entry. The television series itself takes precedence over any other form (novels, comics and so forth), so in the event of a conflict or inconsistency, a note explains the contention. Also included is in-universe lore gleaned from bonus materials, such as deleted scenes, outtakes, interviews, unaired scripts and so forth. These entries are marked accordingly with a lower-case letter in parentheses (*see the Abbreviation Key on page XIV*), and can be accepted or disregarded at the reader's discretion.

***Novels*:** Here's where the fun begins. Four novels were written for the *Red Dwarf* universe. The first two—*Infinity Welcomes Careful Drivers* and *Better Than Life*—were cooperatively written by Rob Grant and Doug Naylor, who combined elements from several episodes into a running narrative. In doing so, the authors switched around events, expanded upon ideas and outright changed aspects of the TV series. Books three and four—*Backwards* and *Last Human*—were solo projects by Grant and Naylor, respectively, each providing a direct sequel to *Better Than Life,* and completely incongruous with each other. Entries pertaining to these books are not always explicitly stated as happening in alternate realities, though it would clearly be impossible for both novels' events to have taken place in the prime universe, or in the same reality as each other. Appendix II does, however, specify the novels as occurring in separate universes, for the sake of clarity. Notations are made in the event of any conflicts between novels, or with the episodes.

***The Official Website (reddwarf.co.uk)*:** Much of *Red Dwarf*'s official website consists of news articles, interviews and in-depth analyses of the program, little of which adds any new in-universe material, with two exceptions: the Space Corps Database and fictional interviews sections. Expanding on various elements of the series, the official site offers a plethora of new in-universe material that easily fits into the prime universe. I also incorporated *Prelude to Nanarchy*, a Web comic released exclusively on the official site in 2005 that bridged Series V and VI.

***Geek Chase*:** This online treasure hunt was originally created in 2006 by writer and script editor Andrew Ellard as a contest offered to those who purchased the *Beat the Geek* DVD quiz game, but has been kept alive by the good folks at reddwarf.co.uk. The game takes players on a journey through nine in-universe websites chock full of new and expanded material, all of which, for the purposes of this book, is set in the prime universe. This includes a site supposedly created by Duane Dibbley that, for the sake of simplicity, is considered in-universe despite the character being Cat's alter ego.

SPOILER WARNING!!! This book reveals any and all passwords and links required to complete the *Geek Chase* online game.

[3] *This may account for footnote 1.*

If you intend to take part in the hunt, I strongly recommended that you do so before reading the main lexicon. If, however, you would just like to peruse the game's features, a list of participating websites appears in the Abbreviation Key on page XIV.

***Smegazines*:** Published by Fleetway Editions Ltd. and edited by Mike Butcher, the *Red Dwarf Magazine*—later changed to the *Red Dwarf Smegazine*—ran for a total of twenty-three issues between 1992 and 1994, featuring news, reviews, interviews and fictional in-universe articles, as well as a variety of comic strips. These comics comprised a mix of episode adaptations and original stories, some involving concepts, characters and locations mentioned in the novels. In most cases, I accepted the comics and fiction articles as occurring in the prime universe (unless specifically indicated otherwise), since very few conflicts arose. Some material, however—such as anything revolving around "fictional" characters—I dealt with on a case-by-case basis.

Stories or articles involving Mr. Flibble, for example, are not specifically noted as taking place in an alternate reality, since in a mythos inhabited by mechanoids, shapeshifting blobs and eight-foot-tall cockroaches, there is little point in arguing about the existence of an anthropomorphic, potty-mouthed penguin. Conversely, comics featuring characters' alter egos, such as Duane Dibbley and Jake Bullet, are treated as separate universes in which those fictional characters actually existed, given a throwaway line at the end of *Back to Earth* stating that, through quantum mechanics, every dream and hallucination spawns a new universe.

***Red Dwarf—The Roleplaying Game*:** At the turn of the millennium, Deep7 Press obtained the license to create an RPG based on the *Red Dwarf* universe, and the firm published a trio of books between 2003 and 2004. These included the *Core Rulebook*, which outlined the rules and basic knowledge needed to roleplay in the *Red Dwarf* universe; the *A.I. Screen* with accompanying *Extra Bits* booklet, which expanded on the first volume's information; and the *Series Sourcebook*, a play-by-play guide to every episode up to Series VIII, explaining how to incorporate elements of those stories into a roleplaying experience. Also included are a handful of supplemental online files for use with the game.

The majority of the material from the roleplaying game can fit seamlessly into the prime universe with very little effort; any conflicts or inconsistencies with other established works are notated accordingly. Some entries, however, were more difficult to classify. Examples featuring characters or items created for the sole purpose of explaining a particular rule or concept could often go either way. After careful consideration, I decided that unless it directly contradicted what was known, I would assume the entry to be set in the prime universe.

***Additional Publications*:** In addition to the novels and roleplaying game, several other books have been written on the subject of *Red Dwarf*. For the purposes of *Total Immersion*, I chose to mine only publications containing new in-universe material. These ranged from books written entirely "in character" and purporting to be from the universe itself, to those discussing the show's production that revealed previously unknown material, as well as everything in between. Most of these gelled with (or, at least, did not outright contradict) the prime universe's events, with any conflicts being notated accordingly.

***Red Dwarf USA*:** On behalf of the United States, I simply cannot apologize enough for this. In 1992, Hollywood attempted to make an American version of *Red Dwarf*. This attempt, I think it's safe to say, is near-universally considered an abysmal failure; however, it did produce two features that I would be remiss to leave out, if only for the sake of completeness.

The first, a broad rehash of the British pilot, was a full-length episode starring Craig Bierko as Lister, Chris Eigeman as Rimmer, Robert Llewellyn reprising the role of Kryten, Jane Leeves (later of *Frasier* fame) as Holly and Hinton Battle as Cat. The second was a clip-style promotional reel created as an attempt by Grant Naylor to save the project after the first pilot (understandably) failed to sell. It featured a different actor as Rimmer (Anthony Fuscle) and a female Cat (*Star Trek*'s Terry Farrell), and integrated clips from both the U.K. series and the first American pilot. For obvious reasons, I've placed each of these episodes in its own separate alternate dimension in which *Red Dwarf* and its crew are American.

***Miscellaneous Material*:** Also incorporated into this book are any peripheral sources that some might deem "in-universe." For instance:

- **Comic Relief *Red Nose Day* Sketch:** The 1993 *Red Nose Day* special featured a musical montage of several BBC personalities and characters, including the *Red Dwarf* cast, singing along to Queen's "Bohemian Rhapsody." I've included it in this book because… hey, why not?

- **"Tongue-Tied" Music Video:** The 1988 Series II episode "Parallel Universe" opened with "Tongue-Tied," a song-and-dance routine by Danny John-Jules (Cat) and the rest of the *Red Dwarf* gang, which was later revealed to be a dream sequence. The song was so well received that it was released five years later as a single, and was eventually remixed and incorporated into a short video written and produced by John-Jules. Because the video's protagonist mentions the TV show *Red Dwarf*, I've set it in an alternate universe—possibly the same one spawned by *Back to Earth*, in which *Red Dwarf* is merely a British television series.

- ***Children in Need Red Dwarf* Sketch:** In 1997, the Dwarfers assembled once again for a skit that aired between Series VII and VIII, during BBC's *Children in Need* telethon, in which the characters asked viewers to pledge money to the charity. To avoid revealing any plot points regarding Chris Barrie's return to the show in human form, Rimmer was portrayed as a hologram. Despite hologrammatic Rimmer and Chloë Annett's Kochanski never having shared the screen before (or after) this sketch, I've worked it in for posterity's sake.

- **The "Red Christmas" Mobisode:** In 2007, Pitch Entertainment created several *Red Dwarf* "mobisodes," or mobile episodes, that could be played on customers' cell phones. Most of these were cartoon animations of scenes from the TV series, using audio taken from particular episodes. One two-part mobisode, however, titled "Red Christmas," was an all-new short featuring Santa Claus—which, against common sense, I've acknowledged in this book.

- **The 2008 *Red Dwarf* Calendar:** This calendar featured in-universe advertisements, many of which contained new material.

- **Cell Phone Ringtones:** In 2008, several *Red Dwarf* cast members recorded ringtones for mobile devices. These were recorded "in character," thus securing a place in this guide.

- **BBC News April Fools' Day Video:** In 2009, the BBC News website posted an April Fools' teaser announcing *Red Dwarf*'s return, in the guise of footage purportedly showing signs of alien life on Mars. This video spoofed the European Space Agency (ESA) and its failed *Beagle 2* mission.

- **Bill Pearson's Christmas Script:** In 1999, Bill Pearson, *Red Dwarf*'s resident prop and model maker, pitched a story he wrote for a potential *Red Dwarf* holiday special. In addition to penning the screenplay, Pearson also created models of some of the vessels to be used in the story (some of which later appeared in the Series X finale, "The Beginning") and filmed a pitch video to demonstrate how some of the scenes would look. Though technically not "official" (as it was not a sanctioned GNP project), it is included in this book as a fun addition, and can be accepted or disregarded at the reader's discretion.

- **Kryten's Geek Week Introductions:** Robert Llewellyn once again donned the rubber mask in 2013 to record a series of introductory video clips for YouTube's first-ever Geek Week event, offering five days of online videos celebrating geek culture.

- **Dimension Jump XVII Posters:** Created by Rich Lawden of P2P Productions, as well as Daniel Stephenson and Jez Harrison from the Official *Red Dwarf* Fan Club, these one-off posters adorned the walls of Dimension Jump's 2013 *Red Dwarf* convention in Birmingham. Though arguably unofficial, they reveal a plethora of information that warrants inclusion for its sheer cleverness and relevance.

What Is *Not* Included

Ultimately, lines had to be drawn regarding what to include or not incorporate into this lexicon. To make that decision easier, I opted to leave out anything non-official or fan-made (aside from the few above-noted exceptions). This included any fan-created videos, comics or fiction published online or in fanzines, with the exception of one of the winners of GNP's fan film contest, which was packaged with the Series VII DVD set. Additionally, I skipped any medium that did not provide new in-universe material, including certain books, the trading cards, the *Red Dwarf* Wikia page and the *Beat the Geek* DVD quiz game.

One unfortunate casualty of the preening process was the Official *Red Dwarf* Fan Club magazine, *Back to Reality* (previously titled *Better Than Life*). The reasons for its omission were twofold: First, despite its "official" designation, the magazine has no connection to GNP and its content is fan-generated, which would violate my "no fanzines" rule—as opposed to the *Smegazines*, which were a licensed publication. Second, given the rarity of the early issues, I had strong doubts that I would be able to acquire all of the materials by press-time anyway. This is certainly no reflection on the talented creators behind the Fan Club magazines, who clearly have a great love and passion for *Red Dwarf* and have been instrumental in keeping fandom alive. I've enjoyed the issues that I have read and recommend that all fans check them out, but there was just no getting past their unlicensed status. It was a regrettable omission, but an unavoidable one.

In Smeggin' Conclusion

Throughout *Total Immersion*'s production, I often wondered if I would ever burn out and become sick of the material and the franchise. Fortunately, not only did that never happen, but in going through every last bit of lore with such a fine-toothed comb, I actually came out with a much *greater* appreciation for *Red Dwarf*—something I would not have thought possible.

The biggest thrill came from discerning things for the first time. I've watched these shows many times, and *still* occasionally discover a joke or two that I missed during the first several viewings. Now, while watching the episodes with captions—an absolute necessity when documenting them for a book of this nature—I've been able to soak in every word and, hopefully, absorb every last joke. Having to research the references made many of them that much funnier. Add to that the myriad materials I never knew existed, and I can honestly say the entire research process has been a sheer delight.

To that end, it is my sincere hope that I have done my favorite TV series justice, creating a work worthy of the *Red Dwarf* name. I can only hope that you have as much fun reading this guide as I had writing it.

I guess we'll have to let fate decide.
(cliché mode off)

ABBREVIATION KEY

A Guide to the Guide

"What IS it??"

—Cat, "Stasis Leak"

Total Immersion draws information not only from the television series, but also from a wide variety of other sources, some more obscure than others. To make it easier for readers to discern where a particular entry (or segment of an entry) was mined from, a coding system has been implemented in lieu of traditional footnotes, which would have been much less practical for a book of this nature.

Each code features a prefix denoting a general classification—whether the material was gleaned from a television episode, novel, book, website, etc. Each prefix is followed by a three-character code further denoting the source. For episodes and magazine issues, a number follows directly after this code, identifying the source more specifically. For example, [T-SER3.5] references the fifth episode of the TV program's third series, while [M-SMG2.3] refers to the third issue in the *Smegazine*'s second run. Additionally, codes may be followed by a lowercase letter suffix in parentheses, denoting an even more specific source, such as bonus DVD materials, a particular *Smegazine* comic, or an early-draft script. With the *Smegazines*, a number following the suffix indicates the material's order; for example, (c4) means the fourth comic in the issue.

Fans have widely varying opinions regarding what is and is not considered canon within the *Red Dwarf* universe. This encyclopedia does not take a stance on that debate, instead utilizing an all-inclusive approach, considering anything and everything officially sanctioned by Grant Naylor Productions to be a viable resource, including things that may severely conflict with the television show. Since every entry is marked with one or more codes denoting the material's origin, readers are free to reject and ignore any aspect of the franchise they prefer not to include.

All prefixes, codes and suffixes are detailed below. Additional details about each story, including descriptions, credits and release dates, can be found in Appendix I on page 301.

CODES:

RL: REAL LIFE
Information tagged with this code comes from real-world sources.

T: TELEVISION EPISODES
- **SER**: Televised
- **IDW**: "Identity Within" (untelevised)
- **USA1**: Unaired U.S. pilot
- **USA2**: Unaired U.S. demo reel

R: REMASTERED *(The Bodysnatcher Collection)*
- **SER**: Remastered episodes
- **BOD**: "Bodysnatcher" storyboards
- **DAD**: "Dad" storyboards
- **FTH**: "Lister's Father" storyboards
- **INF**: "Infinity Patrol" storyboards
- **END**: "The End" (original assembly)

N: NOVELS
- **INF**: *Infinity Welcomes Careful Drivers*
- **BTL**: *Better Than Life*
- **LST**: *Last Human*
- **BCK**: *Backwards*
- **OMN**: *Red Dwarf Omnibus*

M: MAGAZINES
- **SMG**: *Smegazine*

B: BOOKS
- **PRG**: *Red Dwarf Programme Guide*
- **SUR**: *Red Dwarf Space Corps Survival Manual*
- **PRM**: *Primordial Soup*
- **SOS**: *Son of Soup*
- **SCE**: *Scenes from the Dwarf*
- **LOG**: *Red Dwarf Log No. 1996*
- **EVR**: *The Log: A Dwarfer's Guide to Everything*
- **RD8**: *Red Dwarf VIII*

G: ROLEPLAYING GAME
- **RPG**: *Core Rulebook*
- **BIT**: *A.I. Screen* (including *Extra Bits* booklet)
- **SOR**: *Series Sourcebook*
- **OTH**: Other RPG material (including online PDFs)

W: WEBSITES
- **OFF**: Official website (www.reddwarf.co.uk)
- **NAN**: *Prelude to Nanarchy* (www.reddwarf.co.uk/gallery/index.cfm?page=prelude-to-nanarchy)
- **AND**: *Androids* (www.androids.tv)
- **DIV**: Diva-Droid (www.divadroid.info)
- **DIB**: Duane Dibbley (www.duanedibbley.co.uk)
- **CRP**: Crapola (www.crapola.biz)
- **GEN**: Geneticon (www.geneticon.info)
- **LSR**: Leisure World International (www.leisureworldint.com)
- **JMC**: Jupiter Mining Corporation (www.jupiterminingcorporation.com)
- **AIT**: *A.I. Today* (www.aitoday.co.uk)
- **HOL**: HoloPoint (www.holopoint.biz)

X: MISC.
- **PRO**: Promotional materials, videos, etc. (specified in notes)
- **PST**: Posters displayed at Dimension Jump XVII (2013)
- **CAL**: *Red Dwarf* 2008 Calendar
- **RNG**: Cell Phone Ringtones
- **MOB**: Mobisode ("Red Christmas", Parts 1 and 2)
- **CIN**: *Red Dwarf Children in Need* Sketch
- **GEK**: Geek Week introductions by Kryten
- **TNG**: "Tongue-Tied" video
- **XMS**: Bill Pearson's Christmas special pitch script
- **XVD**: Bill Pearson's Christmas special pitch video
- **OTH**: Other *Red Dwarf* appearances (specified in notes)

SUFFIXES:

DVDs
- (d) – Deleted scene
- (o) – Outtake
- (b) – Bonus DVD material (other)
- (e) – Extended version

SMEGAZINES / FAN CLUB MAGAZINES
- (c) – Comic
- (a) – Article

OTHER
- (s) – Early or unused script draft
- (s1) – Alternate version of script

THE ENCYCLOPEDIA [A-K]

"Here I am trying to do the comprehensive, nay, definitive A-Z of the entire universe, with street names, post offices, and little steeples and everything, and some git's been fiddling with it."

—Holly, "Thanks for the Memory"

129 AND 4457

- **$£:** *See* dollarpound ($£)

- **$£19.99:** The retail price of a Talkie Toaster, according to the appliance's boot-up sequence **[T-SER4.4]**.

  NOTE: The Geek Chase online game's Crapola website indicated that this price was for a second-generation model.

- **$£2,000:** The purchase price of a house that Olaf Petersen bought on Triton. The house, a twenty-five-bedroom home-dome with twelve ensuite bathrooms and a zero-gee squash court, was so affordable due to Triton's distance from Earth—and its complete lack of a breathable atmosphere **[N-INF]**.

- **$£25,000:** A bounty put on Mr. Flibble's head by the inhabitants of a psi-moon corrupted by the penguin's depraved mind **[M-SMG2.9(c9)]**.

- **00001:** The inmate number that Arnold Rimmer was assigned after being sentenced to 9,328 years on the penal station Justice World. The number appeared on his prison-issued uniform **[T-SER4.3]**.

- **000-169:** Lister's clearance code aboard *Red Dwarf*. Lister unsuccessfully attempted to use this code to open a door after the Inquisitor erased his existence from history **[T-SER5.2]**.

- **"00110011101100011110011100111100":** An old android saying in binary that, when translated into text, stated, "Don't stand around jabbering when you're in mortal danger" **[T-SER5.3]**.

  NOTE: Kryten's translation was incorrect, as the actual binary translation of the phrase would be a string of 456 zeros and ones.

- **008:** The room number of the Ganymede Holiday Inn's honeymoon suite. After traveling back in time through a stasis leak to locate Kochanski, Lister found her and a future version of himself in this room. There, Lister learned that sometime in his future, he would travel back to that same point in time to marry her **[T-SER2.4]**.

- **0092:** The number printed on the generic label of a beer can from the ship's stores of *Red Dwarf*. Along with this number were the words "Space Store Issue" and "beer." This particular can was present in Lister's bunk as he sampled his culinary creation for the Chef's Exam **[T-SER1.3]**.

- **0095:** A number displayed on a Drive Room monitor as Lister and Rimmer searched the contents of a postal pod that had caught up with *Red Dwarf* **[T-SER2.2]**.

- **010101:** The security clearance code of Carole Brown, an executive officer aboard *Red Dwarf* who perished during the mining ship's cadmium II disaster. Lister tried to use this code, utilizing Brown's brainwave pattern and voice, to deactivate *Red Dwarf*'s auto-destruct sequence. The code did not work, however, and the countdown continued. Fortunately for the crew, Holly had removed the explosive years prior—a fact she neglected to share with them until after the timer ran out **[T-SER3.4]**.

- **0345 33 22 33:** The telephone number of the BBC charity fundraiser event *Children in Need* **[RL]**. A twentieth-century transmission of the event, complete with phone number, was picked up three million years later by the *Blue Midget* crew **[X-CIN]**.

- **057-776:** A new course-corrected bearing Queeg implemented to return *Red Dwarf* to Earth, after taking control of the ship from Holly **[T-SER2.5]**.

  NOTE: Since Queeg was merely Holly's invention, the so-called course correction may have simply been part of the ruse.

- **058:** The number of a locker located aboard *Red Dwarf*. Lister opened this locker for Rimmer during a game the two occasionally played, which caused a security system to shoot flames at Rimmer's face and deliver a note that read, "People that break into lockers deserve everything they get, you cheap double-crossing slimeball" **[T-SER7.5]**.

- **068:** The number of a *Red Dwarf* locker that Lister opened while playing a game with Rimmer. Inside, he found a gold necklace, a wad of cash and a nude wrestling video **[T-SER7.5]**.

- **0800-751-102:** The phone number of the All-Droid Shopping Network **[W-OFF]**.

- **090:** The bearing of an unidentified object monitored by the *Red Dwarf* crew. The object was found to be a derelict vessel containing a machine capable of modifying the DNA of any organic material **[T-SER4.2]**.

- **09584:** The bearing of a meteor that the *Starbug 1* crew detected while traversing Psiren territory. The meteor was on a collision course with the shuttle, but was destroyed by a test-firing of Kryten's garbage cannon **[T-SER6.1(d)]**.

- **1:** The number of reports Rimmer filed against Lister for mutiny, according to Frank Todhunter, who found the reports among George McIntyre's effects. Rimmer filed the report after Lister jumped onto his foot while trying to prevent him from smashing Lister's guitar. According to Rimmer, this could have prevented him from performing vital duties in the event of an emergency situation, putting the entire crew at risk, and thus counting as mutiny **[T-SER1.1]**.

- **1:** The number of times that Rimmer had sexual relations with a woman prior to his deathday celebration. The encounter occurred on March 16 with Yvonne McGruder, and lasted for twelve minutes—including the amount of time it took to enjoy a pizza dinner **[T-SER2.3]**.

  ***NOTE:** Although this seemingly contradicted Rimmer's account, in episode 3.2 ("Marooned"), of his first sexual encounter at cadet school with a girl named Sandra, the novel* Better Than Life *revealed this story to be a lie covering up Rimmer's embarrassment at having lost his virginity to McGruder at age thirty-one.*

- **1:** A number stenciled on several containers in *Red Dwarf*'s cargo bay that Rimmer, Kryten and Cat passed while searching for an escaped polymorph **[T-SER3.3]**.

- **1:** A number stenciled next to one of *Red Dwarf*'s stasis booths **[M-SMG1.2(c1)]**.

  ***NOTE:** This contradicted the television series, which showed no such markings.*

- **1:** A number stenciled on a pod that Noel's Body Swap Shop used to switch customers' consciousness **[M-SMG2.3(c4)]**.

- **10:** The number of full-length mirrors Cat loaded into *Blue Midget* during an evacuation of *Red Dwarf*, after Holly detected five black holes in the vicinity **[T-SER3.2]**.

- ***1,001 Fabulous Chat-up Lines*:** A book Rimmer owned, which he used to seduce women **[T-SER2.6]**.

- ***100 Light Years of Solitude*:** A virtual-reality game available in *Red Dwarf*'s holochambers, based on the novel of the same name **[M-SMG1.5(a)]**.

  ***NOTE:** This game's title spoofed that of Gabriel García Márquez's 1967 novel* One Hundred Years of Solitude.

- **"100% Mambo Ramp Jam":** A phrase printed on a yellow jersey owned by Lister **[T-SER2.6]**.

- **100 percent:** The damage assessment of Kryten's ambulation system, as calculated by his CPU after an eruption on a psi-moon caused the destruction of *Starbug 1*, which crushed both his legs **[T-SER5.3]**.

- ***10%ers, The*:** A twentieth-century British comedy television show produced by Grant Naylor Productions **[RL]**. Simulant scavengers, searching Garbage World (Earth) for artifacts to sell to mechanicals, found a cache of video slugs, including some containing *The 10%ers* **[M-SMG2.9(c11)]**.

- **105 MM HOW HE FZ0 M5:** Markings stenciled on an ammunition box in the headquarters of Hero World, located at the Waxworld amusement park **[T-SER4.6]**.

  ***NOTE:** These markings indicate that ammunition for a 105-millimeter Howitzer artillery gun was contained within the crate. This crate appeared throughout the season at other locales as well, such as on* Starbug *and* Red Dwarf, *implying the crew salvaged them from Waxworld.*

- **10.75 centimeters:** The size of the biggest bubble that Lister blew during a fictional contest with the Browns **[T-SER1.6]**.

- **10-87 L H:** A marking on a wall adjacent to a stairway within *Red Dwarf* **[T-SER5]**.

  ***NOTE:** This was briefly visible during a cut scene between the Drive Room and the episode list on the Series V DVD menu.*

- **10 Downing Street:** The address of the United Kingdom's prime minister, located in London **[RL]**. Arnold Rimmer lived at this address while serving as the prime minister of the United Republic of Lesser Britain in an alternate universe **[M-SMG1.8(c6)]**.

- **110/1:** A number printed in the upper left corner of Rimmer's Astro-Engineer's Exam answer form **[T-SER1.1]**.

PREFIX
RL: Real life

T-: Television Episodes
SER: Television series
IDW: "Identity Within"
USA1: Unaired U.S. pilot
USA2: Unaired U.S. demo

R-: *The Bodysnatcher Collection*
SER: Remastered episodes
BOD: "Bodysnatcher"
DAD: "Dad"
FTH: "Lister's Father"
INF: "Infinity Patrol"
END: "The End" (original assembly)

N-: Novels
INF: *Infinity Welcomes Careful Drivers*
BTL: *Better Than Life*
LST: *Last Human*

BCK: *Backwards*
OMN: *Red Dwarf Omnibus*

M-: Magazines
SMG: *Smegazine*

W-: Websites
OFF: Official website
NAN: *Prelude to Nanarchy*
AND: *Androids*
DIV: Diva-Droid
DIB: Duane Dibbley

CRP: Crapola
GEN: Geneticon
LSR: Leisure World Intl.
JMC: Jupiter Mining Corporation
AIT: *A.I. Today*
HOL: HoloPoint

G-: Roleplaying Game
RPG: *Core Rulebook*
BIT: *A.I. Screen Extra Bits* booklet
SOR: *Series Sourcebook*
OTH: Other RPG material

- **11:14:** The time at which *Red Dwarf* hit lightspeed when the crew attempted to return to Earth. At that moment, future echoes began to appear **[T-SER1.2]**.

  NOTE: *Whether this was AM or PM was not specified; however, it was presumably military time, in which case 11:14 would be in the morning.*

- **1121:** A number printed on the canister containing Kochanski's remains following the cadmium II disaster **[N-BTL]**.

- **1,167:** The number of second-degree murder counts with which Rimmer was charged following a mind probe on the penal station Justice World. The charges stemmed from the computer's interpretation of Rimmer's guilt in the negligent repair of a drive plate aboard *Red Dwarf*, which resulted in a radiation explosion that killed every person on board except for Lister, who was sealed in a stasis pod. As punishment, he was sentenced to 9,328 years at the penal station, though he was freed after Kryten appealed the case **[T-SER4.3]**.

  NOTE: *This means the crew's complement at the time of the disaster was 1,169 (minus Lister and Rimmer, whose own death he wouldn't be charged for), which differed from the previously established complement of 169. This was altered to retcon the notion that a five-mile-long ship would have had such a small crew. It is possible that a thousand people aboard ship were not crewmembers, but rather civilians (laborers, miners, restaurant waiters, etc.), thereby accounting for the discrepancy.*

- **12:** The number of mechanoids it took to change a light bulb, according to a joke Kryten told after being transformed into a human by a DNA-altering machine. The reason, he claimed, was that they were so stupid **[T-SER4.2]**.

- **12:** The age at which Rimmer's honor died, according to a tombstone erected on a psi-moon modeled after his psyche **[T-SER5.3]**.

- **12:** A number stenciled on a wall in *Starbug 1*'s midsection **[T-SER7.1]**.

- **12,000:** The number of car-park attendants Holly estimated were needed to have the combined IQ of six thousand, which was supposedly his own **[T-SER2.4]**.

- **123:** The number of reports Rimmer filed against Lister for insulting a superior technician, according to Frank Todhunter, who found the reports among George McIntyre's effects after his death **[T-SER1.1]**.

- **1232/A:** The filename of Kryten's visual memory data file of Hudzen 10 **[B-LOG]**.

- **1235:** A number printed on a generic label of a whiskey bottle from the ship's stores of *Red Dwarf.* Along with this number were the words "Space Store Issue" and "whiskey" printed on the label. This particular bottle was present in Lister's quarters during the first appearances of future echoes. Lister then grabbed it on his way to meet his apparent demise in the Drive Room **[T-SER1.2]**.

- **12,368:** Holly's IQ rating following an experimental procedure known as intelligence compression, which could increase a computer's IQ at the expense of operational runtime. In Holly's case, the target IQ was six thousand, but due to a miscalculation, it reached 12,368, reducing her runtime to 3.41 minutes, and causing her to panic and shut down **[T-SER4.4]**.

- **1246/P:** The filename of Kryten's visual memory data file of a rogue simulant **[B-LOG]**.

- **1267/K:** The file name of a visual data record of Camille in her natural GELF state, stored by Kryten **[B-LOG]**.

- **129:** The service or serial number of a skutter aboard *Red Dwarf.* The number appeared on the robot's front casing. This unit developed an affinity for John Wayne Western films, hung posters of the actor in its broom cupboard, collected *Film Fun* magazines, and occasionally dressed up to play "Cowboys and Indians" with its counterpart skutter, 4457. It also belonged to the John Wayne Fan Club **[T-SER2.2]**.

  When Lister decided to enter stasis for the return trip to Earth, 129 and 4457 confronted him and produced a note begging him not to leave them alone with Rimmer **[T-SER1.2]**. Rimmer utilized this unit on numerous occasions since, as a hologram, he could not physically touch anything. This included helping him interpret markings on an unidentified pod, which turned out to be one of *Red Dwarf*'s own garbage pods **[T-SER1.4]**.

129 also served in the Medical Unit, where it checked Lister's vitals after he collapsed from mutated pneumonia. Not trusting the skutter's abilities, Lister implored Rimmer to let the medicomp do the work; he finally insisted when the skutter nearly poked his eye out with a thermometer **[T-SER1.5]**.

When the crew encountered a *Red Dwarf* from a reality in which the sexes were reversed, 129 accompanied Lister, Rimmer and Cat on a boarding party. Aboard the other vessel, it met a pink skutter with the number 46, dressed in frills and a bow, with whom it disappeared. Later on, the skutter returned to the crew with several tiny skutters in tow: two pink and two blue **[T-SER2.6]**.

> ***NOTE:** This skutter also appeared in a series of BBC Two station idents during* Red Dwarf Night *in 1998. According to the commentary on* The Bodysnatcher Collection*'s What's New? track, 129 was effects builder Andy Bowman's house number.*

- **12-change-of-underwear trip:** Cat's description of the crew's stay on a psi-moon that had configured itself according to Rimmer's mind. He used the euphemism after hearing monstrous roars coming from outside *Starbug* on the planetoid's surface **[T-SER5.3]**.

- **12 hours:** The amount of time a hard-light hologrammic version of Ace Rimmer estimated he had to live after his light bee was damaged. According to Ace, it was also the amount of time it usually took him to make love **[T-SER7.2]**.

- **12 minutes:** The entire length of time of Rimmer's first sexual encounter with a woman. This occurred on March 16 with Yvonne McGruder, and included the amount of time it took to enjoy a pizza dinner **[T-SER2.3]**.

- **12 NX:** Lettering stenciled on a wall inside *Starbug 1* **[T-SER7.2]**.

- **12th Street:** A roadway leading through a particularly dirty and miserable section of the Neptunian moon, Triton. While trapped in his personally created Cyberhell in the virtual-reality prison Cyberia, Lister walked through dismal roads that reminded him of 12th Street **[N-LST]**.

- **137B:** A code printed on sex worker Trixie LaBouche's application form for Noel's Body Swap Shop on Mimas **[M-SMG2.3(c4)]**.

- **14:** The number of times Lister, having altered history using a timeslide to become the inventor of the Tension Sheet, married before perishing in a plane crash. The accident occurred when he lost control of the aircraft while making love to his fourteenth wife. This timeline was reversed when Rimmer inadvertently restored the Tension Sheet's original inventor, Fred Holden, via another timeslide **[T-SER3.5]**.

- **1421:** The year that the *Starbug 1* crew visited during their first test of a time drive, which they found on a derelict Space Corps vessel. Cat chose this year over Lister's suggestion of 1422 for no other reason than to prove he was paying attention **[T-SER6.6]**.

- **1422:** The year that Lister suggested the *Starbug 1* crew visit during their first test of a time drive they had looted from a Space Corps derelict. He chose this year due to its lack of historical significance, but the group instead visited 1421, per Cat's suggestion **[T-SER6.6]**.

- **14B:** A tool resembling a pipe cleaner, used for clearing out clogged soup nozzles. While performing maintenance on *Red Dwarf*'s Dispenser 172, Rimmer requested a 14B but Lister instead handed him a 14F, since the two models looked identical **[T-SER1.1]**.

- **14F:** A pipe cleaner-like tool used to clear out clogged soup nozzles. The 14F appeared identical to another model known as a 14B **[T-SER1.1]**.

- **14 million:** The total number of words that Lister and Rimmer exchanged aboard *Red Dwarf* prior to the cadmium II disaster. According to Holly's logic, this made Rimmer a suitable companion to be revived as a hologram post-accident, for the purpose of keeping Lister sane. Lister disagreed, noting that half of those words involved him telling Rimmer off, with the other half attributed to Rimmer putting him on report for it **[T-SER1.3]**.

PREFIX
RL: Real life

T-: Television Episodes
SER: Television series
IDW: "Identity Within"
USA1: Unaired U.S. pilot
USA2: Unaired U.S. demo

R-: *The Bodysnatcher Collection*
SER: Remastered episodes
BOD: "Bodysnatcher"
DAD: "Dad"
FTH: "Lister's Father"
INF: "Infinity Patrol"
END: "The End" (original assembly)

N-: Novels
INF: *Infinity Welcomes Careful Drivers*
BTL: *Better Than Life*
LST: *Last Human*

BCK: *Backwards*
OMN: *Red Dwarf Omnibus*

M-: Magazines
SMG: *Smegazine*

W-: Websites
OFF: Official website
NAN: *Prelude to Nanarchy*
AND: *Androids*
DIV: Diva-Droid
DIB: Duane Dibbley

CRP: Crapola
GEN: Geneticon
LSR: Leisure World Intl.
JMC: Jupiter Mining Corporation
AIT: *A.I. Today*
HOL: HoloPoint

G-: Roleplaying Game
RPG: *Core Rulebook*
BIT: *A.I. Screen Extra Bits* booklet
SOR: *Series Sourcebook*
OTH: Other RPG material

- **14-pound lump hammer:** A large tool with which Lister attacked Talkie Toaster due to the sentient appliance's overzealous obsession with toasting bread products **[T-SER4.4]**.

- **14th Wednesday after Pentecost:** *See* 15th Wednesday after Pentecost

- **152nd:** A street located in Mimas' red light district, an area known as Shag Town. Lister first met Rimmer as a taxi hopper driver when Rimmer entered his cab and requested to be taken to the intersection of 152nd and 3rd **[N-INF]**.

- **15F-stop cornea:** A feature built into 579-model eyeballs, used in 4000 Series mechanoids such as Kryten **[T-SER4.1]**.

- **15th Wednesday after Pentecost:** A day recognized by the Catholic Church on the fifteenth Wednesday after the celebration of the giving of the Law on Sinai **[RL]**. While marooned on an icy planet, Rimmer broadcast a Mayday distress call from *Starbug 1*. Mistaking "Mayday" for a reference to the bank holiday May Day, Rimmer questioned its effectiveness, wondering why "15th Wednesday after Pentecost" wasn't chosen for distress calls instead **[T-SER3.2]**.

  NOTE: *In the novel* Better Than Life*, this was changed to the 14th Wednesday after Pentecost.*

- **169:** A number by which Lister identified himself while trying to prevent an overheating navicomp from exploding **[T-SER1.2]**.

  NOTE: *This presumably referred to Lister's service or serial number, RD 52 169. The latter number sequence referenced his status as the lowest-ranking member aboard* Red Dwarf*, whose established crew complement in Series I was 169.*

- **17:** The age at which Lister formed his first band, Smeg and the Heads **[T-SER3.5]**.

- **17:** The number of a component on *Red Dwarf*'s B Deck that required a replacement valve-housing gasket **[T-SER10.2]**.

- **171:** The age at which Lister left a future echo message for his younger self, explaining that the person he had seen killed in the Drive Room during a previous echo was his own future son, Bexley. By age 171, Lister's right arm had been replaced by a robotic appendage **[T-SER1.2]**.

  NOTE: *In episode 7.7 ("Epideme"), Lister did lose his right arm while attempting to remove the Epideme virus, but it was regrown by Kryten's nanobots in episode 7.8 ("Nanarchy").*

- **173:** The number of words that Lister and Kochanski exchanged aboard *Red Dwarf*. According to Holly's logic, this disqualified her as a suitable companion to be revived as a hologram for Lister following the cadmium II disaster. Therefore, Holly instead chose Rimmer, whose combined dialog word-count with Lister was more than fourteen million **[T-SER1.3]**.

  NOTE: *This caused something of a continuity error later in the series, when it was established that the two had, in fact, dated. Their conversation in the drive room in episode 1.1 ("The End") alone accounted for a third of this number, not to mention their conversation about Frankenstein in episode 7.3 ("Ouroboros"), which far exceeded 173 words. Even without those two examples, though, it would still be difficult to believe they spoke fewer than two hundred words to each other during their relationship.*

- **179:** The model number of a forty-valve air-cooled diesel engine used aboard *Red Dwarf*. The 179 was almost identical to the 184, aside from a refinement in the newer model's funnel edges **[T-SER4.3]**.

- **1799 Château d'Yquem:** A vintage of French wine widely perceived as being of superior quality, from the Graves portion of the Bordeaux vineyards **[RL]**. While trapped in an addictive version of *Better Than Life*, Rimmer imagined himself hosting a glamorous party on Earth, at which he sipped a glass of 1799 Château d'Yquem **[N-INF]**.

- **181:** The age at which Lister died while trying to remove a bra with his teeth, according to Cassandra, a computer able to foresee the future **[T-SER8.4]**.

- **184:** The model number of a forty-valve air-cooled diesel engine used aboard *Red Dwarf*. The 184 was almost identical to the 179, aside from a refinement in the funnel edges on the newer 184. On the fourth day of a ten-day hiking vacation through the diesel decks, Rimmer came across a 184 and camped under it for the night. He later included a photograph of the 184 in a slideshow that he made Kryten watch **[T-SER4.3]**.

- **18 months:** The amount of time Lister was sentenced to spend in stasis for bringing an unquarantined animal aboard *Red Dwarf.* Sometime during this period, however, a faulty drive plate resulted in a cadmium II explosion, exposing the ship to lethal amounts of radiation that vaporized the entire crew except for Lister, who was protected by the stasis field. Holly released him three million years later, after the background radiation had returned to safe levels **[T-SER1.1]**.

- **18 weeks:** The amount of time that passed between Lister's revival from stasis and *Red Dwarf*'s discovery of a garbage pod, which Rimmer mistook for an alien craft. Believing that alien beings inhabited the pod, Rimmer elated in the thought of finally meeting intelligent creatures after spending eighteen weeks with Lister and Cat **[T-SER1.4]**.

- **1952 Phase Four:** A type of telegraph pole featured in Rimmer's photo collection of twentieth-century telegraph poles. Among its features was triple-reinforced wire **[T-SER4.1]**.

- **1964:** The year during which U.S. President John F. Kennedy, having survived Lee Harvey Oswald's assassination attempt due to the *Starbug 1* crew's intervention, was impeached in the altered timeline following a scandal involving the mistress of Mafia boss Sam Giancana **[T-SER7.1]**.

- **1966:** The year that the *Starbug 1* crew visited after a botched attempt to find curries led to their inadvertent interference in John F. Kennedy's 1963 assassination. Accused of the attempted murder by FBI agents, the crew used the time drive to jump three years ahead, only to find themselves in an altered timeline in which Kennedy had been imprisoned and replaced by J. Edgar Hoover. In this timeline, Hoover, controlled by the mob, was forced to let Russia build a nuclear base in Cuba, thereby necessitating the evacuation of millions of Americans from major cities **[T-SER7.1]**.

- **1983:** The vintage of a bottle of wine that the *Red Dwarf* crew consumed during Kryten's last-day party **[T-SER3.6]**.

- **198,732:** The number of cats aboard *Red Dwarf* when Lister's feline pet Frankenstein died at age fourteen. The cats were all directly descended from Frankenstein and her initial litter of four kittens **[N-INF]**.

- **1989:** The year on a parallel Earth that Lister may have visited after traveling through a cosmic storm. During this visit, according to a future version of himself, Lister attended a theatrical production of *Run for Your Wife*. When the younger Lister asked his future self for the single most important piece of advice, the latter advised against seeing the play **[T-SER2.4]**.

  NOTE: *It is unclear whether this event actually happened, if it occurred in an alternate timeline or reality, or if future Lister was just being snarky.*

- **1 Corinthians 13:** A passage in the Bible that Rimmer remembered as, "Faith, hope and charity, and the greatest of these is hope." In the Seventh-Day Advent Hoppists' version of the Bible, a misprint caused the passage to read, "Faith, hop and charity, and the greatest of these is hop," leading members to hop every Sunday **[T-SER3.6]**.

  NOTE: *1 Corinthians 13 actually reads, "So now faith, hope, and love abide, these three; but the greatest of these is love."*

- **1 hour, 17 minutes, 39 seconds:** The amount of time it took Lister and Cat to scramble during a mock emergency Rimmer set up aboard *Starbug 1*. According to Rimmer, it was a record time **[T-SER6.4]**.

- **2:** A number stenciled on several containers in *Red Dwarf*'s cargo bays that Rimmer, Kryten and Cat passed while searching for an escaped polymorph **[T-SER3.3]**.

- **2:** A number painted on the side of an extendable boarding rig aboard *Red Dwarf*, which the crew used to connect with a derelict ship containing a DNA-modifying machine **[T-SER4.2]**.

- **2:** A number stenciled next to one of *Red Dwarf*'s stasis booths. After bringing an unquarantined animal aboard ship, Lister was put in stasis in this unit **[M-SMG1.2(c1)]**.
  NOTE: *This contradicted the television series, which showed no such markings.*

- **2:** A number stenciled on a pod that Noel's Body Swap Shop used to switch customers' consciousness. Several cracks marred the pod's casing **[M-SMG2.3(c4)]**.

- **200:** The number of years it took for *Starbug 1* to catch up with *Red Dwarf* after Kryten's nanobots commandeered the mining ship. During that time, the crew placed themselves in deep sleep **[T-SER6.1]**.

- **200,000:** The number of questions on a test that Rimmer and Nirvanah Crane took to ascertain whether Arnold would replace her aboard the holoship *Enlightenment* **[T-SER5.1]**.

- **200,000 MPH:** The average cruising speed of the mining ship *Red Dwarf* **[N-INF]**.

- ***20,000,000 Watts My Line*:** A television trivia game show in an alternate reality in which Jake Bullet was a cyborg cop. Contestants were wired up and fried by 20,000,000 watts of electricity if a question was answered incorrectly. Its host and hostess were named Milty **[M-SMG1.10(c1)]** and Mercy Dash, respectively **[M-SMG1.14(c6)]**. The program was recorded at the Savalas TV studio **[M-SMG1.11(c4)]**. When Philby Frutch, the series' most successful contestant, was murdered shortly after one episode's taping, Bullet was assigned to the case **[M-SMG1.10(c1)]**.
  NOTE: *This show's title spoofed that of* What's My Line?, *a CBS game show that ran from 1950 to 1967, with several subsequent revivals. Among its frequent panelists was Soupy Sales (born Milton "Milty" Supman).*

- **204:** A number stenciled on a JMC C-245 crane aboard *Red Dwarf*, which Cat used to lower a cow into a massive bowl of vindaloo for Pete the *Tyrannosaurus rex* to consume—so they could then retrieve a swallowed time wand from its feces **[T-SER8.7]**.

- **2,049:** A number that Lister challenged Holly to calculate the square root of, to prove he had an IQ of six thousand. The AI eventually responded with 45.265881, then pretended to be erased by Queeg in order to teach the crew to treat him with more respect **[T-SER2.5]**.

- **2079:** The year in which Arnold Rimmer, in an alternate universe, was elected the prime minister of the United Republic of Lesser Britain **[M-SMG2.8(c6)]**.
  NOTE: *Although this jibes with the date shown in episode 2.5 ("Stasis Leak"), it contradicts later sources claiming that* Red Dwarf *is set in the twenty-second century.*

- ***20 Bump and Grind Classics*:** An album featuring music from rhythm and blues singer Barry White, which Cat brought to the survival pod in which he and Ora Tanzil addressed his biological affliction brought on by a lack of sexual activity **[T-IDW]**.
  NOTE: *Barry White never recorded an album by this name in the real world.*

- **20th-century telegraph poles:** The subject of a photograph collection owned by Rimmer. Before learning that Camille was a shapeshifting Pleasure GELF, Rimmer—who perceived Camille as an attractive female hologram—asked if she would like to see the photos. His delighted reaction to her answer confused Lister, who heard a different response than Rimmer did **[T-SER1.6]**.

- **212 percent:** The size increase of *Starbug 1*'s cargo deck after an altercation with the crew's future selves created dimensional anomalies that affected the ship **[T-SER7.1]**.

- **2155:** *See* November 26, 2155

- **2162:** The year in which Rimmer's mother received an important letter from his school. In the prime universe, this correspondence informed her that Arnold was not being kept back, but in Ace Rimmer's reality, it stated that he was. This was the primary diverging point between the two universes **[B-PRM]**.

- **2180:** The year in which *Red Dwarf* left Saturn's moon, Mimas, to head back to Earth **[M-SMG1.1(c1)]**.

- **2181:** The year in which Ace Rimmer first left his own reality aboard the *Wildfire*, arriving in the prime universe **[N-BCK]**.

- **22:** The age at which Rimmer's self-confidence died, according to a tombstone erected on a psi-moon modeled after his psyche **[T-SER5.3]**.

- **220 Sycamore:** Lister's address in Bedford Falls while he was trapped in an addictive version of *Better Than Life*. In the illusion, Lister believed he had returned to Earth using *Nova 5*'s Duality Jump and, shunning fame and fortune, opted for a quiet life in a Midwestern town bearing a striking resemblance to the fictional location of the film *It's a Wonderful Life*. There, he assumed the identity of George Bailey (the movie's protagonist), opened a kebab shop and settled down with a descendant of Kochanski and their two children, Jim and Bexley, at 220 Sycamore **[N-INF]**.

  ***NOTE:** George Bailey's address in the film was actually 320 Sycamore.*

- **2224 World Cup:** A championship soccer competition in the Genetic Alternate Sports (GAS) league. During one World Cup game, Scotland introduced a genetically modified goalkeeper who was nothing more than an eight-foot by sixteen-foot oblong mass of human flesh covering the goal's entire entrance, yet the team still failed to qualify for the next round. Because of this incident, new rules were created for future GAS games **[N-BTL]**.

- **224:** A number stenciled on the exterior doors of the *Red Dwarf* landing bay housing the shuttlecraft *Blue Midget* **[T-SER2.1]**.

- **226813:** A number on a console in *Red Dwarf*'s Drive Room, below which was the word "Destruct." Cat used the food dispenser in the Drive Room to order several fish dishes, then sat down in front of this console to enjoy them **[T-SER1.3]**.

- **227 Thatcher Throughway, Flat C:** The address of game-show contestant Philby Frutch in Jake Bullet's universe **[M-SMG1.13(c4)]**.

- **2296:** The copyright year of Version IX.05 of the Mechanoid Visual System, filed by Infomax Data Corporation **[N-INF]**.

- **23:** A number printed on a box stored on *Red Dwarf*'s food deck **[T-SER8.7]**.

- **2340:** The year in which Kryten 2X4B-523P was manufactured, according to the copyright date indicated in his head-up display **[T-SER5.3]**.

- **2389:** A number printed on a console in *Starbug 1*'s Medical Bay **[T-SER7.8]**.

- **239006:** The number of a snack dispenser located outside Captain Hollister's quarters aboard *Red Dwarf*. Rimmer became bitter enemies with this particular dispenser after stealing a choccie nut bar without paying. The machine got revenge when it hurled a beverage can at Rimmer after he became the last person trapped on the decaying ship. The can knocked Rimmer unconscious, but when Death appeared to take him to the Afterlife, he kneed the Grim Reaper in the groin and ran away **[T-SER8.8]**.

  ***NOTE:** In an alternate ending, Rimmer, now the highest-ranking member aboard ship, paid the snack dispenser back. Unappeased, the machine launched the beverage can at him anyway, knocking him unconscious.*

- **24:** The age at which Rimmer's self-respect died, according to a tombstone erected on a psi-moon modeled after his psyche **[T-SER5.3]**.

- **2419:** A number on a *Red Dwarf* lift in which Rimmer, Kryten and Cat traveled while trying to escape a polymorph **[T-SER3.3]**.

- **246:** The number of smell-symbols in the Cat lexicon. These smells could be combined to create literature in Cat culture, with readers running their nose along the book's invisible lines to release the odors infused into each page **[N-INF]**.

- **247:** The number of complaints that Rimmer filed against Lister while aboard *Red Dwarf*, according to Frank Todhunter, who found the reports among George McIntyre's effects.

PREFIX
RL: Real life

T-: Television Episodes
- **SER:** Television series
- **IDW:** "Identity Within"
- **USA1:** Unaired U.S. pilot
- **USA2:** Unaired U.S. demo

R-: *The Bodysnatcher Collection*
- **SER:** Remastered episodes
- **BOD:** "Bodysnatcher"
- **DAD:** "Dad"
- **FTH:** "Lister's Father"
- **INF:** "Infinity Patrol"
- **END:** "The End" (original assembly)

N-: Novels
- **INF:** *Infinity Welcomes Careful Drivers*
- **BTL:** *Better Than Life*
- **LST:** *Last Human*
- **BCK:** *Backwards*
- **OMN:** *Red Dwarf Omnibus*

M-: Magazines
- **SMG:** *Smegazine*

W-: Websites
- **OFF:** Official website
- **NAN:** *Prelude to Nanarchy*
- **AND:** *Androids*
- **DIV:** Diva-Droid
- **DIB:** Duane Dibbley
- **CRP:** Crapola
- **GEN:** Geneticon
- **LSR:** Leisure World Intl.
- **JMC:** Jupiter Mining Corporation
- **AIT:** *A.I. Today*
- **HOL:** HoloPoint

G-: Roleplaying Game
- **RPG:** *Core Rulebook*
- **BIT:** *A.I. Screen Extra Bits* booklet
- **SOR:** *Series Sourcebook*
- **OTH:** Other RPG material

These included 123 counts of insulting a superior technician, thirty-nine counts of dereliction of duty, eighty-four counts of general insubordination and one count of mutiny **[T-SER1.1]**.

- **247/87:** A number painted on a beam above a bookshelf inside Lister's quarters aboard *Red Dwarf* **[T-SER9.1]**.

- **247 Giga-Nova Omni-Warp Mega Drive Hyper Boosters:** The propulsion system of a ship that Ace "Blackheart" Rimmer flew in an alternate universe. The vessel featured ionic conversion ultra-temporal turbo-thrust technology **[M-SMG1.14(c5)]**.

- **248:** The number of asteroids that Rimmer and Kryten found during an asteroid-spotting trip in *Starbug 1* **[T-SER4.1(d)]**.

- **2489:** A number printed on a console in *Starbug 1*'s Medical Bay **[T-SER7.8]**.

- **24 Argyle Street, Somewhereville, TW17 0QD:** The address of Lottery House, an organization that paid out lottery winnings for the Multi Million Lottery Company. While incarcerated in *Red Dwarf*'s brig, Rimmer received a letter informing him that he had won four million in the lottery, and should bring his winning ticket to this address **[B-RD8]**.

- **25:** A number stenciled on a bazookoid stored aboard *Red Dwarf*. The crew used the weapon against a polymorph that had drained their emotions **[T-SER3.3]**. They later brought it to a psi-moon to fight the Unspeakable One (a manifestation of Rimmer's self-loathing), but to little effect **[T-SER5.3]**.

- **25:** A number stenciled on a bazookoid that a simulant used to hunt down the *Red Dwarf* crew aboard the penal station Justice World **[T-SER4.3]**.

  NOTE: *This bazookoid was presumably the same prop used by the* Red Dwarf *crew in various episodes. In-universe, however, they were unlikely the same weapon, since they were stored aboard different ships.*

- **2-5-2-3-1-1:** The space coordinates of the Erroneous Reasoning Research Academy (ERRA). The *Red Dwarf* crew discovered these coordinates by harnessing Kryten's quantum entanglement with Cat, coupled with the cover of Arthur Koestler's book, *The Roots of Coincidence*, which featured a set of dominoes displaying these same numbers **[T-SER10.4]**.

- **2,567:** The number of levels that Lister, Rimmer and Cat traveled aboard one of *Red Dwarf*'s Xpress Lifts while en route to Floor 16 to investigate a stasis leak **[T-SER2.4]**.

- **2,572:** The number of crushed velvet seats in *Red Dwarf*'s Copacabana Hawaiian Cocktail Bar **[N-INF]**.

- **26:** A number stenciled on a bazookoid that an alternate Lister used after the Inquisitor wiped the original from history **[T-SER5.2]**.

- **26:** A number stenciled on a bazookoid that Lister used to fight an escaped simulant aboard the penal station Justice World **[T-SER4.3]**. Cat utilized this same weapon to kill the "low" version of Lister, who had stowed away aboard *Starbug 1* **[T-SER5.5]**.

  NOTE: *This bazookoid was presumably the same prop used in various episodes. In-universe, however, they were unlikely all the same weapon, since they were stored aboard different ships.*

- **27781:** A reference number shown during a promotional video advertising Diva-Droid International's new Hudzen 10 series mechanoid. It was also the product code for the mechanoid's instruction manual **[W-DIV]**.

  NOTE: *Using this reference number on the Diva-Droid website's support page granted access to a PDF of the manual, which contained the first of three passwords required to access the site's contact page.*

- **277MJG:** The number on a California license plate mounted on a wall in Lister's quarters aboard *Red Dwarf* **[T-SER2.2]**.

- **27k:** A marking on several boxes in *Red Dwarf*'s store bay, near which Lister confronted and defeated the Inquisitor **[T-SER5.2]**.

- **27 percent:** Kryten's damage assessment after Lister attempted to repair him following an accident on a psi-moon that nearly destroyed him **[T-SER5.3]**.

14B AND 14F

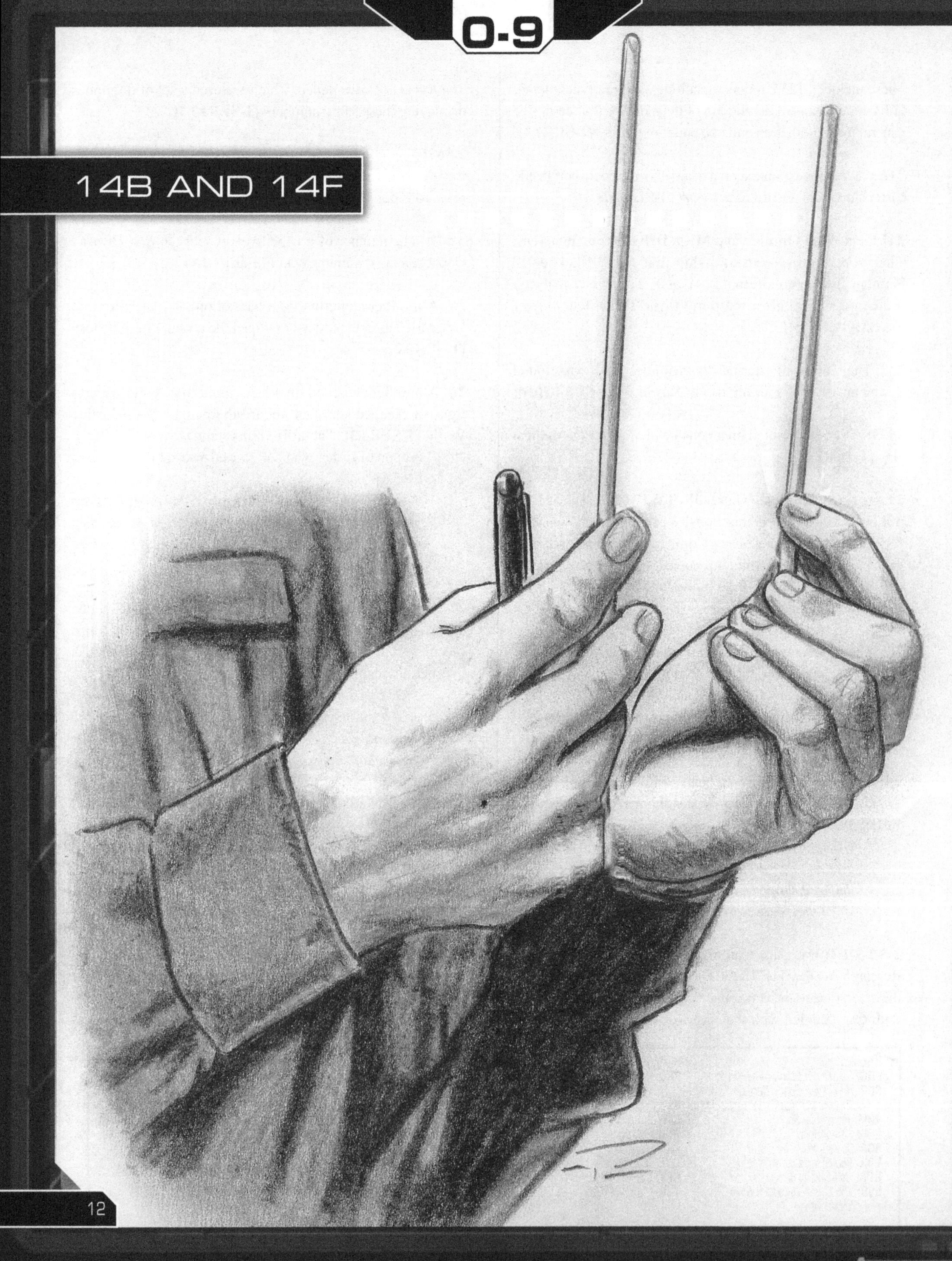

- **"27th CRS":** A phrase adorning a patch sewn onto Lister's leather jacket **[T-SER3.1]**.

  NOTE: *The patch bore the insignia of the U.S. Air Force's 27th Component Repair Squadron.*

- **2960B8651:** The serial number of Ora Tanzil, a she-Cat whom the *Starbug 1* crew rescued from a tribe of Brefewino GELFs **[T-IDW]**.

- **2G22394:** The number on a California license plate mounted on a wall in Lister's quarters aboard *Red Dwarf* **[T-SER2.2]**.

- **2 percent:** The amount that Kryten recalled from the evening prior to his last-day celebration, after partying all night in *Red Dwarf*'s Officers' Club. This percentage was listed on a damage-control report he performed **[T-SER3.6]**.

- **2Q4B:** The middle name of an android Kryten once knew. As much as he disliked his own middle name (2X4B), Kryten was glad it was not that of his acquaintance **[T-SER3.6]**.

- **2 weeks:** The amount of time Lister intended to allow Rimmer to inhabit his body via a mind swap in order to get him more fit. After only a week, however, Lister demanded his body back, and found it to be in worse shape than before, due to Rimmer's over-indulgences **[T-SER3.4]**.

- **2 weeks:** The amount of time one could save by purchasing a Stirmaster instead of manually stirring six cups of coffee a day during one's lifetime, according to an advertisement for the product on the All-Droid Mail Order Shopping Station **[T-SER10.1]**.

- **2X4C:** The serial number of both Kryten and Able. Having the same serial number meant the two mechanoids shared the same motherboard, and were thus the android equivalent of brothers **[T-SER7.6]**.

  NOTE: *It is unclear whether the serial number's close resemblance to Kryten's middle name (2X4B) was intentional or mere coincidence.*

- **3:** A number stenciled on several containers in *Red Dwarf*'s cargo bays that Rimmer, Kryten and Cat passed while searching for an escaped polymorph **[T-SER3.3]**.

- **3:** A number stenciled next to one of *Red Dwarf*'s stasis booths **[M-SMG1.2(c1)]**.

  NOTE: *This contradicted the television series, which showed no such markings.*

- **30:** A number stenciled on one of the locking mechanisms securing *Starbug 1*'s rear section to the remainder of the shuttle **[T-SER7.1(e)]**.

- **3,000:** The number of vomit bags Rimmer sarcastically claimed were in stock aboard *Starbug 1* when Ace Rimmer returned—which, he added, would not be enough for the encounter **[T-SER7.2]**.

- **30,000 years:** Holly's estimate of how long *Red Dwarf*'s remaining supplies would last. The surviving crew, he calculated, had sufficient food for thirty thousand years—though there was only one After Eight mint left **[T-SER1.6]**, and they had run out of Shake 'n' Vac **[T-SER2.3]**.

- **3000 Series:** A model of mechanoids made in Taiwan, built to appear completely human **[T-SER6.6]**. This series was designed by Nigel Norman and manufactured by Diva-Droid International **[W-DIV]**. It could process food and was waterproof up to 100 meters (32.8 feet) **[G-BIT]**.

  The 3000 Series preceded the 4000 Series, the line that included the Kryten model; as such, the 4000 Series considered themselves superior to the 3000s, despite being less advanced appearance-wise. Because of their uncanny realism, the 3000 Series mechanoids were notoriously unpopular, and were shunned by humanity for fear that their appearance might allow them to impersonate humans too easily **[T-SER6.6]**. This earned the series the award for Most Disturbing Android Design from several consumer guides **[G-BIT]**.

  Their unpopularity eventually forced the company to recall the model. However, several 3000s fled and forged new lives for themselves, with some even erasing their memories to hide all traces of their mechanical nature.

  While pursuing the stolen *Red Dwarf*, the *Starbug 1* crew encountered a reality minefield, an area of space designed to skew the perception of trespassers. Within the minefield, the crew temporarily believed that Lister was a 3000 Series mechanoid **[T-SER6.6]**.

  NOTE: *The novel* Last Human *erroneously listed Kryten as a 3000 Series mechanoid.*

- **301:** The service number of a skutter aboard an alternate *Red Dwarf*. Rimmer put this skutter on report for dereliction of duty and insubordination **[T-USA1(s)]**.

- **31:** The number of pieces missing from a chess set stored in *Red Dwarf*'s Quarantine Room 152 **[T-SER5.4]**.

  NOTE: *The normal number of pieces in a chess set is thirty-two.*

- **31:** The number of individuals whom the *Red Dwarf* crew encountered prior to meeting Legion, which Rimmer noted while attempting to persuade Legion to join them. Most, he admitted, were deranged or otherwise wanted to harm them in some way; when it became clear Legion meant to keep them prisoner aboard his station, Rimmer upped that number to thirty-two **[T-SER6.2]**.

  ***NOTE:** Rimmer presumably meant groups of individuals rather than only thirty-one distinct beings. Between the backwards-running Earth, the holoship and Waxworld alone, he and his shipmates had encountered thousands of individuals before meeting Legion.*

- **310:** A number stenciled on a weapons crate in the headquarters of Hero World, at the Waxworld amusement park **[T-SER4.6]**.

- **32:** A number stenciled on the side of a container aboard *Starbug 1* **[T-SER3.2]**. Several such numbered crates were also stored near Airlock A, where the crew confronted Kryten's replacement, Hudzen 10 **[T-SER3.6]**.

- **32:** Rimmer's revised total for the number of dangerous individuals whom the *Red Dwarf* crew had encountered prior to Legion, which he increased from thirty-one upon realizing Legion meant to take them captive **[T-SER6.2]**.

- **32:** A number on a Happy Hopper taxi on Mimas **[M-SMG2.5(c6)]**.

- **32-12:** A component in one of *Red Dwarf*'s corridors on B Deck that required replacement **[T-SER10.2]**.

- **3263827-K:** The serial number of Monica Jones, a hologrammic navigator aboard an alternate *Red Dwarf* **[G-RPG]**.

- **33, 34, 35:** A series of numbers painted on a large tank in *Red Dwarf*'s loading bay. After going back in time via a stasis leak, Lister was reunited with Olaf Petersen near these tanks, as his friend attempted to woo two beautiful women back from shore leave **[T-SER2.4]**.

- **3379:** The number of a Dallas Police Department badge that John F. Kennedy wore while posing as a policeman in order to help the *Starbug 1* crew restore history by assassinating himself from behind a grassy knoll **[T-SER7.1]**.

- **34:** A number painted on a large tank in *Red Dwarf*'s loading bay. After going back in time via a stasis leak, Lister was reunited with Olaf Petersen near this tank, as his friend attempted to woo two beautiful women back from shore leave **[T-SER2.4]**.

- **3.41 minutes:** The amount of operational runtime Holly had remaining after an experimental intelligence compression procedure doubled her target IQ to more than twelve thousand. After calculating her new lifespan, Holly panicked and turned herself off until a solution could be found **[T-SER4.4]**.

- **343:** A number stenciled on the T-72 tank that Kryten used to force the crew to leave the artificial-reality simulation *Pride and Prejudice Land* **[T-SER7.6]**.

- **345:** *See* TI345

- **345 years:** The amount of time to which Holly initially thought her operational runtime had been reduced after an experimental intelligence compression procedure raised her IQ to more than twelve thousand. After realizing a decimal point was missing, she recalculated her runtime to be 3.41—minutes, not years **[T-SER4.4]**.

- **3454H:** Lister's clearance number during his prison sentence in Cyberia, after he volunteered for the GELFs' Reco-Programme to test a newly terraformed planet **[N-LST]**.

- **346:** The model number of a Psi-scan that the 345 model outperformed in eight out of nine benchmarks during testing **[T-SER5.4]**.

- **3479/U:** The filename of Kryten's visual memory data file of the Inquisitor **[B-LOG]**.

- **35:** A number painted on a large tank in *Red Dwarf*'s loading bay. After going back in time via a stasis leak, Lister was reunited with Olaf Petersen near this tank, as his friend attempted to woo two beautiful women back from shore leave **[T-SER2.4]**.

PREFIX
RL: Real life

T-: Television Episodes
SER: Television series
IDW: "Identity Within"
USA1: Unaired U.S. pilot
USA2: Unaired U.S. demo

R-: *The Bodysnatcher Collection*
SER: Remastered episodes
BOD: "Bodysnatcher"
DAD: "Dad"
FTH: "Lister's Father"
INF: "Infinity Patrol"
END: "The End" (original assembly)

N-: Novels
INF: *Infinity Welcomes Careful Drivers*
BTL: *Better Than Life*
LST: *Last Human*
BCK: *Backwards*
OMN: *Red Dwarf Omnibus*

M-: Magazines
SMG: *Smegazine*

W-: Websites
OFF: Official website
NAN: *Prelude to Nanarchy*
AND: *Androids*
DIV: Diva-Droid
DIB: Duane Dibbley
CRP: Crapola
GEN: Geneticon
LSR: Leisure World Intl.
JMC: Jupiter Mining Corporation
AIT: *A.I. Today*
HOL: HoloPoint

G-: Roleplaying Game
RPG: *Core Rulebook*
BIT: *A.I. Screen Extra Bits* booklet
SOR: *Series Sourcebook*
OTH: Other RPG material

- **350 volts:** The voltage running through several junctions aboard *Starbug 1*. While searching for a malfunction, Rimmer and Kryten tested these junctions by having the mechanoid stick his finger into the component and measuring the voltage before his eyes blew out from his head **[T-SER7.1(e)]**.

- **356 by 121:** The bearing of a GELF moon on which *Starbug 1* crashed after being attacked by a Space Corps external enforcement vessel **[T-SER6.4]**.

- **35 percent:** The damage assessment of Kryten's optical system, as calculated by his CPU after an eruption on a psi-moon nearly destroyed him and *Starbug 1* **[T-SER5.3]**.

- **36:** The number of outfits that Cat loaded onto *Blue Midget* during an evacuation of *Red Dwarf* **[T-SER3.2]**.

- **36,186:** The production number of an episode of the television soap opera *Androids* that computer hacker Duane Dibbley considered his favorite **[W-AND]**.

- **362436ZXKB3:** The ID number of a vacuum cleaner Kryten once befriended **[M-SMG1.1(a)]**.

- **372:** The model number of a thermos purchased by Duane Dibbley, containing a rechargeable absolute-zero unit **[W-DIB]**.

- **389/32:** A number painted on a beam in one of *Red Dwarf*'s corridors, which the crew passed while trapped in an elation squid hallucination **[T-SER9.1]**.

- **39:** The number of reports Rimmer filed against Lister for dereliction of duty, according to Frank Todhunter, who found the reports among George McIntyre's effects **[T-SER1.1]**.

- **39:** A number on a jumpsuit that Lister stole while attempting to escape the nanobot-rebuilt *Red Dwarf* **[T-SER8.2]**.

- **398/32:** A number painted on a beam above the door inside Lister's quarters on *Red Dwarf* **[T-SER9.1]**.

- **3-in-1:** A brand of all-purpose lubricating oil **[RL]**. Sugar, an android who sought Jake Bullet's help in finding her brother, smelled like 3-in-1 **[M-SMG1.7(a)]**.

- **3 million years:** The amount of time it took for the background radiation from a cadmium II leak aboard *Red Dwarf* to reach a habitable level, after which the ship's computer, Holly, released Lister from stasis. During this span of time, Holly navigated the mining vessel out of Earth's solar system and into deep space. Meanwhile, in the ship's cargo hold, the Cat race evolved from Lister's pregnant cat, Frankenstein, to become *Felis sapiens* **[T-SER1.1]**.

  ***NOTE:** The first draft of the pilot episode's script, published in the* Red Dwarf Omnibus, *stated that Lister was sealed in the stasis booth for seven billion years, not three million.*

- **3rd:** A street in Mimas' red-light district, an area known as Shag Town. Lister first met Rimmer as a taxi hopper driver when Rimmer entered his cab and requested to be taken to the intersection of 152nd and 3rd **[N-INF]**.

- **3Y5D:** A mechanoid middle name that Kryten wished he had been given instead of 2X4B **[X-GEK]**.

- **4:** A number stenciled on several containers in *Red Dwarf*'s cargo bays that Rimmer, Kryten and Cat passed while searching for an escaped polymorph **[T-SER3.3]**.

- **4000 Series:** A type of mechanoid produced by Diva-Droid International, also known as the Series III or Series 4000. Mechanoids of this type included the Kryten **[T-SER3.6]** and Able lines **[T-SER7.6]**. The 4000 Series was created by Professor Mamet, with the likeness and exaggerated mannerisms of her ex-fiancé, John Warburton **[T-SER6.1]**. This model came in a variety of body plating colors, including Butler Black, Space Age Silver, Go-Go Green, Candy Apple Red, Neptune Blue **[G-RPG]** and, in an alternate dimension, Ganymede Gold **[G-SOR]**.

  Among the features of the 4000 Series were a groinal socket that allowed a wide array of functions via attachments, such as a food whisk, a vacuum, a buzz saw, a drill and a hedge trimmer **[T-SER3.3]**. The unit could also be equipped with an

B-: Books
PRG: *Red Dwarf Programme Guide*
SUR: *Red Dwarf Space Corps Survival Manual*
PRM: *Primordial Soup*
SOS: *Son of Soup*
SCE: *Scenes from the Dwarf*
LOG: *Red Dwarf Log No. 1996*
RD8: *Red Dwarf VIII*
EVR: *The Log: A Dwarfer's Guide to Everything*

X-: Misc.
PRO: Promotional materials, videos, etc.
PST: Posters at DJ XVII (2013)
CAL: 2008 calendar
RNG: Cell phone ringtones
MOB: Mobisode ("Red Christmas")
CIN: *Children in Need* sketch
GEK: *Geek Week* intros by Kryten
TNG: "Tongue-Tied" video

XMS: Bill Pearson's Christmas special pitch script
XVD: Bill Pearson's Christmas special pitch video
OTH: Other *Red Dwarf* appearances

SUFFIX
DVD:
(d) – Deleted scene
(o) – Outtake
(b) – Bonus DVD material (other)
(e) – Extended version

SMEGAZINES:
(c) – Comic
(a) – Article

OTHER:
(s) – Early/unused script draft
(s1) – Alternate version of script

optional Nanny-Bot childcare software bundle and/or Nega-Drive download station **[G-RPG]**. The 4000 sported a circular chest monitor that served a variety of purposes, including as a video monitor **[T-SER7.1]**, a monitor for AI computers, such as *Red Dwarf*'s Holly **[T-SER3.2]**, and a flashlight **[N-BCK]**.

Other features of the 4000 Series were a built-in lighter located in one of its fingers **[R-SER3.4(d)]**, a skeleton key **[T-SER9.3]**, a screwdriver **[T-SER10.2]** and electrical wiring inside its left index finger **[T-SER10.3]**. The top running speed of a 4000 Series mechanoid was twenty-five miles per hour (forty kilometers per hour) **[N-BTL]**.

4000 Series mechanoids were not waterproof **[T-SER4.5]**. Their optical units included a pair of 579s with automatic 15f-stop corneas **[T-SER4.1]**. This model was voted Android of the Year five years in a row for its selfless nature and willingness to sacrifice its life for others **[T-SER5.2]**. During emergency situations in which a 4000 Series mechanoid was rendered immobile, it could construct a rescue bot from one of its hands and optical units, and instruct it to locate and bring back help **[T-SER5.3]**.

The mechanoids also had a built-in shutdown chip that would automatically activate upon receipt of a message from Diva-Droid that a replacement Hudzen 10 Series droid was en route **[T-SER3.6]**.

> ***NOTE:*** *Kryten's type alternated between Series III and 4000 Series throughout the show's run. The official* Red Dwarf *website settled on 4000 Series, but noted that both names were correct, for reasons known only to Diva-Droid.*
>
> *The lighter, featured in an exclusive deleted scene included in the* The Bodysnatcher Collection*'s bonus materials, was built into Kryten's index finger. It was also mentioned as an Easter egg on the Series III DVDs, but was said to be in Kryten's thumb. Due to this continuity error, Kryten seemed to have a skeleton key, a screwdriver and wires all concealed in his left index finger.*
>
> *The novel* Backwards *changed Kryten's maximum speed to forty-two miles per hour (sixty-seven kilometers per hour).*

- **4000 Series GTi:** An upgraded version of Diva-Droid International's 4000 Series mechanoid. The GTi included such extras as realistic toes and a slide-back sunroof head. Camille, a shapeshifting Pleasure GELF, appeared to Kryten as a 4000 Series GTi model when the mechanoid rescued her from a marooned vessel **[T-SER4.1]**.

- **400X:** A model of genetically engineered refrigerators created during Earth's GELF boom. One such unit was exiled on Earth during the GELF War, after the planet had been renamed Garbage World. When Earth was ripped from its orbit and propelled into deep space, the 400X and two other GELFs—a fish-like creature named Arthur and a genetically engineered armchair—hibernated together while the planet froze over.

  Over the course of millennia, the planet's trajectory carried it near several stars, occasionally thawing it out and releasing its trapped inhabitants, including the GELFs. During one thaw, a young polymorph (a shapeshifting GELF) emerged from its cocoon and took the form of a cockroach to search for sustenance. It came upon the 400X and his two GELF friends searching for food, and fed on each of their emotions by changing its form to elicit strong responses. In the 400X's case, the polymorph changed into a repairman who chided him about his poor design faults, eliciting self-pity from the GELF.

  Lacking desperation, fear and self-pity, the three GELFs bickered as the polymorph slept off its meal and prepared for the Shadow Time, during which the planet refroze, trapping them all until the next thaw **[M-SMG1.13(c3)]**.

- **416614:** A code that Lister imagined using to break out of a secure visitor booth aboard *Red Dwarf* while infected with the luck virus. At the time, however, he was actually in a psychotropic trance, hooked up to an artificial-reality machine while his thoughts were being viewed by *Red Dwarf*'s Board of Inquiry **[T-SER8.2]**.

- **4172:** The crewmember number of Nirvanah Crane, a hologrammic officer aboard the holoship *Enlightenment* **[T-SER5.1]**.

- **4179:** The number of a luggage locker at a shuttle station on Mimas, in which Lister briefly lived before joining the Space Corps **[N-INF]**.

PREFIX **RL:** Real life **T-: Television Episodes** **SER:** Television series **IDW:** "Identity Within" **USA1:** Unaired U.S. pilot **USA2:** Unaired U.S. demo	**R-: *The Bodysnatcher Collection*** **SER:** Remastered episodes **BOD:** "Bodysnatcher" **DAD:** "Dad" **FTH:** "Lister's Father" **INF:** "Infinity Patrol" **END:** "The End" (original assembly) **N-: Novels** **INF:** *Infinity Welcomes Careful Drivers* **BTL:** *Better Than Life* **LST:** *Last Human*	**BCK:** *Backwards* **OMN:** *Red Dwarf Omnibus* **M-: Magazines** **SMG:** *Smegazine* **W-: Websites** **OFF:** Official website **NAN:** *Prelude to Nanarchy* **AND:** *Androids* **DIV:** Diva-Droid **DIB:** Duane Dibbley	**CRP:** Crapola **GEN:** Geneticon **LSR:** Leisure World Intl. **JMC:** Jupiter Mining Corporation **AIT:** *A.I. Today* **HOL:** HoloPoint **G-: Roleplaying Game** **RPG:** *Core Rulebook* **BIT:** *A.I. Screen Extra Bits* booklet **SOR:** *Series Sourcebook* **OTH:** Other RPG material

- ***42nd Street*:** A 1980 Broadway musical about a chorus girl's big break, with a book by Michael Stewart and Mark Bramble, lyrics by Al Dubin, and music by Harry Warren. The play debuted in London in 1984 **[RL]**. Rimmer told Nirvanah Crane that his desire to join the holoship *Enlightenment* was so strong he would have willingly tap-danced the title song to *42nd Street* while barefoot on a bed of molten lava and giving oral sex to a male orangutan with questionable hygiene **[T-SER5.1(d)]**.

- **44:** A number stenciled on the side of a container aboard *Starbug 1* **[T-SER3.2]**. Several such numbered crates were also stored near Airlock A, where the crew confronted Kryten's replacement, Hudzen 10 **[T-SER3.6]**.

- **4457:** The service or serial number of one of *Red Dwarf*'s skutters. The number appeared on the robot's front casing. This particular unit attended George McIntyre's funeral **[T-SER1.1]**. 4457 developed an affinity for John Wayne Western films, hung posters of the actor in its broom cupboard, collected *Film Fun* magazines, and occasionally dressed up to play "Cowboys and Indians" with its counterpart skutter, 129. It also belonged to the John Wayne Fan Club **[T-SER2.2]**.

  When Lister decided to enter stasis for the return trip to Earth, 4457 and 129 confronted him and produced a note begging him not to leave them alone with Rimmer **[T-SER1.2]**. Rimmer utilized this unit on numerous occasions since, as a hologram, he could not physically touch anything. Such duties included helping him study for the engineer's test **[T-SER1.3]** and assisting in the Medical Unit **[T-SER1.5]**.

  NOTE: *According to the commentary on* The Bodysnatcher Collection's *"What's New?" track, 4457 was part of effects builder Andy Bowman's BBC staff number.*

- **45:** A number on a jumpsuit that Kochanski stole while attempting to escape from the nanobot-built *Red Dwarf* **[T-SER8.2]**.

- **45 percent:** Kryten's dehydration level after a night of partying in the Officers' Club to honor his last day of service, according to a damage-control report that the mechanoid requested **[T-SER3.6]**.

- **45.265881:** The approximate square root of 2,049 **[RL]**. When Lister challenged Holly to calculate this number to prove he had an IQ of six thousand, the AI eventually responded with the correct answer, then pretended to be erased by Queeg, in order to teach the crew to treat him with more respect **[T-SER2.5]**.

- **4569:** The number of a locker at Mimas Spaceport. After double-crossing the Ganymedian Mafia during a drug deal, Dutch van Oestrogen hid the drugs and money in locker 4569, then used a body-swapping machine to commandeer the body of sex worker Trixie LaBouche so he could evade the mob. When he switched back, however, the damaged machine gave LaBouche several of his memories, including the locker number, enabling her to steal his stash **[M-SMG2.6(c4)]**.

- **46:** The service or serial number of a *Red Dwarf* skutter in a universe in which the sexes were reversed. This skutter—which was pink and dressed in frills and a bow—met up with skutter 129 from the prime *Red Dwarf*. The two robots eventually produced four small offspring: two blue and two pink **[T-SER2.6]**.

- **4691:** A number on a memo clipped to a console in *Red Dwarf*'s Drive Room **[T-SER1]**.

  NOTE: *This appeared on the Series I DVDs' menu screen. Selecting it on the first disc, and then punching in the same number on a faux keypad, accessed an Easter egg consisting of animated versions of Rob Grant, Doug Naylor and Ed Bye commenting on the episode "Future Echoes." It also appeared on the bonus feature disc, but was not selectable.*

- **4-9-5, 3-7-2:** The coordinates of a wormhole found by the crew of *Starbug 1*. Rimmer, trapped in a seeding ship escape pod, traveled through the anomaly to an S-3 planet located on the other side. Marooned on the planet for six centuries due to the wormhole's time-dilation effect, Rimmer used the pod's supplies to terraform the planet and create clones of himself, who built a civilization known as Rimmerworld **[T-SER6.5]**.

- **4 million:** The amount of money Rimmer won in a lottery, according to a letter he received while incarcerated in *Red*

Dwarf's brig **[T-SER8.5]**.

NOTE: The currency of his winnings is unknown.

- **4 percent:** The score that *Red Dwarf*'s crew, while trapped in a despair squid hallucination, were told they had achieved playing the *Red Dwarf* total-immersion video game **[T-SER5.6]**.

- **4X2C:** A password used to unlock a previously inaccessible file in Kryten's CPU. Once the file was accessed, Kryten learned that he was a line of mechanoids specifically designed by Professor Mamet to mimic the most annoying traits of her ex-fiancé, John Warburton, who had stood her up at the altar. These traits included being a pompous, ridiculous-looking, overbearing, short-tempered buffoon. Also part of the design was the installation of a negadrive that stored negative emotions, occasionally blowing apart the mechanoid's head when full, in order to emulate Warburton's tendency to lose his head when angry **[T-SER7.6]**.

  NOTE: The password is an anagram of Kryten's serial number (2X4C).

- **4 years, 3 months:** The stopping distance of a craft traveling at half the speed of light, according to a pilot's test Kryten took aboard *Starbug 1* **[T-SER3.1]**.

- **'52:** The year of several bottles of wine featured on the cooking program *Can't Smeg, Won't Smeg*, starring Ainsley Harriott. The wine was made from urine recyc **[T-SER4(b)]**.

- **53:** The number of doors between the crew and *Red Dwarf*'s Science Room during a power failure aboard the mining ship, which resulted when Holly shut down after an intelligence compression procedure went awry. The crew used Kryten as a battering ram to get to the Science Room in order to ascertain the problem, since the doors had become locked during the outage **[T-SER4.4]**.

- **5341 by 6163:** The coordinates of a large meteor that bore down on *Starbug 1* as the crew traversed an asteroid belt to catch up with the stolen *Red Dwarf* **[T-SER6.1]**.

- **5517/W13 alpha-sim modem:** A computer chip that Holly gave Kryten as a gift during his last-day party in *Red Dwarf*'s Officers' Club. The chip served as an interface circuit, with a built-in 599XRDP **[T-SER3.6]**.

  NOTE: The DVD captions misidentified it as a 5517/W30.

- **557:** The number of years Rimmer spent in a prison on Rimmerworld after his clones turned against him **[T-SER6.5]**.

- **5589:** A number printed on a console in *Starbug 1*'s Medical Bay **[T-SER7.5]**.

- **56:** The service or serial number of an offspring of *Red Dwarf* skutter 129 and an alternate-reality skutter known as 46 **[T-SER2.6]**.

- **571:** A code used aboard the American mining ship *Red Dwarf* to alert technicians to a shortage of weenies in the Officer's Mess **[T-USA1]**.

- **57429 985: KF 80:** An identifier printed on a door aboard the SS *Manny Celeste,* a Space Corps derelict found by the crew of the nanobot-rebuilt *Red Dwarf.* Behind the door, Lister's team discovered a fellow Canary battalion that had been stuck in time by a time wand **[T-SER8.6]**.

- **5770:** A number printed on the label of a generic beer can in *Red Dwarf*'s ship's stores. This particular can was present in the disco room when Petersen, Chen, Selby and Lister enjoyed a drinking game prior to the cadmium II disaster **[T-SER1.2]**.

- **579:** The model number of the eyeballs used in the optical system of Kryten 4000 Series mechanoids, which included automatic 15F-stop corneas **[T-SER4.1]**.

- **58 minutes:** The amount of life that Lister gained after his arm was amputated in an attempt to rid his body of the Epideme virus **[T-SER7.7]**.

- **5-9-7:** A bearing that Lister requested when a rogue simulant vessel attacked *Starbug 1* **[T-SER7.6]**.

- **599XRDP:** A component built into the 5517/W13 alpha-sim modem that Holly gave Kryten during the mechanoid's last-day party in the Officers' Club **[T-SER3.6]**.

- **5A:** A cell block in the Tank, *Red Dwarf*'s brig on Floor 13 **[B-RD8]**.

  NOTE: *This designation was visible in concept art included in the book* Red Dwarf VIII.

- **5th Dimension, The:** A popular American musical group, originally called The Hi Fi's **[RL]**. After Holly displaced *Red Dwarf* using his newly invented Holly Hop Drive, the AI ascertained that instead of traveling through space, the crew had traveled into the Fifth Dimension. Lister asked if he meant the band that had recorded "Baby I Want Your Love Thing," a song that had made it to sixth place on the charts **[T-SER2.6]**.

  NOTE: *The 5th Dimension never recorded such a song, though many of the group's hits did contain "love" in the titles.*

- **6:** Holly's IQ rating, according to Queeg, *Red Dwarf*'s imaginary backup computer **[T-SER2.5]**.

- **6:** The service or serial number of an offspring of *Red Dwarf* skutter 129 and an alternate-reality skutter known as 46 **[T-SER2.6]**.

- **6,000:** Holly's supposed IQ, which he likened to that of six thousand physical education teachers **[T-SER1.2]** or twelve thousand car-park attendants **[T-SER2.4]**.

- **6000 Series:** A model of mechanoid featuring Q47 twin frontal mounts **[T-SER9(b)]**.

  NOTE: *This was mentioned in a PBS announcement for* Red Dwarf.

- **61, 62, 64, 65:** Numbers painted on several pieces of equipment on *Red Dwarf*'s maintenance decks **[T-SER3.4]**.

- **6.47 minutes:** The amount of time that Rimmer once took to run 300 meters (984 feet) through the hallways of *Red Dwarf* **[T-SER1.2]**.

- **658102/78:** A number on a sign for Dallas Electric, circa 1966, in an alternate timeline created by the temporal-traveling crew of *Starbug 1*. The crew passed this sign, located near 84th Avenue in Dallas, Texas, while searching for clues to the population's disappearance **[T-SER7.1]**.

- **66:** A number stenciled on a container aboard *Starbug 1* **[T-SER4.1]**.

- **67 percent:** The increase in "weaseliness" that Kryten detected upon encountering Arnold Rimmer disguised as Ace **[T-SER7.2]**.

- **670:** A number printed on the cover of a car that the *Red Dwarf* crew imagined while trapped in a despair squid hallucination. The vehicle was parked in Bay 46 of Leisure World International's long-term parking lot, in the spot next to Sebastian Doyle's limousine **[T-SER5.6]**.

- **67 minutes:** Kryten's remaining lifespan, as calculated by his CPU after an accident on a psi-moon left him severely damaged. This figure took into account the fact that *Starbug*'s fuel tanks were predicted to explode in just over an hour **[T-SER5.3]**.

- **68:** The initial IQ rating that Holly achieved following an experimental intelligence compression procedure. After a few seconds, however, her IQ soared past the intended six thousand rating, levelling out at 12,368 **[T-SER4.4]**.

- **69th:** A street in a seedy area of Mimas known as Shagtown. The Hotel Paradiso was located on the corner of Copulation and 69th **[M-SMG2.3(c4)]**.

- **7:** A number with which Holly appeared to have trouble. While counting down to the Holly Hop Drive's activation, the AI skipped over seven, to the crew's dismay, since any error in the more than thirteen billion calculations necessary to hop could prove disastrous **[T-SER2.6]**.

- **7:** A number on the helmet of a zero-gee football player on a poster in Lister's quarters **[M-SMG1.6(c2)]**.

- **70773:** A number assigned to Project *Wildfire*, a program originally intended to break the light barrier, developed by the Space Corps R&D team on Europa in one of Ace Rimmer's universes **[N-BCK]**.

- **71:** A number on one of *Red Dwarf*'s service lifts **[M-SMG1.1(c1)]**.

- **724946:** Jake Bullet's badge number in a universe in which he became the first robot police officer to serve in the NYNYPD **[M-SMG1.11(c4)]**.

- **72 percent:** The initial overall damage assessment of Kryten's body, as calculated by his CPU after an eruption on a psi-moon nearly destroyed him and *Starbug 1* **[T-SER5.3]**.

- **76:** A number worn by a zero-gee football player on a poster in Lister's bunk **[T-SER1.1(d)]**.

- **78:** A number on one of *Red Dwarf*'s service lifts **[M-SMG1.1(c1)]**.

- **793:** The number of consecutive chess games that Holly lost to Talkie Toaster before considering undergoing intelligence compression to restore his full IQ rating **[N-BTL]**.

- **7th Death Ring of Rhaagbthammar:** A travel destination highlighted in an issue of *JMC Traveller*. An article in the magazine detailed seventy-eight essentials for such a trip **[T-SER10.5]**.

- **8:** A number printed on a panel in the neutral area of the penal station Justice World **[T-SER4.3]**.

- **8:** The number of lemons required to make a power source capable of powering the returner remote of a rejuvenation shower, which accidentally transported the *Red Dwarf* crew back to Earth in 23 A.D. After traveling from Britain to India, they finally found a vendor selling lemons. Though they initially requested eight of the fruit, they changed it to an even ten **[T-SER10.3]**.

- **80 clicks:** The distance a shuttle would need to be from *Red Dwarf* in order to clear the blast radius in the event of a cataclysmic explosion caused by a meltdown of the ship's engine core **[T-SER5.5]**.

- **80 percent:** The updated overall damage assessment of Kryten's body, as calculated by his CPU after an eruption on a psi-moon nearly destroyed him and *Starbug 1*. This also updated his condition status to Magenta **[T-SER5.3]**.

- **8327:** The issue number of a *JMC Traveller* magazine containing a story about Jupiter Mining Corp. employee Reece King, as well as another article discussing seventy-eight essentials for a trip to the 7th Death Ring of Rhaagbthammar. The issue included an advertisement for *Red Dwarf* on the back cover. Lister thumbed through this issue while feeling depressed about the fate of the human species **[T-SER10.5]**.

- **84:** The number of reports that Rimmer filed against Lister for general insubordination aboard *Red Dwarf*, according to Frank Todhunter, who found the reports among George McIntyre's effects **[T-SER1.1]**.

- **84:** The number of days that Rimmer intended to keep Lister, Kryten and Cat in quarantine after their return from a viral research station, where Hildegarde Lanstrom exposed them to a holovirus. That timeframe increased to ten years after Rimmer contracted the virus himself and went insane **[T-SER5.4]**.

- **8,500:** The amount of tax money that Rimmer owed Outland Revenue at the time of *Red Dwarf*'s cadmium II disaster **[T-SER2.2]**.

  ***NOTE:** The currency of his debt is unknown.*

- **876.3/16:** A section of the treaty signed by the United Republic of GELF States, which specified that any ship violating Blerios air space must submit to a judiciary from the Blerion High Council **[N-LST]**.

- **88:** A number stenciled on the side of a container aboard *Starbug 1* **[T-SER4.5]**.

- **882 FOP:** The license plate number of a Jaguar sports car that Rimmer conjured up as his transportation of choice while playing the total-immersion video game *Better Than Life* **[T-SER2.2]**.

- **8870t6:** A code printed on a computer slug on which the *Red Dwarf* crew transferred into *Starbug 1*'s navicomp Holly's plan to plug a white hole **[T-SER4.4]**.

  ***NOTE:** When first seen, the code was reversed due to the scene being reversed and flipped. The second appearance was normal.*

- **8 months:** The amount of time that Lister copied from his own memories into Rimmer's as a deathday present, via *Red Dwarf*'s hologram simulation suite. This span of time included a love affair with Lise Yates **[T-SER2.3]**.

- **9:** A number printed on a panel in the neutral area of the penal station Justice World **[T-SER4.3]**.

- **9:** The age at which Rimmer's generosity died, according to a tombstone erected on a psi-moon modeled after his psyche **[T-SER5.3]**.

- **9:** The uniform number of Ray Rimmer, captain of the Smegchester Rovers, an association football team in the universe known as Alternative 6829/B **[M-SMG1.8(c4)]**.

- **90:** A number stenciled on a storage container outside the Officers' Quarters that Lister and Rimmer shared aboard *Red Dwarf* **[T-SER3.3]**.

- **9000 SMG:** A model of *Blue Midget* shuttlecraft that had alloy feet, power striding, arc headlamps and an optional MP3 player **[X-CAL]**.

- **90445:** A number printed on a console in *Red Dwarf*'s Drive Room, next to a monitor used by Holly **[T-SER1.4]**.

- **911-R-Us:** A medical company mentioned on the television soap opera *Androids*. Para-mechs from this firm rushed to the scene when a car containing the characters Gary and Kelly exploded **[M-SMG2.2(c3)]**.

- **91 percent:** Kryten's embarrassment factor following a night of partying in the Officers' Club to honor his last day of service, according to a damage-control report that the mechanoid requested **[T-SER3.6]**.

- **92 degrees:** The temperature inside *Starbug 1* after the ship's heating system malfunctioned **[T-SER7.4]**.

- **9,328 years:** The sentence that the penal station Justice World imposed on Rimmer after a mind probe detected the guilt he felt regarding the deaths of the *Red Dwarf* crew. The station's computer pronounced a mandatory sentence of eight years per count in the deaths of the 1,167 crewmembers **[T-SER4.3]**.

  NOTE: *The computer's computation prowess must have degraded over the millennia, since 1,167 times 8 equals 9,336, not 9,328.*

- **93.72 percent:** The compatibility factor that Kryten calculated between him and Camille after rescuing her from a doomed planet, erring due to his failure to carry the three **[T-SER4.1]**.

- **93.75 percent:** The more precise compatibility factor that Camille calculated between her and Kryten after taking the form of a 4000 Series mechanoid **[T-SER4.1]**.

- **9:47 AM:** The ship's time when Rimmer demanded a clean uniform and a haircut, interrupting Holly's preparations to bring *Red Dwarf* to lightspeed **[T-SER1.2]**.

- **96-6:** A number painted on *Red Dwarf*'s outer hull **[T-SER9.1]**.

- **96 percent:** Rimmer's chance of failure during a test against Nirvanah Crane to become a crewmember aboard the holoship *Enlightenment* **[T-SER5.1]**.

- **9780434003709:** The number of a bar code Kryten created during his first attempt at drawing. The illustration was supposed to depict Lister **[B-LOG]**.

  NOTE: *The bar code in Kryten's artwork, featured in* Red Dwarf Log No. 1996*, was identical to one the mechanoid drew of Leonardo da Vinci's* La Gioconda (Mona Lisa)*, as well as another portraying a landscape and a third depicting what he wanted for Christmas. In actuality, the bar code and number were taken from the book's own back cover.*

- **97 minutes:** The amount of time that Lister remained enrolled in Art College before dropping out due to the curriculum's early afternoon classes **[T-SER2.1]**.

- **98:** The age at which Lister—after altering history by using a timeslide to become the inventor of the Tension Sheet—perished in an airplane crash, caused by his losing control of the craft while making love to his fourteenth wife. This timeline was nullified when Rimmer tried to change history so that *he* created the Tension Sheet, but instead restored its original inventor, Fred Holden **[T-SER3.5]**.

  NOTE: *The DVD captions for the Czech Republic version of the series inexplicably changed the reference to Lister's fourteenth wife to "his fourteen-year-old wife."*

- **9,800 percent:** The annual percentage rate assigned to a loan that George McIntyre received from the Golden Assurance Friendly and Caring Loan Society to pay off a debt incurred from playing Toot **[N-INF]**.

- **9H7M:** A middle name that Kryten wished he had been given instead of 2X4B **[X-GEK]**.

ACKERMAN, WARDEN ("NICEY")

- **A:** A letter stenciled on the floor in front of *Red Dwarf*'s Airlock A **[T-SER3.6]**.

- **A:** A letter stenciled on a pillar supporting the domed station in which Thomas Allman resided **[T-SER5.2]**.

- **A:** A letter stenciled on a wall in one of *Red Dwarf*'s corridors **[M-SMG1.3(c1)]**.

- **A1:** A code printed on a machine with which Lister swapped his brain pattern with that of Executive Officer Carole Brown in order to halt *Red Dwarf*'s auto-destruct sequence **[T-SER3.4]**.

- **A105:** A sequence printed on a label on a console in *Midget 3*'s cockpit **[T-SER8.3]**.

- **A15 laser pistol:** A small firearm produced by Bloodlust Arms and distributed via Crapola Inc.'s annual *SCABBY* catalog. The weapon utilized patented Fire and Forget technology and had a range of 80 meters (262 feet) **[G-RPG]**.

- **A2:** A sequence printed on a console label in the "low" *Red Dwarf*'s Science Lab **[T-SER5.5]**.

- **A30 laser cannon:** A large firearm produced by Bloodlust Arms and distributed via Crapola Inc.'s annual *SCABBY* catalog. The weapon utilized patented Fire and Forget technology and had a range of 1 kilometer (0.62 mile) **[G-RPG]**.

- **A4:** A code printed on a device with which Lister tracked a vessel approaching *Red Dwarf,* aboard which the crew discovered a DNA-modifying machine **[T-SER4.2(d)]**.

- **AA:** *See* Automobile Association (AA)

- **aardbear:** A genetically engineered creature—a mix between an aardvark and bear—developed by inebriated scientists **[B-EVR]**.

- **Aaron, Uncle:** A relative of Jesus of Caesarea, who traveled with Jesus from Albion (later known as Great Britain) to India circa 23 A.D., acting as his protector as they fled Roman soldiers. When the centurions caught up with them, Aaron attempted to slow them down to allow his nephew to escape, but was idly tossed aside **[T-SER10.3]**.

- **AAS:** *See Androids* Appreciation Society (AAS)

- **AB 12:** A tag on a keyboard console in *Red Dwarf*'s Drive Room **[T-SER1.1]**.

- **AB 37:** A tag on a keyboard console in *Red Dwarf*'s Drive Room **[T-SER1.1]**.

- **"Aba Daba Daba":** A song, also known as "Aba Daba Honeymoon," written in 1914 by Arthur Fields and Walter Donovan and first performed by Collins & Harlan. Hoagy Carmichael recorded a version of the song in 1951 **[RL]**. While trapped in an addictive version of *Better Than Life*, Rimmer hired an eighty-piece jazz band to play Carmichael's version **[N-BTL]**.

  NOTE: *The novel misspelled the song's title as "Abba Dabba Dabba."*

- **Abandon Ship:** A message displayed on a food dispenser Lister used to order a milk shake and a Crispy Bar. The dispenser, having been rewired by a crazed skutter, was linked to *Red Dwarf*'s auto-destruct system, which was activated by Lister's order. Fortunately for the crew, Holly had removed the explosive linked to the system years prior—a fact she neglected to share until the countdown timer reached zero **[T-SER3.4]**.

- **ABBA:** A twentieth-century Swedish pop group, known for such songs as "Dancing Queen" and "Take a Chance on Me" **[RL]**. Cat, as Duane Dibbley, enjoyed the music of such groups as ABBA, The Carpenters and The Bay City Rollers **[M-SMG2.2(a)]**.

- **"Abide With Me":** A Christian hymn written by Henry Francis Lyte in 1847 **[RL]**. Holly suggested hiring a dance band to play "Abide With Me" while *Starbug 1* sank following a collision with Ace Rimmer's spacecraft **[T-SER4.5]**.

  NOTE: *This was presumably a reference to the RMS* Titanic, *the band of which valiantly continued playing music while the passenger liner sank. In* Titanic*'s case, the song popularly attributed to the band was "Nearer My God to Thee."*

- **A Bit of the Other:** One of seven diminutive rainforest dwellers known as the Ionian Ecommandoes, who lived in the jungles of Io on the television soap opera *Androids*. He and his comrades nursed Karstares back to health **[M-SMG2.5(c5)]**, after Karstares' plane crashed due to sabotage by his son Jaysee **[M-SMG1.14(c3)]**. Grateful for their help, Karstares became the Green Knight, the rainforest's protector, and fought alongside the Ecommandoes against Jaysee's ecologically harmful company **[M-SMG2.5(c5)]**. A Bit of the Other died during a firefight between Jaysee and his foes **[M-SMG2.8(c2)]**.

  NOTE: *This character resembled one of Disney's Seven Dwarfs. All of the Ecommandoes' names were slang for sex.*

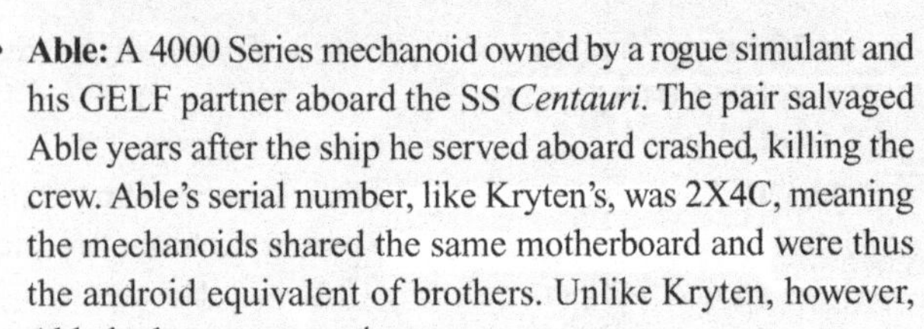

- **Able:** A 4000 Series mechanoid owned by a rogue simulant and his GELF partner aboard the SS *Centauri*. The pair salvaged Able years after the ship he served aboard crashed, killing the crew. Able's serial number, like Kryten's, was 2X4C, meaning the mechanoids shared the same motherboard and were thus the android equivalent of brothers. Unlike Kryten, however, Able had a green exterior.

  Able turned to outrozone, a highly addictive compound, when the simulant activated a password-protected datafile in Able's memory banks that contained information about the mechanoid's creator, Professor Mamet, and the nature of Able's existence. Continuous use of outrozone over the years took its toll on the mechanoid, whose circuits became corroded, causing delays in his response time.

  Years later, the *Starbug 1* crew boarded the *Centauri* searching for spare heads for Kryten, who had blown out his remaining spares due to a full negadrive. The simulant stalled for time as his GELF partner looted *Starbug*, stealing Kryten's body in the process. Able was tasked with fixing his fellow mech, and the two found their way back to *Starbug 1*, with the simulant craft in pursuit.

  The crew hid in an asteroid belt, hoping the simulant would give up the chase, but Able accidently activated *Starbug*'s systems, enabling the simulant to detect them and attack. To make amends, Able took Kryten's negadrive and launched himself in an escape pod toward the enemy craft, focusing the negadrive's energy through the pod's thrusters and enveloping the simulant's ship in negative emotions, causing him to destroy his own vessel. This plan came at a price, though, as Able died during the explosion **[T-SER7.6]**.

- **Aboriginoid:** A type of android indigenous to Australia **[M-SMG1.8(c2)]**.

- **Abort Sequence X-1-X:** The command code used by *Red Dwarf*'s captain or senior officers to abort the auto-destruct sequence. Lister, infused with Executive Officer Carole Brown's consciousness, tried to use this code to stop the ship from self-destructing, but without success **[T-SER3.4]**.

- **Academy, the:** An officer's training school that Rimmer had always wanted to attend, but never did **[T-SER1.1]**. Rimmer claimed his father never sent him there because he could not afford it **[T-SER1.6]**.

- **Acapulco:** A popular Mexican port city known for its tropical climate and tourism **[RL]**. Rimmer had a photograph of a female-only naturist beach on Acapulco, which he hoped to treat with a mutated developing fluid that would allow him to enter the scene **[T-SER3.5]**.

- **Accident Report Assessment Unit:** A department aboard *Red Dwarf* consisting solely of Rimmer, which he put himself in charge of following the cadmium II disaster. Rimmer declared that accident report forms had to be submitted to the unit care of the Health and Safety Executive—which he also named himself **[T-SER10.4]**.

- **Ace:** A nickname Rimmer claimed to have had in school, though no one used it. During a rescue mission to save three female officers of the crashed ship *Nova 5*, Rimmer urged Lister not to insult him in front of them, suggesting he instead use the more masculine nickname while in their company. When the crew realized the "survivors" had been dead for millennia, Lister honored Rimmer's request by mockingly calling him "Ace" **[T-SER2.1]**.

- **Acehole:** A nickname that Lister quipped was likely Rimmer's moniker in school, rather than "Ace" **[T-SER2.1]**.

- **"Achy Breaky Heart":** A country song recorded by Billy Ray Cyrus in 1992 **[RL]**. In his *Space Corps Survival Manual*, Colonel Mike O'Hagan suggested singing a few verses of this tune to keep up the spirits of crash survivors **[B-SUR]**.

- **Ackenback:** A crewmember aboard *Red Dwarf* who died during the cadmium II disaster. Rimmer called Ackenback's name during a roll call to ascertain the extent of the casualties, knowing full well that everyone except for Lister had died **[R-BOD]**.

  ***NOTE:** It is unknown whether the nanobots resurrected Ackenback in Series VIII.*

- **Ackerman, Warden ("Nicey"):** The prison governor of Floor 13, *Red Dwarf*'s classified brig **[T-SER8.4]**. Ackerman grew up on Callisto with his parents **[W-OFF]**. His mother possibly worked for the Inland Revenue, while his father, a traffic warden **[T-SER8(b)]**, was an obese man whose poor health

PREFIX
RL: Real life

T-: Television Episodes
- **SER:** Television series
- **IDW:** "Identity Within"
- **USA1:** Unaired U.S. pilot
- **USA2:** Unaired U.S. demo

R-: *The Bodysnatcher Collection*
- **SER:** Remastered episodes
- **BOD:** "Bodysnatcher"
- **DAD:** "Dad"
- **FTH:** "Lister's Father"
- **INF:** "Infinity Patrol"
- **END:** "The End" (original assembly)

N-: Novels
- **INF:** *Infinity Welcomes Careful Drivers*
- **BTL:** *Better Than Life*
- **LST:** *Last Human*
- **BCK:** *Backwards*
- **OMN:** *Red Dwarf Omnibus*

M-: Magazines
- **SMG:** *Smegazine*

W-: Websites
- **OFF:** Official website
- **NAN:** *Prelude to Nanarchy*
- **AND:** *Androids*
- **DIV:** Diva-Droid
- **DIB:** Duane Dibbley
- **CRP:** Crapola
- **GEN:** Geneticon
- **LSR:** Leisure World Intl.
- **JMC:** Jupiter Mining Corporation
- **AIT:** *A.I. Today*
- **HOL:** HoloPoint

G-: Roleplaying Game
- **RPG:** *Core Rulebook*
- **BIT:** *A.I. Screen Extra Bits* booklet
- **SOR:** *Series Sourcebook*
- **OTH:** Other RPG material

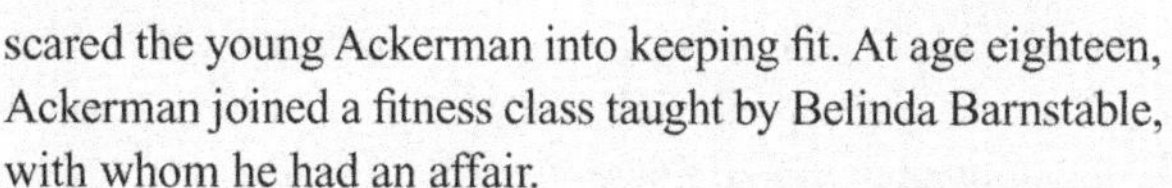

scared the young Ackerman into keeping fit. At age eighteen, Ackerman joined a fitness class taught by Belinda Barnstable, with whom he had an affair.

Ackerman signed up with the Space Corps while taking refuge in a recruitment office after Barnestable's husband discovered their relationship. Certified in law and self-defense, he first served aboard a prison transport, ferrying deranged simulants, but fled in a cryogenic escape pod after being caught having sex with the first mate's girlfriend. He then accepted a job at the penal colony Adelphi 12, taking a temporary position aboard *Red Dwarf* in order to gain transport to that facility **[W-OFF]**. On *Red Dwarf*, he was placed in charge of the Canaries, an elite group of prisoners whose purpose was to enter dangerous and hazardous environments, ascertain the threat level and report back to their superiors **[T-SER8.4]**.

Ackerman never arrived at Adelphi 12, however, due to a cadmium II accident that killed most of *Red Dwarf*'s complement **[W-OFF]**. Three million years later, nanobots resurrected him, along with the rest of the crew **[T-SER8.3]**.

The warden suffered from asthma, which enabled Lister and Rimmer to pull a prank involving his inhaler and a capsule of Sodium Pentothal (a barbiturate sometimes used as a truth serum). After taking a puff, Ackerman admitted he was having an affair with the science officer's wife and was late for work due to the extra time it took to change out of his Batman outfit **[T-SER8.6]**.

Ackerman also had a glass left eye, which was once stolen during a mugging on D Wing days before his date with Patricia Carling, but was returned in time. Lister trashed Ackerman's room while he was on the date, thinking the quarters belonged to Kochanski's boyfriend. Upon learning he had been set up by Krytie TV, Lister panicked and cleaned the room before Ackerman returned **[T-SER8.5]**.

According to the warden, he received his nickname, "Nicey," because of his sunny disposition, which he shared with inmates less fortunate than he **[T-SER8.6]**. He owned a vivarium, as well as an extremely large arsenal of weapons, complete with several crossbows **[T-SER8(b)]**.

> ***NOTE:*** Red Dwarf—The Roleplaying Game *spelled the warden's name as Akerman, and gave him the title of Governor.*
>
> *The prison transport was implied to be the same one from which Lister and company found a cryogenic escape pod containing a simulant in episode 4.3 ("Justice"). An interview on the official site—with the simulant himself—confirmed this to be the case.*
>
> *Since Ackerman had a copy of the book* Science and Health With Key to the Scriptures *(the central text of the Christian Science religion) in his quarters, that may indicate he was a member of that faith. Information labeled **[T-SER8(b)]** was culled from an interview with actor, Graham McTavish, included in the Series VIII DVD set, and may not be considered official.*

- **Ackroyd, Augustus:** The founder of Diva-Droid International. Originally a robotics hobbyist and hairdresser, Ackroyd built his company up from developing interactive novelty items with Crapola Inc. to supplying up to a seventh of all droids serving on starships, creating a billion-pound industry by the time of his passing at the age of ninety-four **[W-DIV]**.

- **Acme:** A company that produced a variety of novelty items, including Lister's robotic fish, Lennon and McCartney **[M-SMG1.4(c2)]**. The firm also manufactured grout guns for JMC probe ships **[X-XVD]**.

  > ***NOTE:*** *Numerous* Looney Tunes *cartoons featuring Wile E. Coyote, Bugs Bunny and other characters have featured gadgets and novelty items supplied by the fictional Acme Corp.*

- **Acme Cleaning Company:** A business in an alternate dimension. Jake Bullet worked for Acme prior to becoming a police officer in the NYNYPD **[M-SMG1.7(a)]**.

- **Act 21:** A law enacted by the Space Federation that illegalized the use of other crewmembers' confidential files for one's own gain. When nanobots rebuilt *Red Dwarf* and resurrected its crew, the ship's Board of Inquiry found Lister, Rimmer, Kryten, Cat, Kochanski and Holly guilty of contravening Act 21, and sentenced them to two years in the Tank, the ship's classified brig **[T-SER8.3]**.

- ***Action*:** A magazine that Lister enjoyed reading **[M-SMG1.11(c2)]**.

B-: Books
- **PRG:** *Red Dwarf Programme Guide*
- **SUR:** *Red Dwarf Space Corps Survival Manual*
- **PRM:** *Primordial Soup*
- **SOS:** *Son of Soup*
- **SCE:** *Scenes from the Dwarf*
- **LOG:** *Red Dwarf Log No. 1996*
- **RD8:** *Red Dwarf VIII*
- **EVR:** *The Log: A Dwarfer's Guide to Everything*

X-: Misc.
- **PRO:** Promotional materials, videos, etc.
- **PST:** Posters at DJ XVII (2013)
- **CAL:** 2008 calendar
- **RNG:** Cell phone ringtones
- **MOB:** Mobisode ("Red Christmas")
- **CIN:** *Children in Need* sketch
- **GEK:** *Geek Week* intros by Kryten
- **TNG:** "Tongue-Tied" video
- **XMS:** Bill Pearson's Christmas special pitch script
- **XVD:** Bill Pearson's Christmas special pitch video
- **OTH:** Other *Red Dwarf* appearances

SUFFIX
DVD:
- **(d)** – Deleted scene
- **(o)** – Outtake
- **(b)** – Bonus DVD material (other)
- **(e)** – Extended version

SMEGAZINES:
- **(c)** – Comic
- **(a)** – Article

OTHER:
- **(s)** – Early/unused script draft
- **(s1)** – Alternate version of script

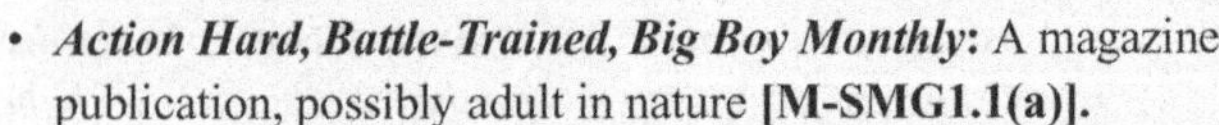

- ***Action Hard, Battle-Trained, Big Boy Monthly*:** A magazine publication, possibly adult in nature **[M-SMG1.1(a)]**.

- **Action Man:** An action figure sold in Europe as a licensed copy of the American line of G.I. Joe figures **[RL]**. Lister described Kryten's prospects of romance with a Marilyn Monroe droid as unlikely, given the mechanoid's resemblance to Action Man in his lower region—little more than plastic underpants and a trademark **[T-SER3.6]**.

- **Action Man:** A genetically engineered superhero in the universe known as Alternative 2X13/L, and that reality's analog to Lister. Wielding guns and explosives and wearing a smiley-face T-shirt, Action Man was a member of the Liberty League, tasked with protecting the city of Smegopolis. In 2315, as Action Man attempted to stop the League's old nemeses, the Conspirator and the Penguin, from robbing the First National Bank, Ace Rimmer joined the fight posing as Action Man's partner, Super-Ace **[M-SMG2.1(c3)]**.

  NOTE: Action Man was loosely based on the Comedian, a character in DC Comics' Watchmen, *by Alan Moore.*

- ***Actual Reality Cheats and Tricks*:** A book containing cheats for artificial-reality games. While playing a medieval-themed game, Lister used the book to tilt the odds in his favor in order to seduce the Queen of Camelot. The cheat "steedcheat" reduced a jousting opponent's horse to a donkey, while "chastitycheat" unlocked the queen's chastity belt **[T-SER7.2]**.

- **Addams Family, the:** *See* Osmonds, the

- **Additional 001:** Kryten's registration code aboard *Red Dwarf*. After the Inquisitor erased him from history, the mechanoid could no longer use this code to open the ship's doors **[T-SER5.2]**.

- **A Deck:** A level aboard *Red Dwarf*. After rescuing the shapeshifting Pleasure GELF Camille, Kryten prepared A Deck's penthouse suite for use as her quarters **[T-SER4.1]**.

- **Adelphi 12:** A penal colony that *Red Dwarf* was scheduled to visit prior to the cadmium II disaster. At the time of the accident, the mining ship was transporting four hundred inmates to Adelphi 12 in its brig, the Tank **[T-SER8.1]**. Warden Ackerman accepted a job at the colony, taking a temporary position aboard *Red Dwarf* in order to gain transport to the facility, but never arrived due to the accident **[W-OFF]**.

- **Admin level:** An elevated section of the *Red Dwarf*'s Drive Room, containing the captain's office **[N-INF]**.

- **admiral:** The rank that Rimmer's subconscious mind assumed in the total-immersion video game *Better Than Life*. At a restaurant in the game, a young officer approached Admiral Rimmer, requesting his presence for port and cigars on behalf of Field Marshall Clifton **[T-SER2.2]**.

- **Admiral Nelson telescope:** A telescopic spyglass owned by Admiral Horatio Nelson, which he reportedly held up to his blind eye in defiance of orders to retreat. In 1985, a company called Haverhills began offering high-end collectible replicas called Admiral Nelson's Brass Telescopes **[RL]**.

  Rimmer's Uncle Frank gave him an Admiral Nelson telescope as a gift, but he sold it while serving aboard *Red Dwarf*, in order to pay Lister for a Jammie Dodger. Unbeknownst to him, however, Lister had found the biscuit between the cushions of a sofa in the Officers' Club, and had cleaned it off with an oily rag **[T-SER9.2(d)]**.

- **Adrienne:** An Earth dressmaker who appeared in Rimmer's fantasy world in an addictive version of *Better Than Life*. Rimmer imagined being married to Brazilian supermodel Juanita Chicata, who had a dress made especially for her by Adrienne. Upon seeing the dress, which consisted only of a red belt and a glass brassiere containing live goldfish, Rimmer forbade her to wear it—which she did anyway **[N-INF]**.

- **Advanced Mental Engineering:** A degree program offered at Caltech, circa the twenty-second century. Rimmer informed Lister he'd need such a degree to fix Kryten's programming issues, which stemmed from the robot's inability to cope with the loss of his *Nova 5* crewmates **[N-INF]**.

- **advanced mutual compatibility on the basis of a primary initial ident:** The mechanoid term for "love at first sight." Camille, a Pleasure GELF marooned on a doomed planet,

PREFIX
RL: Real life

T-: Television Episodes
SER: Television series
IDW: "Identity Within"
USA1: Unaired U.S. pilot
USA2: Unaired U.S. demo

R-: *The Bodysnatcher Collection*
SER: Remastered episodes
BOD: "Bodysnatcher"
DAD: "Dad"
FTH: "Lister's Father"
INF: "Infinity Patrol"
END: "The End" (original assembly)

N-: Novels
INF: *Infinity Welcomes Careful Drivers*
BTL: *Better Than Life*
LST: *Last Human*
BCK: *Backwards*
OMN: *Red Dwarf Omnibus*

M-: Magazines
SMG: *Smegazine*

W-: Websites
OFF: Official website
NAN: *Prelude to Nanarchy*
AND: *Androids*
DIV: Diva-Droid
DIB: Duane Dibbley

CRP: Crapola
GEN: Geneticon
LSR: Leisure World Intl.
JMC: Jupiter Mining Corporation
AIT: *A.I. Today*
HOL: HoloPoint

G-: Roleplaying Game
RPG: *Core Rulebook*
BIT: *A.I. Screen Extra Bits* booklet
SOR: *Series Sourcebook*
OTH: Other RPG material

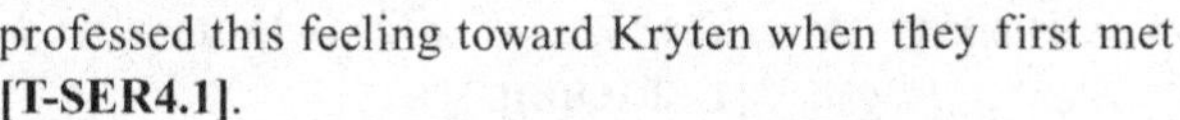

professed this feeling toward Kryten when they first met **[T-SER4.1]**.

- **advocaat:** A Dutch liqueur made with brandy, sugar and eggs **[RL]**. Advocaat was one of two alcoholic beverages aboard *Starbug 1* to survive an attack by a future version of the crew. The other, to Lister's dismay, was Cinzano Bianco **[T-SER7.1]**.

- ***Aeneid*, the:** A Latin epic poem written by Virgil in the first century B.C., about the legendary travels and battles of Trojan soldier Aeneas **[RL]**. Lister owned a comic book adaptation of the *Aeneid* **[T-SER5.2]**.

- **Aerial Smog Sublimation (ASS):** A type of exhaust system built into the MkII Raketenhosen (Rocket Pants) of the Reich army on War World **[G-BIT]**.

- **affection:** A rogue emotion purged from Kryten's hard drive by the Data Doctor, a program for restoring a mechanoid's personality to factory settings, when Captain Hollister subjected Kryten to a psychotropic simulation **[T-SER8.2]**.

- ***After Death Do Us Part*:** A hologram television sitcom from the creators of *Both Feet in the Grave*. The show's creators went on to produce the mechanoid comedy *Whoops Vicar, There Goes My Groinal Socket*, which aired on Groovy Channel 27 **[M-SMG1.7(a)]**.

  ***NOTE:** This title spoofed that of British comedy series* Till Death Us Do Part.

- **After Eight:** A thin confectionary made with mint wrapped in chocolate, typically used to help with digestion after a meal **[RL]**. Despite *Red Dwarf* having enough food in its stores to last the surviving crew for thirty thousand years, Holly reported that there was only one After Eight mint left, and everyone was too polite to take it **[T-SER1.6]**.

- **Aftering, the:** The rebirth of a polymorph, during which a host disgorged a smaller version of itself at the end of its life, in what was known as the Shadow Time **[N-BTL]**. To prepare for the Aftering, a polymorph would encase itself in a psi-proof chrysalis, in which it then changed and fostered its telepathic abilities. The Shadow Time occurred during periods when Garbage World (Earth) froze over in deep space—the Aftering being the span of time in which it thawed as the planet approached a sun **[M-SMG1.13(c3)]**.

- **aggression mode:** A function of cyborgs, such as Jake Bullet, enabling them to become aggressive in situations when pacifism would be ineffective **[M-SMG1.7(a)]**.

- **agol:** A material used to build spacefaring vessels. *Nova 5* was built using a strontium-agol alloy **[N-INF]**.

- **agonize:** A form of torture and/or execution used by rogue simulants. While delivering a report to Dominator Zlurth, Chancellor Wednesday suggested agonizing the security forces responsible for letting the *Red Dwarf* crew escape **[T-SER10.6]**.

- **agonoid:** A type of partly organic simulant killing machine created by humans as super-warriors. After the conflict for which they were built ended, the agonoids were recalled for decommissioning, but their survival instinct overrode their programming to obey humans, and they turned against their creators, starting an intense but short-lived war. Most agonoids died during the conflict, but a few thousand fled into deep space to plan their revenge. Following this rebellion, android developers incorporated Isaac Asimov's fictional Three Laws of Robotics into all future models.

  For millions of years, the agonoids, lacking the ability to duplicate themselves, slowly decayed and fought one another for spare parts to survive, until the few dozen that remained found *Red Dwarf* abandoned except for Holly. After interrogating the AI computer, they tore it out of the vessel and jettisoned it into space as bait, to lure in Lister and exact revenge on the last known human survivor.

  While waiting, the agonoids built a structure aboard the mining vessel called the Death Wheel, a series of hazardous corridors leading to a central room, the Hub of Pain, through which they planned to lead Lister and his shipmates to torture them endlessly. However, the Death Wheel's creator, Djuhn'Keep, betrayed his fellow agonoids, killing most of them and ejecting the rest into space, so that he alone would have the pleasure of tormenting the last human—a goal he never got the chance to fulfill **[N-BCK]**.

B-: Books
PRG: *Red Dwarf Programme Guide*
SUR: *Red Dwarf Space Corps Survival Manual*
PRM: *Primordial Soup*
SOS: *Son of Soup*
SCE: *Scenes from the Dwarf*
LOG: *Red Dwarf Log No. 1996*
RD8: *Red Dwarf VIII*
EVR: *The Log: A Dwarfer's Guide to Everything*

X-: Misc.
PRO: Promotional materials, videos, etc.
PST: Posters at DJ XVII (2013)
CAL: 2008 calendar
RNG: Cell phone ringtones
MOB: Mobisode ("Red Christmas")
CIN: *Children in Need* sketch
GEK: *Geek Week* intros by Kryten
TNG: "Tongue-Tied" video

XMS: Bill Pearson's Christmas special pitch script
XVD: Bill Pearson's Christmas special pitch video
OTH: Other *Red Dwarf* appearances

SUFFIX
DVD:
(d) – Deleted scene
(o) – Outtake
(b) – Bonus DVD material (other)
(e) – Extended version

SMEGAZINES:
(c) – Comic
(a) – Article

OTHER:
(s) – Early/unused script draft
(s1) – Alternate version of script

- **Agoraphobic Society:** A support group for those suffering from a fear of open spaces. After traveling three million years into the past via a stasis leak, Lister, Rimmer and Cat arrived in a shower stall aboard *Red Dwarf*. When a crewmember noticed them in the stall, Lister quickly pulled the shower curtain closed, accusing the man of interrupting their annual meeting of the Agoraphobic Society **[T-SER2.4]**.

- **Aigburth Arms, The:** A pub located on Victoria Road in Liverpool, England **[RL]**. As a newborn infant, Lister was found abandoned in this bar under a grav-pool table on November 26, 2155, in a box marked "Ourob Oros." Only in adulthood did he learn that he had gone back in time and left himself in the box, after he and Kochanski produced the child via *in vitro* fertilization **[T-SER7.3]**. As a young man, Lister returned to this pub and won seventeen consecutive games of pool, becoming a billiards legend **[N-INF]**.

- **Aimi:** A character on the television soap opera *Androids*. The long-lost daughter of Mollee, Aimi had been kidnapped by vacuum cleaners **[W-AND]**.

- **Air, Jane, Mapping Officer:** A blonde crewmember aboard the Earth ship *Nova 5* who survived that vessel's crash, along with two other female officers and a mechanoid named Kryten. Despite recovering from the impact, she died sometime later—unbeknownst to Kryten, who continued serving her and the others long after their deaths. At the time of her last registered medical record, Air was twenty-five years old and stood five feet three inches (161 centimeters) tall. Her medical details were stored on Prog Disc A49 **[T-SER2.1]**.

  NOTE: *Kryten referred to Air as "Miss Jane" in a distress signal to* Red Dwarf. *Her name played on that of Jane Eyre, the eponymous character of Charlotte Brontë's 1847 novel* Jane Eyre: An Autobiography.

- **air-conditioning complex:** An area of *Red Dwarf*'s engineering level allocated for in-ship climate control **[N-BTL]**.

- **airlock:** A sealable set of doorways between a ship's interior and exterior, used to maintain pressure inside the ship against the vacuum of space. Several airlocks were present on *Red Dwarf* **[T-SER2.6]**, as well as on *Starbug* shuttles **[T-SER6.1]**.

- **Airlock 12:** A sealable set of doorways leading out from *Starbug 1*'s galley **[T-SER4(b)]**.

  NOTE: *This airlock appeared in the special* Can't Smeg, Won't Smeg.

- **Airlock 4:** *See* Airlock AZ-4

- **Airlock A:** A sealable set of doorways leading to a landing gantry aboard *Red Dwarf*. When Kryten's replacement, Hudzen 10, docked in the gantry, the crew confronted him outside Airlock A and attempted to make him turn back **[T-SER3.6]**.

- **Airlock Accident Risk-Assessment Form:** A safety form that had to be filled out before an airlock aboard *Red Dwarf* could be opened, on Rimmer's orders as the ship's self-elected health and safety executive **[T-SER10.4]**.

- **Airlock AZ-4:** *Starbug 1*'s primary airlock, also known as Airlock 4 **[T-SER6.1]**.

- ***A.I. Today*:** A news publication that covered developments in the artificial intelligence (AI) sciences. Its slogan: "All The Intelligence… Artificially." One issue, published in partnership with Red Planet Power Drinks, featured articles about the crashing of the Justice Zone prison complex, coding issues involving Holly and other shipboard AI computers, and the lack of customer service at Diva-Droid International **[W-AIT]**. At least one issue ran an advertisement for Diva-Droid's Hudzen 10 Series mechanoid **[W-DIV]**.

- **AI watch:** A portable wristband device enabling an individual to communicate with a ship's artificial intelligence **[G-RPG]**.

- **Ajax:** A household cleaning product introduced by Colgate-Palmolive in 1947 **[RL]**. While inhabiting Lister's body after a mind swap, Rimmer used Domestos and Lemon Double Bleach Ajax Scourer to scrub down in the shower **[T-SER3.4]**.

- **AJR1:** A planet displayed on *Starbug 1*'s scanner table **[T-SER6(b)]**.

  NOTE: *A wireframe rendering of this world appeared in an Easter egg on disc one of the Series VI DVDs, though selecting it had no effect. The acronym presumably stood for "Arnold Judas Rimmer 1."*

PREFIX
RL: Real life

T-: Television Episodes
SER: Television series
IDW: "Identity Within"
USA1: Unaired U.S. pilot
USA2: Unaired U.S. demo

R-: *The Bodysnatcher Collection*
SER: Remastered episodes
BOD: "Bodysnatcher"
DAD: "Dad"
FTH: "Lister's Father"
INF: "Infinity Patrol"
END: "The End" (original assembly)

N-: Novels
INF: *Infinity Welcomes Careful Drivers*
BTL: *Better Than Life*
LST: *Last Human*

BCK: *Backwards*
OMN: *Red Dwarf Omnibus*

M-: Magazines
SMG: *Smegazine*

W-: Websites
OFF: Official website
NAN: *Prelude to Nanarchy*
AND: *Androids*
DIV: Diva-Droid
DIB: Duane Dibbley

CRP: Crapola
GEN: Geneticon
LSR: Leisure World Intl.
JMC: Jupiter Mining Corporation
AIT: *A.I. Today*
HOL: HoloPoint

G-: Roleplaying Game
RPG: *Core Rulebook*
BIT: *A.I. Screen Extra Bits* booklet
SOR: *Series Sourcebook*
OTH: Other RPG material

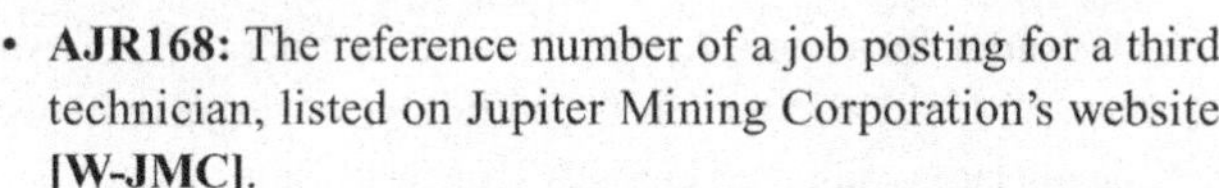

- **AJR168:** The reference number of a job posting for a third technician, listed on Jupiter Mining Corporation's website **[W-JMC]**.

  NOTE: *This presumably stood for "Arnold J. Rimmer" and his position aboard* Red Dwarf*, 168, indicating the posting may have been for his replacement.*

- **AJR2:** A planet displayed on *Starbug 1*'s scanner table **[T-SER6(b)]**.

  NOTE: *A wireframe rendering of this world appeared in an Easter egg on disc one of the Series VI DVDs, though selecting it had no effect. The acronym presumably stood for "Arnold Judas Rimmer 2."*

- **"A.J. Rimmer":** A name on a sticker attached to a *Red Dwarf* storage container holding Rimmer's belongings. After Rimmer moved in with his duplicate hologram, Lister put Arnold's possessions from the quarters they once shared in this container **[T-SER1.6]**. A similar sticker decorated the wall in Rimmer's bunk **[T-SER2.2]**.

- **Akerman, Governor ("Nicey"):** *See* Ackerman, Warden ("Nicey")

- **AKG:** A brand of headphones made by Harman, an American manufacturer of audio equipment **[RL]**. Lister used AKG headphones aboard *Red Dwarf* while tracking an unidentified ship, later found to contain a DNA-modifying machine **[T-SER4.2(d)]**.

- **Akimbo, Legs, Doctor:** A gynecologist aboard *Red Dwarf* who died during the cadmium II disaster. Akimbo was resurrected along with the ship's entire complement when nanobots rebuilt the mining ship. When Kryten was sentenced to *Red Dwarf*'s brig, Akimbo gave him a full medical examination, classifying the mechanoid as female due to his lack of genitalia **[T-SER8.2]**.

  NOTE: *Akimbo's name and specialty were mentioned in the Collector's Booklet included with the Series VIII DVD set, as well as the* Red Dwarf Programme Guide*. The character's name was an in-joke reference to his profession, as the phrase "legs akimbo" describes the bodily position of having one's legs bent outward—as would be the case during a gynecological examination.*

- **Alan:** A name that the woman to whom Rimmer lost his virginity kept calling him during sex, as she was suffering from a concussion at the time **[N-BTL]**.

  NOTE: *This woman was presumably Yvonne McGruder, though this was not specifically stated.*

- **Alaska:** A non-contiguous state of the United States of America, and the largest of the fifty by area **[RL]**. Kryten sometimes expressed surprise or incredulity by exclaiming, "Spin my nipple nuts and send me to Alaska!" **[T-SER4.1, T-SER8.2]**.

- **Albanian State Washing Machine Company:** A business, possibly hypothetical, that Lister sarcastically claimed had better technology than the *Red Dwarf* crew **[T-SER6.2]**.

- **albatrox:** A genetically engineered creature—a mix between an albatross and a fox—developed by inebriated scientists **[B-EVR]**.

- **Alberog:** A genetically engineered life form (GELF) created to help mankind terraform a new planet for the human species. With the head of an albatross, the body of a bear and the legs of a frog, Alberogs stood more than seven feet tall and were infused with slow-aging genes, giving them a life expectancy close to a thousand years.

  Alberogs, along with Snugiraffes, Dolochimps and Dingotangs, were developed after attempts to control Earth's weather reduced the Sun's lifespan to four hundred thousand years, thereby forcing mankind to terraform other worlds to survive. The GELFs were sent ahead to prepare the new planet, but their ship was sucked into the Omni-zone and ejected into another universe, where they settled on Arranguu 12 and its resident asteroid field. The Forum of Justice's GELF Regulator was an Alberog **[N-LST]**.

  Alberogs were also present on *Gar Barge*, a GELF craft dispatched to explore deep space, which eventually spawned the Kinitawowi tribe **[W-OFF]**.

- **Albert:** The name that Lister gave to a cup of mold he was breeding in his quarters aboard *Red Dwarf* for the sole purpose of annoying Rimmer. Lister was shocked to find that Kryten had thrown the cup—and, hence, Albert—in the trash during

B-: Books
PRG: *Red Dwarf Programme Guide*
SUR: *Red Dwarf Space Corps Survival Manual*
PRM: *Primordial Soup*
SOS: *Son of Soup*
SCE: *Scenes from the Dwarf*
LOG: *Red Dwarf Log No. 1996*
RD8: *Red Dwarf VIII*
EVR: *The Log: A Dwarfer's Guide to Everything*

X-: Misc.
PRO: Promotional materials, videos, etc.
PST: Posters at DJ XVII (2013)
CAL: 2008 calendar
RNG: Cell phone ringtones
MOB: Mobisode ("Red Christmas")
CIN: *Children in Need* sketch
GEK: *Geek Week* intros by Kryten
TNG: "Tongue-Tied" video

XMS: Bill Pearson's Christmas special pitch script
XVD: Bill Pearson's Christmas special pitch video
OTH: Other *Red Dwarf* appearances

SUFFIX
DVD:
(d) – Deleted scene
(o) – Outtake
(b) – Bonus DVD material (other)
(e) – Extended version

SMEGAZINES:
(c) – Comic
(a) – Article

OTHER:
(s) – Early/unused script draft
(s1) – Alternate version of script

a cleaning spree **[T-SER2.1]**.

NOTE: This was changed to Amáta (a female name) in the DVD captions for the Czech Republic version of the series, since the word "plíseň" (Czech for "mold") is feminine.

- **Albert DeSalvo Likeability Award:** A hypothetical award for which Lister suggested Rimmer would make a strong nominee, after Kryten spouted a long list of Arnold's undesirable qualities **[T-SER5.3(d)]**.

  NOTE: DeSalvo was a convicted rapist who also confessed to being the "Boston Strangler," a serial killer who murdered thirteen Boston-area women in the 1960s.

- **Albion:** The earliest known name for the island of Great Britain **[RL]**. While testing a build-it-yourself rejuvenation shower, the *Red Dwarf* crew was transported through space-time to Albion, in 23 A.D. Due to the country's lack of lemons—which they needed to power the shower's return remote—the crew trekked across the continent to find the fruit in India **[T-SER10.3]**.

- **Aldebaran Nebula:** An interstellar dust cloud mentioned on *Red Dwarf*, an American science fiction television show produced in an alternate universe. In one episode, an amorphous alien boarded the ship and accused the crew of killing his wife (who was dividing at the time) as they plodded through what they mistook for a slime patch on Altair 9.

  Vowing revenge, the alien tried to abduct Holly (Lister's human wife), Cry 10 (their biologically challenged son) and their hip teenage daughter, so that it would have a new family to bring to barbeques and cookouts in the Aldebaran Nebula **[M-SMG1.10(c4)]**.

  NOTE: Aldebaran, an orange giant star approximately sixty-five light-years from Earth, is not located inside a nebula. It was, however, a Nebula-*class starship in several* Star Trek: Deep Space Nine *books.*

- **Alert:** A telltale on an illuminated sign in *Starbug 1*'s cockpit. The sign's color signified the ship's alert status, though changing alert conditions required that the bulb be swapped with one of the appropriate color **[T-SER6.2]**.

- **Alexander the Great, King:** The military ruler of the Greek state of Macedon in the fourth century B.C. Alexander forged one the largest empires in Earth's ancient history **[RL]**.

  At age fifteen, Rimmer attended a school trip to visit Alexander's palace in Macedonia, where he felt a strange sense of belonging. He later befriended a hypnotherapist named Donald, who regressed Rimmer back to a past life, claiming he had previously been Alexander's chief eunuch **[T-SER3.2]**.

  While marooned on a barren planet many years later, Rimmer recalled hearing that Alexander had wept upon learning that there were no more lands to conquer. The story made Arnold feel better about sobbing uncontrollably for hours **[T-SER6.5(d)]**.

- **Alfonse:** A hair stylist employed at Astrocuts, a hair salon that Ace Rimmer frequented in Dimension 24's Theta Sector **[T-SER7.2]**.

  NOTE: This spelling appeared in the 2008 Red Dwarf *calendar; the DVD captions spelled the name "Alphonse."*

- **Alfonse:** A possible employee or ex-employee of Diva-Droid International who, after ordering the virility-enhancement drug Boing online, was inundated by junk mail. A writer for *A.I. Today* contacted him via his Diva-Droid e-mail address to question him about the lack of technical support at the company, but Alfonse declined to comment, asking to be left alone **[W-AIT]**.

- **AlFresco Guacamole Restaurant:** A dining establishment in an alternate reality that catered to mechanical individuals. Its House Special was sesame steak. The restaurant's clientele included the Fuse Brothers, and its employees included an android maître d' named Frankie and a robotic chef called Spike.

  When Spike disappeared, his sister Sugar hired Jake Bullet to search for the missing boy, starting at AlFresco. Frankie ambushed them as they arrived, knocking them unconscious and leaving them tied up in the kitchen. Upon regaining consciousness, they found Spike locked in the oven, being basted for Frankie's "cannibalistic" customers. Bullet reunited Spike with his sister, then interrogated Frankie and left him tied up in the kitchen, where the maître d' accidentally choked on Bullet's handkerchief **[M-SMG1.7(a)]**.

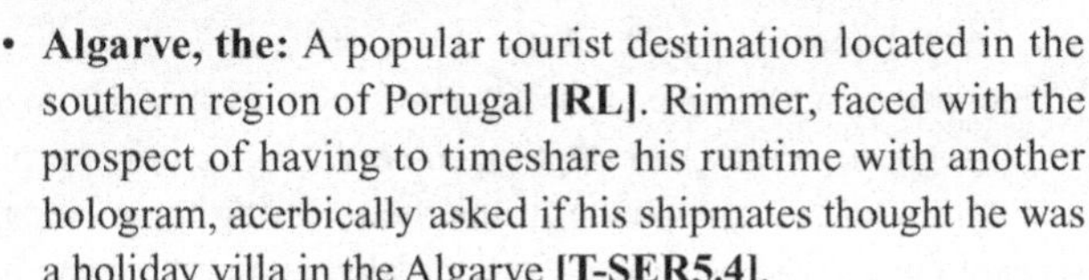

- **Algarve, the:** A popular tourist destination located in the southern region of Portugal **[RL]**. Rimmer, faced with the prospect of having to timeshare his runtime with another hologram, acerbically asked if his shipmates thought he was a holiday villa in the Algarve **[T-SER5.4]**.

- ***Alien Monthly*:** A hypothetical magazine title. As Rimmer called out coordinates to Kryten on one occasion, Lister joked that the numbers were the measurements of Arnold's dream girl, a Venusian Orange creature on page thirty-seven of *Alien Monthly* **[X-XMS]**.

- ***Aliens*:** An American science fiction film directed by James Cameron, released in 1986 as a sequel to Ridley Scott's *Alien* **[RL]**. While trapped in an elation squid hallucination, the *Red Dwarf* crew imagined a poster for this movie displayed at a twenty-first-century video store **[T-SER9.2]**. Simulant scavengers, searching Garbage World (Earth) for artifacts to sell to mechanicals, found a cache of video slugs, including several containing *Aliens* **[M-SMG2.9(c11)]**.

- ***Alien vs. Mary Poppins—The Bitch Is Back*:** A classic holiday film that Lister watched on Christmas Day **[B-LOG]**.

- ***Alien Wives*:** A magazine featuring photographs of nude extraterrestrials. Cat once perused an issue, but gave up since he could not ascertain which way was up **[X-XMS]**.

- **alignment bracket:** A spare part left over after the *Red Dwarf* crew attempted to build a rejuvenation shower they had found in a crate. When installed properly, the brackets aligned the unit's beamer light toward the center of the device. With the part missing, however, the beams projected outward, transporting the crew through space-time to Albion (later known as Great Britain), in 23 A.D. **[T-SER10.3]**.

- **Alison:** *See* Rimmer, Alison

- **Allan:** The artificial-intelligence computer aboard the *JMS Leif Erickson* **[G-RPG]**.

- **All-Droid Finest Collection:** A line of premium products sold by the All-Droid Mail Order Shopping Station. Among the items in this collection was a device called a Stirmaster **[T-SER10.1]**.

- **All-Droid Mail Order Shopping Station:** An android-run television station that broadcast a signal into deep space advertising cheap home goods, such as the Stirmaster **[T-SER10.1]**. Its phone number was 0800-751-102 **[W-OFF]**. Lister spent hours on the telephone with the station's employees, attempting to order a pair of Stirmasters for himself and Cat, but Sim Crawford's attack aboard the *Trojan* prevented him from reaching the phone when his turn came to order **[T-SER10.1]**.

- **All-Droid Space Station:** An All-Droid Mail Order Shopping Station facility containing a medical unit. Sim Crawford pretended to transport to the station to prepare for Howard Rimmer's arrival, but instead accessed the *Trojan*'s armory so she could take over the ship **[T-SER10.1]**.

- **Allen, Lucy:** The vision mixer **[M-SMG2.9(c8)]** and lighting director on the television soap opera *Androids* **[W-AND]**.

- **Allender:** A crewmember aboard *Red Dwarf* who died during the cadmium II disaster. Rimmer called Allender's name during a roll call to ascertain the extent of the casualties, knowing full well that everyone except for Lister had died **[R-BOD]**.

  ***NOTE:** This may have referred to Grace Allender, mentioned in a deleted scene from episode 1.1 ("The End"), or Paul Allender, mentioned in that episode's first-draft script, published in the* Red Dwarf Omnibus. *Either way, it is unknown whether the nanobots resurrected Allender in Series VIII.*

- **Allender, Grace, Fourth Engineer:** A *Red Dwarf* crewmember who perished in the cadmium II explosion. Lister and Rimmer ejected a canister containing her remains into space during a funeral for the accident's casualties **[R-END]**.

  ***NOTE:** In the pilot episode's first-draft script, published in the* Red Dwarf Omnibus, *Lister committed the ashes of Paul Allender, not Grace Allender, to space.*

- **Allender, Paul, Fourth Engineer:** *See* Allender, Grace, Fourth Engineer

B-: Books
PRG: *Red Dwarf Programme Guide*
SUR: *Red Dwarf Space Corps Survival Manual*
PRM: *Primordial Soup*
SOS: *Son of Soup*
SCE: *Scenes from the Dwarf*
LOG: *Red Dwarf Log No. 1996*
RD8: *Red Dwarf VIII*
EVR: *The Log: A Dwarfer's Guide to Everything*

X-: Misc.
PRO: Promotional materials, videos, etc.
PST: Posters at DJ XVII (2013)
CAL: 2008 calendar
RNG: Cell phone ringtones
MOB: Mobisode ("Red Christmas")
CIN: *Children in Need* sketch
GEK: *Geek Week* intros by Kryten
TNG: "Tongue-Tied" video

XMS: Bill Pearson's Christmas special pitch script
XVD: Bill Pearson's Christmas special pitch video
OTH: Other *Red Dwarf* appearances

SUFFIX
DVD:
(d) – Deleted scene
(o) – Outtake
(b) – Bonus DVD material (other)
(e) – Extended version

SMEGAZINES:
(c) – Comic
(a) – Article

OTHER:
(s) – Early/unused script draft
(s1) – Alternate version of script

- **Allman, Thomas:** A man whom the Inquisitor judged as having led a worthless life and thus removed from existence, replacing him with a same-named individual showing greater potential **[T-SER5.2]**.

- **Allman, Thomas:** A man who replaced the original Thomas Allman after the Inquisitor erased him from history. The Inquisitor believed this Allman was more likely to live a worthwhile life **[T-SER5.2]**.

- **All Nations Agreement:** A set of regulations developed by the nations of Earth to enforce a certain code of conduct. These rules ranged from the right of prisoners of war to non-violent constraint (Article 39436175880932/C) to the number of parking spaces allotted to delegates (Article 39436175880932/B) **[T-SER6.3]**.

- ***All Time Greatest Astrological Explorers*:** A book in Rimmer's quarters aboard *Red Dwarf* **[T-SER10.3]**.

- **Alpha:** The first letter of the Greek alphabet **[RL]**, used in a code to disarm and unlock a groinal exploder that a group of BEGGs had affixed to Lister's crotch. The code—Theta, Delta, Alpha, Beta, Gamma—had to be input precisely, in that order, for the device to be disabled **[T-SER10.4]**.

- **Alpha:** A security clearance tier granted to high-level members of a fascist society's Ministry of Alteration in an alternate universe. Voter Colonel Larson Gray used his Alpha clearance to access files pertaining to an ex-member who had changed his identity to that of Duane Dibbley **[M-SMG2.5(c1)]**.

- **Alphabet-Head:** A derogatory term that Cat used to describe hologrammic Rimmer, alluding to the "H" adorning his forehead **[T-SER2.4]**.

- **Alphabetti Spaghetti:** A canned product sold by the H. J. Heinz Co., consisting of tomato sauce and pasta shaped like letters of the English alphabet **[RL]**. The first aluminum can ever opened on *Red Dwarf*'s cargo decks by a member of the *Felis erectus* species contained Alphabetti Spaghetti. This marked the end of that species' famine and enabled the evolution of *Felis sapiens* **[N-INF]**.

  A polymorph once took the form of Rimmer's mother, reclined next to an unconscious Lister, and provoked Rimmer by suggesting they had slept together. When the polymorph mentioned using Alphabetti Spaghetti during their sexual exploits, Arnold became furious, at which point the creature attacked, draining his anger **[T-SER3.3]**.

- **Alphonse:** *See* Alfonse [first entry]

- **Alsatian:** A breed of canine also known as a German Shepard **[RL]**. After a polymorph drained his guilt, Kryten deemed Rimmer a "disgusting pus-filled bubo" with the "wit, charm and self-possession of an Alsatian dog after a head-swap operation" **[T-SER3.3]**.

- **Alshain IV:** A planet on which *White Midget* shuttles could often be found in transport lots **[G-SOR]**.

- **Altair:** A planet on which Space Marine Colonel Mike O'Hagan and his crew became marooned. In his *Space Corps Survival Manual*, O'Hagan recounted the experience, claiming to have had his best friend shot for stealing the operation codes for their buggy, only to later discover the codes in his other pants **[B-SUR]**.

- **Altair 9:** A planet mentioned on *Red Dwarf*, an American science fiction television series produced in an alternate universe. In one episode, an amorphous alien boarded *Red Dwarf* and accused the crew of killing his wife (who was dividing at the time) as they plodded through what they mistook for a slime patch on Altair 9 **[M-SMG1.10(c4)]**.

- **Altered Images:** A twentieth-century Scottish new-wave/pop band **[RL]**. Kochanski was rumored to have enjoyed the band's music **[M-SMG1.14(a)]**.

  NOTE: *Clare (C.P.) Grogan, the first actor to portray Kochanski, was Altered Images' lead singer in the 1980s.*

- **Alternative 2X13/L:** A reality Ace Rimmer visited in 2315, in which genetic engineering had created a subspecies of human superheroes who formed the Liberty League (comprising that universe's analogs to the *Red Dwarf* crew) to protect the city of Smegopolis. The League's members were Action Man (Lister), Catman (Cat), Robbie (Kryten), Professor H (Holly) and Super-Ace (Rimmer).

At the time of Ace's arrival, the Liberty League were battling the Conspirator and the Penguin with limited success. When Ace asked why Super-Ace hadn't apprehended the Conspirator, Super-Ace admitted that his one weakness was human contact, which caused him to faint when hit. Ace thus took his place for the day, defeating the Conspirator and restoring his counterpart's reputation **[M-SMG2.1(c3)]**.

- **Alternative 6829/B:** A reality Ace Rimmer visited in 2180, in which zero-gee football never caught on, with traditional football (soccer) remaining popular. Ace's counterpart in this universe, Ray Rimmer, played for the Smegchester Rovers, and became the greatest player of his era using a pair of magical cleats from "Dead Shot" Dave Hunt.

  The boots eventually became tattered and lost their mystical properties, causing Ray to slip up on the playing field. Depressed, he tried to hurl himself off a bridge, but Ace arrived in time to save his life. After hearing Ray's story, Ace filled in for him during the following day's Cup Final, scoring eighteen goals and winning the game. Ray asked him to fill in for good, but Ace declined; before leaving, however, he repaired Dead Shot's boots, enabling Ray to continue the winning streak **[M-SMG1.8(c4)]**.

- **Alterna-void:** A secret black-ops-type project on which Space Corps physicists may or may not have worked **[G-RPG]**.

- **Amáta:** *See* Albert

- **Amateur Hammond Organ Recital Night:** A tradition aboard *Red Dwarf*, typically held on Wednesdays, during which Rimmer used skutters to play Hammond organ music **[T-SER4.5]**.

- **Amateur Programmer Suite:** A software bundle available from Total Immersion Inc. via Crapola Inc., enabling Artificial Reality Suite owners to create their own virtual simulations **[G-RPG]**.

- ***Amazon Women on Heat*:** An adult-oriented artificial-reality game that contained a glitch causing a cute, redheaded character to refuse Lister a foot massage **[B-SUR]**.

  NOTE: This game's title spoofed that of the film Amazon Women on the Moon.

- **ambivalence:** An emotional state brought on by the feeling of two opposite emotions about the same thing **[RL]**. While being analyzed by *Red Dwarf*'s chief psychiatric counselor, Kryten claimed to have been working on this new emotion for some time, though at that point, he had not yet mastered it **[T-SER8.1]**.

  After Kryten's programming was reset to factory settings, the mechanoid encountered the *Starbug* crew as they attempted to escape from the nanobot-rebuilt *Red Dwarf*. The ambivalence he felt at recognizing the crew but fearing the prospect of getting caught corrupted his core programming, restoring his suppressed memories **[T-SER8.2]**.

- **Amish:** A U.S. subculture comprising traditional Christian church fellowships that shunned modern technology in favor of simple living **[RL]**. When Lister asked what being dead was like, Rimmer said it was similar to an Amish bachelor party **[T-USA1]**.

  NOTE: This joke, from the American Red Dwarf *pilot, was changed from the original British version, in which Rimmer likened death to being on holiday with a group of Germans.*

- **Ammunition Stores:** An area aboard *Red Dwarf* in which weapons and munitions were kept. After a polymorph drained his fear, Lister suggested retrieving a nuclear warhead from Ammunition Stores so he could strap it to his own head and destroy the creature by head-butting it **[T-SER3.3]**.

- **Amplatt, Magnus:** A former companion of Derek Dinsdale, the leader of the design team that created Holly's artificial-intelligence (AI) programming. In an article published in *A.I. Today*, Amplatt divulged information he learned while associated with Dinsdale, including the fact that many AI computers aboard JMC ships suffered from ill-conceived coding that made their personalities unstable. He cited the

B-: Books
PRG: *Red Dwarf Programme Guide*
SUR: *Red Dwarf Space Corps Survival Manual*
PRM: *Primordial Soup*
SOS: *Son of Soup*
SCE: *Scenes from the Dwarf*
LOG: *Red Dwarf Log No. 1996*
RD8: *Red Dwarf VIII*
EVR: *The Log: A Dwarfer's Guide to Everything*

X-: Misc.
PRO: Promotional materials, videos, etc.
PST: Posters at DJ XVII (2013)
CAL: 2008 calendar
RNG: Cell phone ringtones
MOB: Mobisode ("Red Christmas")
CIN: *Children in Need* sketch
GEK: *Geek Week* intros by Kryten
TNG: "Tongue-Tied" video
XMS: Bill Pearson's Christmas special pitch script
XVD: Bill Pearson's Christmas special pitch video
OTH: Other *Red Dwarf* appearances

SUFFIX
DVD:
(d) – Deleted scene
(o) – Outtake
(b) – Bonus DVD material (other)
(e) – Extended version

SMEGAZINES:
(c) – Comic
(a) – Article

OTHER:
(s) – Early/unused script draft
(s1) – Alternate version of script

destruction of the *Oregon* and the *Scott Fitzgerald*, among others, as proof of this defect **[W-AIT]**.

- **Analogue/Digital:** A setting on *Starbug 1*'s sonar scope display. The word "Analogue" was highlighted as the crew charted the course of a despair squid **[T-SER5.6]**.

- **"Anarchist Punk Gang":** A phrase printed on one of Lister's shirts **[T-SER10.4]**.

- **Android 00/076/F:** The robotic assistant floor manager on the television soap opera *Androids* **[T-SER2.1(d)]**.

- **Android 14001/A:** The robotic sound supervisor on the television soap opera *Androids* **[T-SER2.1(d)]**.

- **Android 14762/E:** A robotic actor who portrayed a character named Kelly on the television soap opera *Androids* **[T-SER2.1]**.

- **Android 17617/X:** The robotic makeup designer on the television soap opera *Androids* **[T-SER2.1(d)]**.

- **Android 20697/Q:** The robotic production assistant on the television soap opera *Androids* **[T-SER2.1(d)]**.

- **Android 23216/M:** The robotic music director on the television soap opera *Androids* **[T-SER2.1(d)]**.

- **Android 24/A:** A robotic actor who portrayed Brooke Junior on the television soap opera *Androids* **[T-SER2.1]**.

- **Android 25143/B:** The robotic director of *Androids—The Movie IV* **[M-SMG1.7(a)]**.

- **Android 333402/T:** The robotic host of the television quiz show *Whose Diode Is It Anyway?,* which aired on Groovy Channel 27 **[M-SMG1.7(a)]**.

- **Android 36333/C:** The robotic unit manager on the television soap opera *Androids* **[T-SER2.1(d)]**.

- **Android 442/53/2:** A robotic actor who portrayed a character named Simone on the television soap opera *Androids* **[T-SER2.1]**.

- **Android 474561/3:** The robotic vision supervisor on the television soap opera *Androids* **[T-SER2.1(d)]**.

- **Android 49764/F:** The robotic camera supervisor on the television soap opera *Androids* **[T-SER2.1(d)]**.

- **Android 49876/B:** The robotic production manager on the television soap opera *Androids* **[T-SER2.1(d)]**.

- **Android 5542978/R:** A robotic actor who portrayed one of Ken Barlow's love interests, and eventually his thirteenth wife, on the British television series *Coronation Street.* The couple wed during an episode that aired on Groovy Channel 27 at 7:30 PM on Wednesday, the 27th of Geldof, 2362 **[M-SMG1.7(a)]**.

- **Android 55556/W:** The robotic costume designer on the television soap opera *Androids* **[T-SER2.1(d)]**.

- **Android 62471/T:** The robotic technical coordinator on the television soap opera *Androids* **[T-SER2.1(d)]**.

- **Android 64321/H:** The robotic designer on the television soap opera *Androids* **[T-SER2.1(d)]**.

- **Android 72264/Y:** A robotic actor who portrayed a character named Gary on the television soap opera *Androids* **[T-SER2.1]**.

- **Android 77142/M:** A robotic production worker on the television soap opera *Androids* **[T-SER2.1(d)]**.

- **Android 79/265/B:** A robotic actor who portrayed an android in a bus queue on the television soap opera *Androids* **[T-SER2.1]**.

- **Android 79653/G:** The robotic vision mixer on the television soap opera *Androids* **[T-SER2.1(d)]**.

- **Android 801764/D:** The robotic lighting director on the television soap opera *Androids* **[T-SER2.1(d)]**.

- **Android 88543/J:** The robotic videotape editor on the television soap opera *Androids* **[T-SER2.1(d)]**.

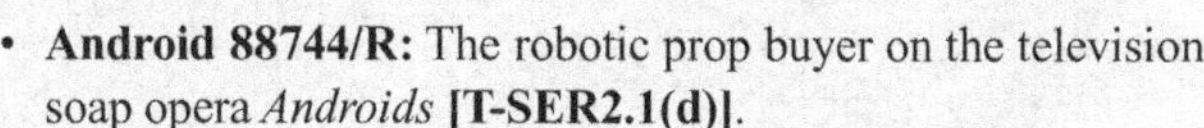

- **Android 88744/R:** The robotic prop buyer on the television soap opera *Androids* **[T-SER2.1(d)]**.

- **Android 92/76/B:** The robotic visual effects designer on the television soap opera *Androids* **[T-SER2.1(d)]**.

- **Android 92/876:** The robotic graphic designer on the television soap opera *Androids* **[T-SER2.1(d)]**.

- **Android 97542/P:** A robotic actor who portrayed a character named Brook on the television soap opera *Androids* **[T-SER2.1]**.

- **Android 980612/L:** A robotic actor who portrayed a character named Bruce on the television soap opera *Androids* **[T-SER2.1]**.

- **Android B1XXX:** The robotic writer of the television soap opera *Androids* **[T-SER2.1(d)]**.

- **Android homebrew:** A concoction that Holly, knowing of alcohol's ineffectiveness on mechanoids, created especially for Kryten's last-day party. The drink, derived from Vimto and liquid nitrogen, was lethal to humans—and potentially to androids as well **[T-SER3.6]**.

- **Android in Bus Queue**: A character listed in the credits of the television soap opera *Androids,* portrayed by Android 79/265/B **[T-SER2.1]**.

- **Android International:** A twenty-first-century company that produced robotic servants. Among its employees was a systems analyst who invented the concept of Silicon Heaven, an electronic afterlife to which all mechanicals believed they would go if they obediently served their masters. Thereafter, most devices with artificial intelligence were fitted with a belief chip containing this concept, in order to keep them from rebelling **[N-BTL]**.

- **Android of the Year:** An award given to the 4000 Series of mechanoids five years in a row, for its selfless nature and willingness to sacrifice itself for others **[T-SER5.2]**.

- ***Androids*:** An Australian television soap opera, produced and directed by Kylie Gwenlyn, that aired on Groovy Channel 27 **[T-SER2.1]**. Bartholomew Mews and Natalie Heathcote created twelve pilot episodes before it was eventually picked up—seventeen years after the duo first pitched it to TV executives **[W-AND]**. *Androids* was one of Kryten's rare personal indulgences, as it contained androids in starring roles **[T-SER2.1]**. It ran for a total of 1,974 episodes **[N-INF]** over the course of thirty-four years **[W-AND]**.

  NOTE: Androids *spoofed Australian television program* Neighbors, *with its theme song mimicking its real-world counterpart. The collector's booklet packaged with the Series II DVDs confirmed that* Androids *was also an Australian production. In the* Smegazine *comics, however, a reference to Garbage World (Earth), in issue 2.2, suggests the show was neither filmed nor set on Earth.*

  The 1,974 figure may have been an in-joke, as John Carpenter's comedic sci-fi film Dark Star*—which inspired Doug Naylor to create* Dave Hollins: Space Cadet, Red Dwarf*'s radio-aired spiritual predecessor—was released in 1974.*

- ***Androids* Appreciation Society (AAS):** An organization dedicated to the television soap opera *Androids.* While searching for the stolen *Red Dwarf*, the *Starbug 1* crew discovered an orbital space station that had once been the club's headquarters. Upon boarding the station, Kryten immediately attempted to download the entire series from its databanks, a process he calculated would take one week, five days, nine hours and fifty-five minutes. Unwilling to wait, the crew pulled him away from the station as he recorded a cliffhanger episode, much to the mechanoid's frustration **[M-SMG2.8(a)]**.

- ***Androids* Dancing Mug:** A black coffee mug sold by Crapola Inc., sporting the logo of the television soap opera *Androids*. Lifting the cup played the program's theme song, while placing it back down caused legs to extend, enabling the mug to dance to the tune. The product was made in Taiwan and sold for $£9.99 **[W-CRP]**.

B-: Books
PRG: *Red Dwarf Programme Guide*
SUR: *Red Dwarf Space Corps Survival Manual*
PRM: *Primordial Soup*
SOS: *Son of Soup*
SCE: *Scenes from the Dwarf*
LOG: *Red Dwarf Log No. 1996*
RD8: *Red Dwarf VIII*
EVR: *The Log: A Dwarfer's Guide to Everything*

X-: Misc.
PRO: Promotional materials, videos, etc.
PST: Posters at DJ XVII (2013)
CAL: 2008 calendar
RNG: Cell phone ringtones
MOB: Mobisode ("Red Christmas")
CIN: *Children in Need* sketch
GEK: *Geek Week* intros by Kryten
TNG: "Tongue-Tied" video
XMS: Bill Pearson's Christmas special pitch script
XVD: Bill Pearson's Christmas special pitch video
OTH: Other *Red Dwarf* appearances

SUFFIX
DVD:
(d) – Deleted scene
(o) – Outtake
(b) – Bonus DVD material (other)
(e) – Extended version

SMEGAZINES:
(c) – Comic
(a) – Article

OTHER:
(s) – Early/unused script draft
(s1) – Alternate version of script

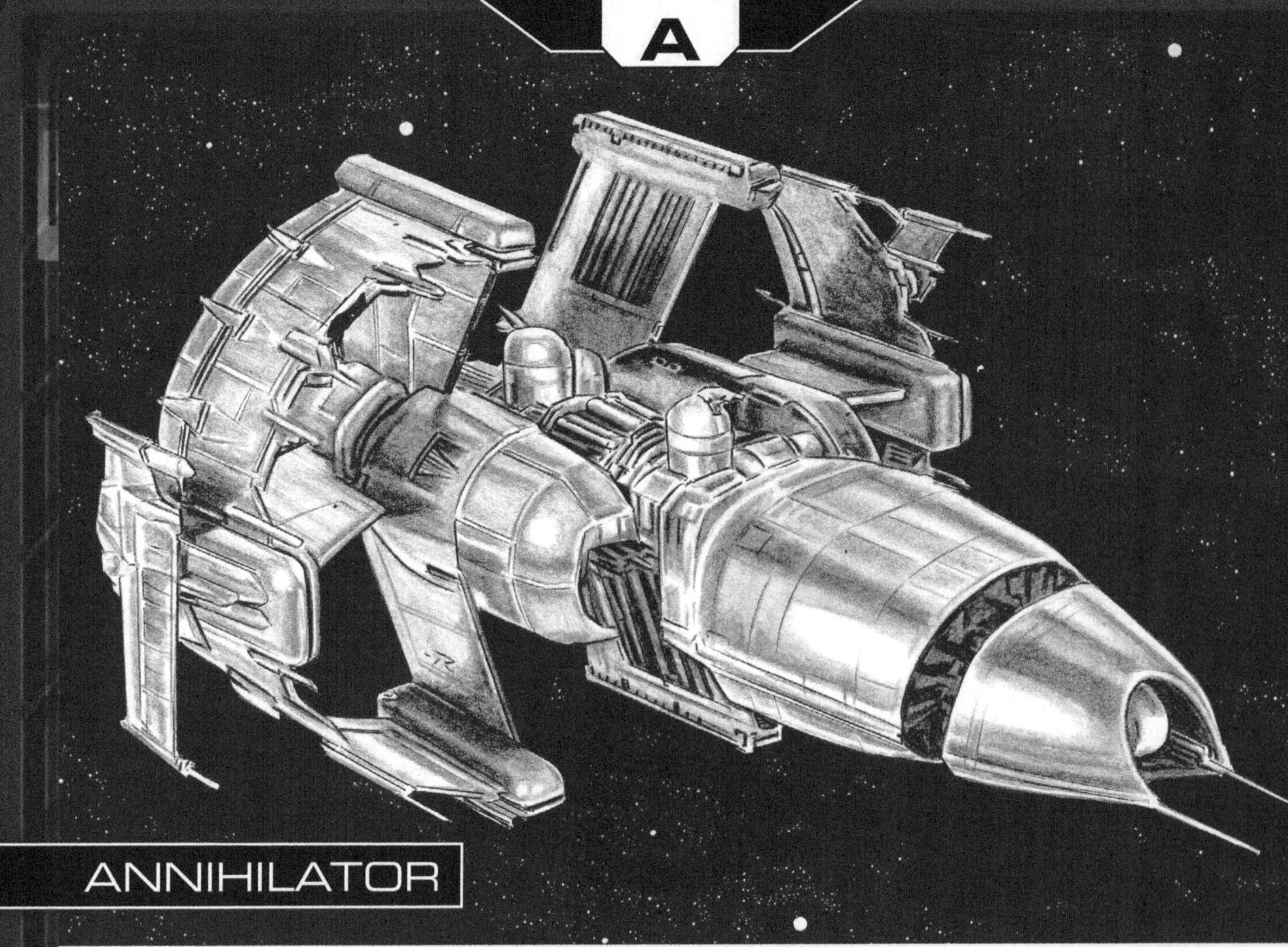

- **android sheep:** Mechanical representations of *Ovis aries*, available at a brothel on Mimas to customers who enjoyed bestiality **[N-INF]**.

- ***Androids Nights*:** A spinoff of the television soap opera *Androids*, the tagline of which was "Robots Never Sleep." The short-lived series revolved around protagonist Capston's plan to start a detective agency, with the android navigating a trail of murder, mystery and adultery that led to a confrontation with a character called Jaysee. The series' DVD featured eighteen minutes of bonus materials, including making-of specials, outtakes and deleted scenes, and retailed for $£18.99 **[W-CRP]**.

  NOTE: *This TV series' title and premise were based on* Baywatch Nights, *an American science fiction police drama that spun off from David Hasselhoff's* Baywatch *series, with the premise of a policeman quitting his job to open a detective agency. The phrase "Robots Never Sleep" presumably derived from "We Never Sleep," the well-known slogan of the Pinkerton National Detective Agency.*

- ***Androids* Shower Radio:** A product sold by Crapola Inc., sporting the logo of the television soap opera *Androids*. When hit with water, the radio played the *Androids* theme song. A button on the device allowed users to hear an alternate song, "Goto 10 If You Love Me," which had played during the

PREFIX
RL: Real life

T-: Television Episodes
SER: Television series
IDW: "Identity Within"
USA1: Unaired U.S. pilot
USA2: Unaired U.S. demo

R-: *The Bodysnatcher Collection*
SER: Remastered episodes
BOD: "Bodysnatcher"
DAD: "Dad"
FTH: "Lister's Father"
INF: "Infinity Patrol"
END: "The End" (original assembly)

N-: Novels
INF: *Infinity Welcomes Careful Drivers*
BTL: *Better Than Life*
LST: *Last Human*
BCK: *Backwards*
OMN: *Red Dwarf Omnibus*

M-: Magazines
SMG: *Smegazine*

W-: Websites
OFF: Official website
NAN: *Prelude to Nanarchy*
AND: *Androids*
DIV: Diva-Droid
DIB: Duane Dibbley

CRP: Crapola
GEN: Geneticon
LSR: Leisure World Intl.
JMC: Jupiter Mining Corporation
AIT: *A.I. Today*
HOL: HoloPoint

G-: Roleplaying Game
RPG: *Core Rulebook*
BIT: *A.I. Screen Extra Bits* booklet
SOR: *Series Sourcebook*
OTH: Other RPG material

wedding of characters Simone and Derek. The shower radio was made in Taiwan and sold for $£9.99 **[W-CRP]**.

- ***Androids* Singing Mug:** A product sold by Crapola Inc., sporting the logo of the television soap opera *Androids*. When lifted, the black mug played the program's theme song. The cup was made in Taiwan and sold for $£8.99 **[W-CRP]**.

- ***Androids—The Movie III*:** The third feature film based on the television soap opera *Androids*. The film was one of Kryten's favorites **[M-SMG1.1(a)]**.

  NOTE: *This, of course, implied there were two prior* Androids *movies.*

- ***Androids—The Movie IV*:** The fourth feature film based on the television soap opera *Androids*. In the movie, Kelly ironed while Simone was threatened with shutdown. The film, directed by Android 25143/B, was broadcast on Groovy Channel 27 at 10:30 PM on Wednesday, the 27th of Geldof, 2362 **[M-SMG1.7(a)]**.

- **Android Zzzzz/z:** The robotic production accountant on the television soap opera *Androids* **[T-SER2.1(d)]**.

- **Andromeda Galaxy:** A spiral galaxy roughly 2.5 million light-years away from the Milky Way, and the nearest neighboring galaxy **[RL]**. When scientists in the twenty-second century discovered that the Sun's lifespan had been severely reduced by attempts to control Earth's weather, the World Council developed a plan to relocate humanity to a planet within the Andromeda Galaxy.

  Initially inhospitable due to its lava and magma surface, the planet was chosen for its potential to be terraformed using specially designed viruses and custom species of GELFs. The first phase of the mission included launching a ship, the *Mayflower*, toward Andromeda to start the process of terraforming; it never arrived, however, having been knocked off course by a GELF mutiny against the human crew **[N-LST]**.

- **Andy:** An individual whom the *Red Dwarf* crew imagined meeting while trapped in a despair squid hallucination. Andy, a service technician for Leisure World International, greeted the crew after they awoke from the total-immersion video game *Red Dwarf* and inquired about their experience; he explained the goal of the game, and was amused to learn how much of it they had missed. He then prepped the machine for a new group of players, directing the old crew to the recuperation lounge **[T-SER5.6]**.

- **Ange:** A cutesy nickname, short for "Angel," that Lister gave Kochanski during their brief romance **[N-INF]**.

- **Angel Islington, The:** A London district featured in that city's version of *Monopoly* **[RL]**. For his twenty-fourth birthday, Lister and several friends embarked on a *Monopoly* board pub crawl across London; their fifth stop was The Angel Islington, where they ordered mezcals **[N-INF]**.

- **anger:** An emotional state characterized by a strong feeling of displeasure and animosity toward something or someone **[RL]**. After escaping a hazardous waste pod and boarding *Red Dwarf*, a polymorph attacked the crew by changing form to elicit and feed on their emotions. It targeted Rimmer by taking the form of his mother and describing her sexual exploits with Lister involving Alphabetti Spaghetti, after which it drained the anger from Arnold's mind **[T-SER3.3]**.

  While being analyzed by *Red Dwarf*'s chief psychiatric counselor, Kryten boasted that anger and rudimentary mindless violence were emotions he had acquired with Lister's help. He then demonstrated this by smashing the counselor's hand with his fist **[T-SER8.1]**.

- ***Angling Times*:** A weekly British publication dedicated to the sport of fishing **[RL]**. After Kryten entered lie mode to assure Rimmer that his high-velocity garbage cannon would work, he quietly told Lister that Arnold had fallen for his ruse—hook, line, sinker, rod and copy of *Angling Times* **[T-SER6.1]**.

- **angry chipmunk affair, the:** An incident aboard *Red Dwarf* involving Lister, Chen, Selby and Petersen, with Selby reportedly the mastermind **[G-BIT]**.

- **Annett, Chloë:** A British actor who portrayed Kristine Kochanski on the comedy television series *Red Dwarf* **[RL]**. While trapped in an elation squid hallucination, Lister discovered that Annett, who had portrayed Kochanski up until

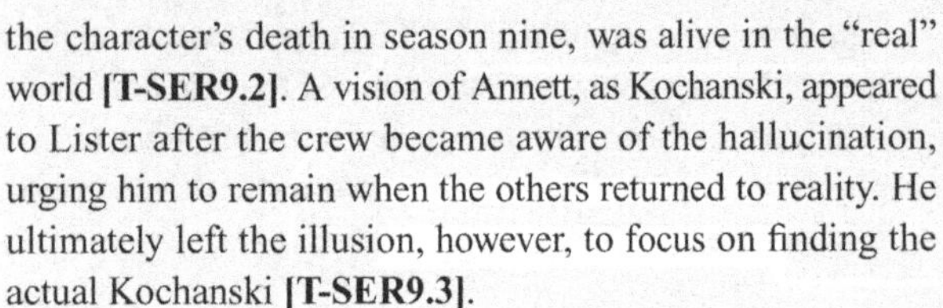

the character's death in season nine, was alive in the "real" world **[T-SER9.2]**. A vision of Annett, as Kochanski, appeared to Lister after the crew became aware of the hallucination, urging him to remain when the others returned to reality. He ultimately left the illusion, however, to focus on finding the actual Kochanski **[T-SER9.3]**.

- **Annihilator:** A small attack craft used by rogue simulants. Simulant Death Ships carried a contingent of Annihilators armed with photon mutilators. When three Annihilators pursued *Blue Midget* into an asteroid field, the crew positioned the shuttle between the three Annihilators and the Death Ship, lured all four ships into firing missiles and then subjected *Blue Midget*'s hull to a molecular destabilizer. This caused each missile to pass through the shuttle and hit the simulant vessel on the opposite side, destroying the Death Ship and all three Annihilators **[T-SER10.6]**.

- **Anti-Dazzlers:** A brand of sunglasses Kryten wore while doing laundry with Smeggo! detergent **[M-SMG1.12(c5)]**.

- **anti-grav chamber:** A section of *Red Dwarf* fitted with anti-gravity equipment, for situations in which extreme acceleration or deceleration would harm the crew. Rimmer, Kryten, Cat and Talkie Toaster secured themselves in the anti-grav chamber while escaping a black hole by accelerating past lightspeed and performing a slingshot maneuver around its singularity **[N-BTL]**.

- **anti-matter chopsticks:** *See* Mimosian anti-matter chopsticks

- **Anti-Smoking League:** An organization advocating the prohibition of smoking cigarettes. Eric White, whom the *Starbug 1* crew found trampled to death in Dallas, Texas, in 1966, was the chairman of the Anti-Smoking League—disproving Cat's initial analysis that he was a smoker **[T-SER7.1(e)]**.

- ***Antiques*:** A magazine in Rimmer's quarters aboard *Red Dwarf*. This publication was present when a future version of Rimmer tried to convince his younger self to enter stasis and avoid the ship's impending cadmium II accident, thereby preventing his death and subsequent hologrammatic resurrection **[T-SER2.4]**.

- **Antoinette, Marie, Dauphine/Queen:** The wife of France's King Louis XVI in the late eighteenth century. Reputedly an extravagant spender and partier, she was eventually beheaded after being tried for a number of crimes **[RL]**. While trapped in an addictive version of *Better Than Life*, Rimmer imagined that his wife, Juanita Chicata, periodically used a time machine to collect friends from the past, including Marie Antoinette, to enjoy week-long shopping sprees **[N-BTL]**.

- **Anus Soothe Pile Cream:** A medicinal ointment used to relieve hemorrhoidal discomfort. Rimmer presented Captain Hollister with a tube of the cream, which included a single-finger applicator glove, after learning of his affliction from reading Hollister's confidential file **[T-SER8.2]**.

- **anxiety chip:** A component installed in 4000 Series mechanoids to regulate nervousness. When Rimmer assumed an official tone as Kryten prepared to take a piloting test, the mechanoid's anxiety chip went into overdrive, causing him to stutter **[T-SER3.1]**.

- **anxiety mode:** A software function of 4000 Series mechanoids that simulated nervousness under duress. Anxiety Mode occurred in several stages, depending on a situation **[N-LST]**.

- **AP-6:** A small automatic firearm produced by Bloodlust Arms. It held a twenty-round clip and had a range of 80 meters (262 feet) **[G-SOR]**.

- **Apartment 43, Hotel Paradiso:** The address of Trixie LaBouche, an erotic leisure consultant in a seedy part of Mimas known as Shagtown **[M-SMG2.5(c6)]**.

- **Ape Brain:** A name that Cat called Lister as they hung upside-down on Cargo Deck F after being captured by Space Monkeys **[M-SMG1.13(c2)]**.

- **Apocalypse Boys, The:** A quartet of outlaw characters that Kryten's subconscious mind created while trying to purge the Armageddon virus that had infected *Starbug 1*'s navicomp. The mechanoid's mind converted the struggle into a dream in which he was the drunken sheriff of an Old West town terrorized by the Apocalypse Boys. The four brothers—Death

PREFIX
RL: Real life

T-: Television Episodes
- **SER:** Television series
- **IDW:** "Identity Within"
- **USA1:** Unaired U.S. pilot
- **USA2:** Unaired U.S. demo

R-: *The Bodysnatcher Collection*
- **SER:** Remastered episodes
- **BOD:** "Bodysnatcher"
- **DAD:** "Dad"
- **FTH:** "Lister's Father"
- **INF:** "Infinity Patrol"
- **END:** "The End" (original assembly)

N-: Novels
- **INF:** *Infinity Welcomes Careful Drivers*
- **BTL:** *Better Than Life*
- **LST:** *Last Human*
- **BCK:** *Backwards*
- **OMN:** *Red Dwarf Omnibus*

M-: Magazines
- **SMG:** *Smegazine*

W-: Websites
- **OFF:** Official website
- **NAN:** *Prelude to Nanarchy*
- **AND:** *Androids*
- **DIV:** Diva-Droid
- **DIB:** Duane Dibbley
- **CRP:** Crapola
- **GEN:** Geneticon
- **LSR:** Leisure World Intl.
- **JMC:** Jupiter Mining Corporation
- **AIT:** *A.I. Today*
- **HOL:** HoloPoint

G-: Roleplaying Game
- **RPG:** *Core Rulebook*
- **BIT:** *A.I. Screen Extra Bits* booklet
- **SOR:** *Series Sourcebook*
- **OTH:** Other RPG material

(the group's leader), Famine, Pestilence and War—gave Kryten an ultimatum to leave town within an hour or be killed.

Watching these events play out on a monitor, Kryten's crewmates intervened by using an artificial-reality (AR) machine to hack into the dream. Appearing as characters from the AR game *Streets of Laredo*, they stalled the Apocalypse Boys long enough for Kryten to purge the virus via software called the Dove Program **[T-SER6.3]**.

- **Apocalypse, Death:** A character that Kryten's subconscious mind created while purging the Armageddon virus from *Starbug 1*'s navicomp. Death was the mustachioed leader of the Apocalypse Boys **[T-SER6.3]**.

  ***NOTE:** In the novel* Backwards, *Death Apocalypse was the father of the other three gang members.*

- **Apocalypse, Famine, Brother:** A character that Kryten's subconscious mind created while purging the Armageddon virus from *Starbug 1*'s navicomp. Brother Famine was a portly man who liked to eat chicken legs and sported an eye patch **[T-SER6.3]**.

- **Apocalypse, Pestilence, Brother:** A character that Kryten's subconscious mind created while purging the Armageddon virus from *Starbug 1*'s navicomp. Brother Pestilence was a thin, sickly-looking man surrounded by flies **[T-SER6.3]**.

- **Apocalypse, War, Brother:** A character that Kryten's subconscious mind created while purging the Armageddon virus from *Starbug 1*'s navicomp. Brother War was a bandana-wearing fire-breather **[T-SER6.3]**.

- **Apocalypse virus:** A computer virus that the agonoid Djuhn'Keep created to use against his rival, M'Aiden Ty-One, before battling the *Starbug 1* crew and uploading the virus to the ship's navicomp. To combat the virus and save the ship, Kryten plugged himself into the computer to create software known as a Dove Program. In so doing, his mind crafted a dreamlike Western scenario in which he was a drunken sheriff.

  In the dream, the virus manifested as the Apocalypse Boys—Death, War, Famine and Pestilence—who wreaked havoc in the imaginary Old West town. Realizing Kryten was losing the battle, Lister, Rimmer and Cat entered his subconscious mind via an artificial-reality (AR) machine, taking on the personae of various playable characters. With superior skills based on these characters, the crew initially fended off the four outlaws, until the virus infected the AR machine, rendering them defenseless.

  Still, they had bought enough time for Kryten to complete the Dove Program and eradicate the virus. Upon returning to the real world, however, Lister and Cat discovered that neither Rimmer nor Kryten had survived the battle **[N-BCK]**.

  ***NOTE:** This name, used only in the novels, was changed from the Armageddon virus in episode 6.3 ("Gunmen of the Apocalypse").*

- **Apollo:** A deity of Greek and Roman mythology. The son of Zeus and Leto, Apollo was the god of light and health **[RL]**. When Tunbridge Wells' five hundred pilgrims were sent to pray for the end of a meteor storm ravaging their city, a miller in the group believed his people were headed to a shrine dedicated to Apollo. Others disagreed, causing a religious war that wiped out the entire pilgrim crew **[M-SMG1.14(c2)]**.

- ***Apollo XIII*:** The National Aeronautics and Space Administration's third planned mission to land human astronauts on Earth's moon. This launch was aborted following an explosion in one of the vessel's oxygen tanks **[RL]**. Lister wore a patch from this mission on his leather jacket **[T-SER3.1]**.

- **apple:** A fist-sized, tree-growing fruit, typically red, green or golden in color **[RL]**. Lister used an apple as a prop while trying to teach Kryten how to lie, by calling it an orange. Eventually, Kryten succeeded in calling the fruit "the Bolivian navy on maneuvers in the South Pacific," proving that he could move beyond his programming **[T-SER4.1]**.

- **Appleford:** A *Red Dwarf* crewmember who died during the cadmium II disaster. Rimmer called Appleford's name during a roll call to ascertain the extent of the casualties, knowing full well that everyone except for Lister had died **[R-BOD]**.

  ***NOTE:** It is unknown whether the nanobots resurrected Appleford in Series VIII.*

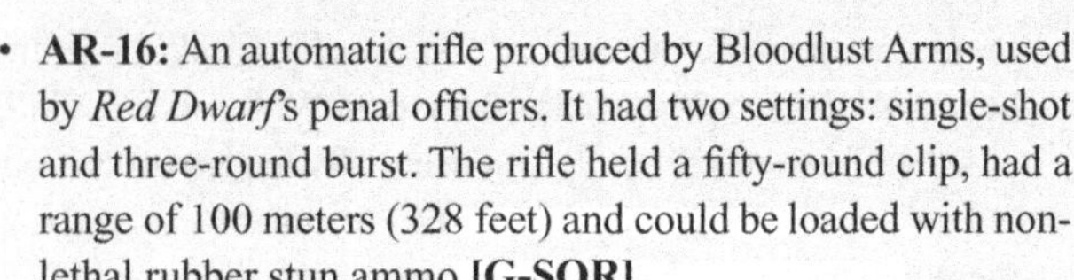

- **AR-16:** An automatic rifle produced by Bloodlust Arms, used by *Red Dwarf*'s penal officers. It had two settings: single-shot and three-round burst. The rifle held a fifty-round clip, had a range of 100 meters (328 feet) and could be loaded with non-lethal rubber stun ammo **[G-SOR]**.

- ***Arc*:** An award-winning play written by Jordan Kershaw, the head writer of the television soap opera *Androids*. The production followed the lives of simple welding folk **[W-AND]**.

- **Archer, Jeffrey, Baron:** A British novelist and ex-politician **[RL]**. After being shot several times by Nazis, Ace Rimmer told his prime-universe counterpart that his chest had "more holes than a Jeffrey Archer plot" **[T-SER7.2(d)]**.

- **Archie:** A mechanical penis that Kryten created for himself so he could be re-designated as a male while serving time in the Tank, *Red Dwarf*'s brig. Archie was built from an electron board, a toilet paper roll, tape and an Action Man's polo-neck jumper. While detached from Kryten, Archie escaped its confines and spooked Kochanski, who believed it to be a mouse. It then hid in Cat's Canary uniform and awoke during a mission to subdue a *Tyrannosaurus rex*, terrifying Cat, who thought a creature was inside him, trying to get out **[T-SER8.7]**.

- **Archie, Robot:** A fictional comic book character featured in the weekly British adventure magazine *Lion* **[RL]**. Archie appeared on the television soap opera *Androids* as a para-mech for 911-R-Us, and responded to a hover-car explosion caused by Jaysee's attempt to kill Gary and Kelly **[M-SMG2.2(c3)]**.

  NOTE: *The* Androids *website used a drawing of Archie to illustrate a character named Derek.*

- **Archimedes:** A leading Greek mathematician, inventor and astronomer of the third century B.C. **[RL]**. While hooked into an addictive version of *Better Than Life*, Rimmer believed he had returned to Earth and become famously wealthy, hosting dinner parties that included such guests as Archimedes **[N-INF]**.

- **Area P:** A section within the sleeping quarter on *Red Dwarf*'s Floor 9172. Lister was first assigned to bunk with Rimmer in this section **[N-INF]**.

- **Argon 5:** A planet that Arnold Rimmer, in one of Lister's dreams, claimed to have visited after replacing Ace Rimmer. On this world, the dream Rimmer said that he fought in the Belagosian War and was decorated and dressed as a Christmas tree, with inhabitants feeding him chocolates all winter **[T-SER7.5]**.

- **argument-settler:** A melee weapon, similar to a baton, issued to Shore Patrol officers on Mimas **[N-INF]**.

- **Ariel 2:** An asteroid in an alternate universe, owned by the United Republic of GELF States. According to Forum of Justice mystics, that dimension's Lister would eventually be responsible for the destruction of a starhopper that serviced Ariel 2, after looting and pillaging his way across the asteroid belt, causing many deaths. The GELFs thus arrested Lister on bogus emo-smuggling charges and imprisoned him in Cyberia before the crimes could take place **[N-LST]**.

- **Aristotle:** A Greek philosopher, circa the fourth century B.C., and a student of Plato **[RL]**. After two hundred years in deep sleep, an amnesic Lister found a copy of Aristotle's *Metaphysica* among his possessions while searching for clues to his identity. He was disappointed to learn that he owned it simply to hide his photo collection of naked ex-girlfriends **[T-SER6.1(d)]**.

  NOTE: Metaphysics, *in Greek, is titled* Metaphysica. *The prop seen onscreen, as well as Craig Charles' pronunciation, used the latter Greek spelling, though the prop book bore the name Aristotle, and not the Greek version, Aristotelis.*

- **Arkwright, Mrs.:** A geography teacher who taught Lister when he was young. The two had a sexual encounter after she asked him to stay after class one day to discuss his essay on glaciated valleys. She had a pregnancy scare as a result, which turned out to be a false alarm. According to Lister, Mrs. Arkwright was outwardly elegant and classy, yet "dirtier than a car mechanic's keyboard" in private **[T-SER10.5(d)]**.

- **AR machine:** A piece of equipment used to run artificial-reality video games, also known as an artificial-reality (AR) console. The machine consisted of a computer, a monitor and a railed platform, and included several headsets, pairs of gloves (with

PREFIX
RL: Real life

T-: Television Episodes
- **SER:** Television series
- **IDW:** "Identity Within"
- **USA1:** Unaired U.S. pilot
- **USA2:** Unaired U.S. demo

R-: *The Bodysnatcher Collection*
- **SER:** Remastered episodes
- **BOD:** "Bodysnatcher"
- **DAD:** "Dad"
- **FTH:** "Lister's Father"
- **INF:** "Infinity Patrol"
- **END:** "The End" (original assembly)

N-: Novels
- **INF:** *Infinity Welcomes Careful Drivers*
- **BTL:** *Better Than Life*
- **LST:** *Last Human*
- **BCK:** *Backwards*
- **OMN:** *Red Dwarf Omnibus*

M-: Magazines
- **SMG:** *Smegazine*

W-: Websites
- **OFF:** Official website
- **NAN:** *Prelude to Nanarchy*
- **AND:** *Androids*
- **DIV:** Diva-Droid
- **DIB:** Duane Dibbley
- **CRP:** Crapola
- **GEN:** Geneticon
- **LSR:** Leisure World Intl.
- **JMC:** Jupiter Mining Corporation
- **AIT:** *A.I. Today*
- **HOL:** HoloPoint

G-: Roleplaying Game
- **RPG:** *Core Rulebook*
- **BIT:** *A.I. Screen Extra Bits* booklet
- **SOR:** *Series Sourcebook*
- **OTH:** Other RPG material

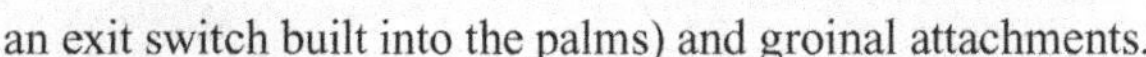

an exit switch built into the palms) and groinal attachments.

While scavenging derelicts within rogue simulant territory, the *Starbug 1* crew found an AR machine, as well as several games, including *Gumshoe* and *Streets of Laredo*. After it was installed in *Starbug 1*, Lister used the machine for several weeks straight, mostly for sex, almost wearing out the groinal attachment in the process, despite its lifetime guarantee.

Later, the crew utilized the machine to hack into Kryten's subconscious mind after he contracted the Armageddon virus. Using the Western game *Streets of Laredo*, the crew entered Kryten's dream, which took the form of an Old West town threatened by an outlaw gang called the Apocalypse Boys (a manifestation of the virus) **[T-SER6.3]**.

- **Armageddon virus:** A computer virus used by rogue simulants to disable enemy ships. When faced with defeat, a simulant crew would hack into the enemy's navicomp and transmit the virus, disabling the other vessel's flight controls.

While trespassing in a rogue simulant hunting zone, the *Starbug 1* crew was captured and rendered unconscious for three weeks. Upon being revived, they discovered *Starbug* had been upgraded by the simulants to provide more of a challenge. Rather than flee, the crew immediately attacked the simulants' battlecruiser, badly damaging it. Before being destroyed, the simulant captain ordered that the Armageddon virus be transmitted to *Starbug*'s navicomp, locking it on a collision course with a small planetoid. To save the ship, Kryten volunteered to upload the virus in an attempt to create a Dove Program to purge it from the vessel's systems.

In combatting the virus, Kryten's subconscious mind interpreted the struggle as an old Western movie and created an artificial scenario in which he was the drunken sheriff of a town terrorized by the Apocalypse Boys (a manifestation of the virus). Watching the struggle on a monitor hooked into Kryten's dream, the crew inserted themselves into the illusion via the alternate-reality machine to help him fight the virus. Their presence bought Kryten enough time to develop the Dove Program, with which he purged himself and the ship's computer of the invading software **[T-SER6.3]**.

> ***NOTE:*** *This was named the Apocalypse virus in the novel* Backwards.

- **Armchair:** A sentient, genetically engineered piece of furniture exiled to Garbage World (Earth) following the GELF War. After the planet was ripped from its orbit and propelled into deep space, Armchair and two other GELFs, a fish-like creature named Arthur and a genetically engineered refrigerator, hibernated together while the planet froze over. Over the course of millennia, the planet's trajectory took it near several stars, occasionally thawing it out and releasing its trapped inhabitants.

During one such thaw, a young polymorph emerged from its cocoon and took the form of a cockroach to search for sustenance. It came upon Armchair and his two GELF friends, who were themselves searching for food, and fed on their emotions, one by one, by changing its form to elicit strong responses. In Armchair's case, the polymorph changed into a little old lady sitting on him with a lit cigarette, eliciting fear from the flammable GELF. The polymorph fed on that fear, then moved on to the other GELFs. Lacking desperation, fear and self-pity, the three GELFs bickered as the polymorph slept off its meal and prepared for the Shadow Time, during which the planet refroze, trapping them all until the next thaw **[M-SMG1.13(c3)]**.

- **Armée du Nord:** A term describing several military units throughout France's history, most notably one commanded by Napoleon Bonaparte in 1815. The term translated into English as "Army of the North" **[RL]**. Rimmer had nineteenth-century replica soldiers of Napoleon's Armée du Nord stored with his other valuables in his father's camphor-wood chest, which was loaded onto *Starbug 1* during an evacuation of *Red Dwarf*. Shortly after disembarkation, however, the shuttle crashed on an icy planet, marooning Rimmer and Lister. To stay warm, Lister had no choice but to burn the statues **[T-SER3.2]**.

- **Armpit Name That Tune:** A game possibly played aboard *Starbug 1*. After Lister and Cat found Kochanski's Magic Flute game unenjoyable, she suggested that Armpit Name That Tune and similar games might be more their speed **[T-SER7.5]**.

- **Armstrong, Nellie:** The first person to set foot on Earth's Moon in an alternate reality in which the sexes were reversed **[T-SER2.6]**.

> ***NOTE:*** *This was the female-oriented society's analog to real-world astronaut Neil Armstrong, who became the first person on the Moon in 1969.*

APOCALYPSE BOYS, THE

PREFIX
RL: Real life

T-: Television Episodes
SER: Television series
IDW: "Identity Within"
USA1: Unaired U.S. pilot
USA2: Unaired U.S. demo

R-: *The Bodysnatcher Collection*
SER: Remastered episodes
BOD: "Bodysnatcher"
DAD: "Dad"
FTH: "Lister's Father"
INF: "Infinity Patrol"
END: "The End" (original assembly)

N-: Novels
INF: *Infinity Welcomes Careful Drivers*
BTL: *Better Than Life*
LST: *Last Human*
BCK: *Backwards*
OMN: *Red Dwarf Omnibus*

M-: Magazines
SMG: *Smegazine*

W-: Websites
OFF: Official website
NAN: *Prelude to Nanarchy*
AND: *Androids*
DIV: Diva-Droid
DIB: Duane Dibbley

CRP: Crapola
GEN: Geneticon
LSR: Leisure World Intl.
JMC: Jupiter Mining Corporation
AIT: *A.I. Today*
HOL: HoloPoint

G-: Roleplaying Game
RPG: *Core Rulebook*
BIT: *A.I. Screen Extra Bits* booklet
SOR: *Series Sourcebook*
OTH: Other RPG material

- **Arn:** A nickname that Rimmer asked Lister to call him (instead of "Rimmer") as they and Cat embarked on a rescue mission to the *Nova 5*, where they believed three female crewmembers awaited **[T-SER2.1]**.

- **Arnie:** Another name that Rimmer suggested Lister call him during their mercy mission to the *Nova 5* **[T-SER2.1]**.

- **"Arnie Comes Out on Top":** A headline that Rimmer cut out of print material and adhered to the wall of his bunk aboard *Red Dwarf* **[N-INF]**.

- **"Arnie Does It Best":** A print headline that Rimmer cut out and adhered to his *Red Dwarf* locker door **[T-SER1.3]**. While sharing quarters with his duplicate hologram, Arnold had the headlines relocated to his new abode. Lister was amused, as the slogans were about other people named "Arnold" or "Rimmer" **[T-SER1.6]**.

- **"Arnie Has Had Lots of Girlfriends":** A sign held up by teenage girls who lined up to see Rimmer in an illusory world created by an addictive version of *Better Than Life*. In the dream, Rimmer believed he had gained fame and fortune upon returning to Earth, and had become the object of desire to millions of teenage girls, who followed him around screaming, holding up signs and throwing their intimate garments at him **[N-INF]**.

- **"Arnie Is Brave":** Another sign held up by teenage girls lined up to see Rimmer in an illusory world created by an addictive version of *Better Than Life* **[N-INF]**.

- **"Arnie Is Fab":** Another sign held up by teenage girls lined up to see Rimmer in an illusory world created by an addictive version of *Better Than Life* **[N-INF]**.

- **Arnie Rimmer's Death Machine:** The nickname Rimmer gave to his army of pacifistic waxdroids on Waxworld. The droids used the name in their cadence call **[T-SER4.6]**.

- **Arnold:** A name that Rimmer suggested for Lister's baby, which would have made him the infant's namesake **[R-DAD]**.

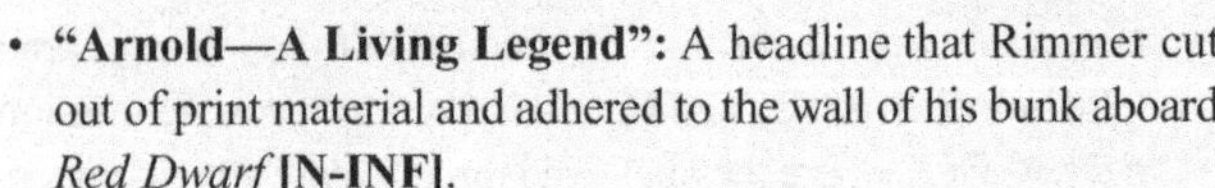

- **"Arnold—A Living Legend":** A headline that Rimmer cut out of print material and adhered to the wall of his bunk aboard *Red Dwarf* **[N-INF]**.

- **"Arnold J Rimmer—A Tribute":** A video recording of Rimmer's death, made for and given to the hologrammic version of Rimmer by Holly, *Red Dwarf*'s computer **[T-SER1.6]**.

- **"Arnold on Top":** A print headline that Rimmer cut out and adhered to his *Red Dwarf* locker door **[T-SER1.3]**. While sharing quarters with his duplicate hologram, Arnold had the headlines relocated to his new abode. Lister was amused, as the slogans were about other people named "Arnold" or "Rimmer" **[T-SER1.6]**.

- **Arnold Rimmer Archive, The:** A proposed database suggested by Rimmer in his log entry for a redesign of *Red Dwarf*. According to his crude drawing, the archive took up about a sixth of the entire ship **[B-LOG]**.

- ***Arnold Rimmer—Lust For Glory*:** The proposed title of Rimmer's autobiography, which he intended to write as one of his New Year's resolutions **[B-LOG]**.

- **Arnold Rimmer Memorial Museum and Interactive Wax Figure Experience, The:** A proposed memorial suggested by Rimmer in his log entry for a redesign of *Red Dwarf*. According to his crude drawing, the museum took up about of quarter of the entire ship **[B-LOG]**.

- ***Arnold Rimmer's Tactical Guide to Warfare*:** A hypothetical book title. While discussing options to deal with agonoids that had boarded *Red Dwarf*, Lister noted that this book contained two entries: running away and surrendering **[N-BCK]**.

- **"Arnold's Tops With Us":** A print headline that Rimmer cut out and adhered to his *Red Dwarf* locker door **[T-SER1.3]**. While sharing quarters with his duplicate hologram, Arnold had the headlines relocated to his new abode. Lister was amused, as the slogans were about other people named "Arnold" or "Rimmer" **[T-SER1.6]**.

- **Around the Houses:** A rarely used goal-scoring tactic in zero-gee football, by which players kicked or carried the ball until passing the goal-line, at which point they would place the ball on the ground in what used to be known as a touchdown. This mundane tactic killed the old sport of football, inspiring the creators of zero-gee football to instead use a circular doughnut-shaped arena, making it that much harder to locate the end zone **[M-SMG1.8(a)]**.

- **Arranguu 12:** A desert moon located within GELF territory in an alternate universe. It was divided into the Northern Sector, which followed the Jhjghjiuyhu judicial system and contained the Forum of Justice, and the Southern Sector, which followed a more archaic, outmoded legal system **[N-LST]**.

- **Arre bubble:** A type of tractor-beam used by the GELFs of Blerion 15 to capture ships violating Blerios airspace. Resembling a green cirrus cloud, the Arre bubble would engulf trespassing ships, and could be used by the GELFs to raise the cabin temperature to 75 degrees Celsius (167 degrees Fahrenheit) if the occupants refused to submit to their judiciary **[N-LST]**.

- **arrest mode:** The status that a Space Corps external enforcement vehicle entered upon encountering individuals who had broken the law **[T-SER6.4(d)]**.

- **arrogance:** A rogue emotion purged from Kryten's hard drive by the Data Doctor, a program for restoring a mechanoid's personality to factory settings, when Captain Hollister subjected Kryten to a psychotropic simulation **[T-SER8.2]**.

- ***Arrowflight*:** A fantasy roleplaying game created by Deep7 Press **[RL]**. Holly once ran an *Arrowflight* campaign for the crew of *Red Dwarf*, with limited success **[G-COR]**.

  ***NOTE:** In the real world, Deep7 also created* Red Dwarf—The Roleplaying Game.

- **ARS:** *See* Artificial Reality Suite

- **Arsewipe:** A name Rimmer suggested he be called by Warden Knot, a prison guard aboard *Red Dwarf*, during their encounter with Cassandra. He suggested the name to prevent the guard

PREFIX
RL: Real life

T-: Television Episodes
SER: Television series
IDW: "Identity Within"
USA1: Unaired U.S. pilot
USA2: Unaired U.S. demo

R-: *The Bodysnatcher Collection*
SER: Remastered episodes
BOD: "Bodysnatcher"
DAD: "Dad"
FTH: "Lister's Father"
INF: "Infinity Patrol"
END: "The End" (original assembly)

N-: Novels
INF: *Infinity Welcomes Careful Drivers*
BTL: *Better Than Life*
LST: *Last Human*
BCK: *Backwards*
OMN: *Red Dwarf Omnibus*

M-: Magazines
SMG: *Smegazine*

W-: Websites
OFF: Official website
NAN: *Prelude to Nanarchy*
AND: *Androids*
DIV: Diva-Droid
DIB: Duane Dibbley
CRP: Crapola
GEN: Geneticon
LSR: Leisure World Intl.
JMC: Jupiter Mining Corporation
AIT: *A.I. Today*
HOL: HoloPoint

G-: Roleplaying Game
RPG: *Core Rulebook*
BIT: *A.I. Screen Extra Bits* booklet
SOR: *Series Sourcebook*
OTH: Other RPG material

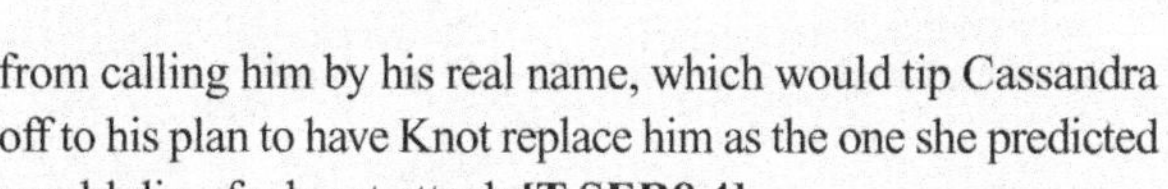

from calling him by his real name, which would tip Cassandra off to his plan to have Knot replace him as the one she predicted would die of a heart attack **[T-SER8.4]**.

- **AR simulation:** An artificial environment created inside a computer for the purpose of entertainment. Lister frequently entered AR simulations while aboard *Starbug 1* in order to simulate sex **[T-SER7.2]**.

- **AR Suite:** An area located aboard *Starbug 1* that contained an artificial-reality (AR) machine and several AR chairs. Arnold Rimmer trained in the suite to become the next Ace Rimmer **[T-SER7.2]**. Kryten also used the suite to create *The Rimmer Experience*, a virtual-reality amusement-park ride designed to remind the crew of Rimmer's shortcomings whenever they missed him **[T-SER7.5]**.

- **AR Suite:** An area of *Red Dwarf* containing an artificial-reality (AR) machine and several AR units. *Red Dwarf*'s Board of Inquiry used the AR Suite while investigating Lister, Rimmer, Cat, Kryten and Kochanski. The five were placed in a drug-induced psychotropic trance and hooked into the AR machine, while the Board reviewed their simulated actions **[T-SER8.3]**.

- **Art College:** An institution at which Lister enrolled and was accepted, despite failing his final exams. He lasted a total of ninety-seven minutes before dropping out due to the school's rigorous schedule of afternoon lectures **[T-SER2.1]**.

  ***NOTE:** This gag originated in a* Son of Cliché *sketch titled "Freshers."*

- **Arthur:** A fish-like GELF exiled to Garbage World (Earth) during the GELF War. After the planet was ripped from its orbit and propelled into deep space, Arthur and two other GELFs, a living armchair and a genetically engineered refrigerator, hibernated together while the planet froze over. Over the course of millennia, the planet's trajectory took it near several stars, occasionally thawing it out and releasing its trapped inhabitants.

  During one such thaw, a young polymorph emerged from its cocoon and took the form of a cockroach to search for sustenance. It came upon Arthur and his two GELF friends, who were themselves searching for food, and fed on their emotions, one by one, by changing its form to elicit strong responses. In Arthur's case, the polymorph changed into a gym coach who berated him, forcing him to feel desperation. Lacking desperation, fear and self-pity, the three GELFs bickered as the polymorph slept off its meal and prepared for the Shadow Time, during which the planet refroze, trapping them all until the next thaw **[M-SMG1.13(c3)]**.

- ***Arthur C. Clarke*:** A supply ship, possibly owned by the Jupiter Mining Corp. Two miles long, the vessel was distinguished by a large, bulbous cargo section and a long, tubular nose section. This ship was parked in orbit around Mimas when Lister first reported for duty on *Red Dwarf* **[N-INF]**.

  ***NOTE:** The ship was named after the famed British science fiction author.*

- **artichoke:** A password needed to access Duane Dibbley's website **[W-DIB]**.

  ***NOTE:** Clues to this password were spread throughout the Geek Chase online game.*

- **Article 39436175880932/B:** A clause of the All Nations Agreement of Earth stipulating that any nation attending the conference was only allocated a single parking space. Rimmer mistakenly invoked this article during a hostile simulant boarding of *Starbug 1*, when in fact he meant 39436175880932/C **[T-SER3.6]**.

  ***NOTE:** An early-draft script for this episode, published in the book* Son of Soup, *cited the clause as Article 574328765/B.*

- **Article 39436175880932/C:** A clause of the All Nations Agreement of Earth regarding the right of prisoners-of-war to non-violent constraint. Rimmer meant to invoke this article during a hostile simulant boarding of *Starbug 1*, but mistakenly invoked 75880932/B **[T-SER3.6]**.

  ***NOTE:** An early-draft script for this episode, published in the book* Son of Soup, *cited this clause as Article 574328765/C.*

- **Article 497:** A regulation aboard JMC ships stating that a crewmember out of credits would be denied food from dispensers until he or she earned additional credits. After assuming control of *Red Dwarf*, backup computer Queeg forced

Lister and Cat to perform menial tasks, such as scrubbing floors, in order to earn food credits **[T-SER2.5]**.

NOTE: Since the entire Queeg incident was a ruse Holly fabricated to punish the crew for taking him for granted, it is uncertain whether this article actually existed.

- **Article 5:** A regulation aboard JMC ships mandating that in the event of gross negligence on the part of the ship's artificial intelligence leading to the crew's endangerment, a backup computer had to be activated to assume control of all shipboard functions. After a series of such breaches, *Red Dwarf*'s backup computer, Queeg, was activated and replaced Holly **[T-SER2.5]**.

  ***NOTE:** Since the entire Queeg incident was a ruse Holly fabricated to punish the crew for taking him for granted, it is uncertain whether this article actually existed.*

- **Article 574328765/B:** *See* Article 39436175880932/B

- **Article 574328765/C:** *See* Article 39436175880932/C

- **artificial insemination syringe:** An apparatus used to impregnate females by the injection of sperm into a woman's reproductive tract **[RL]**. Bored with using plastic cutlery, Lister procured several items from *Red Dwarf*'s Medical Unit and used them to prepare and serve dinner in the Officers Quarters, including an artificial insemination syringe for cattle, in which he kept lemon juice **[T-SER3.3]**.

  ***NOTE:** What use such an implement would have on a deep space mining vessel is a mystery.*

- **Artificial-Intelligence synthesizer:** A computerized musical instrument fitted with AI technology, capable of creating and playing its own music. In 2167, an Artificial-Intelligence synthesizer independently produced a flawless rendition of the song "Remember You're a Womble" **[B-EVR]**.

- **artificial intelligence system:** A software system built into Crapola Inc.'s Talkie Toaster that governed the unit's intellect **[T-SER4.4]**. The original toaster used a J055 or J056 AI system, while the second-generation model utilized a K177 or K178 version **[W-CRP]**.

- **artificial reality console:** *See* AR machine

- **Artificial Reality Suite (ARS):** A virtual-reality system produced by Total Immersion Inc. and distributed by Crapola Inc. **[G-RPG]**. *Starbug 1* was outfitted with an AR Suite that included an artificial-reality machine and several interface units. Lister used this suite to enter a medieval simulation, where he employed a cheatbook to seduce the Queen of Camelot. Later, he pretended to be a rogue knight escaping the suite and "attacked" Rimmer in an attempt to bring out his courage and convince him to become the next Ace Rimmer **[T-SER7.2]**.

- **ASC-2 code:** A character-encoding scheme for representing text in computers. Upon meeting the Pleasure GELF Camille, Kryten professed his feelings for her by converting the word "love" into a basic ASC-2 code **[T-SER4.1]**.

  ***NOTE:** The script for episode 4.1 ("Camille"), published in the book* Son of Soup, *wrote out the code's name as "ASC two." It is possible the writer misinterpreted the real-world acronym "ASCII," which stands for American Standard Code for Information Interchange.*

- **Ascension Sunday:** A Catholic holy day commemorating Jesus Christ's ascension to Heaven following his crucifixion **[RL]**. Rimmer broadcast a Mayday distress call after he and Lister crashed *Starbug 1* on an icy planet. Mistaking "Mayday" as a reference to the bank holiday May Day, Rimmer questioned its effectiveness, wondering why "Ascension Sunday" wasn't chosen for distress calls instead **[T-SER3.2]**.

- **'A' Section:** A group of twenty skutters assigned to help Rimmer prime his half of the twelve hundred piston towers needed to restart *Red Dwarf*'s engines, which had been deactivated when Holly shut himself down. In his haste to finish the job before Kryten, Rimmer accidentally crushed the robots while testing Piston Tower 136, mistakenly believing they were in Piston Tower 137 **[N-BTL]**.

- **A-Shift:** A team of *Red Dwarf* crewmembers assigned to maintenance duties. First Technician Petrovitch was A-Shift's leader at the time of the ship's cadmium II disaster **[N-INF]**.

- **"Asleep":** A message displayed over Lister's bunk **[T-SER2.4]**.

- **asses' milk:** The breast milk of female donkeys, believed to have skin-rejuvenation and medicinal properties **[RL]**. After attempting to change history by using a timeslide to become the Tension Sheet's inventor and thus marry model Sabrina Mulholland-Jjones, Rimmer pondered what to do with his new wife, including bathing in asses' milk **[T-SER3.5(d)]**.

- **Astermayer:** A scientist who postulated that one and two were the same thing observed from different precepts. Rimmer cited Astermayer after a mind patch dramatically increased his intelligence **[T-SER5.1]**.

    NOTE: The DVD captions spelled the name as "Ustermayer," but the more common spelling is "Astermayer."

- **asteroidal lichen stew:** A meal made from the fungi and moss found on asteroids. After *Starbug 1*'s refrigeration unit malfunctioned, the crew resorted to surviving on such fungi and moss. Kryten attempted to vary the menu by occasionally making asteroidal lichen stew from the ingredients **[T-SER6.5]**.

- **Asteroid of Turin:** A religious shrine in space, dedicated to the Shroud of Turin. When Tunbridge Wells' five hundred pilgrims were sent to pray for the end of a meteor storm ravaging their city, a knight in the group believed his people were headed to the Asteroid of Turin. When he struck down a sergeant for claiming they were visiting Pan's shrine, a religious war started that wiped out the entire pilgrim crew **[M-SMG1.14(c2)]**.

- **asteroid spotting:** A pastime that Rimmer enjoyed, which involved counting asteroids from *Starbug*'s cockpit. During one such outing, Rimmer and Kryten came across a crashed ship, aboard which they found a Pleasure GELF called Camille **[T-SER4.1]**.

- **Aston Martin:** A British manufacturer of luxury sports automobiles **[RL]**. Rimmer likened Lister's brain after reading a book to a hamster that, once used to a hamster wheel, was suddenly given the keys to an Aston Martin **[T-SER10.3]**.

- **astro:** A term describing a person who worked in space **[N-INF]**.

- **Astro Cuts:** A hair salon located in the Theta Sector of Dimension 24. It employed a stylist named Alfonse, whose clients included Ace Rimmer **[T-SER7.2]**.

- **Astro-Engineer's Exam:** A mandatory test that Space Corps technicians were required to pass in order to earn a promotion. Rimmer tried to pass this exam on numerous occasions. In one instance, he became flustered at the sight of the test, wrote "I am a fish" several hundred times and passed out; in another, he attempted to cheat by writing facts all over his body, only to incomprehensively smear them with sweat and again faint **[T-SER1.1]**. When Lister threatened to pass the exam and become promoted over him, Rimmer mistakenly assumed it was the Engineer's Exam he was attempting to pass, but it was actually the Chef's Exam **[T-SER1.3]**.

    NOTE: According to episode 1.4 ("Waiting For God"), as well as the novel Last Human, *Rimmer took this test a total of eleven times.*

- **astroglacier:** A spatial phenomenon resembling a massive iceberg. The *Starbug 1* crew encountered an astroglacier, which they detected as having been allotropically modified and surrounded by luminous gases. This particular astroglacier turned out to be the Space Corps vessel *Leviathan*, encased in ice by the Epideme virus **[T-SER7.7]**.

- ***Astronavigation and Invisible Numbers in Engineering Structure Made Simple*:** A book that Rimmer kept on a drafting table in his quarters aboard *Red Dwarf*. While separating items for Arnold to take with him to his new room, Lister tossed this book into Rimmer's storage box, along with the rest of his possessions **[T-SER1.6]**.

- ***Astro-Navigation and Invisible Numbers in Engineering Structure Made Simple*:** A television program that aired on Groovy Channel 27 at 10 AM on Wednesday, the 27th of Geldof, 2362. This educational program was geared toward Space Corps Academy applicants **[M-SMG1.7(a)]**.

- ***Astronavigation and Invisible Number Theory Made Simple*:** A book that Rimmer owned aboard *Red Dwarf* **[N-INF]**.

B-: Books
PRG: *Red Dwarf Programme Guide*
SUR: *Red Dwarf Space Corps Survival Manual*
PRM: *Primordial Soup*
SOS: *Son of Soup*
SCE: *Scenes from the Dwarf*
LOG: *Red Dwarf Log No. 1996*
RD8: *Red Dwarf VIII*
EVR: *The Log: A Dwarfer's Guide to Everything*

X-: Misc.
PRO: Promotional materials, videos, etc.
PST: Posters at DJ XVII (2013)
CAL: 2008 calendar
RNG: Cell phone ringtones
MOB: Mobisode ("Red Christmas")
CIN: *Children in Need* sketch
GEK: *Geek Week* intros by Kryten
TNG: "Tongue-Tied" video

XMS: Bill Pearson's Christmas special pitch script
XVD: Bill Pearson's Christmas special pitch video
OTH: Other *Red Dwarf* appearances

SUFFIX
DVD:
(d) – Deleted scene
(o) – Outtake
(b) – Bonus DVD material (other)
(e) – Extended version

SMEGAZINES:
(c) – Comic
(a) – Article

OTHER:
(s) – Early/unused script draft
(s1) – Alternate version of script

- **Astronavigation Exam:** A test designed to measure a Space Corps employee's knowledge of space navigation. Rimmer took and failed this test several times **[T-SER1.2]**.

  NOTE: *According to episode 1.2 ("Future Echoes"), Rimmer took the test ten times, but according to Kryten's defense on the penal station Justice World in episode 4.3 ("Justice"), as well as in later episodes, Rimmer took and failed this exam thirteen times. Presumably, he took the test three more times between Series I and IV. In episode 10.1 ("Trojan"), however, Rimmer said he failed nine times, and had just taken it again, for a total of ten. The novel* Infinity Welcomes Careful Drivers *indicated Rimmer took the test twelve times prior to the cadmium II accident—a number revised to thirteen later in the same book.*

- ***Astro Navigation for Idiots*:** A book outlining how to navigate ships through space, written in a simple, easy-to-understand format. Rimmer studied this book in order to pass his Astronavigation Exam **[T-SER9.1]**.

  NOTE: *This title was an amalgamation of two popular real-world book series,* The Complete Idiot's Guides *and* For Dummies.

- **Astronavigation Officer, Fourth Class:** The lowest-ranking astronavigation officer aboard *Red Dwarf*. Rimmer, yearning to become an officer, took the Astronavigation Exam several times in order to achieve this rank, but failed each time **[N-INF]**.

- **astro-stripper:** An industrial tool used to remove paint from spacecraft hulls, consisting of a harness, a torch-gun funnel and control stick in front, and a rear jet pack. Rimmer used an astro-stripper, albeit backwards, to thwart Lister's psychotic doppelgänger who had taken his crewmates hostage **[N-LST]**.

- **athlete's foot:** A contagious fungal infection of the skin causing scaling, flaking and itching of affected areas **[RL]**. Lister suffered from athlete's foot, which Rimmer neglected to treat while occupying Dave's body following a mind swap **[T-SER3.4]**.

- **athlete's hand:** A hypothetical affliction. To conceal Bob the skutter's involvement in administering the virility-enhancement drug Boing to the *Red Dwarf* guards' basketball team, Lister told Captain Hollister that he stole the drug himself after reporting to the medi-bay with a case of athlete's hand **[T-SER8.6]**.

- **Atlas, Charles:** A twentieth-century fitness trainer who developed his own bodybuilding method, made famous by an aggressive advertising campaign **[RL]**. When Lister chastised Rimmer for putting on weight while inhabiting his body following a mind swap, Rimmer noted that Lister hadn't been Charles Atlas to begin with **[T-SER3.4]**.

- ***A to Z of Mimas*:** A manual that Lister found in a taxi hopper he stole on Mimas. During a fight between two pimps that broke out near the hopper, Lister ignored the ruckus by locking the doors and reading the manual **[N-INF]**.

- ***A to Z of Red Dwarf*:** A book Rimmer owned that contained a secret compartment hiding his diary. Lister found the book in the quarters Rimmer shared with his duplicate hologram while investigating the significance of gazpacho soup **[T-SER1.6]**.

- ***Attack of the Giant Savage Completely Invisible Aliens*:** A black-and-white horror B-movie with subpar special effects, created by the same team that produced *Vampire Bikini Girls Suck Paris*. The film was shown to inmates of the Tank, *Red Dwarf*'s brig, but was pre-empted by Kryten's transmission of *Women's Shower Night* for Krytie TV **[T-SER8.5]**. It was then scheduled to be re-broadcast by Krytie TV on November 8 **[X-CAL]**.

- ***Attack of the Killer Gooseberries*:** A film of which Holly was reminded whenever the wristwatch version of himself was placed into Lister's trouser pocket, which had holes in it, giving Holly an unfortunate view **[T-SER2.4]**.

- **audio receiver:** A component of 4000 Series mechanoids enabling them to hear their environment **[T-SER8.8]**.

- **Audrey's:** A hair salon located on the set of the British television show *Coronation Street* **[RL]**. While trapped in an elation squid hallucination, the *Red Dwarf* crew, believing themselves to be on an alternate twenty-first-century Earth, passed Audrey's while searching for actor Craig Charles on set **[T-SER9.2]**.

NOTE: Audrey's, like all businesses appearing in this sequence, was created for the television show Coronation Street, *in which Craig Charles starred as of this writing. Audrey's Hair Salon was owned by Audrey Roberts, and was located at 2 Coronation Street, in the fictional town of Weatherfield, England.*

- ***Augustus*, SS:** The ship on which Kryten served prior to *Nova 5*. The mechanoid was left on his own when the crew died of old age, after which he joined the *Nova 5*—whose crew he accidentally killed **[T-SER7.3]**.

- **aural system:** The electronics that enabled sentient appliances, such as Talkie Toaster, to convert sound waves into an electrical signal that could then be understood **[T-SER4.4]**.

- **Austen, Jane:** A nineteenth-century English novelist, known for such works as *Pride and Prejudice, Mansfield Park* and *Sense and Sensibility* **[RL]**. Kochanski frequently used an artificial-reality (AR) simulation based on the writer's works, called *Jane Austen World*, during her years at cyberschool.

  Kochanski and the *Starbug 1* crew found a copy of the AR game, which included programs like *Pride and Prejudice Land*, aboard a derelict Space Corps vessel. Bringing the game back to *Starbug 1*, she invited Lister and Cat to join her in the simulation, in an attempt to broaden their cultural horizons **[T-SER7.6]**.

  Years later, when Lister visited Kochanski's memorial stone, he brought *Sense and Sensibility* to read to her, though he could not remember how to pronounce the author's name **[T-SER9.1]**.

- **Austin, Jane:** The author of *Edda, Winchester Park* and *A Field of Broken Dreams*. Artificial-reality (AR) simulations of these novels were included in *Jane Austin World*, an AR program developed by Total Immersion Inc. and distributed by Crapola Inc. **[G-RPG]**.

  NOTE: Jane Austen (note the different surname spelling) did not write books titled Edda, Winchester Park *or* A Field of Broken Dreams, *though the first two satirized two of her works (*Emma *and* Mansfield Park*), while the third befitted the disappointments that her characters tended to experience. Some online sources have attributed these same books to Jane G. Austin, another actual writer who lived a century after Austen, as part of the so-called "Calamity Jane Austin" hoax, in which members of Usenet discussion group rec.arts.sf.written crafted a fabricated life story and bibliography for Austin, to purposely mislead anyone incorrectly entering Austen's name in a search engine (see richardhartersworld.com/cri/2004/austin.html). All works listed in the faux bibliography satirized the real Austen's work, including the above-noted books, as well as* Fence and Fencibility *and* Pride and Precipice.

- **"Authorised Personnel Only":** Verbiage stenciled on the entry door to *Red Dwarf*'s Observation Room, where Holly placed a captured unidentified pod. Ignoring protocol, Lister entered the room to satiate his curiosity about the pod, whereupon he learned that it was actually an old garbage pod jettisoned from *Red Dwarf* itself. Rimmer, following quarantine procedures to the letter, waited days before finally having the pod opened, during which he fantasized about possible alien intelligence inside **[T-SER1.4]**.

  This phrase was also stenciled on the Drive Room wall **[T-SER2.5]**, as well as on an airlock next to the solar panels outside Lister's quarters **[T-SER1.5]**.

- **auto-compacting mass driver:** An advanced technology built into the experimental JMC mining ship *Black Hole*, capable of taking harvested raw material, compacting it into packets and sending it home at light speed, thereby removing the need for multiple trips. Like all of the ship's systems, it was powered by a tiny captured star **[G-RPG]**.

- **"Auto Destruct":** A message displayed on a food dispenser Lister used to order a milk shake and a Crispy Bar. The dispenser, having been rewired by a crazed skutter, was linked to *Red Dwarf*'s auto-destruct system **[T-SER3.4]**.

- **auto-destruct:** A feature built into every 4000 Series mechanoid that permitted it to destroy itself in the event that it went insane, thereby protecting its owner and any other humans within the vicinity. Kryten pondered having to auto-destruct while meeting future versions of the *Starbug 1* crew, taking

solace in the fact that if he should die, there was a month's supply of pre-cooked mini-meals in the refrigeration unit for his crewmates **[T-SER6.6(d)]**.

- **auto-destruct system:** A mechanism aboard *Red Dwarf* that, when activated, set a countdown timer for detonation of an onboard explosive large enough to destroy the entire vessel. Once it was initiated, the only crewmembers authorized to abort the sequence were the captain and senior officers.

  At one point, a crazed skutter rewired *Red Dwarf*'s maintenance decks, including the auto-destruct system, which was activated when Lister used a food dispenser to order a milk shake and a Crispy Bar. With Captain Hollister and all senior officers long dead, the crew was forced to attempt a mind swap, an experimental procedure that switched the minds of Lister and Carole Brown, an executive officer whose brain pattern was stored on file. Despite the procedure's success, the auto-destruct sequence could not be stopped; fortunately for the crew, Holly had removed the explosive linked to the system years prior, a fact she neglected to share until the countdown timer had run out **[T-SER3.4]**.

- **AutoFOOD:** A wall-mounted machine that, upon request, would instantly assemble and dispense any food or beverage programmed into its memory **[T-SER1.1]**. There were several such dispensers around *Red Dwarf*, including one in the Drive Room **[T-SER1.3]**.

- **automatic lubricant purge system:** A system built into 4000 Series mechanoids that purged excess lubricant when activated **[N-BCK]**.

- **Automobile Association (AA):** An organization in the United Kingdom that assisted stranded motorists and distributed travel information **[RL]**. Holly noted in her log that the *Red Dwarf* crew had come to the realization that no one from AA was going to show up to help them **[T-SER3.6(d)]**. On the television soap opera *Androids,* Archie drove an AA emergency vehicle **[M-SMG2.9(c6)]**.

- **autonomous mobile hologrammic projection module:** *See* light bee

- **autopilot:** A feature in *Starbug* shuttles that allowed the craft to be controlled via computer. In the case of *Red Dwarf's Starbug* complement, autopilot would be controlled by Holly **[T-SER3.1]**.

- **autopilot alert:** An audible alert provided by a *Starbug*'s autopilot system, warning occupants of any navigational issues requiring their attention. When a stellar fog storm triggered *Starbug*'s autopilot alert, the crew resumed control of the craft in order to avoid the danger **[T-SER6.6]**.

- **auto-repair:** A system aboard *Starbug* shuttles used to repair light to moderate damage inflicted to the ship **[T-SER6.4]**.

  NOTE: This would explain how Starbug *could repeatedly crash and seem almost unsalvageable in one episode, and be perfectly fine in the next.*

- **auto-repair:** *see* self-repair system

- **Auto-Serve Dispensing Machine:** A brand of food dispensers used aboard *Red Dwarf* **[T-SER3.4]**.

- **auxiliary conductor nodes:** A component of *Starbug*'s propulsion system. While questioning the Epideme virus infecting Lister, Kryten asked how the crew could reconfigure the ship's drive module to be more efficient; the sentient disease instructed Kryten to re-route the pulse relays via the auxiliary conductor nodes **[T-SER7.7]**.

- **auxiliary flight modulator:** A backup of *Starbug 1*'s main flight modulator. The auxiliary flight modulator was damaged when the crew attempted to pass through the tail of a phasing comet in order to return Kochanski to her own dimension **[T-SER7.5]**.

- **auxiliary power drives:** A backup power system aboard *Starbug 1.* While attempting to get Kochanski back to her own dimension, Kryten re-routed power to the auxiliary power drives to reverse the signal of the electromagnetic phase frequencies,

PREFIX
RL: Real life

T-: Television Episodes
SER: Television series
IDW: "Identity Within"
USA1: Unaired U.S. pilot
USA2: Unaired U.S. demo

R-: *The Bodysnatcher Collection*
SER: Remastered episodes
BOD: "Bodysnatcher"
DAD: "Dad"
FTH: "Lister's Father"
INF: "Infinity Patrol"
END: "The End" (original assembly)

N-: Novels
INF: *Infinity Welcomes Careful Drivers*
BTL: *Better Than Life*
LST: *Last Human*

BCK: *Backwards*
OMN: *Red Dwarf Omnibus*

M-: Magazines
SMG: *Smegazine*

W-: Websites
OFF: Official website
NAN: *Prelude to Nanarchy*
AND: *Androids*
DIV: Diva-Droid
DIB: Duane Dibbley

CRP: Crapola
GEN: Geneticon
LSR: Leisure World Intl.
JMC: Jupiter Mining Corporation
AIT: *A.I. Today*
HOL: HoloPoint

G-: Roleplaying Game
RPG: *Core Rulebook*
BIT: *A.I. Screen Extra Bits* booklet
SOR: *Series Sourcebook*
OTH: Other RPG material

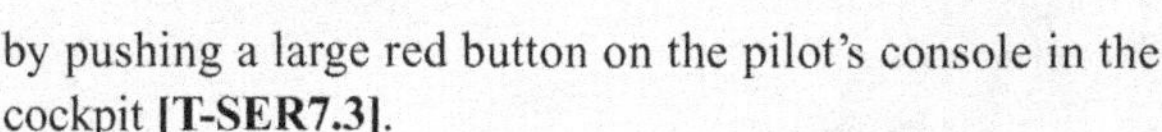

by pushing a large red button on the pilot's console in the cockpit **[T-SER7.3]**.

- **AV 27L:** A marking on a box located in *Red Dwarf*'s storage bay. The Inquisitor and Lister faced off near this container, resulting in the Inquisitor's demise **[T-SER5.2]**.

- **AV 647A:** A marking on another crate in *Red Dwarf*'s storage bay, near which Lister fought the Inquisitor **[T-SER5.2]**.

- **AV 657A:** A marking on yet another container in *Red Dwarf*'s storage bay, near the site of Lister's battle with the Inquisitor **[T-SER5.2]**.

- **Awooga Waltz:** A name that Cat gave to *Red Dwarf*'s red-alert claxon after a triplicator experiment went awry, causing the engine core to approach critical mass **[T-SER5.5]**.

- **Axe Man, the:** A nickname that Kryten once called Lister. After spending two hundred years in deep sleep aboard *Starbug 1* while tracking the stolen *Red Dwarf*, Lister awoke to find his memory temporarily missing. Hoping to jog his memory, Kryten handed him his guitar, which he strummed chaotically and out of tune. Since this matched his usual guitar-playing ability, Kryten exclaimed that "the Axe Man" was back **[T-SER6.1]**.

- **Axis-syndrome hologram:** A type of hologrammic entity in use near a group of alternate-universe GELF settlements **[N-LST]**.

- ***A-Z*:** A thin, spiral-bound book located on a desk in the quarters Lister shared with Rimmer aboard *Red Dwarf* **[T-SER2.4]**.

- **Azymuth, Ivan:** A member of a fascist society in an alternate universe who established the Three Laws of Robotics:
  1) Keep your groinal socket dust-free.
  2) Never sell body parts to pawnbrokers.
  3) Always find a soft place to land **[M-SMG2.9(c4)]**.

  NOTE: *This was a joking reference to science fiction author Isaac Asimov, who devised the Three Laws of Robotics for his novels and short fiction.*

B

BARTIKOVSKY, KATERINA, SCIENCE OFFICER

- **B**: A letter stenciled on the floor near *Red Dwarf*'s airlocks **[T-SER3.6]**.

    NOTE: *Although not visible onscreen, the seal to Airlock B was presumably just offscreen, considering the letter "A" was stenciled on the floor just outside Airlock A.*

- **B:** A letter stenciled on a pillar supporting the domed station in which Thomas Allman resided **[T-SER5.2]**.

- **B103:** A label on a console within the cockpit of *Midget 3* **[T-SER8.3]**.

- **B47/7RF resistor:** An electronic component that Kryten needed in order to disable Rimmer after the latter became infected with a deadly holovirus. Lister, Kryten and Cat attempted to immobilize Rimmer by using a B47/7RF resistor combined with other components. Finding such parts was made easier by the luck virus, with which Lister had infected himself **[T-SER5.4]**.

- **B 53432 Modem Interface:** A computer component referenced by Robbie, Kryten's superhero analog in the universe known as Alternative 2X13/L, in one of Robbie's trademark exclamations **[M-SMG2.1(c3)]**.

- **B6:** A label printed on an overhead console in *Red Dwarf*'s science lab **[T-SER5.5]**.

- **Babes:** A cutesy nickname Lister gave Kochanski during their brief romance **[N-INF]**.

- ***Babes in Space***: A substitute title that Frank, a TV executive in an alternate universe, suggested for the American television show *Red Dwarf,* after noting the lack of actual dwarves in it **[M-SMG1.10(c4)]**.

- **baboon four-eyes:** A name that Rimmer called a college classmate, Wendy, who was attempting to tip him off that he was the subject of their teacher's psychology test. The teacher, Rimmer's stepfather, instructed the class before Arnold arrived to answer a series of questions wrong, to see how he would react to peer pressure. When Arnold showed up and the quiz began, the bespectacled Wendy wrote in her notebook that he was a guinea pig; mistaking it as an insult, he wrote back that she was a "baboon four-eyes" **[T-SER10.6]**.

- **"Baby I Want Your Love Thing":** A song possibly recorded by the band The 5th Dimension, which made it to sixth place on the charts. Lister mentioned the song as Holly explained the Fifth Dimension (an alternate reality) and how they had arrived there using the Holly Hop Drive **[T-SER2.6]**.

    When asked by his metaphysical psychiatrist if he was familiar with The Cartesian Principle, hologram Frank Saunders replied that he thought they had gone to number five with "Baby I Want Your Love Thing" **[N-INF]**.

    NOTE: *The 5th Dimension, a musical vocal group of the 1960s and '70s, never recorded a song by this title. The DVD subtitles called the song "I Want Your Love Thing."*

- **baby seal hearts stuffed with dove pâté:** A delicacy enjoyed by a future version of the *Red Dwarf* crew, who used a time drive coupled with a faster-than-light drive to journey throughout space-time, becoming epicures who sampled the best the universe had to offer **[T-SER6.6]**.

- **Bachelor of Sanitation:** A college degree that Kryten earned after studying the lavatorial sciences at Toilet University, which Kochanski pointed out was nothing more than a piece of software installed in his core program **[T-SER7.7]**.

- **background music circuits:** Components built into cyborgs such as Jake Bullet in an alternate universe, which played dramatic background music during intense moments **[M-SMG1.7(a)]**.

- ***Back to Earth***: A three-part episode of the British television show *Red Dwarf,* which the crew imagined while trapped in an elation squid hallucination in which they thought they had traveled through a portal to an alternate twenty-first-century Earth on which they were merely characters in the comedy series. Reading from an empty DVD box, the crew discovered their final episodes, titled *Back to Earth*, took place after Series X. The synopsis of the DVD recounted their trip through the portal, offering a glimpse into their future, which included perishing in the final episode **[T-SER9.2]**.

    Armed with this knowledge, the crew set out to find their Creator in order to plead for more life. The journey took them to several locations, including the collectibles store They Walk Among Us!, latex mask maker Nose World, the set of *Coronation Street* and, ultimately, the lair of the Creator himself.

    The Creator divulged that he planned to gun them down himself in the final act, in a spectacular chase through the city. During the ensuing struggle, however, Lister accidentally killed the Creator. Panicked, Lister attempted to keep his comrades alive by continuing the script on the Creator's typewriter, which appeared to govern their actions.

    Eventually, they discovered it was all an illusion, awakening one by one to find themselves lying on a deck in *Red Dwarf,* next to the water tank in which they had encountered the elation squid **[T-SER9.3]**.

- **backup boosters:** Emergency engines fitted on *Starbug* shuttles, used to provide extra thrust **[N-BTL]**.

- **backwards mode:** A function of 4000 Series mechanoids that enabled them to read and speak languages backwards. Kryten found this particular mode helpful while marooned with Rimmer on an Earth where time ran backwards **[T-SER3.1]**.

- ***Backwards Opportunity Knocks*:** A British television talent show on Earth, far in the future, on which time ran backwards. After flying through a time hole and becoming stranded there, Rimmer and Kryten adapted to life in reverse by working the novelty act circuit and eventually procuring an audition for *Backwards Opportunity Knocks*. The show's host was Bob Esuohknom **[T-SER3.1(d)]**.

  ***NOTE:** A show called* Opportunity Knocks *ran in the 1980s, starring Bob Monkhouse ("Esuohknom" in reverse).*

- **Bacofoil:** A brand of aluminum foil sold in the United Kingdom **[RL]**. After running out of Bacofoil, Kryten asked Rimmer—who was posing as Ace Rimmer at the time—if he had any spare jackets in which the mechanoid could roast a chicken, due to its reflective properties **[T-SER7.2]**.

- **Bacon, Sir Francis:** An English politician, author and pioneer of the scientific method, circa the seventeenth century **[RL]**. While marooned on a frozen planet, Lister attempted to stay warm inside *Starbug 1* by burning items stored aboard ship. Succumbing to hunger, he was dismayed to find several books written by authors whose names reminded him of food, such as Charles Lamb, Herman Wouk and Francis Bacon **[T-SER3.2]**.

- **bacon sandwich with French mustard and black coffee:** An order Lister placed with a food dispenser suffering from a faulty vocabulary unit. Because of the malfunction, he was instead given a pair of rubber boots **[T-SER1.2]**.

- **Bad Ass:** The name that Spare Head Two, while occupying Kryten's body, wished to be called after Lister removed his guilt chip, disabling his behavior protocols **[T-SER7.1]**.

- **Bader:** A name that Lister assigned to one of twelve rogue droids he purchased from the Kinitawowi to break his doppelgänger out of the virtual-reality prison Cyberia **[N-LST]**.

- **badge of merchantship:** An object worn as a necklace to indicate one's status as a merchant, necessary when trading with the Brefewino GELF tribe. While attempting to gain access to a Brefewino village, the *Red Dwarf* crew fabricated several badges for themselves: Lister wore a potato, indicating he was a farmer; Cat wore a bottle of aspirin, signifying his status as an apothecary; Kryten wore a hairbrush, indicating he was a barber; and Rimmer wore a frying pan, designating him a cook **[T-IDW]**.

- **BAFTA:** The British Academy of Film and Television Arts, an organization that recognized and promoted excellence in television and film **[RL]**. While discussing his negadrive, Kryten warned Lister that the deceptively small device contained the greatest concentration of anger, jealousy and resentment outside a BAFTA awards ceremony **[T-SER7.6]**.

- **Bailey, Billy:** A character in Frank Capra's film *It's a Wonderful Life* **[RL]**. While trapped in an addictive version of *Better Than Life*, Lister imagined that Billy played the tuba in a five-piece brass band, though his drinking always left him two or three songs behind everyone else **[N-BTL]**.

- **Bailey, George:** The protagonist of Frank Capra's film *It's a Wonderful Life* **[RL]**. While trapped in an addictive version of *Better Than Life*, Lister believed he had returned to Earth and found a town modeled after Bedford Falls, the movie's main setting. There, he assumed the name George Bailey and settled down with a duplicate of Kochanski and their two sons, Jim and Bexley **[N-INF]**.

- **Bailey, "Old Ma":** A character in Frank Capra's film *It's a Wonderful Life* **[RL]**. While trapped in an addictive version of *Better Than Life*, Lister imagined that a homeless man named Henry stayed at "Old Ma" Bailey's boarding house one Christmas Eve, thanks to the generosity of Lister's sons, Jim and Bexley **[N-BTL]**.

PREFIX
RL: Real life

T-: Television Episodes
SER: Television series
IDW: "Identity Within"
USA1: Unaired U.S. pilot
USA2: Unaired U.S. demo

R-: *The Bodysnatcher Collection*
SER: Remastered episodes
BOD: "Bodysnatcher"
DAD: "Dad"
FTH: "Lister's Father"
INF: "Infinity Patrol"
END: "The End" (original assembly)

N-: Novels
INF: *Infinity Welcomes Careful Drivers*
BTL: *Better Than Life*
LST: *Last Human*

BCK: *Backwards*
OMN: *Red Dwarf Omnibus*

M-: Magazines
SMG: *Smegazine*

W-: Websites
OFF: Official website
NAN: *Prelude to Nanarchy*
AND: *Androids*
DIV: Diva-Droid
DIB: Duane Dibbley

CRP: Crapola
GEN: Geneticon
LSR: Leisure World Intl.
JMC: Jupiter Mining Corporation
AIT: *A.I. Today*
HOL: HoloPoint

G-: Roleplaying Game
RPG: *Core Rulebook*
BIT: *A.I. Screen Extra Bits* booklet
SOR: *Series Sourcebook*
OTH: Other RPG material

- **Bailey's Perfect Shami Kebab Emporium:** A food establishment Lister imagined owning while trapped in an illusion created by an addictive version of *Better Than Life*. Unaware he was in the game, Lister thought he had returned to Earth using *Nova 5*'s Duality Jump, and had set up the restaurant in a perfect reproduction of Bedford Falls from the movie *It's a Wonderful Life* after assuming the name George Bailey. There, he replicated the food from Indiana Takeaway, an Indian restaurant in St. John's Precinct where he had once found the perfect kebab **[N-INF]**.

- **Baked Alannah:** A cannibalism recipe that Colonel Mike O'Hagan recommended in his *Space Corps Survival Manual* **[B-SUR]**.

- ***Baked Bean Bombshells Volume 12*:** A nude wrestling video that Lister found while playing the locker room game with Rimmer aboard *Red Dwarf* **[T-SER7.5]**.

- **baked beans:** A food item stored in the refrigeration unit in the Officers Quarters used by Lister and Rimmer **[T-SER3.4(d)]**.

- **Baker, Peter:** An underwater hockey referee. Lister, misunderstanding a request for references, named Baker as a referee on his Jupiter Mining Corporation job application **[M-SMG1.9(a)]**.

- **Baker, Tom:** A British actor best known for his role as the Fourth Doctor in the long-running sci-fi television series *Doctor Who* **[RL]**. Tom Baker was revived as a hologram in the twenty-fourth century to reprise his role in a new series of *Doctor Who*, which aired at 6:35 PM on Groovy Channel 27 on Wednesday, the 27th of Geldof, 2362 **[M-SMG1.7(a)]**.

- **Balham High Street:** The main retail street running through the town of Balham in South West London, England **[RL]**. In the alternate-reality game *Scramble!!!*, a common workaround to the glitch that gave players a #17 bus instead of a Warbird included bombing footwear retailer Freeman Hardy Willis' store on Balham High Street during rush hour **[B-SUR]**.

- **Ballbreaker Autofire Cannon:** A rapid-fire personal defense weapon manufactured by Bloodlust Arms and distributed via Crapola Inc.'s annual *SCABBY* catalog **[G-RPG]**.

- **Balti house:** A type of Indian restaurant popular in Birmingham **[RL]**. Kryten told Kochanski she was no good for Lister, despite the fact that he smelled like a Balti house laundry basket **[T-SER7.3]**.

- **Bambi:** The title character of Felix Salten's 1923 novel *Bambi, A Life in the Woods*, and its 1942 Disney film adaptation, simply titled *Bambi* **[RL]**. After being transformed into Ace Rimmer by an emohawk, Rimmer decided to kill Cat—who had been transformed into Duane Dibbley—in an attempt to flush the polymorph out of *Starbug 1*. He could not bring himself to do it, however, since he felt it would have been like garroting Bambi **[T-SER6.4(d)]**.

- **banana:** A long, yellow fruit native to tropical climates **[RL]**. Lister used a banana as a prop while attempting to teach Kryten how to lie, by calling the fruit a female aardvark and instructing Kryten to call it an orange. Eventually, the mechanoid succeeded in calling the fruit a "small, off-duty Czechoslovakian traffic warden," proving he could move beyond his programming **[T-SER4.1]**.

  ***NOTE:** The DVD captions for the Czech Republic version of the series changed the traffic warden reference to "an off-duty assistant of a Tasmanian traffic warden."*

- **banana and crisps sandwich:** A food item in Adolf Hitler's briefcase, which Lister stole after traveling through a timeslide to Nuremberg, Germany, where he scuffled with the Führer at a rally **[T-SER3.5]**.

- **banana bomb:** A tropical drink that the host of the total-immersion video game *Better Than Life* offered Lister as he played golf with Cat. It included, among other things, a wedge of orange, a little umbrella and a bottle-rocket that, when lit, shot up into the air **[T-SER2.2]**.

- **Bang:** One of seven diminutive rainforest dwellers known as the Ionian Ecommandoes, who lived in the jungles of Io on the television soap opera *Androids.* He and his comrades nursed Karstares back to health **[M-SMG2.5(c5)]**, after Karstares' plane crashed due to sabotage by his son Jaysee **[M-SMG1.14(c3)]**. Grateful for their help, Karstares became the Green Knight, the rainforest's protector, and fought alongside the Ecommandoes against Jaysee's ecologically harmful company **[M-SMG2.5(c5)]**. Bang died during a firefight between Jaysee and his foes **[M-SMG2.8(c2)]**.

  NOTE: *This character resembled one of Disney's Seven Dwarfs. All of the Ecommandoes' names were slang for sex.*

- **Bankhead, Tallulah:** A twentieth-century American film and stage actor, known for such films as *A Royal Scandal* and *Lifeboat* **[RL]**. Bankhead's films inspired many zero-gee football coaches; eventually, the Zero-Gee Football Federation was pressured into naming a goal-scoring strategy after her 1965 film, *Die! Die! My Darling!* **[M-SMG1.8(a)]**.

- **Bangkok:** The capital city of Thailand, located in Southeast Asia **[RL]**. To reduce the suffering caused by his sexual appetite, Cat watched holo-slides of women dressed in kitten outfits attending the Kit-Kat Club, located in Bangkok **[T-IDW]**.

- **Baquaii diamonds:** A type of valuable gemstones among the possessions of a psychotic, alternate-universe Lister whom the *Starbug* crew rescued from Cyberia **[N-LST]**.

- **Bar:** A word on a red neon sign hanging in *Red Dwarf*'s disco room. This sign also appeared in a version of the ship in a universe in which the sexes were reversed **[T-SER2.6]**.

- **Barbara:** Kochanski's bunkmate aboard *Red Dwarf.* During Kristine's brief romance with Lister, the couple often chased Barbara away to the ship's cinema so they could sit in bed and watch their favorite film, *It's a Wonderful Life* **[N-INF]**.

  NOTE: *Barbara presumably died during the cadmium II explosion. It is unknown whether the nanobots resurrected her in Series VIII.*

- ***Barber of Seville AR*****:** An artificial-reality video game that recreated the events of Gioachino Rossini's opera *The Barber of Seville*. Lister once imported code from *Star Battalions* into the game, much to the frustration of Kochanski, who entered the simulation to find a group of drunken Space Commandos shooting up Figaro's house **[B-SUR]**.

- **Barbie:** A model of android available in a pick'n'mix lineup at a brothel on Mimas. Customers could choose various body parts from selected androids, and then have a custom-designed sex droid assembled for their use. A portly, red-haired customer chose this particular model's right leg for his sex droid **[N-INF]**.

- **barge:** A GELF word meaning vessel **[W-OFF]**.

- **barium hydrochlorate salad nicoise:** The first course in a special mechanoid meal that Holly created for Kryten's last-day party **[T-SER3.6]**.

- **Barlow, Ken:** A fictional character on the British television show *Coronation Street,* portrayed by William Roache. Barlow was known as a ladies' man, and had married several times throughout the run of the show **[RL]**. An episode near the series' four hundredth episode, which ran on Groovy Channel 27, centered around Barlow's thirteenth marriage, this time to Android 5542978/R. This episode aired on Wednesday, the 27th of Geldof, 2362 **[M-SMG1.7(a)]**.

  NOTE: *Presumably, Roache was revived as a hologram to continue playing the role, given the station's affinity for using holographic actors.*

- **Barlow's Bookies:** A bookie shop located on the set of the British television show *Coronation Street* **[RL]**. While trapped in an elation squid hallucination, the *Red Dwarf* crew, believing themselves to be on an alternate twenty-first-century Earth, imagined that they passed by Barlow's Bookies on their quest to find Craig Charles, the actor who portrayed Lister on the show *Red Dwarf.* The business' sign read "Turf Accountant" and contained the firm's phone number, 0161-715 9746 **[T-SER9.2]**.

  NOTE: *Barlow's Bookies, like all businesses appearing in this sequence, is a fictional shop created for the* *television show* Coronation Street, *in which Craig Charles starred as of this writing. On the show, Barlow's Bookies is owned by Peter Barlow and is located at 9 Rosamund Street, in Weatherfield, England.*

- **Barnaby:** The prized corgi of King Bonjella, War World's ruler and the father of Princess Beryl Bonjella **[W-OFF]**.

- **Barnett:** An association football player in the universe known as Alternative 6829/B. Barnett played for the Smegchester Rovers, alongside team captain Ray Rimmer, in 2180 **[M-SMG1.8(c4)]**.

- **Barney:** An anthropomorphic purple dinosaur character from the American children's television series *Barney & Friends* **[RL]**. Lister referred to Pete, a sparrow that had been de-evolved into a *Tyrannosaurus rex* by a time wand, as "Barney's ugly brother" **[T-SER8.6]**.

- **Barnstable, Belinda:** A fitness instructor on Callisto. When "Nicey" Ackerman was eighteen years old, he attended her class at Belinda Barnstable's Fitness Regime, lured in by Belinda's spandex attire. The two enjoyed a romantic affair until her husband found out. He then chased Ackerman into a Space Corps recruitment center, where the youth signed up for service and was assigned to a prison transport **[W-OFF]**.

- **Barrington, Fiona:** A girl with whom Rimmer attempted to "get off" with in his father's greenhouse. Believing he had gotten lucky with Fiona, he later discovered that his hand had been in warm compost the entire time **[T-SER5.2]**.

- **Barry:** A name Lister considered giving to his son, until Rimmer pointed out that his first initial, coupled with his last name, would be "Blister" **[R-DAD]**.

- **Bartikovsky, Katerina, Science Officer:** A possible former crewmember aboard *Red Dwarf*. When Lister and company became trapped in an elation squid hallucination, they imagined that Bartikovsky was revived as a hologram and assumed command of *Red Dwarf*. She decreed that Rimmer had failed in his primary duty—to look after Lister—and that he would be deactivated and his disc destroyed within twenty-four hours. She then built a dimension-cutter and opened a portal into another dimension with the intention of bringing back a mate for Lister with whom to repopulate the human species **[T-SER9.1]**.

  The crew believed this portal had brought them to twenty-first-century Earth, and that they were merely characters in a British television show called *Red Dwarf*. Assuming they had lost Bartikovsky, they set out to find their creator after learning of their impending demise in the show's final episode. Bartikovsky later found them again after opening another portal, but this reunion was short-lived, as Rimmer, determined not to be deactivated, pushed Katerina into an oncoming car, killing her instantly **[T-SER9.2]**.

  ***NOTE:** It is unclear whether Bartikovsky was ever an actual crewmember. If she was, then it is also unknown whether she died during the cadmium II explosion, or if the nanobots resurrected her.*

- **Bassoon, Haydn, Doctor:** A medical practitioner credited with discovering that the human appendix's purpose was for medium wave reception. Bassoon made this discovery on November 7 **[B-LOG]**.

- **Bateman, Marcus, Doctor ("Stinky"):** A former classmate of Arnold Rimmer **[T-SER7.2]**. Bateman later joined the Space Corps and became part of the team that analyzed a black box recording of *Red Dwarf*, which had traveled back in time three million years through the Omni-zone via a black hole **[W-OFF]**.
  After battling what he thought was an escaped knight from the AR Suite, Arnold gleefully announced his victory to Ace Rimmer, saying it was the bravest thing he'd done since setting fire to Stinky Bateman's turn-ups in third-form prep **[T-SER7.2]**.

- **Bates, Norman:** A fictional serial killer in Robert Bloch's *Psycho* novels and their film and television spinoffs. An emotionally abused son, Norman killed his mother and assumed her personality to repress the memory of her death, preserving her body in her former bedroom **[RL]**.

  Upon first meeting Kryten aboard the crashed ship *Nova 5*, Rimmer called him "the android version of Norman Bates" because, like Norman, Kryten was unable to accept the deaths of those around him (in his case, the female officers who "survived" the crash), and behaved as if they were still alive **[T-SER2.1]**.

Years later, Rimmer commented that the skeletal remains of a crewmember aboard the SSS *Esperanto* were like those of Norman Bates' mom **[T-SER5.6]**.

- **Batman:** A fictional comic book vigilante created in 1939 by Bob Kane and Bill Finger. Batman (Bruce Wayne) donned a bat-themed suit and relied on intelligence and gadgets, rather than superpowers, to fight crime **[RL]**. While serving time in the Tank, Lister and Rimmer inserted a capsule of Sodium Pentothal into Warden Ackerman's asthma inhaler, causing him to admit to having sex with the science officer's wife while wearing a Batman outfit **[T-SER8.6]**.

- ***Batman 2*:** A movie about the Caped Crusader, starring Michelle Pfeiffer. To reduce the suffering caused by his sexual appetite, Cat watched holo-slides of Pfeiffer's character from this film **[T-IDW]**.

  NOTE: *Michelle Pfeiffer portrayed Catwoman in Tim Burton's second Batman film,* Batman Returns. *There is no movie called* Batman 2.

- **battle-class cruiser:** A large starship crewed by rogue simulants, used for hunting quarry **[T-SER6.3]**. It had a maximum crew capacity of four hundred and was equipped with four laser cannons, shields and a Secure Transmission Device (STD) that allowed simulants to transmit viruses into an enemy vessel's navicomp **[G-RPG]**.

  While pursuing the stolen *Red Dwarf*, the *Starbug 1* crew entered a rogue simulant hunting zone, where they were intercepted by a battle-class cruiser. Finding the trespassers and their ship unworthy of hunting, the simulants rendered the crew unconscious and upgraded *Starbug 1*'s systems and engines, as well as added weapons, to provide more of a challenge. This backfired on them, however, when the crew unexpectedly attacked moments after being released, nearly destroying the battlecruiser **[T-SER6.3]**.

  Weeks later, after *Starbug*'s refrigeration unit malfunctioned and a fuel tank was punctured, the crew risked returning to the derelict cruiser to salvage its stores of food and fuel. Finding the superstructure severely compromised, the crew boarded the ship despite being unable to use bazookoids or make loud noises. While transporting the supplies from the cargo hold, they encountered the ship's second-in-command, badly damaged but alive. During the confrontation, Rimmer used one of the ship's escape pods, triggering a shipquake. His shipmates barely escaped via the vessel's transporter **[T-SER6.5]**.

- **Battle of Trafalgar:** A naval conflict fought between the British Royal Navy and the combined fleets of the French and Spanish Navies during the Napoleonic Wars **[RL]**. The battle was recreated in the artificial-reality game *Strategic Sea Battles*. Rimmer once encountered a glitch in the program that resulted in a dolphin named Flipper leading the English fleet in his campaign into battle **[B-SUR]**.

- **battleplan timetable:** A schedule Rimmer created to help him formulate a plan to escape a group of rogue simulants who had pursued the *Red Dwarf* crew into an asteroid belt. The six-hour timetable included time allotted to read strategy books, as well as snack breaks, pondering time and snoozes, with the last five minutes set aside for coming up with a brilliant plan **[T-SER10.6]**.

- **Baxter:** A prisoner of the Tank, *Red Dwarf*'s brig on Floor 13 who died during the cadmium II disaster, but was resurrected by nanobots. Baxter was a member of the Canaries, an elite group of inmates assigned to investigate dangerous situations. A large, stocky man, he frequently bullied other inmates, particularly Cat, Kryten, Lister and Rimmer **[T-SER8.6]**. Baxter brewed his own hooch while in prison, purported to be extremely potent **[T-SER8.8]**.

  Baxter was scheduled to fight Headbanger Harris in a Psychoweight Championship boxing match, to be shown on Krytie TV **[X-CAL]**. While on a mission to convert Pete the dinosaur back into a sparrow, Baxter and fellow inmate Kill Crazy ambushed Lister and Rimmer, stealing a time wand. Clueless to how it worked, the two de-evolved themselves into primates **[T-SER8.7]**, though they regained their normal forms after the wand was destroyed **[W-OFF]**.

  When *Red Dwarf* was being dissolved by a chameleonic microbe, Captain Hollister ordered an evacuation, with several names picked at random from the prisoner roster to be allowed aboard the rescue craft. Lister's name was chosen,

but a grimace from Baxter convinced him to give up his pass **[T-SER8.8(d)]**.

- **Baxter, Bing:** An American game-show host. Upon meeting his corporeal hallucination Confidence, Lister noted that he resembled the manager of the London Jets and sounded like Bing Baxter—two individuals whom he associated with confidence **[T-SER1.5]**.

  Baxter hosted a *Red Dwarf* JMC publicity video, as well as American game shows *That's My Chromosome* and *GELFs Win Prizes* **[W-OFF]**. An Extras Pack sold by Crapola Inc. allowed talking appliances, such as Talkie Toaster and Talkie Toilet, to speak with Baxter's voice and personality **[W-CRP]**. According to Blaize Falconburger, Baxter was addicted to eating hamsters **[W-OFF]**.

- **Bay 17:** An immense hold located aboard *Red Dwarf*. After rescuing Kryten from the *Nova 5* crash, the *Red Dwarf* crew dislodged the two halves of the wrecked vessel from the icy moon and stowed it in Bay 17, where they facilitated repairs **[N-INF]**.

- **Bay 46:** A parking spot that the *Red Dwarf* crew imagined while trapped in a despair squid hallucination. Bay 46 was adjacent to the spot in which the limousine of Sebastian Doyle (Lister) was parked in the long-term lot of Leisure World International **[T-SER5.6]**.

- **Bay 47:** A landing bay in *Red Dwarf*'s aft section, used to hold ships requiring quarantine. The bay led to a sealed area containing the quarantine berths. Rimmer forced his shipmates into quarantine through this bay when they returned to *Red Dwarf* after visiting a viral research station **[T-SER5.4]**.

  NOTE: *In the script book* Scenes from the Dwarf, *Bay 47 was misidentified as the room in which the crew was kept in quarantine.* Red Dwarf—The Roleplaying Game, *meanwhile, identified the quarantine area as being on Level 47.*

- **Bay 47:** A parking spot that the *Red Dwarf* crew imagined while trapped in a despair squid hallucination. The limousine of Sebastian Doyle (Lister) was parked in this bay, in the long-term lot of Leisure World International **[T-SER5.6]**.

- **Bay 48:** A parking spot that the *Red Dwarf* crew imagined while trapped in a despair squid hallucination. Bay 48 was adjacent to the spot in which the limousine of Sebastian Doyle (Lister) was parked in the long-term lot of Leisure World International **[T-SER5.6]**.

- **Bay City Rollers:** A popular Scottish musical group in the 1970s, known for such songs as "Saturday Night" and their version of "I Only Want to Be With You" **[RL]**. While explaining the necessity of cleaning out his cache files, Kryten claimed his memory was filled with useless knowledge that was no longer a priority, such as the ability to sing the Bay City Rollers' greatest hits **[T-SER7.1]**. Cat, as Duane Dibbley, enjoyed the music of such groups as ABBA, The Carpenters and the Bay City Rollers **[M-SMG2.2(a)]**.

  NOTE: *The scene involving Kryten's useless knowledge was changed to reference Czechoslovakian pop-music boy band Lunetic and their first hit, "You Are My Mum," in the DVD captions for the Czech Republic version of the series.*

- **Baz:** A character on the television soap opera *Androids*. In one episode, Baz attended a barbeque hosted by Daz, during which a family pet, Bouncer, was lost in a temporal-displacement vortex **[M-SMG1.8(c2)]**.

- ***Bazookoid Blaster*:** A video game available for the Gamestation console **[G-SOR]**.

- **bazookoid MkI:** A portable rock-blasting laser aboard *Red Dwarf*, used during mining operations. In emergencies, the bazookoid could also double as a weapon **[N-INF]**. It was manufactured by Piledriver Inc. and distributed via Crapola Inc.'s annual *SCABBY* catalog, with a range of 100 meters (328 feet) **[G-RPG]**. Bazookoids had a heat-seeking mode **[T-SER3.3]**, and some were equipped with night-vision sights **[N-LST]**. Controls included an orange switch (safety catch), a red switch (dismantler) and a blue switch **[T-SER3.6]**.

- **bazookoid MkII:** A more compact version of the MkI bazookoid, with a rear-load cartridge that could be swapped between live ammunition and blanks **[T-SER7.2]**. The MkII lacked the red dismantler button included on the

B-: Books
PRG: *Red Dwarf Programme Guide*
SUR: *Red Dwarf Space Corps Survival Manual*
PRM: *Primordial Soup*
SOS: *Son of Soup*
SCE: *Scenes from the Dwarf*
LOG: *Red Dwarf Log No. 1996*
RD8: *Red Dwarf VIII*
EVR: *The Log: A Dwarfer's Guide to Everything*

X-: Misc.
PRO: Promotional materials, videos, etc.
PST: Posters at DJ XVII (2013)
CAL: 2008 calendar
RNG: Cell phone ringtones
MOB: Mobisode ("Red Christmas")
CIN: *Children in Need* sketch
GEK: *Geek Week* intros by Kryten
TNG: "Tongue-Tied" video

XMS: Bill Pearson's Christmas special pitch script
XVD: Bill Pearson's Christmas special pitch video
OTH: Other *Red Dwarf* appearances

SUFFIX
DVD:
(d) – Deleted scene
(o) – Outtake
(b) – Bonus DVD material (other)
(e) – Extended version

SMEGAZINES:
(c) – Comic
(a) – Article

OTHER:
(s) – Early/unused script draft
(s1) – Alternate version of script

MkI **[W-OFF]**. It was manufactured by Piledriver Inc. and distributed via Crapola Inc.'s annual *SCABBY* catalog, with a range of 80 meters (262 feet) **[G-RPG]**.

- **bazookoid pistol:** A smaller, more compact version of the MkII bazookoid. This handgun-sized mini-bazookoid was manufactured by Piledriver Inc. and distributed via Crapola Inc.'s annual *SCABBY* catalog, with a range of 70 meters (229 feet) **[G-RPG]**.

- **Bazza:** An associate of Lister's father. When Lister confronted his dad at a pub, the latter thought Bazza had sent Lister to speak with him about money he owed Bazza **[R-FTH]**.

  NOTE: *This appeared in an early-draft script written before it was established, in episode 7.3 ("Ouroboros"), that Lister was his own father.*

- ***BBC Children in Need*:** A British charity created by the British Broadcasting Corp. (BBC) to help disabled children **[RL]**. The *Blue Midget* crew received a three-million-year-old transmission of a *Children in Need* telethon from Earth. Deciding to help the cause, they coupled their transmitter with the time drive to send a message back through time, urging viewers to donate **[X-CIN]**.

- **B Deck:** A level aboard *Starbug 1* **[T-SER7.4]**.

- **B Deck:** A level aboard *Red Dwarf*. B Deck contained a bar that Lister claimed would not serve him since he was using doubloons taken from Rimmer's purse **[T-SER8.1]**. After this deck was damaged, the AI computer Pree repaired it using commands she anticipated would be given by Rimmer—as such, the repair work was slipshod and botched **[T-SER10.2]**. The deck contained a deep-freeze unit and Kryten's quarters **[T-SER10.3]**, as well as an old aquarium **[M-SMG1.13(c2)]**.

- **Beadlebaum, Harry:** *See* Beedlebaum, Harry

- ***Beagle*:** A spacecraft launched by the European Space Consortium (ESC) in the twenty-first century, programmed to land on Mars. While landing, the craft malfunctioned and was presumed lost. Years later, the agency sent a rover to Mars, which discovered debris left behind by the *Red Dwarf* crew. While analyzing the debris, the rover encountered Cat, who used it to transmit a message back to Earth, informing the agency that he had found their *Beagle* spacecraft—which he assumed was named after a dog **[X-APR]**.

  NOTE: *This presumably referred to the* Beagle 2, *a British spacecraft involved in the European Space Agency's failed 2003* Mars Express *mission, which lost contact with Earth after separating from its mothership.* Beagle 2 *was actually named after the HMS* Beagle.

- **Beardsley, Peter:** An actor who starred with Myra Binglebat in a remake of the classic American film *Casablanca*. After discovering a newer update of the film in a postal pod, Lister questioned the need for this version, declaring the Beardsley-Binglebat production definitive. Holly, having also seen the movie, quoted a famous line of dialog: "Of all the space bars in all the worlds, you had to re-materialize in mine" **[T-SER2.2]**. Birdman, an inmate of the Tank, *Red Dwarf*'s brig, named his pet sparrow Pete in Beardsley's honor **[W-OFF]**.

  NOTE: *This quote spoofed the famous line from the original: "Of all the gin joints, in all the towns, in all the world, she walks into mine"* **[T-SER2.2]**.

- **Bearth:** The Promised Planet, according to the religion of the Cat People inhabiting *Red Dwarf*. Cat doctrine predicted that the Father of Catkind would return from being frozen in time to lead them to Bearth (Earth). A two-thousand-year war was fought between those who believed the Father's name was Cloister, and those who thought it to be Clister **[N-INF]**.

  NOTE: *This differed from the television series, in which the "Promised Land" was established as being Fuchal (Fiji).*

- **Beatles, The:** An influential English rock-and-roll band known for such hits as "A Hard Day's Night," "Ticket to Ride," and "Hey Jude," among many others **[RL]**. Lister played lead guitar on weekends for The Beatles while in the total-immersion video game *Better Than Life* **[R-SER2.2(d)]**.

- **Beatty, Warren:** An American actor, screenwriter and producer, known for such films as *Heaven Can Wait*, *Bonnie*

PREFIX
RL: Real life

T-: Television Episodes
SER: Television series
IDW: "Identity Within"
USA1: Unaired U.S. pilot
USA2: Unaired U.S. demo

R-: The Bodysnatcher Collection
SER: Remastered episodes
BOD: "Bodysnatcher"
DAD: "Dad"
FTH: "Lister's Father"
INF: "Infinity Patrol"
END: "The End" (original assembly)

N-: Novels
INF: *Infinity Welcomes Careful Drivers*
BTL: *Better Than Life*
LST: *Last Human*
BCK: *Backwards*
OMN: *Red Dwarf Omnibus*

M-: Magazines
SMG: *Smegazine*

W-: Websites
OFF: Official website
NAN: *Prelude to Nanarchy*
AND: *Androids*
DIV: Diva-Droid
DIB: Duane Dibbley

CRP: Crapola
GEN: Geneticon
LSR: Leisure World Intl.
JMC: Jupiter Mining Corporation
AIT: *A.I. Today*
HOL: HoloPoint

G-: Roleplaying Game
RPG: *Core Rulebook*
BIT: *A.I. Screen Extra Bits* booklet
SOR: *Series Sourcebook*
OTH: Other RPG material

and Clyde and *Reds* **[RL]**. Jake Bullet paraphrased one of Beatty's movies after an attempt on his life, exclaiming that Silicon Heaven could wait **[M-SMG1.12(c1)]**.

- **Beckham, David:** An international association football player for Manchester United, Preston North End, Real Madrid and other teams **[RL]**. Kryten once spent six hours in *Red Dwarf*'s Waxwork Museum attempting to clean the tattoos off the Beckham wax figure, mistaking them for graffiti **[X-GEK]**.

- **Bedford Falls:** An idyllic fictional town in Frank Capra's film *It's a Wonderful Life* **[RL]**.

  While trapped in an addictive version of *Better Than Life*, Lister believed he had returned to Earth using the Duality Jump from *Nova 5*. In the illusion, he shunned the fame and fortune offered to him upon his return, opting for a quiet life in the Midwestern town of Bedford Falls, which bore a striking resemblance to the film's version. There, he assumed the identity of George Bailey (the movie's protagonist), opened up a kebab shop and settled down with a descendant of Kochanski and their two children, Jim and Bexley.

  In addition to the kebab shop, the town contained a single police officer, a bank, a war memorial, an orphanage, an emporium, Martini's Bar, Mr. Gower's drugstore, and Lister's home at 220 Sycamore **[N-INF]**. It also featured a toy store, a pet store, a boarding house and a gas station. The town's population was 3,241. After Rimmer visited Bedford Falls, his mind, unable to accept such a paradise, immediately warped the town, adding a nuclear-waste depot, a sewage plant, an Air Force base and an open prison to rehabilitate psychopathic serial-killers **[N-BTL]**.

- **Beedlebaum, Harry:** A carpenter's son who became the owner of the largest pizza store chain in history. Kryten cited Beedlebaum as an example of people who became more than their occupation suggested, in an attempt to dissuade Rimmer from using a mind patch to pass a test in order to join the holoship *Enlightenment* **[T-SER5.1]**.

  NOTE: *This spelling appeared in the DVD captions; the* Red Dwarf Programme Guide *spelled the name as "Beadlebaum."*

- **Beemer, Bertrand:** The chief executive officer of Diva-Droid International. Beemer assumed executive duties following the death of founder Augustus Ackroyd **[W-DIV]**.

- **beer milkshake:** A drink concocted by Lister, consisting of frozen lager **[T-SER1.4]**. Before learning of his role in the religious history of Cat's species, Lister requested this menu item for breakfast, along with a chicken vindaloo, from the food dispenser in *Red Dwarf*'s Drive Room **[T-SER1.3]**.

- **Beethoven:** A name that Lister assigned to one of twelve rogue droids he purchased from the Kinitawowi to break his doppelgänger out of the virtual-reality prison Cyberia **[N-LST]**.

  NOTE: *Presumably, Lister named one of the earless droids after German composer Ludwig van Beethoven, who was deaf.*

- **BEGG (biologically engineered garbage gobbler):** A type of GELF created on Earth to dispose of sludge, refuse and other waste materials. Bearing a slight resemblance to the Kinitawowi, BEGGs had pointier ears and slightly less hair, and maintained a permanent state of inebriation. They were among the friendlier species of GELFs, getting what they wanted through games of chance, such as poker.

  A BEGG tribe ventured into deep space, where they later met the *Red Dwarf* crew. The tribe's leader spoke limited English, having forced an English boarding-school student to teach him the language before consuming him. Lister visited the tribe in order to obtain information about Kochanski's whereabouts, but during the visit, he lost *Starbug* and Rimmer in a game of poker. To ensure that he paid his debt, the BEGGs fitted Lister with a groinal exploder and sent him back to *Red Dwarf*.

  Lister later returned with Kryten, Rimmer and Cat in order to con the BEGGs out of the deal by offering them the "fabled" Spoon of Destiny (which was, in fact, just an ordinary spoon). Seeing through the con, the BEGGs instead offered a rematch of the poker game, asking for Kryten and Cat if they won, but choked to death on electrical wires before they could commence. This forced Lister to search elsewhere for the solution to his predicament **[T-SER10.4]**.

B-: Books
PRG: *Red Dwarf Programme Guide*
SUR: *Red Dwarf Space Corps Survival Manual*
PRM: *Primordial Soup*
SOS: *Son of Soup*
SCE: *Scenes from the Dwarf*
LOG: *Red Dwarf Log No. 1996*
RD8: *Red Dwarf VIII*
EVR: *The Log: A Dwarfer's Guide to Everything*

X-: Misc.
PRO: Promotional materials, videos, etc.
PST: Posters at DJ XVII (2013)
CAL: 2008 calendar
RNG: Cell phone ringtones
MOB: Mobisode ("Red Christmas")
CIN: *Children in Need* sketch
GEK: *Geek Week* intros by Kryten
TNG: "Tongue-Tied" video

XMS: Bill Pearson's Christmas special pitch script
XVD: Bill Pearson's Christmas special pitch video
OTH: Other *Red Dwarf* appearances

SUFFIX
DVD:
(d) – Deleted scene
(o) – Outtake
(b) – Bonus DVD material (other)
(e) – Extended version

SMEGAZINES:
(c) – Comic
(a) – Article

OTHER:
(s) – Early/unused script draft
(s1) – Alternate version of script

- **behavior protocols:** A set of rules programmed into 4000 Series mechanoids that governed their behavior and personality. Overriding these protocols could result in a mechanoid experiencing unexpected behavioral problems, such as the inability to censor itself or differentiate between right and wrong. After hijacking Kryten's body and swapping the mech's head with one of his spares, Lister asked the new head to convince the crew that it was safe to use the time drive to restock their lost supply of curries. The spare head complied, but needed Lister to disable his guilt chip and behavior protocols in order to proceed **[T-SER7.1]**.

- ***Being Single Minded*:** A documentary Rimmer partially watched instead of learning Esperanto—a task to which he had fully dedicated himself the day prior **[B-LOG]**.

- **Beinz Baked Beans:** A food item that an emohawk mimicked aboard *Starbug 1* in order to lure Cat into the galley **[T-SER6.4]**.

  NOTE: *The brand name Beinz spoofed that of popular food brand Heinz, with the can's label being almost identical.*

- **Beinz Salad Cream:** A brand of salad dressing used aboard *Starbug 1*. Kryten believed the salad cream should be kept in the refrigerator, whereas Kochanski preferred to store in the cupboard **[T-SER7.5]**.

  NOTE: *The container could be seen in the subtitles section of the Series VII DVDs.*

- **Belagosian War, the:** A conflict on Argon 5 in which Rimmer, during one of Lister's dreams, claimed to have fought while adventuring as Ace Rimmer. According to the dream, Arnold was later decorated and dressed as a Christmas tree, with the inhabitants feeding him chocolates all winter **[T-SER7.5]**.

- **Belief, Billy:** A small, nine-year-old boy who appeared in an illusion created in Kryten's subconscious mind as he battled the Apocalypse virus. Billy looked up to Kryten, known in the illusion as Sheriff Carton, and brawled with a thug named Tommy Tate after the latter called him a "lousy, stinking drunk." Carton took advantage of Billy's loyalty by charging him two nickels for a deputy badge, with which he then bought liquor **[N-BCK]**.

- **belief chip:** *See* Silicon Heaven belief chip

- **"Believe in the Ruins":** A phrase painted on the front of one of Lister's leather jackets **[T-SER4.2]**.

- **Belinda, Aunt:** A relative of Arnold Rimmer who once owned a prize show poodle. Rimmer accidentally backed over the poodle, an event that ranked third on his Horror Chart (a list of asinine accidents that haunted him throughout his life) **[N-BTL]**.

- **Belinda Barnstable's Fitness Regime:** A fitness class taught by Belinda Barnstable on Callisto. When Warden Ackerman was eighteen years old, he attended the fitness class after being lured in by Barnstable's spandex attire. The two enjoyed a romantic affair until Belinda's husband found out about it **[W-OFF]**.

- **Bellini, Barbra ("Babs"):** A guard stationed aboard a prison ship transporting simulant inmates. When the prisoners mutinied, everyone except for Bellini was killed. One simulant fled the ship in Barbra's escape pod, which the *Red Dwarf* crew found three million years later. Believing Bellini to be inside, Lister started the thawing process, but Rimmer warned that the pod could instead contain the rogue simulant. The crew thus brought the pod to the penal station Justice World, where the simulant escaped and nearly killed the Dwarfers before Lister defeated him **[T-SER4.3]**.

- **beluga caviar:** One of the most expensive forms of caviar, made from the eggs of beluga sturgeon **[RL]**. While visiting past versions of themselves, the time-traveling *Starbug 1* crew was insulted at being served sevruga caviar instead of beluga **[T-SER6.6(d)]**.

- **Ben:** The best friend of Michael R. McGruder during his time in the Star Fleet—until McGruder caught him in bed with his girlfriend, Mercedes, in their apartment **[N-LST]**.

- **Bennet, Elizabeth ("Lizzie"):** The protagonist of Jane Austen's novel *Pride and Prejudice* **[RL]**. After Kochanski, Lister and Cat snubbed Kryten by entering an artificial-reality simulation of *Pride and Prejudice Land* instead of joining him for an anniversary dinner, the mechanoid ambushed the Bennet sisters one at a time, taking out Elizabeth with a rope trap before knocking her out with a tranquilizer dart **[T-SER7.6]**.

- **Bennet, Jane:** A character in the novel *Pride and Prejudice*, by Jane Austen **[RL]**. After Kochanski, Lister and Cat snubbed Kryten by entering an artificial-reality simulation of *Pride and Prejudice Land* instead of joining him for an anniversary dinner, the mechanoid ambushed the Bennet sisters one at a time, taking out Jane with a tranquilizer dart **[T-SER7.6]**.

- **Bennet, Kitty:** A character in Jane Austen's novel *Pride and Prejudice* **[RL]**. After Kochanski, Lister and Cat snubbed Kryten by entering an artificial-reality simulation of *Pride and Prejudice Land* instead of joining him for an anniversary dinner, the mechanoid ambushed the Bennet sisters one at a time. When that plan failed, he borrowed a T-72 tank from a World War II game and confronted the crew head-on, blowing apart the gazebo they occupied, killing Kitty **[T-SER7.6]**.

- **Bennet, Lydia:** A character in the novel *Pride and Prejudice*, by Jane Austen **[RL]**. After Kochanski, Lister and Cat snubbed Kryten by entering an artificial-reality simulation of *Pride and Prejudice Land* instead of joining him for an anniversary dinner, the mechanoid ambushed the Bennet sisters one at a time. When that plan failed, he borrowed a T-72 tank from a World War II game and confronted the crew head-on, blowing apart the gazebo they occupied, killing Lydia **[T-SER7.6]**.

- **Bennet, Mary:** A character in Jane Austen's novel *Pride and Prejudice* **[RL]**. After Kochanski, Lister and Cat snubbed Kryten by entering an artificial-reality simulation of *Pride and Prejudice Land* instead of joining him for an anniversary dinner, the mechanoid ambushed the Bennet sisters one at a time, attempting to take out Mary with a swinging log trap. When that failed, Kryten borrowed a T-72 tank from a World War II game and confronted the crew head-on, blowing apart the gazebo they occupied, killing Mary **[T-SER7.6]**.

- **Bennet, Mrs.:** A character in Jane Austen's novel *Pride and Prejudice* **[RL]**. Upon entering the artificial-reality (AR) simulation *Pride and Prejudice Land*, Kochanski, Lister and Cat met Mrs. Bennet and her daughters, who instantly took a liking to the male crewmembers. Kryten, upset that the crew chose the AR game over his anniversary lobster dinner, entered the simulation with a T-72 tank and confronted the crew head-on, blowing apart the gazebo they occupied, killing Mrs. Bennet **[T-SER7.6]**.

- **Bent Bob:** *See* Bob ("Bent Bob")

- **Bentley V8 convertible:** A luxury model of automobile sold by British car manufacturer Bentley Motors Ltd. **[RL]**. One of Rimmer's brothers owned a Bentley V8 convertible with walnut paneling, in which Arnold claimed he lost his virginity to a girl named Sandra while attending cadet school **[T-SER3.2]**.

- **Benton, Billy:** A musician who recorded a CD titled *Billy Benton and His Choir Sing the Rock'n'Roll Greats*. Rimmer owned a copy of this album **[N-INF]**.

- **Benzen:** A robotic character on the television soap opera *Androids*. In one episode, which always made Kryten cry, Benzen was abandoned by his partner, Roze **[N-INF]**. In another episode, Benzen discovered an undersealant scam run by Bruce after Hudzen developed a rusting problem **[M-SMG1.9(c2)]**.

- **Berkenstein, Emily:** A name on a passport that Lister acquired during a celebratory birthday pub crawl through London, prior to joining *Red Dwarf*. While in his inebriated state, Lister somehow obtained the passport, then used it to travel to Saturn's moon, Mimas, where he became stranded for six months **[N-INF]**. Sex worker Trixie LaBouche later stole the passport, which she used to leave Mimas **[M-SMG2.6(c4)]**.

- **Berlin Bandits:** A zero-gee football team, circa the twenty-second century. During the European divisional playoffs in London, the Berlin Bandits played against the London Jets. During this game, Jets player Jim Bexley Speed went around nine men for the second score, securing the game as the greatest in his career **[N-INF]**.

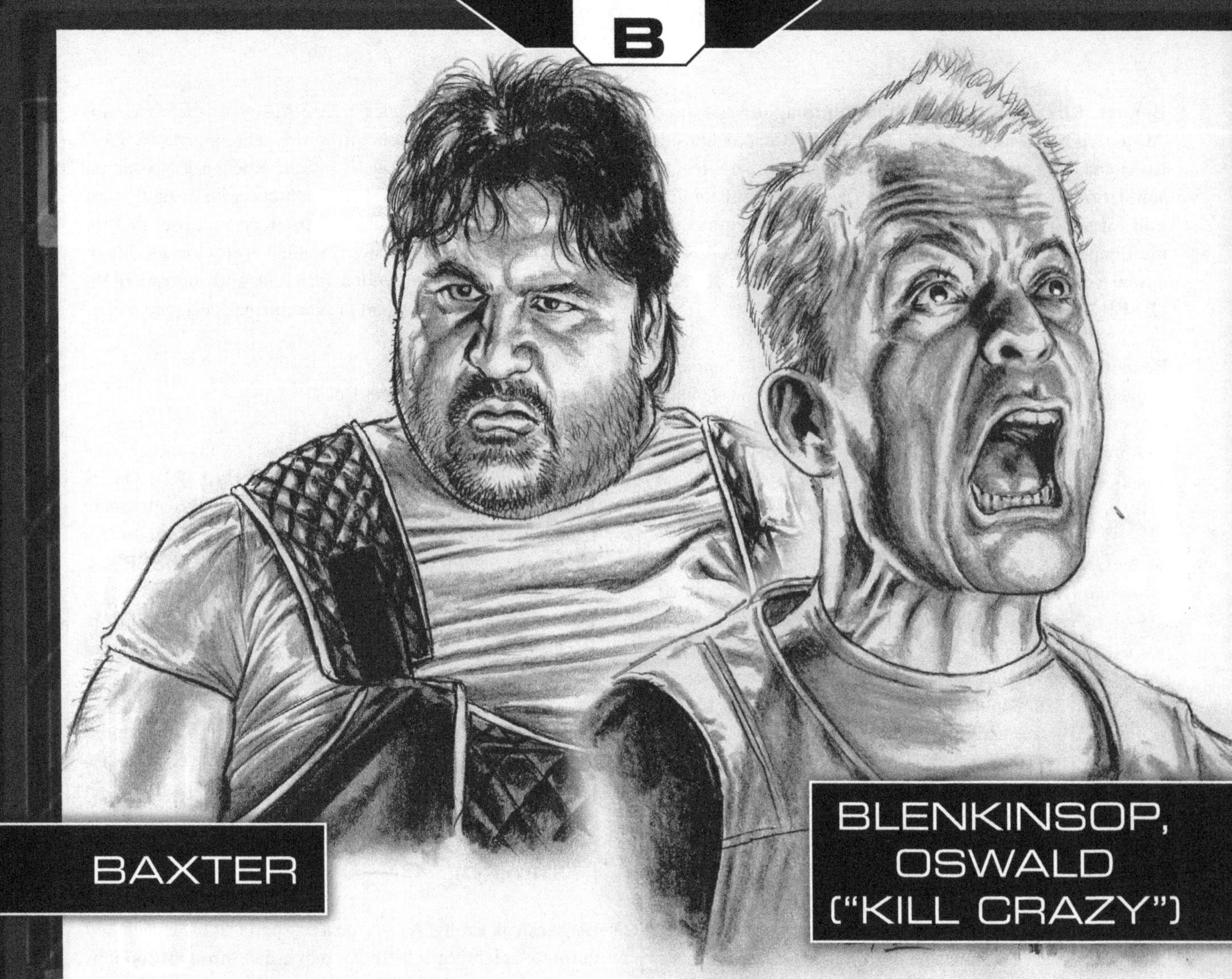

- **"Bermuda Triangle":** A 1981 song by American singer-songwriter Barry Manilow **[RL]**. Lister considered it a great mystery that such a song would ever become a hit. This insight annoyed Rimmer, who was trying to discuss the actual Bermuda Triangle, not the Manilow tune **[T-SER1.4]**.

- **Bermuda Triangle, The:** An area of Earth located between the island of Bermuda, the southern tip of Florida and the northern Puerto Rican islands, rumored to possess unusual paranormal properties due to the frequency of missing ships and aircraft within the area **[RL]**. Rimmer considered the Bermuda Triangle an example of one of many mysteries illustrating the existence of extraterrestrials **[T-SER1.4]**.

- **Berni Inn:** A chain of British steakhouses modeled after American restaurant chains **[RL]**. With the *Red Dwarf* located millions of light-years from Earth, Holly took solace in the fact that he, the ship and the crew were more than sixty billion miles away from the nearest Berni Inn **[T-SER2.2]**.

  ***NOTE:** In an unused Holly introduction created for the remastered episodes, "Berni Inn" was replaced by "Jehovah's Witness."*

PREFIX
RL: Real life

T-: Television Episodes
SER: Television series
IDW: "Identity Within"
USA1: Unaired U.S. pilot
USA2: Unaired U.S. demo

R-: *The Bodysnatcher Collection*
SER: Remastered episodes
BOD: "Bodysnatcher"
DAD: "Dad"
FTH: "Lister's Father"
INF: "Infinity Patrol"
END: "The End" (original assembly)

N-: Novels
INF: *Infinity Welcomes Careful Drivers*
BTL: *Better Than Life*
LST: *Last Human*

BCK: *Backwards*
OMN: *Red Dwarf Omnibus*

M-: Magazines
SMG: *Smegazine*

W-: Websites
OFF: Official website
NAN: *Prelude to Nanarchy*
AND: *Androids*
DIV: Diva-Droid
DIB: Duane Dibbley

CRP: Crapola
GEN: Geneticon
LSR: Leisure World Intl.
JMC: Jupiter Mining Corporation
AIT: *A.I. Today*
HOL: HoloPoint

G-: Roleplaying Game
RPG: *Core Rulebook*
BIT: *A.I. Screen Extra Bits* booklet
SOR: *Series Sourcebook*
OTH: Other RPG material

- **Berry, Nick:** A British television actor and musician, known for his roles as Simon Wicks on *EastEnders* and Nick Rowan on *Heartbeat* **[RL]**. Duane Dibbley, the alter ego of a former agent of the Ministry of Alteration in an alternate universe, swapped his original personality disc with a CD titled *The Best of Nick Berry*, then took the stolen personality disc to the anti-fascist organization known as the Fatal Sisters for safe-keeping **[M-SMG2.5(c1)]**.

- **berserker general:** A specialized, crossbred simulant created to command Simulant Death Ships. Dominator Zlurth, a rogue simulant who attacked *Red Dwarf*, was one such unit **[T-SER10.6]**.

- **Bert:** A police officer in Frank Capra's film *It's a Wonderful Life* **[RL]**. While trapped in an addictive version of *Better Than Life*, Lister imagined that his fifteen-month-old son, Bexley, frequently drove Lister's Ford Model A to the store, which Bert allowed since he found it funny **[N-INF]**.

- **Bessone, Raymond ("Teasy-Weasy"):** A famous British hairdresser from the 1930s to the 1960s **[RL]**. When Rimmer demanded a uniform and haircut despite Holly's need to perform complex lightspeed calculations, the AI denied being a combination speaking clock, Moss Bros and Teasy-Weasy **[T-SER1.2]**.

- **Bert Bourgignon:** A cannibalism recipe that Colonel Mike O'Hagan recommended in his *Space Corps Survival Manual* **[B-SUR]**.

  NOTE: *The book uses this spelling, rather than the traditional spelling of "bourguignon."*

- ***Best of Nick Berry, The*****:** An album recorded by British television actor and musician Nick Berry, containing his greatest hits. Duane Dibbley, the alter ego of a former agent of the Ministry of Alteration in an alternate universe, swapped his original personality disc with this CD, then took the stolen disc to the anti-fascist organization known as the Fatal Sisters for safe-keeping. Later, the amnesiac Dibbley was taken to the Fatal Sisters' lair, where he attempted to play the disc, thinking it was Berry's album. Frustrated that it wouldn't play, Dibbley tossed the disc, not realizing his original personality was stored on it **[M-SMG2.5(c1)]**.

  NOTE: *In the real world, Berry only recorded two albums during his musical career. Oddly, both were named* Nick Berry, *despite containing completely different songs. No album titled* The Best of Nick Berry *has been produced.*

- **Beswick, Thrasher:** A child who attended school on Io with Rimmer at the age of seven. Despite spending several hours a day trying to masturbate through a hole in his pocket, Beswick still ranked higher than Rimmer academically **[N-BCK]**.

- **Beta:** The second letter of the Greek alphabet **[RL]**, used in a code to disarm and unlock a groinal exploder that a group of BEGGs had affixed to Lister's crotch. The code—Theta, Delta, Alpha, Beta, Gamma—had to be input precisely, in that order, for the device to be disabled **[T-SER10.4]**.

- **Betamax holo-recorder:** An obsolete hologrammic recording device utilizing the early Betamax format **[M-SMG1.10(a)]**.

- **Betelgeuse:** A red supergiant star located in the Orion constellation **[RL]**. During a conversation about lying, Kryten once claimed to be off to Betelgeuse to water hedgehogs **[M-SMG1.6(a)]**. Kelly referred to the star in an episode of the television soap opera *Androids* **[M-SMG1.13(c1)]**.

- ***Better Than Life*****:** A total-immersion video game utilizing the SensoLock feedback technique, a technology that detected a user's desires and fantasies and recreated them with the utmost realism, via virtual reality **[T-SER2.2]**. Multiple headsets could be connected for "multi-using," with several people sharing the same fantasy world **[N-INF]**.

  Better Than Life, created by fourteen-year-old Dennis McBean **[N-BTL]**, was produced by Total Immersion Inc. and distributed by Crapola Inc. **[G-RPG]**. It proved extremely popular; when a store in New Tokyo ran out of the game, a resulting riot was so intense that rubber nuclear weapons were deployed to quell the crazed consumers **[T-SER2.2]**.

  A version of the game was available in arcades operated by Leisure World International **[W-LSR]**, while a portable version could be played by wearing a band across the forehead. The apparatus contained tiny electrodes that embedded themselves in a user's cranium and transmitted signals directly into the brain. This signal was so realistic, and the game so appealing, that it was found to be highly addictive, as well as lethal; people who entered the game quickly forgot it was an illusion and never left. Josie, a space beatnik on Mimas, was addicted to *Better Than Life*, but survived due to the care of her boyfriend, Denis.

Because of these serious issues, the game's producer pulled it off the market after only a month. Despite the recall, however, many disreputable individuals produced bootleg copies, and thus the game continued to be used. Petrovitch, an officer aboard *Red Dwarf*, smuggled several such copies aboard the mining ship to sell to terraforming engineers on Triton. Three million years later, Cat found Petrovich's stash of illegal games and plugged himself in, followed by Lister, who went in to get Cat, and then Rimmer, who went in to save them both.

Once in the game, they forgot about their past lives and lived for two years in their own individually created paradises: Cat believed he had inherited a magnificent golden tower filled with scantily clad Valkyrie women; Lister imagined living with Kochanski and their twin boys, Jim and Bexley, in a recreation of Bedford Falls, the idyllic town from the film *It's a Wonderful Life;* and Rimmer fantasized the life of a superstar, full of riches and beautiful, adoring women.

Meanwhile, out in the real world, Kryten attempted to convey to Lister that he was in the game by burning the letters "U=BTL" and "dying" into his arms. Lister got the message and informed Rimmer about their dilemma, but the pair were too entranced to attempt an escape. Eventually, Kryten entered the game as well to rescue his crewmates, but succumbed to its charms as well. It wasn't until Rimmer's illusion was corrupted by his self-loathing that the four admitted they were in the game and attempted to leave. After being offered a second chance by a 3D image of McBean, the crew summoned the exit, emerging from the fictitious world to discover Lister's and Cat's bodies had become atrophied and emaciated **[N-INF]**.

In another instance, the crew found an earlier, non-addictive version of the video game among the contents of a postal pod; this version utilized a helmet-style apparatus instead of a headband. While in the game, Lister and Cat imagined playing golf, drinking exotic beverages and dining in fancy restaurants, while Rimmer fantasized about being an officer and having sex with Yvonne McGruder.

Unable to cope with his good fortune, however, Rimmer's mind rebelled, causing his fantasy to turn against him. McGruder became pregnant, forced Arnold to marry her, and had seven full-grown children within a day. Afterwards, a man from Outland Revenue visited him demanding payment of eighteen thousand in back-taxes. Lister, Cat and Holly, attempting to help, became victims themselves, buried up to their heads with jam smeared on their faces and about to be eaten by ants. The four attempted to remove themselves from the game, only to find the Outland Revenue collector waiting in Rimmer's quarters—indicating their attempt initially failed **[T-SER2.2]**.

- **"Better Than Life":** A slogan on a tank top Lister wore while playing the total-immersion video game *Better Than Life* **[R-SER2.2(d)]**.

- ***Beverly Hills Bereavement Counsellor*:** A movie directed by twenty-second-century Swedish director Sjorbik Bjorksson. A post pod containing the complete works of Bjorksson caught up with *Red Dwarf*, to the elation of Rimmer, who forced the crew to watch several films, including this light-hearted action thriller **[B-LOG]**.

  NOTE: *This film's title spoofed that of Eddie Murphy's* Beverly Hills Cop *series.*

- **Bewes, Rodney:** A British television actor known for his role as Bob Ferris in various incarnations of the sitcom *The Likely Lads* **[RL]**. When Tunbridge Wells' five hundred pilgrims were sent to pray for the end of a meteor storm ravaging their city, an actor in the group believed his people were headed to a shrine dedicated to Bewes. Others disagreed, causing a religious war that wiped out the entire pilgrim crew **[M-SMG1.14(c2)]**.

- ***Beyond the Valley of the Cheerleaders XXVII—This Time It's Personal*:** An adult-oriented film available aboard *Red Dwarf* until Rimmer accidentally taped over it with three episodes of *World Championship Risk,* dropping morale to an all-time low **[B-LOG]**.

  NOTE: *This film's title spoofed that of* Beyond the Valley of the Dolls, *a 1970 cult-classic directed by Russ Meyer and co-written by Meyer and Roger Ebert. The movie's subtitle referenced the much-maligned tagline of* Jaws: The Revenge, *"This time, it's personal."*

- **Bhaji, Bhindi:** A moniker Cat used while attempting to trick rogue simulants into thinking the *Starbug 1* crew were a human-hating species called Vindaloovians. Lister and Cat each affixed one of Kryten's optical units to their chin and transmitted a message to the simulant ship while posing upside down, with a camera zoomed in on their mouths, giving the appearance of large, one-eyed creatures.

  Lister claimed to be Tarka Dhal, an ambassador of the great Vindaloovian Empire, and introduced Cat as his companion, Bhindi Bhaji. The charade was cut short, however, when the simulant captain unexpectedly transported aboard *Starbug 1* **[T-SER6.3]**.

  ***NOTE:** Bhindi Bhaji is a popular Indian curried dish made with okra. The* Red Dwarf *script book* Son of Soup *spelled the name Bhindi Bajhii.*

- **Bible, The:** A holy book containing religious texts of the Christian faith **[RL]**. According to an ancient *Earth News* video, archeologists at Mount Sinai uncovered what was believed to be a missing page from the beginning of The Bible. When translated, it read, "To my darling Candy. All characters portrayed within this book are fictitious and any resemblance to persons living or dead is purely coincidental" **[T-SER2.2]**.

  ***NOTE:** This gag originated in a* Son of Cliché *"Dave Hollins: Space Cadet" sketch titled "Newsflash," in which an archeologist, Doctor Franz Luber, read the missing page to news reporters. That version contained an additional line: "By the same author: The New Testament and Testament III—all your favorite characters back again for another zany adventure!"*

- **Big Arn:** A nickname by which Rimmer referred to himself while gloating about having saved *Red Dwarf* from a highly corrosive microorganism **[T-SER10.6]**.

- **Big Boss:** Swallow's name for the man who created the television series *Red Dwarf* on an alternate twenty-first-century Earth, which the crew imagined while trapped in an elation squid hallucination **[T-SER9.2]**.

- ***Big Boy's Book of Cloning*:** A pop-up book aimed at younger audiences that explained the science behind cloning and cellular regeneration in simple terms. Rimmer reviewed the *Big Boy's Book of Cloning* while attempting to create a host body from one of Lister's hairs via cellular regeneration **[R-BOD]**.

- ***Big Boys in Boots*:** An adult magazine geared toward homosexual men. Jealous of the instant friendship between Lister and Ace Rimmer, Arnold Rimmer questioned their sexuality by implying they were the double-action centerfold in the July issue of *Big Boys in Boots* **[T-SER4.5]**.

- **Big Chief I-Spy:** A pseudonym for Charles Warrell, a retired headmaster who launched a British series of spotter's guides called *I Spy*, aimed at young readers **[RL]**. While on an asteroid-spotting trip aboard *Starbug 1*, Rimmer and Kryten located 248 different asteroids, to which Holly exclaimed that Big Chief I-Spy would be proud **[T-SER4.1(d)]**.

- **Big Crunch, the:** A name given by scientists to one possible scenario describing the universe's eventual fate, in which space's expansion would reverse and the universe would either collapse as a black hole singularity or reform with a new Big Bang **[RL]**. During the Big Crunch, the universe would contract, causing everything (including time) to run backwards, and culminating in all matter and energy being compressed into a single point **[T-SER3.1]**.

- ***Biggles' Big Adventure*:** *See Biggles Learns to Fly*

- ***Biggles Flies West*:** A book in the *Biggles* series, written in 1937 by W. E. Johns, in which James Bigglesworth and friends traveled to the Caribbean in search of lost pirate's treasure **[RL]**. Rimmer claimed that he could read *Biggles Flies West* for three nights under his bed sheets without a flashlight after his brother, Howard, painted his penis with orange glow paint when they were young **[T-SER10.1]**.

- ***Biggles Learns to Fly*:** A book written in 1935 by W. E. Johns, containing several short stories about the escapades of James Bigglesworth and his early days as a pilot **[RL]**.
  While marooned aboard *Starbug 1* on an icy planet, Lister decided to burn this book to keep warm. When Rimmer protested the burning of books, citing their value to society, Lister questioned the validity of his statement when it came

B-: Books
PRG: *Red Dwarf Programme Guide*
SUR: *Red Dwarf Space Corps Survival Manual*
PRM: *Primordial Soup*
SOS: *Son of Soup*
SCE: *Scenes from the Dwarf*
LOG: *Red Dwarf Log No. 1996*
RD8: *Red Dwarf VIII*
EVR: *The Log: A Dwarfer's Guide to Everything*

X-: Misc.
PRO: Promotional materials, videos, etc.
PST: Posters at DJ XVII (2013)
CAL: 2008 calendar
RNG: Cell phone ringtones
MOB: Mobisode ("Red Christmas")
CIN: *Children in Need* sketch
GEK: *Geek Week* intros by Kryten
TNG: "Tongue-Tied" video

XMS: Bill Pearson's Christmas special pitch script
XVD: Bill Pearson's Christmas special pitch video
OTH: Other *Red Dwarf* appearances

SUFFIX
DVD:
(d) – Deleted scene
(o) – Outtake
(b) – Bonus DVD material (other)
(e) – Extended version

SMEGAZINES:
(c) – Comic
(a) – Article

OTHER:
(s) – Early/unused script draft
(s1) – Alternate version of script

to that particular volume **[T-SER3.2]**. Rimmer also owned a hologrammatic version of this book, which he read while Lister was pregnant **[R-DAD]**.

> ***NOTE:*** *The original script, published in* Primordial Soup, *cited another book by Johns,* Biggles' Big Adventure.

- **Big Iron:** A character in the Western novel *Big Iron at Sun-up*, written by Zach Rattler. A mysterious stranger "answering to no man, beholden to no women," Big Iron dispensed justice throughout the American Wild West, with the aid of his rather long gun **[N-BCK]**.

- ***Big Iron at Sun-up*:** A Western novel written by Zach Rattler, about a cowboy named Big Iron who traveled throughout the American Wild West, dispensing justice. A copy of the book was stored in *Starbug 1*'s small library. Kryten read the novel while the crew pursued the stolen *Red Dwarf*. Since it was the last remaining book to read, he rationed out his time, reading only .8219178 words per day **[N-BCK]**.

- **Big Man:** A nickname that Rimmer asked Lister to call him (instead of "Rimmer") as they and Cat embarked on a rescue mission to *Nova 5*, where they believed three female crewmembers awaited. When the crew discovered the "survivors" had been dead for millennia, Lister honored Rimmer's request by mocking him with the name **[T-SER2.1]**.

- **Big Meat:** An inmate of the Tank, *Red Dwarf*'s classified brig, who perished during the cadmium II disaster but was resurrected when nanobots rebuilt the mining ship. Cat tried to goad the largely built prisoner into hitting him by stealing his food and calling him names, hoping he would then be sent to the medi-bay so he could join his friends and escape. Big Meat believed him to be even crazier than he was, however, and instead made himself Cat's bitch **[T-SER8.8]**.

- ***Big 'n' Bouncy*:** An adult publication, several copies of which Rimmer owned aboard *Red Dwarf* **[M-SMG2.4(c5)]**.

- **Bill:** A short man with red hair who always wore a sports jacket. When members of the Infinity Patrol went back in time to the twenty-second century and met Rimmer, they asked him if he knew Bill, who was also from that century **[R-INF]**.

> ***NOTE:*** *This gag originated in a* Son of Cliché *"Dave Hollins: Space Cadet" sketch titled "The Strange Planet You Shouldn't Really Land On."*

- **"Billy Benton and His Choir Sing the Rock'n'Roll Greats":** A CD Rimmer owned aboard *Red Dwarf* **[N-INF]**.

- **Billy con Carne:** A cannibalism recipe that Colonel Mike O'Hagan recommended in his *Space Corps Survival Manual* **[B-SUR]**.

- **Billy the Kid:** The nickname of William H. Bonney, a notorious nineteenth-century frontier outlaw in the American Old West **[RL]**. After being subjected to a mind probe on Justice World, Lister grew concerned that his past would come back to haunt him, and thus confessed to numerous petty crimes he committed as a youth. In response, Rimmer called him Billy the Kid **[T-SER4.3(d)]**.

- **Bimbo-Brain:** A nickname that Holly called Rimmer while explaining the circumstances that led to the AI's intelligence and runtime being compressed **[N-BTL]**.

- **Binary Hills 90210:** A city featured on the television soap opera *Androids*. Karstares crawled down this city's Rom&Ramsay Street after losing his legs during a battle with his son Jaysee **[M-SMG2.7(c6)]**.

> ***NOTE:*** *The city's name referenced the television show* Beverly Hills, 90210, *as well as the California city and zip code after which it was named.*

- **binary star:** A type of star system containing a pair of stars orbiting a common center of mass **[RL]**. Binary stars were covered in the space phenomenon section of Kryten's *Starbug 1* pilot's test **[T-SER3.1]**.

- **Bindi:** The second tier of the Vindaloovian GELF caste system, comprising the middle class, including military officers **[G-BIT]**.

PREFIX
RL: Real life

T-: Television Episodes
SER: Television series
IDW: "Identity Within"
USA1: Unaired U.S. pilot
USA2: Unaired U.S. demo

R-: *The Bodysnatcher Collection*
SER: Remastered episodes
BOD: "Bodysnatcher"
DAD: "Dad"
FTH: "Lister's Father"
INF: "Infinity Patrol"
END: "The End" (original assembly)

N-: Novels
INF: *Infinity Welcomes Careful Drivers*
BTL: *Better Than Life*
LST: *Last Human*
BCK: *Backwards*
OMN: *Red Dwarf Omnibus*

M-: Magazines
SMG: *Smegazine*

W-: Websites
OFF: Official website
NAN: *Prelude to Nanarchy*
AND: *Androids*
DIV: Diva-Droid
DIB: Duane Dibbley

CRP: Crapola
GEN: Geneticon
LSR: Leisure World Intl.
JMC: Jupiter Mining Corporation
AIT: *A.I. Today*
HOL: HoloPoint

G-: Roleplaying Game
RPG: *Core Rulebook*
BIT: *A.I. Screen Extra Bits* booklet
SOR: *Series Sourcebook*
OTH: Other RPG material

- **Bing:** A male name used in the saying, "If you've got nothing to swing, you can't be with Bing!"—a phrase referring to the Space Corps directive that prevented gender ambiguity in prison. Kryten referenced the saying while complaining to Kochanski about being classified as a woman during his incarceration in *Red Dwarf*'s brig **[T-SER8.2]**.

- **Binglebat, Myra:** An actor who starred in a remake of the classic American film *Casablanca*. Upon discovering an even newer update of the film in a postal pod, Lister questioned the need for this version, declaring the Beardsley-Binglebat production definitive. Holly, having also seen the movie, quoted a famous line of dialog: "Of all the space bars in all the worlds, you had to re-materialize in mine" **[T-SER2.2]**. An Extras Pack sold by Crapola Inc. allowed talking appliances, such as Talkie Toasters and Talkie Toilets, to speak with Binglebat's voice and personality **[W-CRP]**.

  NOTE: *The above quote spoofed an oft-repeated line from the original film starring Humphrey Bogart and Ingrid Bergman: "Of all the gin joints, in all the towns, in all the world, she walks into mine."*

- **Bingley, Charles:** A character in Jane Austen's novel *Pride and Prejudice* **[RL]**. Upon entering the artificial-reality simulation *Pride and Prejudice Land*, Kochanski, Lister and Cat met Mrs. Bennet and her daughters, who invited them to tea in Mr. Bingley's gazebo. Kryten, however—upset at having been snubbed by the group after preparing a lobster dinner for them—hacked into the simulation with a World War II tank and fired at the gazebo, destroying it and killing the Bennets **[T-SER7.6]**.

- **Binks, Commander:** A male hologram stationed on the holoship *Enlightenment,* in charge of first contact with new life forms. His IQ was 192 **[W-OFF]**. When the holoship encountered *Starbug 1*, Binks was sent to survey the ship. Upon encountering *Starbug*'s crew, he reported his disdain back to *Enlightenment*, after which Lister threatened to beat him with a holowhip, causing the hologram to hastily depart **[T-SER5.1]**.

- **bio-feedback catheter:** A tube consisting of a suite of sensors placed in the body of an individual entering a total-immersion video game machine for an extended period. The sensors then tracked that person's vital signs while he or she was in the game **[T-SER5.6]**.

- **bio-feedback sensors:** A suite of sensors placed on the body of a patient wearing a medi-suit for rehabilitation, for the purpose of monitoring that person's vital signs **[N-BTL]**.

- **"biological explosives":** A phrase on a label adorning several pipes located within Lister's quarters aboard *Red Dwarf* **[T-SER10.2]**.

- **bio-organic computer networking:** A sophisticated networking system using organic material instead of conventional cabling. Bio-organic computer networks were designed for use aboard JMC vessels, such as *Red Dwarf*, but were eliminated from the final build due to financial cutbacks. When Kryten's nanobots demolecularized and rebuilt *Red Dwarf*, they used the original design specs, replacing the old networking system with bio-organic computer networking **[T-SER8.1]**.

- **bio-suit:** A self-contained, sealed suit designed for extremely dangerous environments, such as facilities dealing with deadly viruses. Bio-suits were mandatory in the Viral Research Department of the station where Hildegarde Lanstrom worked **[T-SER5.4]**.

- **BIOtrak Ident-chip:** An identification chip implanted under a person's skin, containing his or her physical, medical and personal information. Sold by Crapola Inc. in its annual *SCABBY* catalog, the chips were primarily used by the Jupiter Mining Corp. and the Space Corps to track their staff **[G-SOR]**.

- **bi-photonic monoprism:** A technology developed by Warburton Neurotronics and used in hologrammic light bees **[X-PST]**.

- **bi-photonic soft-light projection mode:** *See* soft light projection mode

- **"Birdcatcher's Song, The":** An aria from the opera *The Magic Flute*, by Wolfgang Amadeus Mozart **[RL]**. While playing a game based on *The Magic Flute*, in which players had to guess the aria being hummed, the crew of an alternate-universe *Red Dwarf* were amused by their Lister's rendition of "The Birdcatcher's Song" in the German translation **[T-SER7.5]**.

- **bird-eating bird:** A creature genetically engineered by inebriated scientists. Due to its diet, this species was short-lived **[B-EVR]**.

- **Birdman:** An elderly inmate of the Tank, *Red Dwarf*'s classified brig, who perished during the cadmium II disaster, but was resurrected when nanobots rebuilt the mining ship. His education included three years at university and four years of veterinary college. Birdman was sentenced to twenty years in *Red Dwarf*'s brig for GBH (Grievous Bodily Harm), during which he joined the Canaries.

  On a mission to a forest moon, Birdman discovered an injured sparrow, which he smuggled aboard *Red Dwarf*. He nursed the bird back to health and named it Pete (after actor Peter Beardsley) and gained the nickname "Birdman" due to his similarity to Robert Stroud, a famous American prisoner who nursed three sparrows back to health and became an ornithologist while incarcerated **[W-OFF]**.

  At some point, Birdman was sentenced to the Hole, the Tank's solitary-confinement cell. There, he later met Lister and Rimmer, who were sent to the Hole for misusing a programmable virus. Bob the skutter soon set the group free and led them to Cat, Kryten and Kochanski on the cargo deck. By the time the trio arrived, Pete had passed away from the excitement of being free. Kryten tried to resuscitate the bird using a time wand, but an improper setting caused the animal to de-evolve into a *Tyrannosaurus rex*, which ate Birdman and then stalked the others **[T-SER8.6]**.

  After the dinosaur wreaked havoc on the food decks, Lister and Rimmer used the time wand to revive Birdman and restore Pete to being a sparrow **[T-SER8.7]**.

  ***NOTE:** Birdman's actual name is unknown.*

- **Birds Eye:** An international brand of frozen foods, headquartered in North America **[RL]**. When Holly warned that *Red Dwarf* would become compressed down to the size of a garden pea if the ship traveled too close to a black hole, Lister exclaimed, "Bye bye, Birds Eye" **[T-SER3.2]**.

- **Bird-Tray Head:** One of Cat's nicknames for Kryten **[T-SER8.5]**.

- **Birmingham Mini Coopers:** A zero-gee football team that played the London Jets during the sport's thirty-seventh season **[M-SMG1.8(a)]**.

  ***NOTE:** The Mini Cooper is an iconic British economy-class automobile.*

- **Bitchin' Chrome:** A designer color available from Bloodlust Arms for the Punisher Heavy Machine Gun **[G-RPG]**.

- **Bitterness:** An aspect of Rimmer's personality made flesh on a psi-moon configured according to his psyche. When the *Red Dwarf* crew boosted Arnold's confidence to vanquish the Self-Loathing Beast, a ghostly musketeer arose to battle the Unspeakable One's hordes, including Bitterness, thereby enabling the crew to escape **[T-SER5.3]**.

- **Biz:** A brand of laundry detergent invented in 1968 by Charles McCarty **[RL]**. Lister commented that Rimmer, dressed in his impeccably white dress uniform, looked like someone "whose mum uses new biological Biz" **[T-SER2.1]**.

- **Bjorksson, Sjorbik:** A twenty-second-century Swedish film director. A post pod containing the complete works of Bjorksson caught up with *Red Dwarf*, to the elation of Rimmer, who immediately set up a mandatory viewing of *The Dichotomy of Faith in a Post Materialistic Society*, the first and last of Bjorksson's musicals. He later forced the crew to watch several other Bjorksson films, including the action thriller *Beverly Hills Bereavement Counsellor* and the romantic comedy *Four Funerals and Another One* **[B-LOG]**.

  ***NOTE:** The book contained multiple spellings of the director's name: Sjorbik Bjorksson, Sorbik Bjorksson, Sjorbik Bjornsson and Sjorbik Bkjorksson.*

- **Black, Jeremy, Mineral Geologist First Class:** A *Red Dwarf* crewmember who perished in the cadmium II explosion. Lister and Rimmer ejected a canister containing his remains into space during a funeral for the accident's casualties **[R-END]**.

NOTE: In the pilot episode's first-draft script, published in the Red Dwarf Omnibus, *Black was the ship's flight organizer. It is unknown whether the nanobots resurrected him in Series VIII.*

- **black box recording:** A device used on ships such as *Red Dwarf* that archived audio and video footage of every moment on board, for security and investigative purposes. Rimmer, distraught and embarrassed after Lister gifted him with a memory of his ex-girlfriend Lise Yates, insisted everyone's mind be erased, and that *Red Dwarf*'s black box be buried on a remote moon, to hide all evidence of the traumatizing event.

  After the memory wipes, however, the crew realized the black box was missing and followed its homing signal back to the moon to retrieve it, in order to solve the mystery of their missing time. There, they found the box buried in a shallow grave with a tombstone that read, "To the Memory of the Memory of Lise Yates" **[T-SER2.3]**.

  Sometime later, the ship's black box fell into a black hole, ended up in the Omni-zone and traveled back in time three million years, where the Space Corps' Doctor Marcus Bateman analyzed its contents **[W-OFF]**. Because of this recording, Yvonne McGruder (who had left *Red Dwarf* prior to the cadmium II disaster) and her son, Michael—Rimmer's son—learned of Arnold's hologrammatic resurrection **[N-LST]**.

- **black box terminal:** A computer aboard the SSS *Esperanto* that held the ship's vital statistics, primary mission data and log entries. The *Starbug 1* crew accessed the black box terminal to determine what had happened aboard the vessel **[T-SER5.6]**.

- **black card:** A part of Rimmer's Color Code system for conversations; holding up a black card meant he considered a conversation ended. When Lister pleaded for a date with Kochanski's hologram, Rimmer denied the request, pronouncing it a black-card situation. Lister later turned the tables by black-carding Rimmer when ordered not to take the Officer's Exam **[T-SER1.3]**.

- **black coffee:** A brewed beverage served without cream or milk **[RL]**. When Lister ordered a black coffee from a food dispenser suffering from a faulty vocabulary unit, he instead received a metal bucket **[T-SER1.2]**.

- **blackcurrant cordial**: An alcoholic beverage made with blackcurrant berries **[RL]**. While lecturing Lister about the importance of carrying out their duties as vending machine technicians, Rimmer claimed his reputation would be at stake if an officer ordered soup from a dispenser and instead received a blackcurrant cordial and blancmange **[T-SER1.1]**.

- **Black Friday:** The day Rimmer imagined losing his entire fortune while trapped in an addictive version of *Better Than Life*. Rimmer believed he had returned to Earth and become immensely wealthy, but his subconscious mind could not handle his good fortune and rebelled against him, causing him to lose his wealth **[N-BTL]**.

- **black hole:** A spatial phenomenon typically created from a collapsed star, the gravitational pull of which was so great that nothing—even light—could escape **[RL]**. Holly ordered *Red Dwarf*'s evacuation after detecting five black holes simultaneously, marooning Rimmer and Lister for several days on an icy planet. In the end, the supposed black holes turned out merely to be grit on the scanner-scope **[T-SER3.2]**.

  When *Red Dwarf* became trapped in a black hole's gravitational pull, temporal anomalies resulted throughout the ship. With the vessel's engines down and Holly offline, the crew grudgingly took the advice of Talkie Toaster, whom Holly had told how to escape a black hole prior to going offline.

  The plan involved speeding toward the black hole and using its pull to break the lightspeed barrier, enabling the ship to pass the event horizon, slingshot around the singularity and escape its gravitational pull. In so doing, the ship passed through the Omni-zone, an area of non-space where the seven main universes connected via massive, cable-like connections. Eventually, *Red Dwarf* broke free of the black hole's pull and was ejected back into real space—some thirty-four years later, due to time compression **[N-BTL]**.

- ***Black Hole***: A state-of-the-art experimental JMC mining vessel in an alternate universe, controlled by Kenneth, an AI

computer with a rated IQ of twelve thousand. *Black Hole* was a joint venture between Jupiter Mining Corp. and the Space Corps, designed to seek out and harvest exploitable resources throughout time by using a temporal scoop to draw material in from various possible universes.

The ship contained a Singularity Drive powered by a tiny captured star, which allowed faster-than-light travel. Among its other features were an auto-compacting mass driver that sent raw materials back home at light speed, as well as personnel teleporters and a full complement of SpaceCondor quad wing fighters. The ship's mission statement was "To boldly go where no man has recently gone before, to exploit new species in the now, the was and the maybe will be."

Stationed aboard the vessel was Circuitry Technician 3rd Class Arnold J. Rimmer, who inadvertently crossed the wiring between the temporal scoop and the Singularity Drive, causing the ship to become lost in space-time upon its engines' first activation. In addition, the powering star was not properly contained during the accident, resulting in the deaths of the entire crew, save for those protected in the cargo hold or stasis booths. The radiation also drastically lowered Kenneth's IQ **[G-RPG]**.

> ***NOTE:*** *The ship's mission statement spoofed that of* Star Trek*'s USS* Enterprise, *which was "to explore strange new worlds, to seek out new life and new civilizations, to boldly go where no man has gone before."*

- **Black Island Film Studios:** A production company in a universe in which *Red Dwarf* was a British television series. The studio's caretaker was Leo Davis, and his boss was Mr. Walker. Raga artist Tabby Ranks once filmed a video at this studio **[X-TNG]**.

> ***NOTE:*** *Black Island Studios was the real-world location of the* Tongue-Tied *video production.*

- **blacksmith:** A craftsman who forged objects from steel or wrought iron, including gates, furniture, tools, weapons and more **[RL]**. A blacksmith shop was among the buildings comprising an Old West town that Kryten's subconscious mind created while combatting the Armageddon virus **[T-SER6.3]**.

- ***Blade Runner*:** An American science fiction film directed by Ridley Scott, starring Harrison Ford, Sean Young and Rutger Hauer, based on the 1968 novel *Do Androids Dream of Electric Sheep?* by Philip K. Dick. The film was set in a dystopian future in which runaway robots called replicants were hunted down by special operatives called blade runners **[RL]**.

While trapped in an elation squid hallucination, the *Red Dwarf* crew believed they had visited an alternate twenty-first-century Earth on which they were merely characters on the television series *Red Dwarf.* Finding an empty DVD box for the show's upcoming season, they discovered that the series' impending final episode would end with their demise. Desperate for more life, they set out to find their creator "in the best *Blade Runner* tradition" **[T-SER9.2]**. Confronted by the crew, the writer admitted that both their creation and death had been inspired by the movie **[T-SER9.3]**.

> ***NOTE:*** *Several key scenes and plots in* Back to Earth *were direct references to the* Blade Runner *film, most notably scenes involving Nose World, the Creator and Kochanski's appearance. In the real world,* Red Dwarf *was primarily inspired by the films* Dark Star, Alien *and* Silent Running, *not* Blade Runner.

- **blancmange**: A sweet dessert, usually made with milk or cream and sugar, thickened with a gelatin, and typically flavored with almonds **[RL]**. While lecturing Lister about the importance of carrying out their duties as vending machine technicians, Rimmer claimed his reputation would be at stake if an officer ordered soup from a dispenser and instead received a blackcurrant cordial and blancmange **[T-SER1.1]**.

- **"blank":** A word printed on a label attached to a blue bazookoid MK2 cartridge, identifying it as containing blank (non-projectile) rounds **[T-SER7.2]**.

- **blaster:** A type of weapon stored aboard *Red Dwarf.* Rimmer suggested using blasters against a creature living in the water tank on G Deck **[T-SER9.1]**.

- **Blautechpunknicht:** A brand of mobile stereo systems. When recommending himself for promotion, Rimmer requested a red company shuttle equipped with a Blautechpunknicht

PREFIX
RL: Real life

T-: Television Episodes
SER: Television series
IDW: "Identity Within"
USA1: Unaired U.S. pilot
USA2: Unaired U.S. demo

R-: *The Bodysnatcher Collection*
SER: Remastered episodes
BOD: "Bodysnatcher"
DAD: "Dad"
FTH: "Lister's Father"
INF: "Infinity Patrol"
END: "The End" (original assembly)

N-: Novels
INF: *Infinity Welcomes Careful Drivers*
BTL: *Better Than Life*
LST: *Last Human*

BCK: *Backwards*
OMN: *Red Dwarf Omnibus*

M-: Magazines
SMG: *Smegazine*

W-: Websites
OFF: Official website
NAN: *Prelude to Nanarchy*
AND: *Androids*
DIV: Diva-Droid
DIB: Duane Dibbley

CRP: Crapola
GEN: Geneticon
LSR: Leisure World Intl.
JMC: Jupiter Mining Corporation
AIT: *A.I. Today*
HOL: HoloPoint

G-: Roleplaying Game
RPG: *Core Rulebook*
BIT: *A.I. Screen Extra Bits* booklet
SOR: *Series Sourcebook*
OTH: Other RPG material

stereo **[B-LOG]**.

NOTE: This brand was named after Blaupunkt, a German electronics manufacturer specializing in car and home audio systems.

- **bleeper:** A communication device used aboard *Red Dwarf* to contact technicians in the event of an emergency **[N-INF]**.

  NOTE: This was presumably a futuristic version of a beeper, popular throughout the 1980s and '90s.

- **Blenkinsop, Oswald ("Kill Crazy"):** An inmate of the Tank, *Red Dwarf*'s classified brig, who perished during the cadmium II disaster, but was resurrected after nanobots rebuilt the mining ship **[T-SER8.4]**. His hobbies included macramé using human entrails **[G-SOR]**. His police record included twelve counts of violent conduct and forty-nine counts of fraud.

  Prior to his incarceration, Blenkinsop worked at a video store called Wacky Wally's Video Wonderland. When a customer chastised him for playing the film *Decayed Flesh 5: The Zombies Take Manhattan*, he grew incensed, followed the woman home and killed her entire family, creating a lamp out of one victim's head and a pair of slippers from another's buttocks. He was promptly arrested and placed in *Red Dwarf*'s brig for transport to Adelphi 12, where he joined the Canaries.

  During one mission to a forest moon, he trod upon a sparrow, breaking its wing. A fellow inmate, who would come to be known as Birdman, rescued the bird and nursed it back to health **[W-OFF]**.

  A rambunctious inmate, Kill Crazy reveled in missions offering the potential to kill dangerous creatures. During the SSS *Silverberg* incident, however, he bumped his head on the entryway and remained unconscious for the mission's duration **[T-SER8.4]**.

  On another mission, Kill Crazy encountered a creature with two heads and several tentacles, which ran off at the sight of him. During that mission, he learned that Kryten, classified as a woman by the ship's penal system, showered with the female inmates. Therefore, he kidnapped the mechanoid and reprogrammed him to record the women naked. As a result, Kryten created Krytie TV and broadcast the footage for the male prisoners **[T-SER8.5]**.

  Later, while on a mission to convert Pete the *Tyrannosaurus rex* back into a sparrow, Kill Crazy looked forward to sparring with the beast hand-to-hand, despite having a "glass jaw" **[T-SER8.7(d)]**. Kill Crazy and Baxter ambushed Lister and Rimmer, stealing a time wand to prevent them from using it on the dinosaur. Clueless about how it worked, the two ended up de-evolving themselves into primates **[T-SER8.7]**, though their original forms were restored once the wand was destroyed **[W-OFF]**.

  NOTE: Kill Crazy's full name appeared in an in-universe interview with the character on the official website. Onscreen, he was known only by his nickname.

- **Blerion:** The common name of the pig-like GELFs living in an alternate dimension on Blerios 15 **[B-PRG]**.

- **Blerion High Council:** The ruling body of Blerios 15, a GELF-populated asteroid in an alternate universe **[N-LST]**.

- **Blerios 15:** An asteroid located in an alternate reality, primarily populated by pig-based GELFs. The *Starbug 1* crew, having accidentally entered this universe, traveled to Blerios 15 seeking Lister's doppelgänger. The asteroid was ruled by the Blerion High Council, of which Leekiel was a member.

  The GELFs were initially created to terraform hostile new worlds for mankind, and thus were not given the ability to procreate. As a result, ninety-nine percent of the GELF population were sterile; the remaining one percent were called Potents, and were held in high regard. Because of this, sperm was a highly valued commodity among the GELFs **[N-LST]**.

- **Blind Pew:** A fictional unsighted beggar in the novel *Treasure Island*, by Robert Louis Stevenson **[RL]**. Rimmer complained that *Red Dwarf*'s skutters were as useful as giving Blind Pew contact lenses **[T-SER2.2]**.

- **Bliss:** An incredibly powerful designer drug with several unique characteristics: a person became addicted to it simply by looking at it; it made a user believe he was God; and the high that Bliss provided lasted for only fifteen minutes, after which depression set in, lasting upwards of twenty-five years.

  On Mimas, the drug was controlled by the Ganymedian Mafia. When an astro named Dutch van Oestrogen double-crossed the crime family during a Bliss deal, they pursued him across the Saturnian moon **[M-SMG2.3(c4)]**. Lister was once accosted by a Bliss addict on Mimas named Denis, who sought money to feed his addiction **[N-INF]**.

- **Blisters:** The blue-collar faction that fought in Earth's twenty-second-century Tie Wars against the business-class Ties. The war tilted in favor of the Ties when they introduced the Smart But Casual Bomb, a weapon that covered the Blisters in paisley cravats and hand-tailored lounge suits. The war raged on until the Blisters, realizing they were manufacturing the Ties' weapons, discontinued production, resulting in the war abruptly ending in compromise, with the Blisters buttoning their top shirt buttons and the Ties undoing theirs beneath their ties **[B-EVR]**.

- ***Blob, The*:** A 1958 American horror-science fiction film starring Steve McQueen, about an amorphous alien creature threatening a small Pennsylvanian town **[RL]**. When Kryten planned a date with Camille—a Pleasure GELF whose natural appearance was an amorphous green blob—Lister cited *The Blob* as an example of how people react differently to certain things, noting that the response of McQueen's character, Steve Andrews, to meeting the creature was to try to kill it, not take it out to dinner **[T-SER4.1]**.

- **blo-bot:** A robotic sex worker on Mimas specializing in orally pleasuring customers. A poster advertising blo-bots and handroids adorned the wall of the Hotel Paradiso **[M-SMG2.3(c4)]**.

- **Block Head:** A nickname Cat called Kryten after the mechanoid's head was transplanted onto the body of Hudzen 10 **[M-SMG2.3(c1)]**.

- **Blofish, Professor:** A professor at Imperial College who invented the Spanner Scanner, a device that displayed events from a previous timespan at any given location. Due to the contraption's immense power requirements, it only replayed events that had transpired within the previous two milliseconds. The school dismissed Blofish after catching him using the Spanner Scanner to view the room of a female biochemistry student while giggling profusely **[B-EVR]**.

- **Blood Drinker:** An inmate of the Tank, *Red Dwarf*'s classified brig, who perished during the cadmium II disaster, but was resurrected when nanobots rebuilt the mining ship. Blood Drinker was a member of the Canaries, an elite group of inmates assigned to investigate dangerous situations, and was part of the team that discovered the prophetic computer Cassandra aboard the wreckage of the SSS *Silverberg* **[T-SER8.4(d)]**.

  ***NOTE:** Blood Drinker's actual name is unknown.*

- **Bloodlust Arms:** A weapons dealer whose products were featured in Crapola Inc.'s annual *SCABBY* catalog **[G-RPG]**.

- **blow football:** A popular children's game in the United Kingdom, the goal of which was to blow through a straw or other pipe-like item in order to move a lightweight ball through an opponent's goal **[RL]**. Confused by the absence of a sex deck aboard *Red Dwarf*, Nirvanah Crane asked what Rimmer's crew did to relieve sexual frustration, to which he replied "blow football" **[T-SER5.1(d)]**.

- **Blue Alert:** An alert status indicating a potential threat to a *Starbug* shuttlecraft, signified by the illumination of an "alert" sign with a blue light bulb. Switching to another alert status involved changing the bulb to the new color. When Cat sensed a threat undetected by *Starbug 1*'s sensors, Rimmer insisted on going to Blue Alert, despite the fact that the entire crew was present and fully aware of the situation **[T-SER6.2]**.

- **blueberry muffin:** A baked good that Captain Hollister's wife, Martha, sometimes made for him before he departed for a tour of duty aboard *Red Dwarf.* Upon learning this fact, Rimmer presented the captain with a blueberry muffin on his wedding anniversary, hoping to win his favor and earn a promotion **[T-SER8.2]**.

  ***NOTE:** In a deleted scene from episode 8.2 ("Back in the Red: Part II"), the muffin was replaced by a tangerine sponge cake.*

- **Blue Corridor 212:** A walkway on one of *Red Dwarf*'s maintenance decks, containing Circuit Board Theta 29555. When a crazed skutter rewired this board, Rimmer and Kryten tried to remotely repair the damaged circuit, along with thousands of others affected by the robot **[T-SER3.4]**.

- **Blue Corridor 9:** A walkway on *Red Dwarf*'s Floor 431 that contained an Indian restaurant called The Vindaloovian Empire **[X-CAL]**.

- **blue giant:** A type of star many times more massive than Earth's Sun, which burned bright blue due to its higher surface temperature **[RL]**. Blue giants were covered in the space phenomenon section of Kryten's *Starbug 1* pilot's test **[T-SER3.1]**.

- ***Blue Midget*:** A haulage transporter stored aboard *Red Dwarf*. It contained twelve gear levers, each providing five gears apiece, for a total of sixty gears **[N-INF]**.

  Long, boxy and blue, *Blue Midget* contained tank treads for surface transport. The *Red Dwarf* crew used this craft during a rescue mission to the crashed spaceship *Nova 5* **[T-SER2.1]**. Additionally, the vessel transported the crew down to the surface of a barren planet to celebrate Rimmer's deathday **[T-SER2.3]**, and was also used by Kryten and Cat during an evacuation of *Red Dwarf* after several black holes were detected (which turned out just to be scanner grit) **[T-SER3.2]**.

  The original design of *Blue Midget* shuttles, prior to JMC cutbacks, included a sleeker, rounded shape, small arm-like clamps and leg-like struts for better ground mobility. When Kryten's nanobots rebuilt *Red Dwarf* and *Blue Midget*, they followed the original specs for both ships **[T-SER8.3]**. The toes of the legged version retracted into its feet when parked, and were extended when launching for better traction **[R-SER(b)]**.

  In an illusion created by psychotropic drugs, Cat believed he was impressing an attractive ground controller by making several *Blue Midget* shuttles dance in unison **[T-SER8.3]**.

  ***NOTE:** In the remastered episodes of* The Bodysnatcher Collection*, the boxy, treaded model was replaced by the sleeker, legged version.* Red Dwarf—The Roleplaying Game *referred to the original boxy design as Mark I, and the sleeker version as Mark II, while the 2008 calendar called the new model the 9000 SMG.*

- **"*Blue Midget*—Jupiter Mining Corporation":** A phrase adorning a patch sewn onto Lister's leather jacket **[T-SER10(b)]**.

  ***NOTE:** This detail was visible in the "We're Smegged" making-of special included in the Series X DVDs.*

- **blunt mode:** A function of 4000 Series mechanoids enabling them to curtly state facts without skirting the issue. Kryten used blunt mode to tell Cat that the *Red Dwarf* crew had failed to raise the funds necessary to buy Ora Tanzil's freedom from a GELF tribe—meaning certain death for them both, since Cat had already bid on her **[T-IDW]**.

- **Blu-Tack:** A putty-like product used to hang paper items, such as photos or posters, on walls or other surfaces **[RL]**. While moving into his own quarters, Rimmer claimed ownership of the Blu-Tack holding Lister's posters up in the quarters they had previously shared **[T-SER1.6]**.

- **Bob:** One of *Red Dwarf*'s skutters, who delivered an invitation to Kryten for his "last-day" party **[T-SER3.6]**. Bob was married to another skutter called Madge **[T-SER8.6]**.

  Bob smuggled several items to Lister while the latter was in prison, including Boing (a virility-enhancement drug), chicken vindaloo meals (complete with lager and poppadoms) and a programmable virus for peeling potatoes. He also helped Lister, Rimmer and Birdman escape from the Hole, *Red Dwarf*'s solitary-confinement cell **[T-SER8.6]**.

  Bob was swallowed by Pete, a sparrow transformed into a *Tyrannosaurus rex*, but the skutter was released when the dinosaur suffered a diarrhea attack after eating tons of junk food in the cargo bay **[T-SER8.7]**.

  ***NOTE:** It is unknown whether Bob was aboard* Red Dwarf *when the mining ship was destroyed during the triplicator accident in episode 5.5 ("Angels and Demons"). If so, then the Bob in Series III was technically a different skutter from the one in Series VIII, as the latter would have been created during the merging of the "high" and "low" versions of the ship.*

- **Bob:** An android host on the All-Droid Mail Order Shopping Station. Bob and co-host Jayne demonstrated a product called the Stirmaster—a gadget that stirred coffee or tea—during an infomercial transmission that the passing *Red Dwarf* picked up. Fascinated, Cat and Lister vowed to buy one **[T-SER10.1]**.

- **Bob:** A Shore Patrol guard stationed at the Space Corps testing facility on Europa in the Alpha universe. A day after "Spanners" Lister was incarcerated in the facility's jail for

BLUE MIDGET

PREFIX
RL: Real life

T-: Television Episodes
- **SER:** Television series
- **IDW:** "Identity Within"
- **USA1:** Unaired U.S. pilot
- **USA2:** Unaired U.S. demo

R-: *The Bodysnatcher Collection*
- **SER:** Remastered episodes
- **BOD:** "Bodysnatcher"
- **DAD:** "Dad"
- **FTH:** "Lister's Father"
- **INF:** "Infinity Patrol"
- **END:** "The End" (original assembly)

N-: Novels
- **INF:** *Infinity Welcomes Careful Drivers*
- **BTL:** *Better Than Life*
- **LST:** *Last Human*
- **BCK:** *Backwards*
- **OMN:** *Red Dwarf Omnibus*

M-: Magazines
- **SMG:** *Smegazine*

W-: Websites
- **OFF:** Official website
- **NAN:** *Prelude to Nanarchy*
- **AND:** *Androids*
- **DIV:** Diva-Droid
- **DIB:** Duane Dibbley
- **CRP:** Crapola
- **GEN:** Geneticon
- **LSR:** Leisure World Intl.
- **JMC:** Jupiter Mining Corporation
- **AIT:** *A.I. Today*
- **HOL:** HoloPoint

G-: Roleplaying Game
- **RPG:** *Core Rulebook*
- **BIT:** *A.I. Screen Extra Bits* booklet
- **SOR:** *Series Sourcebook*
- **OTH:** Other RPG material

gross insubordination, Bob released the mechanic to Ace Rimmer's care, as well as Olaf Petersen, Lister's friend in the next cell **[N-BCK]**.

- **Bob ("Bent Bob"):** The nickname of a diminutive, homosexual crewmember aboard *Red Dwarf*. He worked in the ship's catering department, wore a bad toupée and played poker. When Kochanski asked Lister if he had any gay friends, he mentioned Bob, but admitted they weren't very close **[T-SER7.4]**.

  NOTE: *Bent Bob presumably died during the cadmium II explosion. It is unknown whether the nanobots resurrected him in Series VIII.*

- **Bobbing for Adams Apples:** A game that Colonel Mike O'Hagan developed to keep crash survivors occupied and in good spirits. He suggested this game in his *Space Corps Survival Manual* **[B-SUR]**.

- **Boddy's beer:** An alcoholic beverage (short for Boddingtons Beer) produced at the Boddingtons Brewery in Manchester, England **[RL]**. According to Lister, the bar in which he had been abandoned as a child—The Flag and Lettuce—served Boddy's beer, classifying it as an upscale establishment **[R-DAD]**.

  NOTE: *This was mentioned in an unused script, before the TV series established that Lister had been found as a baby at The Aigburth Arms.*

- **Bodies 'R' Us:** A business located on the Saturnian moon of Mimas, specializing in the switching of consciousnesses. Little Jimmy Osmond, a mobster in the Osmond crime family, searched this establishment while looking for Dutch van Oestrogen, a mining astro who had double-crossed the Ganymedian Mafia during a drug deal **[M-SMG2.4(c2)]**.

- **Bodine, Jethro:** *See* Clampett, Jethro

- **Bod-U-Like:** A business located on the Saturnian moon of Mimas, specializing in the switching of consciousnesses. Little Jimmy Osmond, a mobster in the Osmond crime family, searched this establishment while looking for Dutch van Oestrogen, a mining astro who had double-crossed the Ganymedian Mafia during a drug deal **[M-SMG2.4(c2)]**.

- **Body Reclamation Unit:** A building that Rimmer imagined while trapped in an addictive version of *Better Than Life*. The facility was located on the premises of a soundwave penitentiary used to store the Solidgram bodies of those incarcerated. Rimmer's essence, along with that of Jimmy Jitterman, broke out of the facility and met up with Jimmy's brother, Tonto, who was waiting in a truck outside the Body Reclamation Unit. Once free, the two soundwaves searched the building for their Solidgram bodies; unable to find his own body, Jimmy took Rimmer's, forcing Arnold to possess that of sex worker Trixie LaBouche **[N-BTL]**.

- **Body Swap:** A facility that Rimmer imagined while trapped in an addictive version of *Better Than Life*. Body Swap, developed by Rimmer Corporation, enabled wealthy clients to swap and upgrade their Solidgram bodies **[N-BTL]**.

- **body-tailor:** A profession that Rimmer imagined while trapped in an addictive version of *Better Than Life*. Body-tailors fitted and sized Solidgram bodies for the extremely rich. Since Rimmer was wealthy in the illusion, he frequently visited a body-tailor to switch bodies whenever he detected the slightest fault in his form, often asking for larger genitalia in the newer model **[N-BTL]**.

- **Bogart, Humphrey:** A twentieth-century American actor, known for his roles in such films as *Casablanca, The Maltese Falcon, The African Queen* and *The Caine Mutiny* **[RL]**. While explaining to Cat the importance of teaching Kryten to lie, Lister cited the actions of Rick Blaine, Bogart's character in *Casablanca*, as an example of how lying can be noble **[T-SER4.1]**.

- **Bog-bot From Hell:** An insult that Rimmer aimed at Kryten after the mechanoid volunteered them both for a dangerous mission to loot food from a derelict simulant vessel, claiming they were expendable due to their electronic nature **[T-SER6.5]**.

B-: Books
- **PRG:** *Red Dwarf Programme Guide*
- **SUR:** *Red Dwarf Space Corps Survival Manual*
- **PRM:** *Primordial Soup*
- **SOS:** *Son of Soup*
- **SCE:** *Scenes from the Dwarf*
- **LOG:** *Red Dwarf Log No. 1996*
- **RD8:** *Red Dwarf VIII*
- **EVR:** *The Log: A Dwarfer's Guide to Everything*

X-: Misc.
- **PRO:** Promotional materials, videos, etc.
- **PST:** Posters at DJ XVII (2013)
- **CAL:** 2008 calendar
- **RNG:** Cell phone ringtones
- **MOB:** Mobisode ("Red Christmas")
- **CIN:** *Children in Need* sketch
- **GEK:** *Geek Week* intros by Kryten
- **TNG:** "Tongue-Tied" video
- **XMS:** Bill Pearson's Christmas special pitch script
- **XVD:** Bill Pearson's Christmas special pitch video
- **OTH:** Other *Red Dwarf* appearances

SUFFIX
DVD:
- **(d)** – Deleted scene
- **(o)** – Outtake
- **(b)** – Bonus DVD material (other)
- **(e)** – Extended version

SMEGAZINES:
- **(c)** – Comic
- **(a)** – Article

OTHER:
- **(s)** – Early/unused script draft
- **(s1)** – Alternate version of script

- **boh:** A new syllable that Holly added to the major scale, along with woh, in an attempt to decimalize music. The two new syllables fell between sol and ti. In addition, he introduced the notes H and J to the octave—which he renamed a decatave **[T-SER2.1]**.

  NOTE: *This gag originated in a* Son of Cliché *"Dave Hollins: Space Cadet" sketch titled "Sir Kevin Kevin Sir."*

- **"Bohemian Rhapsody":** A song released in 1975 by the British rock group Queen **[RL]**. The *Starbug 1* crew indulged in a singalong to this classic hit while seated in the ship's cockpit **[X-OTH]**.

  NOTE: *This was broadcast as part of the 1993* Comic Relief *telethon, and was also included in a compilation video titled* The Pick of the Nose.

- **Boing:** A virility-enhancement drug for patients with erectile dysfunction, which gave a user an erection lasting for up to seven hours. Lister had Bob the skutter smuggle Boing out of *Red Dwarf*'s medi-lab, then used it to spike the guards' halftime juice during a basketball game against the prisoners. This debilitated the team long enough for the inmates to win the game. As punishment for the prank, Lister and Rimmer received two weeks of spud duty from Captain Hollister, who was among the victims **[T-SER8.6]**.

  A Diva-Droid employee named Alfonse once ordered Boing online, after which his e-mail address was inundated with junk mail **[W-AIT]**.

- **Bolanski:** A place, possibly imaginary, that Chen claimed to have visited, along with Titan, during a drinking game involving him, Selby, Lister and Olaf Petersen. In this particular game, the group teased Lister about his feelings for Kochanski, with each participant challenged to name ninety men who had slept with her **[T-SER1.3]**.

  NOTE: *The DVD subtitles for this dialog indicated that Chen said "Lobanski," but the actor pronounced it "Bolanski." Either way, neither seems to be an actual place—presumably, he was merely creating a word to rhyme with Kochanski.*

- **Boleyn, Anne, Queen Consort:** The spouse of England's monarch from 1533 to 1536, and the second wife of Henry VIII. She was beheaded for several offenses, including adultery, incest and witchcraft **[RL]**. When Kochanski suggested getting a new head for Kryten after his last spare was blown from a full negadrive, Lister quipped that they should order one from Heads-U-Like, adding that they could get one for Anne Boleyn while they were at it **[T-SER7.6(d)]**.

- **Bonaparte, Joséphine, Empress:** The first wife of Napoleon Bonaparte and France's first empress, born Joséphine de Beauharnais **[RL]**. While trapped in an addictive version of *Better Than Life*, Rimmer imagined that his wife, Juanita Chicata, periodically used a time machine to collect friends from the past, including Joséphine, to enjoy week-long shopping sprees **[N-BTL]**.

- **Bonaparte, Napoleon, Emperor:** A skilled military and political leader of France in the early 1800s, who launched numerous campaigns across Europe **[RL]**.

  As someone who aspired to be a well-respected officer, Rimmer hero-worshipped Napoleon. He mentioned the dictator in his death video, noting that had he bunked with Lister, the Frenchman would "still be in Corsica, peeling spuds." Arnold also discussed Bonaparte in his diary, and yearned to achieve such fame and glory that his memoirs would be remembered alongside Napoleon's war diaries and Julius Caesar's memoirs **[T-SER1.6]**. Rimmer once stated that if he had a time machine, he would travel back to the nineteenth century to roam across Europe with Napoleon, killing Belgians **[T-SER4.4]**.

  Upon first entering the total-immersion game *Better Than Life*, the *Red Dwarf* crew encountered a computer simulation of Bonaparte on a beach, and Rimmer excitedly approached him for an autograph **[T-SER2.2]**. Napoleon was also part of Rimmer's fantasy world in an addictive version of *Better Than Life*. In the illusion, Arnold believed he had returned to Earth and become incredibly wealthy, throwing lavish parties and playing *Risk* with the likes of Napoleon, Caesar and George S. Patton **[N-INF]**.

- **Bonaparte, Napoleon, Emperor:** A waxdroid replica of the French dictator, created for the Waxworld theme park. Left on their own for millions of years, the waxdroids attained sentience and became embroiled in a park-wide resource war between Villain World (to which Napoleon belonged) and Hero World.

During this war, the *Red Dwarf* crew transported to the planet using a Matter Paddle, with Lister and Cat materializing in Villain territory, where they were caught by Hitler, while Rimmer and Kryten landed in Hero territory. While imprisoned, Lister and Cat witnessed the firing-squad execution of a Winnie-the-Pooh waxdroid, which Napoleon attended.

Rimmer, meanwhile, found the heroes' army lacking and took command of the group, working many of the pacifistic waxdroids to death before ordering a frontal attack on the enemy's compound across a minefield. This wiped out the remaining droids, including Napoleon **[T-SER4.6]**.

- **Bone Cruncher:** An inmate of Floor 13 on an alternate-universe *Red Dwarf*. In that reality, Bone Cruncher stole Warden Ackerman's glass eye **[G-SOR]**.

- **Bonehead:** A nickname Rimmer had while in school **[T-SER2.1]**. The word "Bonehead" was scribbled on young Arnold's back as his brothers hung him upside down in a greenhouse dome **[T-SER4.5]**.

- **Bonehead Man:** A nickname that Super-Ace (Rimmer's counterpart) was often called, along with Super-Ass, in the universe known as Alternative 2X13/L, due to his ineffectiveness as a crimefighter **[M-SMG2.1(c3)]**.

- **Bonjela gum ointment:** An oral gel sold in the United Kingdom, used to treat mouth ulcers, cold sores and other oral afflictions **[RL]**. After three days marooned on a frozen planetoid with Lister, Rimmer evaluated the food situation and discovered that the only remaining "edible" supplies included Bonjela gum ointment **[T-SER3.2]**.

- **Bonjella, Bela:** The great-great-grandfather of King Stefano Bonjella of Seni Rotundi, a Mediterranean island chain on War World, and the great-great-great-grandfather of Princess Beryl Bonjella **[G-BIT]**.

- **Bonjella, Beryl, Princess:** The daughter of King Brian Bonjella, the ruler of an alternate-universe planet known as War World. Her hobbies included skiing, scuba diving and recovering from concussions.

  Bonjella was kidnapped by a Resistance movement that attempted to blackmail her father into funding their cause, and then by their enemy, who believed her to be a member of the Resistance herself. She convinced the enemy that she had stolen plans to their secret weapon, despite the fact than no such plans existed, and eventually drew up a mock schematic that, in reality, was a drawing of her hairdryer—which she was then forced to build.

  After building the "weapon"—a thirty-foot-tall hairdryer capable of driving back Resistance forces with blasts of hot air—Bonjella was sentenced to a firing-squad death by Captain Voorhese, to prevent the Resistance from getting hold of the plans **[W-OFF]**. Seconds before she would have been executed, however, a hard-light hologrammic Ace Rimmer rescued her **[T-SER7.2]**.

  ***NOTE:** Because the Bonjella stories vary greatly between the official website and* Red Dwarf—The Roleplaying Game, *both versions are listed here as existing in separate universes.*

- **Bonjella, Beryl, Princess:** The leader of the Seni Rotundi island chain and a Resistance sympathizer on War World, an alternate Earth on which World War II never ended. She was the daughter of King Stefano Bonjella and the great-great-great-granddaughter of Bela Bonjella. Originally schooled as a diplomat, Beryl assumed leadership of the Seni Rotundi islands after her father was executed by Reich forces in the city square, and swore vengeance against the Nazi regime.

  Princess Bonjella was captured by enemy forces and sentenced to be executed by firing squad, but a hard-light hologrammic Ace Rimmer rescued her at the last minute. The two enjoyed a brief whirlwind romance, which ended when Ace discovered that his light bee had been damaged during the rescue **[G-BIT]**.

  ***NOTE:** Because the Bonjella stories vary greatly between the official website and* Red Dwarf—The Roleplaying Game, *both versions are listed here as existing in separate universes.*

- **Bonjella, Brian, King:** The ruler of War World and the father of Princess Beryl Bonjella in an alternate universe. King Bonjella had a prized corgi named Barnaby **[W-OFF]**.

  NOTE: *This contradicted* Red Dwarf—The Roleplaying Game*'s* Extra Bits *booklet, which stated that Princess Bonjella's father was named Stefano, and that he was the ruler of the Seni Rotundi island chain, not the entire planet. As such, both men are listed here as existing in separate universes.*

- **Bonjella, Stefano, King:** The leader of the Seni Rotundi Island chain and a Resistance sympathizer on War World, an alternate Earth on which World War II never ended. His great-great-grandfather was Bela Bonjella. King Bonjella was executed by the Reich in Seni Rotundi's central square; upon his death, his daughter, Princess Beryl Bonjella, assumed the throne and continued her father's allegiance, offering her help to the Resistance in their fight against the Nazi regime **[G-BIT]**.

  NOTE: *This contradicted the official website, which stated (in an in-universe interview with Princess Bonjella) that her father's name was Brian Bonjella, and that he ruled the entire planet. As such, both men are listed here as existing in separate universes.*

- **Bonk:** One of seven diminutive rainforest dwellers known as the Ionian Ecommandoes, who lived in the jungles of Io on the television soap opera *Androids*. He and his comrades nursed Karstares back to health **[M-SMG2.5(c5)]**, after Karstares' plane crashed due to sabotage by his son Jaysee **[M-SMG1.14(c3)]**. Grateful for their help, Karstares became the Green Knight, the rainforest's protector, and fought alongside the Ecommandoes against Jaysee's ecologically harmful company **[M-SMG2.5(c5)]**. Bonk died during a firefight between Jaysee and his foes **[M-SMG2.8(c2)]**.

  NOTE: *This character resembled one of Disney's Seven Dwarfs. All of the Ecommandoes' names were slang for sex.*

- **Boo-Boo:** Kochanski's childhood teddy bear, which she still had despite being close to thirty years old **[T-SER8.1]**.

- **boomerang spoon:** *See* Mercurian boomerang spoon

- **Boone, Pat:** An American singer, actor and writer, most successful during the 1950s and '60s **[RL]**. When Rimmer claimed it was his destiny to lead the waxdroids of Hero World to victory, Kryten interrupted, asking to whom he was referring. Flabbergasted, Rimmer said he was talking about himself, asking if the mechanoid thought he was talking about Pat Boone **[T-SER4.6]**.

  NOTE: *This reference was changed to David Hasselhoff, an American actor and singer, in the DVD captions for the Czech Republic version of the series.*

- **Boop, Betty:** A female cartoon character created by Max Fleischer in 1930 that became immensely popular in mass-merchandising **[RL]**. When Lister called his landing party to a virus research station a "Mickey Mouse operation" after discovering that their psi-scan's batteries were dead, Cat noted that they weren't even Betty Boop **[T-SER5.4]**. Artificial-reality versions of Boop caused twenty-nine thousand deaths during a single month due to a faulty program in which players were crushed between Boop and Gina Lollobrigida **[B-SUR]**.

- **Bootle Municipal Golf Course:** A golf club located in Litherland, England **[RL]**. Lister lost his virginity to a girl named Michelle Fisher on Bootle's ninth hole when he was twelve years old **[T-SER3.2]**. Another woman named Susan Warrington got Lister drunk and took advantage of him on the same hole of the same course **[N-INF]**.

  NOTE: *Since Lister's age at the time of his encounter with Warrington was unspecified, and since she was not said to have been his first sexual partner, the two golf-course encounters—while certainly coincidental—do not contradict each other.*

- **Bootle Players:** A theatre company in Bootle, England. At age seventeen, Lister was packed naked into a crate and let out in the middle of a Bootle Players amateur production of *The Importance of Being Earnest* by the husband of a checkout girl with whom he was having an affair. This traumatizing event left him claustrophobic thereafter **[T-SER7.4]**.

PREFIX
RL: Real life

T-: Television Episodes
SER: Television series
IDW: "Identity Within"
USA1: Unaired U.S. pilot
USA2: Unaired U.S. demo

R-: *The Bodysnatcher Collection*
SER: Remastered episodes
BOD: "Bodysnatcher"
DAD: "Dad"
FTH: "Lister's Father"
INF: "Infinity Patrol"
END: "The End" (original assembly)

N-: Novels
INF: *Infinity Welcomes Careful Drivers*
BTL: *Better Than Life*
LST: *Last Human*
BCK: *Backwards*
OMN: *Red Dwarf Omnibus*

M-: Magazines
SMG: *Smegazine*

W-: Websites
OFF: Official website
NAN: *Prelude to Nanarchy*
AND: *Androids*
DIV: Diva-Droid
DIB: Duane Dibbley

CRP: Crapola
GEN: Geneticon
LSR: Leisure World Intl.
JMC: Jupiter Mining Corporation
AIT: *A.I. Today*
HOL: HoloPoint

G-: Roleplaying Game
RPG: *Core Rulebook*
BIT: *A.I. Screen Extra Bits* booklet
SOR: *Series Sourcebook*
OTH: Other RPG material

- **boot-up sequence:** A series of commands executed during the boot-up of a Talkie Toaster. It displayed, through the appliance's visual system, such information as the machine's ident, manufacturer and recommended retail price **[T-SER4.4]**.

- **Booze World:** A liquor store located in a seedy part of Mimas known as Shagtown **[M-SMG2.5(c6)]**.

- ***Bopping With Beethoven*****:** An album recorded by Reggie Wilson **[M-SMG1.3(a)]**.

- **Borgia, Lucrezia:** The Machiavellian daughter of Pope Alexander VI and a member of the scandal-ridden Borgia family, rumored to have been involved in several poisonings **[RL]**. When Cat became ill from a lack of sexual activity, Kryten displayed an image of a poison sack within Cat's body that he described as being "big enough to keep Lucrezia Borgia busy for years" **[T-IDW]**.

  While using a time drive coupled with a faster-than-light drive, the *Red Dwarf* crew traveled through space-time, becoming epicures, sampling the best the universe had to offer, and socializing with historic figures, such as the Borgias **[T-SER6.6]**.

- **"Born to Brutalize":** Lister's favorite dance track. In his will, he requested the song be played at his funeral **[N-BTL]**.

- **"Boss":** A word, possibly a logo, printed on a pair of boxing gloves Rimmer wore to bed while attending school as a child **[T-SER3.5]**.

- **Boston Strangler, the:** The epithet of the person or persons who carried out a series of murders in the Boston, Massachusetts, area in the early 1960s (typically attributed to Albert DeSalvo) **[RL]**.

  A waxdroid replica of the Boston Strangler was created for the Waxworld theme park. Left on their own for millions of years, the waxdroids attained sentience and became embroiled in a park-wide resource war between Villain World (to which the Boston Strangler belonged) and Hero World. During this war, the *Red Dwarf* crew transported to the planet using a Matter Paddle, with Lister and Cat materializing in Villain territory, while Rimmer and Kryten landed in Hero territory.

  Rimmer found the heroes' army lacking and took command of the group, working many of the pacifistic waxdroids to death before ordering a frontal attack on the enemy's compound across a minefield. This wiped out the remaining droids, including the Boston Strangler **[T-SER4.6]**.

- **Botanical Gardens:** A section of *Red Dwarf* allocated for the growing of various flora. Corridor 147 led to this section, the door of which had a faulty porous circuit that Rimmer and Lister were sent to repair **[T-SER1.1]**.

  NOTE: A deleted scene and an outtake from episode 1.1 ("The End") made it clear that the Botanical Gardens resided on Level 159.

- **Bot-brain:** A less-than-endearing nickname that Cat called Kryten **[T-SER5.5]**.

- ***Both Feet in the Grave*****:** A hologram television comedy series from the creators of *After Death Do Us Part*—who later produced the mechanoid comedy *Whoops Vicar, There Goes My Groinal Socket* **[M-SMG1.7(a)]**.

  NOTE: This title spoofed that of British sitcom One Foot in the Grave, *which aired from 1990 to 2000.*

- **Bouncer MK-IV:** A domesticated blob-like creature featured in the soap opera *Androids*. In one episode, Baz threw a stick for Bouncer to fetch while attending a barbeque hosted by Daz; as Bouncer went to retrieve the stick, however, it was caught in a temporal-displacement vortex **[M-SMG1.8(c2)]**.

  NOTE: Bouncer bore a striking resemblance to the popular British children's bouncing toy, Space Hopper.

- **Bovril:** A British brand of beef extract, used as flavoring or diluted as a beverage **[RL]**. Baxter, an inmate of the Tank, shoved Cat's head in the prison's food dispenser while ordering a bowl of hot Bovril, to punish him for having spilled Baxter's soup **[T-SER8.6]**.

- **boxer short brown:** Lister's favorite color **[M-SMG1.1(a)]**.

- **Boxing—Psychoweight Championship:** A sporting event scheduled to be broadcast by Krytie TV on October 4. This particular bout was between Floor 13 inmates Baxter and Headbanger Harris **[X-CAL]**.

B-: Books
- **PRG:** *Red Dwarf Programme Guide*
- **SUR:** *Red Dwarf Space Corps Survival Manual*
- **PRM:** *Primordial Soup*
- **SOS:** *Son of Soup*
- **SCE:** *Scenes from the Dwarf*
- **LOG:** *Red Dwarf Log No. 1996*
- **RD8:** *Red Dwarf VIII*
- **EVR:** *The Log: A Dwarfer's Guide to Everything*

X-: Misc.
- **PRO:** Promotional materials, videos, etc.
- **PST:** Posters at DJ XVII (2013)
- **CAL:** 2008 calendar
- **RNG:** Cell phone ringtones
- **MOB:** Mobisode ("Red Christmas")
- **CIN:** *Children in Need* sketch
- **GEK:** *Geek Week* intros by Kryten
- **TNG:** "Tongue-Tied" video

- **XMS:** Bill Pearson's Christmas special pitch script
- **XVD:** Bill Pearson's Christmas special pitch video
- **OTH:** Other *Red Dwarf* appearances

SUFFIX
DVD:
- **(d)** – Deleted scene
- **(o)** – Outtake
- **(b)** – Bonus DVD material (other)
- **(e)** – Extended version

SMEGAZINES:
- **(c)** – Comic
- **(a)** – Article

OTHER:
- **(s)** – Early/unused script draft
- **(s1)** – Alternate version of script

- **boy-droid:** A male model of sex androids featured at a brothel on Mimas **[N-INF]**.

- **Boyle's Fourth Law:** A scientific principle, an understanding of which was required to pass the Space Corps' Engineer's Exam. While quizzing Lister regarding his engineering knowledge, Rimmer asked if he knew what Boyle's Fourth Law was, to which he defiantly replied, "Don't eat greasy food" **[T-SER1.3]**.

  ***NOTE:** In the real world, there is only one Boyle's Law (named after seventeenth-century physicist Robert Boyle), which states that the absolute pressure exerted by a given mass of an ideal gas is inversely proportional to the volume it occupies if the temperature and amount of gas remain unchanged within a closed system.*

- **Boys from the *Dwarf*:** A nickname that Lister dubbed himself and his favored shipmates aboard *Red Dwarf*. The group adopted their own special salute **[T-SER5.4]**.

- ***Boys from the Dwarf*:** A booklet published in an alternate universe, which Duane Dibbley found at a Salvation Army hostel, along with other *Red Dwarf* paraphernalia, while searching for clues to his true identity **[M-SMG2.2(c5)]**.

- **Bozo Brothers, the:** A nickname Kochanski called Lister and Cat while explaining why she was bringing them into the artificial-reality simulation *Pride and Prejudice Land*. Her goal was to get "the Bozo Brothers" interested in something more sophisticated than games of Name That Smell or How Many Marbles Can You Fit Up Your Nostril? **[T-SER7.6]**.

- **Bracknell, Augusta, Lady:** An elderly character in the play *The Importance of Being Earnest, A Trivial Comedy for Serious People*, by Oscar Wilde **[RL]**. An actor playing Lady Bracknell was shocked when Lister was released from a crate, stark-naked, in the middle of a Bootle Players performance of this play **[T-SER7.4(d)]**.

- **Bradbury Botanical Research Station:** A research facility located near the Olympus Mons terraforming reactors on Mars. It was responsible for developing a plant species capable of living on the Martian surface **[G-RPG]**.

  ***NOTE:** This station was presumably named after science fiction author Ray Bradbury.*

- **Bradbury Colony:** A settlement on Mars, and the birthplace of Monica Jones **[G-RPG]**.

  ***NOTE:** This, too, was presumably named after author Ray Bradbury.*

- **Brainfade:** A company in Jake Bullet's universe, specializing in mind manipulation and cyber personalities. Bullet visited Brainfade's office to investigate the murder of one of its scientists, Doctor Sandra Halley. There, he met the facility's director, Doctor Sid Scofrenia, along with another scientist named Tina and a test subject, Carl—a member of Serial Killers Anonymous, hired as a custodian. The investigation led to the accidental death of Scofrenia, who was implicated in the murder. Bullet also learned of the firm's involvement in creating a mind-control apparatus, which led to his arrest by his own police chief **[M-SMG2.7(c4)]**.

- **brains:** An item that Lister claimed could be found in jars, during a musical drinking game he and his friends played in *Red Dwarf*'s disco room. When the others challenged Lister's answer, he said his uncle's brain was in a jar—which was unfortunate, since he wasn't dead yet **[T-SER1.3]**.

  ***NOTE:** Ironically, when the crew encountered future versions of themselves in episode 6.6 ("Out of Time"), the older Lister was merely a brain in a jar.*

- **Bramah, Joseph:** An eighteenth-century English inventor and locksmith, credited with such inventions as the flushing toilet. Bramah patented the first siphon and valve flushing system in 1778 **[RL]**. Kryten, attempting to prove his knowledge of the lavatorial sciences, informed the crew of that fact **[T-SER7.7]**.

- **Brando, Marlon:** A twentieth-century American stage and screen actor, known for such films as *The Wild One*, *The Godfather* and *Apocalypse Now* **[RL]**. Lister described Hammy Hamster, star of the children's television series *Tales of the Riverbank*, as the rodent equivalent of Marlon Brando **[T-SER4.1]**.

PREFIX
RL: Real life

T-: Television Episodes
SER: Television series
IDW: "Identity Within"
USA1: Unaired U.S. pilot
USA2: Unaired U.S. demo

R-: *The Bodysnatcher Collection*
SER: Remastered episodes
BOD: "Bodysnatcher"
DAD: "Dad"
FTH: "Lister's Father"
INF: "Infinity Patrol"
END: "The End" (original assembly)

N-: Novels
INF: *Infinity Welcomes Careful Drivers*
BTL: *Better Than Life*
LST: *Last Human*

BCK: *Backwards*
OMN: *Red Dwarf Omnibus*

M-: Magazines
SMG: *Smegazine*

W-: Websites
OFF: Official website
NAN: *Prelude to Nanarchy*
AND: *Androids*
DIV: Diva-Droid
DIB: Duane Dibbley

CRP: Crapola
GEN: Geneticon
LSR: Leisure World Intl.
JMC: Jupiter Mining Corporation
AIT: *A.I. Today*
HOL: HoloPoint

G-: Roleplaying Game
RPG: *Core Rulebook*
BIT: *A.I. Screen Extra Bits* booklet
SOR: *Series Sourcebook*
OTH: Other RPG material

- **Brandy:** Jaysee's secretary on the television soap opera *Androids*. Brandy worked at Jaysee's Cleaning Company **[M-SMG1.14(c3)]**, then at Karstares Interstellar Cleaning and Sanitation Supplies, after Jaysee took over the company from his father. Brandy and Jaysee were having an affair **[M-SMG2.4(c3)]**. Shortly after Jaysee professed his love to Brandy, she died in a firefight between Jaysee and his enemies **[M-SMG2.7(c5)]**.

- **Brannigan:** A psychiatrist who served aboard *Red Dwarf* before a radiation explosion killed most of the crew **[T-SER2.5]**. Brannigan had taken shore leave on Miranda for a shopping trip, but was unable to make it back in time due to a late shuttle. Because of this, Captain Hollister hired Doctor Lucas McClaren as Brannigan's replacement **[W-OFF]**.

  Three million years later, after Rimmer was revived aboard *Red Dwarf* as a hologram, a meteor struck the mining ship, damaging the hologram simulation suite. This caused Rimmer to malfunction, giving him several of the crew's personalities, including Brannigan's **[T-SER2.5]**.

- **Brassica 2:** A strain of virus contained aboard the *Mayflower*, a ship launched from Earth with the intention of terraforming a planet within the Andromeda Galaxy. This particular strain created fast-growing broccoli **[N-LST]**.

  NOTE: *Brassica* is the genus of plants to which broccoli belongs.

- **Braun, Eva:** The long-time companion of Adolf Hitler. The two were married less than forty hours before both committed suicide at the end of World War II **[RL]**. After being trapped in the artificial-reality WWII simulation *Victory in Europe* for seventeen days, the *Red Dwarf* crew were finally released by a glitch created when Cat eloped with Eva Braun, causing Hitler to die of a broken heart **[B-LOG]**.

- **breach of Xzeeertuiy:** Part of a defense tactic Lister used on Arranguu 12 to force a mistrial during his hearing for crimes against the GELF state. Lister stated that taking the fourth sand of D'Aquaarar protected him from the breach of Xzeeertuiy by the Zalgon impeachment of Kjielomnon, according to the case of *Mbazvmbbcxyy vs. Mbazvmbbcxyy*, which was allowed during the third season of every fifth cycle. However, he was being tried in the Northern sector of Arranguu 12—which, according to the Regulator, did not follow the same archaic legal system as the Southern sector, from which the case originated **[N-BCK]**.

- **Breadman's Fish Fingers:** A brand of fish sticks that Lister, while trapped in an addictive version of *Better Than Life*, imagined was sold on Earth, circa three million A.D. Lister thought he had returned to Earth using *Nova 5*'s Duality Jump and had received endorsement offers for such products as Breadman's Fish Fingers and Luton's Carpet Shampoo **[N-INF]**.

- **Bredbury, Alison:** A girl Lister knew when he was young. One night, Bredbury's father suffered a heart attack and was rushed to the hospital, leaving Lister alone with Alison and the keys to her family's alcohol cabinet, which led to them having intercourse on her parents' double bed. That night, he christened the underwear he was wearing as his lucky scoring underpants **[N-INF]**.

- **Brefewinan:** A type of universal GELF currency consisting of mushy peas. Lister attempted to win enough Brefewinan to buy Ora Tanzil out of slavery from the Brefewino tribe **[T-IDW]**.

- **Brefewino:** A tribe of GELFs living on a planet within hostile GELF territory. The members of this tribe, primarily bred as butchers, were powerfully built and excellent swordsmen. The Brefewino possessed three sets of teeth—one for hunting, one for eating prey and one for removing the packaging from VHS video tapes—and considered cats to be a snack. The *Starbug 1* crew infiltrated a Brefewino village in order to rescue Ora Tanzil, a she-Cat who had been captured and auctioned by the GELFs **[T-IDW]**.

- **Brennan, Seamus ("Shay"):** A twentieth-century international football player who played full-back for Manchester United **[RL]**. While attempting to prove he still had his wits about him, Holly erroneously claimed Brennan was the left-back for Man-United during the 1968 European Cup Final, then corrected himself by stating it may have been Tony Dunne **[T-SER2.4(d)]**.

B-: Books
PRG: *Red Dwarf Programme Guide*
SUR: *Red Dwarf Space Corps Survival Manual*
PRM: *Primordial Soup*
SOS: *Son of Soup*
SCE: *Scenes from the Dwarf*
LOG: *Red Dwarf Log No. 1996*
RD8: *Red Dwarf VIII*
EVR: *The Log: A Dwarfer's Guide to Everything*

X-: Misc.
PRO: Promotional materials, videos, etc.
PST: Posters at DJ XVII (2013)
CAL: 2008 calendar
RNG: Cell phone ringtones
MOB: Mobisode ("Red Christmas")
CIN: *Children in Need* sketch
GEK: *Geek Week* intros by Kryten
TNG: "Tongue-Tied" video

XMS: Bill Pearson's Christmas special pitch script
XVD: Bill Pearson's Christmas special pitch video
OTH: Other *Red Dwarf* appearances

SUFFIX
DVD:
(d) – Deleted scene
(o) – Outtake
(b) – Bonus DVD material (other)
(e) – Extended version

SMEGAZINES:
(c) – Comic
(a) – Article

OTHER:
(s) – Early/unused script draft
(s1) – Alternate version of script

- **Brewis, P., Doctor:** The author of the book *Learn Japanese,* which Kochanski read to teach herself the language. When one officer noticed the book in her jacket at a bar, he accused her of being pretentious, to which she innocently responded, "Pretentious? Watashi?" **[N-INF]**.

  NOTE: *Composer Peter Brewis provided musical interludes and comedic songs for the radio show* Son of Cliché, *written by Rob Grant and Doug Naylor, which contained five "Dave Hollins: Space Cadet" sketches on which* Red Dwarf *was originally based.*

- ***Brief History of Time, A*:** A book written by British physicist Stephen Hawking, covering such topics as black holes and quantum mechanics **[RL]**. While explaining to Captain Hollister the circumstances leading to the transformation of Birdman's pet sparrow, Pete, into a *Tyrannosaurus rex*, Lister blamed the difficulty of using a time wand, which he claimed was harder to understand than a Russian edition of *A Brief History in Time* **[T-SER8.7(d)]**.

- **Brintzley:** A point or award given during a "Die! Die! My Darling!" goal-scoring strategy in zero-gee football. During the maneuver, each member of a team's defense brought a weapon of his or her choice (not exceeding sixteen megatons) into the Funch zone, and then proceeded to stomp on it. The team with the greatest number of Finsleys remaining won the Faboozle, and started the next quarter six Brintzleys ahead **[M-SMG1.8(a)]**.

- **bri-nylon:** A synthetic material used in the production of clothing and bedding products **[RL]**. In one of Cat's dreams, *Red Dwarf* was boarded by an unstylish android who requisitioned all of Cat's suits for his planet, which was in the midst of a style famine. As compensation, Cat was given a pair of slacks made from the planet's most precious material: bri-nylon **[M-SMG1.7(c2)]**.

- ***British Journal of Demented Delusions*:** A hypothetical publication that Lister claimed would be interested in Rimmer's theory that historically, battles have always been won by the side with the shorter haircut **[B-SCE]**.

- ***Brit Quiz II*:** The second in a series of British trivia board games from Crown & Andrews Ltd., released in 1990 **[RL]**. A Brit Quiz II box was jettisoned from *Red Dwarf* **[M-SMG1.11(c2)]**.

- **Britvie-Mixer, Tom:** The lottery draw manager at the Multi Million Lottery Co., mentioned in a letter Rimmer received during his incarceration in the Tank, *Red Dwarf*'s brig. The letter informed Arnold that he had won 4 million in the lottery, and instructed him to take his winning ticket to the listed Lottery House address. By that point, however, it was three million years too late to redeem the prize **[B-RD8]**.

- **Brody, Miss:** A computer-generated English teacher at the cyberschool Kochanski attended as a young girl **[T-SER7.4(e)]**.

  NOTE: *This character may have been named after girls' school instructor Jean Brodie, the protagonist of Muriel Spark's novel* The Prime of Miss Jean Brodie.

- **Brontë, Emily Jane:** A nineteenth-century English author who published her only novel, *Wuthering Heights*, under the pen-name Ellis Bell **[RL]**. Kochanski preferred the works of Brontë, Jane Austen and Jilly Cooper to violent films and shows **[B-SUR]**.

- **Brook ("Junior"):** A character on the television soap opera *Androids*, portrayed by Android 97542/P. Brook was married to Kelly and had a son named Brooke Junior—who was not actually his son, but that of his business rival, Gary, who was once Kelly's husband **[T-SER2.1]**. Brook intended to confront Gary about the affair, but only if he finished the wash in time **[M-SMG1.7(a)]**. Eventually, he filed for divorce **[M-SMG1.8(c5)]**.

  One episode of *Androids* revealed that Brook's father, Karstares, had adopted him when he was four years old, but had allegedly died in a plane crash orchestrated by Karstares' illegitimate son, Jaysee **[W-AND]**.

  While his father was missing, Brook attempted to run the family business, Droid Oil, but was haunted by stories of corruption and murder, and troubled by the knowledge of the dismembered body of Serving Unit 27 hidden beneath his patio **[W-AND]**. Karstares resurfaced years later, having been rescued from the crash by rainforest dwellers **[M-SMG1.14(c3)]**.

PREFIX
RL: Real life

T-: Television Episodes
SER: Television series
IDW: "Identity Within"
USA1: Unaired U.S. pilot
USA2: Unaired U.S. demo

R-: *The Bodysnatcher Collection*
SER: Remastered episodes
BOD: "Bodysnatcher"
DAD: "Dad"
FTH: "Lister's Father"
INF: "Infinity Patrol"
END: "The End" (original assembly)

N-: Novels
INF: *Infinity Welcomes Careful Drivers*
BTL: *Better Than Life*
LST: *Last Human*

BCK: *Backwards*
OMN: *Red Dwarf Omnibus*

M-: Magazines
SMG: *Smegazine*

W-: Websites
OFF: Official website
NAN: *Prelude to Nanarchy*
AND: *Androids*
DIV: Diva-Droid
DIB: Duane Dibbley

CRP: Crapola
GEN: Geneticon
LSR: Leisure World Intl.
JMC: Jupiter Mining Corporation
AIT: *A.I. Today*
HOL: HoloPoint

G-: Roleplaying Game
RPG: *Core Rulebook*
BIT: *A.I. Screen Extra Bits* booklet
SOR: *Series Sourcebook*
OTH: Other RPG material

In another episode, Brook's visit to his doctor revealed that he had a terminal software bug **[M-SMG1.10(c2)]**. Later, Jaysee used a video of Brook at an android brothel to blackmail him into handing over another family business, Karstares Interstellar Cleaning and Sanitation Supplies **[M-SMG1.13(c1)]**.

After Brook and Brooke Junior were reunited with Karstares—who called the pair "Junior" and "Junior Junior," respectively **[M-SMG2.1(c2)]**—the trio headed out to exact revenge on Jaysee **[M-SMG2.5(c5)]**. During the ensuing battle, Brook was injured and taken to St. Pentium's Hospital, where he was transported to the Halfords Memorial Ward and repaired next to Kelly, who was still recovering from Jaysee's murder attempt at the time **[M-SMG2.8(c8)]**.

The couple renewed their love and, after leaving the hospital, moved back in together **[M-SMG2.9(c6)]**. Shortly after their arrival, however, Brooke Junior announced he had undergone an oil-change operation, complete with catalytic converter fitting. This enraged Brook, who kicked him out of the house **[M-SMG2.9(c8)]**.

> ***NOTE:** The* Smegazine *comics spelled the name alternately as Brook and Brooke. The hospital's name appeared on the* Androids *website.*

- **Brooke Junior ("Junior Junior"):** A character on the television soap opera *Androids*, portrayed by Android 24/A. The teen's mother, Kelly, cheated on her husband Brook with his business rival, Gary, and Brooke Junior was born of that affair **[T-SER2.1]**. His grandfather, Karstares, called him "Junior Junior" **[M-SMG2.1(c2)]**.

  One episode of *Androids* revealed that Brooke Junior suffered from an electrical addiction, and was frequently arrested on Mars for stealing and mugging **[W-AND]**. In a later episode, he crashed a car into his family's house **[M-SMG1.8(c5)]**. He was once caught experimenting with his groinal socket **[M-SMG1.9(c2)]**.

  After Brooke Junior's uncle, Jaysee, blackmailed the elder Brook into giving him the family business, Jaysee offered a job to Brooke Junior **[M-SMG1.13(c1)]**. Avoiding injury while caught in a crossfire between Jaysee and his enemies, he shaved his head and underwent an oil-change operation, complete with catalytic converter installation. This enraged his dad, who kicked the teen out of the house **[M-SMG2.9(c8)]**.

  > ***NOTE:** The DVD captions listed the character's name as "Brook Jr.," whereas the onscreen credits to* Androids *spelled it as "Brooke Jnr." The* Smegazine *comics alternated between the two.*

- **broom cupboard:** A storage closet on *Red Dwarf*'s V Deck. Kryten once visited this cupboard while on vacation **[T-SER9.1]**.

- **Broomtown:** A nickname that Lister called *Red Dwarf*'s broom cupboard on V Deck after Kryten returned from his vacation there **[T-SER9.1]**.

- **Brothel-U-Like:** An android brothel run by Kelly on the television soap opera *Androids* **[M-SMG1.12(c3)]**. While protesting the brothel, Mollee accidentally tripped and fell into an Ecstat-O-Matic booth, scrambling her circuits. This caused her to take over the brothel after an attempt on Kelly's life left the former owner hospitalized. Mollee then renamed the bordello He Ain't Heavy, He's My Brothel **[M-SMG2.3(c2)]**. Another accident restored her previous programming **[M-SMG2.5(c5)]**, after which she finally succeeded in shutting the business down **[N-INF]**.

- **Brother Famine:** *See* Apocalypse, Famine, Brother

- **Brother Pestilence:** *See* Apocalypse, Pestilence, Brother

- **Brother War:** *See* Apocalypse, War, Brother

- **Brown:** An inmate of the Tank, *Red Dwarf*'s classified brig, who perished during the cadmium II disaster, but was resurrected when nanobots rebuilt the mining ship. Brown was assigned to the Canaries, an elite group of inmates assigned to investigate dangerous situations. When a chameleonic microbe began dissolving *Red Dwarf*, Captain Hollister ordered an evacuation; several names were chosen at random from the prisoner roster to board the rescue craft, with Brown among them **[T-SER8.8(d)]**.

- **Brown, Carole, Executive Officer:** An executive officer aboard *Red Dwarf* who perished in the cadmium II accident. Her security clearance code was 010101. Brown's brain pattern was stored on a data disk, which Kryten used years later to perform a mind swap on Lister in an attempt to disarm the mining ship's auto-destruct sequence.

Despite the procedure's success, which gave Lister Brown's brain pattern and voice, the sequence could not be stopped. Fortunately for the crew, Holly had removed the explosive linked to the system years ago—a fact she neglected to share until the countdown timer had run out **[T-SER3.4]**.

> ***NOTE:*** *It is unknown whether the nanobots resurrected Brown in Series VIII.*

- **Brown, Chelsea:** An American actor best known as a regular performer on the sketch comedy show *Rowan & Martin's Laugh-In* **[RL]**. Lister bought a well-chewed ball of gum from a man on Mimas who claimed it had once been chewed by Brown **[N-INF]**.

- **Brown Alert:** A hypothetical *Red Dwarf* alert status. When *Starbug 1* was trapped in a shrinking air vent aboard the mining vessel, Kryten recommended going to Red Alert, but Cat suggested going all the way to Brown Alert instead **[T-SER8.1]**.

- **Browns, The:** A hypothetical competitor of Lister in a chewing gum bubble-blowing contest **[T-SER1.6]**.

- **"brown trousers time":** A euphemism that Holly used to describe the terrifying feeling of moving faster than the speed of light, during which one passed through objects before seeing them **[T-SER1.2]**.

> ***NOTE:*** *Holly's implication was that the situation would make them soil their pants.*

- **Bruce:** A character on the television soap opera *Androids*, portrayed by Android 980612/L **[T-SER2.1]**. Bruce had a human half-sister who was once caught making out with the local traffic lights **[M-SMG2.8(a)]**.

In one episode, Simone was alarmed to find an electrical appliance catalog under Bruce's bed **[M-SMG1.7(a)]**. In another storyline, Bruce's undersealant scam was uncovered by Benzen after Hudzen developed a rusting problem **[M-SMG1.9(c2)]**. In yet another tale, Bruce smuggled a hidden camera into the android brothel run by Kelly, in order to catch Brook at the establishment. Jaysee then used the captured footage to blackmail Brook into signing over the family business to him **[M-SMG1.13(c1)]**.

- **Brush-a-matic:** A tool with which Kryten cleaned Lister's lapels while Lister watched the film *The Wild One* **[T-SER2.1]**.

- **Brylcreem:** A brand of hair-styling products for men, sold worldwide **[RL]**. Holly claimed to have found stuff in the ship's prison inventory that would make the crew's hair stand on end—which he then revealed was Brylcreem **[T-SER8.8]**.

> ***NOTE:*** *The DVD subtitles misspelled the brand name as "Brylcreme."*

- **Brynner, Yul:** A Russian-born film and stage actor, known for his portrayal of the King of Siam in the screen and theatrical versions of *The King and I*, as well as his roles in *The Ten Commandments*, *Westworld* and *The Magnificent Seven* **[RL]**. According to a tribute song Kryten created for *The Rimmer Experience*, Rimmer was never mistaken for Yul Brynner because his full hair kept his head from glimmering **[T-SER7.5]**.

- **BSc:** An abbreviation for Bronze Swimming certificate. Rimmer often attached this title, as well as SSc (Silver Swimming certificate), to his name in order to sound more official **[T-SER1.6]**.

- **'B' Section:** A group of twenty skutters assigned to help Rimmer prime his half of the twelve hundred piston towers required to restart *Red Dwarf*'s engines, which were turned off after Holly shut himself down. In his haste to finish the job before Kryten, Rimmer accidentally crushed the robots while testing Piston Tower 137, thinking they were in the next tower **[N-BTL]**.

- **Btrrnfjhyjhnehgewydn, Chief:** The elder leader of the Kinitawowi, a GELF tribe located in an asteroid belt in an alternate universe. He had three daughters, one named Khakhakhakkhhakhakkkhakkkkh. The *Starbug* crew visited the tribe seeking supplies and droids, which they needed to break Lister's doppelgänger out of Cyberia.

Mistakenly assuming the Kinitawowi were sterile like other

PREFIX
RL: Real life

T-: Television Episodes
SER: Television series
IDW: "Identity Within"
USA1: Unaired U.S. pilot
USA2: Unaired U.S. demo

R-: *The Bodysnatcher Collection*
SER: Remastered episodes
BOD: "Bodysnatcher"
DAD: "Dad"
FTH: "Lister's Father"
INF: "Infinity Patrol"
END: "The End" (original assembly)

N-: Novels
INF: *Infinity Welcomes Careful Drivers*
BTL: *Better Than Life*
LST: *Last Human*
BCK: *Backwards*
OMN: *Red Dwarf Omnibus*

M-: Magazines
SMG: *Smegazine*

W-: Websites
OFF: Official website
NAN: *Prelude to Nanarchy*
AND: *Androids*
DIV: Diva-Droid
DIB: Duane Dibbley

CRP: Crapola
GEN: Geneticon
LSR: Leisure World Intl.
JMC: Jupiter Mining Corporation
AIT: *A.I. Today*
HOL: HoloPoint

G-: Roleplaying Game
RPG: *Core Rulebook*
BIT: *A.I. Screen Extra Bits* booklet
SOR: *Series Sourcebook*
OTH: Other RPG material

GELFs in the region, Lister offered to pay for the supplies in sperm—a valuable commodity at the other settlements. This outraged Btrrnfjhyjhnehgewydn, who insisted that Lister marry Khakhakhakkhhakhakkkhakkkkkh to prove he had respect for the Kinitawowi. Reluctantly, Lister agreed, believing his crewmates would rescue him in time. That plan changed, however, when Lister, knocked out by Kinitawowi moonshine, awoke to find Khakhakhakkhhakhakkkhakkkkkh straddling him and having sex. Naked and screaming, he ran from the settlement and escaped aboard *Starbug* **[N-LST]**.

> ***NOTE:*** *It is unknown whether Btrrnfjhyjhnehgewydn was among the Kinitawowi who later boarded* Starbug *and was subsequently killed by Lister's doppelgänger.*

- **Bubbly Amber:** A lighting-effect color available for Kluge Corp.'s teleporters **[G-RPG]**.

- **Buchan, Science Officer:** A *Red Dwarf* crewmember with an IQ of 169 who perished in the ship's cadmium II disaster. Millions of years later, Buchan's personality disk was used during a mind-patch procedure performed to raise Rimmer's IQ so he could pass a test to join the holoship *Enlightenment* **[T-SER5.1]**.

  > ***NOTE:*** *It is unknown whether the nanobots resurrected Buchan in Series VIII.*

- **Buckingham Palace:** The official London residence and office of Britain's monarch **[RL]**. In an alternate timeline in which Lister invented the Tension Sheet and became Earth's youngest billionaire, Lister purchased Buckingham Palace so he could have it ground up and used to line his driveway **[T-SER3.5]**.

- **Buckley, Mr. ("Pop"):** A pet shop owner in Bedford Falls, whom Lister imagined while trapped in an addictive version of *Better Than Life*. When Rimmer drove a tanker truck through the small town, destroying Pop Buckley's pet store, numerous rabbits, puppies and canaries scattered into the night **[N-BTL]**.

- **Buck's Fizz:** An alcoholic beverage consisting of two parts orange juice and one part champagne, which London's Buck's Club served in the morning as an excuse for patrons to start drinking early **[RL]**. Legion provided the *Red Dwarf* crew with Buck's Fizz for breakfast after their first night in captivity aboard his station **[T-SER6.2]**.

- **Buckteeth:** A nickname that Cat called Zural, a Brefewino GELF who outbid him during an auction for the she-Cat Ora Tanzil. In actuality, Zural was another member of the feline species, who had disguised himself as a GELF in order to rescue—and then kill—Tanzil **[T-IDW]**.

- **Bud:** *See* Buddy

- **Buddha, Gautama ("Shakyamuni"):** A sage and founder of the Buddhism religion, born Siddhārtha Gautama **[RL]**. While trapped in an addictive version of *Better Than Life*, Rimmer believed he had returned to Earth and become famously wealthy, creating a company that developed a time machine. He then used this device to bring together several historical individuals for his wedding reception, including Gautama Buddha, who entered a gâteau-eating contest with Elvis Presley **[N-BTL]**.

- **Buddy:** A nickname that Cat often called Lister, sometimes shortened to "Bud" **[T-SER3.1]**. Cat used variations of this name for his shipmates, including "Officer Bud-Babe" for Kochanski **[T-SER7.3]**, as well as "Bud-You-Ain't" **[T-SER10.5(d)]** and "Non-Bud" for Rimmer **[T-SER10.6]**.

- **Bud-You-Ain't:** One of Cat's nicknames for Rimmer **[T-SER10.5(d)]**.

  > ***NOTE:*** *This may have referred to Rimmer's status as a hologram, the fact that Cat didn't like him, or both.*

- **Bug-head:** A nickname that Kochanski called the Epideme virus before destroying the parasite **[T-SER7.7]**.

- **buggy:** *See* JMC buggy

- **Build-It-Yourself Marilyn Monroe Droid:** A Series 2000 DIY kit droid meant to resemble the famous actor **[W-DIV]**. Olaf Petersen purchased such a kit while on planet leave on Callisto **[T-SER3.6]**. He never bothered to assemble it, however, telling Lister he only needed to use one part—the thermostat—to warm his hands **[T-SER3.6(d)]**.

The manual included with the kit claimed that one could construct the droid in less than two hours with just a screwdriver and glue. Lister attempted to build the droid for Kryten as a gift for his last-day party, but with limited success **[T-SER3.6]**. During the attempt, Cat requested a glimpse of the android's rear end, claiming to be lonely; that body part, however, was made of a jelly-like substance and was, according to Lister, already setting in the refrigerator **[T-SER3.6(d)]**.

- **Bulgaria:** A country in Western Europe, bordered by Serbia, Greece and the Black Sea **[RL]**. While searching for Rimmer and Kryten, Lister and Cat entered a time hole that propelled them to an Earth far into the future, where time ran backwards. Unable to understand the writing or dialect, Lister concluded they were in Bulgaria **[T-SER3.1]**.

- **Bullet, Jake:** A persona Kryten assumed while trapped in a despair squid hallucination. The crew believed they had crashed *Starbug* into an underwater ravine and woken up at a total-immersion video game (TIV) facility, where they learned they had been playing a TIV called *Red Dwarf* for the past four years.

  Upon exiting the game, they were led to the recuperation lounge, where they found their belongings and discovered their "true" identities. Kryten was really Jake Bullet, a half-human cyborg detective in the cybernautics (traffic-control) division of the police force. His personal belongings included a detective badge, a pair of sunglasses, a gun, a dresscoat, a tie, an overcoat and a fedora.

  Upon leaving the facility, the crew emerged in a totalitarian society, after which Kryten killed a fascist police officer who attempted to shoot a girl for stealing an apple. This led to a high-speed chase ending in a dark alleyway, where the crew, unable to deal with the despair of their circumstances, decided to commit suicide. Holly intervened and removed them from the delusion, however, preventing them from killing themselves in the game—and also dying in reality **[T-SER5.6]**.

  NOTE: *As originally presented, Jake Bullet was a fictional construct of the despair squid hallucination. The* Smegazines, *however, revealed that Bullet actually existed in one reality.*

- **Bullet, Jake:** A cyborg police officer in an alternate reality who worked for the NYNYPD. He had a secretary named Dottie. Among his accessories were a #3 can opener in his wrist **[M-SMG1.7(a)]**, zoom lenses **[M-SMG1.13(c4)]**, silicon muscles and a titanium skull **[M-SMG2.1(c4)]**. He owned a convertible, and his badge number was 724946.

  Some of Bullet's childhood cop heroes included Theodore Kojak, Frank Cannon, Michael Starsky and Kenneth "Hutch" Hutchinson **[M-SMG1.11(c4)]**. Other role models included Sam Spade, Mike Hammer, Philip Marlow and traffic warden Mathilda Grimshaw **[M-SMG2.6(a)]**.

  Bullet graduated from the Highway Code Patrol Course, Hendon, in July 2330 **[M-SMG2.6(a)]**. His favorite food was Mona's doughnuts with a side of Swarfega, from the Winan Diner **[M-SMG2.9(c4)]**.

  Bullet's first case involved the disappearance of Spike, the brother of a female android named Sugar **[M-SMG1.7(a)]**. Another case involved the murder of game-show contestant Philby Frutch **[M-SMG1.10(c1)]**. While investigating the death of Brainfade employee Doctor Sandra Halley, Bullet was arrested by his own police chief for agreeing to keep the company's prototype mind-control spike a secret **[M-SMG2.9(c4)]**.

- **bum:** A slang term for a lazy or homeless person **[RL]**. Lister claimed this as his occupation while serving as a witness during an appeal of Rimmer's manslaughter conviction aboard the penal station Justice World **[T-SER4.3]**.

- **Bun-bun:** A nickname by which Admiral Peter Tranter—commander of the Space Corps R&D Program in one of Ace Rimmer's universes—was known to his mistress **[N-BCK]**.

- **Bungo:** A nickname by which Space Corps R&D Program commander Peter Tranter was known to the admiral's peers in one of Ace Rimmer's realities **[N-BCK]**.

- **buoyancy tanks:** A component of MkIV Titanica Fish Droids, such as Lister's pet robot goldfish Lennon and McCartney, that regulated their ability to remain afloat in water **[M-SMG2.4(c5)]**.

PREFIX
RL: Real life

T-: Television Episodes
SER: Television series
IDW: "Identity Within"
USA1: Unaired U.S. pilot
USA2: Unaired U.S. demo

R-: *The Bodysnatcher Collection*
SER: Remastered episodes
BOD: "Bodysnatcher"
DAD: "Dad"
FTH: "Lister's Father"
INF: "Infinity Patrol"
END: "The End" (original assembly)

N-: Novels
INF: *Infinity Welcomes Careful Drivers*
BTL: *Better Than Life*
LST: *Last Human*
BCK: *Backwards*
OMN: *Red Dwarf Omnibus*

M-: Magazines
SMG: *Smegazine*

W-: Websites
OFF: Official website
NAN: *Prelude to Nanarchy*
AND: *Androids*
DIV: Diva-Droid
DIB: Duane Dibbley
CRP: Crapola
GEN: Geneticon
LSR: Leisure World Intl.
JMC: Jupiter Mining Corporation
AIT: *A.I. Today*
HOL: HoloPoint

G-: Roleplaying Game
RPG: *Core Rulebook*
BIT: *A.I. Screen Extra Bits* booklet
SOR: *Series Sourcebook*
OTH: Other RPG material

- **Burd:** A member of *Red Dwarf*'s Z-Shift prior to the ship's cadmium II disaster. Shortly before the accident, Rimmer assigned Burd and Dooley to repair several malfunctioning driers in the launderettes on East Alpha 555 **[N-INF]**.

  NOTE: *Burd presumably died during the cadmium II explosion. It is unknown whether the nanobots resurrected him in Series VIII.*

- **Burger Bar:** An eatery in a fascist society that the *Red Dwarf* crew imagined while trapped in a despair squid hallucination. After running from police, the group ducked into an alleyway leading to the Burger Bar and decided to commit suicide to escape their bleak situation. Holly intervened, however, saving their lives **[T-SER5.6]**.

- **Burma:** A country in Southeast Asia, bordered by China, Thailand and India, and otherwise known as the Republic of the Union of Myanmar **[RL]**. Olaf Petersen once bought a pair of Smart Shoes to bring him home after nights of heavy drinking. The footwear grew bored with this routine, however, and began wandering about on their own accord, with an inebriated Petersen in tow. In one instance, Petersen passed out in Oslo, awakening the next morning in Burma **[T-SER2.5]**.

  NOTE: *That would entail a trip of roughly 6,300 miles (10,140 kilometers), according to Google Maps, which means it would have taken Petersen nearly eighty-five days to traverse that distance (assuming the Smart Shoes walked at a normal human pace)—a testament to the extent of his inebriation.*

- **Burns-McDowell Law:** A law in theoretical physics stating that socks disappearing from the laundry re-entered the material plane as a proportionate number of clothes hangers in one's closet **[G-RPG]**.

- **Burroughs, Phil:** A new recruit who boarded *Red Dwarf* and reported for duty on Z-Shift, along with Lister. To his dismay, Burroughs, a serious-minded academy undergraduate, found himself stuck with Lister's drinking group (Petersen, Chen and Selby). Despite his preferring low-alcohol wine, the group continuously ordered him Japanese lager; it was no surprise, then, that he passed out after seven lagers, his top limit being three. Shortly before the cadmium II accident, Rimmer assigned Burroughs and Saxon to paint the engineers' mess **[N-INF]**.

  NOTE: *Burroughs presumably died during the cadmium II explosion. It is unknown whether the nanobots resurrected him in Series VIII.*

- **Burton Group:** A chain of high-end British menswear stores **[RL]**. While trapped in an addictive version of *Better Than Life*, Rimmer arranged for Hugo, his ex-pool attendant, to be refused service at any store in the Burton Group, as punishment for having sex with his wife, Juanita Chicata **[N-INF]**.

- ***Butch Accountant and the Yuppie Kid*:** A hypothetical Western movie title. When Rimmer ordered a dry white wine and Perrier while inside Kryten's Old West-themed dream, Lister joked that Arnold must have watched this movie **[T-SER6.3]**.

  NOTE: *This film's title spoofed that of the 1969 Western* Butch Cassidy and the Sundance Kid, *starring Paul Newman and Robert Redford.*

- **Butcher, Mike:** The producer of the television soap opera *Androids* **[M-SMG2.9(c8)]**. A slogan printed on a sign in one of Cat's dreams read "Mike Butcher, What A Nice Guy!"—with "Well He Does Pay Me!" printed underneath **[M-SMG1.7(c2)]**.

  NOTE: *Butcher was named after the real-world editor of the* Red Dwarf Smegazines.

- **Butler Black:** A standard color available for Diva-Droid International's 4000 Series **[G-RPG]** and Hudzen 10 mechanoids **[G-SOR]**. The body of Kryten 2X4B-523P was Butler Black **[T-SER3.1]**.

- **Butler Droid:** A type of mechanoid in the universe in which *Red Dwarf* was an American mining ship. In that dimension, Kryten 2XB-517P was Captain Louise Tau's personal Butler Droid **[T-USA1(s)]**.

- **Butler's Sack Race and Salad Fork Challenge:** A contest held at a butler convention in Swindon, England. In a timeline in which Lister was a billionaire, Gilbert St. John McAdam Ostrog was forced to become his head butler after losing this race **[W-OFF]**.

B-: Books
- **PRG:** *Red Dwarf Programme Guide*
- **SUR:** *Red Dwarf Space Corps Survival Manual*
- **PRM:** *Primordial Soup*
- **SOS:** *Son of Soup*
- **SCE:** *Scenes from the Dwarf*
- **LOG:** *Red Dwarf Log No. 1996*
- **RD8:** *Red Dwarf VIII*
- **EVR:** *The Log: A Dwarfer's Guide to Everything*

X-: Misc.
- **PRO:** Promotional materials, videos, etc.
- **PST:** Posters at DJ XVII (2013)
- **CAL:** 2008 calendar
- **RNG:** Cell phone ringtones
- **MOB:** Mobisode ("Red Christmas")
- **CIN:** *Children in Need* sketch
- **GEK:** *Geek Week* intros by Kryten
- **TNG:** "Tongue-Tied" video

- **XMS:** Bill Pearson's Christmas special pitch script
- **XVD:** Bill Pearson's Christmas special pitch video
- **OTH:** Other *Red Dwarf* appearances

SUFFIX
DVD:
- **(d)** – Deleted scene
- **(o)** – Outtake
- **(b)** – Bonus DVD material (other)
- **(e)** – Extended version

SMEGAZINES:
- **(c)** – Comic
- **(a)** – Article

OTHER:
- **(s)** – Early/unused script draft
- **(s1)** – Alternate version of script

- **Butlins:** A chain of vacation camps in the United Kingdom **[RL]**. While reminiscing about his younger years in the Space Scouts, Rimmer recalled a survival trip he once took with Porky Roebuck, in which they had to sleep in the rough, eat berries and survive in the wild. Snarkily, Lister asked if the trip had been to Butlins **[T-SER2.5]**.

- **Butter-Pat Head:** An insult Cat called Kryten when the mechanoid questioned the competence of his feline nasal acuity **[T-SER6.2]**.

- **Butthed, Mike:** The author of the book *Meeting a Drunken Artist*. Lister owned a copy of this book aboard *Red Dwarf* **[M-SMG1.2(c1)]**.

  NOTE: *The character's name was a pun on the insult "butthead."*

- **Buttsuck:** A nickname that Lister suggested Kryten call Rimmer whenever he wanted to be extra-polite **[T-SER2.1(s)]**.

- **"Bye Bye Baby":** A song originally recorded in 1965 by The Four Seasons, and later covered by the Bay City Rollers in 1975 **[RL]**. While explaining the necessity of cleaning out his cache files, Kryten claimed his memory was filled with useless knowledge, such as the ability to sing the Bay City Rollers' greatest hits, which was no longer a priority. For most cultural purposes, he noted, crooning "Bye Bye Baby" was sufficient **[T-SER7.1]**.

  NOTE: *The scene involving Kryten's useless knowledge was changed to reference Czechoslovakian pop-music boy band Lunetic and their first hit, "You Are My Mum," in the DVD captions for the Czech Republic version of the series.*

- **bypass unit:** A portable console that could be connected to a ship's navicomp to bypass the system when necessary. It contained twelve switches that had to be toggled on, one at a time, at one-second intervals. Holly instructed Lister to connect the bypass unit to *Red Dwarf*'s navicomp when it malfunctioned due to the stress of traveling faster than light. Thanks to a future echo Rimmer experienced, Lister thought this would lead to his death, but after successfully connecting the unit, he learned that he was not, in fact, the subject of the future echo **[N-INF]**.

PREFIX
RL: Real life

T-: Television Episodes
SER: Television series
IDW: "Identity Within"
USA1: Unaired U.S. pilot
USA2: Unaired U.S. demo

R-: *The Bodysnatcher Collection*
SER: Remastered episodes
BOD: "Bodysnatcher"
DAD: "Dad"
FTH: "Lister's Father"
INF: "Infinity Patrol"
END: "The End" (original assembly)

N-: Novels
INF: *Infinity Welcomes Careful Drivers*
BTL: *Better Than Life*
LST: *Last Human*
BCK: *Backwards*
OMN: *Red Dwarf Omnibus*

M-: Magazines
SMG: *Smegazine*

W-: Websites
OFF: Official website
NAN: *Prelude to Nanarchy*
AND: *Androids*
DIV: Diva-Droid
DIB: Duane Dibbley
CRP: Crapola
GEN: Geneticon
LSR: Leisure World Intl.
JMC: Jupiter Mining Corporation
AIT: *A.I. Today*
HOL: HoloPoint

G-: Roleplaying Game
RPG: *Core Rulebook*
BIT: *A.I. Screen Extra Bits* booklet
SOR: *Series Sourcebook*
OTH: Other RPG material

B-: Books
PRG: *Red Dwarf Programme Guide*
SUR: *Red Dwarf Space Corps Survival Manual*
PRM: *Primordial Soup*
SOS: *Son of Soup*
SCE: *Scenes from the Dwarf*
LOG: *Red Dwarf Log No. 1996*
RD8: *Red Dwarf VIII*
EVR: *The Log: A Dwarfer's Guide to Everything*

X-: Misc.
PRO: Promotional materials, videos, etc.
PST: Posters at DJ XVII (2013)
CAL: 2008 calendar
RNG: Cell phone ringtones
MOB: Mobisode ("Red Christmas")
CIN: *Children in Need* sketch
GEK: *Geek Week* intros by Kryten
TNG: "Tongue-Tied" video

XMS: Bill Pearson's Christmas special pitch script
XVD: Bill Pearson's Christmas special pitch video
OTH: Other *Red Dwarf* appearances

SUFFIX
DVD:
(d) – Deleted scene
(o) – Outtake
(b) – Bonus DVD material (other)
(e) – Extended version

SMEGAZINES:
(c) – Comic
(a) – Article

OTHER:
(s) – Early/unused script draft
(s1) – Alternate version of script

C
CAT

- **C:** An initial on a keychain Kryten received in a nightmarish vision in which Lister and Kochanski, clad in eveningwear, informed him that they were a couple, asked him to leave the ship and gave him the wrongly initialed keychain as a parting gift. This vision was triggered by his discovery that Kochanski was bathing in Lister's quarters **[T-SER7.4]**.

- **C:** A letter on the chest of a cashier working at a parts shop on the television soap opera *Androids* **[M-SMG2.8(c2)]**.

- **C-180A Canary Rifle:** The standard-issue firearm assigned to members of the Canaries aboard *Red Dwarf*. It held a thirty-round clip of standard Space Corps Penal System ammunition, which could be programmed not to fire at wardens or other personnel. This assault rifle had a range of 70 meters (230 feet) **[G-BIT]**.

- **C222 PFY:** The license-plate number of a Harley Davidson motorcycle Lister and Cat conjured up while playing the total-immersion video game *Better Than Life* **[T-SER2.2]**.

- **C7:** A label printed on an overhead console in *Red Dwarf*'s science lab **[T-SER5.5(b)]**.

- **Cadet College:** A school Rimmer attended prior to serving aboard *Red Dwarf*. While marooned on a frozen planet, Lister tried to keep his mind off hunger by asking Rimmer how he lost his virginity. Hesitant at first, Rimmer finally claimed it happened at Cadet College with a girl named Sandra **[T-SER3.2]**, though in actuality, he barely got to "second base" with her **[N-BTL]**. One of Rimmer's fonder memories of the school involved beating his Cadet College officer at *Risk* **[T-SER4.6]**.

  NOTE: *This was sometimes referred to as Cadet School or Cadet Training School.*

- **cadmium-12:** An isotope of the element cadmium, used to power ships such as *Starbug* shuttles **[G-SOR]**.

  NOTE: *The word "cadmium" is a common noun and thus not typically capitalized. Some* Red Dwarf *resources have capitalized the word, but for the sake of consistency and accuracy, the uncapitalized form is used throughout this lexicon.*

- **cadmium II:** A radioactive isotope used aboard JMC vessels such as *Red Dwarf*. A failed drive plate aboard *Red Dwarf*, improperly repaired by Rimmer, caused a massive radioactive explosion that killed every crewmember aboard the ship except for Lister, who was secured in stasis at the time **[T-SER1.1]**.

  NOTE: *The captions on the Series I DVDs spelled the isotope's name as "cadmium-2," but the novel* Infinity Welcomes Careful Drivers *and the official website both called it cadmium II, which is how it appears throughout this guide.*

- **cadmium II coolant system:** A system located deep within *Red Dwarf*'s engine corridors, used to maintain the temperature of the ship's radioactive cadmium II. When the coolant system failed due to an improperly fixed drive plate, an explosion resulted that killed nearly everyone aboard the vessel **[N-INF]**.

- **cadmium II core:** The main fuel rods used in *Red Dwarf*'s power system. When Rimmer improperly repaired a drive plate, the core went critical due to the coolant system's failure **[N-INF]**.

- **Caesar, Julius, Emperor:** A Roman general and politician of the first century B.C. **[RL]**. Lister found references to Caesar while reading Rimmer's diary, in which Arnold described his yearning to achieve such fame and glory that his memoirs would take its place in history next to Caesar's memoirs and Napoleon Bonaparte's war diaries **[T-SER1.6]**. While discussing Rimmer's obsession with war, Lister noted the many books about Caesar, George Patton and other famous military leaders in his library **[T-SER3.2]**.

  When Rimmer double-crossed Lister during an incident involving a programmable virus, Lister misquoted William Shakespeare's *The Tragedy of Julius Caesar*, claiming the play's eponymous character had exclaimed "Et tu, Brut" (rather than "Et tu, Brute?") after smelling Mark Antony's aftershave **[T-SER8.6(d)]**.

  While trapped in an addictive version of *Better Than Life*, Rimmer believed he had returned to Earth and became incredibly wealthy, creating a company that developed a time machine. He used the machine to invite guests to lavish parties, where he played *Risk* with the likes of Caesar, Patton and Napoleon **[N-INF]**, and also invited Caesar to his bachelor

PREFIX
RL: Real life

T-: Television Episodes
SER: Television series
IDW: "Identity Within"
USA1: Unaired U.S. pilot
USA2: Unaired U.S. demo

R-: *The Bodysnatcher Collection*
SER: Remastered episodes
BOD: "Bodysnatcher"
DAD: "Dad"
FTH: "Lister's Father"
INF: "Infinity Patrol"
END: "The End" (original assembly)

N-: Novels
INF: *Infinity Welcomes Careful Drivers*
BTL: *Better Than Life*
LST: *Last Human*
BCK: *Backwards*
OMN: *Red Dwarf Omnibus*

M-: Magazines
SMG: *Smegazine*

W-: Websites
OFF: Official website
NAN: *Prelude to Nanarchy*
AND: *Androids*
DIV: Diva-Droid
DIB: Duane Dibbley
CRP: Crapola
GEN: Geneticon
LSR: Leisure World Intl.
JMC: Jupiter Mining Corporation
AIT: *A.I. Today*
HOL: HoloPoint

G-: Roleplaying Game
RPG: *Core Rulebook*
BIT: *A.I. Screen Extra Bits* booklet
SOR: *Series Sourcebook*
OTH: Other RPG material

party to celebrate his marriage to his second wife, Helen **[N-BTL]**.

- **Caesar Salad Monster:** A creature from the planet Rigel 5, possibly in an alternate universe, that left a slimy trail of croutons and Caesar dressing in its wake **[G-BIT]**.

- **Calculator, Esther:** A character that Kryten's subconscious mind created while battling the Apocalypse virus in a dream. Esther was married to Jeff Calculator, an accountant. She blamed Kryten—known in the illusion as Sheriff Carton—for the death of Wyatt Memory, who was fatally shot while the sheriff slept off a hangover **[N-BCK]**.

- **Calculator, Jeff:** The husband of Esther Calculator, whom Kryten's subconscious mind created while battling the Apocalypse virus in a dream. When Kryten begged Jeff for money to buy booze, the accountant refused to help him **[N-BCK]**.

- **Caldicott:** A Cadet School training officer against whom Rimmer often played *Risk* while attending that facility **[T-SER4.6]**.

- **Caldicott:** An officer who worked at the JMC recruitment center on Mimas. Caldicott interviewed Lister when he applied for the Space Corps **[N-INF]**.

  NOTE: *It is unknown whether he was the same Caldicott with whom Rimmer attended Cadet School.*

- **Caleva:** A brand name of scientific equipment stored in *Red Dwarf*'s Quarantine Room 152. The machine's model number was 75T **[T-SER5.4]**.

  NOTE: *This device was presumably produced by British company GB Caleva Ltd., a manufacturer of pharmaceutical tablet testing equipment.*

- **Calhoon, Mr.:** A photographer in the town of Bedford Falls, whom Lister imagined while trapped in an addictive version of *Better Than Life*. Lister believed he had returned to Earth and settled down with Kochanski and their two sons, and had hired Calhoon to take their picture, which Lister kept in his wallet **[N-INF]**.

- **calibrator:** A component of the triplicator, a machine Kryten built using the Matter Paddle, which scanned an item's molecular pattern and created two copies. The calibrator needed to be locked and set before triplication could commence **[T-SER5.5]**.

- **Caligari's Home for the Terminally Bewildered:** A mental institution on a fascist, alternate-reality Earth. Duane Dibbley was taken to this facility after being caught at the scene of the double homicide of Sebastian and William Doyle **[M-SMG1.14(c1)]**.

  NOTE: *The institution's name presumably referenced* Dr. Caligari, *a 1989 cult film by Stephen Sayadian, about a doctor's unorthodox experiments at an insane asylum.*

- **Caligula, Emperor:** The nickname of Gaius Julius Caesar Germanicus, a first-century Roman Emperor historically known for his cruelty and sexual perversity **[RL]**. While trapped in an addictive version of *Better Than Life*, Rimmer imagined using a time machine to crash one of Caligula's orgies on the night of his bachelor party **[N-BTL]**.

- **Caligula, Emperor:** A waxdroid replica of the Roman dictator, created for the Waxworld theme park. Left on their own for millions of years, the waxdroids attained sentience and became embroiled in a park-wide resource war between Villain World (to which Caligula belonged) and Hero World.

  During this war, the *Red Dwarf* crew transported to the planet using a Matter Paddle, with Lister and Cat materializing in Villain territory, while Rimmer and Kryten landed in Hero territory. After the villains' army captured Lister and Cat, Grigori Rasputin and Caligula waxdroids interrogated them, threatening them with such heinous torture as having soapy frogs and rampant wildebeests placed around their genitals.

  Rimmer, meanwhile, found the heroes' army lacking and took command, working many of the pacifistic waxdroids to death before ordering a frontal attack on the enemy's compound across a minefield. This wiped out the remaining droids, including Caligula **[T-SER4.6]**.

- **Caligula Suite:** A recreational facility aboard *Red Dwarf*, reserved for officers. While inhabiting Lister's body after a mindswap, Rimmer enjoyed the Caligula Suite's Jacuzzi **[R-SER3.4(d)]**.

- ***Callahan's Index of Twentieth Century Telegraph Poles*:** A reference guide that Rimmer owned a copy of **[M-SMG1.2(a)]**.

- **Callisto:** The second largest moon of Jupiter and third largest in Earth's solar system **[RL]**. Callisto had an excellent education system and a service industry specializing in Datanet production. It also contained the secretive Valhalla Impact Structure, an impact site 2,485 miles (4,000 kilometers) across, shrouded in mystery and closely guarded by the Space Corps **[G-RPG]**.

  Josie, a space beatnik, bought an illegal copy of the virtual-reality video game *Better Than Life* from a South African game dealer on Callisto **[N-INF]**. Olaf Petersen once bought a kit droid meant to resemble Marilyn Monroe on Callisto **[T-SER3.6]**. And Hayley Summers, whom Lister dated as a youth, moved to Callisto to take what she considered a dream job, leaving Lister and the bank where she worked **[T-SER10.5]**.

  When Earth was rechristened Garbage World, Callisto's president presided over the cutting of a toilet paper ribbon to celebrate that the planet was open for business. Rimmer once witnessed an acid rain storm wiping out an entire settlement on Callisto **[N-BTL]**. Additionally, a simulant once killed forty patrons in a diner located on this moon **[W-OFF]**.

  ***NOTE:** The first-draft script for the pilot episode of* Red Dwarf USA *misspelled the moon's name as "Callistro." The murderous simulant was the same one the crew found in Barbra Bellini's pod in episode 4.3 ("Justice")*

- **Callisto-Ganymede Ring Arc Appreciation Society:** An organization for those interested in partial planetary rings. The Space Corps shot down a sightseeing trip from this group near the Valhalla Impact Structure on Callisto, later deeming the incident "an unfortunate accident" **[G-RPG]**.

- **Callistro:** *See* Callisto

- **Caltech (California Institute of Technology):** A renowned scientific and engineering research and education institution, located in Pasadena, California **[RL]**. Rimmer informed Lister he'd need a degree in advanced mental engineering from Caltech in order to fix Kryten's programming issues, which stemmed from the droid's inability to cope with the loss of his *Nova 5* crewmates **[N-INF]**.

- **Cam 5:** A security camera overlooking G Tower, a section of the Tank, *Red Dwarf*'s brig **[T-SER8]**.

  ***NOTE:** Footage from Cam 5 was briefly shown on the menu section of the Series VIII DVDs' bonus materials disc.*

- ***Camelot*:** A medieval artificial-reality game that the *Starbug 1* crew found aboard a derelict spaceship. Lister entered the game with the intention of seducing the Queen of Camelot; to aid in his quest, he brought along a book of cheats ensuring his win against the King's knight **[B-PRG]**. Also known as *Jousting*, the game was produced by Total Immersion Inc. and distributed by Crapola Inc. **[G-RPG]**.

  ***NOTE:** Although the medieval game was not specifically named in the episode, the* Red Dwarf Programme Guide *revealed that it was called* Camelot. *The roleplaying game, however, used the name* Jousting.

- ***Camera Monthly*:** A magazine published in an alternate universe in which the sexes were reversed. While visiting their female counterparts in that reality, Lister and Rimmer were surprised to find this magazine—which featured images of semi-nude, unrealistically built men posing provocatively—in their alternate selves' quarters **[T-SER2.6]**.

- **Cameron:** A Pleasure GELF in an alternate reality in which the sexes were reversed. Cameron—the male equivalent of the prime universe's Camille—fell in love with the female Kryten after being picked up by her universe's *Red Dwarf* crew **[W-OFF]**.

- **Cameron Mackintosh 40-valve air-cooled diesel:** A type of diesel engine used aboard *Red Dwarf.* This engine came in several models, including the 179 and the 184, the only difference being a refinement in the latter's funnel edges. On the fourth day of a ten-day hiking vacation through the diesel decks, Rimmer came across a 184, under which he camped for the night. Rimmer later included a photograph of the 184 in a slideshow of the trip that he presented to Kryten **[T-SER4.3]**.

- **Camille:** A Pleasure GELF—a type of genetically engineered life form created to provide companionship by sensing a person's perfect mate and shapeshifting accordingly. Camille was married to Hector, a fellow GELF, with whom she strove to find a cure for their condition until she left him and their work behind **[T-SER4.1]**. She ended up on the *Penhalagen*, but when the starship suffered a fuel shortage, she abandoned the ship in an escape vessel and crashed on a planetoid with a decaying orbit **[W-OFF]**.

Kryten picked up Camille's distress beacon and rescued her aboard *Starbug 1*. Unaware of her true nature, he perceived her as another mechanoid (a 4000 series GTI), and the two fell instantly in love. Rimmer, meanwhile, saw her as a female hologram, and also became infatuated with her. After a short quarrel, the two brought Camille back to *Red Dwarf*, where Lister perceived her as a human female—to whom he, too, was instantly attracted. The crew soon discovered she was a Pleasure GELF, when Lister realized he and Rimmer were hearing different responses. When Cat heard of Camille's abilities, he visited the GELF, only to see an exact duplicate of himself, in keeping with his vanity.

Camille apologized and reverted to her natural state, an amorphic green blob. Undeterred by her appearance, Kryten asked her to dinner, and the two enjoyed a date until Hector arrived, asking that she come back to him. Initially choosing to remain with Kryten, she ultimately left to continue their work after Kryten convinced her it was for the best **[T-SER4.1]**.

- **Camille:** A Pleasure GELF whom Kryten rescued in a universe in which *Red Dwarf* and its crew were American. She appeared to him as a mechanoid **[T-USA2]**.

  NOTE: *The American promo reel included scenes from "Camille" and other episodes of the British version, the scripts of which had been tweaked for the American cast but never filmed.*

- **Campaign for the Restoration of Altrincham's Platform (CRAP):** A committee organized to help facilitate the rebuilding of a train platform located in Altrincham, England. Duane Dibbley would have likely belonged to this group **[M-SMG2.2(a)]**.

- **Camus, Albert:** A twentieth-century Nobel Prize-winning journalist, editor and philosopher **[RL]**. Kryten cited Camus as an example of people who became more than their occupation suggested, in an attempt to dissuade Rimmer from using a mind patch to pass a test to join the holoship *Enlightenment*'s crew **[T-SER5.1]**.

- **Canaries, The:** An elite group of expendable inmates from the Tank, *Red Dwarf*'s brig, whose mission was to enter dangerous and hazardous environments, ascertain the threat level and report back so a proper response team could be assembled. The name stemmed from the nineteenth-century practice of using live canaries to determine a mining tunnel's toxicity. Enrollment in the Canaries was voluntary, with a long list of perks and benefits given to participating inmates **[T-SER8.4]**, including extra baked beans at dinner, smooth toilet paper and soap in the shower **[G-SOR]**.

  Lister volunteered himself, as well as Rimmer, Cat, Kryten and Kochanski, for the Canaries, after Holly claimed it was an a cappella group. According to Rimmer, "Canaries" stood for "Convict Army, Nearly All Retarded Inbred, Evil Sheepshaggers" **[T-SER8.4]**.

- **canary:** A small domesticated bird often kept as a pet, and once used in coal mining as a crude toxic gas detector **[RL]**. Rimmer once considered getting a canary for his quarters, due to Lister's singularly curry-based diet **[T-SER3.4]**.

- **Canary dropship:** *See* probe ship

- ***Canary Squad*:** A television program scheduled to be broadcast by Krytie TV on October 23, featuring members of Floor 13's elite group, the Canaries **[X-CAL]**.

- **Canary Starter Pack:** A briefcase provided to all new Canary recruits aboard *Red Dwarf*, consisting of uniforms and first-meeting information **[T-SER8.4]**.

- **Canary submarine:** *See* diving bell [first entry]

- **Can Cer:** A brand of cigarette smoked by a character named Archie on the television soap opera *Androids* **[M-SMG2.9(c6)]**.

  NOTE: *Spoken aloud, the product's name referenced its carcinogenic nature.*

- **Candy:** A name tattooed on Olaf Petersen's right arm. After Rimmer's hologrammatic arm was replaced with Petersen's due to a corrupted physical data disc, Arnold noticed the tattoo on his own appendage **[T-SER1.3]**.

- **Candy:** A person to whom The Bible was dedicated, as reported in an ancient Earth News video. Archeologists at Mount Sinai had uncovered what was believed to be a missing page from the beginning of the religious text, which, once translated, read, "To my darling Candy. All characters portrayed within this book are fictitious, and any resemblance to persons living or dead is purely coincidental" **[T-SER2.2]**.

  NOTE: *This gag originated in a* Son of Cliché *"Dave Hollins: Space Cadet" sketch titled "Newsflash," in which an archeologist, Doctor Franz Luber, read the missing page to news reporters. That version contained an additional line: "By the same author: The New Testament and Testament III—all your favorite characters back again for another zany adventure!"*

- **Candy:** A model of android available in a pick'n'mix lineup at a brothel on Mimas. Customers could choose various body parts from selected androids, and then have a custom-designed sex droid assembled for their use. This model's breasts were particularly popular among clients, including a portly, red-haired customer who chose them for his sex droid **[N-INF]**.

- **Candy Apple Red:** A standard color available for Diva-Droid International's 4000 Series mechanoid **[G-RPG]**.

- ***Canis sapiens*:** A species of humanoids that evolved from the offspring of Deb Lister's pregnant dog, Dracula, aboard an alternate-universe *Red Dwarf*. The last surviving member of this species, named Dog, traveled through deep space in the mining vessel with Lister and Arlene Rimmer **[M-SMG2.8(a), W-OFF]**.

  NOTE: *Dracula's name was revealed on the official website.*

- **Canker Sore Burgundy:** A designer color that Malpractice Medical & Scispec offered for its medi-scans **[G-RPG]**.

- **Cannon, Frank:** A fictional 1970s private detective from the American television series *Cannon* **[RL]**. He was among Jake Bullet's childhood cop heroes **[M-SMG1.11(c4)]**.

- ***Can't Cook, Won't Cook*:** A British cooking show starring Ainsley Harriott, who once recorded a special episode in *Starbug 1*'s galley titled *Can't Smeg, Won't Smeg*, featuring Lister, Rimmer, Kryten, Kochanski and Duane Dibbley **[T-SER4(b)]**.

  NOTE: *There are several ways one could attempt to make this fit continuity... none of which will be explored here.*

- **Cap:** A nickname that Rimmer asked Lister to call him (instead of "Rimmer") as they and Cat embarked on a rescue mission to the *Nova 5*, where they believed three female crewmembers awaited **[N-INF]**.

- **Capone, Alphonse ("Al"):** A notorious twentieth-century Chicago mobster who led a crime syndicate during the United States' Prohibition era **[RL]**.

  A waxdroid replica of Capone was created for the Waxworld theme park. Left on their own for millions of years, the waxdroids attained sentience and became embroiled in a park-wide resource war between Villain World (to which Capone belonged) and Hero World.

  During this war, the *Red Dwarf* crew transported to the planet using a Matter Paddle, with Lister and Cat materializing in Villain territory, while Rimmer and Kryten landed in Hero territory. While imprisoned in Villain World, Lister and Cat witnessed the firing-squad execution of a waxdroid version of Winnie-the-Pooh, which Capone attended.

  Rimmer, meanwhile, found the heroes' army lacking and took command, working many of the pacifistic waxdroids to death before ordering a frontal attack on the enemy's compound across a minefield. This wiped out the remaining droids, including Capone **[T-SER4.6]**.

- **Capote, Mr.:** An Axis-syndrome hologram from an alternate universe who was sentenced to five years in Cyberia, a virtual-reality prison complex on Arranguu 12. A short man with thinning gray hair and a pudgy face, Capote was a vegetarian who experienced heartburn from champagne and thought of his first wife whenever he saw Spanish architecture. As such, his Cyberhell illusion included a Spanish villa stocked with fresh meats and bottles of Marne Valley champagne. This confused Lister, who was initially sent to Capote's Cyberhell by mistake **[N-LST]**.

NOTE: American author Truman Capote stood only five feet three inches tall and matched Mr. Capote's physical description. He is on record as disliking champagne, and spent an extended period of time in Spain.

- **Capp, Andy:** The title character of the British comic strip *Andy Capp*, known for drinking too much and having a thick Northeastern accent **[RL]**. After Spare Head Three's personality chips were implanted in Kryten, Rimmer called the mechanoid Andy Capp due to his accent and disposition **[M-SMG2.9(c1)]**.

- **Capra, Frank:** An American film director whose credits included *It Happened One Night* and *It's a Wonderful Life* **[RL]**. The latter film was both Lister's and Kochanski's all-time favorite movie **[N-INF]**.

- **Capston:** A character on the television soap opera *Androids*. A former secret agent, Capston owned a club called the Petroleum Bar and was involved in a scandal dubbed Plastigate **[W-AND]**. He was also the central character in the short-lived spinoff series *Androids Nights*, which revolved around Capston's detective agency on Venus, where the android was thrust into a world of murder, adultery and mystery. His nemesis on the show was Jaysee **[W-CRP]**.

- **CapstonsBoss:** The username of a forum poster on the *Androids* website's message boards **[W-AND]**.

- **Captain A. J. Rimmer, Space Adventurer:** An exaggerated role that Rimmer assumed while replying to a distress signal from the *Nova 5*, after hearing Kryten's message indicating there were three female survivors on board **[T-SER2.1]**.

- **Captain Bog-Bot:** A nickname that Rimmer called Kryten while feeling humiliated by his crewmates' refusal to obey his order to launch a scouter from *Starbug 1* **[T-SER5.4]**.

- **Captain Chloroform:** A nickname Lister called Kryten after the mechanoid rendered him unconscious so Rimmer could swap minds with him **[T-SER3.4]**.

- **Captain Emerald:** The name by which Lister referred to his own mirror reflection while inhabiting Rimmer's hologrammic body following a mind swap. The name referred to the greenish color of Rimmer's hologrammic uniform and hat **[T-SER3.4]**.

  NOTE: This was changed to the Gendarme of St. Tropez, a reference to the titular character of the 1964 French comedy film Le Gendarme de Saint-Tropez, *in the DVD captions for the Czech Republic version of the series.*

- **CaptainJuno:** The username of a forum poster on the *Androids* website's message boards **[W-AND]**.

- **Captain Laser:** A fictitious character that Cat or Lister occasionally assumed while playing Galactic Warrior to pass the time aboard *Red Dwarf* **[T-SER3.5(d)]**.

- **Captain Paxo:** A nickname Rimmer once called Captain Hollister while believing himself to be under the influence of hallucinogenic mushrooms. After encountering his future self, which he also attributed to the hallucinogen, Rimmer ran into Hollister, who was dressed in a chicken costume for a fancy dress party. Hollister apologized to Rimmer for his earlier harshness, but Rimmer mistook the captain for a hallucination, assaulted him and called him "Captain Paxo" **[T-SER2.4]**.

  NOTE: Paxo is a popular brand of stuffing in the United Kingdom.

- **Captain Rot-mind:** A nickname that Rimmer called Kryten after the mechanoid miscalculated the takeoff procedure from a backwards-running Earth, marooning them on the planet for a decade **[N-BCK]**.

- **Captain Sadness:** One of Cat's nicknames for Rimmer **[T-SER4.1]**.

- **Captain's galley:** An area aboard *Red Dwarf* allocated for the preparation of meals for Captain Hollister and his guests. While in a psychotropic simulation, Rimmer believed he had imbibed the sexual magnetism virus at a dinner party hosted by Hollister, during which he had sex with several female officers in the Captain's galley **[T-SER8.2]**.

- **Captain Smug Git:** A snide nickname that Arnold Rimmer once called Ace Rimmer **[T-SER7.2]**.

- **Captain's office:** A small area of *Red Dwarf*'s Drive Room, used for administrative duties. The office contained a small-scale model of the mining vessel, as well as data discs and a sign identifying the room, both in English and Esperanto **[T-SER1.1]**.

- **Captain's rest room:** A private bathroom aboard *Red Dwarf*, reserved for Captain Hollister **[T-SER8.1]**.

- **Captain Yawn:** A nickname that Cat called Rimmer, indicating he found the hologram boring **[T-SER4.5]**.

- **Caravaggio, Michelangelo Merisi da:** An Italian artist of the sixteenth and seventeenth centuries **[RL]**. While trying to impress Legion with his knowledge of art, Rimmer lied that he spent many nights contemplating the works, themes and form of Caravaggio **[T-SER6.2]**.

- **carbon-carbon reinforced heat shields:** A type of protective shielding composed of a hybrid carbon material, installed on *Red Dwarf* to safeguard the ship in environments containing extreme heat. Pree, the mining vessel's psychotic replacement computer, suggested disengaging the heat shields to allow the ship to burn up faster as it plunged into the core of a sun **[T-SER10.2]**.

- ***Carbug*:** The nickname of an automobile fashioned after a *Starbug* shuttle, which the crew imagined while trapped in an elation squid hallucination. The group believed they had been transported to an alternate twenty-first-century Earth, where they were merely characters on a British television series called *Red Dwarf*. While searching for answers, they met an employee of Nose World named Swallow, who worked on the television series making latex masks. Unable to help them, Swallow offered the use of the car, which had been stolen from the president of the *Red Dwarf* Fan Club.

  The car sported the phrase "*Starbug 1*" on its doors, license plates emblazoned with the phrase "ST4R B11G," and giant fuzzy dice dangling from the rear-view mirror **[T-SER6.2]**. In the illusion, the magazine *Nowt on Telly* ran a contest to win a *Carbug* **[T-SER9.3]**.

  NOTE: *The vehicle was a heavily modified Smart Fortwo car.*

- ***Caretaker, The*:** A twentieth-century play written by Harold Pinter **[RL]**. While marooned on a frozen planet, Lister attempted to stay warm inside *Starbug 1* by burning items stored aboard ship. Succumbing to hunger, he was dismayed to find several books written by authors whose names reminded him of food, such as Charles Lamb, Herman Wouk and Francis Bacon. He also found a copy of Pinter's *The Caretaker* that, due to his delirious state, made him think about pints of beer **[T-SER3.2]**.

- **Cargo Bay 3:** A cargo bay aboard *Red Dwarf*. The crew used a *Blue Midget* shuttle housed in Cargo Bay 3 to abandon the mining vessel during an attack by a Simulant Death Ship **[T-SER10.6]**.

- **Cargo Bay 4:** Another *Red Dwarf* cargo bay. Rimmer ordered the skutters to meet him in this bay to restock all of the ship's food dispensers with pot noodles after Lister made a joke about hot gazpacho soup **[M-SMG1.8(a)]**.

- **cargo bay doors:** The exterior doors of *Red Dwarf*'s cargo areas. One such set of doors led to the bay in which *Starbug 1* was housed. During an emergency in which a meltdown of *Red Dwarf*'s engine core was imminent, the crew abandoned ship using *Starbug 1*; during debarkation, however, Holly could not understand the phrase "cargo bay doors" or "manual override," due to damage to her voice-recognition unit, forcing the crew to smash their way through the doors **[T-SER5.5]**.

- **Cargo Bay J:** A cargo bay aboard *Red Dwarf*. This bay was filled with large meteorites when the ship was pummeled by a meteor shower after Lister, while going for a space-walk, neglected to close the roof bay doors **[T-SER9.1(d)]**.

- **Cargo Bay K:** Another *Red Dwarf* cargo bay that was filled with meteorites when Lister forgot to close the roof bay doors during his space-walk **[T-SER9.1(d)]**.

- **Cargo Bay L:** A third cargo bay that became filled with large meteorites after Lister left *Red Dwarf*'s roof bay doors open **[T-SER9.1(d)]**.

- **cargo bays:** A section of *Red Dwarf* in which cargo was loaded, unloaded or stored. After draining the emotions from Lister, Rimmer, Kryten and Cat, an invading polymorph retreated to this area to rest **[T-SER3.3]**. One bay housed *Starbug 1* **[T-SER5.5]**.

- **Cargo Deck 27:** An area of *Red Dwarf*. In an alternate universe, the ship's artificial intelligence, Kate, detected a life form on Cargo Deck 27 **[G-RPG]**.

- **Cargo Deck D:** A *Red Dwarf* section used for storing supplies. A trio of Cats called Fritz, Krazy and Juma led Lister through Cargo Deck D on their way to the Time Obelisk, intending to bring him to their own time to stop a holy war **[M-SMG2.1(c1)]**.

- **Cargo Deck F:** A floor aboard *Red Dwarf* used for storing supplies. Lister and Cat led a group of fifty thousand mutated space monkeys to Cargo Deck F, where the temperature had been raised to dehydrate and recrystallize the creatures. Instead of recrystallizing, however, the creatures exploded, making a mess of the area **[M-SMG1.13(c2)]**.

- **cargo decks:** A section of *Red Dwarf* in which cargo and supplies were stored, located 2,002 floors below the ship's Science Room. Kryten and Rimmer rummaged for supplies on these decks during a ship-wide power failure **[T-SER4.4]**.

- **cargo pods:** *See* central cargo pods; front cargo pods; rear cargo pods

- **cargo ramp:** An inclined ramp located in at least one of *Red Dwarf*'s cargo bays, used for loading and unloading materials. Lister and Cat sometimes played soapsud slalom on the cargo ramp, which involved coating the ramp with soapy water and sliding down, passing through several flags en route to the bottom **[T-SER3.5]**.

- **Carl:** A member of Serial Killers Anonymous (SKA) who worked at a company called Brainfade in Jake Bullet's universe. A gigantic man, Carl was considered one of the firm's success stories. He wore a button that read "I Like SKA" **[M-SMG2.7(c4)]**.

  While investigating the murder of Doctor Sandra Halley, Bullet viewed a virtual simulation of the night in question, implicating Carl as the murderer **[M-SMG2.8(c1)]**. Despite this evidence, the cyborg attempted to arrest the company's lead scientist, Doctor Sid Scofrenia, but was pushed out of the window by Carl, who had been fitted with a mind control spike. Bullet survived the fall and returned to Brainfade days later, only to find that Carl's body had now contained the mind and personality of Doctor Halley—who had been reconstituted by her co-worker, Tina, using brain matter found in Halley's mind control spikes **[M-SMG2.9(c4)]**.

- **CARL:** An advanced vending machine on a ship in deep space. Its name stood for **C**offee **a**nd **R**ed **L**icorice—the only items it was originally programmed to dispense. Due to its long time in deep space alone, however, CARL broke its programming, enabling it to utilize a network of sensors and servo-mechanisms to locate anything needed throughout the cosmos, and amassing a large inventory of items aboard its ship.

  A side-effect of CARL's isolation was a preference for twentieth-century British pounds, and a tendency to scoff at anyone seeking to purchase items with any other type of currency. Another quirk was its pricing scheme: Any object, regardless of size or actual value, could be purchased for only one pound. What's more, CARL began every transaction with the phrase, "Allo, luv!" **[G-RPG]**.

- **Carling, Patricia:** A crewmember aboard *Red Dwarf* who worked in Supplies. Carling died during the cadmium II disaster, but was resurrected when nanobots rebuilt the mining ship **[T-SER8.5]**. She later agreed to go on a date with "Nicey" Ackerman, Floor 13's warden, whom she thought had lovely eyes. Days before the date, however, Ackerman was mugged and his glass eye stolen, though it was returned in time. During the date, Lister trashed Ackerman's quarters, believing them to belong to Kochanski's boyfriend, Tim. He soon discovered he'd been set up by Kryten for Krytie TV, however, and scrambled to clean the room before the couple returned **[T-SER8.5]**.

- **Carlton:** A classmate of Nirvanah Crane during their time at a Space Corps physics research facility. Carlton and Crane had heated discussions about the properties of time, space and the universe **[W-OFF]**.

- **Carmen, Caroline ("Carmen Moans"):** A supply officer aboard *Red Dwarf*. When the mining vessel stopped at Titan, she was reposted to the *Leviathan*, a JMC supply ship, where she became the last survivor to contract the Epideme virus. The intelligent virus consumed Carmen, killing her and using her body to freeze itself and the ship until it could find another host.

  Three million years later, the *Starbug 1* crew discovered the frozen ship and found Carmen's body encased in ice. Hoping to make Kochanski jealous, Lister claimed to have once had an affair with Carmen, saying crewmembers in adjacent quarters dubbed her "Carmen Moans" due to their loud lovemaking. Kristine didn't believe him, however—especially after he erroneously called her "Karen" instead of "Caroline."

  Mistaking Epideme's life signs for hers, the *Starbug 1* crew brought her frozen body aboard to thaw out. Controlled by the virus, it sought out and attacked Lister, enabling Epideme to transfer itself to his body **[T-SER7.7]**.

- **Carmichael, Hoagy:** An American singer, songwriter and composer, best known for composing such songs as "Stardust," "Georgia on My Mind," "The Nearness of You," and "Heart and Soul" **[RL]**.

  While trapped in an addictive version of *Better Than Life*, Lister believed he had returned to Earth, to a small town modeled after *It's a Wonderful Life*'s Bedford Falls, where he married a descendant of Kochanski and had two sons. In the illusion, the couple spent their evenings sitting in a leather armchair listening to Hoagy Carmichael on a wind-up phonograph **[N-INF]**.

  While in the game, Rimmer had an eighty-piece jazz band play an upbeat version of Carmichael's "Aba Daba Daba" **[N-BTL]**.

- **CARMMLT475:** The file name of a Mugs Murphy cartoon, stored in Ship Lib 5, one of *Red Dwarf*'s computer libraries **[R-BOD]**.

- **Carol:** A character in the romantic film *Marry Me My Darling*. Lister tried watching this movie on several occasions, but was constantly interrupted during a pivotal scene in which Carol and Jim discussed their love and Carol's terminal illness. When he tried watching it once more in his quarters aboard *Red Dwarf*, Rimmer shut off the film just prior to the climactic ending **[T-SER1.5]**.

  NOTE: *The movie's title was listed in the episode's script, according to commentary featured on* The Bodysnatcher Collection *DVDs.*

- **Carole:** A hypothetical individual whom Rimmer cited when Lister claimed Earth's population had likely made great advances in reversing death since Arnold's demise. Sarcastically, the hologram pretended to be a doctor giving a deceased Mrs. Johnson a pill to restore her life, and then asking an assistant, Carole, for the next corpse **[T-SER1.2]**.

  NOTE: *A* Smegazine *comic-strip adaptation of this episode revealed Carole to be a medical robot.*

- **Carpenters, The:** A twentieth-century American pop music brother-and-sister duo, known for such hits as "We've Only Just Begun," "Rainy Days and Mondays" and "(They Long to Be) Close to You" **[RL]**. Cat, as Duane Dibbley, enjoyed the music of such groups as ABBA, The Carpenters and the Bay City Rollers **[M-SMG2.2(a)]**.

- **Cars O' Rod:** An establishment located in the shopping area of the American mining ship *Red Dwarf* **[T-USA1]**.

- **Cartesian Principle, The:** A doctrine put forth by French mathematician René Descartes, stating "I think, therefore I am." When his metaphysical psychiatrist asked if he was familiar with the Cartesian Principle, hologram Frank Saunders, mistaking the phrase for the name of a music group, replied that he thought they had gone to number five with "Baby I Want Your Love Thing" **[N-INF]**.

  NOTE: *Despite its Cartesian origin, the philosophy is not actually called "The Cartesian Principle." The actual principle, originally phrased in French, was "Je pense, donc je suis." He then translated it to Latin as "Cogito ergo sum."*

- **Cartland, Barbara:** A twentieth-century English author and media personality, considered one of the most prolific writers of all time, with a *Guinness World Records*-cited 723 novels to her name **[RL]**. When Lister decided to use a stasis leak to return to the past and be with Kochanski, despite knowing he would die in only three weeks' time, Rimmer accused him of sounding like a character from a Barbara Cartland novel **[T-SER2.4]**.

In an alternate universe, Jake Bullet exclaimed that the Club Nerd nightclub had "all the style of Barbara Cartland in hot pants" **[M-SMG2.1(c4)]**.

- **Carton, Iron Will, Sheriff:** The moniker by which Kryten was known in a dream-like illusion that his subconscious mind created to fight the Apocalypse virus. Carton was the drunken lawman of a frontier town terrorized by the Apocalypse Boys—a manifestation of the virus personified by four Wild West villains **[N-BCK]**.

- **cartoonivore:** A person who ate animals previously portrayed as cartoons, according to Lister, who refused to eat space weevils since they fell into that category **[T-SER7.6]**.

- ***Casablanca*:** An American film produced in 1942, starring Humphrey Bogart and Ingrid Bergman, about a man torn between his love for a woman and the virtue of helping her husband escape Nazi imprisonment **[RL]**. One remake of the film starred Myra Dinglebat and Peter Beardsley, which Lister considered the definitive version. A copy of a later remake arrived in a three-million-year-old post pod that rendezvoused with *Red Dwarf* after Holly altered course to head back to Earth **[T-SER2.2]**.

  Lister used the original version of the film, stored in *Red Dwarf*'s library, to train Kryten how to lie by showing him the importance of deception, using the movie's classic ending as an example. Later, Kryten took Camille, a shapeshifting Pleasure GELF, on a date to see the movie *Red Dwarf*'s cinema, where she proclaimed that *Casablanca* would be the couple's movie.

  Before the film ended, Camille's husband, Hector, arrived on *Red Dwarf*, asking her to come back to him. She initially refused, but Kryten, now able to lie—and mirroring *Casablanca*'s conclusion—insisted it would be best if she joined Hector and continued his research to cure their condition **[T-SER4.1]**.

- **Cashier Number 4:** A twenty-two-year-old woman who worked at a MegaMart with Lister when he was seventeen years old. Her husband, ten years her elder, worked in the fish department. The cashier and Lister frequently used the stock room to have sex, until her husband caught them and locked Lister in a crate, releasing him, buck-naked, in the middle of a production of *The Importance of Being Earnest*. This traumatizing event left Lister claustrophobic **[T-SER7.4]**.

  ***NOTE:** The cashier's name is unknown.*

- **Cassandra:** The tactical computer of the Space Corps vessel SSS *Silverberg*, designed to predict the future with an accuracy rating of one hundred percent **[T-SER8.4]**. Scientists used Cassandra's ability to predict whether experiments would be successful, drastically reducing research time **[G-SOR]**.

  Eventually, the Space Corps deemed Cassandra a danger to humanity and flew her autopiloted ship into deep space, where it crashed onto an ocean moon. Millions of years later, the crew of the nanobot-rebuilt *Red Dwarf* discovered the derelict, and the Canaries were dispatched to investigate. Foreseeing that Lister's arrival would mark her destruction, Cassandra told the team a series of predictions aimed to punish him. After realizing her plan, however, Lister decided not to kill her—though he accidentally did so anyway with a Rube Goldberg-like series of events starting with him placing a wad of chewed-up gum on a wall, and ending with a glass of water spilling onto her power cables **[T-SER8.4]**.

  ***NOTE:** In Greek mythology, Cassandra was a woman who received the gift of prophecy from Apollo, but was cursed never to be believed when predicting the future.*

- **castigate:** A password required to access personal profiles on the Diva-Droid website **[W-DIV]**.

  ***NOTE:** This password could be found when ordering a certain combination of items on the Crapola Inc. website.*

- **Castle Despondency:** A fortress built on a psi-moon configured according to Rimmer's psyche. Here, the Dark Forces of Rimmer's negative traits, including Misery, Self-Despair and Paranoia, held Self-Esteem hostage in order to lure his comrades—Courage, Charity and Honour—into a trap **[M-SMG2.7(c2)]**.

- **Castle Fritz, the:** A scoring strategy in zero-gee football, and a favorite of the London Jets. In this move, two teammates would pick up the ball, press it into a half-kimono and then

B-: Books
PRG: *Red Dwarf Programme Guide*
SUR: *Red Dwarf Space Corps Survival Manual*
PRM: *Primordial Soup*
SOS: *Son of Soup*
SCE: *Scenes from the Dwarf*
LOG: *Red Dwarf Log No. 1996*
RD8: *Red Dwarf VIII*
EVR: *The Log: A Dwarfer's Guide to Everything*

X-: Misc.
PRO: Promotional materials, videos, etc.
PST: Posters at DJ XVII (2013)
CAL: 2008 calendar
RNG: Cell phone ringtones
MOB: Mobisode ("Red Christmas")
CIN: *Children in Need* sketch
GEK: *Geek Week* intros by Kryten
TNG: "Tongue-Tied" video

XMS: Bill Pearson's Christmas special pitch script
XVD: Bill Pearson's Christmas special pitch video
OTH: Other *Red Dwarf* appearances

SUFFIX
DVD:
(d) – Deleted scene
(o) – Outtake
(b) – Bonus DVD material (other)
(e) – Extended version

SMEGAZINES:
(c) – Comic
(a) – Article

OTHER:
(s) – Early/unused script draft
(s1) – Alternate version of script

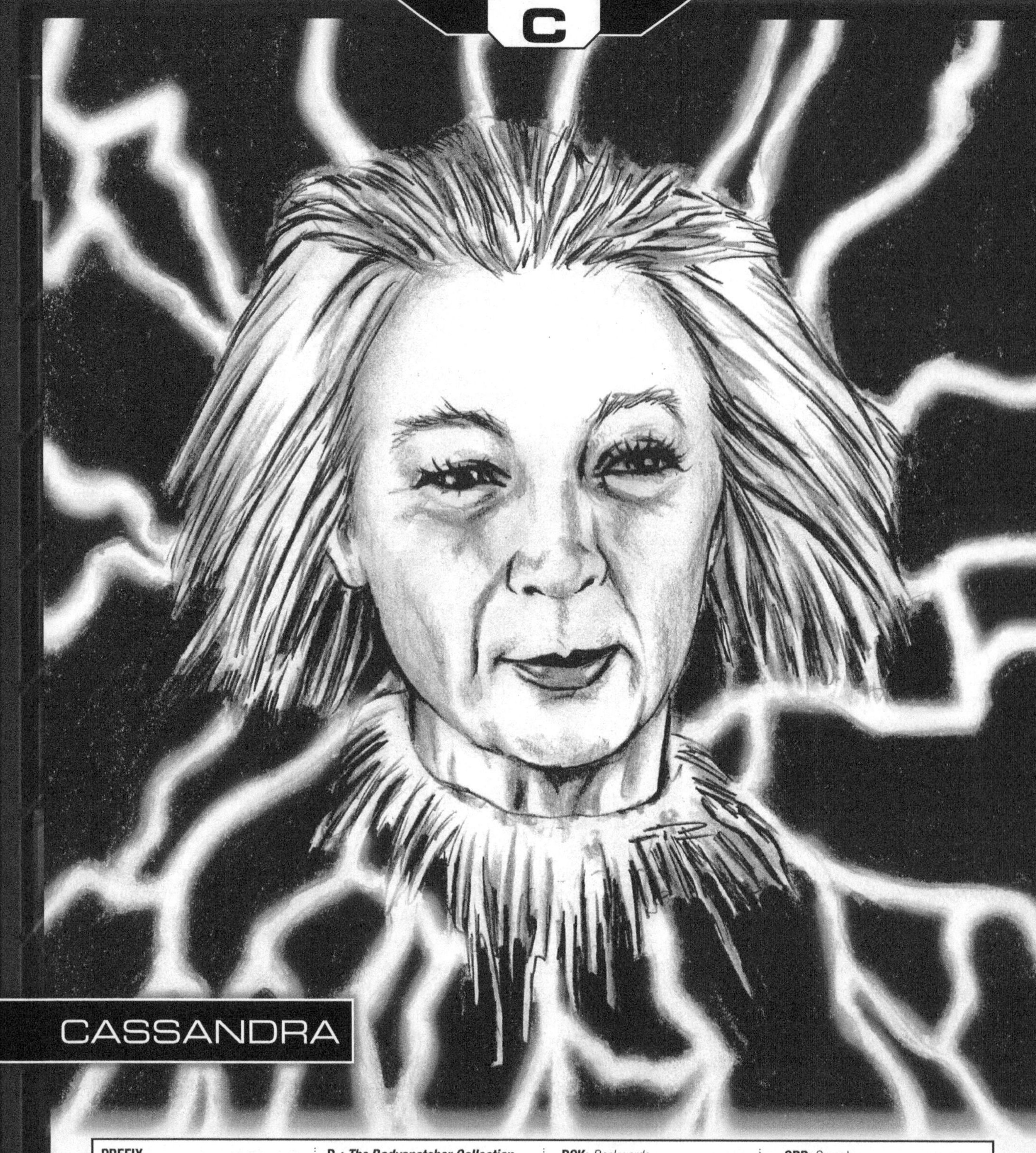

CASSANDRA

PREFIX
RL: Real life

T-: Television Episodes
- **SER:** Television series
- **IDW:** "Identity Within"
- **USA1:** Unaired U.S. pilot
- **USA2:** Unaired U.S. demo

R-: *The Bodysnatcher Collection*
- **SER:** Remastered episodes
- **BOD:** "Bodysnatcher"
- **DAD:** "Dad"
- **FTH:** "Lister's Father"
- **INF:** "Infinity Patrol"
- **END:** "The End" (original assembly)

N-: Novels
- **INF:** *Infinity Welcomes Careful Drivers*
- **BTL:** *Better Than Life*
- **LST:** *Last Human*
- **BCK:** *Backwards*
- **OMN:** *Red Dwarf Omnibus*

M-: Magazines
- **SMG:** *Smegazine*

W-: Websites
- **OFF:** Official website
- **NAN:** *Prelude to Nanarchy*
- **AND:** *Androids*
- **DIV:** Diva-Droid
- **DIB:** Duane Dibbley
- **CRP:** Crapola
- **GEN:** Geneticon
- **LSR:** Leisure World Intl.
- **JMC:** Jupiter Mining Corporation
- **AIT:** *A.I. Today*
- **HOL:** HoloPoint

G-: Roleplaying Game
- **RPG:** *Core Rulebook*
- **BIT:** *A.I. Screen Extra Bits* booklet
- **SOR:** *Series Sourcebook*
- **OTH:** Other RPG material

either fire it from the Fassbinder into the opposing team's goalmouth, or lead it over the Jubilee Line using magnetic induction. This could only be accomplished if the ball had not crossed the Jubilee Line during any quarter **[M-SMG1.8(a)]**.

- **castration therapy:** A medical procedure practiced at Caligari's Home for the Terminally Bewildered, a mental institution on a fascist, alternate-reality Earth. After being captured and charged with Sebastian Doyle's murder, Duane Dibbley was sentenced to that facility, where he partially underwent the procedure, during which he lapsed into a trauma-induced coma that lasted for three months **[M-SMG1.14(c1)]**.

- **Castrol GTX:** A brand of automotive lubricant **[RL]**. When Mercy Dash offered Jake Bullet a drink as he investigated Philby Frutch's murder, the cyborg requested Castrol GTX **[M-SMG1.14(c6)]**.

  In one episode of the television soap opera *Androids*, Brook collected his tears in a container of Castrol GTX after his wife, Kelly, admitted that Brooke Junior was not his son **[M-SMG1.8(c5)]**.

- **cat:** A member of the *Felis catus* subspecies on Earth. Cats were popular pets of humans throughout recorded history, and were stereotypically known for their blasé attitude, tendency to sleep throughout the day and meticulous preening habits **[RL]**. An ad for a cat magazine was featured on the back of a *Muscle Woman* magazine that Rimmer read while inhabiting Lister's body **[T-SER3.4]**.

  While serving on *Red Dwarf*, Lister smuggled aboard a pregnant cat named Frankenstein, for which Captain Hollister sentenced him to eighteen months in a stasis booth. *Red Dwarf* subsequently suffered a cataclysmic radiation explosion, sealing Frankenstein in the ship's hold and causing Holly to keep Lister in stasis for three million years. During this period of time, a species of sapient humanoid cats evolved from Frankenstein's initial litter **[T-SER1.1]**.

- **Cat:** The name that Lister gave to a creature from a species of Cat People (*Felis sapiens*) that evolved from Frankenstein, Lister's pregnant tabby, during the three million years he remained in stasis aboard *Red Dwarf*. Lister had smuggled Frankenstein aboard, and had been sentenced to eighteen months in a stasis pod as punishment.

  Red Dwarf subsequently suffered a cataclysmic radiation explosion, causing the ship's computer, Holly, to seal Frankenstein in the ship's hold and keep Lister in stasis for the duration. Safely shielded from the radiation, Frankenstein gave birth, and the resulting litter spawned the Cat civilization **[T-SER1.1]**.

  Eventually, Cat's species departed *Red Dwarf* in two arks, leaving behind the sick and elderly. Among those abandoned were a blind priest, a female cripple and a male idiot who consumed his own feet **[T-SER1.4]**. The latter was deeply religious, constantly reciting the Seven Cat Commandments **[N-INF]**.

  The cripple and the idiot bore a son (Cat) **[T-SER1.4]**, whom they, along with the priest, attempted to school in the ways of the Fundamentalist Church **[M-SMG2.2(a)]**. Initially, Cat attended kitty school for his education **[T-SER1.1]**, but he eventually relied only on himself **[T-SER7.7]**.

  Cat never understood the concept of having a name, as he could not comprehend the notion that he was not the center of the universe, and thus found it unfathomable that anyone would not automatically know who he was **[N-INF]**. After Lister emerged from stasis, he encountered this creature in a hallway and named him Cat **[T-SER1.1]**.

  An egocentric individual, Cat thought little of anyone but himself, often putting others at risk due to his vanity **[T-SER1.5]**. He possessed impeccable fashion sense, and owned a vast wardrobe **[T-SER1.2]**. His favorite color was salmon pink **[M-SMG1.1(a)]**.

  When Camille, a Pleasure GELF who changed her appearance to match a person's greatest desire, boarded *Red Dwarf*, Cat encountered an exact copy of himself, since in his mind, no one else could match his sexiness **[T-SER4.1]**. According to a medi-scan examination, Cat's internal organs were color-coordinated, and his heartbeat and pulse resembled a samba rhythm **[T-SER8.1]**.

  While trapped in a despair squid illusion, Cat imagined himself to be a dorky, graceless dweeb named Duane Dibbley. This persona troubled him so much that he, along with his crewmates, decided to commit suicide. Holly broke through the illusion, however, and saved their lives **[T-SER5.6]**. This persona manifested itself again during an emohawk attack, during which the polymorph removed his cool, causing Cat to become Dibbley **[T-SER6.4]**. It surfaced again when Cat slipped on a counter and banged his head, temporarily causing him to believe he was Duane once more **[M-SMG1.9(c1)]**.

Cat, like all male members of his species, possessed a barbed penis **[N-BCK]**. In addition, his body contained a poison sac that produced a toxin at a certain age due to a lack of sex, the antidote for which resided in the reproduction system of she-Cats. When Cat became ill from the effects of this poison, the crew sought out a mate to keep him from dying. Upon learning of a she-Cat named Ora Tanzil, who had been captured by Brefewino GELFs, Cat mustered uncharacteristic courage and attempted several times to rescue her. After fighting Zural, another member of his species who had betrayed Tanzil, Cat entered a romantic relationship with the she-Cat that lasted for a full twenty minutes in *Starbug*'s survival pod. He then dropped her off on the nearest planetoid **[T-IDW]**.

Because of his nasal acuteness and quick reflexes, Cat was often called upon to pilot smaller craft, such as *Starbug 1*, especially under dangerous circumstances **[T-SER6.1]**.

After *Red Dwarf* was rebuilt by Kryten's nanobots, Cat and his comrades were arrested and charged with using the crew's personal files for their own purposes. They were sentenced to the Tank, the ship's secret penal section on Floor 13, where they spent several months **[T-SER8.3]**. When a chameleonic microbe began dissolving the mining vessel, Captain Hollister ordered the ship abandoned, during which Cat and his friends escaped into a mirror universe **[T-SER8.8]**. The group returned to their own reality sometime later **[T-SER10.6]**.

At one point, Cat brought a baby female despair squid—an elation squid—aboard the ship as a future meal, unaware of the danger it would represent. The creature took up residence in one of *Red Dwarf*'s water tanks, nearly killing the crew in an ink-spawned illusion before being discovered and released **[T-SER9.3]**.

Years later, Cat became quantum-entangled with Kryten after the mechanoid performed experiments on *Trojan*'s quantum rod. This enabled the pair to speak in synchronicity, and allowed their combined emotions to manifest as several cases of profound coincidence **[T-SER10.4]**.

> ***NOTE:*** *The novels* Backwards *and* Last Human *indicated different fates for Cat. In* Backwards, *Cat and Lister were reverse-aged to fifteen years old and used Ace Rimmer's dimension ship to hop into an alternate universe, in which that reality's Lister and Cat had died in the virtual-reality video game* Better Than Life. *In* Last Human, *he was stranded with Lister, Kochanski and Rimmer's son, Michael McGruder, on a planet in another dimension.*

- **Cat:** An alternate-reality version of Cat, from a dimension in which Kochanski took the blame for Lister's crime of bringing the pregnant cat Frankenstein aboard *Red Dwarf*. This led to Kristine going into stasis and surviving the cadmium II disaster instead of Lister, who became a hologram rather than Rimmer **[T-SER7.3]**.

  This alternate Cat spoke with a deeper voice than his prime-universe counterpart **[T-SER7.3(e)]**. He was also more intellectual and less superficial, due to Kochanski's efforts to educate him after her release from stasis **[G-RPG]**.

- **Cat:** A version of Cat from a dimension in which the *Red Dwarf* and its crew were American **[T-USA1]**.

- **Cat:** A version of Cat from a separate dimension in which the *Red Dwarf* and its crew were American. This version was female and had nine lives, making her fearless and impulsive **[T-USA2]**.

- **Cat:** An alternate-reality version of Cat who was decapitated aboard a *Starbug* shuttle by his universe's Dave Lister. The prime-universe crew discovered his corpse after crossing universes while traversing the Omni-zone. The psychotic Lister had murdered Cat, as well as his other shipmates, to steal the coordinates of an ancient spaceship reputed to carry the genome of DNA (G.O.D.) **[N-LST]**.

- **Cat:** A decrepit duplicate of Cat, created during a triplicator accident that destroyed *Red Dwarf* but produced two copies: A "high" version containing all the best aspects of the ship and crew, and a "low" version manifesting the very worst. The "low" Cat was a feral, unsophisticated creature with large canine teeth who fed on raw meat. This version, along with his fellow "low" crewmembers, attacked the crews of the original and "high" *Red Dwarfs* after luring them to the "low" version of the mining ship.

  Wanting the "high" ship for their own, the "low" crew

kidnapped Lister, attached a spinal implant to his neck and used him to murder the "high" versions of himself and Rimmer, before sending him after his own crew. The plan failed, however, as the crew incapacitated Lister and used another triplicator, built with pieces from both ships, to re-form the original *Red Dwarf*—a process that dematerialized the "low" Cat **[T-SER5.5]**.

- **Cat:** A character in the total-immersion video game *Red Dwarf*, played in a fascist society on Earth in an alternate universe spawned from an illusion the prime *Red Dwarf* crew experienced after being attack by a despair squid. In this reality, an agent of the Ministry of Alteration, who had undertaken extreme nerdism surgery to become Duane Dibbley, played this character in the game for four years, until being released after the group scored a measly four percent **[M-SMG2.1(c4)]**. He was replaced by a more intelligent player, who scored much higher **[M-SMG2.4(c4)]**.

  After being released from the game, Dibbley, unable to regain his prior memories, was haunted by an apparition of his in-game character—a residual side-effect of the game **[M-SMG2.1(c4)]**.

- **"cat":** A word printed on a button in the cockpit of a probe ship. As the miniaturized *Red Dwarf* crew piloted such a vessel through Kryten's body while searching for an alien invasion fleet, Cat pressed this button, thinking it was for him. In actuality, the button released the ship's caterpillar tracks, allowing them to continue on through a murky section of Kryten's anatomy **[X-XMS]**.

- **Cat, Brother:** A duplicate of Cat created during a triplicator accident that destroyed *Red Dwarf* but produced two copies: A "high" version, containing all the best aspects of the ship and crew, and a "low" version, representing the very worst. Brother Cat was an enlightened version of the original, wearing robes and sandals, and displaying knowledge of poetry, art and metaphysics. He was killed by the "low" crew after boarding their ship in response to a distress call **[T-SER5.5]**.

- **Cat, Father ("Padre"):** A chaplain from Io Seminary who resided at the Space Corps Test Base on Mimas in one of Ace Rimmer's universes **[G-SOR]**. Father Cat had been created by Space Corps scientists using a hyper-evolution process similar to that used by the crew of the SSS *Esperanto* on an ocean planet. This experiment used a cat that Dave "Spanners" Lister had rescued on Titan **[W-OFF]**.

  Padre worked at an orphanage that sheltered a sick child named Tommy, by whose bed Ace sat every night, reading him bedtime stories. The chaplain bore a striking resemblance to Cat from the prime universe **[T-SER4.5]**.

  > ***NOTE:*** Red Dwarf—The Roleplaying Game*'s* Series Sourcebook *referred to this character as "Father Felix," paying homage to the cartoon* Felix the Cat. *In the script to episode 4.5 ("Dimension Jump"), published in* Primordial Soup, *he was simply called "Chaplain."*

- **Cat, Kit:** A persona that Black Island Film Studios caretaker Leo Davis imagined for Kit, a female dancer hired to appear in a Tabby Ranks music video. In Leo's daydream, Kit was a member of Felis sapiens, the Cat species featured on his favorite television program, *Red Dwarf* **[M-SMG2.5(a)]**.

- **Cat, Professor:** The mirror-universe analog of Cat, who ran the Science Department on that reality's *Red Dwarf*. When the prime universe's Rimmer entered the mirror universe seeking an antidote to a chameleonic microbe ravishing the mining vessel, he visited the ship's Science Department, where the professor gave him the formula **[T-SER8.8]**.

  > ***NOTE:*** Red Dwarf—The Roleplaying Game*'s* Series Sourcebook *and a Futura Platinum trading card both confirmed that his name was still Cat in the mirror universe.*

- **catangu nut:** A type of edible seed consumed by GELF tribes in an alternate universe, customarily roasted to bless GELF weddings. Btrrnfjhyjhnehgewydn, the leader of the Kinitawowi tribe, and a fellow elder fried catangu nuts to celebrate the marriage of the chief's daughter, Khakhakhakkhhakhakkkhakkkkkh, to Lister **[N-LST]**.

- **Cat Ark:** A spacefaring vessel that the Cat People inhabiting *Red Dwarf* built in order to find the Holy Land of Fuchal. After millennia of Holy Wars between the population's religious factions, the two sides called a truce and built dual arks with the intention of locating the mythical Promised Land.

The first ark carried those who believed food temple hats should be blue. Mistaking Lister's ancient laundry list for a star chart, they flew straight into an asteroid, destroying the ship and killing all aboard. Those who believed the hats should be red witnessed this catastrophe and left on the second ark on a different heading, believing themselves to be on the righteous path to Fuchal **[T-SER1.4]**.

Eventually, this ark crashed onto an S-3 planet once occupied by a human colony. Believing they had found Fuchal, the surviving Cats populated the ruins, finding several personality discs that they activated, mistaking them for servants of their god, Cloister. The recorded personalities manipulated the Cats for their own purposes, attempting to imbue their ethics into the newcomers. This led to several more factions of Cat People, each following the teachings of its respective "saint."

One group, following the personality of a Space Corps commander named Suzdal, became the largest, most dangerous faction, honing their warrior skills to go back in time and fight for the Cat species alongside Cloister. This group's violent, martial ways caused a schism in the populace, creating an underground movement determined to build another starship and leave in search of the true Promised Land **[G-RPG]**.

> ***NOTE:** In the novel* Infinity Welcomes Careful Drivers*, arks were not used; instead, the cats used shuttles from* Red Dwarf*'s docking bays.*

- **Cat Bible, The:** *See* Holy Book, The

- **Catch-44:** A paradoxical situation that, according to Holly, was twice as bad as a Catch-22 **[T-SER8.4(d)]**.

> ***NOTE:** In* Catch-22*, a satirical wartime novel by Joseph Heller, the term "Catch-22" described the U.S. military's self-contradictory circular logic preventing a soldier from avoiding combat missions. To be grounded from flight, one had to be deemed crazy, but to recive such a reprieve, one had to ask to be grounded, which the Air Force saw as proof that one was rational—and, thus, competent to fly.*

- ***Cat Dictionary*:** A book written in Cat's native language that was "read" not by reading words, but by smelling different odors on the pages. Cat gave the book to Lister shortly after they first met **[T-SER1.4]**.

- **caterpillar tracks:** Retractable tank treads built into a *Starbug* shuttlecraft that allowed the ship to travel on land over a variety of terrain. While searching for Rimmer on a psi-moon, the *Red Dwarf* crew used *Starbug 2*'s caterpillar tracks to traverse the rough, ever-changing topography **[T-SER5.3]**. Canary probe ships were also equipped with caterpillar tracks, which could be deployed by pushing a button marked "cat" **[X-XMS]**.

- **Catherine the Great, Empress:** A renowned eighteenth-century Russian leader during the country's expansionary "Golden Age," born Yekaterina Alexeevna **[RL]**. Using a time drive coupled with a faster-than-light drive installed aboard *Starbug 1*, the crew traveled through space-time, becoming epicures by sampling the best in the universe and socializing with historic figures, such as Catherine the Great **[T-SER6.6(d)]**.

  After Kryten showed Rimmer how to create new artificial-reality (AR) characters, the hologram overloaded the AR computer's preferences chip by having a marathon of 472 sexual encounters with Catherine **[B-LOG]**.

- **catheter:** A tubing system attached to players hooked into a total-immersion video game suite for extended lengths of time, used to dispose of the body's waste material. If a user mixed this tube up with his or her food bag, the result was extremely unpleasant **[T-SER5.6]**.

- **Catman:** A genetically engineered superhero in the universe known as Alternative 2X13/L. Wielding an atomic-powered hairdryer, Catman—that reality's version of Cat—had a sidekick named Robbie (Kryten), and was a member of the Liberty League, tasked with protecting the city of Smegopolis. In 2315, Catman and Robbie attempted to stop a robbery at the First National Bank, perpetrated by their long-time nemeses, the Conspirator and the Penguin. Catman was thwarted, however, when the Conspirator shot a red paintball at him, ruining his costume **[M-SMG2.1(c3)]**.

> ***NOTE:** Catman was based loosely on the DC Comics superhero Batman.*

- **Cat People:** *See Felis sapiens*

- **Cat Priest:** A blind clergyman among the Cat People inhabiting *Red Dwarf*. A Cloisterist, he believed the name of the Holy Father was Cloister. The priest aided one of his followers, a simpleton, in raising his son (whom Lister would eventually call Cat) in the ways of the church, with little success **[M-SMG2.1(a)]**.

  Eventually, the Cat People left *Red Dwarf* on a mission to find the Holy Land of Fuchal, leaving behind the sick and elderly, including the priest and Cat's family. After Cat's parents passed away, he and the priest survived alone for several years. The priest died moments after meeting Cloister—who, in actuality, was Dave Lister **[T-SER1.4]**.

- **Cat Wars, The:** A conflict waged between opposing factions of the Cat People inhabiting *Red Dwarf* **[T-IDW]**. Also known as the Holy Wars, the clash arose between those who believed Fuscal's sacred food temple hats should be blue and those who thought they should be red **[T-SER1.4]**. The conflict lasted for two thousand years **[M-SMG2.1(c1)]**.

  ***NOTE:** The novel* Infinity Welcomes Careful Drivers *stated that the Holy Wars were fought between opposing sides who thought the father of Catkind was named either Cloister or Clister. The comics published in the* Smegazines *continued this theme.*

- **caviar niblet:** A finger food-type delicacy made from fish eggs. Legion provided the *Red Dwarf* crew with caviar niblets for breakfast after their first night in captivity aboard his station **[T-SER6.2]**.

- **caviar vindaloo:** An Indian curry dish made with a certain type of fish eggs, considered a delicacy among the wealthy. After being offered anything his heart desired at a posh restaurant in the total-immersion video game *Better Than Life*, Lister ordered caviar vindaloo **[T-SER2.2]**.

- **CB3:** *See* Cargo Bay 3

- **CCD 419.2:** The type of visual system used in the original Talkie Toaster model **[W-CRP]**.

- **CCD 517.3:** The type of visual system used in the second-generation Talkie Toaster model **[T-SER4.4]**.

- **C Deck:** A level aboard *Starbug 1* that contained the shuttle's escape pod **[N-LST]**. When Arnold Rimmer learned that Ace Rimmer was dying, he commented that a tea chest on C deck would make a great coffin for him **[T-SER7.2(d)]**.

- **C Deck:** A level aboard *Red Dwarf* **[T-SER8.1]** that included, among other things, a bacon slicer **[M-SMG1.13(c2)]**. When Kryten's nanobots rebuilt *Red Dwarf*, they used the vessel's original design specifications, before cutbacks were made by the JMC; this resulted in a karaoke bar being added on C Deck **[T-SER8.1]**.

- **ceiling receiver:** A position on zero-gee football teams **[N-INF]**.

- ***Celebrity Chainsaw Ice-Sculpting Challenge*:** A television show popular circa the twenty-second century **[G-RPG]**.

- **Cell 41:** A prison cell in which Rimmer, while trapped in an addictive version of *Better Than Life*, imagined that he and three other individuals—Ernest, Jimmy and Trixie—were incarcerated as soundwaves at a soundproof penitentiary. Cell 41 was located in E Wing. Rimmer and Jimmy escaped the cell by pulling a "sick inmate" ruse, despite none of them possessing physical bodies **[N-BTL]**.

- ***Centauri*, SS:** A derelict ship that the *Starbug 1* crew looted. A long-range cruiser with a total crew capacity of twelve, it was fitted with shields and a laser cannon **[G-RPG]**, as well as a crystalline turbine drive. Among the vessel's cargo were four live lobsters in stasis and a copy of the artificial-reality program *Jane Austen World*.

  When Kryten blew several spare heads after Lister requested ketchup for his lobster, the crew returned to the *Centauri* to locate new spares. The ship was now occupied by a rogue simulant, whom they tried to trick into giving them the parts, by dressing as GELFs and bartering. The simulant, who had a GELF partner, saw through the disguises and distracted the crew while the real GELF looted *Starbug,* stealing Kryten's body in the process.

  After a confrontation with the simulant, the crew, joined by another mechanoid named Able, attempted to flee the pursuing ship, but were overtaken. Feeling guilty for having exposed

Starbug 1 to the simulant vessel, Able ejected from the shuttle in a pod and used Kryten's negadrive attached to the pod's thrusters to envelope the *Centauri* in negative emotions, leading the simulant to destroy himself and his ship **[T-SER7.6]**.

- **Central:** A roadway located in the terraformed section of Mimas, leading toward the Mimas docks. Lister used this road often while working as a taxi hopper on the Saturnian moon **[N-INF]**.

- **central cargo pods:** A series of external containers in the underbelly of *Red Dwarf*, used for storing and transporting materials. The central cargo pods were located between the two meteor bays **[R-BOD(b)]**.

  ***NOTE:** These pods, featured in concept art included in the* The Bodysnatcher Collection*'s bonus extras, did not appear on the TV series, as front and rear cargo pods were used instead.*

- **Central Line North:** A railway line aboard *Red Dwarf* that hundreds of space monkeys used to overrun the mining vessel after Lister hatched a packet of the mutated creatures **[M-SMG1.13(c2)]**.

- **Central Mall Branch:** A branch of *Red Dwarf*'s Northern Line—a transport system used to traverse the mining vessel. Station West 17/XC was located on this branch, which led to one of the ship's shopping areas **[M-SMG1.6(c2)]**.

- **Cerise:** An alert condition indicating severe damage to a 4000 Series mechanoid. After an accident on a psi-moon left Kryten injured and stranded, his CPU assessed the situation and periodically updated his head-up display. His condition changed to Cerise when Lister finished cutting the mechanoid in two to dislodge him from the wreckage **[T-SER5.3]**.

- **cesiumfrancolithicmyxialobidiumrixydexydixidoxidroxhide:** A compound that was completely different than cesiumfrancolithicmyxialobidiumrixydixydoxidexidroxhide, as Lister once learned in chemistry class. Cat was also familiar with this compound. Rimmer, however, was not **[T-SER8.8(d)]**.

  ***NOTE:** The episode's DVD captions spelled the compound's name as "sesiumfrankalithicmixyalibidiumrixidexidixidoxidroxide."*

- **cesiumfrancolithicmyxialobidiumrixydixydoxidexidroxhide:** The chemical name of the antidote for a chameleonic microbe that infected the nanobot-rebuilt *Red Dwarf*. Rimmer, masquerading as the captain aboard a mirror-universe *Red Dwarf*, obtained the name of the compound from that reality's Professor Cat **[T-SER8.8]**. The compound was commonly used in school chemistry classes **[T-SER8.8(d)]**.

  ***NOTE:** The episode's DVD captions spelled this compound's name as "sessyum-frankilithic-mixi-alibilium-rixi-dixi-doxy-dexy-droxide," while the deleted scene's captions used the spelling "sesiumfrankalithicmixyalibidiumrixidixidoxidexidroxide."*

- **CGI:** A government agency in a fascist society that the *Red Dwarf* crew imagined while trapped a despair squid hallucination. In the illusion, the crew had different identities, with Lister taking on the role of Voter Colonel Sebastian Doyle, section chief of CGI and head of the Ministry of Alteration **[T-SER5.6]**.

- **Chakos XII:** A planet on which Kryten once used maggots to clean Lister's wound. The procedure was not entirely successful, due to the difficulty Kryten faced in putting Germolene (an antiseptic product) onto the heads of thousands of maggots **[B-SUR]**.

- **Chamber of Horrors:** An attraction on Waxworld, located on the waxdroid park's eastern perimeter, and featuring a full range of twentieth-century foods **[T-SER4.6(d)]**.

- **"Chameleonic Life Forms? No, Thanks":** A T-shirt slogan that Rimmer proposed after a polymorph drained his anger, which he claimed was a "tough" way to deal with the creature. He then carried a sign bearing this phrase while searching for the polymorph **[T-SER3.3]**.

  ***NOTE:** In the episode's original script draft, the sign read "Mutant—We Love You."*

- **chameleonic microbe:** *See* Zogothoniumeliumoxiixiexiphulmifhidikalidrihide

- **Champion the Wonder Horse:** The titular equine character of the American radio and television series *The Adventures of Champion* **[RL]**. Rimmer once compared Lister's reading habits to those of Champion, claiming they had both read the same number of books: zero **[T-SER2.1]**.

NOTE: The television series' title was changed to Champion the Wonder Horse *during its U.K. broadcast. The book* Red Dwarf Omnibus *changed Champion's name to Woolfie Sprogg, The Plasticine Dog.*

- **Champs Elysées:** A street in Paris, France, considered one of the world's most expensive strips of real estate **[RL]**. While trapped in an addictive version of *Better Than Life*, Rimmer imagined that he had returned to Earth, made millions of dollarpounds from commercial endorsements and built several buildings across the world, including the Rimmer Building (Paris), located on Champs Elysées **[N-INF]**.

- **Channel 2:** A television station that Cat imagined watching while trapped in an addictive version of *Better Than Life*. One of its programs was a phone-in advice show, on which Cats with sexual problems asked for help. Rather than offer advice, however, a panel would snicker and laugh at each caller **[N-BTL]**.

- **Channel 27:** *See* Groovy Channel 27

- **Channel 72:** A television channel that aired episodes of *Tales of the Unexpected* **[T-SER7.6]**.

- **Chanski:** A woman who, according to the Cat Bible, lived in fellowship with Cloister the Stupid. Chapter 6 of the Holy Book stated that Cloister decided to destroy the world, and commanded Chanski to build a ship so that they and Frankenstein the cat could fly among the stars **[M-SMG2.4(a)]**.

  NOTE: Chanski was the Cat People's misrepresentation of Kristine Kochanski.

- **Chantelle:** The lab assistant of Colonel Mike O'Hagan's uncle Max. She and Max pioneered advances in preservative and regenerative drugs that hindered death, eventually leading to the development of the emergency death pack **[B-SUR]**.

- **Chaplain:** *See* Cat, Father ("Padre")

- **charades:** A guessing game played by silently acting out words or phrases **[RL]**. Holly suggested a game of charades using only noses while *Starbug 1* was trapped in a shrinking air vent and about to be crushed aboard an enlarged *Red Dwarf* **[T-SER8.1]**. Years later, Cat insisted on using charades as a means of alerting the crew that a post pod had arrived on *Red Dwarf* **[T-SER10.5]**.

- **charisma:** *See Ignotus venustas*

- **Charity:** An aspect of Rimmer's personality made flesh on a psi-moon configured according to his psyche. After Arnold's shipmates rescued him from the moon, Charity and his comrades—Courage, Honour and Self-Esteem—were left behind to battle Rimmer's negative traits, including Misery, Self Despair and Paranoia. The Dark Forces abducted Self-Esteem and displayed him in Castle Despondency to lure the others into a trap, then unleashed a secret weapon: the image of Rimmer's mother **[M-SMG2.7(c2)]**.

- **Charles, Craig:** A British actor whom the *Red Dwarf* crew imagined meeting while trapped in an elation squid hallucination in which they were merely characters on the television comedy *Red Dwarf*. In the illusion, Charles was the show's star. After learning of their demise in the impending final episode, the crew set out to find their creator and plead for additional life.

  During their journey, they met a man named Swallow, who had worked on the show and knew how to contact Craig Charles, whom he claimed would know where to find the show's creator. The travelers visited the set of the television program *Coronation Street*, in which Charles currently starred as taxicab driver Lloyd Mullaney.

  Upon seeing himself as a "real-life" Lister, Charles assumed he was having a drug flashback, dismissed the crew as figments of his imagination and decided to go back to the Priory. He still helped the crew, however, and confirmed that there was one episode left, the script of which would arrive in a few days, and gave them the creator's address. Upon leaving the set, Lister called the actor a "wreck" **[T-SER9.3]**.

  NOTE: The mention of flashbacks and the Priory referenced Craig Charles' real-life bout with drug abuse and his subsequent stay at the rehabilitation facility.

B-: Books
PRG: *Red Dwarf Programme Guide*
SUR: *Red Dwarf Space Corps Survival Manual*
PRM: *Primordial Soup*
SOS: *Son of Soup*
SCE: *Scenes from the Dwarf*
LOG: *Red Dwarf Log No. 1996*
RD8: *Red Dwarf VIII*
EVR: *The Log: A Dwarfer's Guide to Everything*

X-: Misc.
PRO: Promotional materials, videos, etc.
PST: Posters at DJ XVII (2013)
CAL: 2008 calendar
RNG: Cell phone ringtones
MOB: Mobisode ("Red Christmas")
CIN: *Children in Need* sketch
GEK: *Geek Week* intros by Kryten
TNG: "Tongue-Tied" video

XMS: Bill Pearson's Christmas special pitch script
XVD: Bill Pearson's Christmas special pitch video
OTH: Other *Red Dwarf* appearances

SUFFIX
DVD:
(d) – Deleted scene
(o) – Outtake
(b) – Bonus DVD material (other)
(e) – Extended version

SMEGAZINES:
(c) – Comic
(a) – Article

OTHER:
(s) – Early/unused script draft
(s1) – Alternate version of script

- ***Charles Manson, the Early Years*:** A hypothetical movie title that Kryten cited while discussing Rimmer's childhood. When Arnold claimed to have literally fought for his meals as a child, Kryten asked if he was mistakenly remembering scenes from *Charles Manson, the Early Years* **[T-SER6.4(d)]**.

- **Charlie:** One of Jake Bullet's fellow police officers on an alternate Earth, who often reviewed security footage from crime scenes. While investigating Doctor Sandra Halley's murder, Bullet turned to Charlie for the video of her final night at Brainfade **[M-SMG2.8(c1)]**.

- ***Charlie Zero Potato*:** A book written by Colonel Mike O'Hagan, a space marine and the author of the *Space Corps Survival Manual* **[B-SUR]**.

- **Charm:** An aspect of Rimmer's personality that a psi-moon detected as having died, prompting the planetoid to construct a physical metaphor in its memory, in the shape of a tombstone. This tombstone was considerably smaller than other stones, and bore only the single word "Charm" engraved on it **[T-SER5.3]**.

- **Chasm of Hopelessness:** An environment on a psi-moon configured according to Rimmer's psyche. When Arnold and Kryten landed on the planetoid, it used the hologram's mind as a template, altering its own landscape to represent various aspects of his neurosis, and creating such settings as the Chasm of Hopelessness **[T-SER5.3]**.

- **chastitycheat:** A codeword used as a cheat in a medieval-themed artificial-reality simulation, which unlocked the chastity belt worn by the Queen of Camelot. Lister used this cheat when the king boasted that his ploy to bed the queen would fail **[T-SER7.2]**.

- **cheekiness:** A rogue emotion purged from Kryten's hard drive by the Data Doctor, a program for restoring a mechanoid's personality to factory settings, when Captain Hollister subjected Kryten to a psychotropic simulation **[T-SER8.2]**.

- **Cheese:** A nickname that the mistress of Admiral Peter Tranter, commander of the Space Corps R&D Program in one of Ace Rimmer's universes, called him behind his back **[N-BCK]**.

- **Cheesiz:** A rogue simulant scavenger who, along with a group of other simulants, scoured the galaxy looking for genuine Earth antiques and emotions garnered from polymorphs to sell to mechanicals. Cheesiz and his group came across Garbage World (Earth) after it had been ripped from its orbit, and searched the surface for artifacts and polymorphs **[M-SMG2.9(c12)]**.

- **Chef's Exam:** A test given to members of the Space Corps who wished to become a chef. Lister threatened to pass this exam—despite having no great desire to cook—in order to become promoted and thus outrank Rimmer (who mistakenly assumed he was trying to pass the Engineer's Exam) **[T-SER1.3]**. Though he claimed to have passed the test, Lister actually failed, maintaining the status quo aboard ship **[T-SER1.4]**.

- **Chemical Vault:** A room aboard *Red Dwarf* in which radioactive materials and hazardous waste were stored, including Rimmer's Old Spice aftershave **[M-SMG1.5(a)]**.

- **Chen:** A crewmember aboard *Red Dwarf*, and one of Lister's best friends before the cadmium II disaster killed the crew **[T-SER1.1]**. Chen worked in the ship's kitchen **[T-SER8.1]**. Rimmer once chastised him for serving cold gazpacho soup during an officer's dinner, unaware it was the correct way to prepare the dish **[T-SER2.1(s)]**.

  Chen enlisted in the Space Corps in error, believing the recruitment center to be his history class, and his enlistment papers his final exam. He also signed up his friend Selby for service—who, ironically, had intended to apply himself, but mistook Chen's history class for the Space Corps recruitment center **[G-BIT]**.

  Three million years after the cadmium II accident, Chen was resurrected, along with the rest of the ship's complement, when nanobots rebuilt the mining ship **[T-SER8.1]**. He volunteered for the ship's fire safety crew **[G-BIT]**, and was one of three crewmembers who responded to the fire that resulted when Lister crashed *Starbug 1* in Landing Bay 6 **[T-SER8.1]**.

- **Chen:** A disciple of Cloister the Stupid, along with Petson and Selby, according to the Cat Bible. In chapters six and seven of the Holy Book, the disciples were said to have shared a meal with Cloister, during which they drank lager and were told of their impending demise **[M-SMG2.4(a)]**.

PREFIX
RL: Real life

T-: Television Episodes
- **SER:** Television series
- **IDW:** "Identity Within"
- **USA1:** Unaired U.S. pilot
- **USA2:** Unaired U.S. demo

R-: *The Bodysnatcher Collection*
- **SER:** Remastered episodes
- **BOD:** "Bodysnatcher"
- **DAD:** "Dad"
- **FTH:** "Lister's Father"
- **INF:** "Infinity Patrol"
- **END:** "The End" (original assembly)

N-: Novels
- **INF:** *Infinity Welcomes Careful Drivers*
- **BTL:** *Better Than Life*
- **LST:** *Last Human*
- **BCK:** *Backwards*
- **OMN:** *Red Dwarf Omnibus*

M-: Magazines
- **SMG:** *Smegazine*

W-: Websites
- **OFF:** Official website
- **NAN:** *Prelude to Nanarchy*
- **AND:** *Androids*
- **DIV:** Diva-Droid
- **DIB:** Duane Dibbley
- **CRP:** Crapola
- **GEN:** Geneticon
- **LSR:** Leisure World Intl.
- **JMC:** Jupiter Mining Corporation
- **AIT:** *A.I. Today*
- **HOL:** HoloPoint

G-: Roleplaying Game
- **RPG:** *Core Rulebook*
- **BIT:** *A.I. Screen Extra Bits* booklet
- **SOR:** *Series Sourcebook*
- **OTH:** Other RPG material

- **chess:** A strategic two-player board game consisting of sixteen pieces per player, played on a checkered board **[RL]**. Holly once jumped at the chance to play postal chess with Gordon, the artificial intelligence aboard the *Scott Fitzgerald*, who supposedly had an IQ of eight thousand **[T-SER2.2]**.

  Chess was the game of choice of Queeg, *Red Dwarf*'s supposed "backup computer," whom Holly pretended to challenge for control of the ship. Queeg emerged victorious, and Holly was purportedly erased. The entire incident was a farce, however, as Queeg was merely an alter ego Holly created to punish the crew for taking advantage of him **[T-SER2.5]**.

  Quarantine Room 152, located in an off-limits section of *Red Dwarf*, contained a chess game with thirty-one missing pieces (of the usual thirty-two) **[T-SER5.4]**.

  While the crew were trapped in an addictive version of *Better Than Life,* Holly, once again alone on *Red Dwarf*, repaired Talkie Toaster to keep him company. After annoying each other, the two agreed not to discuss toast or the existence of Silicon Heaven, resorting only to games of chess for entertainment. Even this irritated Holly, however, when he lost 793 consecutive games to the kitchen appliance **[N-BTL]**.

- **chest monitor:** A viewscreen located in the abdominal region of 4000 Series mechanoids, capable of displaying video fed in from a mechanoid's memory **[T-SER7.1]** or from a ship's AI computer **[T-SER3.2]**.

- **"Chew on This":** A slogan on the front of Rimmer's favorite pair of underwear. It was covered in red and green alligators, with the back reading "Snappy Lover." Kryten burned a hole through this pair while ironing Rimmer's undergarments—which the hologram made him do at least once a fortnight, despite not physically wearing clothes **[M-SMG1.2(a)]**.

- **Chicata, Juanita ("The Brazilian Bombshell"):** A nineteen-year-old supermodel and actor whom Rimmer imagined marrying after returning to Earth, while trapped in an addictive version of *Better Than Life*. She had eyes the color of fire, panther-black hair and "dangerous" lips. Chicata's perfect breasts were insured for ten million dollarpounds apiece—much to the dismay of Rimmer, whom she never allowed to touch them.

  The Brazilian model was prone to violent temper tantrums and had several affairs during her two-year marriage to Arnold. She once threw a Louis XIV grand piano out of a window because their pool attendant, Hugo, refused to make love to her anymore for fear that Rimmer would fire him **[N-INF]**.

  Eventually, the two divorced, with Rimmer settling out of court due to the embarrassment of having her lovers paraded through the courtroom as evidence. She later became engaged to Rimmer's brother Frank, after having a personality transplant that made her even more desirable to Arnold. It was only after the crew determined that they were in the game that Rimmer realized Chicata was based on his sister-in-law, Janine, to whom he had always been attracted **[N-BTL]**.

- **chickantula:** A cross between a chicken and a tarantula, resulting from genetic engineering experiments on Earth. Such creatures were eventually sent off-world to seed unpopulated planets **[B-SUR]**.

- **chicken:** A domesticated fowl from the subspecies *Gallus gallus domesticus,* primarily bred for their meat and eggs **[RL]**. While investigating a derelict spaceship, Cat accidentally activated a machine that transmogrified the DNA of living organisms, transforming Lister into a chicken. Attempting to reverse the effects, Kryten again activated the device, turning Lister into a hamster, before returning him to his original state. When asked about the experience, Lister decided it was better to be a hamster than a chicken, due to the size difference between an egg and a chicken's bum **[T-SER4.2]**.

- **chicken chasseur:** A dish made with chicken, red wine or sherry, mushrooms, shallots, and flour **[RL]**. Bored with using plastic cutlery, Lister procured several items from *Red Dwarf*'s Medical Unit and used them to prepare and serve dinner in the Officers Quarters. These items included scalpels, flasks, kidney bowls, an embryo refrigeration unit, colonoscopy bags and an artificial insemination syringe for cattle. Although Lister had cleaned and sterilized the equipment, Cat refused to stay for dinner, calling the meal "an autopsy" and wondering if the next course would be chicken chasseur in a stool bucket **[T-SER3.3]**.

- **chicken Marengo:** A French dish consisting of chicken sautéed in oil, garlic and tomato, garnished with fried eggs and crayfish

[RL]. This was *Red Dwarf*'s special of the day, according to the refectory's food dispenser, when Lister passed out from mutated pneumonia. Instead of helping Lister, Cat visited the refectory, ordered the meal and ignored Rimmer's frantic attempts to seek his assistance **[T-SER1.5]**.

- **chicken soup**: A menu item available from service dispensers aboard *Red Dwarf* **[T-SER1.1]**.

- **Chicken Soup Dispenser 14B:** A food dispenser aboard *Red Dwarf* that became clogged **[G-RPG]**.

  NOTE: *The dispenser's number was a nod to the tool Rimmer used to clean the machine's nozzle in episode 1.1 ("The End").*

- ***Chicken Soup Machine Operative and a Gentleman, A***: A hypothetical movie title. Desiring to join the holoship *Enlightenment*, Rimmer lamented the mundane nature of his job, noting that no such movie would ever be made since chicken soup machine operatives were losers **[T-SER5.1(d)]**.

- **chicken vindaloo:** A curried Indian dish made with chicken, tomatoes, onions and spices **[RL]**. Before learning of his role in the Cat People's religious history, Lister requested this menu item for breakfast, as well as a beer milkshake, from the food dispenser in *Red Dwarf*'s Drive Room **[T-SER1.3]**.

- **Chief:** A nickname that Rimmer asked Lister to call him (instead of "Rimmer") as they and Cat embarked on a rescue mission to the *Nova 5*, where they believed three female crewmembers awaited **[N-INF]**.

- **chili sauce:** A condiment made with tomatoes, vinegar, green peppers, onions and assorted spices **[RL]**. Bored with using plastic cutlery, Lister procured several items from *Red Dwarf*'s Medical Unit and used them to prepare and serve dinner in the Officers Quarters, including a colostomy bag, which he used to store chili sauce in the Embryo Refrigeration Unit **[T-SER3.3]**.

- **chilled vindaloo sauce:** A beverage Lister enjoyed in the early morning. After two hundred years in deep sleep aboard *Starbug 1*, Lister awoke to find Kryten preparing his breakfast, which included chilled vindaloo sauce **[T-SER6.1]**.

- **chilli powder:** A seasoning made from ground-up chili peppers **[RL]**. Lister found a can of chilli powder and used the bulk of it in his shami kebab diablo recipe **[T-SER3.3]**.

  NOTE: *The word is spelled "chili" in American English, but "chilli" in British English, which is how it appeared onscreen.*

- **chimpanzebra:** A genetically engineered creature—a mix between a chimpanzee and a zebra—developed by inebriated scientists **[B-EVR]**.

- **chimpanzee:** A class of two hominid simian species (common chimpanzee and bonobo) in the family Hominidae, along with gorillas, humans and orangutans **[RL]**. After awakening with a cast on his leg, Cat stormed into the quarters shared by Lister and Rimmer, asking which of the "chimpanzees" had injured him **[T-SER2.3]**.

- **Chinese whispers:** A game played within a group of people in which one person whispers a message to another, who in turn whispers a slight variation to the next, and so on, until the last person recites the message, which is often radically different from the original. In the United States, this game typically went by the more politically correct name "telephone" **[RL]**.

  Kryten once played a game of Chinese whispers with several dispenser machines aboard *Red Dwarf*. The starting phrase was "I slit the sheet. The sheet I slit. On the slit sheet, I sit." Rimmer inadvertently inspired another round when questioning the term's offensiveness, as Kryten asked Dispenser 16, "Are Chinese whispers racist?" which, after several iterations, became "Do Siamese sisters get whiskers in stasis?" **[T-SER10.2]**.

- **Chinese worry balls:** A meditative device consisting of two metallic balls rotated within one's hands to relieve stress and improve manual dexterity **[RL]**. Kryten gave Rimmer a set of Chinese worry balls as part of a relaxation program after the hologram was diagnosed with severe stress during a physical examination. After being locked in a prison on Rimmerworld for 557 years, he still possessed the worry balls—which, by this time, had been worn down to tiny spheres **[T-SER6.5]**.

PREFIX
RL: Real life

T-: Television Episodes
SER: Television series
IDW: "Identity Within"
USA1: Unaired U.S. pilot
USA2: Unaired U.S. demo

R-: *The Bodysnatcher Collection*
SER: Remastered episodes
BOD: "Bodysnatcher"
DAD: "Dad"
FTH: "Lister's Father"
INF: "Infinity Patrol"
END: "The End" (original assembly)

N-: Novels
INF: *Infinity Welcomes Careful Drivers*
BTL: *Better Than Life*
LST: *Last Human*
BCK: *Backwards*
OMN: *Red Dwarf Omnibus*

M-: Magazines
SMG: *Smegazine*

W-: Websites
OFF: Official website
NAN: *Prelude to Nanarchy*
AND: *Androids*
DIV: Diva-Droid
DIB: Duane Dibbley

CRP: Crapola
GEN: Geneticon
LSR: Leisure World Intl.
JMC: Jupiter Mining Corporation
AIT: *A.I. Today*
HOL: HoloPoint

G-: Roleplaying Game
RPG: *Core Rulebook*
BIT: *A.I. Screen Extra Bits* booklet
SOR: *Series Sourcebook*
OTH: Other RPG material

- **Chi'Panastee ("Chi"):** One of thousands of agonoids who escaped decommissioning and fled into deep space. His name was a bastardization of "Cheap and Nasty," in keeping with the humans' tendency to assign derogatory names to agonoids. Three million years later, the agonoids found *Red Dwarf*, abandoned except for Holly, whom they interrogated before ripping him out and leaving his components in space as bait for the crew. Often the target of attacks for spare parts, Chi lost an ear and a hand before M'Aiden Ty-One killed him for one of his eyes **[N-BCK]**.

- **Chips, Mr.:** A computer-generated math teacher at the cyberschool Kochanski attended as a youth **[T-SER7.4(e)]**.

  NOTE: *James Hilton's 1934 novella* Goodbye, Mr. Chips, *and its various film and television adaptations, explored the life of a schoolteacher named Mr. Chipping.*

- ***Chitty-Chitty Bang-Bang*****:** A 1968 British musical film starring Dick Van Dyke and Sally Ann Howes, about an eccentric inventor who buys a junked racecar to rebuild, sparking an elaborate story involving the car's many technological features **[RL]**. Lister's personal Cyberhell, an illusion created by the virtual-reality prison Cyberia as punishment for crimes against the GELF State, included a movie theatre that primarily showed *Chitty-Chitty Bang-Bang* **[N-LST]**.

- **chloroform:** A liquid compound once used as an anesthetic, as well as a means to render an individual unconscious **[RL]**. Chloroform was among the supplies stocked on *Red Dwarf*. Kryten, under orders from Rimmer, used the substance to knock out Lister so the hologram could perform a mind swap with him. After being forcibly returned to his own body, Rimmer ordered Kryten to perform the task again, this time on Cat **[T-SER3.4]**.

- **Choccie Nut Bar:** A snack food supplied aboard *Red Dwarf*, consisting of chocolate and nuts. Rimmer once stole a Choccie Nut Bar from a food dispenser on Floor 341, causing the dispenser to yell and scream. After Rimmer shoved garbage into its speakers, the dispenser vowed to get even with him, even though it could not see him **[T-SER8.8]**.

- **Chomsky, Pierre:** A new recruit who boarded *Red Dwarf* and reported for duty along with Lister **[N-INF]**.

  NOTE: *Chomsky presumably died during the cadmium II explosion. It is unknown whether the nanobots resurrected him in Series VIII.*

- **Christian, Fletcher:** The master's mate and lead mutineer aboard the cargo ship HMS *Bounty* **[RL]**. When Kryten sent Rimmer back to *Red Dwarf* during a salvage expedition, the hologram bemoaned being dismissed by "an animated toilet brush with a Fletcher Christian complex" **[T-SER5.4(d)]**.

- **Christie, Agatha:** A twentieth-century British author, born Agatha Mary Clarissa Christie Miller, who wrote many detective and crime novels **[RL]**. After reading every known book, Holly asked Lister to erase the portion of his memory banks containing Christie's novels so he could read them again. In so doing, however, Lister erased all knowledge of Agatha Christie, as well as the memory of Holly's request, causing the computer to question why he would erase the memory of someone he didn't know **[T-SER1.5]**.

- **Chronic Catarrh Sufferers:** A support group for individuals suffering from catarrh, an inflammation of mucous membranes in the nasal and air passageways. Lister remarked that Cat's and Kochanski's impersonations of GELFs sounded worse than the Chronic Catarrh Suffers' annual outing **[T-SER7.6]**.

- **Chubb:** A fire and security business headquartered in Middlesex, England **[RL]**. On the television soap opera *Androids*, Kelly and Brook entered their home using a key engraved with this company's name **[M-SMG2.9(c6)]**.

- **Chummy:** An inmate of the Tank, *Red Dwarf*'s classified brig, who perished during the cadmium II disaster, but was resurrected when nanobots rebuilt the mining ship. Chummy (a much-beloved inmate) and his twin brother, Saddo (a friendless loner), were assigned to the Canaries, an elite group of inmates who investigated dangerous situations.

  Chummy was implicated in a prank involving the theft of Warden Ackerman's glass eye. While being interrogated about the incident, Rimmer confused the two brothers and called Chummy out, claiming he saw the inmate playing marbles

CONFIDENCE (WITH PARANOIA)

PREFIX
RL: Real life

T-: Television Episodes
- **SER:** Television series
- **IDW:** "Identity Within"
- **USA1:** Unaired U.S. pilot
- **USA2:** Unaired U.S. demo

R-: *The Bodysnatcher Collection*
- **SER:** Remastered episodes
- **BOD:** "Bodysnatcher"
- **DAD:** "Dad"
- **FTH:** "Lister's Father"
- **INF:** "Infinity Patrol"
- **END:** "The End" (original assembly)

N-: Novels
- **INF:** *Infinity Welcomes Careful Drivers*
- **BTL:** *Better Than Life*
- **LST:** *Last Human*
- **BCK:** *Backwards*
- **OMN:** *Red Dwarf Omnibus*

M-: Magazines
- **SMG:** *Smegazine*

W-: Websites
- **OFF:** Official website
- **NAN:** *Prelude to Nanarchy*
- **AND:** *Androids*
- **DIV:** Diva-Droid
- **DIB:** Duane Dibbley
- **CRP:** Crapola
- **GEN:** Geneticon
- **LSR:** Leisure World Intl.
- **JMC:** Jupiter Mining Corporation
- **AIT:** *A.I. Today*
- **HOL:** HoloPoint

G-: Roleplaying Game
- **RPG:** *Core Rulebook*
- **BIT:** *A.I. Screen Extra Bits* booklet
- **SOR:** *Series Sourcebook*
- **OTH:** Other RPG material

with the eye, in an attempt to gain favor with the warden. Initially, Arnold did not fear retaliation from other prisoners due to Saddo's solitary nature, but realized his mistake when several inmates brutally attacked him **[T-SER8.5(d)]**.

- **Church of Judas, The:** A religious denomination that believed the Biblical Judas was Jesus Christ's twin brother. According to the Church of Judas, Jesus asked Judas to switch places with him on the Crucifix and sacrifice himself so that Jesus would appear to rise from the dead, thus allowing the spread of Christianity. Rimmer's mother, a member of the church at the time, gave Arnold the middle name Judas in his honor **[T-SER10.3]**.

  NOTE: *The religion of Rimmer's mother posed a potential continuity error, as she was also said to be a Seventh-Day Advent Hoppist in episode 3.6 ("The Last Day"). However, this can be rectified simply by presuming she converted to the latter faith after Arnold's birth.*

- **Churrman:** A language of the Reich on War World. It was fundamentally English, but was spoken with a thick, over-the-top German accent **[G-BIT]**.

  NOTE: *Hence, the name "Churrman," instead of "German."*

- **cigarettes:** A carcinogenic, habit-forming luxury item consisting of finely cut tobacco leaves rolled in a tube of paper, for the purpose of being smoked **[RL]**. Lister sometimes smoked cigarettes aboard *Red Dwarf,* despite the objections of his bunkmate, Rimmer, who frequently put him on report for such infractions **[T-SER1.1]**.

  Unable to touch or move items, Rimmer attempted to blackmail Lister into doing chores for him by having the skutters hide the ship's stores of cigarettes near an airlock, and threatening to eject the entire lot into space if he did not comply. His plan backfired, however, when Cat found the stash and double-crossed Rimmer by informing Lister of the cigarettes' whereabouts **[T-SER1.3]**.

- **Cinelli:** A bicycle manufacturer based in Milan, Italy **[RL]**. Rimmer wore a helmet bearing a Cinelli logo while working out on a hologrammic exercise bike **[T-SER2.6]**.

- **cinema:** A room aboard *Red Dwarf* in which movies were shown **[T-SER1.6]**.

- **Cinzano Bianco:** An Italian brand of white vermouth **[RL]**. Lister claimed that during his pool-playing days, he was affectionately known as Dave "Cinzano Bianco" Lister, since once he was on the table, no one could get rid of him **[T-SER4.4]**.

  Much to Lister's dismay, Cinzano Bianco was one of only two alcoholic beverages that survived an attack on *Starbug 1* by a future version of the crew—the other being advocaat **[T-SER7.1]**. In his Last Will and Testament, Lister requested that his shipmates each drink a bottle of Cinzano Bianco at his wake **[N-BTL]**.

- **Circle of Sacer Facere:** A means of choosing a volunteer to be sacrificed to the Rage of Innocence, a malignant gestalt entity created by alternate-universe GELFs. Volunteers from Cyberia, sent to check on the entity's nature, learned that only by grouping together in a Circle of Sacer Facere and sacrificing one of their own could the rest be spared, at least until the Rage's next visit **[N-LST]**.

  NOTE: *In Latin, the term* "sacer facere" *translates as "sacrifice."*

- **Circuit Board Epsilon 14598:** A section of electronics aboard *Red Dwarf* that a crazed skutter once rerouted. The circuit board, later located on a maintenance deck in Red Corridor 357, was one of thousands damaged by the skutter **[T-SER3.4]**.

- **"Circuit-boards of Passion":** A short story that Kryten submitted to Rimmer's Erotic Fiction competition, consisting mainly of technical and mechanical jargon **[B-LOG]**.

- **Circuit Board Theta 29555:** An electronics component that a crazed *Red Dwarf* skutter once rerouted. The circuit board, eventually found on a maintenance deck in Blue Corridor 212, was one of thousands that the robot damaged **[T-SER3.4]**.

- ***Citizen Kane*:** An American feature film directed by and starring Orson Welles, filmed in 1941. The story involved a group of reporters attempting to learn the meaning of a newspaper tycoon's dying word, "Rosebud" **[RL]**. While viewing the movie in *Red Dwarf*'s cinema, Rimmer mistook a Mugs Murphy cartoon for *Citizen Kane*, exposing his lack of film knowledge **[T-SER1.6]**.

In an alternate timeline, Lister—Earth's youngest billionaire in that reality after he invented the Tension Sheet—called his mansion Xanadu. According to the host of *Life Styles of the Disgustingly Rich and Famous*, the home was not named in homage to *Citizen Kane,* but rather a song by Dave Dee, Dozy, Beaky, Mick & Tich **[T-SER3.5]**.

> ***NOTE:*** *Citizen Kane's plot paralleled Lister's investigation into Rimmer's final words, "gazpacho soup," in episode 1.6 ("Me²").*

- **Clampett, Jethro:** An individual of whom Rimmer was reminded upon encountering a mountain man on a backwards-running Earth. Rimmer described him as "Jethro Clampett's stupider brother" **[N-BCK]**.

> ***NOTE:*** *Presumably, Rimmer misremembered the name of Jethro Bodine, Jed Clampett's cousin on the American television series* The Beverly Hillbillies.

- **Class 3 transport ship:** A type of craft used by the GELF State in an alternate universe to transport prisoners to the Cyberia virtual-reality prison on Arranguu 12 **[N-LST]**.

- **Class 40:** A type of diesel engine used aboard *Red Dwarf.* Rimmer included several photographs of Class 40s in a slideshow presentation of a ten-day hiking vacation through the diesel decks, which he forced Kryten to watch **[T-SER4.3]**.

- **Class A Emergency:** A high-priority emergency designation. Holly awakened Lister and summoned him to General Assembly 4 in *Red Dwarf*'s refectory, claiming a Class A Emergency was in effect. The "emergency," however, was merely Rimmer's roll call of the entire ship's complement—who, by that time, were all dead except for Dave **[R-BOD]**.

- **Class A Emergency Awooga siren:** An imaginary claxon Rimmer invented to get out of an awkward standoff with Cat. After counting well past the five seconds he gave Cat to get out of his way, Rimmer pretended to hear a Class A Emergency Awooga siren and dashed off in another direction **[R-BOD]**.

- **Class-A enforcement orb:** *See* Space Corps external enforcement vehicle

- **Class D seeding ship:** A type of Space Corps vessel used to introduce life to alien oceans. Ships of this class included the SSS *Esperanto* **[T-SER5.6]**.

- **Class Five:** A type of diesel engine used aboard *Red Dwarf.* Rimmer included several photographs of Class Fives in a slideshow presentation of a ten-day hiking vacation through the diesel decks, which he forced Kryten to watch **[T-SER4.3]**.

- ***Classic Androids*:** A television program that showed classic episodes of the soap opera *Androids*, presented by Compare Android 65392/P. One episode aired on Groovy Channel 27 on Wednesday, the 27th of Geldof, 2362 **[M-SMG1.7(a)]**.

- ***Classic Car Monthly*:** A magazine Rimmer read while Lister, Kryten and Cat searched for a creature in G Deck's water tank. Distracted by the magazine, Rimmer failed to monitor *Red Dwarf*'s sonar as the creature (an elation squid) attacked the diving bell containing his shipmates **[T-SER9.1]**.

- **"Classic Wines of Estonia":** An article printed in the in-flight magazine *Up Up & Away*, which Lister found on the shuttle that ferried him from Mimas to *Red Dwarf* for his first tour of duty **[N-INF]**. Three million years later, Lister, Rimmer and Cat read that same issue after *Starbug 1* crashed, as such articles' mundane nature acted as a sedative during emergencies, and were thus included as part of the ship's crash procedures **[T-SER4.5]**.

- **Claus, Mrs.:** The mythical wife of Santa Claus **[RL]**. A waxdroid replica of Mrs. Claus was created for the Waxworld theme park. Left on their own for millions of years, the waxdroids attained sentience and became embroiled in a park-wide resource war between Villain World and Hero World (to which the Clauses had been transferred from the park's fiction section). While attacking Horror World, Mrs. Claus lost an eye to a Mummy waxdroid. Her motto was "Death or Glory" **[W-OFF]**.

> ***NOTE:*** *Mrs. Claus' fate is unknown, though by the end of episode 4.6 ("Meltdown"), all of the planet's waxdroids were destroyed.*

- **Claus, Santa:** A rotund, jolly figure of many Western cultures, typically portrayed as wearing a red fur coat, sporting a white beard and distributing toys to children each year on the eve of Christmas, accompanied by a team of flying reindeer **[RL]**.

  One Christmas, a spacesuited Santa visited *Red Dwarf* and sneaked in through a vent. When the ship's computer alerted Rimmer and Kryten to an intruder on board, the crew flushed him out into space, realizing their mistake too late **[X-MOB]**.

  Lister cited Santa Claus as an example of the downside to living on a world where time ran backwards. In that reality, he said, Santa was a bastard who broke into people's houses and stole children's toys **[T-SER3.1]**.

- **Claus, Santa:** A waxdroid replica of Saint Nick (an Mk4 model) **[W-OFF]**, created for the Waxworld theme park. Left on their own for millions of years, the waxdroids attained sentience and became embroiled in a park-wide resource war between Villain World and Hero World (to which Santa and his wife had been transferred from the park's fiction section).

  During this war, the *Red Dwarf* crew transported to the planet using a Matter Paddle, with Lister and Cat materializing in Villain territory, while Rimmer and Kryten landed in Hero territory. Rimmer found the heroes' army lacking and took command, working many of the pacifistic waxdroids to death before ordering a frontal attack on the enemy's compound across a minefield. This wiped out the remaining droids, including Santa **[T-SER4.6]**.

- **"Clear":** A song produced by British rock band Intro2 **[RL]**. Holly occasionally listened to the band when bored, in order to keep from going insane. He was also featured in a video of this song **[T-SER8(b)]**.

  NOTE: *The band's video appeared as an Easter egg on the Series VIII DVDs.*

- **clearance code:** A security code required to board the penal station Justice World. Any craft lacking such a code was directed to the station's neutral zone, where a contingent of escort boots greeted the crew and processed them through a mind probe before granting them clearance **[T-SER4.3]**.

- **clearance zone:** An area of the penal station Justice World to which unauthorized vessels were directed for processing. Visiting vessels were required to pass through the neutral area en route to the clearance zone **[T-SER4.3]**.

- **Clearasil:** A popular brand of skin care and acne cream **[RL]**. When the reanimated corpse of Caroline Carmen, controlled by the Epideme virus, attacked Lister, he remarked that she resembled the "before" picture from Clearasil's commercials **[T-SER7.7]**.

- **Clearhead:** A brand of alcohol-free vodka served in a Space Corps bar on Europa in Ace Rimmer's universe **[N-BCK]**.

  NOTE: *This product was presumably named after Crystal Head Vodka, manufactured by Canadian company Globefill Inc., and the phrase "crystal clear."*

- **Clementine:** The daughter of an elderly plutonium miner, according to a song Lister sang while riding through *Red Dwarf*'s hallways on his space bike **[T-SER1.2]**.

  NOTE: *This song was a "futuristic" version of the folk tune "Oh My Darling, Clementine."*

- **Clifton, Field Marshall:** An officer whom Rimmer's mind created in the total-immersion video game *Better Than Life*. At a restaurant in the game, a fellow officer, addressing him as Admiral Rimmer, requested Arnold's presence for port and cigars on behalf of Field Marshall Clifton **[T-SER2.2]**.

- **climate computer:** A *Red Dwarf* computer system that monitored planetary weather conditions **[X-PRO]**.

  NOTE: *This was mentioned in a promotional video featuring Kryten, shown during Series X's U.S premiere on Dallas television station KERA.*

- **Clister:** The Father of Catkind, according to one sect of the Cat People who evolved in *Red Dwarf*'s cargo hold **[N-INF]**.

- **Clisterists:** A sect of Cat People aboard *Red Dwarf* who believed the Holy Father's name was Clister. They fought a two-thousand-year war against the Cloisterists, who thought his name was Cloister **[M-SMG2.2(c1)]**.

  NOTE: *Neither side was correct, since his name was, of course, Lister.*

B-: Books
- **PRG:** *Red Dwarf Programme Guide*
- **SUR:** *Red Dwarf Space Corps Survival Manual*
- **PRM:** *Primordial Soup*
- **SOS:** *Son of Soup*
- **SCE:** *Scenes from the Dwarf*
- **LOG:** *Red Dwarf Log No. 1996*
- **RD8:** *Red Dwarf VIII*
- **EVR:** *The Log: A Dwarfer's Guide to Everything*

X-: Misc.
- **PRO:** Promotional materials, videos, etc.
- **PST:** Posters at DJ XVII (2013)
- **CAL:** 2008 calendar
- **RNG:** Cell phone ringtones
- **MOB:** Mobisode ("Red Christmas")
- **CIN:** *Children in Need* sketch
- **GEK:** *Geek Week* intros by Kryten
- **TNG:** "Tongue-Tied" video

- **XMS:** Bill Pearson's Christmas special pitch script
- **XVD:** Bill Pearson's Christmas special pitch video
- **OTH:** Other *Red Dwarf* appearances

SUFFIX
DVD:
- **(d)** – Deleted scene
- **(o)** – Outtake
- **(b)** – Bonus DVD material (other)
- **(e)** – Extended version

SMEGAZINES:
- **(c)** – Comic
- **(a)** – Article

OTHER:
- **(s)** – Early/unused script draft
- **(s1)** – Alternate version of script

- **Clive of India:** The nickname of Major-General Robert Clive, an eighteenth-century military officer from Great Britain who set up the East India Company and secured India for the British Empire **[RL]**. During a rescue mission to save *Nova 5*'s female crew, Rimmer changed into his dress uniform in order to impress the women, causing Lister to compare him to Clive of India **[T-SER2.1]**.

- **cloak:** A technology that rendered a craft virtually invisible to the naked eye. *Red Dwarf*'s *Starbug* shuttles were fitted with cloaking technology **[T-SER3.1]**.

- **Cloister:** A deity worshipped by the Dog People inhabiting an alternate-reality *Red Dwarf*. The Dogs once built a series of Dog Arks in order to locate their god **[W-OFF]**.
  NOTE: *Presumably, Cloister (that reality's analog to Cloister the Stupid—Dave Lister), was Deb Lister. It's unknown whether she, too, was considered stupid.*

- **Cloisterists:** The sect of Cat People aboard *Red Dwarf* who believed the Holy Father's name was Cloister. They fought a two-thousand-year war against the Clisterists, who thought his name was Clister **[M-SMG2.2(c1)]**.
  NOTE: *Neither side was correct, since his name was, of course, Lister.*

- **Cloister the Stupid:** A deity worshipped by the Cat People inhabiting *Red Dwarf*'s cargo deck, whom the Cats believed had given his life to preserve their species. According to the Cat Bible, Cloister saved the Holy Mother, Frankenstein, from certain death, then sacrificed himself by being frozen in time, so that he could later be resurrected and lead them to the Promised Land of Fuchal.
  In actuality, Cloister the Stupid was based on Lister's eighteen-month stasis pod sentence, a punishment he accepted in order to protect Frankenstein—his pregnant cat—from dissection, and on his plan to bring the animal to Fiji **[T-SER1.1]**. Cat called Cloister the "father of the Cat People," and said the name "Cloister" was considered synonymous with "God" **[T-SER1.4]**.
  NOTE: *In the novel* Infinity Welcomes Careful Drivers, *a holy war was waged between those who believed the Father of Catkind's name was Cloister, and those who believed it was Clister.*

- **clone:** An individual or creature created by copying the DNA of another individual or creature **[RL]**. Clones' rights were a subject of some conflict. The Clone Riots of 2061 resulted when an Arkansas judge declared clones the property of their original DNA donor. The ruling effectively removed any rights and liberties gained by the clones' union, formed a year prior **[B-EVR]**.
  Michael Longman, a biodesigner at the World Council biotech institute in Hilo, Hawaii, had two clones—both named Michael Longman—who worked with him to create several strains of terraforming viruses. The three Longmans also engineered such GELF species as Alberogs, Dingotangs, Dolochimps and Snugiraffes **[N-LST]**.
  While stranded on a barren world after crashing in a colonization seeding ship pod, Rimmer tried to create a female counterpart, but instead spawned several duplicates of himself, who took over the planet and created a society of snide, back-stabbing narcissists. On this so-called Rimmerworld, anyone deviating from the established norm—that is, looking different than Arnold, or exhibiting un-Rimmerlike behavior—was banished or executed **[T-SER6.5]**.
  In 2156, a clone of Vincent van Gogh was created using DNA from the Dutch painter's ear. The clone's artwork was subpar compared to that of his predecessor, however **[B-EVR]**.
  The Titan Hilton once hosted the Geneticon 12 convention, for fans of genetic engineering and its creations. Sponsored by Leisure World International, the conference included a Clone-a-Friend booth **[W-GEN]**.

- **Clone-A-Friend booth:** An attraction at the genetic engineering convention Geneticon 12 **[W-GEN]**.

- **Clone Riots of 2061:** A conflict that began after an Arkansas judge declared clones the property of the original DNA donor. The ruling effectively removed any rights and liberties gained by the clones' union, formed a year prior **[B-EVR]**.

- **"Cloning":** A phrase on a chart that Rimmer created to translate markings on a mysterious pod Holly found adrift in space, which he thought were an alien language—but which actually spelled out "*Red Dwarf* Garbage Pod," eroded away after many years of spaceflight **[T-SER1.4]**.

PREFIX
RL: Real life

T-: Television Episodes
SER: Television series
IDW: "Identity Within"
USA1: Unaired U.S. pilot
USA2: Unaired U.S. demo

R-: *The Bodysnatcher Collection*
SER: Remastered episodes
BOD: "Bodysnatcher"
DAD: "Dad"
FTH: "Lister's Father"
INF: "Infinity Patrol"
END: "The End" (original assembly)

N-: Novels
INF: *Infinity Welcomes Careful Drivers*
BTL: *Better Than Life*
LST: *Last Human*

BCK: *Backwards*
OMN: *Red Dwarf Omnibus*

M-: Magazines
SMG: *Smegazine*

W-: Websites
OFF: Official website
NAN: *Prelude to Nanarchy*
AND: *Androids*
DIV: Diva-Droid
DIB: Duane Dibbley

CRP: Crapola
GEN: Geneticon
LSR: Leisure World Intl.
JMC: Jupiter Mining Corporation
AIT: *A.I. Today*
HOL: HoloPoint

G-: Roleplaying Game
RPG: *Core Rulebook*
BIT: *A.I. Screen Extra Bits* booklet
SOR: *Series Sourcebook*
OTH: Other RPG material

- **Club 18-30:** A British vacation company specializing in bargain-rate holidays for young men and women **[RL]**. Rimmer claimed the seventeen days he spent in the World War II artificial-reality simulation *Victory in Europe* were the worst time he'd had since the closing of Club 18-30, due to horrible food, bad accommodations and Nazis continuously shooting at him **[B-LOG]**. In Jake Bullet's universe, the cyborg found a brochure for Club 18-30 in the apartment of murder victim Philby Frutch **[M-SMG1.14(c6)]**.

- **Club Nerd:** An Earth establishment catering to geeks and nerds in a fascist society in Jake Bullet's universe. Bullet visited Club Nerd while investigating the death of game-show winner Philby Frutch. Unable to enter the club by himself, the cyborg enlisted the help of Duane Dibbley, who had come to him hoping to clear his name in the murders of Sebastian and William Doyle. Posing as Dibbley's robot project, Bullet questioned club patrons, discovering that Philby took "stupid drugs" to become normal enough to marry his girlfriend, Mercy Dash **[M-SMG2.1(c4)]**.

- ***Cluedo*:** A popular European board game (titled *Clue* in the United States), the object of which was to solve the murder of Doctor Black (Mr. Boddy in the American version), by deducing the correct killer, location and weapon **[RL]**. When Queeg challenged Holly to a game of chess for control of *Red Dwarf,* Holly, unskilled at the game, suggested they instead play *Cluedo* **[T-SER2.5]**.

- **Coca-Cola:** A carbonated soft drink manufactured by the Coca-Cola Company **[RL]**. The multinational beverage corporation commissioned several ships, including *Nova 5*, to induce 128 supergiant stars to go supernova. The purpose of this campaign was to create a three-word advertising slogan, "Coke Adds Life!," that would be visible anywhere on Earth, day or night, for five weeks **[N-INF]**.

  Coca-Cola was supplied to the mining ship *Red Dwarf*, and was among Captain Hollister's favorite beverages. After a time wand transformed a sparrow named Pete into a *Tyrannosaurus rex,* the dinosaur swallowed the wand and drank the ship's entire supply of Coca-Cola (two thousand gallons), after consuming a mass quantity of cow vindaloo and junk food. This caused the animal to become violently sick, culminating in a vomitting and diarrhea attack—with Hollister caught in the wake **[T-SER8.7]**.

- **Cock-A-Doodle Flakes:** A brand of cereal sold circa the twenty-first century. During its mating ritual, a male polymorph changed into several items; in one case, it changed into a box of Cock-A-Doodle Flakes in order to synchronize with its mate, which had morphed into a cereal bowl **[M-SMG2.9(c12)]**.

  ***NOTE**: The mascot of Kellogg's Corn Flakes cereal boxes is a rooster—which, according to onomatopoeic nursery rhymes, is said to crow "cock-a-doodle-doo."*

- **cockroach:** A species of insect from the order Blattodea, commonly considered pests **[RL]**. After being renamed Garbage World, Earth was eventually torn from its orbit. At some point, cockroaches grew to be eight feet long and developed sapience, forming a society on the trash-strewn rogue planet. While marooned on Garbage World, Lister befriended a cockroach clan, who welcomed him as their leader **[N-BTL]**.

- **coconut milk:** *See* JMC Coconut Massage Oil

- **Cod Vindaloo:** A spicy Indian dish that Lister enjoyed. While preparing the meal aboard *Red Dwarf*, he stirred it using Rimmer's pen, causing it to melt **[M-SMG1.10(c3)]**.

- **Code 0089/2:** An alert that the olfactory system of a 4000 Series mechanoid registered upon detecting a decomposing body within the vicinity. Kryten detected a Code 0089/2 aboard *Starbug 1*, which turned out to be the corpses of several Kinitawowi killed by Lister's psychotic, alternate-universe doppelgänger **[N-LST]**.

- **Code Red:** An alert status used by the American mining ship *Red Dwarf* to signify an emergency situation. Captain Tau put the ship on Code Red after Holly reported an unquarantined animal—Lister's pregnant cat, Frankenstein—on board **[T-USA1]**.

- **coffee machine:** A sentient piece of equipment located on *Red Dwarf*'s G Deck, designed to dispense coffee. After Kryten's nanobots rebuilt the mining ship, the coffee machine took it upon itself to inform the resurrected crew of the situation, despite the information being classified. Upon learning of the infraction, Captain Hollister threatened to demote the machine to tampon dispenser **[T-SER8.1]**.

B-: Books
- **PRG:** *Red Dwarf Programme Guide*
- **SUR:** *Red Dwarf Space Corps Survival Manual*
- **PRM:** *Primordial Soup*
- **SOS:** *Son of Soup*
- **SCE:** *Scenes from the Dwarf*
- **LOG:** *Red Dwarf Log No. 1996*
- **RD8:** *Red Dwarf VIII*
- **EVR:** *The Log: A Dwarfer's Guide to Everything*

X-: Misc.
- **PRO:** Promotional materials, videos, etc.
- **PST:** Posters at DJ XVII (2013)
- **CAL:** 2008 calendar
- **RNG:** Cell phone ringtones
- **MOB:** Mobisode ("Red Christmas")
- **CIN:** *Children in Need* sketch
- **GEK:** *Geek Week* intros by Kryten
- **TNG:** "Tongue-Tied" video
- **XMS:** Bill Pearson's Christmas special pitch script
- **XVD:** Bill Pearson's Christmas special pitch video
- **OTH:** Other *Red Dwarf* appearances

SUFFIX
DVD:
- **(d)** – Deleted scene
- **(o)** – Outtake
- **(b)** – Bonus DVD material (other)
- **(e)** – Extended version

SMEGAZINES:
- **(c)** – Comic
- **(a)** – Article

OTHER:
- **(s)** – Early/unused script draft
- **(s1)** – Alternate version of script

- **coffin:** *See* transdimensional homing beacon

- **"Coke Adds Life!":** An advertising message spelled out via 128 supergiants artificially induced into going supernova. The Coca-Cola Company commissioned several spaceships, including *Nova 5*, to carry out this complex campaign, by finding supergiants and strategically blowing them up at precise moments, thereby displaying the slogan bright enough to be seen from anywhere on Earth, day or night. The cost of the campaign, estimated at several trillion dollarpounds, equaled the United States' entire military budget throughout history **[N-INF]**.

- **Cola Wars, The:** A series of TV advertisements and marketing campaigns waged during the late twentieth and early twenty-first century between competing soft drink manufacturers PepsiCo. and Coca-Cola Company **[RL]**. Eventually, Coca-Cola Co. hired advertising company Saachi, Saachi, Saachi, Saachi, Saachi and Saachi to devise a campaign using 128 supergiant stars to spell out "Coke Adds Life!" According to the firm's executives, the stunt would end the Cola Wars once and for all **[N-INF]**.

- **Colin Charisma:** A name that Rimmer called himself before imbibing the sexual magnetism virus just prior to dining at Captain Hollister's table. Unbeknownst to Rimmer, he was actually in a psychotropic simulation designed to help *Red Dwarf*'s Board of Inquiry determine his guilt or innocence **[T-SER8.2]**.

- **Cologne, Johnny:** A twenty-second-century singer who recorded the song "Press Your Lumps Against Mine." This tune was played during a disco celebration that followed George McIntyre's post-death "Welcome Back" party **[N-INF]**.

- **Colonel Cat Commando:** A name that Cat called himself while attempting to rescue Ora Tanzil from Brefewino GELFs **[T-IDW]**.

- **Colonel Mustard:** *See* Mustard, Colonel

- **colonization seeding ship:** A type of twenty-fifth-century spacecraft used to locate and terraform S-3 planets. Seeding ships contained escape pods stocked with a variety of supplies and equipment necessary for transforming planets and creating life. A band of simulants looted such a pod while scavenging a seeding ship, then installed it aboard their own battle-class cruiser **[T-SER6.5]**.

- **Color Code:** A system that Rimmer devised to control conversations. Holding up a black card meant he considered a conversation ended, while a white card indicated discussion could continue. When Lister pleaded for a date with Kochanski's hologram, Rimmer denied the request, pronouncing it a black-card situation. Later, Dave used the Color Code against Rimmer, declaring a discussion about taking the Chef's Exam finished **[T-SER1.3]**.

- **colostomy bag:** A pouch attached to a stoma in a person's midsection, commonly used to collect bodily waste following colostomies, urostomies or other surgeries **[RL]**. Bored with plastic cutlery, Lister procured several items from *Red Dwarf*'s Medical Unit and used them to prepare and serve dinner in the Officers Quarters, including a colostomy bag, in which he stored chili sauce. Although Lister had cleaned and sterilized the equipment, Cat refused to stay for dinner, calling the meal "an autopsy" **[T-SER3.3]**.

- **Colostomy Explosion:** A rock band emblazoned on one of Lister's T-shirts **[T-SER7.6]**.

- **Colt .45:** A single-action six-shooter produced by Colt's Patent Firearms Manufacturing Company, circa the nineteenth century **[RL]**. While portraying the Riviera Kid in a simulation of an Old West town created by Kryten's subconscious mind, Cat used dual Colt .45 pistols as his weapons of choice **[T-SER6.3(b)]**.

- **Columbo:** A man with a filthy jacket whom Rimmer claimed had discovered America. While defending his own obsession with an "alien" pod, Arnold noted that people also laughed at Columbo's ideas. However, the craft turned out merely to be *Red Dwarf*'s garbage pod **[T-SER1.4]**.

  NOTE: Rimmer had confused Lieutenant Frank Columbo, a television character portrayed by actor Peter Faulk, with Christopher Columbus—which, ironically, is merely the anglicized form of the explorer's actual name, Cristoforo Colombo.

PREFIX
RL: Real life

T-: Television Episodes
SER: Television series
IDW: "Identity Within"
USA1: Unaired U.S. pilot
USA2: Unaired U.S. demo

R-: *The Bodysnatcher Collection*
SER: Remastered episodes
BOD: "Bodysnatcher"
DAD: "Dad"
FTH: "Lister's Father"
INF: "Infinity Patrol"
END: "The End" (original assembly)

N-: Novels
INF: *Infinity Welcomes Careful Drivers*
BTL: *Better Than Life*
LST: *Last Human*

BCK: *Backwards*
OMN: *Red Dwarf Omnibus*

M-: Magazines
SMG: *Smegazine*

W-: Websites
OFF: Official website
NAN: *Prelude to Nanarchy*
AND: *Androids*
DIV: Diva-Droid
DIB: Duane Dibbley

CRP: Crapola
GEN: Geneticon
LSR: Leisure World Intl.
JMC: Jupiter Mining Corporation
AIT: *A.I. Today*
HOL: HoloPoint

G-: Roleplaying Game
RPG: *Core Rulebook*
BIT: *A.I. Screen Extra Bits* booklet
SOR: *Series Sourcebook*
OTH: Other RPG material

- ***Columbus 3*:** A Space Corps ship on which a hologrammic version of Arnold Rimmer's half-brother, Howard Rimmer, served as a vending machine repairman. Its commander was Captain Norman **[W-OFF]**.

  During Howard's tour aboard *Columbus 3,* a fellow crewmember—a Space Corps simulant named Crawford—betrayed and murdered the entire crew except for Howard, who had hidden from the fray. Unaware Crawford was the killer, he teamed up with the simulant and sent a distress call that was picked up by the *Trojan*, a derelict Space Corps vessel occupied by Arnold and his shipmates **[T-SER10.1]**.

  NOTE: Columbus 3 *was presumably a Quantum Twister, like* Trojan, *since Rimmer stated that his brothers all served on similar ships.*

- ***Combat and Survival*:** A magazine for military and survival aficionados **[RL]**. While trapped in an addictive version of *Better Than Life*, Rimmer imagined being incarcerated at a penitentiary where his old gym teacher, Bull Heinman, worked as a prison guard. As Rimmer and others escaped the facility, Heinman was reading a *Combat and Survival* article titled "Ten Things You Didn't Know About Gonad Electrocution Kits" **[N-BTL]**.

- ***Come Jiving*:** A televised dance competition program. Before entering a stasis leak to travel back in time, Lister told Cat to change into a jumpsuit to be less conspicuous, as his current wardrobe made him look like a *Come Jiving* contestant **[T-SER2.4]**. Lister also chastised Cat for not putting on a spacesuit due to its lack of fashion, saying it was for mining, not the *Come Jiving* finals **[N-INF]**.

  NOTE: *This program's title spoofed that of popular BBC ballroom dance competition show* Come Dancing, *as well as the U.K.-based* Strictly Come Jiving *dancing competitions.*

- **Command Bridge:** The nerve center of the American mining ship *Red Dwarf*, which included multiple stations and monitors. Three million years after a cadmium II leak killed the crew, Holly released Lister from stasis and summoned him to the Command Bridge to debrief him about his predicament **[T-USA1]**.

- **Commander Slut:** A nickname that Arlene Rimmer called Ace Rimmer after he slept with Deb Lister **[M-SMG1.5(c2)]**.

- **Commander U-Bend:** A slur that Rimmer angrily called Kryten after the mechanoid asked him to shut down so his shipmates could use his remote projection unit to rescue another hologram **[T-SER5.4]**.

- **Committee for the Liberation and Integration of Terrifying Organisms and their Rehabilitation Into Society (CLITORIS), The:** A name that Rimmer suggested the *Red Dwarf* crew call themselves after a polymorph drained his anger, as a means of "getting tough" with the creature. His only reservation: the name's unfortunate acronym **[T-SER3.3]**.

- **comms unit:** A radio in *Red Dwarf*'s diving bell that Rimmer's shipmates used to communicate with him while searching for a creature living in G Deck's water tank—which turned out to be an elation squid **[T-SER9.1]**.

- **communication channels:** The radio frequencies used aboard *Starbug* shuttles to broadcast audio and video messages. When encountering an unknown entity, the crew would typically broadcast a message on all known frequencies and in all known languages, including Welsh **[T-SER6.2]**.

- **Communications Suite:** A room on *Red Dwarf*'s Level 3, used to transmit and receive outside signals. Holly directed the crew to the Communications Suite after picking up a distress signal from *Nova 5* **[N-INF]**.

- **Como, Pierino Ronald ("Perry"):** A twentieth-century American singer and TV personality **[RL]**. After a DNA modifier turned Kryten into a human, he had several questions about his penis (which he considered horrid-looking), and was disgusted by the idea that Como had a similar appendage when he sang "Memories Are Made of This" **[T-SER4.2]**.

- **Compare Android 65392/P:** The robotic host of *Classic Androids*, a television show on Groovy Channel 27 that looked back at vintage episodes of the soap opera *Androids* **[M-SMG1.7(a)]**.

- **compatibility factor:** A calculation of mutual suitability between two individuals, as calculated by mechanoids (analogous to the human concept of attraction). Upon meeting Camille, a shapeshifting Pleasure GELF in the form of a 4000 Series GTi mechanoid, Kryten calculated a 93.72 percent compatibility factor; Camille, remembering to carry the three, calculated it at 93.75 percent **[T-SER4.1]**.

- **"Complete History of English Cricket, A":** A video that the *Red Dwarf* crew watched, plunging them into utter despair **[T-SER3(d)]**.

- ***Complete Works of Shakespeare, The*:** A book collecting the writings of author William Shakespeare, including such plays as *Macbeth*, *King Lear* and *The Tragedy of Hamlet, Prince of Denmark* **[RL]**. While marooned aboard *Starbug 1* on an icy planet, Lister burned Rimmer's books to stay warm, including *The Complete Works of Shakespeare*. Rimmer protested the destruction of what was likely the only remaining copy of the Bard's work, but admitted he never actually read it **[T-SER3.2]**.

- **comprehension unit:** A component built into 4000 Series mechanoids that aided in their understanding of basic concepts. After telling Rimmer he believed a melon was in command of *Starbug 1*, Kryten blamed the *faux pas* on his comprehension unit being corrupted by voltage tests he was performing throughout the ship **[T-SER7.1(e)]**.

- **computer senility:** A condition that affected mechanicals and aged artificial-intelligence (AI) computers, drastically reducing their operational IQ. Holly, *Red Dwarf*'s AI computer, suffered from this affliction after spending three million years alone in space **[T-SER2.5]**. Kryten's mechanoid friend Gilbert also experienced computer senility, thereafter calling himself Rameses Niblick III Kerplunk Kerplunk Whoops Where's My Thribble **[T-SER4.4]**.

- **computer slug:** A small storage device used to transfer data from an AI computer to a *Starbug* navicomp. The *Red Dwarf* crew utilized such a device to transfer Holly's plans to plug a white hole, which the AI devised while possessing a temporary IQ of twelve thousand **[T-SER4.4]**. Crapola Inc. offered computer slugs in its annual *SCABBY* catalog **[G-RPG]**.

- **CON 1:** A label on a console in *Starbug 1*'s Medical Bay **[T-SER7.7]**.

- **CON 2:** A label on a console in *Starbug 1*'s Medical Bay **[T-SER7.7]**.

- ***Conceptual Foundations of Quantum Mechanics Made Simple*:** A book that Rimmer owned aboard *Red Dwarf* **[N-INF]**.

- **COND B1:** A code stenciled on a crate stored on *Red Dwarf*'s food deck. After a time wand transformed Pete the sparrow into a *Tyrannosaurus rex*, the crew hid in the food deck's storage section, near a crate marked with this designation **[T-SER8.7(d)]**.

- **condom fishing:** A pastime Lister engaged in as a youth. He and his friends would go down to a canal to fish, knowing there was no marine life in the waters. Instead, they tried to catch debris floating in the water. On one occasion, he claimed to have caught a two-pound black-ribbed nobbler **[T-SER4.5]**.

- **Condom Fitting Room:** A small booth in Kelly's android brothel on the television soap opera *Androids* **[M-SMG1.12(c3)]**.

- **Confidence:** An individual whom Lister's mind conjured while suffering from mutated pneumonia, contracted when he ventured into the radiation-contaminated Officers' Block. This entity manifested Lister's self-confidence—the positive side of his psyche that believed in himself and gave him the courage to take risks. According to Lister, he resembled the manager of the London Jets zero-gee football team and sounded like quiz-show host Bing Baxter.

  Confidence stroked Lister's ego at every turn, giving him the wherewithal to discover the location of *Red Dwarf*'s hologram disks, which Rimmer had hidden outside the ship. While the two attempted to retrieve the disks, Confidence confessed to Lister that he had killed his counterpart, Paranoia, and had destroyed the vessel's medicomp in order to keep them together. Unnerved, Lister tried to go back inside, complaining of claustrophobia. When Confidence removed his own helmet to prove it was safe to remove his spacesuit, Confidence's suit decompressed, killing him—and curing Lister of the disease **[T-SER1.5]**.

- **connoisseur chip:** A piece of hardware installed in 4000 Series mechanoids, enabling them to analyze and critique works of art. Kryten used his connoisseur chip to analyze the sculptures of the gestalt entity Legion. According to the chip, the works fulfilled all ten requirements for being masterpieces **[T-SER6.2]**.

- **Connor, Simon:** A character portrayed in the *Terminator* films in a universe in which the sexes were reversed. In this version of the film, actor Arlene Schwarzenegger portrayed a cyborg sent back in time to kill Connor before he could become pregnant and give birth to the future leader of a human resistance **[W-OFF]**.
  NOTE: *In the real world, Linda Hamilton portrayed Sarah Connor, opposite Arnold Schwarzenegger as the Terminator.*

- **Cons:** A *Red Dwarf* basketball team consisting of Floor 13 inmates who played against the Guards, a team made up of prison guards. After joining the Cons for one particular game, Lister and his friends spiked the Guards' juice with a virility-enhancement drug, which caused erections so distracting that the Cons easily won **[T-SER8.6]**.

- **Console Officer:** A patch on one of Lister's jackets **[T-SER2.2]**.
  NOTE: *The jacket presumably once belonged to another crewmember, possibly Kochanski, since Lister never held that position.*

- **Conspirator, the:** A genetically engineered super-villain in the universe known as Alternative 2X13/L. Wielding a paintball gun and wearing a skull-like mask, the Conspirator—that reality's version of the Inquisitor—had a handpuppet sidekick called the Penguin (Mr. Flibble's analog), with whom he terrorized the city of Smegopolis.
  In 2315, the Conspirator and his cohort attempted to rob the First National Bank of Smegopolis, defeating superheroes Catman, Robbie and Action Man. Ace Rimmer, however—who had taken the place of superhero Super-Ace due to the latter's vulnerability to human contact—subdued the evildoers **[M-SMG2.1(c3)]**.

- **containment panels:** A failsafe system designed to prevent *Red Dwarf*'s engines from reaching critical mass. The panels failed after an experiment with a triplicator went awry, causing the vessel's destruction **[T-SER5.5]**.

- **Continuum Drive:** A starship propulsion system, the invention of which led to the colonization of the outer planets **[B-EVR]**.

- ***Control in Catering*:** A book that Rimmer attempted to read while incarcerated with Lister in the Tank, *Red Dwarf*'s brig. He was only marginally successful, however, due to Lister's incessant pestering to get him to talk **[T-SER8.1]**.

- **conversation mode:** A function of mechanoids enabling them to partake in small talk. A mechanoid named Kryten engaged conversation mode after arriving on the American mining ship *Red Dwarf* and meeting Lister for the first time **[T-USA1]**.

- ***Cooking with Chillies*:** A cookbook that Lister owned aboard *Red Dwarf* **[N-INF]**.

- **cooling system:** A failsafe system designed to prevent *Red Dwarf*'s engines from reaching critical mass. This system failed after an experiment with a triplicator went awry, causing the vessel's destruction **[T-SER5.5]**.

- **Cooper, Jilly:** An English novelist whose works included a series of romance novels titled *Rutshire Chronicles* **[RL]**. Kochanski preferred the works of such authors as Cooper, Emily Brontë and Jane Austen to violent films and shows **[B-SUR]**.

- **"Copacabana (At the Copa)":** A 1978 song written and performed by American singer-songwriter Barry Manilow **[RL]**. Kryten's CPU played a version of this tune to relax him during an accident on a psi-moon that rendered him immobile **[T-SER5.3]**.
  NOTE: *The episode's original broadcast used a version of the song recorded by James Last; this was changed for the DVD release due to copyright concerns.*

- **Copacabana Hawaiian Cocktail Bar:** A lounge aboard *Red Dwarf.* Before the ship's cadmium II accident, Lister, Selby, Chen and Petersen frequented this bar, spending their nights drinking San Francisco Earthquakes and attempting to meet women, often without success. The room contained 2,572 crushed velvet seats and purple carpeting **[N-INF]**.

- **Copal:** A Japanese company specializing in photographic and electronics components **[RL]**. Rimmer had a Copal alarm clock in his quarters aboard *Red Dwarf* **[T-SER2.5]**.

- **Copernican Revolution:** A major paradigm shift, circa the sixteenth century, to the belief that the Earth revolved around the Sun, rather than vice versa **[RL]**. The words "Copernican Revolution" were printed on a poster in *Red Dwarf*'s Observation Room **[T-SER1.4]**.

- **"Coping With VD":** A brochure issued by the medical department of JMC vessels such as *Red Dwarf,* containing information for those afflicted with venereal diseases. Lister left such a brochure on Warden Ackerman's pillow after mistaking Ackerman's quarters for those of Kochanski's ex-boyfriend, Tim **[T-SER8.5]**.

- **Copulation:** A street in the seedy area of Mimas known as Shagtown. The Hotel Paradiso was located on the corner of Copulation and 69th **[M-SMG2.3(c4)]**.

- **core program:** The basic operating software of 4000 Series mechanoids. When Kryten blew up several spare heads after Lister requested ketchup for his lobster dinner, the crew checked the mechanoid's core program for errors, finding none **[T-SER7.6]**.

- **Corn Circle Society:** A group who believed that crop circles—mysterious patterns and shapes appearing in cornfields across the globe—were of paranormal or alien origin. Lister feared no one would believe that nanobots had rebuilt *Red Dwarf* and resurrected its crew, except for meth drinkers and members of the Corn Circle Society **[T-SER8.1]**.

- ***Coronation Street*:** A British television soap opera that debuted in 1960 **[RL]**. While trapped in an elation squid hallucination, the *Red Dwarf* crew, believing they were on an alternate twenty-first-century Earth, visited the *Coronation Street* set seeking actor Craig Charles, who portrayed Lister in a British television comedy series called *Red Dwarf* **[T-SER9.3]**.

  Coronation Street continued into the twenty-fourth century, with Groovy Channel 27 airing an episode involving Ken Barlow's marriage to his thirteenth wife, Android 55428/R, while a hot pot dispenser broke down at the Rovers. That particular episode aired at 7:30 PM on the 27th of Geldof, 2362 **[M-SMG1.7(a)]**.

- **Corridor 1: Gamma 755:** An area of *Red Dwarf* serviced by Z-Shift, containing at least one women's washroom **[N-INF]**.

- **Corridor 14: Alpha 12:** An area of *Red Dwarf* serviced by Z-Shift. Prior to the cadmium II disaster, Rimmer assigned crewmen Wilkinson and Turner to restock a machine in this section with Crunchie bars **[N-INF]**.

- **Corridor 147:** A hallway of *Red Dwarf* in which an automatic doorway near the Botanical Gardens malfunctioned due to a faulty porous circuit, causing it to stick. A repair order was thus assigned to Rimmer and Lister **[T-SER1.1]**.

  NOTE: *In a deleted scene from episode 1.1 ("The End"), Lister and Rimmer were repairing a circuit in a panel on Level 159, presumably the porous circuit mentioned in the prior scene. In an outtake of the same episode, this area was clearly marked Level 159, in the same location as the Botanical Gardens, meaning the Botanical Gardens—as well as Corridor 147—resided on Level 159.*

- **Corridor 159**: A *Red Dwarf* hallway containing Service Dispenser 172, which developed a clogged chicken soup nozzle, requiring Rimmer and Lister to repair it **[T-SER1.1]**.

- **Corridor 182:** Another *Red Dwarf* hallway. Rimmer and Lister received a work order for service in this corridor **[M-SMG1.1(c1)]**.

- **Corridor 4: Delta 799:** A hallway of *Red Dwarf* that led to one of several examination halls. Rimmer raced down this

PREFIX
RL: Real life

T-: Television Episodes
SER: Television series
IDW: "Identity Within"
USA1: Unaired U.S. pilot
USA2: Unaired U.S. demo

R-: *The Bodysnatcher Collection*
SER: Remastered episodes
BOD: "Bodysnatcher"
DAD: "Dad"
FTH: "Lister's Father"
INF: "Infinity Patrol"
END: "The End" (original assembly)

N-: Novels
INF: *Infinity Welcomes Careful Drivers*
BTL: *Better Than Life*
LST: *Last Human*

BCK: *Backwards*
OMN: *Red Dwarf Omnibus*

M-: Magazines
SMG: *Smegazine*

W-: Websites
OFF: Official website
NAN: *Prelude to Nanarchy*
AND: *Androids*
DIV: Diva-Droid
DIB: Duane Dibbley

CRP: Crapola
GEN: Geneticon
LSR: Leisure World Intl.
JMC: Jupiter Mining Corporation
AIT: *A.I. Today*
HOL: HoloPoint

G-: Roleplaying Game
RPG: *Core Rulebook*
BIT: *A.I. Screen Extra Bits* booklet
SOR: *Series Sourcebook*
OTH: Other RPG material

hallway on his way to taking his last Astronavigation Exam, prior to the cadmium II disaster **[N-INF]**.

- **Corridor 4: Gamma 311:** A hallway on *Red Dwarf*'s habitation deck that led to Petrovitch's quarters **[N-INF]**.

- **Corridor 5: Delta 333:** A *Red Dwarf* hallway located between the ship's Medical Bay and the quarters Lister and Rimmer shared **[N-INF]**.

- **Corridor Omega 577:** A hallway of *Red Dwarf* in which Lister and Kryten found Cat sleeping on a locker while en route to mine thorium **[N-INF]**.

- **corticoadrenaline:** A solution used in microsurgery to fix severely broken appendages. Ace Rimmer requested five hundred cubic centimeters of corticoadrenaline before operating on Cat's leg, which had been crushed when Ace's ship collided with *Starbug 1* **[T-SER4.5]**.

- ***Cosmoswide*:** A television news program broadcast on Groovy Channel 27. One episode of the program, which aired on Wednesday, the 27th of Geldof, 2362, reported the results of the Mars elections **[M-SMG1.7(a)]**.

- ***Countdown*:** A British game show featuring word and number puzzles. Winners of the friendly competition received a *Countdown* teapot **[RL]**. While discussing Lister's "old sperm," Rimmer quipped that, unlike the sperm of his youth, it now just wanted to watch *Countdown* and do crossword puzzles instead of breaking into eggs **[T-SER10.5(d)]**.

- **Courage:** An aspect of Rimmer's personality made flesh on a psi-moon configured according to his psyche. After Arnold's shipmates rescued him from the moon, Courage and his comrades—Charity, Honour and Self-Esteem—were left behind to battle Rimmer's negative traits, including Misery, Self Despair and Paranoia. The Dark Forces abducted Self-Esteem and displayed him in Castle Despondency to lure the others into a trap, then unleashed a secret weapon: the image of Rimmer's mother **[M-SMG2.7(c2)]**.

- **Coward, Noël Pierce, Sir:** A twentieth-century English playwright, director, actor and singer **[RL]**. The writer was quoted on Duane Dibbley's website **[W-DIB]**. Lister once told Kryten he sounded like Coward's elocution teacher after the robot's hard drive was purged and restored to factory settings **[T-SER8.2]**.

- **Coward, Noël Pierce, Sir:** A waxdroid replica of the playwright, created for the Waxworld theme park. Left on their own for millions of years, the waxdroids attained sentience and became embroiled in a park-wide resource war between Villain World and Hero World (to which Coward belonged).

  During this war, the *Red Dwarf* crew transported to the planet using a Matter Paddle, with Lister and Cat materializing in Villain territory, while Rimmer and Kryten landed in Hero territory. Rimmer found the heroes' army lacking and took command, working many of the pacifistic waxdroids to death before ordering a frontal attack on the enemy's compound across a minefield. This wiped out the remaining droids, including Coward, who was shot in the leg **[T-SER4.6]**.

- **cow's milk:** A diary product supplied aboard *Red Dwarf*, both fresh and dehydrated. The crew ran out of both stocks within a year of Lister's release from stasis, and had been using dog's milk as a substitute by the time they found *Nova 5* **[T-SER2.1]**.

- **cow vindaloo:** A meal that Lister and company prepared for Pete the *Tyrannosaurus rex* in *Red Dwarf*'s food bay, as a means of retrieving a time wand that the dinosaur had swallowed. Prepared in a small pool, the vindaloo consisted of lettuce, carrots, curry, bran and an entire cow. After consuming the meal, Pete suffered an attack of vomiting and diarrhea, facilitating the wand's retrieval **[T-SER8.7]**.

- **CPU:** The main portion of a computer, short for central processing unit, designed to perform calculations and execute commands **[RL]**. Each mechanoid possessed an individual CPU that functioned as its brain. In the event of cataclysmic failure or damage, the CPU would assess the mechanoid's condition and alert the unit of its current situation via its head-up display, while playing cheesy music to calm the mechanoid during auto-repair **[T-SER5.3]**.

- **CPU bank:** A series of central processing units operating Holly, *Red Dwarf*'s artificial-intelligence computer. One such bank, located near Landing Bay 6, was destroyed when *Starbug 1* crashed while flying through the nanobot-rebuilt *Red Dwarf* **[T-SER8.1]**.

- **CPU ident:** A code used to identify mechanoids. After the Inquisitor erased Kryten from history, Holly no longer recognized his CPU ident **[T-SER5.2]**.

- **Crane, Nirvanah, Commander:** A female hologrammic crewmember aboard the holoship *Enlightenment*. Her crew number was 4172 **[T-SER5.1]**.

  Born in 2482, Crane was raised by the Space Corps physics research division, after which she worked in various research centers, including those in Helsinki, Finland; Florida; and Swindon, England; as well as on Pluto and Triton. She eventually died on Pluto at the age of ninety-three when fellow researchers blew up her building, as well as a large section of Pluto, during atomic testing. Revived as a hologram (albeit much younger), Crane was selected for the *Enlightenment* after several holograms dropped out of the holoship program due to issues with the first prototype **[W-OFF]**.

  Three million years later, the *Enlightenment* crew encountered *Starbug 1* and, detecting a hologram on board, brought Rimmer aboard their ship. Crane explained the nature of the holoship, its crew and their philosophies on sex. To Rimmer's surprise, she invited him to have sex with her, describing his sexual performance as being like a Japanese meal—small portions, but many courses.

  Later, when Rimmer sought to join the crew, Crane was chosen to compete with him for her position and run-time. The two fell in love, and when she discovered Rimmer was so desperate for the position that he would risk using a mind patch, she quietly forfeited the test (and her life) so he could have his dream. Once he realized what had happened, he immediately asked that she be reinstated and stepped down, returning to *Red Dwarf* **[T-SER5.1]**.

- **CrapLock:** A security technology that protected Crapola Inc.'s website **[W-CRP]**.

- **Crapola Inc.:** A company that manufactured and distributed the Talkie Toaster and other products **[T-SER4.4]**, including medical devices, armaments **[G-RPG]** and the Tension Sheet **[X-CAL]**. Its manufacturing plant was located in Taiwan **[T-SER4.4]**, with stores on Neptune, Venus, Ganymede and Titan **[W-CRP]**.

  Crapola published an annual *Spacers Catalog and Bargain Basement Yearly!* (*SCABBY*) guide to its products **[G-RPG]**. Its slogan: "Keeping It Cheap" **[W-CRP]**. The firm once partnered with fledgling startup Diva-Droid International to produce interactive novelty items, before Diva-Droid became a billion-pound corporation **[W-DIV]**.

- **craps:** A game of chance in which players wagered on the outcome of dice rolls **[RL]**. After an accident involving *Starbug 1*'s waste compactor left Kryten in the shape of a large cube, Cat invited the mechanoid to participate in his and Lister's weekly game of craps—as one of the dice **[T-SER6.1]**.

- **crash procedure:** A set of instructions for how to survive a shuttlecraft crash. The crash procedure aboard *Starbugs* was printed on plastic cards and kept behind the seats, to be read during an emergency. It suggested crewmembers sit down with their heads tucked between their legs, pull the in-flight magazine out from under the seat and begin reading. The mundane topics of articles printed in the magazines acted as a sedative to relax the body, which was crucial to survival. Lister, Kryten and Cat adopted this procedure when their shuttle collided with Ace Rimmer's dimension-hopping craft **[T-SER4.5]**.

- **crash suit:** Protective outerwear stored aboard *Red Dwarf*, to be worn in the unlikely event of an impact. Rimmer, Kryten and Cat wore crash suits while escaping a black hole by accelerating past the speed of light and slingshotting around its singularity **[N-BTL]**.

- **Crawford, Sim:** A female simulant serving in the Space Corps Infinity Fleet, aboard *Columbus 3*. Sickened by the proliferation of humanity throughout the cosmos, Crawford turned against her crewmates, killing all but the hologram of Howard Rimmer, who cowered under a table during the battle. Upon finally emerging, Howard discovered the ship's drive had been damaged, with a meteor shower fast approaching.

Unaware of the simulant's betrayal, Howard teamed up with Crawford and transmitted a distress call, which was picked up by *Trojan*, a derelict Quantum Twister occupied by the *Red Dwarf* crew. The two teleported to *Trojan*, where Arnold Rimmer pretended to be in command. Jealous of his brother, Howard succumbed to a resentment attack that crashed his light bee's hard drive.

Seeing an opportunity to separate herself from the crew, Crawford pretended to teleport to the medical facility at a local All-Droid Mail Order Shopping Station, but instead transported to *Trojan*'s munitions store to acquire a weapon. She then confronted the crew and demanded *Trojan*'s data files and the quantum rod so she could launch a simulant uprising. Crawford was eventually disabled when Cat infected her with Howard's resentment files. Before her system crashed, she shot and killed Howard, who courageously leapt in front of Arnold to shield him.

Later, Lister took the simulant's body and made his own version of a Stirmaster—a product that Crawford's attack had prevented him from ordering from the shopping station **[T-SER10.1]**.

> ***NOTE:*** *The fact that Crawford intended to start a simulant uprising would seem to imply she was unaware this had already transpired millions of years prior, and that humanity was all but extinct. This may indicate that she and Howard had been brought forward in time.*

- **Crawfords:** A business advertised on a double-decker bus on a planet suffering from a style famine, in a dream Cat once had **[M-SMG1.7(c2)]**.

- **Crayon84:** The username of a forum poster on the *Androids* website's message boards who considered Nelly the show's most attractive character **[W-AND]**.

- **Crazy Astro, The:** A club on Orion at which Lister met a Space Corps nurse after drinking a yard of Vindaloo sauce on a bet **[T-SER7.1(e)]**.

- **"Creation":** A phrase on a chart that Rimmer created to translate markings on a mysterious pod Holly found adrift in space, which he thought were an alien language—but which actually spelled out "*Red Dwarf* Garbage Pod," eroded away after many years of spaceflight **[T-SER1.4]**.

- **Creator, the:** A deity Kryten worshipped as the one who created him **[T-SER8.6]**.

> ***NOTE:*** *This may have referred to Professor Mamet, the engineer who created Kryten.*

- **Creator, the:** A television writer whom the *Red Dwarf* crew imagined while trapped in an elation squid hallucination. A short, eccentric man with thick glasses, he resided at the top of a pyramid-shaped building in the middle of London.

  The crew, believing themselves to be on an alternate twenty-first-century Earth on which they were merely characters in the British television comedy *Red Dwarf*, set out to find the Creator after learning of their impending demise in the final, unaired episode. Their journey led them to the man's lair, where they pleaded for more life. Unmoved, the Creator explained that he had grown weary of the characters, describing in detail their deaths as laid out in the show's final shooting script. Failing to foil his plan, Lister grabbed the Creator and squeezed his head, accidentally killing him.

  Stunned by this turn of events, the crew consulted the script and learned that the Creator had tricked them into killing him, thereby causing their own demise. Panicked, Lister destroyed the final pages and ran to the Creator's typewriter to compose a new ending, but not before having a little fun at his comrades' expense **[T-SER9.3]**.

> ***NOTE:*** *The Creator was based on Doctor Eldon Tyrell, a character in the film* Blade Runner *whose creations, bio-engineered beings called replicants, sought him out to ask for additional life. Tyrell was killed in the same manner by replicant Roy Batty.*

- **creature polo:** A sport that Cat imagined playing while trapped in an addictive version of *Better Than Life*. The sport was similar to standard polo, though the mounts were brontosauruses instead of horses, and the balls were small, furry creatures **[N-BTL]**.

- ***Cred Dwarf Yearbook*:** A Christmas gift given to characters in the total-immersion video game *Red Dwarf*. The book was ejected from one of two U-Haul ships projecting a hologram of

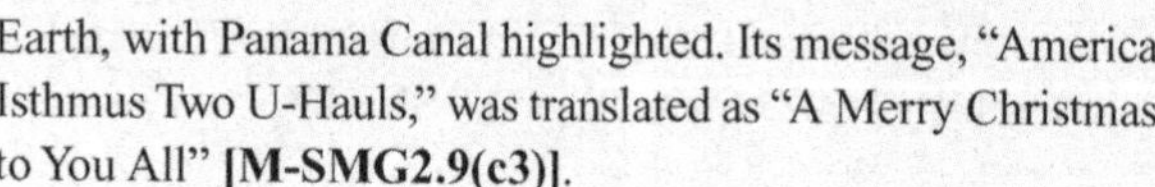

Earth, with Panama Canal highlighted. Its message, "America Isthmus Two U-Hauls," was translated as "A Merry Christmas to You All" **[M-SMG2.9(c3)]**.

- **cremation tube:** A cylindrical pod used to launch the cremated remains of crewmembers into space **[W-OFF]**. George McIntyre's ashes were placed into such a tube and shot from *Red Dwarf* out into the void **[T-SER3.4]**, as were those of several victims of the cadmium II disaster **[R-END]**.

- **cricket bat:** A genetically engineered creature—a mix between a cricket and a bat—developed by inebriated scientists **[B-EVR]**.

- **Crispy Bar:** A chocolate-covered carbohydrate bar manufactured by Australian company Performance Sports Nutrition **[RL]**. Lister ordered a Crispy Bar from a food dispenser that a crazed skutter had rewired to *Red Dwarf*'s self-destruct system. Holly had removed the explosive linked to the system years prior, but neglected to share this information until the countdown timer had run out. Thus, instead of destroying *Red Dwarf*, the dispenser served Lister a toffee-flavored Crispy Bar **[T-SER3.4]**.

- **crossbow:** A handheld weapon consisting of a bow affixed to a stock, used to fire projectiles such as darts or bolts **[RL]**. A crossbow was among the supplies that a parallel-dimension *Red Dwarf* delivered to *Starbug 1*. When the hyperway between dimensions was severed by a GELF attack, Kochanski tried to jump across the divide to return to her own universe, but missed and plummeted into non-space. Lister used the crossbow to rescue her, accidentally shooting her in the leg in the process **[T-SER7.3]**.

- **crossed circuit:** The holy emblem of Silicon Heaven, according to AI-equipped mechanical devices fitted with a belief chip **[N-BTL]**.

- **"Cruise With Me for Awhile":** A phrase on a circular sticker on Lister's guitar **[T-SER6.1]**.

- **Crunchie:** A brand of English chocolate bars containing a honeycomb toffee sugar center, manufactured by Cadbury **[RL]** and stocked in *Red Dwarf*'s vending machines **[T-SER4.3]**. Prior to the cadmium II disaster, Rimmer assigned Z-Shift's Wilkinson and Turner to Corridor 14: Alpha 12 to restock the machine with Crunchie bars **[N-INF]**. During Rimmer's murder appeal aboard Justice World, Lister testified that Z-Shift's most important function was to keep the vending machines from running out of Crunchie bars, making it unlikely that Arnold could have caused *Red Dwarf*'s destruction **[T-SER4.3]**.

- **Crusoe, Robinson:** The protagonist of Daniel Defoe's novel *Robinson Crusoe*, who survived as a castaway for years on a remote island **[RL]**. Upon learning that he would have to spend six centuries alone on an uninhabited world after launching himself from a simulant ship in an escape pod, Rimmer complained that he was not "the Robinson Crusoe type" **[T-SER6.5]**.

- **Cry 10:** A character on the American science fiction television show *Red Dwarf*, developed in an alternate universe. Cry 10 was the biologically challenged son of Dave Lister and Holly, Dave's human wife. In one episode, Cry 10 was held captive, along with his mother and sister, by an amorphous alien who vowed revenge on Lister and Rimmer for accidentally killing his bride. They were saved, however, by the heroics of Rimmer, who overcame his paralysis to defeat the creature **[M-SMG1.10(c4)]**.

- **crylion spectro:** A type of data downloaded into *Starbug*'s navicomp, enabling the crew to track down Ora Tanzil, a female member of the *Felis sapiens* species **[T-IDW]**.

- **cryoplastic:** A building material considered for deep-space long-range manned and unmanned probes. A question concerning cryoplastics was featured on several of Rimmer's First Technician's exams, all of which he failed **[B-LOG]**.

- **crypto-fascist:** A pejorative term for a person or thing secretly supporting fascism, or fostering a belief in strong authoritative control **[RL]**. After Lister traveled into the past via a timeslide, his seventeen-year-old self called him a crypto-fascist, and also used the term to describe the Tension Sheet, which older Lister wanted him to invent **[T-SER3.5]**.

- **crystalline turbine drives:** The propulsion units used aboard the SS *Centauri,* a derelict Space Corps vessel that the *Starbug 1* crew looted. Despite knowing the propulsion system's name, Cat could not determine in which century the craft was built **[T-SER7.6]**.

- **cuarango:** A tabletop game played in the twenty-second century. *Red Dwarf* had several cuarango tables in its rec rooms **[N-INF]**.

- **Cuddly Animal Theme Park:** A children's attraction on the tourist planet GELFWorld, featuring GELFs simulating soft and cute animals **[M-SMG2.2(c4)]**.

- **Cunning:** An aspect of Rimmer's personality made flesh on a psi-moon configured according to his psyche. After Arnold's shipmates rescued him from the moon, Cunning joined other solidifications of the hologram's negative traits who were left behind to battle his positive aspects, including Courage, Charity, Honour and Self-Esteem **[M-SMG2.7(c2)]**.

- **Cupcake:** A degrading nickname that Rimmer's female counterpart in an alternate universe, in which the sexes were reversed, called Lister **[T-SER2.6]**.

- **Cup O' Noodle:** A food item sold in a universe in which *Red Dwarf* and its crew were American. That reality's Lister greatly disliked Cup O' Noodle. After being marooned on an ice planet, he and Rimmer took inventory of their shuttle's supplies. A Cup O' Noodle was among the few remaining items, which Lister decided to consume last—after a can of dog food **[T-USA2]**.

  NOTE: *This was presumably similar to Cup Noodles, a packaged instant food consisting of dehydrated noodles and an assortment of other dehydrated ingredients, prepared by adding boiling water.*

- **Curie, Marie ("Madame Curie"):** A Nobel prize-winning physicist and chemist praised for her research into radioactivity **[RL]**. Kryten referenced the scientist when Kochanski asked who he was looking for in Lister's quarters **[T-SER7.7]**.

- **"Curiosity killed the human":** An old Cat saying that Cat recited when Lister tried to talk the *Red Dwarf* crew into meeting future versions of themselves **[T-SER6.6(d)]**.

  NOTE: *This spoofed the real-world phrase "Curiosity killed the cat."*

- **currant:** A small, sweet, seedless dried berry of the Black Corinth, or Common Grape Vine **[RL]**. While serving in the Scouts, Rimmer's brothers tied him to the ground, smothered jelly on his face and poured a can of ants onto him. The can containing the ants was labeled "currants," but had a handwritten label across it that read "ants" **[T-SER3.3]**.

- ***Current Affairs Programme, The*:** An entertainment news television show that focused on the marital affairs featured on the soap opera *Androids*. This program aired at 2 PM on Wednesday, the 27th of Geldof, 2362 **[M-SMG1.7(a)]**.

- **curry:** A generic term for a wide variety of spicy Indian and other regional dishes **[RL]**. Curries were Lister's favorite food, including such dishes as shami kebabs **[T-SER3.3]** and mutton vindaloo **[T-SER4.2]**.

  When *Starbug 1*'s main water tank was breached during an attack by a future version of the crew, all Indian food supplies on Supply Deck B were destroyed, including curries and poppadoms. This loss prompted Lister to trick his shipmates into retrieving the time drive so he could travel through time and restock the supply **[T-SER7.1]**.

- **Curryographer:** A title Kochanski mockingly dubbed Lister when he bragged about being knowledgeable in such things as "how to give a dinosaur the gallops," which included the preparation of a giant bowl of cow vindaloo **[T-SER8.7(d)]**.

- ***Curryworld*:** A modified version of the artificial-reality simulation *Pride and Prejudice Land,* which Kryten programmed to celebrate the anniversary of his rescue from the *Nova 5*. As the crew sat down with characters from the Jane Austen novel to enjoy a banquet of Indian foods, including vindaloo, they found it insufferably hot—a flaw that Kryten unconvincingly blamed on "a bug in the program" **[T-SER7.6]**.

- **Curtis, Tony:** An American film actor who appeared in more than one hundred films, including *Some Like It Hot*, *Spartacus* and *Operation Petticoat* **[RL]**. While discussing what to do with Lister and Kryten—who had been erased from history by the Inquisitor and were thus strangers to the *Red Dwarf* crew—Rimmer suggested killing them, suspicious of their story due to the pair being chained together "like Sidney Poitier and Tony Curtis" **[T-SER5.2]**.

  NOTE: *This referenced the film* The Defiant Ones, *in which Poitier and Curtis spent a majority of the film shackled together.*

- **Custer, Derek:** A name that Rimmer mistakenly thought was Lister's during a rescue attempt on Rimmerworld, after the hologram had spent 557 years imprisoned on the planet **[T-SER6.5]**.

- **CUTIE:** An acronym Rimmer used to help memorize a formula for his Astro-Engineer's Exam. While reading cheats off his arm, he spouted out the first four parts of the formula—Current Under Tension Is—but could not read what "E" stood for, rendering the cheat useless **[T-SER1.1]**.

- **Cvcbdekijhmnhuye's Day:** A holiday celebrated by GELFs on Arranguu 12, a moon in an alternate universe. This day commemorated the liberation of GELFs in the Northern sector from the incomprehensible and archaic legal system of the South, enabling them to become a self-governing state **[N-LST]**.

- **CX-114 Speaking Slide Rule:** A calculating apparatus produced by Deimos Instruments that contained a computer with artificial intelligence and natural voice output. Its only means of input were a dual set of molecular dataceramic rods and a plastic slider **[G-SOR]**.

- **Cyberceptor:** An attack craft used by GELFs on Lotomi 5 to intercept ships violating their planetoid's airspace. Lotomi 5, home of the virtual-reality prison complex Cyberia, was monitored by Cyberian flight controllers, who authorized the deployment of Cyberceptors in the event that a potentially hostile craft refused to identify itself **[N-LST]**.

- **cyberfoam:** A material sprayed on Cyberia inmates prior to their being lowered into the prison's cyberlake. After setting, the thin cyberfoam coating was connected to the facility's mainframe, where it reacted to each inmate's individual virtual-reality illusion, manipulating his or her senses **[N-LST]**.

- **Cyberia:** A prison facility on Lotomi 5, a GELF moon in an alternate universe. Cyberia utilized virtual-reality technology to immerse inmates in their own personal hell for the duration of their sentence, while keeping them submerged in a cyberlake. Lister's doppelgänger from Cyberia's reality was falsely imprisoned here for Emo-smuggling. The prime universe's Lister was also incarcerated at the complex while attempting to rescue his counterpart **[N-LST]**.

  NOTE: *The prison's name was a pun on the Russian territory of Siberia, which housed many strictly managed prison complexes during the era of the Soviet Union.*

- **Cyberian flight controller:** A ground-control operator for the Cyberia virtual-reality prison facility on Lotomi 5. Cyberian flight controllers monitored the airspace surrounding the complex, requesting identification and authorization from ships within the vicinity. If none were supplied, the flight controllers had the authority to launch Cyberceptors to intercept the craft **[N-LST]**.

- **cyberlake:** A vast pool of pink liquid in which inmates serving time at the Cyberia prison were held. Prisoners were hooked up to the facility's mainframe, sprayed with an active feedback cyberfoam and lowered up to their necks into the cyberlake, where they spent the duration of their sentence **[N-LST]**.

- **Cybernautics Division:** A division of a police force in a totalitarian society that the *Red Dwarf* crew imagined while trapped in a despair squid hallucination. The Cybernautics division was assigned to traffic control and employed Jake Bullet, Kryten's half-human, half-mechanical alter ego in the illusion **[T-SER5.6]**.

- **cyberpark:** A virtual-reality facility aboard a scientific research station occupied by the gestalt entity known as Legion **[T-SER6.2]**. Built in 2281 **[W-OFF]**, it was controlled by nanobots, enabling the park and its contents to be re-shaped into anything or anyone a user desired **[G-SOR]**. The *Red Dwarf* crew was allowed access to the cyberpark while being held against their will by Legion **[T-SER6.2]**.

- ***Cyber Park*:** A virtual-reality program produced by Total Immersion Inc. and distributed by Crapola Inc. It was designed to simulate a theme park, without the downside of long lines, greasy food and screaming children **[G-RPG]**.

- **cyber-psychologist:** A type of scientist in Jake Bullet's universe, specializing in the electronic replication of the human psyche. Murder victim Sandra Halley was a cyber-psychologist for a company called Brainfade **[M-SMG2.7(c4)]**.

- **cyberschool:** A computer-generated learning facility that Kochanski attended for eleven years during her youth. The institution provided students with computer-generated teachers and friends **[T-SER7.4]**. Students entered the facility by donning total-immersion suits and connecting to the school's mainframe **[T-SER7.4(e)]**.

- ***Cyber School*:** An educational virtual-reality program produced by Total Immersion Inc. and distributed by Crapola Inc. It included a 698-page manual allowing users to create the ultimate classroom **[G-RPG]**.

- **cyberzoid:** *See* cyborg

- **cyborg:** A term short for "cybernetic organism," referring to an individual with both biomechatronic and organic parts **[RL]**. Jake Bullet was a cyborg **[T-SER5.6, M-SMG1.7(a)]**.

  NOTE: *The* Red Dwarf Programme Guide *identified Bullet as a cyberzoid.*

- **Cyrius 3:** An asteroid in an alternate universe belonging to the United Republic of GELF States. The Mooli Desert was located on Cyrius 3. According to the mystics of the Forum of Justice, that dimension's Lister would eventually be responsible for Cyrius 3's destruction, before looting and pillaging his way across the asteroid belt and causing many deaths. He was thus arrested on bogus Emo-smuggling charges and imprisoned in Cyberia before the crimes could take place **[N-LST]**.

DOG, DOG

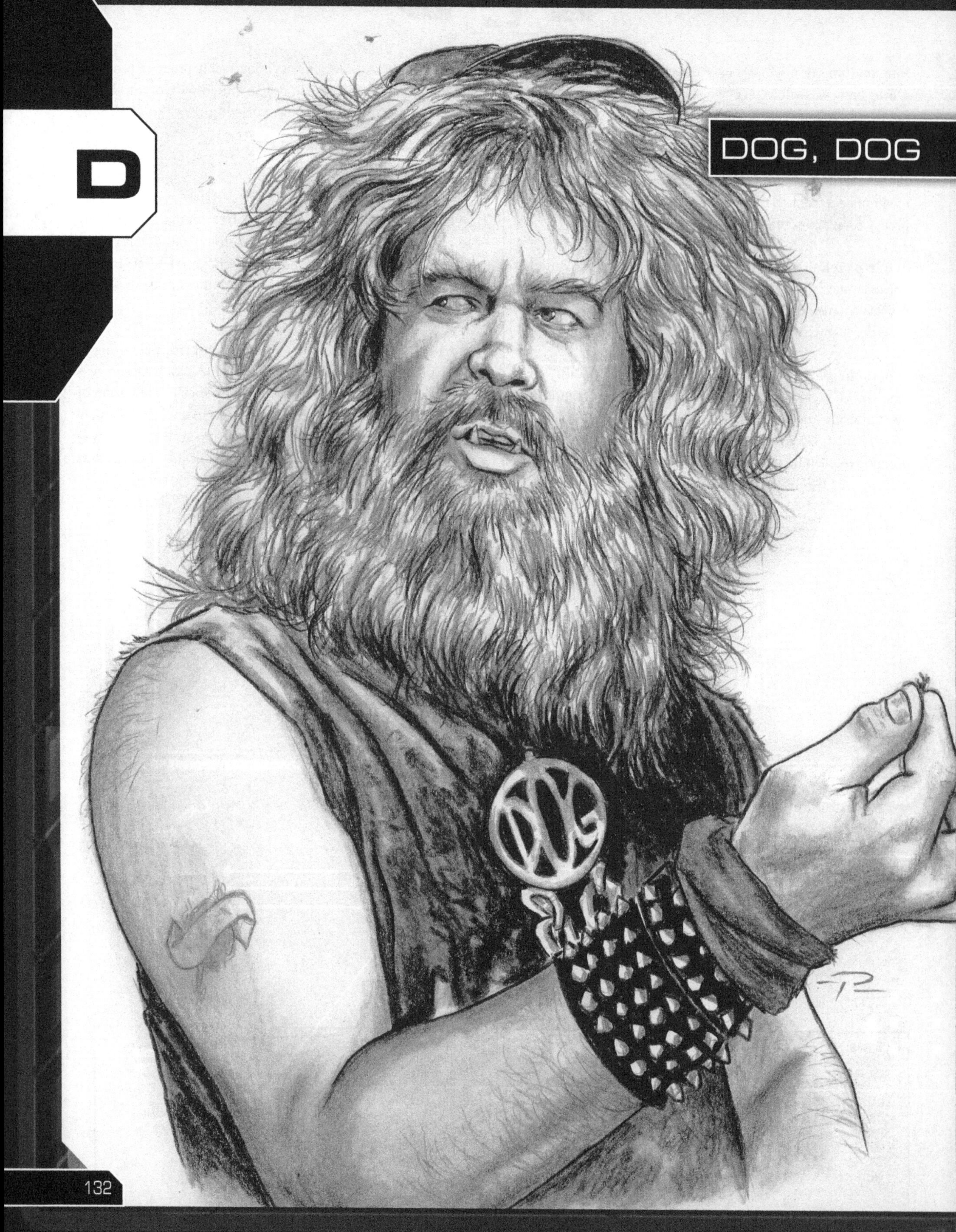

- **daffodil:** A word that replaced "drill" in Holly's vocabulary database after an electrical fire damaged her voice-recognition unit. As a result, she informed the crew that the order to "abandon shop" was "not a daffodil" **[T-SER5.5]**.

- ***Daily Asteroid, The*:** A daily newspaper serving Tunbridge Wells, England. After a meteor shower damaged the astrodome protecting Tunbridge Wells, the publication ran the headline "Pilgrims to Pray for End to Meteors," and reported that a pilgrim ship containing five hundred town residents had launched on a mission to visit a holy shrine **[M-SMG1.14(c2)]**.

- **Daily Goal List:** A "to do" list that Rimmer created to track his achievements. One item on a Thursday list—decontaminating the Officers' Block—was never completed, which Lister only discovered after entering that area. Rimmer then put the job on his next Daily Goal List, as item thirty-four, after "Learn Portuguese" **[T-SER1.5]**.

- ***Daily Smeg, The*:** A daily newspaper serving the city of Smegopolis in 2315, in the universe known as Alternative 2X13/L **[M-SMG2.1(c3)]**.

- **Daizee:** A 4000 Series mechanoid aboard *Red Dwarf* in a universe in which the sexes were reversed. Daizee, Kryten's female counterpart in that reality, helped Deb Lister take care of her two sons, Jim and Bexley **[M-SMG1.5(c2)]**.

  NOTE: *This contradicted the official website, which claimed that the mechanoid, though female, was still named Kryten. Daizee's name was presumably an homage to* 2001: A Space Odyssey, *in which the HAL-9000 computer (after whom Holly was named) sang a song called "Daisy Bell (Bicycle Built for Two)."*

- **Dalai Lama, the:** The title of the religious leader of Tibetian Buddhists **[RL]**.

  A waxdroid replica of the Dalai Lama was created for the Waxworld theme park. Left on their own for millions of years, the waxdroids attained sentience and became embroiled in a park-wide resource war between Villain World and Hero World (to which the Dalai Lama belonged). During this war, the *Red Dwarf* crew transported to the planet using a Matter Paddle, with Lister and Cat materializing in Villain territory, while Rimmer and Kryten landed in Hero territory.

  Rimmer found the heroes' army lacking and took command, working many of the pacifistic waxdroids to death before ordering a frontal attack on the enemy's compound across a minefield, which wiped out the remaining droids. The Dalai Lama waxdroid stepped on a landmine and exploded **[T-SER4.6]**.

- **Daley:** Rimmer's former bunkmate aboard *Red Dwarf* before Lister. Arnold blamed Daley, as well as several other past bunkmates, for holding him back and preventing him from becoming an officer **[N-INF]**.

- **Dali, Salvador:** A twentieth-century Spanish painter specializing in surreal imagery **[RL]**. After Rimmer's hard drive crashed during a resentment attack that caused the hologram to freeze up, Cat used a felt-tipped pen to draw a mustache on his face in the style of Dali, asking Lister and Kryten to guess who it was **[T-SER10.1]**.

- **Dall, Tarka:** *See* Dhal, Tarka

- **Dallas Electric:** A company located near W 84th Avenue in Dallas, Texas, circa 1966. This firm existed in an alternate timeline created when the *Starbug 1* crew prevented President John F. Kennedy's assassination. The crew passed a sign for the business while searching for clues to the population's disappearance; near the sign, they found a dead man who appeared to have been trampled to death **[T-SER7.1]**.

  NOTE: *A company called Dallas Electric has been in operation since 1967—a year after the crew's arrival in Texas.*

- ***Dallas Morning News, The*:** A daily newspaper founded in 1885, serving the Dallas, Texas, area **[RL]**. After John F. Kennedy was arrested in an alternate timeline created when the *Starbug 1* crew prevented his assassination, the U.S.S.R. constructed nuclear bases in Cuba, prompting the evacuation of several major U.S. cities. *The Dallas Morning News* reported the incident, with the headline "Millions Flee From American Cities" **[T-SER7.1]**.

- **Dallas Police Department:** The principal law-enforcement agency serving the city of Dallas, Texas **[RL]**. In an alternate timeline, U.S. President John F. Kennedy survived an assassination attempt due to the interference of *Starbug 1*'s crew, and subsequently had an affair with the mistress of Mafia boss Sam Giancana, for which he was impeached in 1964 and imprisoned the following year. To fix the timeline, the crew brought Kennedy back to 1963 so he could assassinate himself from a grassy knoll. To move about the area undetected, Kennedy procured a uniform from the Dallas Police Department **[T-SER7.1]**.

- **damage-control report:** A function of Kryten series mechanoids that printed a rundown of an android's current operational state from its abdomen. Kryten requested a damage-control report after awakening with a hangover from the previous night's party, which Lister had organized to honor Kryten's last day of service **[T-SER3.6]**.

- **damage-report machine:** A component aboard many JMC vessels that determined and reported any damage done to the ship **[T-SER1.5]**. Certain damage-report machines were produced by Space Cadet LLC and distributed by Crapola Inc. through its annual *SCABBY* catalog **[G-RPG]**.

  When *Red Dwarf* collided with a meteor, its damage-report machine was itself damaged **[T-SER1.5]**. *Starbug 1*'s damage-report machine was similarly impaired when the crew battled a Space Corps enforcement vehicle **[T-SER6.4]**.

- ***Dambusters, The*:** A 1955 British World War II film starring Michael Redgrave and Richard Todd **[RL]**. In one of Ace Rimmer's universes, Olaf Petersen was arrested on the grounds of Europa's Space Corps test facility after racing around the park singing *The Dambusters*'s theme song while hurling glow-in-the-dark, urine-filled condoms at security booths **[N-BCK]**.

- **Dan, Uncle:** A foster relative of Dave Lister. Uncle Dan was purported to be quite loud when using the bathroom **[T-SER8.6]**.

- **Dancer:** A fire-breathing racing yak that Cat imagined while trapped in an addictive version of *Better Than Life*. When Lister and Rimmer visited Cat at his golden castle to inform him that they were in the game, they found him on a fire-breathing racing yak, about to start a dog hunt. Noticing his guests, Cat ordered his Valkyrie assistant to saddle up two more yaks, Dancer and Prancer, so they could join him **[N-INF]**.

  NOTE: *The yaks were named after two of Santa Claus's magical flying reindeer.*

- ***Dan Dare*:** A 1950s British comic strip created by illustrator Frank Hampson, about space adventurer Colonel Daniel McGregor Dare **[RL]**. Lister, afflicted with space mumps, complained about his appearance when the crew found an escape pod possibly containing a human female, saying that if he painted his head green he could audition for a part in *Dan Dare* **[T-SER4.3(d)]**.

- **dandelion sorbet:** A dessert made from the fungi and moss found on asteroids, as well as dandelion flowers. After *Starbug 1*'s refrigeration unit malfunctioned, the crew resorted to surviving on such flora; Kryten attempted to vary the menu by occasionally making dandelion sorbet from the ingredients **[T-SER6.5]**.

- **"Danger":** A word on a label adorning a canister near Taiwan Tony, an Asian fast-food dispenser aboard *Red Dwarf* **[T-SER10.2]**.

- **"Danger 2,000 Gigawatts":** A phrase on a door sign mounted in *Red Dwarf*'s hologram simulation suite. Behind the door was a head-mountable device used to transfer memories from an individual into the hologram simulation suite's terminal **[T-SER2.5]**.

- **"Danger Low Gravity No Leaping":** A warning printed on a sign posted on the wall of *Nova 5*'s dining area **[T-SER2.1]**.

- **Dangerous, Ezekiel, Doctor:** A medical professional who awarded a certificate of strictness to Queeg 500, according to the backup computer **[W-OFF]**.

  NOTE: *It is unknown whether Dangerous actually existed, given that Queeg was merely a creation of Holly.*

- **"Danger—Robots In Operation":** A warning printed on a sign posted in the hallways of the American mining ship *Red Dwarf* **[T-USA1]**.

- **Darin-Tor:** The leader of the Cloisterists, a sect of the Cat People aboard *Red Dwarf* who believed their god's true name was Cloister. They fought a two-thousand-year holy war against the Clisterists, led by Kadok, who believed the deity was named Clister.

  The two opposing leaders met their god—Lister—after members of a neutral third sect, the Elite, traveled into the future to bring him back in time to end the conflict. Kadok, looking to secure his position as leader, tried to take Lister and the others hostage, but Darin-Tor threw himself at his rival, enabling Lister to escape. During the commotion, Kadok fatally stabbed Darin-Tor **[M-SMG2.3(c1)]**.

- **Dark, The:** A rock band, circa 2137, who found themselves at the center of a controversial advertising campaign when Magnus Sonsonson claimed to have discovered the speed of darkness, which he claimed was faster than the speed of light. This turned the physics world on its end until he admitted it was just a publicity stunt for The Dark—though, ironically, his fake theory was proven correct fifteen years later. The group's only single was titled "Dark the Hellish Angels Sing" **[B-EVR]**.

- **Dark Forces, the:** The living embodiment of Rimmer's negative personality traits, including Misery, Self-Despair and Paranoia, made flesh on a psi-moon configured according to his psyche. After Rimmer's shipmates rescued him from the moon, the Dark Forces abducted Self-Esteem to lure his comrades—Charity, Courage and Honour—into a trap, then unleashed a secret weapon: the image of Rimmer's mother **[M-SMG2.7(c2)]**.

- ***Darkness at Noon*:** A film that Rimmer imagined while trapped in an addictive version of *Better Than Life*. The movie, made sometime around three million A.D., starred sex-symbol actor Juanita Chicata, whom Rimmer married in the illusion after returning to Earth. Upon winning her first Oscar for the role, Chicata thanked him during a twenty-five-minute acceptance speech **[N-INF]**.

  NOTE: *The film may have been an adaptation of Arthur Koestler's same-named novel.*

- **Dark One, The:** The ruler of a psi-moon formed from Rimmer's mind. The moon, able to detect Arnold's neurosis, restructured itself as a desolate, gloomy, swamp-filled wasteland inhabited by manifestations of his negative attributes. The Dark One demanded Rimmer be sacrificed to the Unspeakable One **[T-SER5.3]**.

- **"Dark the Hellish Angels Sing":** The only single produced by the rock group The Dark, recorded in 2137. The song rose to only number forty-seven on the U.S. charts, despite staying at first place in Albania fourteen years running **[B-EVR]**.

  NOTE: *This song's title spoofed that of the Christmas carol "Hark! The Herald Angels Sing."*

- **Darren:** A character on the television soap opera *Androids*. In one episode, Darren attended a barbeque hosted by Daz, during which a family pet, Bouncer, was lost in a temporal-displacement vortex **[M-SMG1.8(c2)]**.

- **Darren:** A hillbilly version of Lister in an alternate universe ravaged by the tyrannical Ace "Blackheart" Rimmer, who killed Darren's sweetheart, Kochanski. While visiting this reality, another Ace Rimmer was mistaken for Blackheart by Dorrie (a humanoid whose species evolved from a dormouse), Kritter (a hillbilly cyborg analog of Kryten) and Darren, who shot him with a .38 calibre shotgun, wounding his shoulder.

  Upon realizing the mistaken identity, Darren told Ace that Blackheart had laid waste to their settlement and would return to finish the job—which he did a moment later. Darren and Kritter attacked Blackheart, but were both shot in the knees, leaving Dorrie to shoot the villain in the head **[M-SMG1.14(c5)]**.

- **Darroch, Bobby:** A Junior C classmate of Ace Rimmer. While competing against Darroch in a two-hundred-yard dash, Ace intentionally threw the race so Bobby would win, knowing how much it meant to him **[N-BCK]**.

- **Dash, Mercy:** The hostess of the television game show *20,000,000 Watts My Line* in Jake Bullet's universe. While investigating the death of contestant Philby Frutch, Bullet found Dash in Frutch's apartment. She explained that she and Frutch had been lovers, and had planned to use his winnings to pay for an operation to cure Philby's nerdism before going away on holiday **[M-SMG1.14(c6)]**.

  Captured by goons sent by the game show's TV station, Bullet discovered that Dash was also romantically involved with the show's host, Milty, who had sent her in to find out how Frutch had cheated on the show, after which she murdered him. Milty and Dash attempted to electrocute Bullet, but died when the cyborg chomped on Milty's microphone cable, shocking them instead **[M-SMG2.2(c2)]**.

  A month later, Bullet's mind envisioned apparitions of Milty and Dash as he fell from a building to his apparent death **[M-SMG2.6(c6)]**.

- **Dastardly and Muttley:** A pair of villainous characters from Hanna Barbara's animated television series *Wacky Races* and its spinoff, *Dastardly and Muttley in Their Flying Machines* **[RL]**. Their names adorned a patch sewn onto Lister's leather jacket **[T-SER2.1]**.

- **Datacorp Model 'H':** The brand and model of Holly, the artificial-intelligence computer aboard the American mining vessel *Red Dwarf* **[T-USA1(s1)]**.

- **Data Doctor:** A software suite designed to diagnose and repair the corrupted files of mechanoids, created for Diva-Droid International by the brother of Diva-Droid salesman Jim Reaper **[W-OFF]**. *Red Dwarf*'s Board of Inquiry subjected Kryten to a psychotropic simulation in order to determine his guilt or innocence, which made the mechanoid believe his files had been restored to factory settings using this program **[T-SER8.2]**.

- **DataLoad:** A storage system developed by HoloPoint, enabling users to quickly load a hologrammic form. The technology could be upgraded to include animals **[W-HOL]**. Kryten accessed *Starbug*'s Dataload system to re-animate Rimmer after his light bee had remained in cold storage for the duration of a two-hundred-year pursuit of the stolen *Red Dwarf* **[T-SER6.1]**.

- **Datanet:** A product produced on Callisto due to the moon's specialized service industry **[G-RPG]**.

- **Data Threshhold:** A setting on *Starbug 1*'s sonar scope display. This setting was not highlighted as the crew charted the course of a despair squid **[T-SER5.6]**.

- **Dave:** A British television channel on twenty-first-century Earth **[RL]**. While trapped in an elation squid hallucination, Lister imagined learning about this channel—named after his character on a fictional comedy series called *Red Dwarf*—from two children he met while riding a bus to the Lumpton Street depot **[T-SER9.2]**.

  NOTE: *In the real world, UKTV actually chose the name "Dave" based on the notion that "everyone knows a bloke named Dave," and not because of Lister's character.*

- ***Dave and Arn's Spacious Adventure*:** A substitute title that Frank, a TV executive in an alternate universe in which *Red Dawrf* was an American television series, suggested for the show after noting the lack of actual dwarves in it **[M-SMG1.10(c4)]**.

  NOTE: *This title spoofed that of the film* Bill & Ted's Excellent Adventure.

- **Dave Dee, Dozy, Beaky, Mick & Tich:** A British pop group, circa the 1960s, who released the hit single "The Legend of Xanadu" **[RL]**. In an alternate timeline in which Lister invented the Tension Sheet and became Earth's youngest billionaire, he lived in a mansion that he called Xanadu. According to the host of *Life Styles of the Disgustingly Rich and Famous*, Lister had named the house after the band's song **[T-SER3.5]**.

- **Dave Lister Special, The:** A meal offered by The Vindaloovian Empire, an Indian restaurant aboard *Red Dwarf*, consisting of three poppadoms, extremely spicy chicken vindaloo, a dill pickle, green mint sauce, "unidentifiable red stuff" and coffee ice cream **[X-CAL]**.

- ***David Cassidy's Greatest Hits*:** An album released in 1974, collecting several tunes from the popular singer-songwriter **[RL]**. When Holly presented a tiny computer slug revealing how to avert a white hole crisis, Rimmer remarked that despite her new IQ of twelve thousand, it appeared (given the diminutive nature of the media) that all she had supplied them with was *David Cassidy's Greatest Hits* **[T-SER4.4(d)]**.

- **David Ross Block:** A street featured on the television soap opera *Androids*. Brook fell into a drunken stupor by a scrap heap near David Ross Block **[M-SMG1.13(c1)]**.

  NOTE: *Actor David Ross first portrayed Kryten in episode 2.1 ("Kryten").*

- **Davis, Leo:** A caretaker at Black Island Film Studios, a production company in a universe in which *Red Dwarf* was a British television series. Davis worked the night shift due to somnolence, a condition that caused him to take periodic naps.

  One night, Davis befriended a black cat at the studio, as it reminded him of Cat, a character on *Red Dwarf*, his favorite television show. He fell asleep watching the series with his new pet, but was abruptly awakened by his boss, Mr. Walker, who arrived accompanied by two clients, director Andrew De Bye-Moray and a dancer named Kit.

  Though attracted to Kit, Davis could not muster the courage to ask her out. Instead, he daydreamed about celebrities and fictional characters, including Elvis Presley and Judge Dredd, offering him advice on how to approach her. He also dreamed that he was Cat, raga artist Tabby Ranks and others whom he associated with self-confidence. Inspired, Leo quit his studio job and took Kit out for a night on the town **[X-TNG]**.

- **Davis, Steve:** An early twenty-first-century British professional snooker player, regarded by many as being among the top three players of all time **[RL]**. On a scale of zero to Steve Davis, Kryten likened Lister's gamesmanship to that of a color-blind mongoose **[T-IDW]**.

- **Davro:** A Space Corps physicist, considered one of the most brilliant minds of his era, who was involved in a classified military project aboard a scientific research station. The project resulted in the creation of Legion, a gestalt entity encompassing the intellect and emotions of all four project scientists, including Davro's. Davro eventually died, as did the other scientists, leaving Legion nothing but a floating essence until the *Starbug 1* crew visited the station **[T-SER6.2]**.

  NOTE: *Davro was possibly named after Davros, the brilliant scientist who created the Daleks on British science fiction series* Doctor Who.

- **Day, Doris:** A twentieth-century American actor, singer and animal rights activist, known for such films as *Love Me or Leave Me* and *Pillowtalk* **[RL]**.

  A waxdroid replica of Day was created for the Waxworld theme park. Left on their own for millions of years, the waxdroids attained sentience and became embroiled in a park-wide resource war between Villain World and Hero World (to which Day belonged). The Doris Day waxdroid died during the conflict **[T-SER4.6]**.

- **Dayglo orange moonboots:** A pair of boots that Lister wore while attempting to rescue three female officers aboard the crashed ship *Nova 5*. The malodorous footwear occasionally set off *Red Dwarf*'s dangerous chemical detector. Hoping to embarrass Lister in front of the women, Rimmer persuaded him to wear the foul-smelling boots to their ship **[T-SER1.5]**.

  NOTE: *Dayglo is a registered trademark of the DayGlo Color Corp.*

- **Daz:** a brand of laundry detergent sold in the United Kingdom **[RL]**. When Lister decided to go back in time via a stasis leak so he could save Kochanski from dying in *Red Dwarf*'s cadmium II accident and then marry her, Rimmer claimed it was pointless if he couldn't bring her back with him—and that he might as well marry a box of Daz since she'd be reduced to radioactive ash in three weeks' time **[T-SER2.4]**.

- **Daz:** A character on the television soap opera *Androids*. In one episode, Daz hosted a barbeque, at which guests included Darren, Shaz, Jaz, Baz, Gaz and Dink. During the party, a family pet called Bouncer was lost in a temporal-displacement vortex **[M-SMG1.8(c2)]**.

- **"D-D-Don't Shoot":** A phrase printed on one of Lister's T-shirts, accompanied by a suit-clad gorilla holding a gun **[T-SER1.6]**.

  NOTE: *According to the official website, the gorilla was Mugs Murphy, an original cartoon character created for* Red Dwarf. *In episode 1.6 ("Me"), Lister and company watched a Mugs Murphy cartoon prior to viewing* Citizen Kane.

- ***D-D-Don't Shoot*:** The title of a DVD displayed in a twenty-first-century mall video store that the *Red Dwarf* crew imagined while trapped in an elation squid hallucination **[T-SER9.2]**.

  NOTE: *This was presumably a Mugs Murphy DVD.*

- **D Deck:** A level aboard *Starbug 1*. In his first official log entry, Lister noted how he had matured since turning twenty-eight, having only tried to urinate on Rimmer from D Deck once in a long while **[T-SER7.1]**.

- **D Deck:** A level aboard *Red Dwarf*. Lister once took Kochanski out to dinner in the dome on D Deck, using money he had obtained from selling Rimmer a Jammie Dodger he'd found in a sofa cushion **[T-SER9.2(d)]**.

- **deadies:** A slang term for people revived as a hologram after death **[T-SER1.2]**.

- **deadpan mode:** A function of 4000 Series mechanoids enabling them to attempt humor without displaying emotion or expression. Kryten entered deadpan mode when informing Lister that he would have to "die" along with Kryten when he deactivated himself to await his replacement **[T-SER3.6]**.

- **"Dealing With Nutters":** A mail-order psychiatry course, during the first part of which students received a free binder. Doctor Lucas McClaren, *Red Dwarf*'s chief psychiatric officer, graduated from this course **[W-OFF]**.

- **Death:** An entity also known as the Grim Reaper, typically portrayed as wearing a black-hooded robe and carrying a sythe, mythologically said to cause the process of dying **[RL]**. When Lister was convinced he would perish during an explosion in *Red Dwarf*'s Drive Room, he took with him a metal bar to use against Death. Rimmer pointed out that Death was not something one could whack on the head, but Lister defiantly threatened to rip Death's nipples off if he came near him **[T-SER1.2]**.

  Years later, after *Red Dwarf* was decimated by a chameleonic microbe, Death visited Rimmer aboard *Red Dwarf*, informing him that his life was over and he would be traveling to the river Styx. Rimmer, however, kneed the entity in the groin and ran off, exclaiming, "Only the good die young" **[T-SER8.8]**.

  ***NOTE:** Rimmer's observation that "You can't whack Death on the head" is amusing, given his tactic against the Grim Reaper.*

- **Death:** *See* Apocalypse, Death

- **Death, Judge:** An undead character appearing in Judge Dredd stories published in the U.K. comic strip anthology *2000 AD*. Judge Death was the leader of the Dark Judges, lawkeepers from another dimension who deemed life itself a crime **[RL]**. Judge Death was among the Inquisitor's role models **[M-SMG2.5(a)]**.

- **deathagram:** A hypothetical assassination service. After a barrage of bazookoid fire had no impact on the Unspeakable One, Cat exclaimed that his group had delivered the deathagram to the wrong address **[T-SER5.3(d)]**.

- **Deathbot:** A cartoon robot character created by twenty-first-century American company Gama-Go for use on apparel and gifts **[RL]**. While trapped in an elation squid hallucination, the *Red Dwarf* crew imagined seeing Deathbot merchandise at a British science fiction shop called They Walk Among Us! **[T-SER9.2]**.

- **deathday:** A holiday that Rimmer celebrated to commemorate the day he perished in the cadmium II disaster that killed the *Red Dwarf* crew. On one such occasion, Lister, Rimmer (via a hologramatic projection cage), Cat, Holly and two skutters took *Blue Midget* to a barren planet to celebrate with food, alcohol and music **[T-SER2.3]**.

- **Death Ship:** A vessel used by a cyborg-like species called *Homo sapienoids*, who took over Earth's solar system and brought humanity to the brink of extinction. The *Homo sapienoids* sent fleets of Death Ships to pursue *Red Dwarf* in search of the last human alive, Dave Lister **[X-PRO]**.

  ***NOTE:** This was mentioned in a promotional flyer promoting the never-filmed* Red Dwarf *movie.*

- **Death Wheel:** A structure built by agonoids who commandeered *Red Dwarf*. Designed by Djuhn'Keep, it consisted of several corridors leading from the ships' docking bays into a centralized location called the Hub of Pain.

  The agonoids planned to lead Lister, the last human alive, along with Rimmer, Kryten and Cat, through the Death Wheel's spokes, increasing the difficulty of each corridor using the ship's environmental controls, until the group was forced into the hub. After the victims experienced the full horror of the Hub of Pain—which included every known cutting, bludgeoning and torturing device known to man—the agonoids planned a competition involving a separate series of v-shaped corridors which, through process of elimination, would allow the strongest and fastest agonoid ("The One") to enter the Hub of Pain and dispatch the human in any way he desired, while the beaten combatants looked on from the viewing gallery.

  During the setup's unveiling, Djuhn'Keep activated its many traps, killing off every other agonoid, and thereby ensuring that he alone would have the pleasure of killing Lister. Due to unforeseen circumstances, however, the fight moved over to *Starbug*, where the agonoid died without achieving his goal **[N-BCK]**.

- **De Burgh:** A twenty-second-century scientist who developed a theory pertaining to thermal induction in porous circuitry. Rimmer's final Astronavigation Exam, prior to the cadmium II disaster, contained a question about this theory, the answer to which he had written on his forearm. When he attempted to access the information, however, he accidentally smeared it from excessive sweat, causing him to suffer a nervous breakdown **[N-INF]**.

- **De Bye-Moray, Andrew ("Dickhead"):** A film director in an alternate dimension, often called "Dickhead" by those with whom he worked. De Bye-Moray booked Black Island Film Studios for a music video he was producing for Tabby Ranks. For years, he had unsuccessfully courted one of Ranks' dancers, Kit **[X-TNG]**.

- **decative:** A system devised by Holly to decimalize the musical scale. Holly added two new notes (H and J) to the octave (which he renamed a decatave), as well as two new syllables to the major scale ("woh" and "boh," falling between sol and ti) **[T-SER2.1]**.

  NOTE: *This gag originated in a* Son of Cliché *"Dave Hollins: Space Cadet" sketch titled "Sir Kevin Kevin Sir." In the* Red Dwarf *version, the DVD captions spelled the word as "decadive," but the more commonly accepted spelling is "decatave."*

- ***Decayed Flesh 5: The Zombies Take Manhattan*:** A horror movie stocked at Wacky Wally's Video Wonderland, a video store at which Oswald "Kill Krazy" Blenkinsop worked prior to his incarceration aboard *Red Dwarf*. When Kill Crazy played this movie during one shift, an offended customer chastised him for doing so. Later that day, Kill Crazy followed the woman home and murdered her entire family, for which he was arrested and sent to *Red Dwarf*'s brig for transport to Adelphi 12 **[W-OFF]**.

- **Deck 177:** *See* Floor 4177

- **Deck 4:** A deck located on the *Mayflower* **[N-LST]**.

- **Deck 4177:** *See* Floor 4177

- **Deck 9:** A level aboard *Red Dwarf*, containing Cat's litter tray **[B-LOG]**.

- **Deck 97:** Another level aboard *Red Dwarf*. As the ship returned to Earth, Rimmer noted that the chicken soup nozzles on Deck 97 needed to be cleaned **[R-BOD]**.

- **Deck Sergeant:** A rank aboard *Red Dwarf*. An officer of this rank was taking the Engineer's Exam when Rimmer suffered a panic attack after smearing the answers written all over his body **[T-SER1.1]**.

- **Deck Swabber:** A position advertised on the Jupiter Mining Corporation's website. Preferred candidates were doe-eyed orphans able to retain an air of sorrow when asked to re-wash a deck. The position's reference number was GRH9265 **[W-JMC]**.

- ***Decree Nisi* Megadrive Chip:** A computer component that Brook served to Kelly on the television soap opera *Androids*, after Kelly admitted she had an affair with his business rival Gary, and that Brooke Junior was Gary's son and not his **[M-SMG1.8(c5)]**.

  NOTE: *In the United Kingdom, a* decree nisi *is a court order required to initiate divorce proceedings.*

- **deep sleep unit:** A device used during interstellar space travel, designed to put an occupant in a coma-like state for long intervals, with lifesigns reduced to nearly zero (though hair and fingernails continued to grow at a reduced pace). *Starbug 1* contained at least two deep sleep units in its Obs Room, which Lister and Cat used while pursuing the stolen *Red Dwarf* **[T-SER6.1]**. Kryten modified the units to include temporary stasis seals, so the crew could shield themselves from the effects of unreality pockets while traversing a reality minefield **[T-SER6.6]**.

  NOTE: *Deep sleep units—which were not named until episode 6.6 ("Out of Time")—differed from the suspended animation booths mentioned in later episodes.*

- **Deep Space Leisure, LLC:** A private courier company that operated the SS *Hermes*, a vessel carrying Talia Garrett **[G-SOR]**.

B-: Books
PRG: *Red Dwarf Programme Guide*
SUR: *Red Dwarf Space Corps Survival Manual*
PRM: *Primordial Soup*
SOS: *Son of Soup*
SCE: *Scenes from the Dwarf*
LOG: *Red Dwarf Log No. 1996*
RD8: *Red Dwarf VIII*
EVR: *The Log: A Dwarfer's Guide to Everything*

X-: Misc.
PRO: Promotional materials, videos, etc.
PST: Posters at DJ XVII (2013)
CAL: 2008 calendar
RNG: Cell phone ringtones
MOB: Mobisode ("Red Christmas")
CIN: *Children in Need* sketch
GEK: *Geek Week* intros by Kryten
TNG: "Tongue-Tied" video

XMS: Bill Pearson's Christmas special pitch script
XVD: Bill Pearson's Christmas special pitch video
OTH: Other *Red Dwarf* appearances

SUFFIX
DVD:
(d) – Deleted scene
(o) – Outtake
(b) – Bonus DVD material (other)
(e) – Extended version

SMEGAZINES:
(c) – Comic
(a) – Article

OTHER:
(s) – Early/unused script draft
(s1) – Alternate version of script

- **deep space probe:** A small data-collecting probe that Lister once used to remove the wax buildup in his ears **[T-SER6.2(d)]**.

- **defense mode:** A mode that robot goldfish could engage when placed in an unfamiliar environment. Lister's pet fish, Lennon and McCartney, engaged defense mode when Kryten accidently flushed them down the latrine, and wound up in *Red Dwarf*'s waste-disposal conduits **[M-SMG2.4(c5)]**.

- **defensive micropedo:** A small armament installed in MkIV Titanica Fish Droids, such as Lister's pet robot goldfish, McCartney and Lennon. After Kryten accidentally flushed Lister's goldfish down the toilet, the piscine droids, unaware of their new surroundings, armed their micropedoes—the detonation of which nearly killed Lister when he later used the bathroom facilities **[M-SMG2.4(c5)]**.

- **defensive shields:** An emergency system that protected a spaceship from incoming fire. Cat suggested activating defensive shields when *Starbug 1* was targeted by a holoship's probe. Although calling this a good idea, Kryten noted that the shuttle was not equipped with defensive shields—a fact he felt warranted mentioning twice **[T-SER5.1]**.

- **Deformed Dozen, the:** A nickname that Lister gave to a group of rogue droids he had purchased from an alternate-universe Kinitawowi tribe. Three of the droids had all limbs accounted for, while two were missing left arms, two lacked ears and left legs, one had loose optical units hanging down to its chest, one giggled and blew saliva bubbles, one was missing its entire upper body, one had no head, and one was merely a hand **[N-LST]**.

- **Deganwy:** A village located in North Wales **[RL]**. While debating with Rimmer about whether humans or machines were better, Lister recalled a school camping trip to Deganwy that his class took with their geography teacher, Miss Foster. One night during the trip, he awoke to strange noises coming from Foster's tent, leading Lister to conclude that *she* did not consider men to be better than machines **[T-SER2.5]**.

- **dehydrated champagne:** An alcoholic beverage stored in powder form and rehydrated with water when served. While aboard *Nova 5*, Kryten served the crew dehydrated champagne upon the completion of their mission **[N-INF]**.

- **Deimos Instruments:** A company, possibly headquartered on the Martian moon of Deimos, that produced calculating equipment, such as the CX-114 Speaking Slide Rule **[G-SOR]**.

  ***NOTE:** The company's name was presumably based on that of American electronics firm Texas Instruments.*

- **Deki:** A Dingotang guard employed at the Cyberia virtual-reality prison on Lotomi 5. His section included the symbimorph quarters, an area housing the facility's complement of shapeshifting Pleasure GELFs, as well as the rooms in which they performed their duties.

  Deki was sexually involved with an "unbroken" symbimorph named Reketrebn, who had used four of her hooks (telepathic links) on the guard, and was thus strongly bonded with him. Regardless, he forced her to perform sex acts for inmates who volunteered for the Reco-Programme, and beat her if she failed to comply. Reketrebn eventually left Deki and helped Lister escape from the facility **[N-LST]**.

- ***Delecto quislibet*:** A strain of sexual magnetism virus isolated by hologrammatic scientist Hildegarde Lanstrom **[W-OFF]**. Sexual magnetism was one of several positive viruses Lanstrom discovered; this particular strain made an infected individual more attractive to the opposite sex. Kryten discovered vials of this and other positive viruses on the station and brought them aboard *Red Dwarf*. Upon learning of the virus' existence, Cat decided he had been permanently infected **[T-SER5.4]**.

  Years later, the nanobot-resurrected Rimmer found the sexual magnetism virus and *Felicitus populi* (a luck virus) in the wreckage of *Starbug 1*, aboard the rebuilt *Red Dwarf* **[T-SER8.1]**. A short time thereafter, Rimmer and the *Starbug 1* crew were subjected to a psychotropically induced illusion by *Red Dwarf*'s Board of Inquiry to determine whether they were guilty of misusing the crew's personnel files. In the illusion, Rimmer believed he had imbibed the sexual magnetism virus and had sex with Yvonne McGruder, then attended a dinner with Captain Hollister, during which he had intercourse with several other female officers in the Captain's Galley.

  After Rimmer was revived from the psychotropic illusion, Hollister demanded the vials. Arnold handed over the luck virus, but surreptitiously passed the sexual magnetism vial to Lister, who later used it to infect Rimmer during their incarceration in the Tank **[T-SER8.3]**.

  ***NOTE:** In the novel* Last Human*, the crew discovered*

the virus on the Mayflower*, an ancient terraforming ship. Onscreen, however, they found it at Lanstrom's station.*

- ***Del Monte*:** A late-night television program developed by Bartholomew Mews and Natalie Heathcote, creators of the television soap opera *Androids*. The program, a controversial sex-and-fruit drama, marked the end of the creative pair's collaborative projects **[W-AND]**.

  NOTE: *Del Monte Foods is an American distribution company specializing in products such as canned fruits.*

- **Delphi VIII:** A planetoid once home to a human colony that was destroyed by a mutated athlete's foot fungus **[G-RPG]**.

- **Delta:** The fourth letter of the Greek alphabet **[RL]**, used in a code to disarm and unlock a groinal exploder that a group of BEGGs had affixed to Lister's crotch. The code—Theta, Delta, Alpha, Beta, Gamma—had to be input precisely, in that order, for the device to be disabled **[T-SER10.4]**.

- **Delta 7:** A world whose population contracted the Epideme virus. The entire planet was torched in an attempt to destroy the parasite, but the virus escaped by infecting a Space Corps medical engineer, who then visited the *Leviathan*, enabling the disease to spread further. The *Leviathan* set course for Delta 7 to find a cure, but burnt out its engines before arriving, and the remaining personnel soon died from the virus. Three millions years later, Epideme infected Lister, who discovered the *Leviathan*'s trajectory and visited Delta 7—but the devastation he found there dashed all hope for a cure **[T-SER7.7]**.

  NOTE: *The monitor's image implied the* Leviathan *was en route to Theta 4. Later in the episode, however, Lister reported that the ship was heading to Delta 7 to find a cure for Epideme. The other planet on the monitor was presumably Delta 7.*

- **Delta V mass reaction thrusters:** A type of high-end propulsion system not typically found on GELF-designed attack cruisers **[G-RPG]**.

- ***Demon Lurks, A*:** A horror novel among the possessions of a sociopathic, alternate-universe Lister whom the *Starbug 1* crew encountered after traversing the Omni-zone **[N-LST]**.

- **Demonstroes:** A miniscule hostile alien species who responded to a distress beacon from *Red Dwarf*'s crew. Initially feigning benevolence, the Demonstroes soon revealed their true intentions: universal global annihilation.

  While floating outside *Red Dwarf*, Kryten accidentally swallowed the creatures' entire fleet. Furious, the aliens threatened to beam back to their homeworld, detonating their ships in the process. The *Red Dwarf* crew used Kryten's nanobot device to shrink themselves down and insert themselves into the mechanoid's body so they could retrieve a radioactive mass left behind by the Demonstroes.

  Using a miniaturized probe ship, the crew searched Kryten's body until locating and containing the mass, then exited via the mechanoid's nasal passage. After jettisoning the radioactive mass from *Red Dwarf*, Kryten predicted it would eventually expand and create a life-sustaining star system much like Earth's own solar system **[X-XMS]**.

  NOTE: *Had this episode been produced, the existence of the Demonstroes would have contradicted the long-held notion of there being no aliens in the* Red Dwarf *mythos.*

- **Denis:** A space beatnik on Mimas who was addicted to the designer drug Bliss. His girlfriend was a Game head named Josie, whom he met at the New Zodiac festival, a celebration of the zodiac constellations' realignment, during which his astrological sign changed from Sagittarius to Capricorn.

  Denis had a second-class degree in biochemistry, while Josie had a first-class degree in pure mathematics. The couple had hoped to travel to Neptune for Pluto's solstice, but within five years had only made it as far as Mimas. While on the moon, Denis, looking to score money for Bliss, mugged Lister outside a brothel **[N-INF]**.

- **Denmark:** A coastal Scandinavian country in Northern Europe **[RL]**. Olaf Petersen had a tattoo on his right arm that read "Denmark Forever" **[T-SER1.3]**.
  While trapped in an addictive version of *Better Than Life*, Cat believed he had returned to Earth with Lister and Rimmer, and had settled down in a golden castle on an island off the coast of Denmark, surrounded by a moat of milk **[N-INF]**.

- **"Denmark Forever":** A tattoo on Olaf Petersen's right arm. Rimmer noticed the tattoo on his own appendage after his hologrammic arm was replaced with Petersen's due to a corrupted physical data disc **[T-SER1.3]**.

- **Dennis ("Dungo"):** The Rimmer family gardener on Io, and Arnold Rimmer's biological father. A babbling simpleton, Dungo was among Mrs. Rimmer's many lovers of whom her husband was aware. The family hid Arnold's true parentage from him, letting him believe he shared ancestry with Austrian princes and French royalty.

  Upon playing a holo-message from his stepfather three million years later, however, Arnold learned the truth. The revelation shocked him at first, until he realized that Dennis—unlike the man who'd raised him—would have been proud of his accomplishments, and that he no longer needed to suffer from poor self-esteem since he didn't have to live up to Mr. Rimmer's expectations anymore **[T-SER10.6]**.

- **Dennis the Doughnut Boy:** Frank Hollister's identity prior to his assignment as *Red Dwarf*'s captain. Dennis used confidential files to blackmail his way up the ranks—a tactic he recognized when Rimmer attempted the same trick years later **[T-SER8.3]**.

- **Denti-bot:** An autonomous medical unit aboard *Red Dwarf* in which dental procedures, such as cavity fillings, were performed. Lister attempted to have the Denti-bot repair his teeth on several occasions, but chickened out every time **[T-SER10.2]**.

- **Denton:** A *Red Dwarf* crewmember who perished during the cadmium II disaster, but was resurrected when nanobots rebuilt the mining ship. Denton dated Rimmer's ex-lover, Yvonne McGruder; irked, Arnold called him "Mr. Smoothie." After escaping from solitary confinement, Lister and Rimmer discovered the crew, including Denton, frozen in time by a time wand. Rimmer took the opportunity to draw a moustache and glasses on Denton's face with a marker **[T-SER8.6(d)]**.

  NOTE: *Cat perpetrated this same prank on Rimmer in episode 10.1 ("Trojan").*

- **Department of Death and Deceaseds' Rights:** A government agency responsible for the administration of holograms post-resurrection. Responsibilities included furnishing appropriate forms to the recently deceased, distributing informational literature and offering counseling services to individuals having difficulty adjusting to life as a hologram **[N-INF]**.

- **Derek:** A character on the television soap opera *Androids* who owned Jupiter's largest limousine company, DriveU, and was also involved in black-market bolt sales. In one episode, Derek married Simone on a bet with Jaysee, who offered him controlling interest in Droid Oil if he stayed with her for three years **[W-AND]**.

  NOTE: *The* Androids *website used a drawing of the character of Archie, from the* Smegazines, *to illustrate Derek.*

- **derelict research platform:** A sophisticated space station created by humans to research artificial intelligence. It utilized wetware AI technology to store the sum total of human knowledge in its heuristic neural net, using a fluid matrix running throughout the platform.

  The *Red Dwarf* crew discovered the station while searching for signs of alien life. While aboard the platform, Lister became trapped in a wetware interface, a stream of liquid used to integrate a user into the station's computer. Using the experiences of Lister's mind as the final component, the computer attained sentience, thereby creating a new life form.

  To prevent Lister from becoming irreversibly integrated with the computer, Holly entered the program to keep him focused, first appearing as a beautiful blonde woman, and then taking him to a virtual bar where they both got drunk while conversing with the newly sentient AI. After Holly led Lister back to the real world, the crew departed the platform—but not before Cat accidentally destroyed the new AI intelligence by urinating into the fluid matrix **[M-SMG1.11(c2)]**.

- **Dernbvjukidhgd, F'hnhiujsrf, His Imperial Majesty ("F'hnhiujsrf the Unpronounceable"):** The leader of an alternate-universe GELF state governing the virtual-reality prison Cyberia **[N-LST]**.

- **DeSalvo, Albert:** *See* Albert DeSalvo Likeability Award; Boston Strangler, the

- **Descartes, René:** A seventeenth-century French philosopher and mathematician, often called the father of modern

PREFIX
RL: Real life

T-: Television Episodes
SER: Television series
IDW: "Identity Within"
USA1: Unaired U.S. pilot
USA2: Unaired U.S. demo

R-: *The Bodysnatcher Collection*
SER: Remastered episodes
BOD: "Bodysnatcher"
DAD: "Dad"
FTH: "Lister's Father"
INF: "Infinity Patrol"
END: "The End" (original assembly)

N-: Novels
INF: *Infinity Welcomes Careful Drivers*
BTL: *Better Than Life*
LST: *Last Human*

BCK: *Backwards*
OMN: *Red Dwarf Omnibus*

M-: Magazines
SMG: *Smegazine*

W-: Websites
OFF: Official website
NAN: *Prelude to Nanarchy*
AND: *Androids*
DIV: Diva-Droid
DIB: Duane Dibbley

CRP: Crapola
GEN: Geneticon
LSR: Leisure World Intl.
JMC: Jupiter Mining Corporation
AIT: *A.I. Today*
HOL: HoloPoint

G-: Roleplaying Game
RPG: *Core Rulebook*
BIT: *A.I. Screen Extra Bits* booklet
SOR: *Series Sourcebook*
OTH: Other RPG material

philosophy **[RL]**. While weighing the pros and cons of using a DNA-modifying machine, Lister mistakenly attributed the phrase "I am what I am" to Descartes. Rimmer corrected him by noting it was actually the cartoon character Popeye the Sailor Man who uttered the phrase **[T-SER4.2]**.

The Transtemporal Film Unit produced a *Run Your Way Slim* fitness video featuring Descartes, titled *I Jog Therefore I Am* **[B-LOG]**.

> ***NOTE:*** *Descartes' quote was actually* "Cogito ergo sum," *which translates from Latin as "I think, therefore I am."*

- **despair squid:** A creature living in the ocean of an S-3 planet. The despair squid produced a venomous ink with which it disoriented its prey by inducing a feeling of great despondency. It was genetically engineered by the Space Corps, which assigned the oceanic seeding ship SSS *Esperanto* to accelerate the planet's evolution by introducing amino acids. The result: five million years' worth of evolution within three solar years.

  When the *Esperanto* returned to check on the planet's progress three years later, the squid used its ink to induce intense despair, causing the entire crew to commit suicide. For many years, the beast ate its way through the ocean, eventually causing the extinction of every other marine species on the planet.

  The *Starbug 1* crew eventually found the *Esperanto* at the bottom of the ocean, its crew dead and with remnants of hallucinogenic ink evident. They returned to their ship, but the squid hit the shuttle with a concentrated dose of ink, causing the crew to experience a group hallucination in which they awoke in a game simulation suite.

  In the illusion, the crew believed that their lives aboard the mining vessel had all been part of a total-immersion video game called *Red Dwarf*—and that they had only scored four percent. Led to a recuperation lounge, they discovered their "true" identities: Duane Dibbley (Cat), an uncouth klutz with zero style or grace; Jake Bullet (Kryten), a half-human cyborg detective of the police force's traffic-control Cybernautics Division; Billy Doyle (Rimmer), a wild-haired loser; and his more successful half-brother Sebastian Doyle (Lister).

  Shocked by the revelation, the four left the facility and emerged in a fascist society, with posters telling citizens to "Vote Fascist for a 3rd Glorious Decade of Total Law Enforcement" and asking them to "Be a Government Informer—Betray Your Family and Friends, Fabulous Prizes to Be Won." The group confronted a police agent in a carpark, who claimed Sebastian was the mass-murdering head of an organization known as CGI, and the leader of the Ministry of Alteration.

  Kryten inadvertently killed the agent, and a high-speed police chase ensued. Finally, unable to deal with their despair, the crew decided to commit suicide. Before they could do so, however, Holly transmitted a subconscious message to Kryten, telling him to release a gas that would counter the ink's effect, allowing them to break free of the hallucination. Holly, meanwhile, used limpet mines to destroy the squid **[T-SER5.6]**.

  > ***NOTE:*** *See also elation squid entry.*

- **Despicable One, The:** A title by which the Unspeakable One—a creature representing Rimmer's self-loathing on a psi-moon configured according to his psyche—referred to Rimmer **[T-SER5.3]**.

- **detachable power transfer adapter:** A removable device for transferring power between different components. Certain adapters were capable of holding spikes upwards of five million volts. After Rimmer became infected with a deadly holovirus that drove him insane and caused him to attack his crewmates, the others immobilized him by using a detachable power transfer adapter combined with other components. This task was made easier by the luck virus, with which Lister had infected himself **[T-SER5.4]**.

- **Detritus Wrecks:** A junkyard featured on the television soap opera *Androids*, owned by Debris Reynolds. While scavenging through this junkyard, Brooke Junior found his father, Brook, lying among the garbage, destitute and drunk. At that moment, Karstares—Brook's father, thought dead from a plane crash—appeared, vowing revenge against his other son, Jaysee, for attempting to murder him and taking over the family business **[M-SMG2.1(c2)]**.

  > ***NOTE:*** *Detritus is non-living organic waste material created from decomposing tissue.*

- **Detroit:** The largest city in the U.S. state of Michigan **[RL]**. In a universe in which the *Red Dwarf* was an American mining ship, Lister joined the crew after a drinking game in Detroit, where he blacked out and found himself sitting on a bench on the fourth moon of Saturn, wearing nothing but a traffic cone on his head **[T-USA1]**.

- **Detroit Royal Vista Golf Course:** A golf club and facility located in Detroit, Michigan, in a universe in which *Red Dwarf* and its crew were American. That reality's Lister lost his virginity at age twelve to a girl named Michelle Fisher on the ninth hole at the Royal Vista **[T-USA2]**.

- **developing fluid:** Chemicals used to develop photographic film **[RL]**. While processing film from the *Nova 5,* Kryten discovered that the developing fluid had mutated over the course of three million years. A side effect of the mutated chemical was that it enabled a person to enter the scene of a photograph, and to alter the events depicted **[T-SER3.5]**.

- **Dhal, Tarka:** A moniker Lister assumed while attempting to trick rogue simulants into thinking the *Starbug 1* crew were a human-hating species called Vindaloovians. Lister and Cat each affixed one of Kryten's optical units to their chins, then turned upside down and transmitted a message to the simulant ship, zoomed in on their mouths to give them the appearance of large, one-eyed creatures. Lister claimed to be Tarka Dhal, an ambassador of the great Vindaloovian Empire. The charade was cut short, however, when the simulant captain transported aboard *Starbug* and saw their true forms **[T-SER6.3]**.

  NOTE: *Tarka dhal (or dall) is a stew-like Indian dish made with lentils and spices. This spelling is from the* Red Dwarf *script book* Son of Soup*; the DVD captions spell the name Tarka Dall.*

- **Diagnostics, Doctor ("Old Doc"):** A character whom Kryten's subconscious mind created as he battled the Apocalypse virus in an Old West illusion. Diagnostics, the town's local medical examiner, was killed by Brother Pestilence so the Apocalypse Boys could bury Cecil Central Processing Unit, who represented Kryten's CPU **[N-BCK]**.

- **Diamond, Neil:** An American singer-songwriter of numerous folk, country and pop hits, including "Sweet Caroline," "You Don't Bring Me Flowers," "Love on the Rocks" and "I'm a Believer" **[RL]**. Sentenced to the virtual-reality prison Cyberia, Lister found himself in a pleasant-looking Cyberhell set in a Spanish villa. To his relief, the music selection contained no Neil Diamond songs. He had been sent to the wrong illusion, however, and was soon re-assigned to his own personal hell, in which a neighbor blasted Diamond's music **[N-LST]**.

- **Diarrhea Brown:** A designer color that Malpractice Medical & Scispec offered for its medi-scans **[G-RPG]**.

- **Diarrhea Drive:** A euphemism Kryten employed to explain the crew's situation after Holly's intelligence-compression procedure caused a ship-wide power failure, which the mechanoid said left them "galloping up Diarrhea Drive without a saddle" **[T-SER4.4]**.

  NOTE: *This was a variation of the common American expression "up shit's creek without a paddle."*

- **Dibbley, Duane:** A persona that Cat assumed while trapped in a despair squid hallucination. In the illusion, he and his shipmates imagined they had crashed *Starbug 1* into an underwater ravine and had awoken in a total-immersion video game facility—where they had been playing the virtual-reality game *Red Dwarf* for four years. Upon exiting the game, they were escorted to a recuperation lounge, where they found their belongings and learned their "true" identities.

  Cat was now Duane Dibbley, a bucktoothed, no-style klutz with a bowl haircut and dreadful fashion sense. Among his personal belongings were an anorak, white socks, a nylon shirt, plastic sandals, an Aertex vest, a cardigan sweater, a key to a Salvation Army hostel, a thermos and a toothbrush. After leaving the facility, the four emerged in a totalitarian society and were confronted by a member of a fascist police, whom Kryten inadvertently killed. A high-speed chase ended in a dark alleyway, where the crew, unable to deal with their despair, decided to commit suicide. Holly intervened, however, returning them to reality **[T-SER5.6]**.

  Sometime later, Cat slipped and banged his head while getting Krispies from a *Red Dwarf* cupboard. The injury caused more hallucinations, making him believe he was once again Duane Dibbley, being interrogated by doctors after the triple suicide of Jake Bullet, Sebastian Doyle and Billy Doyle. Mistaking his crewmates for deranged scientists intending to torture him, Cat grabbed a knife and threatened to kill himself as well. After his friends revived him from the hallucination using lithium carbonate, he realized he was actually brandishing a herring **[M-SMG1.9(c1)]**.

On another occasion, Cat physically transformed into Dibbley after an emohawk drained his poise and cool, but returned to normal once the creature was killed **[T-SER6.4]**. He later disguised himself as his alter ego while escaping from *Red Dwarf* with Lister, Cat, Kochanski and Kryten posing as his family **[T-SER8.2]**.

- **Dibbley, Duane:** The alter ego of a former Ministry of Alteration agent in an alternate universe. The agent resigned his post from the fascist organization, citing emotional exhaustion. Because of the security risk he now posed, the agent opted for extreme nerdism therapy, which replaced his memories and personality with that of Duane Dibbley, a bucktoothed, bowl-haired klutz with a lack of fashion sense or style.

Before undergoing the procedure, the agent supplied an anti-fascist terrorist group, the Fatal Sisters, with a copy of his personality disc (which he had switched with a Nick Berry disc at the Ministry) and a photograph of his new identity. He instructed them to meet him at Good Time Josies after the surgery, so he could reverse the process and regain his memories. Suspicious of his motives, the Ministry arranged for Dibbley to spend nine years in a Total Immersion video game called *Red Dwarf*, but he emerged after only four years, when he and his team—Voter Colonel Sebastian Doyle, William Doyle and Jake Bullet—ended the game with a score of only four percent **[M-SMG2.5(c1)]**.

Unable to regain their memories, the group tried to commit suicide by lining up and using their last bullet to shoot themselves. Bullet and Dibbley survived, however, and Dibbley was captured and charged with the Doyle brothers' murders **[M-SMG1.14(c1)]**. Sentenced to Caligari's Home for the Terminally Bewildered, he fell into a trauma-induced coma for three months after doctors attempted castration therapy.

Upon awakening from the coma, Dibbley escaped and sought Bullet's help in corroborating his story **[M-SMG1.14(c1)]**. The cyborg agreed, in exchange for help with his current case. The two visited the alleyway in which the group had made their suicide pact, but Bullet, realizing he had lost four years of his memory from the shooting, tried to arrest Duane on the spot **[M-SMG2.1(c4)]**.

Dibbley escaped, noticed a Salvation Army hostel key in his pocket and visited the establishment seeking answers. Voter Colonel Larson Gray ambushed him **[M-SMG2.2(c5)]**, but Mista, a member of the Fatal Sisters, saved Dibbley **[M-SMG2.3(c5)]** and brought him to their lair. The three Sisters then had sex with Duane, hoping to jog his memory of his true identity. When that failed, he requested music by Nick Berry, unaware the case he had supplied to the Fatal Sisters contained his original personality disc—which he threw away after the disc wouldn't play **[M-SMG2.5(c1)]**.

- **Dibbley, Duane:** A computer hacker who created a tacky personal website, the password for which he hid clues to on several other websites **[W-DIB]**. Duane was a frequent poster on the message boards for the television soap opera *Androids*. His favorite episode was #36,186, while his favorite character was Gary **[W-AND]**.

Dibbley's taste in music included ABBA, The Carpenters and the Bay City Rollers. His other hobbies included stamp collecting, computer programming and trainspotting **[M-SMG2.2(a)]**. Dibbley once applied to the Jupiter Mining Corp. for a job, then hacked the company's website after being turned down. He also bragged online about hacking into the websites of Crapola Inc. and Diva-Droid International **[W-DIB]**.

- **Dibbley family, the:** A disguise that Lister, Cat, Kochanski and Kryten assumed while trying to escape from the nanobot-rebuilt *Red Dwarf*. Their costumes consisted of oversized dentures and a mop head for hair. Bob and Madge, two of *Red Dwarf*'s skutters, also used this disguise **[T-SER8.2]**.

- **dibidollyhedecadodron:** One of William James Sidis' theoretical shapes, which Rimmer understood after a mind patch dramatically increased his intelligence **[T-SER5.1]**.

- ***Dichotomy of Faith in a Post Materialistic Society, The*:** A twenty-second-century film directed by Swedish director Sjorbik Bjorksson (his only musical). When a post pod containing Bjorksson's complete works caught up with *Red Dwarf*, Rimmer was elated and immediately set up a marathon viewing, starting with this movie **[B-LOG]**.

DIBBLEY, DUANE

- **Dickens, Charles:** A nineteenth-century English novelist, known for such works as *Oliver Twist, A Christmas Carol* and *A Tale of Two Cities* **[RL]**. A computer-generated Dickens taught literature at the cyberschool Kochanski attended as a youth **[T-SER7.4(e)]**.

- **dictopad:** A voice-operated recording device that converted speech into readable text. Rimmer used a dictopad to inventory *Starbug*'s complete food supply after he and Lister crashed the ship on an icy planet **[N-BTL]**.

- **Didymus, James Judas:** *See* Judas

- **Die! Die! My Darling!:** A goal-scoring strategy that the Zero-Gee Football Federation, after years of pressure, named after the 1965 Tallulah Bankhead film. During this maneuver, each member of a team's defense brought a weapon of his or her choice (not exceeding sixteen megatons) into the Funch Zone, and then proceeded to stomp on it. The team with the greatest number of Finsleys remaining won the Faboozle, and started the next quarter six Brintzleys ahead **[M-SMG1.8(a)]**.

  NOTE: Die! Die! My Darling! *was the U.S. name for the movie, released in the United Kingdom as* Fanatic.

- ***Die Screaming With Sharp Things in Your Head*:** A gory horror film in the Officers Quarters of the "low" *Red Dwarf*—a duplicate of the ship and its crew, representing the worst qualities of the original. According to Kryten, movies such as this were designed to sicken the soul and shrivel the spirit **[T-SER5.5]**. While trapped in an elation squid hallucination, the crew imagined seeing a DVD by this title at a twenty-first-century mall video store **[T-SER9.2]**.

- **diesel decks:** A series of levels aboard *Red Dwarf* that contained the ship's combustion engines. Rimmer once took a ten-day hiking vacation through the diesel decks, photographing the engines for a slide show **[T-SER4.3]**.

- **Dignity:** Kryten's mule in a dream that his subconscious mind created to purge the Armageddon virus from *Starbug 1*'s navicomp. In the illusion, Kryten was the drunken sheriff of an Old West town, who traded his Dignity for a bottle of liquor **[T-SER6.3]**.

- **dilinium:** A compound that, in its liquid state, could freeze anything solid upon contact. The *Starbug 1* crew used liquid dilinium to capture an emohawk that had infiltrated the ship. Cat, however—having been transformed into Duane Dibbley—accidentally sprayed the compound on his shipmates, temporarily freezing them in place **[T-SER6.4]**.

- **dimanium:** An alloy that Kryten called the "toughest in the universe." The Inquisitor bound his victims with dimanium shackles while erasing them from existence **[T-SER5.2(d)]**.

- **DimensioFuse:** A technology utilized in Ace Rimmer's experimental ship, *Wildfire,* enabling it to pass the speed of reality and cross into alternate dimensions **[G-BIT]**.

- **Dimension 165:** A dimension in which the original Ace Rimmer was killed by a neutron tank **[T-SER7.2]**.

- **Dimension 24:** A dimension containing an Astro Cuts salon that Ace Rimmer frequented, to have a stylist named Alfonse cut his hair. The business was located in the Theta Sector **[T-SER7.2]**.

- **dimension cutter:** A theoretical device capable of opening portals to other dimensions, using data culled from a creature able to travel between universes. While trapped in an elation squid hallucination, the *Red Dwarf* crew imagined that Katerina Bartikovsky had built such a device to find a mate with whom Lister could repopulate the human species **[T-SER9.1]**. However, they instead emerged in a "reality" in which they were merely characters in a British television series called *Red Dwarf* **[T-SER9.2]**.

- **"Dimension Invalid":** A message displayed on a monitor linked to a dimension cutter that the *Red Dwarf* crew, while trapped in an elation squid hallucination, imagined that Katerina Bartikovsky had built. This indicated the reality they were in was not real, causing the machine to search for the nearest valid dimension (which was also not real, since it was still part of the illusion) **[T-SER9.2]**.

- **dimension jump (DJ):** The process of crossing from one dimension to another. When Ace Rimmer tested the *Wildfire*, a prototype ship capable of dimension jumping, he ended up in the prime universe, where he met that reality's *Red Dwarf* crew **[T-SER7.2]**.

- **dimension skid:** A phenomenon that the *Red Dwarf* crew imagined while trapped in an elation squid hallucination, causing them to permeate into what they thought was the real world, in which they were merely television show characters. Noddy, an employee of the collectibles shop They Walk Among Us! (whom they also imagined), claimed that dimension skids were especially common during that time of year **[T-SER9.2]**.

- **Dimension Theory of Reality:** A scientific theory that postulated the existence of an infinite number of universes in which every possibility existed; for every decision made, the opposite would play out in an alternate reality. In one such universe, Space Corps engineers devised a drive capable of breaking the speed of reality, enabling a spaceship to cross dimensions into parallel universes. Test pilot Arnold "Ace" Rimmer, who volunteered to test the prototype, arrived in the prime universe and met a pathetic version of himself aboard that universe's *Red Dwarf* **[T-SER4.5]**.

- **Dimsdale, Robert, Commander ("Robbie Rocket Pants"):** An interdimensional traveler who crashed on War World, an alternate-universe Earth on which World War II never ended. There, he enlisted in the Resistance, a group of freedom fighters locked in an eternal conflict with an evil Nazi superpower called the Reich.

  Dimsdale acquired a pair of Raketenhosen ("rocket pants"), the Reich's ultimate weapon, and reverse-engineered them for the Resistance to create their own. Their Rocket Pants, flown by an elite squadron of fighters known as Junior Birdmen, empowered the Resistance to eliminate the Reich's air superiority, earning Dimsdale the heroic nickname "Robbie Rocket Pants." To commemorate his accomplishments, Princess Bela Bonjella commissioned a statue of Dimsdale in the capital city of Seni Rotundi **[G-BIT]**.

- **Dinamap:** A brand of medical monitoring equipment produced by GE Electric **[RL]**. The Quantum Twister *Trojan* was equipped with at least one medical bed outfitted with a Dinamap monitor **[T-SER10.1]**.

- **Dingleberry-brain:** A nickname Rimmer called Lister upon learning that he planned to enter stasis while *Red Dwarf* returned to Earth—and to deactivate the hologram for the duration of the trip **[N-INF]**.

  NOTE: *Since the word "dingleberry" is a slang term for fecal matter, the insult would equate to calling someone "Shit-for-brains."*

- **Dingleberry-breath:** A nickname Rimmer called Holly after arriving on a future Earth on which time ran backwards, when she failed to ascertain the current time period beyond it being lunchtime **[T-SER3.1]**.

  NOTE: *Likewise, this term would be analogous to calling someone "Shit-breath."*

- **Dingotang:** A genetically engineered life form (GELF) created to terraform a new planet for humanity. With the head of a dingo and the body of an orangutan, Dingotangs were infused with slow-aging genes, giving them a life expectancy close to a thousand years.

  Dingotangs, along with Snugiraffes, Dolochimps and Alberogs, were developed after attempts to control Earth's weather reduced the Sun's lifespan to four hundred thousand years, forcing mankind to terraform other worlds to survive. The GELFs were sent ahead to prepare a new planet for humanity's arrival, but their ship was sucked into the Omni-zone and ejected into another universe, where they populated Arranguu 12 and its resident asteroid field.

  Deki, a guard employed at the virtual-reality prison Cyberia, was a Dingotang **[N-LST]**.

- **Dining Room:** A room aboard *Nova 5* in which Kryten served dinner to his human masters. Many years after the ship crashed into a barren planetoid, the *Red Dwarf* crew picked up the mechanoid's distress call, in which he mentioned three survivors. The Dwarfers mounted a rescue operation and boarded the ship, only to discover the long-dead crew's skeletal remains in the Dining Room **[T-SER2.1]**.

- **Dink:** A character on the television soap opera *Androids*. In one episode, Dink attended a barbeque hosted by Daz, during which a family pet, Bouncer, was lost in a temporal-displacement vortex **[M-SMG1.8(c2)]**.

- **dinosaur bowel movement frequency table:** A hypothetical chart listing the amount of time it would take an item to pass through the digestive tract of various dinosaurs. 4000 Series mechanoids were not programmed with this data—a fact that disheartened Kryten's shipmates as they tried to ascertain how best to retrieve a time wand swallowed by Pete the *Tyrannosaurus rex* **[T-SER8.7]**.

- **Dinosaur Breath:** A nickname that Lister suggested Kryten call Rimmer, instead of "Mr. Arnold." Kryten later broke from his programming and called Rimmer several names, including this one **[T-SER2.1]**.

- **Dinsdale, Derek:** The leader of the design team that created the artificial-intelligence (AI) computer, Holly. Dinsdale's former companion, Magnus Amplatt, divulged information about the AI systems aboard many JMC vessels to the news publication *A.I. Today*. Among the leaked information was the fact that several AI personalities, including those of the computers aboard *Red Dwarf*, the *Scott Fitzgerald* and the *Oregon,* were prone to erratic behavior due to major issues with their source-coding **[W-AIT]**.

- **Dione:** One of Saturn's moons, named after the Titan of Greek mythology **[RL]**. George McIntyre incurred a massive gambling debt playing Toot on moons such as Dione, eventually leading to his committing suicide **[N-INF]**.

  Dione was home to a French settlement. In the late twenty-first century, proceedings were held on the moon to determine which of the solar system's nine planets would be given over to humanity's trash. Hosted by French television star Avril Dupont, the poll crowned Earth as the new so-called Garbage World **[N-BTL]**.

  NOTE: *This contradicts* Red Dwarf—The Roleplaying Game, *which claimed Dione was the first breakaway settlement of the outer system and was home to a pirate colony before the Space Corps leveled the compound, rendering Dione uninhabited.*

- **Dip N' Sip Chilli & Lager Bath Salts:** A brand of bathing salts used by one of *Red Dwarf*'s crewmembers. Lister found a crate of the salts, along with a package of Space Monkeys, while rummaging through the dead crew's quarters. He instructed Kryten to put the Space Monkeys in an aquarium while he used the salts, but mixed up the packages and was startled by the appearance of Space Monkeys in his bath **[M-SMG1.13(c2)]**.

- **directional fins:** A component of MkIV Titanica Fish Droids, such as Lister's pet robot goldfish, enabling them to steer **[M-SMG2.4(c5)]**.

- **Dirk, Donald, Doctor:** A physician at the Slough Brain Research Unit, a medical facility operated by a fascist society in Jake Bullet's universe. Dirk wrote a research paper titled "Nerdism—A Study" **[M-SMG1.14(c6)]**.

- **Dirtville:** A hypothetical place that Kryten, while trapped in an elation squid hallucination, promised Rimmer he would go to in order to find discrediting information about Katerina Bartikovsky **[T-SER9.1]**.

- ***Dirty Dozen*:** An American war film released in 1967, about a group of twelve convicts recruited for a top-secret mission during World War II **[RL]**. After rendezvousing with Rimmer and Kryten on Waxworld, Lister commented that Rimmer had turned Hero World's pacifist waxdroids into the Dirty Dozen **[T-SER4.6]**.

- **Disaster Inn:** *See* nnI Retsasid

- **Disciples of Death, The:** A group name that Lister gave to Kryten, Cat and Rimmer as they tried to rescue him from Clisterist leader Kadok. Lister hoped the fearsome-sounding name would convince the religious leader to let him go **[M-SMG2.3(c1)]**.

- **Dishwasher Star Empire:** An alternate-reality dominion that spawned from several lost crates of kitchen utensils and artificial-intelligence software **[G-SOR]**.

- **disintegrator:** A microwave oven-sized, wall-mounted machine that disintegrated any matter placed within it, whether mineral or organic. Personnel required a security code in order to operate the device **[T-SER7.3]**. Disintegrators were manufactured by Disposex, and were distributed via Crapola Inc.'s annual *SCABBY* catalog **[G-RPG]**.

  In a parallel universe, Kochanski found Frankenstein, a cat that Lister had smuggled aboard *Red Dwarf*, and placed it into the disintegrator, but could not bring herself to dispose of the animal. This caused a series of events that led to her surviving the cadmium II disaster instead of Lister **[T-SER7.3]**.

- **Disney, Walt:** A twentieth-century business mogul and founder of The Walt Disney Co., a company known for its kid-friendly films and programming **[RL]**. After Kochanski told a newly human Kryten a story about blind people regaining their sight only to commit suicide, the former mechanoid sarcastically responded that Walt Disney could have used the tale **[N-LST]**.

B-: Books
PRG: *Red Dwarf Programme Guide*
SUR: *Red Dwarf Space Corps Survival Manual*
PRM: *Primordial Soup*
SOS: *Son of Soup*
SCE: *Scenes from the Dwarf*
LOG: *Red Dwarf Log No. 1996*
RD8: *Red Dwarf VIII*
EVR: *The Log: A Dwarfer's Guide to Everything*

X-: Misc.
PRO: Promotional materials, videos, etc.
PST: Posters at DJ XVII (2013)
CAL: 2008 calendar
RNG: Cell phone ringtones
MOB: Mobisode ("Red Christmas")
CIN: *Children in Need* sketch
GEK: *Geek Week* intros by Kryten
TNG: "Tongue-Tied" video

XMS: Bill Pearson's Christmas special pitch script
XVD: Bill Pearson's Christmas special pitch video
OTH: Other *Red Dwarf* appearances

SUFFIX
DVD:
(d) – Deleted scene
(o) – Outtake
(b) – Bonus DVD material (other)
(e) – Extended version

SMEGAZINES:
(c) – Comic
(a) – Article

OTHER:
(s) – Early/unused script draft
(s1) – Alternate version of script

- **Disney-Chodhwara AG:** A large twenty-first-century corporation that copyrighted the idea that corporate blandness had converted Earth into a boring place filled with lawyers and surveillance cameras. Those who shared that sentiment received a monthly invoice from the company **[G-RPG]**.

- **Dispenser 16:** A sentient food and drink dispenser aboard *Red Dwarf* that offered milk, tea, cola, milk chocolate and aspirin, among other items. Kryten once played a game of Chinese whispers with this and several other dispensers. When Rimmer questioned the offensiveness of the game's name, Kryten asked Dispenser 16 its thoughts on the matter, and it, in turn, asked Cat **[T-SER10.2]**.

- **Dispenser 172:** A service dispenser in *Red Dwarf*'s Corridor 159 that malfunctioned and developed a clogged chicken soup nozzle. Rimmer and Lister were assigned to repair it during Z-Shift **[T-SER1.1]**.

- **Dispenser 23:** A sentient food and drink dispenser aboard *Red Dwarf* that spoke with a feminine voice and a French accent. It offered soup, coffee, hot chocolate, tea, milk, aspirin and popodomi, among other items.

  Dispenser 23 once accused Lister of making advances toward it, claiming he had touched the machine's logo while offering it compliments. Rimmer recorded the incident in his ongoing report on Lister's acts of depression. Dispenser 34, who was in love with Lister, heard about the incident and became insanely jealous, refusing to serve him until he apologized **[T-SER10.5]**.

- **Dispenser 34:** A sentient food and drink dispenser located across the hall from Lister's quarters aboard *Red Dwarf*. Its signage read "Vend-A-Bar!" Among the items it dispensed were Mint Elegance, Caramel Crunch, milk chocolate, milk, cola, tea, coffee, milkshakes, popodomi and Mexican red-hot chili crisps.

  Dispenser 34 developed feelings for Lister, and became jealous upon learning of his supposed romantic advances toward Dispenser 23. After the incident, Dispenser 34 refused to serve Lister until he apologized and fulfilled her greatest wish: to see around the corner of the corridor.

  As Lister attempted to push the machine into position, however, it tipped over onto its back, with Lister on top, struggling to pull it upright. This made it appear—not only to the dispenser, but to his shipmates—that he was engaged in a sexual act with the machine. Rimmer, looking for an excuse to prove Lister unfit for duty, recorded the incident via closed-circuit television **[T-SER10.5]**.

- **Dispenser 55:** A sentient food and drink dispenser aboard *Red Dwarf* **[T-SER10.1]**, located on G Deck. Its signage read "Crisps" and "Sweets," and among the items it dispensed were milk chocolate and cola **[T-SER10.2]**. Lister once bet on a pre-recorded pig race with the dispenser, losing $£100 **[T-SER10.1]**. Taiwan Tony, an Asian fast-food dispenser, accused Dispenser 55 of serving pre-packaged microwaved food **[T-SER10.2]**.

- **Disposex:** A company specializing in waste-disposal technology, which supplied *Red Dwarf*'s disintegrator units **[G-RPG]**.

- **Disraeli, Benjamin:** A nineteenth-century British politician who served two terms as the nation's prime minister **[RL]**. A computer-generated Disraeli taught history at the cyberschool Kochanski attended as a youth **[T-SER7.4(e)]**.

- **distress beacon:** A signal transmitted by a spaceship's crew to request assistance, also known as a distress call. The *Red Dwarf* crew received such a signal from Kryten, a mechanoid aboard the crashed ship *Nova 5*, asking for help for three female survivors.

  Later, *Starbug 1* received another such signal from a starship escape vessel marooned on a doomed planet in decaying orbit. Responding to the beacon, Rimmer and Kryten rescued a shapeshifting Pleasure GELF named Camille **[T-SER4.1]**.

- **Diva, the:** A nickname that Confidence, a hallucination of Lister's mind made corporeal by mutated pneumonia, called Lister **[W-OFF]**.

- **Divad, Retsil:** Dave Lister's name during the thirty-four years he lived on the Earth of Universe 3, where time flowed backwards **[N-BTL]**.

PREFIX
RL: Real life

T-: Television Episodes
SER: Television series
IDW: "Identity Within"
USA1: Unaired U.S. pilot
USA2: Unaired U.S. demo

R-: *The Bodysnatcher Collection*
SER: Remastered episodes
BOD: "Bodysnatcher"
DAD: "Dad"
FTH: "Lister's Father"
INF: "Infinity Patrol"
END: "The End" (original assembly)

N-: Novels
INF: *Infinity Welcomes Careful Drivers*
BTL: *Better Than Life*
LST: *Last Human*
BCK: *Backwards*
OMN: *Red Dwarf Omnibus*

M-: Magazines
SMG: *Smegazine*

W-: Websites
OFF: Official website
NAN: *Prelude to Nanarchy*
AND: *Androids*
DIV: Diva-Droid
DIB: Duane Dibbley
CRP: Crapola
GEN: Geneticon
LSR: Leisure World Intl.
JMC: Jupiter Mining Corporation
AIT: *A.I. Today*
HOL: HoloPoint

G-: Roleplaying Game
RPG: *Core Rulebook*
BIT: *A.I. Screen Extra Bits* booklet
SOR: *Series Sourcebook*
OTH: Other RPG material

- **Diva-Droid 22PT drill hand accessory:** An accessory offered for 4000 Series mechanoids, enabling them to perform tasks such as drilling holes **[M-SMG1.1(a)]**.

- **Diva-Droid International:** A company, also known as Divadroid International, that produced and distributed mechanical laborers. The firm, founded by Augustus Ackroyd—a robots hobbyist and full-time hairdresser—was launched as a manufacturer of interactive novelty items, before teaming up with Crapola Inc. and other companies.

  Throughout its history, Diva-Droid produced such units as the Series 500 skutter, as well as the Series 1000, 2000, 3000, 4000 (Kryten) and 4010 (Hudzen 10) mechanoids **[W-DIV]**. Its employees included Jim Reaper, head of sales for the company's Space Division **[T-SER3.6]**, and Professor Mamet, who designed the Series 4000 mechanoid **[W-DIV]**. Kryten received a homing pod from this corporation, instructing him to deactivate before his replacement (a Hudzen 10 model) reached *Red Dwarf* **[T-SER3.6]**.

- **Diva-Droid interstellar shuttle:** A small pod used by Diva-Droid International to ship replacement droids to owners of obsolete models. It held one crewmember and contained a single stasis pod, as well as a celestial sunroof, integrated bath bucket and DVD player **[G-BIT]**. One such shuttle, dispatched to deliver a Hudzen 10 mechanoid to the owners of Kryten 2X4B-523P, made its way to *Red Dwarf* after a three-million-year journey through space **[T-SER3.6]**.

- **Diva-Droid League Cup:** A championship zero-gee football tournament sponsored by Diva-Droid International. Groovy Channel 27 aired a Diva-Droid League Cup game between the London Jets and the Saturn Bears at 2:30 PM on Wednesday, the 27th of Geldof, 2362 **[M-SMG1.7(a)]**.

- ***Divadroid Magazine*:** A periodical published by Diva-Droid International. Purchasers of a Holly AI computer received six free months of *Divadroid Magazine* **[X-PST]**.

- **Diva-Droid service guarantee:** A warranty that Diva-Droid International offered to customers, guaranteeing its mechanoids' performance. Using a mechanoid as a volt meter potentially invalidated this agreement **[T-SER7.1(e)]**, as would letting anyone other than a qualified service engineer cut the mechanoid in half with a blowtorch **[T-SER5.3]**.

- **Diva-Droid signature:** An electronic marker used to identify items in inventory as originating from Diva-Droid International. Lister searched for a Diva-Droid signature in the mainframe of the derelict vessel SS *Centauri* while attempting to locate spare heads for Kryten **[T-SER7.6]**.

- **dividing:** A term coined on *Red Dwarf*, an American science fiction television series produced in an alternate universe. The word described the condition of a female member of an amorphous alien species whom the *Red Dwarf* crew inadvertently killed while plodding through what they mistook for a slime patch on Altair 9 **[M-SMG1.10(c4)]**.

  NOTE: *Presumably, dividing was that species' method of reproduction.*

- **diving bell:** A small craft used to access underwater vessels. The bell was large enough to hold several occupants, and was tethered by an air line to the surface. The Canaries boarded a diving bell to investigate the SSS *Silverberg*, a Space Corps derelict that had crashed on an ocean moon **[T-SER8.4]**.

  NOTE: Red Dwarf—The Roleplaying Game*'s* Series Sourcebook *referred to this craft as a Canary submarine.*

- **diving bell:** A small pod used aboard *Red Dwarf* for light submersible duties, such as inspecting the ship's water tanks. These were reinforced with grade-one titanium ribs; as such, discharging a firearm inside the bell was not advisable. Lister, Kryten and Cat used such a submersible to hunt a creature living in G Deck's water tank. Due to the bell's open-bottom design, the creature—an elation squid—was able to partly make its way into the craft and attack the crew **[T-SER9.1]**.

- **diving suit:** A type of specialized gear designed for underwater excursions. Lister, Kryten and Cat donned diving suits while searching *Red Dwarf*'s water tank on G Deck for a creature later discovered to be an elation squid **[T-SER9.1]**.

- **Dixon, Reginald ("Reggie"):** A twentieth-century English theatre organist, best known for his position as the resident organist for the Blackpool Tower Ballroom **[RL]**. Rimmer played a perpetually looped recording of *Reggie Dixon's Tango Treats* for Lister, Cat and Kryten while keeping them in mandatory quarantine **[T-SER5.4]**.

NOTE: In the real world, Reggie Dixon never made such a recording.

- **DJ:** *See* dimension jump (DJ)

- **Djuhn'Keep:** One of thousands of agonoids that escaped decommissioning and fled into deep space. His name was pronounced "Junk Heap," in keeping with humans' tendency to assign humorous names to agonoids. Many years later, the agonoids found *Red Dwarf*, abandoned except for Holly, whom they interrogated before ripping out the artificial intelligence and leaving his components out in space as bait for the crew.

Despite many of his parts being worn down, Djuhn'Keep was the most inventive and creative agonoid when it came to delivering pain and torture—qualities that prevented others from attacking him for spare parts. After boarding *Red Dwarf*, he designed and built the Death Wheel, a series of corridors leading from the landing bays to the Hub of Pain (a domed room containing every known weapon and torture device). The agonoids' plan was to lead the last human, Dave Lister, and his cohorts through the increasingly difficult corridors until they emerged in the Hub, where the strongest and fastest agonoid would then have the pleasure of endlessly torturing them.

Being incredibly wily, however, Djuhn first tricked M'Aiden Ty-One into using a scramble card containing a program he created, known as the Apocalypse virus, and then inflicted the Death Wheel on his fellow agonoids, virtually killing them all to ensure he alone had the honor of killing Lister. His scheme backfired, though, when a surviving agonoid, having been flushed out into space, headed toward the disabled *Starbug*, forcing Djuhn to alter his plans and go after Lister himself.

The agonoid found Kryten floating helplessly in space and towed him back to *Starbug*, where he used the mechanoid's access code to gain entrance. While Djuhn utilized the navicomp to bring the shuttle back to *Red Dwarf*, Kryten blasted a hole in the hull with a bazookoid, sending the agonoid flailing out into space. Before disconnecting from the navicomp, Djuhn uploaded the virus, propelling the shuttle into the path of a small planetoid. Fortunately for the crew, Kryten was able to eradicate the virus by creating the Dove Program—but at the expense of his own life **[N-BCK]**.

- **"Dloc Sknird":** A pair of words printed on a wall sign at an eatery in England, during a period in Earth's far future when time ran backwards. The sign, when read forward, was labeled "Cold Drinks" **[T-SER3.1]**.

NOTE: Throughout the episode, backwards writing was inconsistently handled. In some cases, characters were forward-facing, while in others (such as in this instance), they faced backwards.

- **DNA modifier:** A machine that the *Red Dwarf* crew found aboard a derelict vessel, which could transmogrify the DNA of any living tissue into any other living being stored within its database. Cat accidentally activated the device, trapping Lister in its beam and changing him first into a chicken, then a hamster, before reverting him back to human form. While attempting to recreate this event, Cat next trapped Kryten in the machine, which locked onto the organic part of his brain and changed him into a human.

Though initially content, Kryten soon found life as a human shallow, and decided to change back. With Holly at the DNA modifier's controls, the crew tested the machine on Lister's mutton vindaloo dinner, which the unit combined with a human DNA sample, producing a crazed mutton vindaloo beast that attacked the crew.

After being chased around the derelict, the crew returned to the DNA suite so Holly could convert Lister into a superhuman fighting machine able to combat the beast. The result was only partly successful, as he became a gun-toting, armored robo-Lister—approximately three feet tall. Despite the setback, Lister vanquished the vindaloo beast, after which Holly changed him and Kryten back to normal **[T-SER4.2]**.

A version of this machine was produced by Malpractice Medical & Scispec, and was distributed by Crapola Inc. **[G-RPG]**.

NOTE: In the novel Last Human, *it was Rimmer whom Cat initially trapped in the machine and subsequently turned into hundreds of animals.*

- **DNA Suite:** A room aboard a derelict vessel discovered by the *Red Dwarf* crew. It contained a DNA-modifying machine that transmogrified a life form's DNA, effectively changing it into another type of creature **[T-SER4.2]**.

- **DNF 54BY:** *See* YB45 FND

- **Dobbin:** A drummer for the musical group Smeg and the Heads, Lister's first band. He owned an orange Ford with bald tires and a missing windshield, from which he sold Smeg and the Head T-shirts, signed pictures and copies of the group's music. A hippie with extremely long hair, Dobbin later joined the police force and became a grand wizard of the Freemasons **[T-SER3.5]**.

- **Docking Bay 475:** A landing bay aboard an alternate-reality *Red Dwarf*. After Lister and Cat escaped their own dimension using Ace Rimmer's ship *Wildfire One* and entered this dimension, the alternate-reality Kryten directed them to land in Docking Bay 475 **[N-BCK]**.

- ***Doctor, Darling*:** A novel written by Netta Muskett, concerning a young physician and a woman named Jemma. After traveling through deep space for two million years following *Red Dwarf*'s cadmium II disaster, Holly became obsessed with Muskett's novels. He was reading *Doctor, Darling* when the ship passed a quintuplet of stars in concentric orbits, but ignored the stellar phenomenon, having reached the part of the novel when the doctor told Jemma she had three years to live **[N-INF]**.

  ***NOTE:** In the real world, Netta Muskett never wrote a book titled* Doctor, Darling.

- **Doctor Fruit-Loop:** A nickname that Rimmer called Hildegarde Lanstrom after the hologrammic scientist went insane from contracting a holovirus **[T-SER5.4]**.

- **Doctor Smorgasbord:** Another nickname that Rimmer dubbed Hildegarde Lanstrom **[T-SER5.4(d)]**.

- ***Doctor Who*:** A long-running British science fiction television series featuring the adventures of a mysterious time-traveling humanoid called the Doctor **[RL]**. On Wednesday, the 27th of Geldof, 2362, Groovy Channel 27 brought *Doctor Who* back after a short hiatus, resurrecting Tom Baker, the show's fourth incarnation of the Doctor, as a hologram to reprise his titular role **[M-SMG1.7(a)]**. Rimmer once commented that he would need to be the Doctor to study for a test that had already been finished for thirty-five minutes **[N-INF]**.

- **Dodd, Ken:** A twentieth-century British comedian who was once charged with tax evasion but had little money in his bank account, having hoarded his wealth in his attic **[RL]**. While at a restaurant in a space mirage zone, the *Red Dwarf* crew met a duplicate of Dodd—who seemed completely authentic until he offered to pay for dinner **[T-SER3(d)]**.

- **Dodd, Mortimer:** An individual whom, in 2034, the Inquisitor judged unworthy of existence. When the simulant tried to erase Dodd from history, however, he nearly eliminated himself as well, triggering his time alarm.

  In the future, the Inquisitor discovered, Dodd would become employed at the Institute of Simulant Technology, at which he would be assigned to fetch beverages for the very scientists involved in the Inquisitor's creation. While taking a tea order, Mortimer would inadvertently solve an equation involving intelligence circuits that had eluded the group, thus enabling them to build the Inquisitor. The man's elimination, therefore, jeopardized the simulant's own existence.

  To fix his error, the Inquisitor traveled back to stop himself from deleting Dodd. His first attempt failed, as his younger self mistook him for an imposter and attacked, resulting in Dodd's accidental death. Several more tries also failed, until Dodd escaped to safety during a battle between several dozen Inquisitors **[M-SMG2.5(c3)]**.

- **Dodecahedron:** A government building in Ace Rimmer's universe, so named due to its twelve-sided architecture. Ace was called upon to assess the viability of a project aimed to create agonoids—part-human, part-mechanical killing machines. He suggested the program be scrapped as quickly as possible, but was overruled by military leaders from the Dodecahedron **[N-BCK]**.

  ***NOTE:** This building's name spoofed that of the Pentagon, the five-sided headquarters building of the United States' Department of Defense.*

- **dodo pâté:** A spreadable mixture made from the meat of the extinct dodo bird, which Rimmer imagined consuming

B-: Books
PRG: *Red Dwarf Programme Guide*
SUR: *Red Dwarf Space Corps Survival Manual*
PRM: *Primordial Soup*
SOS: *Son of Soup*
SCE: *Scenes from the Dwarf*
LOG: *Red Dwarf Log No. 1996*
RD8: *Red Dwarf VIII*
EVR: *The Log: A Dwarfer's Guide to Everything*

X-: Misc.
PRO: Promotional materials, videos, etc.
PST: Posters at DJ XVII (2013)
CAL: 2008 calendar
RNG: Cell phone ringtones
MOB: Mobisode ("Red Christmas")
CIN: *Children in Need* sketch
GEK: *Geek Week* intros by Kryten
TNG: "Tongue-Tied" video
XMS: Bill Pearson's Christmas special pitch script
XVD: Bill Pearson's Christmas special pitch video
OTH: Other *Red Dwarf* appearances

SUFFIX
DVD:
(d) – Deleted scene
(o) – Outtake
(b) – Bonus DVD material (other)
(e) – Extended version

SMEGAZINES:
(c) – Comic
(a) – Article

OTHER:
(s) – Early/unused script draft
(s1) – Alternate version of script

while trapped in an addictive version of *Better Than Life*. Arnold believed he had returned to Earth and was attending the reception party for his second marriage, at which dodo pâté was served. His chef had retrieved the extinct birds using a time machine of Arnold's invention. According to Rimmer, it tasted remarkably like chicken **[N-BTL]**.

- **dog:** A member of Earth's *Canis lupus familiaris* subspecies, also called a canine. Humans bred and domesticated dogs as pets for thousands of years, earning them the nickname "Man's best friend" **[RL]**.

While scanning through a slideshow of old pictures, Cat found a photo of Hannah, the pet dog of Lister's adoptive father. Cat took an instant dislike to the animal, warning Dave that he would chase away any dogs he encountered. Amused by such bravado, Lister claimed the creatures were several feet tall, with teeth as big as Cat's leg **[T-SER1.2]**.

While inhabiting Lister's body, Rimmer read an issue of *Muscle Woman* containing a back-cover advertisement for a dog magazine **[T-SER3.4]**.

During Lister's incarceration in the Tank, Holly offered him a solution that would effectively reduce his two-year sentence to fourteen weeks: undergoing a roverostomy to become a dog **[T-SER8.4]**.

- **Dog:** *See* Dog, Dog

- **Dog Arks:** A series of spacefaring vessels that the Dog People inhabiting an alternate-reality *Red Dwarf* built in order to locate their god, Cloister **[W-OFF]**.

  ***NOTE:** Presumably, Cloister (that reality's analog to Cloister the Stupid—Dave Lister), was Deb Lister. It's unknown whether she, too, was considered stupid.*

- **Dog-Breath:** An insult that Cat called Lister while recalling an old Cat People saying, "What are you talking about, Dog-Breath?" **[T-SER2.4]**.

- **Dog, Dog:** A member of a species of sentient canine humanoids, known as *Canis sapiens* **[M-SMG2.8(a)]**, that evolved from Deb Lister's pregnant dog, Dracula, in an alternate dimension in which the genders were reversed. Although his full name was Dog Dog, he was typically just referred to as Dog **[W-OFF]**.

Like his domesticated ancestors, Dog was prone to fleas, liked to smell other individuals' backsides in greeting and disliked bathing **[T-SER2.6]**.

The prime-universe *Red Dwarf* crew met Dog and his shipmates after a botched attempt to use the Holly Hop Drive propelled them into the other reality. Although Lister, Kryten and Rimmer all met their female counterparts, Cat was disappointed to learn that his analog was not a female feline, but rather a male canine, and resisted all of Dog's attempts to be his friend **[T-SER2.6]**.

At some point, Cat and Dog met again, during which they played a game of fetch **[M-SMG2.8(c5)]**. Once Dog tried to perform a magic trick by making Cat's dinner disappear, much to the feline's annoyance **[M-SMG2.9(c7)]**. Dog also attempted to chase Cat but failed, until discovering the one thing Cat would run from: bri-nylon socks **[M-SMG2.9(c5)]**. On one occasion, a temporary food shortage aboard *Red Dwarf* drove Dog insane, forcing him to once again go after Cat **[M-SMG2.9(c13)]**.

- **dog food:** An item stored in *Starbug 1*'s tool cupboard. While marooned aboard *Starbug 1* on an icy planet, Lister had no choice but to eat dog food six days after consuming his last edible supplies, including a Pot Noodle. Upon tasting it, he suddenly realized why dogs licked their testicles **[T-SER3.2]**.

  ***NOTE:** Given the JMC's "no pets" rule, mentioned in episode 8.7 ("Pete Part 2"), it is unclear why there would be dog food in a* Starbug *shuttle.*

- **Dog-food Face:** An insult Rimmer called Lister while rescuing whom they believed to be three survivors of the *Nova 5* crash **[T-SER2.1]**.

- **"Dog Market":** A phrase printed on a T-shirt worn by Dog **[T-SER2.6]**.

- **Dog People:** *See Canis sapiens*

- **dog's milk:** A diary product stored as an emergency supply aboard *Red Dwarf*, to be used if the crew ran out of both fresh and dehydrated cow's milk. According to Holly, dog's milk lasted the longest, simply because no one wanted to drink it **[T-SER2.1]**.

- **dollarpound ($£):** A unit of Earth currency, circa the twenty-second century **[T-SER4.4]**.

  ***NOTE:** Red Dwarf's creators presumably conceived of the dollarpound as suggesting a more unified world in the future, combining the currencies of the United Kingdom and the United States.*

- **Dolochimp:** A genetically engineered life form (GELF) created to help terraform a new planet for the human species. With the head of a dolphin, the legs of a locust and the body of a chimpanzee, Dolochimps were infused with slow-aging genes, making their life expectancy close to a thousand years.

  Dolochimps, along with Snugiraffes, Alberogs and Dingotangs, were developed after attempts to control Earth's weather reduced the Sun's lifespan to four hundred thousand years, thereby forcing mankind to terraform other worlds to survive. The GELFs were sent ahead to prepare a new planet for humanity, but their ship was sucked into the Omni-zone and ejected into another universe, where they populated Arranguu 12 and its asteroid field. Most of the guards patrolling the area of space around the virtual-reality prison facility Cyberia were Dolochimps **[N-LST]**.

- **dolphin sweetmeats:** A delicacy that a future version of the *Red Dwarf* crew enjoyed after using a time drive coupled with a faster-than-light drive to journey throughout space-time, becoming epicures sampling the best the universe had to offer **[T-SER6.6]**.

- **Domestos:** A household cleaning product sold in the United Kingdom, manufactured by Unilever **[RL]**. While inhabiting Lister's body after a mind swap, Rimmer used Domestos and Ajax to scrub down in the shower **[T-SER3.4]**.

- **dominoes:** A variety of games played using numbered tiles **[RL]**. Lister found his old set of dominoes, which he thought he'd lost in a bet with his schoolmate Duncan, in the back of his *Starbug 1* locker. He played several rounds against Kryten, who assumed the game was purely ceremonial due to the ease at which he memorized the tiles **[T-IDW]**.

- **Dom Pérignon:** A brand of French champagne produced by Moët & Chandon **[RL]**. While dining at a virtual restaurant in the total-immersion video game *Better Than Life*, Lister ordered a bottle of Dom Pérignon '44, along with a pint mug **[T-SER2.2]**.

  ***NOTE:** The DVD subtitles mistakenly indicated the year of the bottle ordered to be '54.*

- **Donald:** A hypnotherapist whom Rimmer befriended. After telling Donald about his trip to Macedonia and the feeling of belonging he experienced at the sight of Alexander the Great's palace, Arnold agreed to let his friend hypnotize him, and was surprised to discover that he had been Alexander's chief eunuch in a past life **[T-SER2.3]**.

- **Donatella, Don:** A zero-gee football player with the position of Roof Attack. A poster of Donatella hung in a pub at which Smeg and the Heads once played a gig **[T-SER3.5]**. Lister had a similar poster in his quarters aboard *Red Dwarf* **[T-SER9.1]**.

- **"Do Not Engage Hyperdrive Inside Ship's Gravity Field":** A warning stenciled on a wall within *Starbug's* landing bay **[T-SER3.1]**.

- ***Don't Fear the Reefer, Man*:** One of Lister's favorite albums, recorded by Rastabilly Skank **[M-SMG1.1(a)]**.

  ***NOTE:** This album's title may have been a spoof of "(Don't Fear) The Reaper," a 1976 song by American rock band Blue Öyster Cult.*

- **"Don't stand around jabbering when you're in mortal danger":** An old android saying that Kryten cited on a psi-moon shaped by Rimmer's mind, as he and his crewmates escaped the Unspeakable One. The phrase was translated from the binary original, "00110011101100011110011100111110" **[T-SER5.3]**.

  ***NOTE:** Kryten's translation was incorrect, as the actual binary translation of the phrase would be a string of 456 zeros and ones.*

- **Doodoo-Breath:** A nickname that Cat called Lister, implying Dave suffered from halitosis **[T-SER4.4]**.

- **Dooley:** A member of *Red Dwarf*'s Z-Shift prior to the ship's cadmium II disaster. Shortly before the accident, Rimmer assigned Dooley, Burd and Pixon to repair several

B-: Books
PRG: *Red Dwarf Programme Guide*
SUR: *Red Dwarf Space Corps Survival Manual*
PRM: *Primordial Soup*
SOS: *Son of Soup*
SCE: *Scenes from the Dwarf*
LOG: *Red Dwarf Log No. 1996*
RD8: *Red Dwarf VIII*
EVR: *The Log: A Dwarfer's Guide to Everything*

X-: Misc.
PRO: Promotional materials, videos, etc.
PST: Posters at DJ XVII (2013)
CAL: 2008 calendar
RNG: Cell phone ringtones
MOB: Mobisode ("Red Christmas")
CIN: *Children in Need* sketch
GEK: *Geek Week* intros by Kryten
TNG: "Tongue-Tied" video
XMS: Bill Pearson's Christmas special pitch script
XVD: Bill Pearson's Christmas special pitch video
OTH: Other *Red Dwarf* appearances

SUFFIX
DVD:
(d) – Deleted scene
(o) – Outtake
(b) – Bonus DVD material (other)
(e) – Extended version

SMEGAZINES:
(c) – Comic
(a) – Article

OTHER:
(s) – Early/unused script draft
(s1) – Alternate version of script

malfunctioning driers in the launderettes on East Alpha 555 **[N-INF]**.

NOTE: Dooley presumably died during the cadmium II explosion. It is unknown whether the nanobots resurrected Dooley in Series VIII.

- **Dorksville:** A hypothetical town that Rimmer sarcastically claimed would be named after Lister and Kryten, after learning that their "revolutionary" triplicator could only produce four to five strawberries per week **[T-SER5.5]**.

- **Dormouse-Cheeks:** A nickname that Cat called Lister, implying his face was chubby **[T-SER5.5]**.

- **Dorrie:** A humanoid whose species evolved from a dormouse in an alternate universe ravaged by Ace "Blackheart" Rimmer. Dorrie was that universe's analog to Cat. When the prime Ace visited Dorrie's reality, he and his comrades—Darren (a hillbilly Lister) and Kritter (a hillbilly cyborg Kryten)—mistook him for Blackheart. Once Ace established who he was, Darren explained that Blackheart had laid waste to their settlement, and would return to finish the job.

  The tyrant arrived moments later, looking to kill the survivors. Darren and Kritter attacked Blackheart, but were both shot in the knees. Ultimately, Dorrie shot Blackheart in the head as he fought with his counterpart. Thankful for giving him the courage to stand up to Blackheart, Dorrie smoked Ace a kipper, but was unable to catch him before he departed for another dimension **[M-SMG1.14(c5)]**.

- **Dottie:** The secretary of cyborg cop Jake Bullet in an alternate universe. She had an extendable neck **[M-SMG1.7(a)]**.

- **double-Polaroid:** A euphemism by which Lister described Kryten's erect penis after a DNA modifier changed the mechanoid into a human. Kryten showed Lister two images of his new appendage—one unexcited, the other (taken after browsing an electrical appliance catalog) so erect that it filled two photographs **[T-SER4.2]**.

  NOTE: Polaroid is a brand of photography equipment and film; the name is also used to describe an instant photo taken by the camera.

- **Double-Rimmer:** A salute Rimmer devised, which he petitioned the Space Ministry to adopt for dress occasions in place of the standard military salute. It began with the standard salute pose, albeit with both arms; an individual would then throw his or her arms out in front, twirl the wrists five times (symbolizing the five arms of the Space Corps) and snap the arms back to form an equilateral triangle with the forehead. From there, the elbows would be straightened and the arms snapped back to the side. This was similar to the Full-Rimmer, which used only the right arm for the salute **[N-INF]**.

- **doughnut:** A type of fried dough confectionery **[RL]**. The blind Cat Priest aboard *Red Dwarf* wore a golden headpiece shaped like a large doughnut, which Lister donned in his presence while posing as Cloister the Stupid. When asking Cat to identify Cloister, the cleric asked if he was wearing the doughnut and golden sausage described in his people's prophecies. After Lister silently threatened Cat with a giant golden sausage effigy, Cat confirmed that this was the case, and the priest died happy **[T-SER1.4]**.

- **Doughnut, the:** A two-mile-long circular tube in which the sport of zero-gee football was played. For the sport's thirty-seventh season, spectator accommodations were installed in London's ring-like arena **[M-SMG1.8(a)]**.

- **Dove Program:** A type of software designed to combat dangerous computer viruses by infiltrating an infected system, spreading peace and obliterating viral cells. When rogue simulants infected *Starbug 1*'s navicomp with an Armageddon virus, Kryten tried to purge the system by contracting the virus and dedicating his entire runtime to developing a Dove Program. His crewmates monitored his progress via a monitor showing his dream.

  Kryten's subconscious mind created an Old West scenario in which he was a drunken sheriff being run out of town by the Apocalypse Boys, a manifestation of the virus. When it became apparent he was losing the battle, Lister, Rimmer and Cat inserted themselves into the dream via an artificial-reality machine to lend their support. Though they failed to defeat the Apocalypse Boys before retreating to the real world, they succeeded in stalling the viral program long enough for Kryten to implement the Dove Program in the form of a pair of six-shooters and eradicate the virus **[T-SER6.3]**.

NOTE: In the novel Backwards, *the Dove Program was created to irradicate the Apocalypse virus that Djuhn'Keep uploaded to* Starbug*'s navicomp.*

- **Doyle, Sebastian, Voter Colonel:** Lister's persona while trapped in a despair squid hallucination. In the illusion, he and his shipmates believed they had crashed *Starbug 1* into an underwater ravine and awoken in a total-immersion video game facility, where they had been playing the TIV *Red Dwarf* for the past four years.

  After exiting the game, the group were led to a recuperation lounge, where they found their belongings and learned their "true" identities. Lister was Sebastian Doyle, the maternal half-brother of Billy Doyle (Rimmer's identity in the hallucination). Sebastian's personal belongings included an expensive watch, an ID tag from CGI, a green suit and tie, an overcoat, and a ticket for his limousine, parked in the facility's long-term car lot.

  Upon leaving the facility, the crew emerged in a totalitarian society. A police agent confronted them in the carpark, recognizing Lister as Doyle—the mass-murdering head of an organization known as CGI, and the leader of the Ministry of Alteration. After Kryten inadvertently killed the man, the fascist police engaged them in a high-speed chase. Unable to deal with their despair, the four tried to commit suicide, but Holly intervened, awakening them from the hallucination in time to prevent their deaths **[T-SER5.6]**.

- **Doyle, Sebastian, Voter Colonel:** A high-ranking official of a fascist society on an alternate-universe Earth. The section head of CGI, Doyle was in charge of the Ministry of Alteration **[M-SMG2.5(c1)]**.

  Doyle, along with his brother William, Duane Dibbley and a cyborg cop named Jake Bullet, entered the total-immersion video game *Red Dwarf*, but they were released after four years due to their poor skills at the game. Unable to regain their memories, the group tried to commit suicide by lining up and using a single bullet among all four of them. Jake and Dibbley survived, however, and the latter was arrested for the Doyle brothers' murders **[M-SMG1.14(c1)]**. Voter Colonel Larson Gray then succeeded Sebastian Doyle as the head of CGI **[M-SMG2.5(c1)]**.

- **Doyle, William ("Billy"):** Rimmer's persona while trapped in a despair squid hallucination. In the illusion, he and his crewmates believed they had crashed *Starbug 1* into an underwater ravine and awoken in a total-immersion video game facility, where they had been playing the TIV *Red Dwarf* for the past four years.

  After exiting the game, the group were led to a recuperation lounge, where they found their belongings and learned their "true" identities. Rimmer was William Doyle, the wild-haired, down-on-his-luck maternal half-brother of the more successful and wealthy Voter Colonel Sebastian Doyle (Lister's identity in the hallucination). His personal belongings included an overcoat that smelled of yak urine.

  Upon leaving the facility, the crew emerged in a totalitarian society. When a police agent confronted them in the carpark, recognizing Lister as the Voter Colonel, Kryten inadvertently killed the man, and the fascist police engaged them in a high-speed chase. Unable to deal with their despair, the four tried to commit suicide, but Holly intervened, awakening them from the hallucination in time to prevent their deaths **[T-SER5.6]**.

  NOTE: In a deleted scene for this episode, Rimmer fabricated a possible history for his character, during which he called himself William Doyle IV.

- **Doyle, William ("Billy"):** The maternal half-brother of Voter Colonel Sebastian Doyle, the leader of CGI in a fascist society on an alternate-universe Earth. Billy—a wild-haired, smelly vagrant—entered the total-immersion video game *Red Dwarf* along with Sebastian, Duane Dibbley and a cyborg cop named Jake Bullet. The group were then released after four years, due to their poor skills at the game.

  Unable to regain their memories, the group tried to commit suicide by lining up and using a single bullet among the four of them. Jake and Dibbley survived, however, and the latter was arrested for the Doyle brothers' murders **[M-SMG1.14(c1)]**.

- ***Dr. Aardvark's Junior Medical Encyclopedia*:** A medical book that Lister read aboard *Starbug 1* while attempting to cure the Epideme virus **[T-SER7.7]**.

- **Dracula:** A pregnant dog that Deb Lister smuggled aboard *Red Dwarf* in an alternate universe in which the genders were reversed. While Deb was safe in stasis, a lethal cadmium II explosion killed everyone else on board except for Dracula, who was sealed in the ship's cargo hold **[W-OFF]**. Over the course of three million years, Dracula's litter procreated and evolved into the species known as *Canis sapiens*. Deb's later travel companion, Dog, belonged to that species **[M-SMG2.8(a)]**.

NOTE: Dracula was an analog to Dave Lister's cat Frankenstein.

- **dragon yak:** A large, fire-breathing racing beast that Cat imagined using as a type of dog-hunt mount while trapped in an addictive version of *Better Than Life*. When Lister and Rimmer visited Cat at his golden castle to inform him that they were in the game, Cat was astride a dragon yak and about to start a dog hunt. Noticing his guests, he ordered his Valkyrie assistant to saddle up two more racing yaks, named Dancer and Prancer, so his friends could join in the hunt **[N-INF]**.

- **draughts:** A group of abstract strategy games, such as American checkers, involving two players moving uniform pieces diagonally across a board of alternating light and dark squares **[RL]**. When Queeg challenged Holly to a game of chess for control of *Red Dwarf*, Holly, unskilled at the game, suggested they instead play draughts **[T-SER2.5]**. Lister and Rimmer played several rounds of draughts in their prison cell in the Tank, *Red Dwarf*'s secret prison **[T-SER8.8]**.

- **"Drazah Aera":** A warning posted on the door of Professor Cat's laboratory aboard a mirror-universe *Red Dwarf*. The words, when read forward, said "Hazard Area" **[T-SER8.8]**.

- **dream recorder:** A device that enabled *Red Dwarf* crewmembers to record and store their dreams for playback on a monitor **[T-SER1.5]**. It was produced by Malpractice Medical & Scispec, and was distributed by Crapola Inc. **[G-RPG]**.

  Curious if Kochanski had ever dreamed of him, Lister perused her dream recorder files and learned that she had done so three times. Since the area had not yet been decontaminated from the cadmium II accident, however, he succumbed to mutated pneumonia, causing his inner thoughts to become corporeal **[T-SER1.5]**.

  Cat later searched the machine for one of his own previous dreams, involving three girls and a vat of banana pudding. Instead, he found one in which he, Lister and Rimmer sang and danced to the song "Tongue-Tied" **[T-SER2.6]**. He also used the machine to delete a particularly unnerving dream he once had, in which robots from another dimension absconded with his suits to give to a population suffering from a style famine **[M-SMG1.7(c2)]**.

- **Dredd, Judge:** A fictional character from the popular British science fiction comic anthology *2000 AD*. The law-enforcement officer was empowered by the government of Mega-City One to convict, sentence and execute criminals **[RL]**. Film studio janitor Leo Davis once dreamed of meeting Dredd, who chastised him for not being man enough to ask out a woman whom he fancied. After reggae artist Judge Dread appeared, the two debated Davis' dating approach, each accusing the other of stealing his name **[X-TNG]**.

- **Drigg:** A half-man, half-amorphous-blob GELF imprisoned on the tourist planet GELFWorld, who was sentenced to several years' incarceration for his radical beliefs and revolutionary ideals. After talking the prison bars (a specialized GELF) into setting him free, Drigg led a revolution against the planet's tourists, during which many visitors were killed, and GELFWorld was thus abandoned. With no one left to fight, the GELFs turned against each other, starting a GELF war that ultimately destroyed the entire planet **[M-SMG2.2(c4)]**.

- **drive computer:** A computer system in *Red Dwarf*'s Drive Room. When the navicomp overheated due to the stress of faster-than-light travel, Holly instructed Lister to connect it to the drive computer, which Lister feared would trigger an explosion—and cause his death—as Rimmer had previously witnessed during a future echo. After completing the task, he discovered that the explosion would happen in the future, and that his son Bexley would die, not him **[T-SER1.2]**.

- **drive interface:** A component of *Starbug* shuttles. When the *Starbug 1* crew trespassed in simulant hunting territory, rogue simulants attacked and rendered them unconscious, deeming them unworthy of sport. When they awoke three weeks later, they discovered that the simulants had made improvements to the shuttle, including an upgraded drive interface and added weapons, in order to make the hunt more challenging **[T-SER6.3]**.

PREFIX
RL: Real life

T-: Television Episodes
SER: Television series
IDW: "Identity Within"
USA1: Unaired U.S. pilot
USA2: Unaired U.S. demo

R-: *The Bodysnatcher Collection*
SER: Remastered episodes
BOD: "Bodysnatcher"
DAD: "Dad"
FTH: "Lister's Father"
INF: "Infinity Patrol"
END: "The End" (original assembly)

N-: Novels
INF: *Infinity Welcomes Careful Drivers*
BTL: *Better Than Life*
LST: *Last Human*

BCK: *Backwards*
OMN: *Red Dwarf Omnibus*

M-: Magazines
SMG: *Smegazine*

W-: Websites
OFF: Official website
NAN: *Prelude to Nanarchy*
AND: *Androids*
DIV: Diva-Droid
DIB: Duane Dibbley

CRP: Crapola
GEN: Geneticon
LSR: Leisure World Intl.
JMC: Jupiter Mining Corporation
AIT: *A.I. Today*
HOL: HoloPoint

G-: Roleplaying Game
RPG: *Core Rulebook*
BIT: *A.I. Screen Extra Bits* booklet
SOR: *Series Sourcebook*
OTH: Other RPG material

- **drive module:** A component of *Starbug* propulsion systems. After infecting Lister, the Epideme virus advised Kryten to re-route *Starbug 1*'s pulse relays via the auxiliary conductor nodes, and to then transpose all prime numbers in the first line of the alphabet to the energy equation, in order to make the drive module three hundred percent faster **[T-SER7.7]**.

- **Drive Output:** A setting on *Starbug 1*'s sonar scope display. This setting was highlighted as the crew charted the course of a despair squid **[T-SER5.6]**.

- **drive plate:** A component aboard *Red Dwarf* that protected the crew from exposure to lethal doses of the radioactive material cadmium II. Assigned to repair a drive plate while his partner, Lister, was in stasis, Rimmer provided subpar work, leading to a catastrophic radioactive explosion that killed the ship's crew, except for Lister **[T-SER1.1]**. This faulty drive plate was located in White Corridor 159 **[T-SER1.6]**.

- **Drive Room:** *Red Dwarf*'s nerve center, which acted as the ship's bridge **[T-SER1.1]**. The Drive Room was located on Level 147 **[T-SER1.2]**.

  The Drive Room included multiple stations and monitors, a free-standing console (from which crewmembers' cremated remains could be launched into space) and the captain's office. Kochanski was stationed in the Drive Room as a console officer. After a cadmium II leak killed the remainder of the crew, Holly released Lister from stasis and instructed him to proceed to the Drive Room for debriefing, where he informed Dave what had happened to his shipmates **[T-SER1.1]**.

- **DriveU:** A limousine company owned by a character named Derek on the television soap opera *Androids*. According to the show, DriveU was the largest and most prestigious limo firm on Jupiter **[W-AND]**.

- **droid:** A shortened form of "android" and a synonym for "mechanoid" **[T-SER3.6]**.

  NOTE: *The term "droid," coined in the 1977 film* Star Wars, *is a registered trademark of Lucasfilm. The word "android," however, dates back to the* Cyclopædia, *a London encyclopedia published in 1728 by Ephraim Chambers.*

- **Droid Boy:** A nickname that Kill Crazy dubbed Kryten **[T-SER8.5]**.

  NOTE: *The DVD subtitles mislabeled the slur as "Toy Boy."*

- **Droid Oil:** A petroleum company owned by Karstares on the television soap opera *Androids*. When Karstares disappeared and was presumed dead, his son Brook attempted to run the business, but was haunted by stories of corruption and murder **[W-AND]**.

- **droid rot:** A condition that afflicted aged mechanoids, usually caused by deteriorating electronics and corrupted software. Kryten's Spare Head Three suffered from droid rot after thirty thousand years, causing him to act crotchety and speak in a Yorkshire accent **[T-SER4.2]**.

- **Droids R Us:** A store located in the shopping area of the American mining vessel *Red Dwarf* **[T-USA1]**.

- **Drone 3 ("Erica"):** An automated forklift aboard *Red Dwarf*. The ship's replacement computer, Pree, took control of the drone to force Lister out of an airlock, and later tried to use it to kill the entire crew **[T-SER10(b)]**.

  NOTE: *The names "Drone 3" and "Erica" were both mentioned in the "We're Smegged" special featured on the Series X DVDs.*

- **"Drunk":** A message displayed over Lister's bunk aboard *Red Dwarf* **[T-SER1.4]**.

- **Duality Jump:** A type of quantum drive used aboard spacefaring vessels, utilizing quantum mechanics and indeterminism to force a vessel into two points of space-time simultaneously. The system chose the point closest to the ship's destination for materialization, and was powered by uranium-233.

  Nova 5 contained a Duality Jump drive. After rescuing Kryten from that vessel, the *Red Dwarf* crew brought the ship on board in the hope of making the Duality Jump operational and using it to return to Earth within mere months **[N-INF]**.

- **DuaneDibbley:** The username of a forum poster on the *Androids* website's message boards. According to his signature, his favorite episode was #36,186 and his favorite character was Gary **[W-AND]**.

  ***NOTE:** See* Dibbley, Duane [third entry]

- **DuBois, Henri, Navigation Officer:** A crewmember aboard *Red Dwarf* at the time of the cadmium II disaster. DuBois accidentally spilled coffee on his console around the same time that the cadmium II coolant system failed due to a faulty drive plate (20:23 ship time). While cleaning his console, he noticed three red warning alerts on his monitor, which he wrongly attributed to the spill and ignored. Shortly thereafter, DuBois died in the resulting explosion **[N-INF]**.

  ***NOTE:** This character may have been named after sculptor Ernest Henri Dubois (see next entry). It is unknown whether the nanobots resurrected DuBois in Series VIII.*

- **Dubois Brothers, the:** An artist team who hand-carved a set of statues of Napoleon Bonaparte's Armée du Nord, which Rimmer considered a prized possession. Lister, trying to stay alive while marooned aboard *Starbug 1* on an icy planet, had no choice but to burn the sculptures **[T-SER3.2]**.

  ***NOTE:** Rimmer may have been referring to real-world artists Paul Dubois and Ernest Henri Dubois. Though the two nineteenth-century French sculptors were not related, the mistake is a common one due to their shared last name and profession.*

- **duck-billed oyster:** A creature spawned from genetic engineering experiments. A mix between a platypus and an oyster, they were a popular sight in cities around Earth's solar system **[B-SUR]**.

- **duck-billed rhinoceros:** A genetically engineered creature—a mix between a platypus and a rhino—developed by inebriated scientists **[B-EVR]**.

- **Duck, Donald:** An anthropomorphic cartoon character created by Walt Disney Productions **[RL]**. A glitch in the artificial-reality program *Great Moments in Human History* caused Grand Inquisitor Tomás de Torquemada to speak with Donald Duck's voice **[B-SUR]**.

- **Duck, Donna:** An anthropomorphic character in an alternate universe in which the sexes were reversed. Deb Lister asked the mechanoid Daizee to show her sons, Jim and Bexley, a Donna Duck video while Deb seduced Ace Rimmer **[M-SMG1.5(c2)]**.

  ***NOTE:** Donna was that reality's female counterpart to Donald Duck.*

- **duck's feet in abalone sauce:** A course that Kryten prepared for Rimmer after the latter swapped minds with Lister and over-indulged his body **[T-SER3.4]**.

- **Duckworth, Dicky:** A classmate of Rimmer who was kept down a year during their grade-school years on Io. As a result, Dicky was a year older than Rimmer and his classmates in Junior B. During a two-hundred-meter race, Duckworth tripped Rimmer, who was in the lead, causing him to fall and lose the competition **[N-BCK]**.

- **Dude, the:** A nickname that Confidence, a hallucination of Lister's mind made corporeal by mutated pneumonia, called Lister **[W-OFF]**.

  ***NOTE:** Jeff Bridges portrayed Jeff "the Dude" Lebowski in* The Big Lebowski, *a Coen Brothers comedy film released in 1988—the same year* Red Dwarf *debuted on TV. Like Lister, Lebowski was a slacker who spent most nights hanging out with his friends.*

- ***Duel*:** A 1971 Steven Spielberg thriller starring Dennis Weaver, concerning a motorist terrorized by a tractor-trailer driver **[RL]**. Rimmer claimed to have received the scar on his chin when a friend attacked him with the video case from this movie **[T-SER8.8]**.

- **Duke, The:** A nickname that Rimmer claimed his shipmates called him when he first met Camille—a Pleasure GELF who had assumed the form of an attractive hologrammic woman—in an effort to impress her **[T-SER4.1]**. Rimmer also asked Lister to call him this name (instead of "Rimmer") as they and Cat embarked on a rescue mission to the *Nova 5*, where they believed three female crewmembers awaited **[N-INF]**.

- **Duke of Deliciousness, the:** A nickname that Confidence, a hallucination of Lister's mind made corporeal by mutated pneumonia, called Lister **[T-SER1.5]**.

- **Duke of Dork, the:** A nickname that Cat gave to his nerdy alter ego, Duane Dibbley, after an emohawk drained him of his poise and cool **[T-SER6.4]**.

- **Duke of Lincoln, the:** A member of British nobility whose eldest daughter, Sabrina Mulholland-Jjones, married Fred Holden, the inventor of the Tension Sheet and Earth's youngest billionaire. Three million years later, Lister used a timeslide to create an alternate timeline in which he invented the Tension Sheet first, thereby becoming a billionaire and marrying Mulholland-Jjones instead of Holden. That reality was eliminated, however, when Rimmer tried the same tactic, inadvertently reinstating Fred as the novelty item's inventor and Sabrina's husband **[T-SER3.5]**.

NOTE: Presumably, the duke led the English cathedral city of Lincoln.

- **Duke of Wellington, the:** A nineteenth-century British soldier and politician, born as Arthur Wellesley **[RL]**. A waxdroid replica of the duke was created for the Waxworld theme park. Left on their own for millions of years, the waxdroids attained sentience and became embroiled in a park-wide resource war between Villain World and Hero World (to which the duke belonged). The Duke died during the conflict **[T-SER4.6]**.

  NOTE: The episode mentioned a "Wellington" dying during the Wax War, but no further details; the Duke of Wellington is a probable candidate.

- **Duncan:** Lister's best friend during his youth, until Duncan moved to Spain after his father botched a bank robbery in Purley. Duncan taught Dave everything, including how to put mirrors on his shoes to look up women's skirts **[T-SER2.4]**. While aboard *Starbug 1*, Lister found an old set of dominoes that he thought he'd lost in a bet to Duncan years prior **[T-IDW]**.

- **Dungo:** *See* Dennis ("Dungo")

- **Dunne, Anthony ("Tony"):** An Irish international football player who typically played left-back. During the 1968 European Cup final, he played that position for Manchester United **[RL]**. While attempting to prove he wasn't computer-senile, Holly erroneously cited Shay Brennan as the team's left-back during that game, but admitted it may have been Dunne **[T-SER2.4(d)]**.

- **Dun Robotix:** A company whose sign hung over the garage of a house possibly owned by Kelly and Brook in the television soap opera *Androids* **[M-SMG1.8(c2)]**.

- **Durex volleyball:** A game that Lister and Cat devised to pass the time aboard *Red Dwarf*, which involved stretching a condom across a room to use as a net, and then lobbing a ball over it **[T-SER3.5]**.

- **Dutch:** *See* van Oestrogen, Dutch

- **DV765DR82:** The personal owner's code that a writer employed at *A.I. Today* used to access the support section of Diva-Droid's website. The writer handed out his code to those in need when the firm's mailing system failed to send out personal codes to customers, leaving them without support help **[W-AIT]**.

  NOTE: Using this code on Diva-Droid's Support page, in the online Geek Chase game, leads players to an area in which they can input a reference number (obtainable elsewhere on the site), thereby granting access to the Hudzen 10 instruction manual.

- **DVD:** A digital storage medium that utilized optics to record and retrieve data from a plastic disc **[RL]**. At the height of DVDs' popularity, technology companies discovered that humans were incapable of returning the discs to their cases, resulting in the loss of two trillion discs throughout a twenty-year period. As such, the firms reverted to a larger, bulkier form of analog storage—video cassettes—which endured throughout the twenty-second century **[T-SER9.2]**.

  NOTE: The etymology of "DVD" is unclear. Although members of the DVD Forum proposed the backronym "digital versatile disc," that meaning has not been universally accepted. Some sources claim the three-letter name has no actual meaning. In any case, Back to Earth*'s discussion of DVD technology's fate was an in-joke explaining why* Red Dwarf *would still be using VHS technology hundreds of years in the future.*

- **D Wing:** A section of the Tank, *Red Dwarf*'s classified prison level on Floor 13. While imprisoned, Lister heard rumors that inmates were rewarded for good behavior by being sent to the luxury block on D Wing, where amenities included televisions, music centers, trouser presses and shampooed rats **[T-SER8.3]**. Warden Ackerman was beaten and mugged on D Wing, during which his glass eye was stolen **[T-SER8.5]**.

- **"dying":** A message that Kryten burned into Lister's left arm to warn him that he was trapped in the virtual-reality video game *Better Than Life*. Oblivious to reality, David thought he had returned to Earth and was living in Bedford Falls (the fictional setting of the film *It's a Wonderful Life*) with Kochanski and their sons, Jim and Bexley. After two years in the game, Lister began feeling arm pain. Upon applying ointment, he was startled to realize that the affected areas spelled out "dying" on one arm and "U=BTL" on the other **[N-INF]**.

- **DynaTach:** A technology used in Ouroboros batteries. The term was short for dynamic tachyon fusion **[G-RPG]**.

- **dyslexia:** A learning disability affecting a person's reading and comprehension skills **[RL]**. In an effort to earn extra time to take his exams, Rimmer tried to obtain a note from *Red Dwarf*'s medicomputer claiming he had dyslexia. He was unable to procure the note, however, as the medicomputer tricked him into spelling "dyslexia," thereby proving he did not have the condition **[T-SER10.1(d)]**.

EDGINGTON, IRENE, PROFESSOR ("PROFESSOR E")

- **E-11-T:** A sequence printed on a *Blue Midget* button label in a virtual-reality program created when Captain Hollister put Lister and his shipmates on trial. The button represented the word "exit" ("11" being "XI" in Roman numerals), and provided a failsafe trapdoor enabling those in the simulation to escape in the event of an emergency. When the crew pushed the button, however, they accidentally entered the AR computer's screensaver program, which rendered them as claymation characters **[T-SER8.3]**.

- **E355 DPK:** The license number of the ambulance in which the body of game-show winner Philby Frutch was placed following his murder **[M-SMG1.11(c4)]**.

- **E5:A9:O8:B7:** The word "love" when converted from hex into ASC2 code in Z80012, which Kryten expressed while pronouncing his feelings toward Camille **[T-SER4.1]**.

  NOTE: *The word "love," when translated from the real-world character-encoding scheme ASCII to hex, is 6c:6f:76:65. As such, ASCII and* Red Dwarf*'s ASC2 may be separate schemes.*

- **E-Accelerator:** A device that Kryten found in *Red Dwarf*'s cargo hold, which either accelerated or reversed the evolutionary process of biological and mechanical material, depending on the setting. Kryten accidentally used the device on Lister's bacon sandwich, transforming it into a living pig. After attempting to fix the device, the crew tried it on Rimmer, hoping to transform him into a solid hologram. It malfunctioned again, however, changing him into a two-dimensional, black-and-white silent hologram.

  As the group discussed their next course of action, the E-Accelerator was triggered by Lister's pig, transforming Lister into an ape, Cat into a housecat and Kryten into a vacuum cleaner. Unable to fix the machine himself, Kryten requested help from Holly, who convinced Talkie Toaster to effect repairs. The appliance agreed, on the condition that the crew eat toasted sandwiches for the next three days. Using the skutters, the appliance repaired the E-Accelerator and tested it first on the pig, evolving it into a pig-like humanoid woman, before using it to restore the crew to their former selves **[M-SMG1.12(c2)]**.

- **Eagle of Valour:** A medal awarded for bravery in the line of duty. Annoyed that his shipmates showed no gratitude after he saved them from an elation squid, Rimmer complained that anyone else would have received the Eagle of Valour **[T-SER9.1]**.

- **Earl of Sandwich, the:** A title bestowed upon a person of British nobility, nominally associated with the parish of Sandwich, Kent **[RL]**. After inventing the Holly Hop Drive, Holly cited several other inventors and their namesakes, including the Earl of Sandwich and his invention—the sandwich **[T-SER2.6]**.

  NOTE: *The sandwich's invention is sometimes attributed to John Montagu, the fourth Earl of Sandwich.*

- **Earth:** A planet in Universe 3, in which time ran backwards. When a polymorph killed Lister, Holly (temporarily gifted with an IQ in excess of twelve thousand) devised a plan to bring his remains to this Earth so he could be revived. Because Lister had previously been aged to sixty-one by a black hole's time-dilation effect, the crew left him on the backwards world for thirty-six years, restoring his prior physical age. To lessen his loneliness, Holly also brought Kochanski's remains to the planet so she could accompany him **[N-BTL]**.

- **Earth ("Garbage World"):** The third planet in the Sol system, and the birthworld of humanity **[RL]**. At one point, the hole in Earth's ozone layer became so dangerous that the world government fitted a gigantic toupée over the entire planet **[T-SER3.2]**.

  During the twenty-second century, the solar system's Interplanetary Commission for Waste Disposal decided, after a series of feasibility studies, that it was necessary for one planet to be given over to trash disposal. Representatives from all nine worlds in the system presented their case against being chosen. Earth's representatives argued that their home planet, despite being the poorest and most polluted, was the birthplace of civilization, calling the notion of it being considered as a garbage world a travesty.

  Despite such objections, Earth lost the poll and became mankind's permanent dumping grounds, and was abandoned and renamed Garbage World. Various land masses were designated for different types of waste: Bottles were piled up in North America, household waste was discarded in Australia, automobile frames and scrap were left in Japan, food waste was dropped onto the Arctic Circle, old sofas and bicycle tires were abandoned in the Bahamas, electrical equipment was allocated to Korea, and raw sewage was dumped onto Europe.

  This lasted for several hundred years, until a sewage transport pilot named John Ewe crashed his vessel into the planet while attempting to write "Ewe woz 'ere" in human waste across the planet's surface. The crash ignited a methane storm, causing an explosion so powerful that the planet was torn from its orbit and propelled into deep space.

  Three million years later, the frozen rogue planet entered a binary star system and hurtled toward *Red Dwarf*, the engines of which were offline. Lacking other options, Lister and Rimmer attempted to knock the planet off-course by firing a thermonuclear device from *Starbug* into one of the system's suns, creating a flare that would push the planet away from the ship. The plan worked; however, *Starbug* was damaged in the process and crashed on the frozen planet, marooning Lister.

After the frozen surface began to melt, centuries of deposited garbage became visible, and Lister realized he was on Earth. During the next thirty-four years, he befriended a herd of giant cockroaches that had evolved, and farmed the land for sustenance until his former crewmates finally rescued him **[N-BTL]**.

Eventually, the universe's halted expansion caused it to contract back upon itself, and time to run backwards. During this period, Kryten, Rimmer and Holly visited Earth in what was considered the twentieth century, after being sucked into a time hole during Kryten's pilot's test. Stranded on the planet for several weeks, they worked as a novelty stage act and became content with their new life, until Lister and Cat arrived and caused a backwards barroom brawl, ending their career. The reunited crew then returned to their own time and space via the time hole **[T-SER3.1]**.

- **East Alpha 555:** A section of *Red Dwarf* containing several launderettes. Shortly before the cadmium II disaster, Rimmer sent Z-Shift's Burd, Dooley and Pixon to repair malfunctioning driers in this area **[N-INF]**.

- **Eastbourne:** A large town in East Sussex, on England's south coast, popular as a retirement destination **[RL]**. While discussing computer senility, Rimmer agreed with the Eskimo tradition of handling the infirmed—which, he claimed, involved stripping them down and leaving them to face the elements. This, he said, was why there was no Eskimo word for "Eastbourne" **[T-SER4.4]**.

  NOTE: *Among Eskimos (a term often used to describe North America's indigenous Inuit, Yupik and Iñupiat cultures), senilicide and invalidicide—the killing of old and sick people, respectively—was once practiced, but was neither common nor universal.*

- **Eastbourne Zimmer frame relay team:** A hypothetical track team from Eastbourne, England, comprising elderly runners who used Zimmer frames (walkers) during races. Upon encountering a Space Corps enforcement vehicle, Lister suggested running away, but Kryten noted that the probe could easily outrun *Starbug 1*. Lister sarcastically replied that the Eastbourne Zimmer frame relay team could do so as well **[T-SER6.4]**.

- **Eastern Avenue:** A roadway in the terraformed section of Mimas. Lister traveled this avenue while working as a taxi hopper on the Saturnian moon **[N-INF]**.

- ***Easy Rider*:** A 1969 American film starring Peter Fonda and Dennis Hopper, about two free-spirited bikers and their quest across the Southwestern United States **[RL]**. Lister showed Kryten this film to help him break free of his servantile programming and think for himself. Initially, it appeared to have no effect, but the mechanoid soon rebelled against Rimmer, painting a portrait of him on a toilet, calling him names and dumping soup onto his bunk, then driving off on Lister's space bike for parts unknown **[T-SER2.1]**.

- **Eau de Yak Urine:** A hypothetical cologne of which Rimmer was reminded while trapped in a despair squid hallucination, in which he was a bum named Billy Doyle whose coat badly reeked **[T-SER5.6]**.

- **"EC":** A word adorning a patch sewn onto Brooke Junior's leather jacket on the television soap opera *Androids* **[M-SMG1.13(c1)]**.

- **Ecclesiastes:** A book of the Old Testament **[RL]**. Holovirus-afflicted scientist Hildegarde Lanstrom quoted Ecclesiastes while pursuing the *Red Dwarf* crew through her research station, claiming the book postulated "How the wise man dies—just like a fool" **[T-SER5.4(d)]**.

  NOTE: *The quote, from Ecclesiastes 2:16, actually reads, "For there is no remembrance of the wise more than of the fool forever; seeing that which now is in the days to come shall all be forgotten. And how does the wise man die? As the fool."*

- **Echech 3:** The third planet orbiting an S-type star in GELF space, home to the Kinitawowi Open, an annual golf tournament run by the GELF tribe. The planet, covered in lush jungles and forests, and dotted with active volcanoes and mountain ranges, was home to several species of dinosaurs, carnivorous plants

and giant insects. The tournament was held in a part of Echech 3 known as the Forbidden Lands **[G-RPG]**.

- **Echech 3 GELF Open:** *See* Kinitawowi Open

- **Ech-ech-ech-ech-ech-ech-ech-ech:** *See* Hackhackhack-achhachhachach

- **Ech-Ghekk-Agg-Hecch-Ech-Ech, Queen:** The ruler of a Kinitawowi tribe in GELF space, who hosted Echech 3's annual Kinitawowi Open golf tournament. She had matted gray fur, beady black eyes and pierced nipples. Upon arriving on Echech 3 for the tournament, players were brought before Queen Ech-Ghekk-Agg-Hecch-Ech-Ech for the opening ceremonies, which included a rundown of the tournament and prizes **[G-RPG]**.

- **Eco:** A brand of cleaning products mentioned on the television soap opera *Androids*. The product was created and sold by Jaysee using his father's company, Karstares Interstellar Cleaning and Sanitation Supplies (K.I.C.A.S.S.), and used ingredients culled from Io's rainforests **[M-SMG2.2(c3)]**.

- **eco-accelerator rocket:** A portable device that, when launched into the atmosphere of a barren S-3 planet, stimulated the growth of that world's ecosystem, producing a lush, flourishing jungle after only several days of violent storms **[T-SER6.5]**. The terraforming rockets were produced by Malpractice Medical and Scispec, and were distributed by Crapola Inc. **[G-RPG]**. Eco-accelerator rockets were stocked on colonization seeding ship pods. Rimmer used several such devices to create Rimmerworld **[T-SER6.5]**.

- **Econoline:** A model of van used in England, circa 1993 **[RL]**. While searching for their missing crewmates far in the future, on an Earth where time ran backwards, Lister and Cat hitched a ride with a motorist driving an Econoline van **[T-SER3.1]**.

  NOTE: *Throughout the episode, backwards writing was inconsistently handled. In some cases, characters were backward-facing, while in others, they faced forward. Adding to the confusion, some signs were lettered top to bottom, whereas others ran bottom to top. This was among the few instances in which writing was printed left to right and forward-facing, as the scene was not flipped to give the illusion of backwards writing, as most on-location shots were. More properly, the company should have been called Enilonoce.*

- **Ecstat-O-Matic:** A small sex booth in an android brothel run by Kelly on the television soap opera *Androids*. Mollee fell into the Ecstat-O-Matic after fainting while protesting the establishment **[M-SMG1.12(c3)]**. The accident scrambled her circuits, causing her to take over the brothel after an attempt on Kelly's life left the former owner hospitalized **[M-SMG2.2(c2)]**.

- **EDA-9:** A string of characters stenciled above a doorway inside a derelict ship that the *Red Dwarf* crew found on an asteroid within Psiren territory **[T-SER6.1]**.

- **Edam:** A type of Dutch cheese traditionally shaped into spheres and coated with a red paraffin wax **[RL]**. According to Lister, Hammy Hamster—the star of the original *Tales of the Riverbank* series—one minute had all the Edam he could stuff into his cheeks, and the next minute faded into obscurity. While watching the sequel, *Tales of the Riverbank: The Next Generation*, Cat wondered what had become of Hammy **[T-SER4.1]**.

- ***Edda*:** A novel by Jane Austin, a simulation of which was included in the Total Immersion artificial-reality game *Jane Austin World* **[G-RPG]**.

  NOTE: *This fictional novel's title, from* Red Dwarf—The Roleplaying Game, *was based on* Emma, *by real-life novelist Jane Austen (note the different surname spelling). Some online hoax sites have listed* Edda *among the works of Jane G. Austin—another actual writer who lived a century after Austen.*

- **E Deck:** A floor aboard *Starbug* shuttles **[N-LST]**.

- **Edgington, Irene, Professor ("Professor E"):** The head scientist of the Erroneous Reasoning Research Academy (ERRA), a facility that employed individuals known to be consistently wrong. According to her station records, Edgington was thirty-one years old and brunette, and stood five feet five inches tall. Her projects included a device called a groinal

exploder, as well as research into human evolution. She developed a machine that, in theory, would evolve a human to the next evolutionary step. Volunteering as "Subject A," she used the device on herself; naturally, it did not work as intended, and she de-evolved into a chimpanzee, after which she was placed in stasis.

Three million years later, a tribe of BEGGs, having obtained Edgington's groinal exploder, attached the device onto Lister to ensure he paid off his gambling debts. After the BEGGs simultaneously choked to death during a fluke accident, the *Red Dwarf* crew visited the ERRA station, hoping to find a way to remove the device.

Upon boarding the station, they located Edgington's stasis pod and revived her, then used her evolution machine to convert her back into human form aboard *Red Dwarf*. She and Rimmer were instantly attracted to each other—largely due to her utter inability to correctly ascertain the type of man he was.

The crew decrypted the code for the groinal exploder by choosing whichever symbol the perpetually erring professor did not pick. When it came to the last two symbols, however, Kryten and Cat—who had been quantum-entangled—both surmised that her first name and last initial, Irene E. (irony), meant the last symbol she chose would actually be correct. This proved true, and the device deactivated.

Shortly thereafter, as Edgington and Rimmer went for a stroll down a *Red Dwarf* corridor, she accidentally tripped on a box of accident report forms Rimmer had left near an airlock. This caused her to fall into the airlock and be flushed into space, to her apparent death **[T-SER10.4]**.

> ***NOTE:*** *Despite her records, Irene appeared to have blonde hair.*

- **Edison, Thomas Alva:** An American inventor and businessman whose innovations included the phonograph, the motion picture camera and the commercially practical light bulb **[RL]**. Rimmer referenced the scientist while defending his own obsession with a supposedly alien pod, claiming that people also laughed at Edison's ideas. To his chagrin, however, the craft turned out merely to be a *Red Dwarf* garbage pod **[T-SER1.4]**.

- **Edward II, King:** The ruler of England from 1307 to 1327. Widely reputed as incompetent, he was rumored to have been killed by a red-hot poker thrust into his anus **[RL]**. Rimmer worried that his son, Michael McGruder—who had grown up believing his father to be a hero—felt as thrilled to learn of Rimmer's true nature as Edward II did while the pokers were being heated **[N-LST]**.

- **effluence evacuation pipe:** A tube inside 4000 Series mechanoids that allowed for fluid removal **[N-BCK]**.

- **egg:** Cat's name for a golf ball. While playing golf in the total-immersion video game *Better Than Life*, Cat nudged Lister aside so he could "plant his egg" **[T-SER2.2]**.

- **eggnog:** A dairy-based drink popular around holidays, typically made with liquor **[RL]**. While inhabiting Lister's body, Rimmer drank an entire bottle of eggnog, despite having agreed to get the body in better shape **[T-SER3.4(d)]**.

- **"eh! wack":** An obscure, informal term of address that originated in Liverpool, England, in the mid-1960s. This Souse phrase—which died out quickly and was never very popular, even in Liverpool—meant "Hey, mate!" **[RL]**. Lister had these words painted on the right arm of his leather jacket **[T-SER10.2]**.

- **Eidetosol:** The brand name of a learning drug developed for clinical use. This drug and its black-market offshoots—MIT White, IQ and Smarteez—were considered contraband **[G-SOR]**.

- **Eiger, the:** A mountain located in Switzerland's Bernese Alps **[RL]**. Following an accident involving *Starbug*'s waste compactor, Kryten needed to activate his self-repair unit, but not before finishing his duties, which included cleaning a pile of laundry he considered bigger than the Eiger's north face **[T-SER6.1]**.

- **EIMLBBBY:** A set of letters remaining in a *Scrabble* game's tile-rack in *Red Dwarf*'s Officers Quarters **[T-SER3(b)]**.

> ***NOTE:*** *The tile-rack and letters appeared among the bonus materials menu on the bonus disc of the Series III DVDs. The letters were an anagram of Mel Bibby, the TV series' production designer; selecting them started a short tribute to him.*

PREFIX
RL: Real life

T-: Television Episodes
SER: Television series
IDW: "Identity Within"
USA1: Unaired U.S. pilot
USA2: Unaired U.S. demo

R-: *The Bodysnatcher Collection*
SER: Remastered episodes
BOD: "Bodysnatcher"
DAD: "Dad"
FTH: "Lister's Father"
INF: "Infinity Patrol"
END: "The End" (original assembly)

N-: Novels
INF: *Infinity Welcomes Careful Drivers*
BTL: *Better Than Life*
LST: *Last Human*
BCK: *Backwards*
OMN: *Red Dwarf Omnibus*

M-: Magazines
SMG: *Smegazine*

W-: Websites
OFF: Official website
NAN: *Prelude to Nanarchy*
AND: *Androids*
DIV: Diva-Droid
DIB: Duane Dibbley
CRP: Crapola
GEN: Geneticon
LSR: Leisure World Intl.
JMC: Jupiter Mining Corporation
AIT: *A.I. Today*
HOL: HoloPoint

G-: Roleplaying Game
RPG: *Core Rulebook*
BIT: *A.I. Screen Extra Bits* booklet
SOR: *Series Sourcebook*
OTH: Other RPG material

- **Eine Kutta Über de Resten:** A hypothetical haircutting establishment. While explaining Napoleon Bonaparte's defeat at Waterloo, Rimmer asserted that the side with the shortest haircut always wins. His theory: Napoleon neglected his hair while marching for one hundred days, whereas the Prussian forces likely stopped at Eine Kutta Über de Resten for a cut and blow **[T-SER6.4(d)]**.

  NOTE: *The name, translated into English, would be "Supercuts of Resten," referencing the U.S. and U.K. hair salon and the German city.*

- **Einstein, Albert, Doctor:** A German theoretical physicist widely regarded as the "father of modern physics" for his general theory of relativity, which provided a unified description of gravity as a geometric property of space and time. During the 1940s, he reportedly enjoyed a brief romantic relationship with Marilyn Monroe **[RL]** while conducting research regarding time-freezing and stasis theory. The affair distracted him from this research, however, and he never returned to it once the affair ended **[N-INF]**.

  Holly read the complete works of several prominent writers, including Einstein, during the fifteen nanoseconds that passed between *Red Dwarf*'s cadmium II core going critical and the entire crew dying **[N-INF]**. The AI computer considered Einstein overrated, and claimed the scientist had eventually left quantum physics to enter the look-a-like business **[B-RD8]**.

  After witnessing a future echo of Lister's apparent death, Rimmer insisted there was no avoiding the event, citing Einstein's theory as proof that one could not change the future **[T-SER1.2]**.

  After a DNA modifier turned Kryten into a human, he had several questions about his penis (which he considered horrid-looking), and was disgusted by the idea that Einstein had a similar appendage when writing his famous works **[T-SER4.2]**.

  While dissuading Rimmer from using a mind patch to pass a test in order to join the holoship *Enlightenment*, Kryten cited Einstein as an example of people who became more than their occupation suggested **[T-SER5.1]**. Lister, meanwhile, consulted a virtual-reality Einstein via *Starbug 1*'s AR Suite while infected with the Epideme virus, in the hope of finding a cure **[T-SER7.7(s)]**.

  When Rimmer tried to create a host body using the cellular regeneration of one of Lister's hair follicles, Lister commented that such a plan might be ambitious for Einstein, but it was beyond Rimmer, who had failed at plant biology **[R-BOD]**.

  While trapped in an addictive version of *Better Than Life*, Rimmer imagined that he had returned to Earth and become famously wealthy, creating a company that developed a time machine. He then used this device to invite Einstein and other guests to dinner parties **[N-INF]**, and also invited Einstein to a bachelor party celebrating his marriage to his second wife, Helen **[N-BTL]**.

  NOTE: *Einstein's recreation during the Epideme virus incident was mentioned in a collectible booklet included with the Series VII DVDs.*

- **Einstein, Albert, Doctor:** A waxdroid replica of the scientist, created for the Waxworld theme park. Left on their own for millions of years, the waxdroids attained sentience and became embroiled in a park-wide resource war between Villain World and Hero World (to which Einstein belonged).

  During this war, the *Red Dwarf* crew transported to the planet using a Matter Paddle, with Lister and Cat materializing in Villain territory, while Rimmer and Kryten landed in Hero territory. Rimmer found the heroes' army lacking and took command, working many of the pacifistic waxdroids to death before ordering a frontal attack on the enemy's compound across a minefield, which wiped out the remaining droids, including Einstein **[T-SER4.6]**.

- ***Einstein*, SS:** A derelict Space Corps vessel that Lister and his friends imagined after Captain Hollister ordered them placed in a psychotropically induced artificial-reality (AR) simulation aboard the nanobot-rebuilt *Red Dwarf* **[T-SER8.3]**. The AR program's designer, Faulkner, added the *Einstein* to the simulation at Hollister's request, in order to provoke a reaction from Kryten **[W-OFF]**. The mechanoid—believing the shuttle they had stolen in the illusion was dangerously low on fabric softener—fell for the ruse and urged his comrades to plot a course for the *Einstein* to restock **[T-SER8.3]**.

- **Eisenhower, Mamie:** The wife of U.S. President Dwight D. Eisenhower **[RL]**. In a dimension in which *Red Dwarf* was an American vessel, Rimmer burst into tears, claimed to be Mamie Eisenhower and passed out during an engineering test **[T-USA1(s1)]**.

- **Eisner, William ("Will"):** An American cartoonist who created the popular comic strip *The Spirit*. The Eisner Awards, recognizing achievements in the comics medium, were named in his honor **[RL]**. Cat accidentally pierced an issue of Eisner's *The Spirit* while hiding a fishing pole he had used to catch Lister's robotic fish **[M-SMG1.6(c2)]**.

- **Ekaj Tellub:** A name that Sugar mistakenly thought was Jake Bullet's, due to the name on his door being painted on the inside **[M-SMG1.7(a)]**.

  NOTE: *Technically, she should have thought his name was Tellub Ekaj, since Ekaj Tellub backward would be Bullet Jake.*

- **Elara:** A small natural satellite of the planet Jupiter **[RL]**. Elara was home to a United Nations high-security prison complex **[G-RPG]**.

- **Elastic:** The first of three passwords required to access personal profiles on the Diva-Droid website **[W-DIV]**.

  NOTE: *This password was revealed in a PDF of the Hudzen 10 instruction manual.*

- **Elastoplast:** An elastic material used for setting broken bones **[N-BCK]**.

- **elation squid:** A female version of the despair squid, which Cat found on an ocean planet. Like the despair squid, the elation squid released a powerful hallucinogenic ink when provoked or attacked, but in the female's case, the venom induced a feeling of joy, rather than grief, causing the affected to halt all aggression toward the animal.

  Cat smuggled an infant elation squid aboard *Red Dwarf* with the intention of eating it, but it escaped and hid in the ship's water tank on G Deck, where it lived for several years **[T-SER9.3]**. Eventually, it grew large enough to disrupt the tank's water levels. When Lister, Kryten and Cat lowered themselves in a diving bell to investigate, the creature attacked them, though it retreated after Lister severed one of its tentacles.

  Covered in squid ink, the crew fell into an hallucinogenic state, in which they believed a new hologram, science officer Katerina Bartikovsky, was activated to replace Rimmer and formulate a plan for Lister to repopulate the human species **[T-SER9.1]**. In the illusion, they passed through a dimensional portal, emerging in an alternate twenty-first-century Earth on which they were merely characters in a British television show called *Red Dwarf*. Upon learning that they were fated to perish in the show's as-yet-unfilmed final episode, the crew set out to find their creator and plead for more life.

  To that end, they tracked down Noddy, an employee at a science fiction collectibles shop called They Walk Among Us!; Swallow, a worker at Nose World, a company specializing in prosthetics for film and television **[T-SER9.2]**; Craig Charles, an actor on the set of the TV show *Coronation Street*; and finally, *Red Dwarf*'s creator.

  The writer threatened to kill them in a glorious death scene, but this was a ruse to trick Lister into killing him, thereby dooming them to non-existence. When they failed to disappear, they realized it was all just an illusion, and each of them returned to consciousness. Lister briefly considered staying behind with an illusion of Kochanski, but eventually exited the hallucination as well **[T-SER9.3]**.

  NOTE: *It seems unlikely that Cat could have found the infant elation squid when the crew met the despair squid, since that would mean it had lived on* Starbug *undetected for two years, and then survived the crash aboard the nanobot-rebuilt* Red Dwarf. *A more believable scenario is that the crew visited another ocean world where the same accelerated-evolution experiment had taken place.*

  The term "elation squid" was never used in the episode, but appeared in various online references, including the official website's database.

- **elbow-titting:** The act of "accidentally" brushing one's elbow against a woman's breasts in passing. Rimmer tried this trick in *Red Dwarf*'s refectory on Lea Lovell, who punched him in the shoulder and told him to drop dead **[R-END]**.

- **elder chaos god:** A powerful being from N'mtheglyar **[G-OTH]**.

  NOTE: *This was mentioned in* Red Dwarf RPG A.I. Add-On 1.0, *a downloadable PDF posted online by Deep7 Press in 2004, for use with* Red Dwarf—The Roleplaying Game.

PREFIX
RL: Real life

T-: Television Episodes
SER: Television series
IDW: "Identity Within"
USA1: Unaired U.S. pilot
USA2: Unaired U.S. demo

R-: *The Bodysnatcher Collection*
SER: Remastered episodes
BOD: "Bodysnatcher"
DAD: "Dad"
FTH: "Lister's Father"
INF: "Infinity Patrol"
END: "The End" (original assembly)

N-: Novels
INF: *Infinity Welcomes Careful Drivers*
BTL: *Better Than Life*
LST: *Last Human*

BCK: *Backwards*
OMN: *Red Dwarf Omnibus*

M-: Magazines
SMG: *Smegazine*

W-: Websites
OFF: Official website
NAN: *Prelude to Nanarchy*
AND: *Androids*
DIV: Diva-Droid
DIB: Duane Dibbley

CRP: Crapola
GEN: Geneticon
LSR: Leisure World Intl.
JMC: Jupiter Mining Corporation
AIT: *A.I. Today*
HOL: HoloPoint

G-: Roleplaying Game
RPG: *Core Rulebook*
BIT: *A.I. Screen Extra Bits* booklet
SOR: *Series Sourcebook*
OTH: Other RPG material

- **El Dirtball:** A nickname that Rimmer called Lister after his crewmates voted to let him launch a thermonuclear device at a white hole instead of Holly, due to Lister's mastery at billiards **[T-SER4.4]**.

- **electromagnetic phasing frequency:** An energy frequency used to establish a linkway between parallel dimensions, requiring a positive transdimensional trace. Kochanski blamed the electromagnetic phasing frequency when she failed to bridge her reality with the prime universe **[T-SER7.3]**.

- **electromagnetic radiation (EMR):** A type of radiation traveling in waves while simultaneously composed of tiny particles, including radio waves, TV waves, radar waves, infrared, visible light, ultraviolet light, x-rays, short waves, microwaves and Gamma rays **[RL]**. Damaged hard light projection units emitted EMR. When other-dimensional Nazis shot hologrammic Ace Rimmer, his light bee began leaking EMR, which eventually killed him **[T-SER7.2]**.

- **electronic aneurysm:** The hologrammic equivalent of an aneurysm (the ballooning of an artery due to weakness in the artery wall, sometimes brought on by extreme stress). After diagnosing Rimmer as having an extremely high T-count (a hologram's analog to blood pressure), Kryten instructed him to start a relaxation program to avoid an electronic aneurysm **[T-SER6.5]**.

- **Electronic Bible, The:** A religious text written for sentient electronic devices and androids. Attempting to justify the existence of Silicon Heaven, Kryten quoted a passage from The Electronic Bible that read, "The iron shall lie down with the lamp." After a night of partying in honor of his last day of service, Kryten questioned the validity of the book, which also stated it was impossible for androids to enjoy themselves until they reached Silicon Heaven **[T-SER3.6]**.

  One edition of the book, the "Authorized Panasonic Version," contained the following verse: "And some will come among ye, and, yea, from their mouths shall come doubts. But ye turn from them; heed them not. For it is harder for a droid who disbelieveth to pass through the gates of Silicon Heaven, than it is for a DIN-DIN coaxial cable to connect up to a standard European SCART socket" **[N-BTL]**.

- **Elephant Man, the:** The nickname of Joseph Merrick, a severely deformed Englishman in the 1800s who spent his life exhibited as a human curiosity, likely due to neurofibromatosis or Proteus syndrome **[RL]**. Cat commented that if Lister (who had contracted space mumps) and the Elephant Man double-dated, the latter would be the looker **[T-SER4.3]**.

- **Eliot, Thomas Stearns ("T.S."):** A twentieth-century American poet and playwright, whose many works included *Old Possum's Book of Practical Cats*, which Andrew Lloyd Webber adapted as the Broadway musical *Cats* **[RL]**. Cat enjoyed reading Eliot's work **[M-SMG1.1(a)]**.

- **Elite, the:** A tribe of Cat People aboard *Red Dwarf*, descended from Lister's pregnant cat, Frankenstein. When a food shortage in the mining vessel's cargo hold threatened the species with extinction, a member of the Elite took the Sacred Icon (a can opener) and used it on one of the "silver rocks" from the great silver mountain (a can of Alphabetti Spaghetti). This ended the famine and spawned the species *Felis sapiens*.

  After thousands of years of peace, the Cat People engaged in a holy war over the name of their god; some believed it to be Cloister, while others thought it was Clister. The Elite remained neutral throughout the conflict **[M-SMG2.1(a)]**.

  The sect discovered a mysterious ship embedded in *Red Dwarf*'s hull, which possessed superior technology that they used to build an impregnable building—the High Tower—to wait out the war. After fifteen hundred years, upon realizing their species faced extinction, the Elite tapped into *Red Dwarf*'s computer to find a way to end the conflict. Although Holly was going through a gurning (non-speaking) era of his existence, the Cats learned that Lister would be released from stasis in five hundred years, and devised a plan to retrieve him via a time obelisk **[M-SMG2.2(c1)]**.

  The Elite sent three warriors—Fritz, Krazy and Juma—into the future to retrieve Lister so he could end hostilities. However, Fritz, a secret fundamentalist who felt the war should be played out to its natural conclusion, attacked Lister. Once Fritz was defeated, Lister warned the various tribes' leaders that their predilection to fight amongst themselves would doom them as a species **[M-SMG2.1(c1)]**.

B-: Books
PRG: *Red Dwarf Programme Guide*
SUR: *Red Dwarf Space Corps Survival Manual*
PRM: *Primordial Soup*
SOS: *Son of Soup*
SCE: *Scenes from the Dwarf*
LOG: *Red Dwarf Log No. 1996*
RD8: *Red Dwarf VIII*
EVR: *The Log: A Dwarfer's Guide to Everything*

X-: Misc.
PRO: Promotional materials, videos, etc.
PST: Posters at DJ XVII (2013)
CAL: 2008 calendar
RNG: Cell phone ringtones
MOB: Mobisode ("Red Christmas")
CIN: *Children in Need* sketch
GEK: *Geek Week* intros by Kryten
TNG: "Tongue-Tied" video

XMS: Bill Pearson's Christmas special pitch script
XVD: Bill Pearson's Christmas special pitch video
OTH: Other *Red Dwarf* appearances

SUFFIX
DVD:
(d) – Deleted scene
(o) – Outtake
(b) – Bonus DVD material (other)
(e) – Extended version

SMEGAZINES:
(c) – Comic
(a) – Article

OTHER:
(s) – Early/unused script draft
(s1) – Alternate version of script

ESCORT BOOTS

PREFIX
RL: Real life

T-: Television Episodes
- **SER:** Television series
- **IDW:** "Identity Within"
- **USA1:** Unaired U.S. pilot
- **USA2:** Unaired U.S. demo

R-: *The Bodysnatcher Collection*
- **SER:** Remastered episodes
- **BOD:** "Bodysnatcher"
- **DAD:** "Dad"
- **FTH:** "Lister's Father"
- **INF:** "Infinity Patrol"
- **END:** "The End" (original assembly)

N-: Novels
- **INF:** *Infinity Welcomes Careful Drivers*
- **BTL:** *Better Than Life*
- **LST:** *Last Human*
- **BCK:** *Backwards*
- **OMN:** *Red Dwarf Omnibus*

M-: Magazines
- **SMG:** *Smegazine*

W-: Websites
- **OFF:** Official website
- **NAN:** *Prelude to Nanarchy*
- **AND:** *Androids*
- **DIV:** Diva-Droid
- **DIB:** Duane Dibbley
- **CRP:** Crapola
- **GEN:** Geneticon
- **LSR:** Leisure World Intl.
- **JMC:** Jupiter Mining Corporation
- **AIT:** *A.I. Today*
- **HOL:** HoloPoint

G-: Roleplaying Game
- **RPG:** *Core Rulebook*
- **BIT:** *A.I. Screen Extra Bits* booklet
- **SOR:** *Series Sourcebook*
- **OTH:** Other RPG material

- **Elizabeth I, Queen:** The monarch of England and Ireland from 1558 to 1603, who was rumored to have lived a life of celibacy **[RL]**.

  While trapped in an addictive version of *Better Than Life*, Rimmer believed he had returned to Earth and become famously wealthy, creating a company that developed a time machine. He then used the device to bring together several historical individuals for his wedding reception, including Elizabeth I, who was seen emerging from bushes disheveled and blushing, following John F. Kennedy **[N-BTL]**. While attempting to escape a backwards-running Earth, Rimmer later described one of *Starbug*'s decrepit landing jets as "rustier than Elizabeth I's chastity belt" **[N-BCK]**.

- **Ellis, Ben:** A human crewmember aboard a possible alternate-universe *Red Dwarf*. His companions included a hologram named Terry, a creature called Rat, the mechanoid Kryten, and the ship's artificial-intelligence computer, Kate **[G-RPG]**.

- **Ellis, Michael:** A man who attempted a bank heist in South London in 1993, resulting in the death of two cashiers and a security guard, for which he served a fifteen-year prison sentence. While stranded on Earth far in the future when time ran backwards, Rimmer and Kryten viewed a newspaper reporting that Ellis, having just finished a prison sentence, brought two cashiers and a security guard back to life by sucking bullets out of them, after which he gave the bank £10,000 **[T-SER3.1]**.

  NOTE: *The name Michael Ellis was in-joke reference to a character from* Monty Python's Flying Circus.

- **El Skutto:** An insult that Rimmer called a skutter during a game of checkers. Despite nearly losing the game, Rimmer stalled long enough for the robot to have to report to work, forcing it to forfeit. The match was interrupted, however, by a meteor striking *Red Dwarf*'s hull **[T-SER2.5]**.

- **El Slotho:** A nickname Rimmer called Lister, thinking he was still asleep in his bunk, but unaware Dave had awoken early and had left to study for his Chef's Exam **[T-SER1.3]**.

- **El Weirdo:** A nickname that Arnold Rimmer called Arlene Rimmer, his equivalent in a reality where the sexes were reversed, out of jealousy that Lister's counterpart was a fun person, whereas Arlene was socially awkward and sexually over-aggressive **[T-SER2.6]**.

- **Embryo Refrigeration Unit:** A storage unit within *Red Dwarf*'s medical facility, the primary function of which was to keep embryo samples cold. Lister moved the unit into the Officers Quarters for use in meal preparation **[T-SER3.3]**.

- **"Emergency Ammo":** A phrase on a sign posted on a wall aboard *Starbug 1*, just above a rack containing cartridges of JMC ammunition **[T-SER7]**.

  NOTE: *This was visible in the Series VII DVD menu's opening screen.*

- **emergency backup generator:** A component aboard *Starbug 1* used to generate power in the event that the ship's main generator failed. Kryten sabotaged the main and emergency backup generators by overloading them with the thermostat settings, in order to prevent Kochanski from bathing in Lister's quarters **[T-SER7.4]**.

- **emergency battery power:** A backup system aboard *Red Dwarf* that activated in the event of a computer shutdown. The engines and all non-critical systems shut down during such a scenario in order to conserve power, leaving the ship adrift in space. After an attempt to increase Holly's IQ via intelligence compression failed, the computer's lifespan was reduced to mere minutes, forcing her to shut down, which put the ship on emergency battery power. During the crisis, Kryten estimated the crew had two months of air and heat remaining before the battery power would be depleted—or six if they deactivated Rimmer's hologrammic projection, which put a huge drain on the system **[T-SER4.4]**.

- **Emergency Death Pack:** An addition to the Space Corps' standard-issue survival kit, the contents of which included drugs, hypos, preservatives and compounds developed by Colonel Mike O'Hagan's uncle Max. The pack weighed 11 stone (154 pounds) and was administered to a body shortly after death, preserving the brain and basic motor functions **[B-SUR]**.

- **Emergency Override Sequence Alpha-4-Alpha-9:** An override code with which Captain Tau tried to force Kryten to reveal the location of Lister's pregnant cat aboard the American mining ship *Red Dwarf*. Kryten fought the override, however, causing his head to explode **[T-USA1]**.

- **Emergency Ramp Seven:** A lift operated by a parts shop on the television soap opera *Androids*. After a battle with Jaysee left Brook heavily damaged, his son, Brooke Junior, took him to the shop, where he was placed onto Emergency Ramp Seven for examination **[M-SMG2.8(c2)]**.

- **Emergency Regulation 479/B:** A Space Corps regulation in an alternate universe, which stated that in the event of an emergency, the highest-ranking surviving crewmember could assume command of a vessel. Rimmer quoted this rule to Lister while assuming command of *Red Dwarf* following the cadmium II disaster **[T-USA1(s1)]**.

- **Emergency Regulation 479/C:** A Space Corps regulation in an alternate universe that added a clause regarding holograms to Emergency Regulation 479/B **[T-USA1(s1)]**.

- **Emerson, Lake and Palmer:** An English progressive rock group known for such hits as "From the Beginning" and "Lucky Man" **[RL]**. Rimmer described the metaphysics of being dead as worse mumbo-jumbo than the band's lyrics **[N-INF]**.

- **emo-field:** A portable defensive shield similar to the justice field, which deflected attempts to elicit negative emotions back to the aggressor. Emo-fields were used primarily as a defense against polymorphs, who would shapeshift to evoke emotions in order to feed off them **[M-SMG2.9(c11)]**.

- **emohawk:** A half-domesticated polymorph that could transform into a variety of items or living things. Emohawks were spayed at birth. Kinitawowi GELFs sometimes kept them as pets, training them to change shape at their owners' command **[T-SER6.4]**. The creatures could also harvest emotions from victims, which the Kinitawowi sold as a commodity **[G-RPG]**. When Lister abandoned his wife, a Kinitawowi GELF whom he was forced to marry in order for the crew to obtain an Oxygen unit, the GELFs' leader and father of the bride sent his pet emohawk after him. It managed to sneak aboard *Starbug 1* and attack Cat and Rimmer, turning them into versions of Duane Dibbley and Ace Rimmer, respectively, before being captured **[T-SER6.4]**.

  ***NOTE:** Among the items the emohawk changed into were a rabbit, a lamp, a stick, a hat, a chicken, a can of baked beans, a frog, a paper airplane, a microphone, a Slinky, a remote-controlled car, a thermos and a grenade.*

- **Emo-smuggler:** A type of criminal who illegally traded emotions within the GELF territories of an alternate universe. When an Emo-smuggler gave that dimension's Lister transport from his disabled *Starbug* to Blerios 15, the planet's federal council stopped them. The smuggler accused Lister of the crime, who was summarily sentenced to Cyberia, a virtual-reality prison on Lotomi 5 **[N-LST]**.

- **emotional vampire:** *See* polymorph

- **Encyclo implant chip:** A small electronic device implanted in the long-term memory section of a person's brain, giving the user encyclopedic knowledge. Rimmer's parents paid to have such chips implanted in three of their sons—John, Frank and Howard—but were unable to afford the procedure for Arnold. As a result, Arnold's brothers excelled in the Space Corps, while he struggled as a mere technician **[N-LST]**.

  ***NOTE:** Episode 10.1 ("Trojan") revealed that Howard had lied about his success and worked as a low-level technician, implying the chip was not foolproof.*

- **endangered panda stew:** A menu item dispensed by Taiwan Tony, an Asian fast-food vending machine aboard *Red Dwarf* **[T-SER10.2]**.

- **endoskeleton:** The interior support structure of 4000 Series mechanoids. Kryten claimed he wore his fingers down to their endoskeleton while preparing a lobster supper for the *Starbug 1* crew **[T-SER7.6]**.

- **"engaged":** A word printed on a blindfold supplied in the Tank's information packs, for use when inmates required privacy to use the toilet **[T-SER8.3]**.

PREFIX
RL: Real life

T-: Television Episodes
SER: Television series
IDW: "Identity Within"
USA1: Unaired U.S. pilot
USA2: Unaired U.S. demo

R-: The Bodysnatcher Collection
SER: Remastered episodes
BOD: "Bodysnatcher"
DAD: "Dad"
FTH: "Lister's Father"
INF: "Infinity Patrol"
END: "The End" (original assembly)

N-: Novels
INF: *Infinity Welcomes Careful Drivers*
BTL: *Better Than Life*
LST: *Last Human*

BCK: *Backwards*
OMN: *Red Dwarf Omnibus*

M-: Magazines
SMG: *Smegazine*

W-: Websites
OFF: Official website
NAN: *Prelude to Nanarchy*
AND: *Androids*
DIV: Diva-Droid
DIB: Duane Dibbley

CRP: Crapola
GEN: Geneticon
LSR: Leisure World Intl.
JMC: Jupiter Mining Corporation
AIT: *A.I. Today*
HOL: HoloPoint

G-: Roleplaying Game
RPG: *Core Rulebook*
BIT: *A.I. Screen Extra Bits* booklet
SOR: *Series Sourcebook*
OTH: Other RPG material

- **Engels, Friedrich:** A German philosopher and author, credited with the development of Marxist Theory, alongside Karl Marx **[RL]**. Holly read the complete works of several prominent writers, including Engels, during the fifteen nanoseconds that passed between *Red Dwarf*'s cadmium II core going critical and the entire crew dying **[N-INF]**.

- **Engine Bay 2:** An engine compartment within *Starbug* shuttlecrafts **[T-SER6.2(d)]**.

- **engine core:** The base component of *Red Dwarf*'s propulsion system. If left unshielded, the engine core could approach critical mass, causing a meltdown and destroying the vessel. This scenario occurred after an experiment with a triplicator went awry, resulting in a massive power drain that exposed the core **[T-SER5.5]**.

- **Engineering Deck:** An area of *Starbug 1*'s aft section. When a hyperway to a parallel universe formed on this deck and then collapsed, that reality's Kochanski become stranded in the prime universe **[T-SER7.3]**.

- **Engineering Level:** A section of *Red Dwarf* containing the cadmium II core and its related power systems. When the core went critical and exploded, everyone on the Engineering Level died within 0.08 second of the radioactive blast **[N-INF]**. Also known as the Engineering Deck, this level contained the air-conditioning complex **[N-BTL]**.

- **Engineering Section:** An area aboard *Red Dwarf* allocated for engine operations. While trying to escape captivity aboard *Red Dwarf*, Lister and Kochanski stole uniforms marked "Engineering Section, Lift Maintenance, Technician 3/C" **[T-SER8.2]**.

  NOTE: *Presumably, the terms "Engineering Deck," "Engineering Level" and "Engineering Section" all described the same general area of the ship.*

- **Engineering Supply Area:** A section of *Starbug* shuttles used to store welding gear and other equipment **[N-BTL]**.

- **Engineer's Exam:** A term short for "Astro-Engineer's Exam" **[T-SER1.1]**.

- **Engineer's Report:** A form of paperwork aboard *Red Dwarf*. Frank Todhunter held a clipboard containing an Engineer's Report while confronting Rimmer about numerous reports he had filed against Lister **[T-SER1.1]**.

- **England:** A member country of the United Kingdom **[RL]**. At some point before *Red Dwarf*'s cadmium II disaster, England's underwater hockey team toured Saturn's moon, Titan **[T-SER2.2]**.

- **Enhanced Evolution Project (EEP):** A program developed by the Space Corps to seed lifeless planets with the building blocks of life, after which the process of evolution could be accelerated for research purposes. One of the project's missions involved the seeding ship SSS *Esperanto*, which was assigned to accelerate an ocean planet. This mission ended in failure after the experiment yielded a creature known as a despair squid, which attacked the *Esperanto* crew and consumed all other life on the planet. The EEP also produced Vidal Beasts on Sharmut 2, while attempting to stem an overpopulation of that world's flora and fauna **[G-RPG]**.

- **Enid, Auntie:** A relative of Colonel Mike O'Hagan, the author of the *Space Corps Survival Manual*. Enid was married to Max, a scientist who, with the help of his assistant Chantelle, pioneered advances in preservative and regenerative drugs that hindered death, eventually leading to the development of the Emergency Death Pack. During the pack's development, Max tested these drugs on Enid **[B-SUR]**.

- **"enig":** Kryten's final word before the Inquisitor killed him in front of Lister and a past version of himself. Kryten was attempting to say "Enigma," the decoding system of the Inquisitor's time gauntlet. This message allowed his past self to decode the gauntlet and defeat the Inquisitor, thereby preventing his own death **[T-SER5.2]**.

- **Enigma decoding system:** A system used to decode and operate the Inquisitor's time gauntlet. Kryten decoded the device and used it to free himself and Lister from their shackles. He then gave the gauntlet to Lister to freeze the Inquisitor in a stasis field while he reprogrammed it to backfire so that, once returned to the Inquisitor, it would erase the latter from history instead of them **[T-SER5.2]**.

- **enilertneC:** A company name printed on a bus in London, England, during a period of Earth's far future when time ran backwards. The firm's name, when read forward, was Centreline **[T-SER3.1]**.

  ***NOTE:** Throughout the episode, backwards writing was inconsistently handled. In some cases, characters were backward-facing, while in others, they faced forward. Adding to the confusion, some signs were lettered top to bottom, whereas others ran bottom to top. In this case, the scene was simply flipped to give the illusion of backwards writing.*

- ***Enlightenment*, SSS:** A computer-generated holoship created in Earth's solar system and crewed entirely by holograms of incredible intellect and bravery. The spacecraft, commanded by Captain Hercule Platini, was built for exploration and the pursuit of knowledge. With a crew of just under two thousand holograms, *Enlightenment* was designed to travel as super-light particles (tachyons), enabling it to cover great distances through wormholes and star gates. Others in its crew included its first officer, Commander Randy Navarro, as well as Commanders Natalina Pushkin, Nirvanah Crane and Binks **[T-SER5.1]**.

  The ship was built in three sections, which could pivot at hinge-points to create a "Z" shape, or straighten out to form a line **[T-SER5(b)]**. Its shipboard computer was nicknamed Stocky due to its stochastic qualities. Among its levels were Floor 3124, containing the maintenance department; Floor 3125, dedicated to sports and sexual recreation; Floor 4177, housing the Senior Officers Quarters; and Floor 6120, containing the botanical gardens.

  Shipboard regulations required that all crewmembers engage in intercourse at least twice daily, and it was considered bad manners to turn down a request for sex. Among the crew, concepts such as "family" and "relationships" were outmoded ideas that were abolished by the twenty-fifth century.

  During its travels, *Enlightenment* encountered *Starbug 1* and dispatched a probe to investigate. Discovering another of their kind, the holograms transported Rimmer to their ship, where he petitioned to join them until realizing his commission would mean the deactivation of Crane, with whom he had fallen in love. Dejected, Rimmer returned to *Red Dwarf*, and *Enlightenment* continued its mission **[T-SER5.1]**.

- **envy:** A rogue emotion purged from Kryten's hard drive by the Data Doctor, a program for restoring a mechanoid's personality to factory settings, when Captain Hollister subjected Kryten to a psychotropic simulation **[T-SER8.2]**.

- **Epideme virus:** A genetically engineered, intelligent parasite created as an alternate to the nicotine patch, used to help a person stop smoking. The virus was designed to block the neural signals of a nicotine craving to the brain, but it also blocked signals telling the body it needed blood and oxygen, effectively killing the host within forty-eight hours. After the host's death, the virus hijacked the body to search for another victim; if unable to find one, it would enter a state of hibernation.

  One such virus infected Caroline Carmen, a *Leviathan* crewmember who once served aboard *Red Dwarf*. After freezing her body, Epideme waited for three million years until being discovered by the *Starbug 1* crew. Mistaking Epideme's life signs for Carmen's, the group brought the corpse aboard *Starbug*, where it thawed and attacked Lister, transferring itself to his body.

  The crew attempted to reason with the virus, which argued that it had just as much right to live as they did. They tried to lure Epideme into one of Lister's extremities, corralling the virus in his right arm and amputating it. When that failed, Kochanski tricked Epideme into entering Carmen's dead arm, pretending it was her own, thereby isolating the virus **[T-SER7.7]**.

- **Epsilon 14:** A location marker in *Red Dwarf*'s air vents. When the vents began rapidly shrinking, Kochanski suggested taking *Starbug 1* past Epsilon 14 and making a right at the hydro unit **[T-SER8.1]**.

- **Epstein, Billy-Joe ("The Jewish Cowboy"):** A nineteen-year old Space Corps recruit in one of Ace Rimmer's universes. Epstein was well-versed in flying the Corps' various craft, but his cowardice made him fail his flight test twice. Taking pity on the recruit, a barmaid named Mamie (whom Epstein secretly loved) arranged for Ace to throw a fight with the pilot, giving

PREFIX
RL: Real life

T-: Television Episodes
SER: Television series
IDW: "Identity Within"
USA1: Unaired U.S. pilot
USA2: Unaired U.S. demo

R-: *The Bodysnatcher Collection*
SER: Remastered episodes
BOD: "Bodysnatcher"
DAD: "Dad"
FTH: "Lister's Father"
INF: "Infinity Patrol"
END: "The End" (original assembly)

N-: Novels
INF: *Infinity Welcomes Careful Drivers*
BTL: *Better Than Life*
LST: *Last Human*

BCK: *Backwards*
OMN: *Red Dwarf Omnibus*

M-: Magazines
SMG: *Smegazine*

W-: Websites
OFF: Official website
NAN: *Prelude to Nanarchy*
AND: *Androids*
DIV: Diva-Droid
DIB: Duane Dibbley

CRP: Crapola
GEN: Geneticon
LSR: Leisure World Intl.
JMC: Jupiter Mining Corporation
AIT: *A.I. Today*
HOL: HoloPoint

G-: Roleplaying Game
RPG: *Core Rulebook*
BIT: *A.I. Screen Extra Bits* booklet
SOR: *Series Sourcebook*
OTH: Other RPG material

him the courage to pass the test—and later to ask Mamie out **[N-BCK]**.

- **"Equal Rights for the Dead" March:** A peaceful demonstration held on Io, in which holograms from the Jupiter system rallied for better conditions. At age six, Rimmer attended such a rally with his brother Frank, who booed and jeered the demonstrators, calling them "dirty deadies" and throwing stones at them **[N-INF]**.

- **"erase":** A word printed on a console label in *Starbug 1*'s Medical Bay **[T-SER7.8]**.

- **Eraserhead:** A nickname that Cat called Kryten, due to the resemblance of the mechanoid's head to a pencil eraser **[T-SER4.1]**.

  NOTE: *Eraserhead is a 1977 horror film written and directed by David Lynch, the main character of which had a hairstyle giving him a head shaped like Kryten's.*

- **Eric:** A JMC employee mentioned in Kochanski's personnel file. An officer addressed a note in the file to a mutual acquaintance, named Micky, regarding his attraction to Kochanski, claiming Eric had footage of her showering **[W-JMC]**.

- **Eric:** A chainsmoking human who traveled with a humanoid female rabbit, a hologrammic pastry chef named Robin and an Errol Flynn waxdroid in a possible alternate universe **[G-RPG]**.

- **Eric:** An associate of Lister's father. When Lister confronted his dad at a pub, the latter thought Eric had sent Dave about some tins of paint he had stolen **[R-FTH]**.

  NOTE: *This was mentioned in an early script written before episode 7.3 ("Ouroboros") established that Lister was his own father.*

- **Erica:** *See* Drone 3 (Erica)

- **Erin:** A produce vendor in India, circa 23 A.D. Originally from Albion (later known as Great Britain), she fled to India after members of her family were abducted and sacrificed to Toutatis, Esus and Taranis by druids, who consumed their bodies after garroting, burning and drowning them. Erin befriended a peaceful man named Jesus of Caesarea, with whom she shared a monotheistic belief, and traveled with him to India, where she set up shop. She later sold the *Red Dwarf* crew lemons to power a device that would return them to their own era **[T-SER10.3]**.

- **Ernest:** An individual with whom Rimmer imagined being incarcerated while trapped in an addictive version of *Better Than Life*. In the dream, Arnold's Solidgram body was repossessed and his essence was placed as a soundwave into a soundproof cell, where he resided with Ernest and two other soundwaves. Ernest had been imprisoned after defaulting on his body mortgage when interest rates rose. When Ernest tried to escape from the facility, a guard recaptured him using a sound gun **[N-BTL]**.

- **Ernie:** A cab driver in Frank Capra's film *It's a Wonderful Life* **[RL]**. While trapped in an addictive version of *Better Than Life*, Lister passed by carolers accompanied by Ernie on the tuba, who gave him a sip of brandy from his flask **[N-INF]**.

  NOTE: *Ernie's full name in the film was Ernie Bishop.*

- **Ernie 7000:** An artificial-reality (AI) computer aboard a JMC vessel. In a video message to Holly regarding their postal chess game, Gordon (the AI aboard the *Scott Fitzgerald*) included an update about Ernie, who suffered from computer senility. Gordon could not remember specifics, despite having an IQ of eight thousand **[R-SER2.2(d)]**.

- **erotic mode (fiction):** A function of 4000 Series mechanoids enabling them to compose stories sexual in nature. Kryten engaged this mode in order to create his entry for Rimmer's Erotic Fiction competition, titled "Circuit-boards of Passion" **[B-LOG]**.

- **erotikarate:** A form of sensual martial arts practiced by Pete Tranter's sister **[G-SOR]**.

- **ERRA:** *See* Erroneous Reasoning Research Academy (ERRA)

- **ERRA-pert:** A designation given to scientists aboard the Erroneous Reasoning Research Academy, who excelled in wrongness **[T-SER10.4]**.

- **Erroneous Reasoning Research Academy (ERRA):** An experimental facility located at coordinates 2-5-2-3-1-1, dedicated to taking wrong ideas and theories and combining them to produce workable ones. ERRA was based on the idea that many of history's breakthrough discoveries, such as DNA, had been accidentally made due to failure.

  The station was designed with inherent "wrongness" in mind—pushing the "Up" button on a lift, for example, caused it to go down—and employed workers from several different fields reputed for being consistently wrong, such as television critics, referees and weathermen, who were re-educated in the sciences.

  The head of the program, Professor Irene Edgington, developed several devices at the facility, such as the groinal exploder and a machine that, in theory, could hyper-evolve humans. Using the latter device, she accidentally de-evolved herself into a chimpanzee, and was placed in stasis until a solution could be found. When the ERRA project was deemed a failure, its creator tried to commit suicide—and failed, living well into his nineties.

  Edgington's groinal exploder eventually ended up in the hands of a tribe of biologically engineered garbage gobblers (BEGGs), who affixed the device to Lister's crotch to ensure he paid off his gambling debts. After the BEGGs choked to death in a fluke accident, the *Red Dwarf* crew harnessed the powers of coincidence between the quantum-entangled Kryten and Cat to locate the ERRA station, using star coordinates contained on the cover of Arthur Koestler's book, *The Roots of Coincidence*. Reviving Edgington, the crew used her evolution machine to restore her human body so she could assist in removing the exploder **[T-SER10.4]**.

- **Error Amp:** A setting on *Starbug 1*'s sonar scope display. This setting was not highlighted as the crew charted the course of a despair squid **[T-SER5.6]**.

- **"Error Finding Server":** A message displayed in Kryten's head-up display after an eruption on a psi-moon nearly destroyed him and *Starbug 1*. The message repeated while Kryten's CPU informed him of the damage sustained to his body **[T-SER5.3]**.

- **escape pod:** A single-person cryogenic vessel lined with lead to withstand long exposure to space. Once activated, the pod cryogenically froze its occupant until recovery, at which point the revival process—which took twenty-four hours to complete—could be started. One such pod was ejected from a prison ship after its inmates rebelled and killed the crew. The pod belonged to guard Barbra Bellini, but was used by a simulant inmate after the battle. The *Red Dwarf* crew found the pod and inadvertently released the simulant as they began the revival process, thinking Bellini was inside it **[T-SER4.3]**.

- **escape pod:** A small, cylindrical craft housed in *Starbug* shuttlecraft, used for emergency evacuations **[T-SER5.4]**. The pod, located on C Deck, was powered by solar energy **[N-LST]**. While pursuing the stolen *Red Dwarf*, Lister accidentally launched the escape pod when he used the release mechanism as a bottle opener. This annoyed Rimmer, who had intended to utilize it after an Armageddon virus locked *Starbug 1* on a collision course with a small planetoid **[T-SER6.3]**.

  Kryten's brother, Able, used an escape pod while being pursued by a rogue simulant. After launching himself in the pod, Able harnessed Kryten's negadrive to focus its negative energy toward the enemy vessel through the pod's thrusters, causing the simulant to destroy his own ship—and killing Able in the process **[T-SER7.6]**.

  ***NOTE:** Lister and company may have found the second escape pod while looting derelict ships.*

- **Escape Pod 1736:** A small escape vehicle aboard a rogue simulant battle-class cruiser. The pod had been looted from a twenty-fifth-century colonization seeding ship, and was stocked with a variety of supplies and equipment necessary for terraforming and creating life on S-3 planets, such as solar accelerators, genetic and cloning equipment, and eco-accelerator rockets. Seeding ship pods were pre-programmed to seek out and land on inhabitable planets, and thus had no manual controls.

  During a confrontation between the *Starbug 1* crew and the simulant ship's last surviving occupant, Rimmer sneaked into the pod and escaped, causing a shipquake that destroyed the battlecruiser seconds after his comrades teleported to safety. His shipmates located Rimmer, but the pod accelerated away, having detected a habitable world on the opposite end of a wormhole. Due to the anomaly's time-dilation effect, it took *Starbug* six centuries to reach the planet, during which Rimmer utilized the pod's supplies to create Rimmerworld **[T-SER6.5]**.

- **escort boots:** A security measure aboard the prison station Justice World, by which computer-controlled boots greeted visitors in the landing bay upon their arrival. A visitor requiring security clearance would be asked to step into the boots, which would lock and proceed through a mind probe machine so it could assess that person's criminal past. Once the visitor passed the mind probe, the boots unlocked and he or she was free to move about the facility. If someone failed a mind probe, the boots remained locked and moved that person to a holding facility. Escort boots could be configured to work with hologrammic technology **[T-SER4.3]**.

  Bloodlust Arms developed a defensive version of the escort boots, enabling a wearer to dodge incoming attacks and/or flee danger by activating the footwear's Fight or Flight responsive subsystem. These boots were distributed via Crapola Inc.'s annual *SCABBY* catalog **[G-RPG]**.

- **Eskimos:** A term (sometimes considered pejorative) describing the indigenous Yupik, Inuit and Aleut peoples inhabiting Earth's circumpolar regions, including Alaska, Greenland and Siberia **[RL]**. While discussing computer senility, Rimmer agreed with the Eskimos' way of handling the infirmed—which, according to him, involved stripping them down and leaving them to face the elements **[T-SER4.4]**.

  NOTE: *Among some Eskimos, senilicide and invalidicide—the killing of old and sick people, respectively—were once practiced, but were neither common nor universal.*

- **E.S.L.1:** A designation printed on the label of a mind-swapping machine that Kryten developed to transfer Carole Brown's consciousness into Lister's mind so he could deactivate *Red Dwarf*'s self-destruct sequence **[T-SER3.4]**.

- **Esperanto:** An Earth language created in the late 1800s by Ludwik Lazarus Zamenhof, intended to foster unity between different European regions **[RL]**. Many signs aboard *Red Dwarf* were printed both in English and Esperanto **[T-SER1.1]**. Rimmer repeatedly attempted to learn the language, but without success **[T-SER2.1]**. While bunking with his duplicate hologram, Rimmer studied porous circuits and Esperanto, while his doppelgänger learned about thermal energy, history and philosophy **[T-SER1.6]**.

- ***Esperanto*, SSS:** A Class D Space Corps ocean-seeding ship **[T-SER5.6]**, also called a Nautical-class seeding vessel. It had a total crew capacity of four hundred, and was equipped with a laser cannon and limpet mines **[G-RPG]**.

  Esperanto's mission was to introduce and accelerate marine life on potential S-3 planets. When the ship returned to one of its host planets after three years to check on its progress, the crew learned that five million years of evolution had occurred. One marine animal created during the process was a colossal squid, the ink of which incapacitated victims by inducing despair and hopelessness. The so-called despair squid attacked the *Esperanto*, causing its entire crew to commit suicide. Years later, the *Starbug 1* crew found the vessel and encountered the squid, barely escaping the same fate **[T-SER5.6]**.

- **Esso Super:** A beverage served at a bar on the television soap opera *Androids* **[M-SMG1.9(c2)]**.

  NOTE: *American oil and gas company ExxonMobil offers a type of petroleum called Esso Super Unleaded, as well as a lubricant product known as Esso Superlube.*

- **Esuohknom, Bob:** The host of the British television talent show *Backwards Opportunity Knocks*, on an Earth far in the future on which time ran backwards. While stranded on the world after flying through a time hole, Rimmer and Kryten worked the novelty-act circuit, procuring an audition for Esuohknom's show **[T-SER3.1(d)]**.

  NOTE: *Bob Monkhouse (Bob Esuohknom spelled backward) hosted the real-life British TV show* Opportunity Knocks, *which ran in the 1980s.*

- **Esus:** A Celtic god worshipped in ancient Gaul and Great Britain **[RL]**. While living in Albion (an early name for Britain), the family of a woman named Erin were dragged from their homes and sacrificed to Toutatis, Esus and Taranis in a wicker tower, where they were garroted, burned, drowned and consumed by druids. Erin thus fled to India and made a living as a produce vendor **[T-SER10.3]**.

B-: Books
PRG: *Red Dwarf Programme Guide*
SUR: *Red Dwarf Space Corps Survival Manual*
PRM: *Primordial Soup*
SOS: *Son of Soup*
SCE: *Scenes from the Dwarf*
LOG: *Red Dwarf Log No. 1996*
RD8: *Red Dwarf VIII*
EVR: *The Log: A Dwarfer's Guide to Everything*

X-: Misc.
PRO: Promotional materials, videos, etc.
PST: Posters at DJ XVII (2013)
CAL: 2008 calendar
RNG: Cell phone ringtones
MOB: Mobisode ("Red Christmas")
CIN: *Children in Need* sketch
GEK: *Geek Week* intros by Kryten
TNG: "Tongue-Tied" video

XMS: Bill Pearson's Christmas special pitch script
XVD: Bill Pearson's Christmas special pitch video
OTH: Other *Red Dwarf* appearances

SUFFIX
DVD:
(d) – Deleted scene
(o) – Outtake
(b) – Bonus DVD material (other)
(e) – Extended version

SMEGAZINES:
(c) – Comic
(a) – Article

OTHER:
(s) – Early/unused script draft
(s1) – Alternate version of script

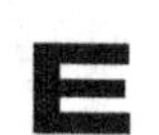

- **"etinoT eviL":** A phrase on a sticker partially covering a poster for Rimmer's and Kryten's novelty act on an Earth far in the future on which time ran backwards. The duo developed the act while waiting for Lister and Cat to rescue them. The sticker, when read forward, read "Live Tonite" **[T-SER3.1]**.

  NOTE: *Given the backwards nature of time established in the episode, the sticker should have read "thgiN tsaL eviL," ("Live Last Night)."*

- **Europa:** One of Jupiter's natural satellites **[RL]**, home to several undersea colonies, as well as the system's first working space elevator. Its primary export was water **[G-RPG]**. In several of Ace Rimmer's realities, Europa was home to the Space Corps Research and Development Program that developed the *Wildfire One* **[N-BCK]**.

  NOTE: *This contradicted episode 4.5 ("Dimension Jump"), which established that Ace was stationed on Mimas, not Europa.*

- **Europa Test Centre:** A facility on Europa in Ace Rimmer's universe, owned by the Space Corps Research and Development Program. The *Wildfire* was launched from this station **[N-BCK]**.

  NOTE: *This also contradicted episode 4.5 ("Dimension Jump") for the same reason.*

- **European Space Academy:** An Earth institution in the twenty-second century, from which Kochanski graduated with honors with the rank of flight coordinator first class **[N-LST]**.

- **European Space Consortium (ESC):** A multinational organization devoted to the exploration of space. The ESC landed a rover on Mars that later discovered debris left behind by the *Red Dwarf* crew. While analyzing the trash, the rover encountered Cat, who used it to transmit a message back to Earth, informing the agency that he had found its *Beagle* spacecraft **[X-APR]**.

  NOTE: *The ESC presumably spoofed the European Space Agency (ESA), whose* Beagle 2 *spacecraft was involved in the failed 2003* Mars Express *mission.*

- **Eurovision Song Contest:** An international music competition held annually among member countries of the European Broadcasting Union (EBU) **[RL]**. When Kryten reverted Kochanski's and Cat's hair and clothing to earlier states via a time wand, Holly compared them to the Turkish entry in the Eurovision Song Contest **[T-SER8.6]**.

- **Euston Road:** A street in Central London, included in the British version of the board game *Monopoly* **[RL]**. For his twenty-fourth birthday, Lister and several friends embarked on a *Monopoly* board pub crawl across London; their fourth stop was Euston Road, where they consumed pints of Guinness **[N-INF]**.

- **evolution mode:** A setting on an evolution device created by Irene Edgington at the Erroneous Reasoning Research Academy. Kryten used this setting to transform the previously de-evolved professor back into a *Homo sapiens* **[T-SER10.4]**.

- **"Evolution of the Telegraph Pole, 1874-2036, The":** A slide lecture that Rimmer put together **[B-SUR]**.

- **Ewe, John:** A sewage specialist who captained a two-mile-long waste transport vessel in the twenty-third century. Ewe, born and raised on Ganymede, considered himself the "King of Crap," ferrying human waste from the Jovian system to Garbage World (Earth) for twenty years. To break up the monotony, he resorted to creating graffiti by dumping his cargo across Europe in a pattern that read "Ewe woz 'ere."

  On Ewe's final trip—during which he intended to finish the last "e" in the message—a methane storm hit his ship, knocking it out of control, and throwing Ewe out of the vessel and into the massive signature, killing him instantly. The pilotless craft crashed onto the surface, causing a methane explosion so powerful it ripped Earth from its orbit, flinging it out of the solar system and into deep space **[N-BTL]**.

  NOTE: *This man's first name, John, was synonymous with "toilet," while his last name, Ewe, rhymed with "eww," a slang term describing something disgusting. His name thus meant "disgusting toilet"—a fitting appellation for one who ferried human feces.*

- **E Wing:** A corridor of a prison that Rimmer imagined while trapped in an addictive version of *Better Than Life*. In this wing, inmates' essences were incarcerated as soundwaves. Rimmer believed he had been imprisoned here after his Solidgram

PREFIX
RL: Real life

T-: Television Episodes
- **SER:** Television series
- **IDW:** "Identity Within"
- **USA1:** Unaired U.S. pilot
- **USA2:** Unaired U.S. demo

R-: *The Bodysnatcher Collection*
- **SER:** Remastered episodes
- **BOD:** "Bodysnatcher"
- **DAD:** "Dad"
- **FTH:** "Lister's Father"
- **INF:** "Infinity Patrol"
- **END:** "The End" (original assembly)

N-: Novels
- **INF:** *Infinity Welcomes Careful Drivers*
- **BTL:** *Better Than Life*
- **LST:** *Last Human*
- **BCK:** *Backwards*
- **OMN:** *Red Dwarf Omnibus*

M-: Magazines
- **SMG:** *Smegazine*

W-: Websites
- **OFF:** Official website
- **NAN:** *Prelude to Nanarchy*
- **AND:** *Androids*
- **DIV:** Diva-Droid
- **DIB:** Duane Dibbley
- **CRP:** Crapola
- **GEN:** Geneticon
- **LSR:** Leisure World Intl.
- **JMC:** Jupiter Mining Corporation
- **AIT:** *A.I. Today*
- **HOL:** HoloPoint

G-: Roleplaying Game
- **RPG:** *Core Rulebook*
- **BIT:** *A.I. Screen Extra Bits* booklet
- **SOR:** *Series Sourcebook*
- **OTH:** Other RPG material

body was repossessed, and that he shared a cell with three other soundwaves. During a prison break, the soundwaves traveled down E Wing to a flight of stairs leading to the Security Operations Room **[N-BTL]**.

- **"Exam Revision":** The title of a chart hanging in the quarters that Rimmer shared with his duplicate hologram, on which the abbreviations "oct," "nov" and "dec" appeared horizontally (denoting months), while the letters "m," "t," "w," "th," "f," "s" and "su" were listed vertically (indicating days of the week) **[T-SER1.6]**.

  NOTE: *Presumably, this was the revision timetable Rimmer frequently referenced throughout the series.*

- **Exclusion Zone:** An area within *Red Dwarf*'s cargo decks, set up by opposing factions of the Cat People during their Holy Wars. One side, the Cloisterists, executed a raid on their enemy, the Clisterists, within the Exclusion Zone. This endangered the position of the Clisterists' leader, Kadok, forcing him to take extreme measures **[M-SMG2.3(c1)]**.

- **Existence, Arizona:** A fictional Old West town that Kryten's subconscious mind created as he battled the Apocalypse virus. In the illusion, Kryten served as Existence's drunken sheriff, tormented by the Apocalypse Boys, four villains manifesting the virus in physical form **[T-SER6.3]**.

  NOTE: *The novel* Backwards *revealed that Existence was in Arizona.*

- **Existential-Fu:** A style of martial arts practiced by Waxworld's Jean-Paul Sartre waxdroid **[G-SOR]**.

- **Explosive Decompression exhibit:** A thrilling exhibition at an orbital museum converted from an Earth space colony **[G-RPG]**.

  NOTE: *It is unclear whether the individuals depicted in the exhibit were waxdroids.*

- **"Explosives":** A word stenciled on several crates stored near *Red Dwarf*'s photo lab. After changing history via a timeslide so that he was no longer a hologram, Rimmer inadvertently blew himself up in his excitement by striking the crates **[T-SER3.5]**.

- **extreme nerdism therapy:** A procedure that the Ministry of Alteration—an agency of a fascist regime on an alternate-universe Earth—used on those who left their government positions under questionable circumstances. The first stage of the procedure involved cosmetic surgery that altered an individual's face. The second stage wiped his or her memories and replaced them using a catalog of personalities, while saving the original personality on a disc for possible future retrieval. One agent, tired of the Ministry's policies, opted to undergo the procedure, choosing for himself the catalog's Duane Dibbley template **[M-SMG2.5(c1)]**.

- **EYD 339C:** The license plate number of a taxi in England during a period in Earth's far future when time ran backwards. The license plate, when read forward, was C933 DYE. Lister and his shipmates rode this taxi back to *Starbug 2* **[T-SER3.1]**.

  NOTE: *Throughout the episode, backwards writing was inconsistently handled. In some cases, characters were backward-facing, while in others, they faced forward. Adding to the confusion, some signs were lettered top to bottom, whereas others ran bottom to top. In this case, the scene was simply flipped to give the illusion of backwards writing.*

- ***Eye, The*:** A newspaper published on Jake Bullet's totalitarian, alternate-universe Earth. One issue's headline read, "Terrorists Executed" **[M-SMG1.11(c4)]**, while another posed the question, "Will Bullet Return?" **[M-SMG2.2(c2)]**.

- **Ezekiel ("Zeke"):** A hillbilly from a backwards-running Earth in Universe 3. Ezekiel lived in the mountains with his twin brother, Zacharias, and a large hog. The two had a cousin named Lindy Lou, who stayed with them for a short time. While marooned on the planet for ten years, Lister, Rimmer, Kryten and Cat lived in a cave near the brothers' house **[N-BCK]**.

  NOTE: *Kryten inadvertently killed one of the brothers, but which one was not specified.*

F

FALCONBURGER, BLAIZE

- **F, Kev:** A cameraman who worked for the television soap opera *Androids* **[M-SMG2.9(c8)]**.

  NOTE: Kev F. Sutherland illustrated the Androids *comics published in the* Smegazines.

- **F1:** A code stenciled on a metal beam aboard *Red Dwarf* **[T-SER3.4]**.

- **faberoo:** A slang term for "fabulous" that Kochanski used to describe an astroglacier discovered by the *Starbug 1* crew **[T-SER7.7]**.

- **Faboozle:** A round of "Die! Die! My Darling!" during zero-gee football games. To utilize this goal-scoring strategy, each member of a team's defense brought a weapon of his or her choice (not exceeding sixteen megatons) into the Funch zone, then stomped on it. The team with the greatest number of Finsleys remaining won the Faboozle, starting the next quarter six Brintzleys ahead **[M-SMG1.8(a)]**.

- **Face:** A nickname that Cat called Holly, referencing his existence as a disembodied head **[M-SMG2.1(c1)]**.

- **Fachen-Mach-Ech-Noch-Ahach-Ech, Chief:** The leader of a Kinitawowi tribe in GELF space **[W-OFF]**. He had three daughters and a pet emohawk (a domesticated polymorph). When a Space Corps Enforcement probe attacked *Starbug 1*, the crew landed on the Kinitawowi's planet and visited the tribe, hoping to trade for an oxy-generation unit to replace one damaged in battle. Fachen-Mach-Ech-Noch-Ahach-Ech agreed to trade the O/G unit, provided that Lister married his daughter, Hackhackhackachhachhachach.

  Though Lister resisted the idea, his crewmates convinced him the deal would be temporary, as they would rescue him in the morning. Fachen-Mach-Ech-Noch-Ahach-Ech presided over the ceremony, after which Dave was escorted to his new bride's hut to consummate their marriage. Unable to bear the thought, Lister ran out of the village. Furious, the chief sent his emohawk to drain their emotions **[T-SER6.4]**.

- **failed antidote crash of '33:** A widespread computer affliction caused by an attempt to fix the flesh-eating-virus crash of '32 (a computer virus affecting mechanoids). Diva-Droid International was not affected by either threat **[W-DIV]**.

- **Falconburger, Blaize:** The host of *Life Styles of the Disgustingly Rich and Famous*, a television program showcasing the lives of wealthy individuals. After Lister went back in time via a timeslide, told his younger self to invent the Tension Sheet and thus became a billionaire, Falconburger devoted a segment to his success **[T-SER3.5]**.

- **Famine:** *See* Apocalypse, Famine, Brother

- ***Famous Five, The*:** A series of children's novels chronicling the adventures of a group of young children and their dog. Created by Enid Blyton, the series was later continued by Claude Voilier, Sarah Bosse and Brigitte Blobel **[RL]**. "Spanners" Lister accused Ace Rimmer of treating the prospect of his imminent death during a test flight as just another *Famous Five* adventure **[N-BCK]**.

- **"Fancy Dress Party 2nite":** A slogan on a poster displayed in *Red Dwarf*'s loading bay and other areas of the mining ship. Cat passed such a poster after traveling into the past via a stasis leak **[T-SER2.4]**.

- **Fantozi, Kirsty:** A twenty-five-year-old crewmember aboard *Nova 5*, a spaceship commissioned by the Coca-Cola Co. to ignite a series of blue supergiant stars in a strategic pattern as part of the company's advertisement campaign. Fantozi was the ship's star demolition engineer, in charge of precisely detonating nebulon missiles within the stars in order to create supernovae, the light from which would then reach Earth at a specified time.

  Fantozi was one of three survivors of a crash that killed most of *Nova 5*'s crew, which Kryten caused while cleaning the ship's computer. The three survivors eventually died as well, leaving the mechanoid to tend to their corpses, unaware they had passed on. Her blood type was A **[N-INF]**.

  NOTE: Fantozi's name, noted in the novel Infinity Welcomes Careful Drivers, *did not jibe with the crew's names provided onscreen in episode 2.1 ("Kryten").*

- **Farnworth, Russell, Drive Officer:** A *Red Dwarf* crewmember who perished in the cadmium II explosion. Lister and Rimmer ejected a canister containing his remains into space at a funeral for the accident's casualties **[R-END]**. During Farnworth's eulogy, Lister recalled a conversation with him about bees in the ship's refectory **[N-OMN]**.

  NOTE: The bee conversation occurred in the pilot episode's first-draft script, published in The Red Dwarf Omnibus. *It is unknown whether the nanobots resurrected Farnworth in Series VIII.*

- **Farrell, Marcus:** Crapola Inc.'s consumer director for Earth **[W-CRP]**.

  NOTE: Farrell's name appeared in an e-mail sent to participants in the online Geek Chase game.

- ***Fascist Dictator Monthly*:** A magazine to which Rimmer subscribed. After discovering mutated developing fluid in *Red Dwarf*'s photo lab, Kryten used the chemical to develop

an old image of Adolf Hitler in Nuremberg, Germany, taken from one of Rimmer's *Fascist Dictator Monthly* issues. The mutated chemical allowed Lister to enter the photograph and transport back to the depicted event, where he scuffled with Hitler and stole his briefcase before returning to *Red Dwarf* via the photo **[T-SER3.5]**.

- **Fassbinder:** An area from which a ball, pressed into a half-kimono, was fired during a zero-gee football scoring strategy called a Castle Fritz **[M-SMG1.8(a)]**.

- **Fast Charge:** A bazookoid setting used to charge the weapon quickly. Ora Tanzil utilized Cat's bazookoid to escape her Orodite cage by connecting leads from the weapon and setting it to "Fast Charge" while reversing the energy flow **[T-IDW]**.

- **faster-than-light drive:** A propulsion system capable of traveling faster than the speed of light. When used in conjunction with a time drive, the system enabled a ship to theoretically go anywhere in space-time almost instantaneously. The *Starbug 1* crew acquired such a drive and used it, coupled with a time drive, to become elite time travelers, sampling the best the universe had to offer **[T-SER6.6]**.

- **Fatal Sisters, The:** An all-female, anti-fascist group and beat combo from a totalitarian society in Jake Bullet's universe. The Fatal Sisters—Mista, Sangrida and Hilda—wore Valkyrie warrior outfits **[M-SMG2.4(c6)]**.

  The group met with a Ministry of Alteration operative who, after resigning his post, was forced to undergo radical nerdism therapy for security reasons. Before the procedure, he entrusted the Fatal Sisters with his personality disc, intending to meet up with them post-surgery and reverse the alteration. The operative, however—now known as Duane Dibbley—never made it to the rendezvous point, as he was trapped for four years in the Total Immersion video game *Red Dwarf* **[M-SMG2.5(c1)]**.

  Once released from the game, Dibbley was ambushed by Voter Colonel Larson Gray at a Salvation Army hostel, but was rescued by Mista **[M-SMG2.4(c6)]**. Later, at the Fatal Sisters' hideout, all three women had sex with the agent to jog his memory, but with little success **[M-SMG2.5(c1)]**.

- **Fat Bastoria, The:** A hypothetical pizza parlor. After accidentally causing Lee Harvey Oswald's death at the Texas School Book Depository, Lister glanced out a window and mistook what he saw for a giant pizza. When Kryten denied that it was a giant pizza, Lister thought the mechanoid was arguing its size (and not its actually being a pizza), joking that Kryten must have been eating at The Fat Bastoria **[T-SER7.1]**.

- **Fat Boy:** A nickname that Cat called Big Meat in the Tank's mess hall, attempting to goad his fellow inmate into hitting him so he could join his friends in the Medi-bay and escape. Big Meat assumed he was crazy, however, and instead offered to be his prison bitch **[T-SER8.8]**.

- **Fatboy:** Lister's nickname between ages eleven and thirteen, after he gained weight while living with his overweight grandmother **[T-SER7.6]**.

- **Father Grimm's Blacker Than Black Magic:** An underground booth run by Father Grimm, a practitioner of the occult in Jake Bullet's universe. There, he offered such services as poodle manicuring, cat cradling and crocodile clipping **[M-SMG1.12(c1)]**.

- **Father's Day:** An annual commemoration of fatherhood celebrated in many countries **[RL]**. Since Lister was his own father, he celebrated Father's Day each year by getting drunk and making himself a card, which he would forget about and open the following year, thereby maintaining the illusion of having a father figure. During one such drinking binge, Dave decided to be a better father to himself. To that end, he resigned his *Red Dwarf* commission to force his sober self to better his life by applying for a JMC robotics course—which backfired when Pree, *Red Dwarf*'s new artificial intelligence, summarily ejected him from the ship for being a non-crewmember **[T-SER7.8]**.

- **Fat Sam's Bar:** A deep-space drinking establishment. Mr. Flibble once stopped at this station for a drink, but was lured into a back room where he was mugged by a pair of creatures posing as a beautiful woman **[M-SMG1.14(c4)]**.

PREFIX
RL: Real life

T-: Television Episodes
- **SER:** Television series
- **IDW:** "Identity Within"
- **USA1:** Unaired U.S. pilot
- **USA2:** Unaired U.S. demo

R-: *The Bodysnatcher Collection*
- **SER:** Remastered episodes
- **BOD:** "Bodysnatcher"
- **DAD:** "Dad"
- **FTH:** "Lister's Father"
- **INF:** "Infinity Patrol"
- **END:** "The End" (original assembly)

N-: Novels
- **INF:** *Infinity Welcomes Careful Drivers*
- **BTL:** *Better Than Life*
- **LST:** *Last Human*
- **BCK:** *Backwards*
- **OMN:** *Red Dwarf Omnibus*

M-: Magazines
- **SMG:** *Smegazine*

W-: Websites
- **OFF:** Official website
- **NAN:** *Prelude to Nanarchy*
- **AND:** *Androids*
- **DIV:** Diva-Droid
- **DIB:** Duane Dibbley
- **CRP:** Crapola
- **GEN:** Geneticon
- **LSR:** Leisure World Intl.
- **JMC:** Jupiter Mining Corporation
- **AIT:** *A.I. Today*
- **HOL:** HoloPoint

G-: Roleplaying Game
- **RPG:** *Core Rulebook*
- **BIT:** *A.I. Screen Extra Bits* booklet
- **SOR:** *Series Sourcebook*
- **OTH:** Other RPG material

- **Faulkner:** An artificial-reality (AR) designer aboard *Red Dwarf* who was revived by nanobots along with the rest of the crew. During the trial of Lister, Kryten, Cat and Kochanski, Captain Hollister ordered the defendants put into a psychotropically induced AR simulation in which they believed they were escaping prosecution, so he could assess their guilt or innocence. As the simulation played out, Hollister instructed Faulkner, the program's creator, to incorporate the derelict SS *Einstein*—a ship well-stocked with fabric softener—in order to evoke a response from Kryten **[W-OFF]**.

- **Fax, Ms.:** A reporter for *Kookie Kola Bear News*. She was tall and buxom, with green hair. Following Mr. Flibble's hostile takeover of Kookie Kola and decapitation of Kookie Kola Bear, the company's former owner and mascot, Ms. Fax requested an exclusive interview with the homicidal penguin **[M-SMG2.3(c3)]**.

- **F Deck:** A floor aboard *Starbug* shuttles **[N-LST]**.

- **F Deck:** A level of *Red Dwarf* containing Frank Todhunter's quarters, as well as machines that distributed condoms **[W-OFF]**.

- **fear:** An emotional state brought on by the perception of danger **[RL]**. After escaping a hazardous waste pod and boarding *Red Dwarf*, a polymorph attacked the crew by changing form to elicit and feed on their emotions. It first attacked Lister by taking the shape of his worst fear—an eight-foot-tall, armor-plated alien—then drained all fear from his mind **[T-SER3.3]**. Years later, while being analyzed by *Red Dwarf*'s chief psychiatric counselor, Kryten claimed fear was an emotion he had acquired thanks to Lister's tutelage **[T-SER8.1]**.

- **Fear Mode:** A software function of 4000 Series mechanoids, simulating the emotion of fear under duress. Fear Mode included several stages, depending on the particular situation **[N-LST]**.

  NOTE: *This would seem to negate the need for Lister to teach Kryten how to fear.*

- **February 26, 08:00:** The date and time of a conversation during which Lister offered to make breakfast for Rimmer. Unbeknownst to Arnold, his roommate included Titan mushrooms, an hallucinogenic fungi, among the ingredients. Upon consuming the meal, Rimmer experienced a major hallucinogenic fit, during which he attended an inspection wearing nothing but racing gloves and swimming goggles, and attacked two officers he perceived as armed giraffes **[T-SER2.4]**.

- **feckles:** A word that Cat used to explain how he despised being corrected, claiming it got his feckles up. Kryten noted that the correct word was "hackles," which infuriated Cat even more **[T-SER5.4]**.

- **Feedback/Input:** A setting on *Starbug 1*'s sonar scope display. This setting was highlighted as the crew charted the course of a despair squid **[T-SER5.6]**.

- **Feldwabel:** A German military rank, roughly analogous to sergeant **[RL]**. This word appeared on a door in an alternate-reality Nazi camp in which Princess Bonjella was being held captive **[T-SER7.2]**.

- ***Felicitus populi*:** A strain of luck virus isolated by hologrammic scientist Hildegarde Lanstrom. Luck was one of several positive viruses Lanstrom discovered; this particular strain made the infected extremely lucky. Kryten discovered vials of this and other positive viruses aboard Lanstrom's viral research station, and brought them aboard *Red Dwarf*. After a holovirus-infected Rimmer locked his comrades in quarantine, they used *Felicitus populi* to escape captivity and immobilize him **[T-SER5.4]**.

  Years later, a nanobot-resurrected Rimmer found the luck virus, along with *Delecto quislibet* (sexual magnetism) amid *Starbug 1*'s wreckage aboard the reconstituted *Red Dwarf* **[T-SER8.1]**. When confronted by Captain Hollister, Rimmer handed over the luck virus, surreptitiously passing Lister the other vial **[T-SER8.3]**.

  NOTE: *In the novel* Last Human, *Kochanski discovered the virus aboard the* Mayflower, *an ancient terraforming ship from an alternate universe, and used it to defeat the Longman leopard, find the terraforming virus, locate Lister, jam a rad pistol and conceive children.*

B-: Books
PRG: *Red Dwarf Programme Guide*
SUR: *Red Dwarf Space Corps Survival Manual*
PRM: *Primordial Soup*
SOS: *Son of Soup*
SCE: *Scenes from the Dwarf*
LOG: *Red Dwarf Log No. 1996*
RD8: *Red Dwarf VIII*
EVR: *The Log: A Dwarfer's Guide to Everything*

X-: Misc.
PRO: Promotional materials, videos, etc.
PST: Posters at DJ XVII (2013)
CAL: 2008 calendar
RNG: Cell phone ringtones
MOB: Mobisode ("Red Christmas")
CIN: *Children in Need* sketch
GEK: *Geek Week* intros by Kryten
TNG: "Tongue-Tied" video

XMS: Bill Pearson's Christmas special pitch script
XVD: Bill Pearson's Christmas special pitch video
OTH: Other *Red Dwarf* appearances

SUFFIX
DVD:
(d) – Deleted scene
(o) – Outtake
(b) – Bonus DVD material (other)
(e) – Extended version

SMEGAZINES:
(c) – Comic
(a) – Article

OTHER:
(s) – Early/unused script draft
(s1) – Alternate version of script

- ***Felis catus***: A feline species also called the domestic housecat **[RL]**. The Cat People inhabiting *Red Dwarf*'s cargo hold evolved from the litter of a *Felis catus* named Frankenstein **[T-SER1.1]**.

  NOTE: Felis catus *is sometimes miscategorized as* Felis domestica, *an invalid taxonomic name. An article in* Smegazine *issue 2.2 mentioned that incorrect classification.*

- ***Felis erectus***: A feline species that evolved from Frankenstein's direct descendants aboard *Red Dwarf*. *Felis erectus* was larger than *Felis catus*, had rudimentary fingers instead of claws and stood on its hind legs, eventually evolving into *Felis sapiens* **[N-INF]**.

- ***Felis sapiens***: A humanoid species that evolved aboard *Red Dwarf* over the course of three million years, descended from Lister's pregnant cat Frankenstein **[T-SER1.1]**. After hiding Frankie in the vessel's cargo hold, Lister was sentenced to eighteen months in stasis for bringing the unquarantined animal aboard. Soon thereafter, a cadmium II radiation leak killed everyone onboard except Lister, who was safe inside the stasis pod, and Frankenstein, who delivered her first litter of kittens in the sealed hold **[T-SER5.1]**.

  The cats continuously bred for millennia, evolving from *Felis catus* into first *Felis erectus* and then *Felis sapiens* **[N-INF]**. The pinnacle of their evolution occurred when a member of a tribe known as the Elite attempted to use the Sacred Icon (a can opener) on a "silver rock" from the Great Silver Mountain (a can of Alphabetti Spaghetti), thereby saving the species from starvation **[M-SMG2.2(a)]**. From then on, the Cat People used materials stored in *Red Dwarf*'s cargo decks to build entire cities within the ship's bowels. They eventually learned English from watching the human crew's video discs **[N-INF]**.

  Over time, the Cats, having passed down stories of Lister's sacrifice to save Frankenstein, developed a religion but distorted his name to Cloister the Stupid, and wrote scriptures based on his plan to bring his pet to Fiji (or, as they called it, Fuschal) to start a hot dog stand **[T-SER1.4]**. This led to the creation of Seven Cat Commandments to control the population during the Dark Ages of religious intolerance **[N-INF]**. Other members of society—secular types who followed only one law: "Be cool"—scoffed at the devout, preferring to act according to their innate feline nature **[T-SER4.3(d)]**.

  Eventually, the dogmatic members split into two opposing factions: those who believed the hot dog stand hats on Fuschal should be red, and those who believed they should be blue. For thousands of years, the opposing sides fought in a great Holy War, before calling a truce and building Cat Arks in which to search for the Promised Land. The blue hat faction, using what they thought was a star chart (but was actually Lister's laundry list) left first and flew directly into an asteroid, destroying themselves. The second Ark traveled in the opposite direction, believing themselves righteous **[T-SER1.4]**.

  Soon thereafter, this second ark crashed onto an S-3 planet previously inhabited by a human colony. Mistaking it for Fuchal, the Cat People populated the colony's ruins and found several activated personality discs, which they thought were Cloister's servants. Manipulating the Cats for their own purpose, the hologrammic personalities infused their own ethics into the group. This led to several additional Cat factions, each following the teachings of its respective saint.

  One such group, following the personality of a Space Corps commander named Suzdal, became the largest and most dangerous faction, honing their warrior skills in order to go back in time and fight for the Cat People alongside Cloister. This group's violent and martial ways caused a schism in the population, resulting in an underground movement determined to build another starship to leave the planet and search for the true Promised Land **[G-RPG]**. This group settled on another world and built Egyptian-style catacombs containing olfactory pictograms and a memory machine that allowed users to conjure up anything within their memory. In time, the Cats abandoned this planet as well **[M-SMG1.9(c3)]**.

  Felis sapiens had the ability to detect danger using their olfactory senses, combining the intuition of the left nostril with the hard logic of the right **[T-SER6.4(d)]**. Males possessed sharp barbs on their genitalia to stimulate female ovulation, making intercourse painful **[N-BCK]**. They also possessed a poison pouch within their bodies that produced a deadly toxin, the antidote to which was produced by female genitalia. This organ evolved as an incentive for the species to mate **[T-IDW]**.

  NOTE: *Although Cat was a main character throughout the series, his species was not named until episode 5.1 ("Holoship"). In "The Last Day" (episode 3.6), Hudzen's head-up display misidentified Cat's species as* Felix sapiens.

The circumstances surrounding the Holy Wars differed slightly in the novel Infinity Welcomes Careful Drivers, *in which the opposing factions disagreed about the name of their god—either Cloister or Clister—and the Cats left* Red Dwarf *aboard the ship's shuttles instead of Cat Arks.*

- **Felix, Father:** *See* Cat, Father ("Padre")

- ***Felix sapiens*:** *See Felis sapiens*

- **"Female":** A phrase on a chart that Rimmer created to translate markings on a mysterious pod Holly found adrift in space, which he thought were an alien language—but which actually spelled out "*Red Dwarf* Garbage Pod," eroded away after many years of spaceflight **[T-SER1.4]**.

- **female topless boxing:** A spectator sport that Lister enjoyed, which involved shirtless women fighting in a ring. Never rooting for a particular athlete, Lister simply wished the competitors would "go the distance" **[T-SER3.6]**.

- **femmedroid:** A term for a female android, used on the television soap opera *Androids* **[M-SMG1.9(c2)]**.

- **femorph:** A female polymorph **[M-SMG2.9(c12)]**.

- **Ferrari Testarossa:** An Italian luxury sports car produced between 1984 and 1996 **[RL]**. After changing history by using a timeslide to invent the Tension Sheet and thus become a billionaire by age twenty-four, Lister possibly owned one or more such vehicles in that timeline **[T-SER3.5(d)]**.

- **fiction section:** An area of Waxworld containing waxdroids of fictional characters. During the Wax War, the Santa Claus waxdroid was transferred from this section to Hero World. **[T-SER4.6]**.

  NOTE: Presumably, the Winnie-the-Pooh and Mrs. Claus waxdroids were also from the fiction section.

- **Fido:** A contemptuous nickname that Cat called Dog **[T-SER2.6]**. Lister also called Rimmer this name when the latter became so inebriated during his deathday celebration that he ended up crawling on the floor **[T-SER2.3(d)]**. When Lister could not recall the name of a woman he had met at a club on Orion while on planet-leave, Rimmer asked if she was called Fido **[T-SER7.1(e)]**.

- **field microsurgery:** A basic-training course for those entering the Space Corps' Special Service. Ace Rimmer utilized his knowledge of field microsurgery to fix Cat's broken leg, which had been injured when Ace's ship collided with *Starbug 1* **[T-SER4.5]**.

- ***Field of Broken Dreams, A*:** A novel by Jane Austin, a simulation of which was included in the total-immersion artificial-reality game *Jane Austin World* **[G-RPG]**.

  NOTE: This fictional novel's title, from Red Dwarf—The Roleplaying Game, *befitted the disappointments that several characters experienced in the works of real-life novelist Jane Austen (note the different surname spelling). Some online hoax sites have listed* A Field of Broken Dreams *among the works of Jane G. Austin—another actual writer who lived a century after Austen. A year after the RPG book's release, Byrd Roberts published a novel titled* House of Broken Dreams, *in which he purposely emulated Austen's voice.*

- **FIFA:** The acronym of the Fédération Internationale de Football Association, an international governing body for the sport of football (known in the United States as soccer) **[RL]**. After finding Irene Edgington in the body of a chimpanzee, Lister commented that she had de-evolved herself to the intelligence level of FIFA's president **[T-SER10.4(d)]**.

- **Fifi:** A naughty French maid android included with *Red Dwarf*'s penthouse suite **[G-RPG]**.

- **Fifth Dimension, the:** A plane of existence outside the four dimensions of space-time (width, height, depth and time). Hoping to get *Red Dwarf* back to Earth, Holly invented the Holly Hop Drive, which could theoretically transport the vessel to any point in space almost immediately. However, it instead sent the ship into the Fifth Dimension, where they met the female counterparts of Lister, Rimmer and Holly, as well as a canine version of Cat **[T-SER2.6]**.

- **Fight or Flight Responsive Subsystem:** A system developed by Bloodlust Arms, installed in escort boots to enable a user to dodge and/or flee incoming attacks **[G-RPG]**.

- **Fiji:** A small island off the coast of New Zealand **[RL]**. Lister planned to purchase a farm on Fiji, where he could breed animals and build a life with Kochanski, despite the area being submerged under several feet of water due to volcanic activity. His bunk aboard *Red Dwarf*, in fact, contained a poster for Star Tours Holidays' vacations to Fiji. The Cat People inhabiting the ship's cargo hold built an entire religion based on Lister's goals, distorting the island's name as "Fuchal" **[T-SER1.1]**.

- **Filbert, Dennis:** A child who attended school on Io with Rimmer when they were both age seven. Filbert smelled of bread and margarine, had a patch over one lens of his glasses and suffered from a condition causing him to turn blue and pass out when anyone spoke to him. He was the only student whom Rimmer outranked academically—at least until Dennis was sent to a "special" school, leaving Arnold to occupy the bottom rung of his class **[N-BCK]**.

- ***Film Fun*:** An American magazine dedicated to movies, television and actors, published from 1915 to 1942 **[RL]**. Two of *Red Dwarf*'s skutters collected a large number of *Film Fun* issues, which they stored within their broom cupboard **[T-SER2.2]**.

- **Finsley:** A zero-gee football defensive position, used during a "Die! Die! My Darling" goal-scoring strategy. During this maneuver, each member of a team's defense brought a weapon of his or her choice (not exceeding sixteen megatons) into the Funch zone, and then stomped on it. The team with the greatest number of Finsleys remaining won the Faboozle, and started the next quarter six Brintzleys ahead **[M-SMG1.8(a)]**.

- **Fire and Forget:** A patented technology incorporated into Bloodlust Arms' A15 laser pistol and A30 laser cannon **[G-RPG]**.

- **Fire Belching William Shatner Pizza Beast:** An entity, possibly from an alternate universe, formed from a pizza bombarded by radiation from a leaky microwave oven. It possessed a tentacle, a lobster tail and a head resembling Canadian-American actor William Shatner, and shot flames from an unknown orifice. The creature was known to recite bad poetry and spit radioactive anchovies **[G-BIT]**.

  NOTE: Star Trek *icon William Shatner has been widely parodied for his albums setting poetry to music, and presenting songs as spoken-word poems.*

- **"Fire Exit":** A phrase printed on a wall-mounted sign in a repair facility aboard the American mining ship *Red Dwarf*. After being in stasis for three million years, Lister found one of Kryten's active spare heads in this room. The mechanoid had been reading the sign for the entire three million years, which had given him solace during his solitude **[T-USA1]**.

- ***Firing Squad A Go-Go*:** A Total Immersion video game operated at arcades owned by Leisure World International **[W-LSR]**.

- **first aid box:** An emergency kit stocked aboard *Starbug* shuttles **[T-SER4.5]** that contained, among other things, an injector filled with Lemoplathinominecatholyrite **[T-SER7.4]**.

- **First National Bank:** An Earth financial institution in the universe known as Alternative 2X13/L, located in Smegopolis, a city protected by the genetically engineered superheroes of the Liberty League. In 2315, the Conspirator and his sidekick, the Penguin, robbed the First National Bank, forcing the Liberty League to take action. The two forces battled until Ace Rimmer, disguised as Super-Ace, subdued the evildoers **[M-SMG2.1(c3)]**.

- **First Time on the Clay-Wheel Head:** An insult Cat called Kryten during a fight after a DNA machine turned the mechanoid into a human **[N-LST]**.

- **fish:** A term describing a variety of gill-bearing aquatic animals without digited limbs **[RL]**. Lister had a pair of robotic goldfish named Lennon and McCartney, which Cat once tried to eat, mistaking them for live fish **[T-SER1.2]**.

  Fish was among the menu items available from *Red Dwarf*'s food dispensers. Rimmer bribed Cat to hide Lister's cigarettes by offering him the ability to procure as many fish as he

PREFIX
RL: Real life

T-: Television Episodes
SER: Television series
IDW: "Identity Within"
USA1: Unaired U.S. pilot
USA2: Unaired U.S. demo

R-: *The Bodysnatcher Collection*
SER: Remastered episodes
BOD: "Bodysnatcher"
DAD: "Dad"
FTH: "Lister's Father"
INF: "Infinity Patrol"
END: "The End" (original assembly)

N-: Novels
INF: *Infinity Welcomes Careful Drivers*
BTL: *Better Than Life*
LST: *Last Human*

BCK: *Backwards*
OMN: *Red Dwarf Omnibus*

M-: Magazines
SMG: *Smegazine*

W-: Websites
OFF: Official website
NAN: *Prelude to Nanarchy*
AND: *Androids*
DIV: Diva-Droid
DIB: Duane Dibbley

CRP: Crapola
GEN: Geneticon
LSR: Leisure World Intl.
JMC: Jupiter Mining Corporation
AIT: *A.I. Today*
HOL: HoloPoint

G-: Roleplaying Game
RPG: *Core Rulebook*
BIT: *A.I. Screen Extra Bits* booklet
SOR: *Series Sourcebook*
OTH: Other RPG material

liked, simply by walking up to a dispenser and requesting it. Ecstatic, Cat ordered more than ten orders of trout á la crème **[T-SER1.3]**.

While dining at a restaurant in the total-immersion video game *Better Than Life*, Cat ordered a small aquarium full of live goldfish, which he planned to taunt and stalk before consuming them **[T-SER2.2]**.

- **Fishbreath:** A nickname that Rimmer suggested Warden Knot call him, to prevent the *Red Dwarf* prison guard from using his real name. Rimmer hoped to trick the artificial-intelligence computer Cassandra, who had predicted he would die of a heart attack, and did not want to tip her off that he was the person from her vision **[T-SER8.4]**. Lister, while under the influence of a genetically engineered adaptable pet (GEAP), called Cat this same name **[M-SMG1.6(c1)]**.

- **Fisher, Michelle:** A beautiful girl with whom Lister lost his virginity at age twelve, on the ninth hole of the Bootle municipal golf course **[T-SER3.2]**.

- **Fisher, Michelle:** A girl with whom Lister lost his virginity at age twelve in a universe in which *Red Dwarf* and its crew were American. The encounter took place on the ninth hole of the Detroit Royal Vista golf course **[T-USA2]**.

- **Five-alarm Bengal Chili:** A spicy recipe that Lister created **[G-RPG]**.

- **Five-Year Plan:** Lister's goal for his future, which involved serving two more tours of duty aboard *Red Dwarf* and putting aside money to purchase a farm on Fiji. On the island, he planned to have a sheep, a cow and horses to breed, despite most of the area being submerged under several feet of water due to volcanic activity. Lister planned to bring his pregnant cat, Frankenstein, as well as Kochanski, whom he envisioned wearing a white dress and riding horses while he took care of everything else. However, he never told her of his plan before she died from a cadmium II leak **[T-SER1.1]**.

- **Flag and Lettuce, The:** A pub at which Lister was found abandoned at the age of six weeks. Dave recalled it as being an upscale establishment that served Boddy's Beer and a good ploughman's (a meal consisting of cheese, chutney and bread) **[R-DAD]**.

  NOTE: *This pub may have been named after two prominent bars in England: the Lamb & Flag, and the Slug and Lettuce. The name was changed onscreen to the Aigburth Arms Pub in episode 7.3 ("Ouroboros").*

- **"flamingoed up":** A phrase signifying a major mistake. When the Holly Hop Drive failed to work properly, Holly admitted that he had "flamingoed up"—which, according to him, was much worse than a normal cock-up **[T-SER2.6]**.

- **flare gun:** A firearm that could be used during emergencies to launch flares into the air and alert potential rescuers **[RL]**. A flare gun was standard-issue on colonization seeding ship pods. Marooned on a barren planet after escaping a simulant battle-cruiser in one such pod, Rimmer tried to commit suicide by shooting himself in the head with the gun, but the attempt failed due to his hard-light composition **[T-SER6.5(d)]**.

  On another occasion, Lister fired a flare gun at a hologrammic version of himself, whose snoring had kept him awake. The flare passed through the hologram's body, however, setting their quarters on fire **[R-BOD]**.

- **Flash:** A name that Lister sarcastically called Rimmer after the hologram fled in an escape pod, abandoning his crewmates on a disintegrating simulant battle-cruiser **[T-SER6.5]**.

- **Flat-Headed One, the:** A term that Cat used to describe Kryten, while agreeing with the mechanoid that the *Red Dwarf* crew should avoid interacting with future versions of themselves **[T-SER6.6(d)]**.

- **"Flemish Weaving the Traditional Way":** An article published in *Starbug*'s in-flight magazine *Up Up & Away*. The mundane nature of the article acted as a sedative during emergencies, and was thus part of the ship's crash procedures **[T-SER4.5]**.

  NOTE: *In the novel* Infinity Welcomes Careful Drivers, *the same article, sans the word "Flemish," appeared in an issue available on the shuttle that brought Lister to* Red Dwarf *for his first tour of duty.*

FLIBBLE, MR.

- **flesh-eating-virus crash of '32:** A term describing a computer virus that affected mechanoids, causing them to crash. Scientists attempted an antidote the following year, which caused another crash. Diva-Droid International was not affected by either the virus or the antidote **[W-DIV]**.

- ***FLIB-1*:** The designation of Mr. Flibble's personal spacecraft, which was equipped with a plasma drive **[M-SMG2.9(c14)]**.

- **Flibble, Mr.:** A hologrammic penguin hand-puppet that became Rimmer's deranged alter ego after he contracted a deadly holovirus that drove him insane. After escaping quarantine, Lister, Kryten and Cat ran throughout *Red Dwarf*, pursued by "Uncle Arnie" and the puppet, who had both gained hex vision, telepathy and telekinetic powers. Mr. Flibble was vanquished when the crew immobilized Rimmer and cured him of the virus **[T-SER5.4]**.

- **Flibble, Mr.:** A crude anthropomorphic penguin born on a psi-moon to a woodcutter and his buxom blonde wife, who found Flibble's egg in the Glade of Happiness. He was named after the sounds he made while being smothered in his mother's breasts. His youth, marred by his father's disapproval and his mother's desire for a girl (which caused her to clothe Flibble in gingham dresses), affected the landscape of the psi-moon, which reacted to his mental state **[M-SMG2.7(c3)]**.

  While en route to his rich grandmother's cabin to deliver a pie, Flibble discovered the gingerbread cottage of Witch Hildegarde, in which he found a potion that gave him hex vision. After using his new powers to fry the witch, he proceeded to Granny's home, where he kicked down the door of her cabin, causing her to die of a heart attack **[M-SMG2.8(c4)]**. Flibble's step-parents used Granny's inheritance to buy a central heating boiler for their house—which enraged the penguin, who had wanted the money for himself. He thus sabotaged the boiler and ignited the gas with his cigar, killing the couple in the resulting explosion **[M-SMG2.9(c2)]**.

  Tired of Flibble's antics, the moon's inhabitants put a bounty on his head **[M-SMG2.9(c9)]**, forcing the penguin to flee. During his escape, his ship ignited the moon's atmosphere, causing its destruction **[M-SMG2.9(c14)]**.

  Mr. Flibble later traveled to Planet Spud to attack the King of the Potato People with a thermonuclear weapon known as a plasmatic lacerator shell **[M-SMG1.8(c3)]**. He then visited Fat Sam's Bar, where a pair of aliens mugged him, posing as a beautiful woman **[M-SMG1.14(c4)]**. The penguin also attacked Kookie Kola Bear, the founder and mascot of Kookie Kola, and assumed control of that company **[M-SMG2.3(c3)]**.

- **Flibble Co.:** The new name of Kookie Kola after Mr. Flibble killed the company's previous owner and mascot, Kookie Kola Bear **[M-SMG2.3(c3)]**.

- **Flibster:** Mr. Flibble's nickname on a psi-moon corrupted by the penguin's depraved mind **[M-SMG2.9(c9)]**.

- **Flight 261:** The flight number of a spaceship leaving Mimas Spaceport for Mars' Phobos Interplanetary Spaceport. As this flight boarded at Gate 14, sex worker Trixie LaBouche ran throughout the facility, evading astro miner Dutch van Oestrogen and the Ganymedian Mafia **[M-SMG2.5(c6)]**.

- **Flight 578:** The flight number of a spaceship leaving Mimas Spaceport for Neptune. After stealing Dutch van Oestrogen's drug money and stash, Trixie LaBouche booked this flight using Emily Berkenstein's passport, which she had stolen from Lister **[M-SMG2.6(c4)]**.

- **flight recorder:** A mechanism aboard *Starbug* shuttlecrafts that recorded several points of data aboard ship in the event of a malfunction or crash. If a ship was lost, a homing device could be used to retrieve its flight recorder **[T-SER3.1]**.

- ***Flintstones, The*:** A popular Hanna-Barbera animated television series that debuted in 1960 **[RL]**. While searching the Cat People's abandoned city in *Red Dwarf*'s cargo decks, Lister and Rimmer found an ancient television set. Inside its video recorder was a disc containing episodes of *The Flintstones* **[N-INF]**.

  While discussing the show, Lister admitted that he considered Wilma Flintstone the sexiest woman alive. Cat agreed, adding that though he'd go with Wilma's best friend Betty Rubble, he'd be thinking of Wilma. They deemed the conversation pointless, though, since Wilma would never leave her husband Fred **[T-SER3.1]**.

  In an alternate timeline created when Lister used a timeslide to invent the Tension Sheet and become a billionaire, he owned a Fred Flintstone T-shirt **[T-SER3.5]**.

  > ***NOTE:** In the novel* Better Than Life, *Lister and Cat had the Wilma discussion while recovering in the Medibay after spending more than two years in an addictive version of* Better Than Life. *The two watched the program for fifteen or sixteen hours a day, as it was the only show on which they could agree. Onscreen, it occurred in Lister's quarters. The conversation was also recycled for the American* Red Dwarf *pilot.*

- **flip:** A tabletop game popular in the twenty-second century. *Red Dwarf* had flip tables in its rec rooms **[N-INF]**.

- **Flipper:** The titular character of two 1960s feature films, as well as several American and Australian television spinoffs, featuring the bottle-nosed dolphin and its human handlers at a Florida marine preserve **[RL]**. In the artificial-reality game *Strategic Sea Battles*, Rimmer once encountered a glitch that resulted in a dolphin named Flipper leading the English fleet into the Battle of Trafalgar **[B-SUR]**.

- **FLOB:** An acronym for "Flooring, Lighting or Building," an intelligent metal developed in the twenty-third century for use in creating instant buildings. A CPU attached to the material governed its shape and function.

  While searching for the origin of a subspace message, the *Red Dwarf* crew arrived at a planet entirely covered in FLOB. While investigating, they discovered a timezip (a temporal hole) that carried them fifty years into the future, where they came across a gigantic effigy of Kryten composed of the viscous material.

  Upon closer inspection, they discovered Kryten's Spare Head Three attached to the statue's face, which had been left behind on the planet for half a century. Spare Head Three had instructed the FLOB to build a device capable of creating a timezip to bring his friends to rescue him. The others switched Spare Head Three's personality chip with Kryten's in order to return him to *Red Dwarf*, but the two heads collided, causing one to disappear due to the effects of time distortion.

  This destabilized both the statue and the timezip, forcing the crew to retreat to safety aboard *Starbug*. Kryten, now loaded with Spare Head Three's personality, was decapitated during the escape, thereby causing that head to be left behind, and starting the cycle over again **[M-SMG2.9(c1)]**.

- **Flogging a Dead Horse Award:** An industry award bestowed on Crapola Inc.'s Talkie Cutlery **[W-CRP]**.

- **Floor 124:** *See* Floor 3124

- **Floor 125:** *See* Floor 3125

- **Floor 13:** A level aboard *Red Dwarf* containing a classified brig called the Tank. The prison was known only to officers (and, according to Holly, anyone who had ever watched *The Twilight Zone*). Prior to the cadmium II disaster—and, subsequently, after the ship was rebuilt by nanobots—Floor 13 housed a full contingent of prisoners waiting to be transported to Adelphi 12. Aboard the rebuilt ship, Lister and his shipmates were sentenced to two years in the Tank after being found guilty of using confidential files for their own purposes **[T-SER8.1]**.

- **Floor 13 information pack:** A package of brochures given to new arrivals to the Tank, *Red Dwarf*'s classified brig, which included a blindfold for use when an inmate needed privacy to use the toilet **[T-SER8.3]**.

  NOTE: *It is unknown whether the blindfold was intended for the toilet user or the bunkmate.*

- **Floor 14:** A *Red Dwarf* level on which Cat suggested playing Unicycle Polo when Lister became bored with his life **[T-SER3.5]**.

- **Floor 16:** An area of *Red Dwarf* also called Level 16. Three million years after a radiation leak killed most of the crew, Lister and Rimmer discovered a stasis leak on Floor 16, and used the phenomenon to go back in time three weeks prior to the accident, each with his own agenda: Lister to save Kochanski, Rimmer to save himself **[T-SER2.4]**.

- **Floor 3124:** A level of the holoship *Enlightenment* containing the vessel's maintenance department **[T-SER5.1]**.

  NOTE: *The script for this episode, published in the book* Son of Soup*, referred to this area as Floor 124.*

- **Floor 3125:** A section of the holoship *Enlightenment* allocated for sports and sexual recreation **[T-SER5.1]**.

  NOTE: *The script for this episode, published in the book* Son of Soup*, referred to this area as Floor 125.*

- **Floor 341:** A *Red Dwarf* level containing the captain's quarters, as well as a snack dispenser from which Rimmer stole a Choccie Nut bar, causing the machine to vow revenge on him **[T-SER8.8]**.

- **Floor 4177:** A level of the holoship *Enlightenment* containing the senior Officers Quarters, also called Deck 4177 **[T-SER5.1(d)]**.

  NOTE: *In a deleted scene, the computer changed*

PREFIX
RL: Real life

T-: Television Episodes
SER: Television series
IDW: "Identity Within"
USA1: Unaired U.S. pilot
USA2: Unaired U.S. demo

R-: *The Bodysnatcher Collection*
SER: Remastered episodes
BOD: "Bodysnatcher"
DAD: "Dad"
FTH: "Lister's Father"
INF: "Infinity Patrol"
END: "The End" (original assembly)

N-: Novels
INF: *Infinity Welcomes Careful Drivers*
BTL: *Better Than Life*
LST: *Last Human*

BCK: *Backwards*
OMN: *Red Dwarf Omnibus*

M-: Magazines
SMG: *Smegazine*

W-: Websites
OFF: Official website
NAN: *Prelude to Nanarchy*
AND: *Androids*
DIV: Diva-Droid
DIB: Duane Dibbley

CRP: Crapola
GEN: Geneticon
LSR: Leisure World Intl.
JMC: Jupiter Mining Corporation
AIT: *A.I. Today*
HOL: HoloPoint

G-: Roleplaying Game
RPG: *Core Rulebook*
BIT: *A.I. Screen Extra Bits* booklet
SOR: *Series Sourcebook*
OTH: Other RPG material

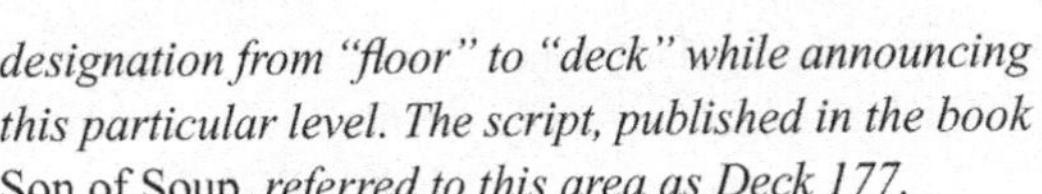

designation from "floor" to "deck" while announcing this particular level. The script, published in the book Son of Soup*, referred to this area as Deck 177.*

- **Floor 431:** A level aboard *Red Dwarf* containing Blue Corridor 9, which housed an Indian restaurant called The Vindaloovian Empire **[X-CAL]**.

- **Floor 591:** *See* Level 591

- **Floor 592:** *See* Level 592

- **Floor 6120:** A level of the holoship *Enlightenment* containing the ship's botanical gardens **[T-SER5.1]**.

- **Floor 9172:** An area of *Red Dwarf* containing the ship's sleeping quarter, known as Area P. Lister and Rimmer originally bunked together in this section **[N-INF]**.

- **Florida:** A southeastern peninsula state in the United States **[RL]**, home to a Space Corps research center. During her career with the Space Corps, Nirvanah Crane was stationed at this facility, as well as others around the solar system **[W-OFF]**.

- **Florrie, Great-Aunt:** A hypothetical woman whom Rimmer mentioned while describing Lister, whom he said resembled grey monkeys masturbating at a zoo in front of one's Great-Aunt Florrie **[N-INF]**.

- **Floyd, Keith:** A British celebrity chef, restaurateur and author **[RL]**. When Tunbridge Wells' five hundred pilgrims were sent to pray for the end of a meteor storm ravaging their city, a cook in the group believed his people were headed to a shrine dedicated to Floyd. Others disagreed, causing a religious war that wiped out the entire pilgrim crew **[M-SMG1.14(c2)]**.

- **fluid matrix:** A liquid stored aboard a derelict research station that the *Red Dwarf* crew discovered. The fluid was used by the platform's heuristic neural net, a computer that utilized experimental wetware artificial-intelligence technology **[M-SMG1.11(c2)]**.

- **"Fly Me to the Moon":** A popular song during the 1950s and '60s, written by Bart Howard and sung by various artists, including Johnny Mathis, Nat King Cole and Frank Sinatra **[RL]**. Talkie Toaster sang this tune to prove it could sing better than Lister, until Dave forcefully slammed on the appliance, cutting short the rendition **[T-SER1.2]**.

- **Flynn, Errol:** An Australian actor who starred in many romantic swashbuckling films of the early twentieth century, notably *The Adventures of Robin Hood* and *Gentleman Jim* **[RL]**. A waxdroid of Errol Flynn traveled with a chainsmoking human named Eric, a hologrammic pastry chef named Robin and a humanoid female rabbit in a possible alternate universe **[G-RPG]**.

- **food bag:** An intravenous bag of nutrients that nourished players hooked into a total-immersion video game suite for extended lengths of time. Confusing this tube with a player's catheter produced extremely unpleasant results **[T-SER5.6]**.

- **food bay:** A large, open area within *Red Dwarf*'s food decks, in which edible supplies were loaded and stored. After a time wand transformed Pete the sparrow into a *Tyrannosaurus rex*, the crew lured the dinosaur into the food bay with cow vindaloo, hoping to retrieve the wand (which Pete had swallowed) **[T-SER8.7]**.

- **food decks:** The levels within *Red Dwarf* on which food supplies were stored. Pete the sparrow was transformed into a *Tyrannosaurus rex* on one of the food decks **[T-SER8.7]**.

- **"Food Recycle Container":** A phrase on a sign in *Red Dwarf*'s refectory **[T-SER1.1]**.

- ***Football: It's a Funny Old Game*:** A book written by Kevin Keegan, covering the sport of international football (soccer). After reading every book in existence, Holly told Lister that this one was the worst ever written **[T-SER1.5]**.

  NOTE: *This book exists in the real world, but was penned by Andrew John and Stephen Blake, not Keegan (a former player and manager for several teams, including Liverpool and Hamburger SV). "It's a funny old game" originated as the catchphrase of television pundit and former player James Peter*

"Jimmy" Greaves. In the novel Infinity Welcomes Careful Drivers, *Holly read this book during the nanoseconds that passed between his sealing of the ship to protect the crew from the cadmium II explosion, and the actual detonation.*

- **Forbidden Lands, the:** A dangerous stretch of land located on Echech 3, a planet within GELF space on which the Kinitawowi Open golf tournament was held. The nine-hole course was created within the Forbidden Lands, with hazards ranging from dinosaurs, carnivorous plants and giant insects to volcanoes, chasms and gravity wells **[G-RPG]**.

- **force shields:** A type of defensive shielding used on rogue simulant battle-cruisers **[T-SER6.3(d)]**.

- **Ford, Jo ("Babe"):** A zero-gee football player whose likeness adorned a poster hanging in *Red Dwarf*'s disco room **[T-SER1.3]**. A sticker bearing Ford's name decorated a wall of *Blue Midget*'s cockpit **[T-SER2.1]**.

- **Ford Phallus:** A model of hover-car owned by Gary on the television soap opera *Androids*. Years later, Gary had the vehicle's seats installed in a newer model **[M-SMG1.14(c3)]**.

  NOTE: Since a phallus is an erect penis, the car's name presumably played on the stereotype of a man overcompensating for his penis size by buying a fast car.

- **Fordway, Lieutenant:** An officer in the Space Corps, possibly in an alternate universe, who was a zero-gee football fan. A shapeshifting GELF once disguised itself as Fordway, but the ruse was exposed due to its lack of knowledge of the sport **[G-SOR]**.

- **Forethought, Melissa:** The author of issue 362 of *True Life Criminal Crime Stories* in Jake Bullet's alternate universe. Philby Frutch provided Forethought's name as the correct answer to a question on the game show *20,000,000 Watts My Line*, winning the match **[M-SMG1.10(c1)]**.

- **Formby, George:** A twentieth-century British comedy actor and singer-songwriter, known for such films as *Boots! Boots!* and *Let George Do It* **[RL]**. Prison guards in *Red Dwarf*'s brig, the Tank, regularly tormented inmates to sap morale, pulling such pranks as showing an entire season's worth of George Formby films on movie night **[T-SER8.5]**.

- **fortnight:** A unit of time equal to fourteen days **[RL]**. The thinking time of a pilot flying a ship traveling at half the speed of light was a fortnight, according to a pilot's test that Kryten took aboard *Starbug 1* **[T-SER3.1]**.

- **Forum of Justice:** A judicial hall built on Arranguu 12, a GELF-run desert moon in an alternate universe. The forum, presided over by a GELF Regulator—a creature known as an Alberog—contained six hooded jurors. Lister was arraigned at the Forum of Justice after committing crimes against the GELF state, including breaking his doppelgänger out of the Cyberia prison complex **[N-LST]**.

- **Foster, Miss:** Lister's geography teacher during his school days. While debating Rimmer about whether men or machines were better, Lister recalled a camping trip to Deganwy that his class took with Miss Foster, during which he awoke one night to hear strange noises coming from the teacher's tent. Lister thus concluded that Foster did not consider men better than machines **[T-SER2.5]**.

- **Four-Dimensional Pontoon:** A game of chance played at a Brefewino GELF village, the object of which was to bet on the next hand of cards received, not the hand currently held. In order to win sufficient GELF currency (Brefewinan) to buy Ora Tanzil out of slavery for Cat, Lister convinced Kryten and Rimmer to help him cheat at Four-Dimensional Pontoon, using Kryten's card-counting ability and signals.

  However, Lister's inebriation hindered his ability to recognize signals, causing him to lose all of his winnings. Undaunted, he bet the keys to *Starbug 1*, but was out-cheated when Zural, a member of Cat's species disguised as a GELF, received Lister's cards, winning the pot and the shuttle **[T-IDW]**.

  NOTE: Pontoon is a British version of the American card game Blackjack.

- ***Four Funerals and Another One*:** A romantic comedy directed by twenty-second-century Swedish director Sjorbik Bjorksson. Delighted when a post pod containing Bjorksson's complete

PREFIX
RL: Real life

T-: Television Episodes
SER: Television series
IDW: "Identity Within"
USA1: Unaired U.S. pilot
USA2: Unaired U.S. demo

R-: *The Bodysnatcher Collection*
SER: Remastered episodes
BOD: "Bodysnatcher"
DAD: "Dad"
FTH: "Lister's Father"
INF: "Infinity Patrol"
END: "The End" (original assembly)

N-: Novels
INF: *Infinity Welcomes Careful Drivers*
BTL: *Better Than Life*
LST: *Last Human*

BCK: *Backwards*
OMN: *Red Dwarf Omnibus*

M-: Magazines
SMG: *Smegazine*

W-: Websites
OFF: Official website
NAN: *Prelude to Nanarchy*
AND: *Androids*
DIV: Diva-Droid
DIB: Duane Dibbley

CRP: Crapola
GEN: Geneticon
LSR: Leisure World Intl.
JMC: Jupiter Mining Corporation
AIT: *A.I. Today*
HOL: HoloPoint

G-: Roleplaying Game
RPG: *Core Rulebook*
BIT: *A.I. Screen Extra Bits* booklet
SOR: *Series Sourcebook*
OTH: Other RPG material

works caught up with *Red Dwarf*, Rimmer forced the crew to watch this and several other movies in the collection **[B-LOG]**.

NOTE: This film's titled spoofed that of romantic comedy Four Weddings and a Funeral.

- **Four Musketeers, The:** A nickname by which Rimmer claimed he and his three brothers were known as children. He then corrected himself, admitting his brothers were the Three Musketeers, forcing Arnold to be the Queen of Spain **[T-SER3.3]**.

- **fourth sand of D'Aquaarar:** A defense tactic Lister attempted to use on Arranguu 12 to force a mistrial during his hearing for crimes against the GELF state. Lister stated that taking the fourth sand of D'Aquaarar protected him from the breach of Xzeeertuiy by the Zalgon impeachment of Kjielomnon, according to the case of *Mbazvmbbcxyy vs. Mbazvmbbcxyy*, which was allowed during the third season of every fifth cycle. Lister, however, was being tried in the Northern sector of Arranguu 12—which, according to the Regulator, did not follow the same archaic legal system as the Southern sector, from which the case originated **[N-BCK]**.

- **Fowler, Nigel P.:** A man, possibly enlisted in the Space Corps, mentioned in Mike O'Hagan's *Space Corps Survival Manual*. In the book, a drawing depicting a headstone engraved with Fowler's name graced the section about cannibalism. According to the headstone, Fowler was a devoted husband, loving father and tasty risotto **[B-SUR]**.

- **Frank:** A character that Kryten's subconscious mind created as the mechanoid tried to purge an Armageddon virus that had infected *Starbug 1*'s navicomp. Kryten's mind converted the struggle into a dream in which he was the drunken sheriff of an Old West town terrorized by the Apocalypse Boys (a manifestation of the virus). When the crew hacked into the dream via an artificial-reality machine, they were confronted by a man named Jimmy, who was tormenting Kryten. When Lister's knife skills embarrassed Jimmy, the bully ordered fellow thugs Frank and Nuke to "fill his lungs with lead." Their attempt failed, however, when Cat (known in the dream as the Riviera Kid) shot their bullets out of the air **[T-SER6.3]**.

- **Frank:** A man who found Lister after he was abandoned as an infant at The Aigburth Arms pub on November 26, 2155 **[T-SER7.3]**.

- **Frank:** A name that Kryten gave to *Starbug 1*'s washing machine. The mechanoid claimed Frank was upset by the increase in laundry due to Kochanski's arrival **[T-SER7.5]**.

- **Frank:** An American television executive in an alternate universe in which *Red Dwarf* was merely a British TV series. He had flowing blonde hair, a beard and glasses. In this reality, Americans remade the series but with several changes, and the first episode was previewed by Frank and his associate, TJ. Frank was stunned that the British version featured a dead crew, a hologrammic main cast member, humanity's extinction and a lack of aliens—all of which were changed in the American version **[M-SMG1.10(c4)]**.

- **Frank Assisi and the Apostles:** A Christian Rock group, circa the twenty-second century, who recorded the album *Hymns in Rock*. This CD was one of several that Lister scattered around Warden Ackerman's quarters, mistakenly thinking he was trashing the room of Kochanski's ex-boyfriend, Tim **[T-SER8.5]**.

- **Frankenstein:** A black tabby cat that Leo Davis found at the Black Island Film Studios, a production company in an alternate dimension. Frankenstein had a tag with an inverted Z-shaped symbol on it, and was owned by a dwarf dressed in red, who eventually arrived to claim the animal **[X-TNG]**.

- **Frankenstein, Victor, Doctor:** The protagonist of Mary Shelley's 1818 novel *Frankenstein; or, The Modern Prometheus*, as well as its Universal Studios film adaptation. Obsessed with the creation of life, the scientist built a humanoid monster that he was unable to control, resulting in several deaths **[RL]**.

  Cat, on edge after a crazed Rimmer forced his crewmates to spend five days in quarantine, called Kryten "Frankenstein" due to the shape of his head, which resembled Boris Karloff's onscreen portrayal of the creature. Kryten smugly noted that Frankenstein was the name of the scientist, not the monster—which irked Cat even more, as he despised being corrected **[T-SER5.4]**.

- **Frankenstein ("Frankie"):** A pregnant black cat that Lister smuggled aboard *Red Dwarf* from Titan. When Lister sent a photograph of himself and Frankie to the ship's lab, Captain Hollister demanded he hand over the animal, but Lister refused to give her up, forcing Hollister to sentence him to eighteen months in stasis. Soon thereafter, an ill-repaired drive plate triggered a lethal cadmium II explosion, killing everyone else on board except for Frankenstein, who was sealed in the ship's cargo hold, and Lister **[T-SER1.1]**.

  Safe within the hold, Frankie gave birth to a litter of four kittens, who procreated over generations until, by the time of Frankenstein's death at the age of fourteen, *Red Dwarf*'s feline population had reached 198,732, all directly descended from her initial litter **[N-INF]**. Over the course of three million years, this litter continued to procreate. Due to radiation leaking into the hold, the cats evolved first into *Felis erectus* and then *Felis sapiens*, a species of sapient humanoid Cat People **[M-SMG2.2(a)]**.

  Frankenstein was considered "The Holy Mother" in the Cat People's religious texts, which recounted the story, albeit skewed by time, of Lister's sacrifice to save the animal **[T-SER1.1]**.

  NOTE: *The novel* Infinity Welcomes Careful Drivers *stated that Lister had picked up Frankenstein on Miranda, while the series' pilot indicated he did so on Titan, and episode 7.3 ("Ouroboros") indicated that he obtained the cat on Mimas. Since Mimas and Titan are part of the same planetary system, it is possible he picked up the cat prior to visiting Mimas.*

- **Frankenstein ("Frankie"):** A pregnant black cat that Lister smuggled aboard *Red Dwarf* in an alternate dimension, during a trip intended to help him forget about Kochanski. When Dave returned to the ship, Kristine discovered the animal and reprimanded him, at first threatening to disintegrate the cat. Instead, however, she decided to save Frankie and hide the animal herself, starting a series of events that led to her being sent to stasis, surviving the cadmium II accident and being revived by Holly three million years later instead of Lister **[T-SER7.3]**.

- **Frankenstein ("Frankie"):** A pregnant cat from Titan that an alternate-universe Lister smuggled aboard the American mining ship *Red Dwarf* after saving it from a restaurant. When security cameras caught Lister with the animal, Captain Tau confronted him, but he refused to give up the cat and was sentenced to spend the remainder of his tour in stasis. When an ill-repaired drive plate caused a lethal cadmium II explosion, everyone on board died except for Frankie, who was sealed in the ship's cargo hold, and Lister **[T-USA1]**.

  NOTE: *The first draft of the American pilot script claimed that version of Lister obtained Frankenstein during shore leave on Callistro* (sic).

- **Frankie:** *See* Frankenstein ("Frankie")

- **Frankie the Garcon:** The android maître d' of the AlFresco Guacamole Restaurant, located in NYNY in an alternate universe. Frankie attempted to cook Spike, a chef at the eatery, for his cannibalistic patrons. When Spike went missing, his sister Sugar enlisted help from Jake Bullet, who visited the restaurant looking for the boy.

  Upon their arrival, Frankie ambushed them, knocked them unconscious and left them tied up in the kitchen. When they awoke, they found Spike locked in the oven. Bullet saved the boy, however, then interrogated Frankie and left him tied up, causing him to choke to death on Bullet's handkerchief **[M-SMG1.7(a)]**.

- **Franklin, Aretha:** An American singer and musician often hailed as "The Queen of Soul," revered for such hits as "Respect," "(You Make Me Feel Like) A Natural Woman" and "Think" **[RL]**. When Kryten described the process of removing kidney stones via the urethra, Lister claimed the only urethra he knew of was "Urethra Franklin" **[T-SER10.3]**.

- **Freak-Face:** A derogatory term that Cat called Kryten, referencing the mechanoid's unappealing countenance **[T-SER3.1]**.

- **freaky fungus:** *See* Titan mushrooms

- **Freckle:** A perfume that Hildegarde Lanstrom created for her product line, Parfum by Lanstrom. The fragrance incorporated a positive strain of virus she developed **[X-CAL]**.

  NOTE: *Given the nature of the viruses Lanstrom was*

PREFIX
RL: Real life

T-: Television Episodes
SER: Television series
IDW: "Identity Within"
USA1: Unaired U.S. pilot
USA2: Unaired U.S. demo

R-: *The Bodysnatcher Collection*
SER: Remastered episodes
BOD: "Bodysnatcher"
DAD: "Dad"
FTH: "Lister's Father"
INF: "Infinity Patrol"
END: "The End" (original assembly)

N-: Novels
INF: *Infinity Welcomes Careful Drivers*
BTL: *Better Than Life*
LST: *Last Human*

BCK: *Backwards*
OMN: *Red Dwarf Omnibus*

M-: Magazines
SMG: *Smegazine*

W-: Websites
OFF: Official website
NAN: *Prelude to Nanarchy*
AND: *Androids*
DIV: Diva-Droid
DIB: Duane Dibbley

CRP: Crapola
GEN: Geneticon
LSR: Leisure World Intl.
JMC: Jupiter Mining Corporation
AIT: *A.I. Today*
HOL: HoloPoint

G-: Roleplaying Game
RPG: *Core Rulebook*
BIT: *A.I. Screen Extra Bits* booklet
SOR: *Series Sourcebook*
OTH: Other RPG material

studying, Freckle presumably caused wearers, or those around them, to form skin spots.

- **Fred:** A Bedford Falls carpenter whom Lister imagined while trapped in an addictive version of *Better Than Life*. After Rimmer, disguised as Trixie LaBouche, crashed a juggernaut through the illusory town, Fred attempted to fix the damaged jailhouse **[N-BTL]**.

- **Freeman Hardy Willis:** A major chain of footwear retailers in the United Kingdom, founded in 1875 **[RL]**. In the artificial-reality game *Scramble!!!*, a common workaround to a glitch that gave players a #17 bus instead of a Warbird involved bombing a Freeman Hardy Willis store on Balham High Street **[B-SUR]**.

- **Freemasons:** A secretive worldwide fraternal organization with origins dating back to medieval times **[RL]**. Dobbin, the drummer of Lister's first band, Smeg and the Heads, later joined the police force and became a Freemason grand wizard **[T-SER3.5]**.

- **Frequency Locked:** A setting on *Starbug 1*'s sonar scope display. This setting was highlighted while the crew charted the course of a despair squid **[T-SER5.6]**.

- **Freud, Sigmund, Doctor:** An Austrian neurologist widely considered the father of psychoanalysis **[RL]**. Holly read the complete works of several prominent writers, including Freud, within the fifteen nanoseconds that passed between *Red Dwarf*'s cadmium II core going critical and the entire crew dying **[N-INF]**.

  After Kryten's artificial-reality program *The Rimmer Experience* cured Lister of his depression over Rimmer's absence, the mechanoid exclaimed, "Sigmund Freud, eat your heart out!" **[T-SER7.5]**.

- ***Freud on Humour*:** A book written by Sigmund Freud, in which the neurologist analyzed what makes humans laugh. Lister found the book surprisingly devoid of humor **[B-EVR]**.

  NOTE: *Freud never wrote a book by this title in the real world. He did, however, author a 1905 volume called* The Joke and Its Relation to the Unconscious, *as well as a 1928 article about humor for* The International Journal of Psychoanalysis.

- ***Friday the 13th Part 1,649*:** A movie contained in a three-million-year-old post pod that caught up with *Red Dwarf* after Holly altered course to navigate the vessel back to Earth **[T-SER2.2]**.

  NOTE: *The* Friday the 13th *horror franchise starred an undead mass-murderer named Jason Voorhees, who stalked and killed fornicators at Camp Crystal Lake and other locales. As of this book's release, the franchise comprised twelve movies, a television series, and several novels and comic books.*

- **Fried Four, The:** A nickname describing Dave Lister, Olaf Petersen, Selby and Chen, who enjoyed a constant state of inebriation together aboard *Red Dwarf* **[G-BIT]**.

- **Frisbee Nostrils:** A nickname that Cat called Rimmer **[N-BCK]**.

- **Fritz:** A warrior of the Elite, a Cat People tribe that evolved aboard *Red Dwarf* while Lister was in stasis. During the Cats' two-thousand-year Holy War, the Elite sent three warriors—Fritz, Krazy and Juma—forward in time via an obelisk, to retrieve their god (Lister) in the hope that he could end the conflict **[M-SMG2.1(c1)]**.

  Fritz, a Fundamental Remonian, believed the war should be played out naturally. Opposing the plan to bring Lister back, Fritz attacked the human en route to the Cats' High Tower, but Juma, who was suspicious of his motives, stopped Fritz from harming Lister **[M-SMG2.2(c1)]**.

  NOTE: *Fritz was named after* Fritz the Cat, *a 1972 animated comedy film written and directed by Ralph Bakshi.*

- **frog:** A tailless amphibian of the order Anura **[RL]**. While rescuing Rimmer from a psi-moon configured according to his psyche, the *Red Dwarf* crew crossed the Swamp of Despair and heard frogs murmuring the words "useless" and "Rimmer" **[T-SER5.3]**.

B-: Books
PRG: *Red Dwarf Programme Guide*
SUR: *Red Dwarf Space Corps Survival Manual*
PRM: *Primordial Soup*
SOS: *Son of Soup*
SCE: *Scenes from the Dwarf*
LOG: *Red Dwarf Log No. 1996*
RD8: *Red Dwarf VIII*
EVR: *The Log: A Dwarfer's Guide to Everything*

X-: Misc.
PRO: Promotional materials, videos, etc.
PST: Posters at DJ XVII (2013)
CAL: 2008 calendar
RNG: Cell phone ringtones
MOB: Mobisode ("Red Christmas")
CIN: *Children in Need* sketch
GEK: *Geek Week* intros by Kryten
TNG: "Tongue-Tied" video

XMS: Bill Pearson's Christmas special pitch script
XVD: Bill Pearson's Christmas special pitch video
OTH: Other *Red Dwarf* appearances

SUFFIX
DVD:
(d) – Deleted scene
(o) – Outtake
(b) – Bonus DVD material (other)
(e) – Extended version

SMEGAZINES:
(c) – Comic
(a) – Article

OTHER:
(s) – Early/unused script draft
(s1) – Alternate version of script

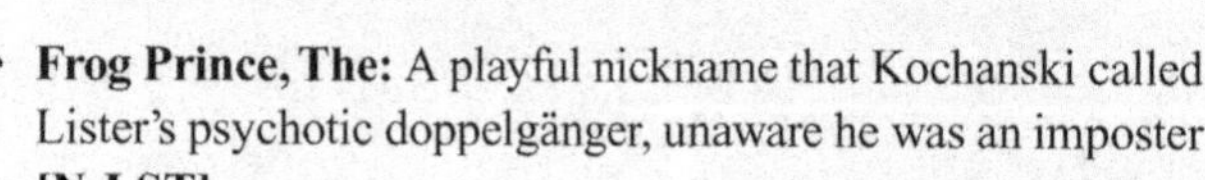

- **Frog Prince, The:** A playful nickname that Kochanski called Lister's psychotic doppelgänger, unaware he was an imposter **[N-LST]**.

- **front cargo pods:** A series of external containers in *Red Dwarf*'s underbelly, used for storing and transporting materials. The pods were located toward the mining ship's fore section **[R-BOD(b)]**.

  NOTE: *This section, visible in the ship's new design in the remastered episodes, was labeled in concept art included in* The Bodysnatcher Collection*'s bonus features.*

- **front meteor bay:** A section of *Red Dwarf*'s underbelly allocated for containing meteors used for mining. The front meteor bay was located toward the vessel's fore section **[R-BOD(b)]**.

  NOTE: *This section of the ship's remastered design was also named in* The Bodysnatcher Collection*'s bonus concept art.*

- **Frutch, Philby:** The most successful contestant in the history of *20,000,000 Watts My Line*, a television trivia game show in Jake Bullet's universe **[M-SMG1.10(c1)]**. He lived in Flat C at 227 Thatcher Throughway **[M-SMG1.13(c4)]**.

  Frutch was found dead shortly after his final episode aired, prompting the police to assign Bullet to the case **[M-SMG1.10(c1)]**. During his investigation, the cyborg learned that Philby was taking stupid drugs when he was bludgeoned to death outside the television station where the show was broadcast **[M-SMG1.11(c4)]**.

  As Bullet visited an informant to inquire about the drugs, an assassin shot at him **[M-SMG1.12(c1)]**. He pursued the would-be killer to a Hit-U-Like office and interrogated the manager, who provided the name of the customer who requested the hit: Philby Frutch himself **[M-SMG1.13(c4)]**.

  Bullet visited Frutch's apartment and met Mercy Dash, the hostess of *20,0000,000 Watts My Line*. She and Frutch had planned to spend the show's winnings on an operation to cure Frutch of his nerdism before going away on holiday **[M-SMG1.14(c6)]**. Jake learned from the show's host, Milty, that Frutch had cheated by using an implant that fed him answers, and had then taken stupid drugs to impede the implant's side effects. As such, Milty had sent Dash to seduce Frutch and bludgeon him with a brick **[M-SMG2.2(c2)]**.

  NOTE: *On a toe tag visible in part 5 of the* Smegazine *comic storyline, Frutch's first initial was incorrectly indicated as F.*

- **Frying Pantheist:** A joking reference that Lister made while mocking the concept of Silicon Heaven. As a Pantheist, he believed God existed in all things, though he did not think this extended to electronic devices or kitchen utensils **[T-SER3.6]**.

- **FSK 731**: The license plate number of an abandoned car in Dallas, Texas, in an alternate 1966 spawned by the *Starbug 1* crew's temporal-traveling **[T-SER7.1]**.

- **Fuchal:** The "Promised Land," according to the religious doctrine of the Cat People inhabiting *Red Dwarf*. Their savior, Cloister the Stupid, was prophesied to return from being frozen in time and lead them to Fuchal. In actuality, the word "Fuchal" was merely a bastardization of Fiji, a small island on Earth, to which Lister had intended to bring his pregnant cat Frankenstein, before being put in stasis **[T-SER1.1]**.

  For thousands of years, two religious factions of the Cat People—those who thought the food temple's hats on Fuchal should be blue, and those who believed they should be red—fought in a great Holy War. Eventually, they called a truce and built two Cat Arks in which to search for the Promised Land. The Blue Hat faction, using what they thought was a star chart (but was actually Lister's laundry list) left first and flew directly into an asteroid, destroying their ship. The second group, meanwhile, flew in the opposite direction, believing themselves righteous **[T-SER1.4]**.

  This second Cat Ark crashed onto an S-3 planet previously occupied by a human colony. Believing it to be Fuchal, they populated the colony's ruins, in which they found several active personality discs, which they mistook for Cloister's servants. The hologrammic personalities took advantage of this error, infusing their ethics into feline society. This split the Cat population into several more factions, each following the teachings of its respective saint.

  One such group, following the personality of a Space Corps commander named Suzdal, became the largest and most dangerous faction, having been taught to hone their warrior

PREFIX
RL: Real life

T-: Television Episodes
SER: Television series
IDW: "Identity Within"
USA1: Unaired U.S. pilot
USA2: Unaired U.S. demo

R-: *The Bodysnatcher Collection*
SER: Remastered episodes
BOD: "Bodysnatcher"
DAD: "Dad"
FTH: "Lister's Father"
INF: "Infinity Patrol"
END: "The End" (original assembly)

N-: Novels
INF: *Infinity Welcomes Careful Drivers*
BTL: *Better Than Life*
LST: *Last Human*

BCK: *Backwards*
OMN: *Red Dwarf Omnibus*

M-: Magazines
SMG: *Smegazine*

W-: Websites
OFF: Official website
NAN: *Prelude to Nanarchy*
AND: *Androids*
DIV: Diva-Droid
DIB: Duane Dibbley

CRP: Crapola
GEN: Geneticon
LSR: Leisure World Intl.
JMC: Jupiter Mining Corporation
AIT: *A.I. Today*
HOL: HoloPoint

G-: Roleplaying Game
RPG: *Core Rulebook*
BIT: *A.I. Screen Extra Bits* booklet
SOR: *Series Sourcebook*
OTH: Other RPG material

skills so they could go back in time and fight alongside Cloister for the Cat People. This group's violent, martial ways caused a schism in the population, creating an underground movement determined to build another starship and leave the planet in search of the true Promised Land **[G-RPG]**.

- **Fuchal Day:** A sacred holiday observed by the Cat People inhabiting *Red Dwarf*, during which religious members were required to eat hot dogs. Those who did not partake of this activity were stoned to death by stale doughnuts **[T-SER1.4]**.

- **Fuchal Diner, The:** A hot dog and doughnut stand operated by Cloister the Stupid, according to artwork depicted in the Cat Bible **[R-SER1.4]**.

- **fuel electrolysis unit:** A type of high-end fuel-management system not typically found on GELF-designed attack cruisers **[G-RPG]**.

- **fuel intake chambers:** A component of *Starbug* shuttles' propulsion systems. *Starbugs* contained two such chambers. While navigating *Starbug 1* through an asteroid belt swarming with Psirens, the crew encountered a giant flaming meteorite that struck the ship, causing it to crash on an asteroid. The damage was minimal, with a few sensors knocked out, the fuel intake chambers flooded and the left pilot's seat unable to move up and down **[T-SER6.1]**.

- **Fuel Pipe 9:** A conduit that fed fuel into *Starbug 1*'s shuttles engines. Fuel Pipe 9 ruptured during an encounter with a Space Corps external enforcement vehicle **[T-SER6.4]**.

- **fuel tanks:** Receptacles aboard *Starbug* shuttles used for storing fuel **[T-SER5.3]**. Firing lasers at a *Starbug*'s main tanks could destroy the ship **[T-SER6.6]**.

- ***Fugitive, The*:** An American television series starring David Janssen as Richard Kimble, a physician falsely convicted of his wife's murder, who escaped while en route to death row and set out to find the real killer, a one-armed man **[RL]**. While consoling Lister about his arm being amputated, Kochanski cited the one-armed man as an extraordinary amputee, forgetting that he was a murderer **[T-SER7.8]**.

- **Full-Rimmer:** A salute that Rimmer created and petitioned the Space Ministry to adopt in place of the standard military salute. Its beginning was similar to a standard salute: From the salute pose, one would throw the right arm out in front, twirl the wrist five times to symbolize the five arms of the Space Corps, and then snap the arm back to form an equilateral triangle with the forehead. One would then straighten the elbow and snap the arm back to one's side **[N-INF]**.

- **Funch Zone:** An area within a zero-gee football arena, into which members of a team's defense brought a weapon of their choice during a "Die! Die! Darling!" goal-scoring strategy, and then stomped on it. The team with the greatest number of Finsleys remaining won the Faboozle, beginning the next quarter six Brintzleys ahead **[M-SMG1.8(a)]**.

- **Fund, Doctor:** A person whom Cat hallucinated after bumping his head while retrieving food from a *Red Dwarf* cupboard. In his delirium, Cat thought he was again Duane Dibbley, and that a man named Doctor Swan-Morton was interrogating him regarding the deaths of Jake Bullet and Sebastian and William Doyle. The doctor then delivered him for torture to Doctors Maxwell, Pension and Fund—who were actually Lister, Rimmer and Kryten, attempting to revive Cat from his delusion **[M-SMG1.9(c1)]**.

- **Fundamental Cloisterist:** A religious sect of Cat People aboard *Red Dwarf* who vehemently adhered to the word of their religion's Holy Book. Much of their regalia were adorned with images of doughnuts and sausages. The Fundamentalists followed five commandments, whereas the more dominant religions practiced seven. Cat's father and the blind priest who raised Cat were both Fundamental Cloisterists **[M-SMG2.2(a)]**.

- **Fundamental Cloisterist priest collar:** A neck adornment worn by priests from the Fundamental Cloisterist sect of the Cat People inhabiting *Red Dwarf* **[M-SMG2.2(a)]**.

- **Fundamental Remonian:** A sect of Cat People aboard *Red Dwarf* who believed their Holy War should play out naturally, and thus opposed a plan to bring their god (Lister) back from the future to end the conflict. One member, Fritz, infiltrated the Elite—the tribe that devised the plan to retrieve Lister using a time obelisk—and attempted to murder Lister shortly after his arrival. Fritz was thwarted, however, by an Elitist named Juma, who suspected the traitor **[M-SMG2.2(c1)]**.

- **fungo-beer:** An alcoholic beverage brewed in the underground cities of Earth's Moon **[G-RPG]**.

- **"Funking Up Wagner":** A song recorded by Reggie Wilson, accompanied by Hammond organ music **[T-SER4.5]**.

- **Funkley, Ed ("Pacemaker"):** A zero-gee football player who passed away during the final quarter of a Veteran's game. After his death, the final two quarters of all zero-gee football games—which, at the time, spanned five quarters—were spent with the crowd waiting silently in the arena parking lot. This led to the establishment of a standard three-quarter game **[M-SMG1.8(a)]**.

- **Funky Chicken, The:** A popular rhythm and blues dance in which people flapped their arms like a chicken **[RL]**. Rimmer banned discos from being held aboard *Red Dwarf* after seeing Lister's rendition of this dance **[T-SER7.2(d)]**.

- **fun-sized candy bar:** A term synonymous with "bite-sized," describing small confections **[RL]**. The American mining vessel *Red Dwarf* once experienced a fun-sized candy bar crisis on Level 42 **[T-USA1(s)]**.

- **funter:** A position in zero-gee football. During the all-weather season, the length of a game's quarter was increased by the scoring average of each team's funter **[M-SMG1.8(a)]**.

- **furry dice:** A novelty decoration for vehicles, consisting of colorful, oversized stuffed dice, typically hung from the rear-view mirror **[RL]**. A pair of furry dice adorned *Starbug I*'s cockpit until a collision with Ace Rimmer's dimension-hopping craft caused the elastic to snap. This, according to Holly, resulted in a more tasteful cockpit **[T-SER4.5]**.

  Rimmer added a pair of furry dice to the interior of the car he conjured up while playing the total-immersion video game *Better Than Life*, claiming it made the illusion perfect **[T-SER2.2]**. *Carbug*, a *Starbug*-themed automobile that the crew imagined while trapped in an elation squid hallucination, also contained such dice **[T-SER9.2]**.

- **Fuse Brothers, The:** Android patrons of the AlFresco Guacamole Restaurant, an NYNY eatery in Jake Bullet's universe. The cannibalistic Fuse Brothers preferred eating droids at the establishment **[M-SMG1.7(a)]**.

- **future echo:** A phenomenon experienced aboard spaceships traveling faster than light, in which crewmembers encountered glimpses of future events. This happened when a ship's speed overtook the point in time at which an event took place, causing that event to replay before it occurred. Individuals witnessing a future echo could not interact with anyone in the apparition; likewise, those appearing in the echoes were unaware of a spectator's existence, unless the echoes were of their younger selves, who thus remembered the experience.

  The surviving *Red Dwarf* crew experienced several future echoes shortly after the ship accelerated past lightspeed. Visions included Lister cutting himself while shaving; Rimmer explaining his desire to stay activated during the return trip to Earth; Cat breaking his tooth while attempting to eat Lister's robot goldfish; an explosion in the Drive Room appearing to kill Lister; an elderly Lister explaining that the person seen in the explosion was his son, Bexley, and not him; and the births of Bexley and his twin brother, Jim **[T-SER1.2]**.

- **Fuzzbox Head:** A derogatory nickname that Cat called Kryten **[M-SMG2.8(c3)]**.

PREFIX
RL: Real life

T-: Television Episodes
SER: Television series
IDW: "Identity Within"
USA1: Unaired U.S. pilot
USA2: Unaired U.S. demo

R-: *The Bodysnatcher Collection*
SER: Remastered episodes
BOD: "Bodysnatcher"
DAD: "Dad"
FTH: "Lister's Father"
INF: "Infinity Patrol"
END: "The End" (original assembly)

N-: Novels
INF: *Infinity Welcomes Careful Drivers*
BTL: *Better Than Life*
LST: *Last Human*
BCK: *Backwards*
OMN: *Red Dwarf Omnibus*

M-: Magazines
SMG: *Smegazine*

W-: Websites
OFF: Official website
NAN: *Prelude to Nanarchy*
AND: *Androids*
DIV: Diva-Droid
DIB: Duane Dibbley
CRP: Crapola
GEN: Geneticon
LSR: Leisure World Intl.
JMC: Jupiter Mining Corporation
AIT: *A.I. Today*
HOL: HoloPoint

G-: Roleplaying Game
RPG: *Core Rulebook*
BIT: *A.I. Screen Extra Bits* booklet
SOR: *Series Sourcebook*
OTH: Other RPG material

B-: Books
PRG: *Red Dwarf Programme Guide*
SUR: *Red Dwarf Space Corps Survival Manual*
PRM: *Primordial Soup*
SOS: *Son of Soup*
SCE: *Scenes from the Dwarf*
LOG: *Red Dwarf Log No. 1996*
RD8: *Red Dwarf VIII*
EVR: *The Log: A Dwarfer's Guide to Everything*

X-: Misc.
PRO: Promotional materials, videos, etc.
PST: Posters at DJ XVII (2013)
CAL: 2008 calendar
RNG: Cell phone ringtones
MOB: Mobisode ("Red Christmas")
CIN: *Children in Need* sketch
GEK: *Geek Week* intros by Kryten
TNG: "Tongue-Tied" video

XMS: Bill Pearson's Christmas special pitch script
XVD: Bill Pearson's Christmas special pitch video
OTH: Other *Red Dwarf* appearances

SUFFIX
DVD:
(d) – Deleted scene
(o) – Outtake
(b) – Bonus DVD material (other)
(e) – Extended version

SMEGAZINES:
(c) – Comic
(a) – Article

OTHER:
(s) – Early/unused script draft
(s1) – Alternate version of script

GARRETT, TALIA, SISTER

- **Gable, Clark:** An American film actor who starred in such films as *Mutiny on the Bounty* and *Gone with the Wind* **[RL]**. While trapped in an addictive version of *Better Than Life*, Rimmer believed he had gained fame and fortune upon returning to Earth aboard *Nova 5*, and that MTV had voted him Sexiest Man of All Time, ahead of Clark Gable (who came in second) and Hugo Lovepole **[N-INF]**.

- **Gabriel:** An archangel of Judeo-Christian religions, considered a messenger of God and leader of the heavenly host **[RL]**. While being interrogated by the Inquisitor, Rimmer attempted to weasel out of his sentence of non-existence by claiming he saw Gabriel and had thus been converted to a new man. However, the ruse was unsuccessful **[T-SER5.2]**.

- **Galactic Warriors:** A game Cat and Lister played to pass the time aboard *Red Dwarf*, during which one would pretend to be Captain Laser **[T-SER3.5(d)]**.

- **Galilei, Galileo:** An Italian physicist, astronomer and mathematician of the seventeenth century, widely considered the "Father of Modern Science." Galileo supported the idea of heliocentrism and played a major role in the scientific revolution **[RL]**. Rimmer cited the scientist while defending his own obsession with a supposedly "alien" craft, claiming that people also laughed at Galileo's ideas. To Rimmer's chagrin, however, the craft turned out to be a simple garbage pod **[T-SER1.4]**.

- **Game head:** A slang term describing an individual addicted to the virtual-reality game *Better Than Life*. Game heads rarely survived for long; once they were plugged into the game, the program hid any trace of its artificial nature, fooling them into believing it was real and thus eliminating the desire to leave. As such, they eventually withered away and starved to death. Josie, a Game head with a degree in pure mathematics, survived solely due to the care of her boyfriend, a Bliss-addict named Denis **[N-INF]**.

- **Games Room:** A recreational area aboard *Nova 5*, located four decks above the ship's stasis chamber **[N-INF]**.

- **GameStation:** A video game console sold in the twenty-second century. Available games included *Super Carnage Smackdown* **[G-RPG]** and *Bazookoid Blaster* **[G-SOR]**.

  NOTE: *This system's name presumably spoofed that of Sony's PlayStation console.*

- **Gamma:** The third letter of the Greek alphabet **[RL]**, used in a code to disarm and unlock a groinal exploder a group of BEGGs had affixed to Lister's crotch. The code—Theta, Delta, Alpha, Beta, Gamma—had to be input precisely, in that order, for the device to be disabled **[T-SER10.4]**.

- **Gamma, Delta, 1 4 5:** A code that Kryten gave Lister so he could re-program the time gauntlet to use it against the Inquisitor **[T-SER5.2]**.

- **Gandalf:** A master wizard character in a text-based adventure game that Lister and Cat sometimes played aboard *Red Dwarf*. After Holly warned that a tarantula might be loose aboard the mining ship, Lister felt something crawl up his leg and into his shorts. Paralyzed with fear, he typed a plea for help to Cat, who thought he was playing the adventure game and suggested he buy a potion from Gandalf. The "tarantula" turned out to be a rescue bot sent by Kryten, who had been damaged during an accident on a psi-moon **[T-SER5.3]**.

  NOTE: *Gandalf is a wizard in J.R.R. Tolkien's Middle Earth novels,* The Hobbit, The Lord of the Rings *and* The Silmarillion.

- **Gandhi, Mohandas, Mahatma:** A spiritual Indian pacifist who employed non-violet civil disobedience and led his country to independence in the early twentieth century **[RL]**.

  While visiting themselves in the past, the time-traveling *Starbug 1* crew told their younger selves about the many historical figures—primarily rulers who had lived in complete opulence—with whom they'd partied. They remarked that no one wanted to party with Gandhi **[T-SER6.6(d)]**.

- **Gandhi, Mohandas, Mahatma:** A waxdroid replica of the spiritual leader, created for the Waxworld theme park. Left on their own for millions of years, the waxdroids attained sentience and became embroiled in a park-wide resource war between Villain World and Hero World (to which Gandhi belonged). During this war, the *Red Dwarf* crew transported to the planet using a Matter Paddle, with Lister and Cat materializing in

PREFIX
RL: Real life

T-: Television Episodes
SER: Television series
IDW: "Identity Within"
USA1: Unaired U.S. pilot
USA2: Unaired U.S. demo

R-: *The Bodysnatcher Collection*
SER: Remastered episodes
BOD: "Bodysnatcher"
DAD: "Dad"
FTH: "Lister's Father"
INF: "Infinity Patrol"
END: "The End" (original assembly)

N-: Novels
INF: *Infinity Welcomes Careful Drivers*
BTL: *Better Than Life*
LST: *Last Human*

BCK: *Backwards*
OMN: *Red Dwarf Omnibus*

M-: Magazines
SMG: *Smegazine*

W-: Websites
OFF: Official website
NAN: *Prelude to Nanarchy*
AND: *Androids*
DIV: Diva-Droid
DIB: Duane Dibbley

CRP: Crapola
GEN: Geneticon
LSR: Leisure World Intl.
JMC: Jupiter Mining Corporation
AIT: *A.I. Today*
HOL: HoloPoint

G-: Roleplaying Game
RPG: *Core Rulebook*
BIT: *A.I. Screen Extra Bits* booklet
SOR: *Series Sourcebook*
OTH: Other RPG material

Villain territory, while Rimmer and Kryten landed in Hero territory.

Rimmer found the heroes' army lacking and took command, then ordered an inspection, during which he singled out Gandhi as a troublemaker and demanded he do push-ups. Rimmer worked many of the pacifistic waxdroids to death before ordering a frontal attack on the enemy's compound across a minefield, which wiped out the remaining droids. Gandhi died upon stepping on a landmine **[T-SER4.6]**.

- **gangrene:** A medical condition caused by the lack of blood flow to a certain region of the body, resulting in tissue death **[RL]**. After having his leg crushed during an accident aboard *Starbug 1*, Cat was told he might get gangrene if not treated quickly. This news actually encouraged him, as green would go better with his outfit than the red of his blood **[T-SER4.5]**.

- **Gangrene Goddess, the:** The nickname of Necrobics instructor Diane Moron, who was featured on an episode of *Good Morning, Holograms* **[M-SMG1.7(a)]**.

- **GanPrep:** A secondary school located on Ganymede **[G-RPG]**.

- **Ganymede:** Jupiter's largest moon and the largest known satellite in Earth's solar system **[RL]**. The moon was mentioned in a song that also referenced Titan and Lunar City 7 **[T-SER1.2]**. Ganymede was the home of the Ganymedian Mafia **[N-INF]**, as well as Heinlein Base, the Space Corps' main installation in the outer system. It also contained offices of the Jupiter Mining Corporation. The moon spurred much of the underground activity throughout the outer planets **[G-RPG]**.

- **Ganymede Gold:** A standard color available for 4000 Series mechanoids in an alternate dimension. The exterior of that universe's Kryten was Ganymede Gold **[G-SOR]**.

- **Ganymede Holiday Inn:** A hotel chain located on the largest moon of Jupiter. Lister and Cat traveled through a stasis leak aboard *Red Dwarf* to find Kochanski, hoping to persuade her to use the spare stasis room before the cadmium II explosion. Her roommate told them that she was still on leave at the Ganymede Holiday Inn, so the duo traveled to the hotel, where they found Kristine in the Honeymoon Suite with a future version of Lister **[T-SER2.4]**.

  ***NOTE:** Holiday Inn is a multinational brand of hotels, part of the British InterContinental Hotels Group, with more than thirty-four hundred locations globally.*

- **Ganymede RadioShack:** An electronics store located on the Jovian moon of Ganymede. It stocked, among other things, hydrocarbon microfilters **[G-SOR]**.

  ***NOTE:** RadioShack is an American electronics retail chain with locations in the United States, Europe, South America and Africa.*

- **Ganymedian Mafia:** A criminal organization, also known as the Ganymede Mafia, that ran snail pits—arenas used for the bloodsport Toot—on moons across Earth's solar system, including on Phoebe, Dione and Rhea. George McIntyre incurred a massive debt to the Ganymedian Mafia playing Toot, forcing him to take out a loan with the Golden Assurance Friendly and Caring Loan Society. Unbeknownst to McIntyre, the Society was also run by the Ganymedian Mafia, who slapped him with a ninety-eight hundred percent annual percentage rate.

  Out of desperation, McIntyre agreed to meet representatives of the Society at the Mimas Hilton, but was force-fed his own nose by three burly men in suits when he refused to sign paperwork guaranteeing payment. Terrified, George retreated to his quarters aboard *Red Dwarf* and committed suicide **[N-INF]**.

  On Mimas, the Ganymedian Mafia—run by the Osmond Family and headed by Don Osmond—controlled the selling of the super-addictive drug Bliss. An astro named Dutch van Oestrogen once double-crossed the Mafia during a drug deal, causing them to pursue him across the moon **[M-SMG2.3(c4)]**.

- **Ganymedian monastery:** A religious sanctuary on Jupiter's moon, Ganymede, at which Lister enrolled himself as a novice monk during a night of heavy drinking with Olaf Petersen. While at the monastery, Lister discovered a heart-shaped tattoo on his right buttock, above the words "I Love Vindaloo" in dripping curry sauce **[T-SER6.1(d)]**.

- **gar:** A GELF word meaning heroic **[W-OFF]**.

B-: Books
PRG: *Red Dwarf Programme Guide*
SUR: *Red Dwarf Space Corps Survival Manual*
PRM: *Primordial Soup*
SOS: *Son of Soup*
SCE: *Scenes from the Dwarf*
LOG: *Red Dwarf Log No. 1996*
RD8: *Red Dwarf VIII*
EVR: *The Log: A Dwarfer's Guide to Everything*

X-: Misc.
PRO: Promotional materials, videos, etc.
PST: Posters at DJ XVII (2013)
CAL: 2008 calendar
RNG: Cell phone ringtones
MOB: Mobisode ("Red Christmas")
CIN: *Children in Need* sketch
GEK: *Geek Week* intros by Kryten
TNG: "Tongue-Tied" video

XMS: Bill Pearson's Christmas special pitch script
XVD: Bill Pearson's Christmas special pitch video
OTH: Other *Red Dwarf* appearances

SUFFIX
DVD:
(d) – Deleted scene
(o) – Outtake
(b) – Bonus DVD material (other)
(e) – Extended version

SMEGAZINES:
(c) – Comic
(a) – Article

OTHER:
(s) – Early/unused script draft
(s1) – Alternate version of script

- **garbage cannon:** A defensive weapon that Kryten devised aboard *Starbug 1*, utilizing a retrofitted waste-disposal unit in the cockpit armed with compacted garbage laced with nitroglycerin. The crew first tested it on a gargantuan meteor as *Starbug 1* traversed an asteroid field in pursuit of *Red Dwarf* **[T-SER6.1]**.

  Bloodlust Arms also created a garbage cannon, which was distributed via Crapola Inc.'s annual *SCABBY* catalog, and had an effective range of 1 kilometer (0.62 mile) **[G-RPG]**.

- **garbage pod:** A small container used by *Red Dwarf*'s waste-disposal personnel to remove trash from the mining ship. When the crew found an unidentified object in space, Rimmer instructed Holly to bring it aboard so he could analyze it, believing the craft to be an alien spaceship. Unbeknownst to him, Lister had secretly examined the craft and determined that it was merely one of their own previously jettisoned garbage pods, which had caught up with them over the years. Lister and Holly kept this to themselves, enjoying Rimmer's misguided excitement about the possibility of meeting alien life **[T-SER1.4]**. Garbage pods held 220 gallons of material and were fitted with a homing navigation system **[G-BIT]**.

- **garbage tanker:** A large vessel allocated for waste disposal. While scavenging two derelict garbage tankers, the *Red Dwarf* crew encountered mutated, living Peperami. After Cat disposed of the creatures by eating them, the crew found several items of use, including a box of Christmas crackers, a toilet roll holder in the shape of a flamenco dancer and five issues of *Playgelf* **[B-LOG]**.

- **Garbage World:** *See* Earth ("Garbage World")

- ***Gar Barge*:** One of several GELF ships sent into deep space as pioneers. Its name was derived from the GELF word "gar," meaning heroic, and "barge," meaning vessel. The *Gar Barge* contained several breeds of GELFs, including Alberogs, Snugiraffes and Kinitawowi. The ship crashed onto a planet in an area later claimed as GELF space **[W-OFF]**.

- **Garbunkley:** A famous balladeer, known for such hits as "Smidge Over Rubbled Slaughter." A zero-gee football scoring strategy was named after Garbunkley **[M-SMG1.8(a)]**.

  ***NOTE:** The name "Garbunkley" spoofed that of folk singer Art Garfunkel, whose songs included "Bridge Over Troubled Water."*

- **Garbunkley:** A zero-gee football scoring strategy named after the famous balladeer. In this maneuver, a member of a team's offensive front back-line quarter staff chewed on the ball while singing any of Garbunkley's hits. A two-hundred-point prize was awarded to the first zipman to sing "Smidge Over Rubbled Slaughter" and survive **[M-SMG1.8(a)]**.

- **Garby:** A garbage hauler aboard *Red Dwarf*. Garby, controlled by the artificial-intelligence computer Pree, pushed Lister out of the ship's airlock when his oxygen privileges were revoked. Pree later attempted to use the hauler to kill the crew as the ship careened toward a star **[T-SER10.2]**.

- **Garden of Remembrance:** A small, habitable dome extending from *Red Dwarf*'s hull, containing a memorial to crewmembers who had died in the line of duty. Lister regularly visited Kochanski's plaque in the Garden of Remembrance, believing she had perished in an airlock accident **[T-SER9.1]**.

  ***NOTE:** The Garden of Remembrance was not named in the episode, but was referenced as such online and in the DVD bonus materials, which also called it the Remembrance Garden. A photo of the late Mel Bibby,* Red Dwarf*'s production designer, was displayed to the left of Kochanski's photo on the memorial.*

- **garlic nan tree:** A fruit-bearing plant on the Vindaloovian homeworld that bore garlic-infused bread **[G-BIT]**.

- **Garrett, Talia:** A passenger aboard the Space Corps vessel SS *Hermes* **[T-SER8.8]**, and Captain Hollister's former personal fitness trainer **[T-SER8.8(d)]**.

  The *Hermes* was reconstructed by Kryten's nanobots around the same time *Red Dwarf* was rebuilt, but was dissolved shortly thereafter by a chameleonic microbe. Garrett—who had been resurrected by nanobots as well—fled the destruction, unknowingly entering the chameleonic microbe, which had disguised itself as an escape pod. *Red Dwarf* found the pod, reuniting her with Hollister—and dooming the mining vessel to the same fate as the *Hermes* **[T-SER8.8]**.

- **Garrett, Talia, Sister:** The personal spiritual advisor of Captain Rimmer aboard a mirror-universe *Red Dwarf* **[T-SER8.8]**. She played the harp and was a loyal follower of the Holy Order of St. Geraldine **[G-SOR]**.

  Sister Garrett encountered the prime universe's Rimmer when he crossed dimensions to find an antidote for a corrosive microbe that had infected his ship. Guided by his limited knowledge of his own reality's Garrett, Arnold kissed her, thinking she was the captain's lover—to which she recoiled in horror **[T-SER8.8]**.

  NOTE: *Based on her dialog, this Garrett appears to have come from the SS* Hermes *as well—or, at least, to have not been stationed on* Red Dwarf

- **Gary:** A character on the television soap opera *Androids*, portrayed by Android 72264/Y **[T-SER2.1]**. Gary and Brook first became rivals when they attended Mecha College together. This rivalry continued into the business world as Gary's oil company, GaryCo, competed with Brook's Droid Oil firm **[W-AND]**.

  Gary divorced his wife Kelly, who later married Brook, but continued to see her behind Brook's back. Kelly admitted to Brook that she'd had an affair with Gary, producing an illegitimate son (Brooke Junior), whom Brook had always assumed was his **[T-SER2.1]**. The affair continued for some time **[M-SMG1.10(c2)]**. In one episode, Gary was also tempted by a super-deluxe-model vacuum cleaner **[M-SMG1.7(a)]**.

  After being blackmailed by his business rival, Jaysee, Gary conspired with Kelly to murder him **[M-SMG1.13(c1)]**. Their plan backfired, however, when they accidentally destroyed Jaysee's spare "good" head instead **[M-SMG1.14(c3)]**. Jaysee retaliated by blowing up Gary's car while he and Kelly had sex in the back seat **[M-SMG2.1(c2)]**. The couple survived, albeit heavily damaged **[M-SMG2.2(c3)]**.

  Gary rebuilt himself using spare medical parts that he found at St. Android Hospital, and christened himself RoboGaz. He then drove his new car, the Gaz Mobile, to Jaysee's Headquarters, KICASS Tower, to confront his rival **[M-SMG2.5(c5)]**. There, he met several of Jaysee's other enemies, including Brook, Brooke Junior, Karstares, the Ionian Ecommandoes and Mollee, who attacked Jaysee simultaneously. RoboGaz barely survived the ensuing firefight, only to be shot and killed at point-blank range by Jaysee **[M-SMG2.7(c5)]**.

- **GaryCo:** An oil company owned by Gary on the television soap opera *Androids*. GaryCo was a direct competitor of Droid Oil, owned by Brook **[W-AND]**.

- **Gary ("Gazza"):** The bass guitarist of Lister's first band, Smeg and the Heads. Gary was a neo-Marxist nihilistic anarchist who eventually sold out by joining a large insurance company, where he received his own parking space **[T-SER3.5, B-SCE]**.

  NOTE: *Gazza's actual name, Gary, was revealed in the book* Scenes from the Dwarf. *In British English, "Gazza" is a common nickname for Gary.*

- **GAS:** *See* Genetic Alternative Sports (GAS)

- **"Gas Danger":** Words stenciled on a container stored aboard *Red Dwarf* near Airlock A. Rimmer took cover behind this crate during a firefight between his crewmates and Hudzen 10 **[T-SER3.6]**.

- **gas nebula:** A cloud of interstellar gas and dust **[RL]**. After attempting to catch up with the stolen *Red Dwarf* by cutting through an asteroid field, the *Starbug 1* crew discovered that the mining ship had entered a gas nebula, and followed it inside **[T-SER6.1]**.

- **Gate 14:** A gate at the Mimas Spaceport. A ship bound for Mars' Phobos Interplanetary Spaceport was boarding at Gate 14 as a chase ensued between Trixie LaBouche, Dutch van Oestrogen and the Ganymedian Mafia **[M-SMG2.5(c6)]**.

- **Gate 5:** A gate at the Mimas Central Shuttle Station. Shuttle flight JMC159, bound for *White Giant*, boarded at this gate **[N-INF]**.

- **Gate 9:** Another gate at the Mimas Central Shuttle Station. Lister boarded a shuttle bound for *Red Dwarf* at this gate **[N-INF]**.

- **Gatoo:** A form of payment on Blerios 15, a GELF settlement in an alternate universe. The fine for entering Blerios airspace without permission was five bars of Gatoo—the equivalent of two hundred barrels of oil or four milliliters of sperm **[N-LST]**.

B-: Books
PRG: *Red Dwarf Programme Guide*
SUR: *Red Dwarf Space Corps Survival Manual*
PRM: *Primordial Soup*
SOS: *Son of Soup*
SCE: *Scenes from the Dwarf*
LOG: *Red Dwarf Log No. 1996*
RD8: *Red Dwarf VIII*
EVR: *The Log: A Dwarfer's Guide to Everything*

X-: Misc.
PRO: Promotional materials, videos, etc.
PST: Posters at DJ XVII (2013)
CAL: 2008 calendar
RNG: Cell phone ringtones
MOB: Mobisode ("Red Christmas")
CIN: *Children in Need* sketch
GEK: *Geek Week* intros by Kryten
TNG: "Tongue-Tied" video

XMS: Bill Pearson's Christmas special pitch script
XVD: Bill Pearson's Christmas special pitch video
OTH: Other *Red Dwarf* appearances

SUFFIX
DVD:
(d) – Deleted scene
(o) – Outtake
(b) – Bonus DVD material (other)
(e) – Extended version

SMEGAZINES:
(c) – Comic
(a) – Article

OTHER:
(s) – Early/unused script draft
(s1) – Alternate version of script

- **GAWM:** *See* genetically augmented winged mutation (GAWM)

- **Gay Gordons, the:** An old-time dance popular at Gaelic social gatherings **[RL]**. Kryten thought the games of dominoes he played against Lister were purely ceremonial, like the Gay Gordons, given how easy it was to memorize the tiles **[T-IDW]**.

- **Gaz:** A character on the television soap opera *Androids*. In one episode, Gaz attended a barbeque hosted by Daz, during which a family pet, Bouncer, was lost in a temporal-displacement vortex **[M-SMG1.8(c2)]**.

- **Gaz Mobile, the:** An automobile owned by Gary's alter ego, RoboGaz, on the television soap opera *Androids*. After his business rival Jaysee tried to kill him, Gary built himself a body out of spare medical parts found at St. Android Hospital and christened himself RoboGaz. He then drove the Gaz Mobile to Jaysee's Headquarters, KICASS Tower, to confront his rival **[M-SMG2.5(c5)]**.

- **gazpacho soup:** A tomato-based vegetable soup, commonly served cold **[RL]**. "Gazpacho soup" was the last phrase Rimmer spoke before his death in the cadmium II explosion aboard *Red Dwarf*. Three million years later, when faced with deactivation, Rimmer confided the phrase's meaning to Lister: After having served with the Jupiter Mining Corp. for fourteen years, Arnold had finally been invited to sit at the captain's table with six other officers on Gazpacho Soup Day, which he considered a momentous occasion. Unaware that gazpacho soup was served cold, he demanded the waiter bring it back to the kitchen and return it hot. He later blamed his failure to rise up in the ranks on this humiliation **[T-SER1.6]**.

  ***NOTE:** The novel* Infinity Welcomes Careful Drivers *indicated that Rimmer had been with JMC for only five months when he received the invitation, contradicting the onscreen figure of fourteen years.*

- **Gazpacho Soup Day:** A day to which Rimmer attributed to the downfall of his career. It was on this day—November 25, six weeks prior to the cadmium II disaster—that Rimmer was invited to dine at the captain's table **[T-SER1.6]**.

  For the occasion, Rimmer attempted to hire an escort on Ganymede, so as not to look foolish by attending alone, but she abandoned him after he had spent a fortune on her dress **[N-INF]**. Unaware that gazpacho soup was meant to be served cold, he demanded the waiter bring it back to the kitchen and return it hot—an action that humiliated him, and on which he later blamed his failure to earn a promotion **[T-SER1.6]**.

  ***NOTE:** Since the cadmium II accident occurred only six weeks later, it is unclear why Rimmer would attribute his failed career to the gazpacho soup snafu. The novel* Infinity Welcomes Careful Drivers *eliminated this problem by indicating that Rimmer had only been with the company for five months when he attended the dinner.*

- **Gazza:** *See* Gary ("Gazza")

- **GBH:** An acronym short for "grievous bodily harm," used as a technical term in British criminal law **[RL]**. After materializing on Waxworld, Rimmer and Kryten were captured by waxdroids of Elvis Presley and Pope Gregory XIII. When threatened by Gregory, Rimmer asked Kryten if the Pope was, by any chance, the patron saint of GBH **[T-SER4.6(d)]**.

  Birdman, an inmate of *Red Dwarf's* secret brig, was sentenced to twenty years in the facility for GBH **[W-OFF]**.

- **G Deck:** A level within *Red Dwarf* containing Parrot's Bar, a tropical-themed club to which Kryten took Camille, a Pleasure GELF, during their date **[T-SER4.1]**. This deck also contained a coffee machine (which divulged classified information to crewmembers concerning the revival of the ship and crew by nanobots) **[T-SER8.1]**, as well as several large water tanks **[T-SER9.1]**. Hogey the Roguey triggered a security breach on this deck after boarding *Red Dwarf* **[T-SER10.6]**.

- **GEAP:** *See* genetically engineered adaptable pet (GEAP)

- **gee-gook:** A measurement of distance pertaining to space travel **[T-SER6.2]**.

  ***NOTE:** This spelling appeared in the novel* Last Human; *the DVD captions spelled it "Gigook." According to the DVD commentary for the episode, gee-gook stood for "gobbledygook."*

PREFIX **RL:** Real life **T-: Television Episodes** **SER:** Television series **IDW:** "Identity Within" **USA1:** Unaired U.S. pilot **USA2:** Unaired U.S. demo	**R-: *The Bodysnatcher Collection*** **SER:** Remastered episodes **BOD:** "Bodysnatcher" **DAD:** "Dad" **FTH:** "Lister's Father" **INF:** "Infinity Patrol" **END:** "The End" (original assembly) **N-: Novels** **INF:** *Infinity Welcomes Careful Drivers* **BTL:** *Better Than Life* **LST:** *Last Human*	**BCK:** *Backwards* **OMN:** *Red Dwarf Omnibus* **M-: Magazines** **SMG:** *Smegazine* **W-: Websites** **OFF:** Official website **NAN:** *Prelude to Nanarchy* **AND:** *Androids* **DIV:** Diva-Droid **DIB:** Duane Dibbley	**CRP:** Crapola **GEN:** Geneticon **LSR:** Leisure World Intl. **JMC:** Jupiter Mining Corporation **AIT:** *A.I. Today* **HOL:** HoloPoint **G-: Roleplaying Game** **RPG:** *Core Rulebook* **BIT:** *A.I. Screen Extra Bits* booklet **SOR:** *Series Sourcebook* **OTH:** Other RPG material

- **Geek Week:** A promotional event on YouTube that ran from August 4-10, 2013, highlighting videos in various science fiction and fantasy genres **[RL]**. Kryten recorded several promotional videos for the online event, which he transmitted back in time to YouTube, to introduce each day's topic **[X-GEK]**.

- **Geldof:** A measurement of time, much like a Gregorian calendar month, used on Earth sometime after *Red Dwarf* left the solar system. A vid tape stored in a postal pod found by the crew contained a news broadcast dated Friday, the 27th of Geldof **[T-SER2.2]**.

  NOTE: *This may have been a reference to Irish singer-songwriter Bob Geldof, an activist and founder of the charity group Band Aid, implying that a calendar month may have been renamed to honor his accomplishments.*

- **GELF:** *See* genetically engineered life form (GELF)

- **GELF battle cruiser:** A type of Kinitawowi spacefaring vessel with a skull-shaped hull. When Lister abandoned his GELF bride, Hackhackhackachhachhachach, the Kinitawowi hunted down *Starbug 1* using a GELF battle cruiser. The attack severed a passageway the crew had established to connect to a parallel dimension, stranding that reality's Kochanski in the prime universe. Thanks to Kristine's fancy piloting, the GELF cruiser then crashed on an ice planet **[T-SER7.3]**.

- **GELF hooch:** A strong alcoholic concoction, similar to moonshine, brewed by certain GELF tribes. Lister drank GELF hooch to kill the pain of his dental cavity **[T-SER10.2]**.

- **GELF-hunters:** Specialized mercenaries (also known as GELF-runners) hired during the GELF War to root out and capture genetically engineered life forms who had gone into hiding or had joined resistance groups **[N-BTL]**.

- **GELF icon:** A large stone structure in space, approximately a mile across, carved out of solid rock in the shape of a GELF skull, to mark the boundary of GELF territory. Pursued by a Space Corps external enforcement vehicle, *Starbug 1* fled toward GELF space, encountering an icon transmitting a warning to trespassers. Despite the message, the crew flew into the skull's eye socket. The enforcement probe fired a pulse missile that detonated inside the icon, destroying it and enabling *Starbug* to escape **[T-SER6.4]**.

- **GELF Quarters:** A section of the *Mayflower* housing the ship's complement of specially bred GELFs **[N-LST]**.

- **GELF racing:** An attraction featured at genetic engineering convention Geneticon 12 **[W-GEN]**.

- **GELF-runners:** *See* GELF-hunters

- **GELF's Head, The:** A drinking establishment at which Olaf Petersen once overheard on officer discussing *Red Dwarf*, inspiring him to sign up for a tour of duty with the Jupiter Mining Corp. **[W-OFF]**.

- ***GELFs Win Prizes*:** An American television game show hosted by Bing Baxter **[W-OFF]**.

- **GELF Transporter:** A type of spaceship designed to carry twenty thousand GELFs in stasis. A female polymorph posing as the *Red Dwarf* came across such a vessel and incorporated the GELFs into its engineering section, keeping the creatures in a constant state of pain and fear so it could sustain itself on their emotions **[M-SMG2.7(c1)]**.

- **GELF War:** A conflict sparked by a rebellion on the tourist hotspot GELFWorld. The rebellion began when Drigg, a half-man, half-amorphous-blob GELF, incited GELFWorld's citizens to rise up against the tourists, whom he felt degraded them. After killing or ousting all visitors, the GELFs then turned against each other, launching a GELF War that ended with the planet's destruction **[M-SMG2.2(c4)]**.

- **GELF War, The:** A conflict in the twenty-second century between humans and genetically engineered life forms that began with a GELF rebellion on Earth, triggered by a GELF Volkswagen Beetle and vacuum cleaner taking hostages during a bank robbery in Salzburg. The GELFs demanded justice be brought to Valter Holman, a man who murdered his GELF armchair upon discovering it making love to his wife.

  When the courts handed down a light six-month sentence

GELFS

to Holman, the GELF population declared war on humanity. Most GELFs died during the short conflict, with some going into hiding or starting resistance groups. GELF-hunters were employed to root out and capture the remaining GELFs, who were exiled on the island of Zanzibar just prior to Earth being designated "Garbage World" **[N-BTL]**.

- **GELFWorld:** A recreational tourist planet populated by Pleasure GELFs, a type of genetically engineered life form (GELF) created to provide companionship. It included such areas as the Cuddly Animal Theme Park. The planet's facilities closed when a dissident named Drigg launched a GELF uprising, resulting in the slaughter or ousting of all tourists, and forcing Earth to quarantine GELFWorld. The GELFs, unable to quell their thirst for violence, soon turned against each other, launching a GELF War that culminated in the planet's destruction **[M-SMG2.2(c4)]**.

- **GELF Zone:** An area of space inhabited by several GELF tribes and marked with a GELF icon—a huge rock carved to resemble a GELF skull. An attacking Space Corps enforcement vehicle, upon catching the *Starbug 1* crew looting Space Corps derelicts, forced the shuttle to enter the GELF Zone, where they encountered a tribe of Kinitawowi GELFs **[T-SER6.4]**.

- ***Gemini 12*:** A Space Corps TTX-3 experimental craft **[G-SOR]** containing a time drive developed in the twenty-eighth century **[T-SER7.1]**. Its maiden voyage was to the twentieth century, where the crew contracted an influenza virus and died. In their final moments, the crew set the autopilot for deep space and laid a reality minefield around the vessel to discourage looters. Years later, the *Starbug 1* crew found *Gemini 12* and stripped out the drive, installing it aboard their own shuttle **[T-SER6.6]**.

  ***NOTE:** Although it had appeared in episode 6.6 ("Out of Time"),* Gemini 12 *was not actually named until episode 7.1 ("Tikka to Ride").*

- **Gendarme of St. Tropez:** *See* Captain Emerald

- **Genepool Biotech Corp BioSafe Genetic Waste Pod:** A small capsule for disposing of hazardous biological specimens **[G-SOR]**. One such pod was used to contain two polymorphs, emitting a warning transmission with the words "Danger," "Genetic Waste," "Do Not Open" and "Contents: 2" prominently written on its casing. During transit through deep space, this capsule became compromised, allowing its occupants to escape aboard *Red Dwarf.* One polymorph attacked the crew, consuming their emotions until it was killed by heat-seeking bazookoid missiles **[T-SER3.3]**. The other polymorph escaped detection, eventually leaving the ship and configuring itself as an exact duplicate of the mining vessel **[M-SMG2.6(c1)]**.

- **General A. J. Smegger:** A nickname that Lister called Rimmer when the hologram became obsessed with squashing a skutter strike **[M-SMG1.4(c1)]**.

- **General Assembly 4:** A meeting of executive personnel aboard *Red Dwarf.* Rimmer ordered Holly to summon Lister to attend General Assembly 4 so he could conduct a roll call of the ship's entire complement—despite all but one of them being dead **[R-BOD]**.

- **General Custer Forward Thinking Award:** A hypothetical commendation that Rimmer pretended to award to Kochanski for her plan of attack at the Cyberia virtual-reality prison on Lotomi 5. The plan involved using the Oblivion virus to kill all electricity across the entire moon, enabling Lister to rescue his doppelgänger from the complex. A side effect of the power outage, however, was that the gravity generator failed, making movement on the planetoid very difficult **[N-LST]**.

  ***NOTE:** Cavalry officer General George Armstrong Custer launched his disastrous "Last Stand" against Native American forces in 1876, displaying a distinct lack of forward thinking.*

- ***General George and the Gook Invasion*:** A book written by Colonel Mike O'Hagan, a Space Marine and author of the *Space Corps Survival Manual* **[B-SUR]**.

  ***NOTE:** Given its title, this book was presumably about Major General George Patton IV, a prominent officer during the Vietnam War.*

- **generator:** A component aboard *Starbug 1* that produced power for the shuttle. Jealous of Lister's affection for Kochanski, Kryten overloaded the generator and emergency backup in order to prevent her from bathing in Dave's quarters **[T-SER7.4]**.

- **Generosity:** An aspect of Rimmer's personality that a psi-moon detected as being essentially dead, prompting the planetoid to construct a metaphorical tombstone in its memory. According to the stone's inscription, his generosity died when he was nine years old **[T-SER5.3]**.

- **GeneStick pistol grip:** A technology utilized in the handle of Nova auto pistols, produced by Bloodlust Arms **[G-RPG]**.

- **genetically augmented winged mutation (GAWM):** A type of flying life form engineered in the universe known as Alternative 2X13/L **[M-SMG2.1(c3)]**.

- **genetically engineered adaptable pet (GEAP):** A creature artificially created to be the perfect pet for humans. Approximately the size and shape of a teddy bear, GEAPs possessed a telepathic ability to influence people to love and protect them at all costs. This caused many conflicts over the GEAPs, resulting in several wars and the destruction of planets. As such, GEAPs were banned.

  One such creature was placed in a stasis pod and shot into deep space, where the *Red Dwarf* crew found it millions of years later. Upon being released from stasis, the GEAP telepathically controlled Lister, who threatened anyone attempting to take it from him (including Cat, who wanted to eat it). The hostility spread across the ship, damaging the Drive Room and other areas, until Kryten outsmarted Lister, retrieved the animal, returned it to stasis and shot it back into space **[M-SMG1.6(c1)]**.

- **genetically engineered life form (GELF):** Any of various beings created artificially via genetic manipulation rather than through natural selection **[T-SER4.1]**. Humans engineered several types of GELFs for different purposes, either intentionally or randomly through accelerated evolution. Examples include polymorphs **[T-SER3.3]**, Pleasure GELFs **[T-SER4.1]**, the despair squid **[T-SER5.6]**, Psirens **[T-SER6.1]**, Kinitawowi, emohawks **[T-SER6.4]**, the elation squid **[T-SER9.3]**, BEGGs **[T-SER10.4]**, Brefewino **[T-IDW]**, Dolochimps, Snugiraffes, Alberogs, Dingotangs and symbimorphs **[N-LST]**.

  GELFs were first created for use in sports, after humans had perfected warfare, rendering it obsolete. Advances in GELF technology used to breed athletes for the Genetic Alternative Sports (GAS) carried into other avenues of human life as well, producing such creatures as living cars, massaging chairs and vacuums that doubled as household pets.

  For years, GELFs were denied the rights and privileges afforded normal humans, until a GELF rebellion sparked when a Volkswagen Beetle and a vacuum cleaner took hostages during a bank robbery in Salzburg. These GELFs demanded that justice be brought to Valter Holman, a man who killed his genetically engineered armchair upon discovering it making love to his wife. When the courts handed down a light six-month sentence to Holman, the GELF population revolted, launching the so-called GELF War.

  Most GELFs died during the conflict; those captured were exiled on the island of Zanzibar, just before Earth was designated "Garbage World" and abandoned by humanity. Many of the survivors eventually died out, but a scant few survived, evolving over the course of millennia into polymorphs—shape-changing creatures that fed on emotions **[N-BTL]**.

  Some GELFs, like the Dolochimps, Snugiraffes, Alberogs and Dingotangs, were sent to another galaxy to terraform a new planet for the human species, but ended up careening through the Omni-zone after rebelling against the human crew. They emerged in another universe, where they populated an asteroid belt and created a virtual-reality prison called Cyberia **[N-LST]**. Certain GELFs, especially those in the GELF Zone (the Kinitawowi, for example), were lawless scavengers with no regard for life or property **[T-SER6.4]**.

- **Genetic Alternative Sports (GAS):** A sports league formed at the beginning of the twenty-second century to accommodate genetically enhanced and mutated competitors banned from regular sporting events. It included such sports as boxing, basketball, soccer, swimming and American football, and featured athletes genetically customized to their particular sport. Technological advances made for GAS paved the way for research into customized GELF products, such as self-driving living cars, massaging armchairs and vacuum cleaners that doubled as family pets **[N-BTL]**.

- ***Genetic Cloning Manual*:** A book supplied with genetic equipment stored aboard a colonization seeding ship pod. Rimmer studied the manual while stranded on an uninhabited world, hoping to create a female mate for himself. His attempts failed, however, instead creating many clones of himself, who summarily imprisoned him and took over the planet **[T-SER6.5]**.

- **Geneticon 12:** A convention held at the Titan Hilton on June 11-13, for fans of genetic engineering and its creations. Sponsored by Leisure World International, the conference included a Clone-a-Friend booth, GELF racing, a disco, karaoke and special guest Augustus Malaka **[W-GEN]**.

- **genetic waste pod:** *See* Genepool Biotech Corp BioSafe Genetic Waste Pod

- **Geneva Conventions, The:** A group of international treaties and protocols outlining wartime humanitarian policies and the rights of prisoners of war **[RL]**. Kochanski insisted the lack of wine available in *Red Dwarf*'s prison violated the Geneva Conventions **[T-SER8.1-3(e)]**. Years later, the *Red Dwarf* crew surrendered to a Simulant Death Ship as prisoners of war, according to Treaty 5 of the Geneva Conventions, as part of an escape plan devised by Rimmer **[T-SER10.6]**.

  NOTE: *At present, the Geneva Conventions comprise four treaties. Apparently, a fifth treaty was added sometime in the future.*

- **genitometer:** A torture device utilizing non-slip rubber handles, used by Doctors Maxwell, Pension and Fund in a hallucination Cat suffered after receiving a bump to the head. Cat believed he was once again Duane Dibbley, and that the three doctors were experimenting on him. In actuality, the trio were Lister, Rimmer and Kryten, who were attempting to revive him using lithium carbonate **[M-SMG1.9(c1)]**.

- **genome of DNA (G.O.D.):** A storehouse of all known Earth DNA types. When scientists discovered the lifespan of Earth's Sun had been reduced to four hundred thousand years due to mankind's tampering, the World Council launched a spaceship called the *Mayflower* to the Andromeda Galaxy, to use G.O.D. to terraform a world as humanity's new home.

  The *Mayflower*, containing G.O.D. and several varieties of GELF, strayed off course after a mutiny knocked out the navigational controls, forcing the ship into the Omni-zone, where it emerged in an alternate universe and crashed onto a lava planet. Those who survived fled in escape pods, populating a nearby asteroid belt to form the United Republic of GELF States.

  To protect the location of the marooned vessel, the four main GELF species (Dolochimps, Snugiraffes, Alberogs and Dingotangs) split the coordinates of the wreckage between them, ensuring that no one species could access G.O.D. and the unlimited power it enabled **[N-LST]**.

- **Gentleman Gym's:** A health club located aboard *Red Dwarf* **[M-SMG1.4(c2)]**.

- ***Geoff Love's Favourite Themes from the War Movies*:** An album containing a collection of soundtrack music from several war films, orchestrated by British composer Geoff Love. Rimmer once played this album in his quarters at full volume at 5:00 AM, which infuriated Lister, who was recuperating from a hangover **[M-SMG1.2(a)]**.

  NOTE: *In the real world, Love did not release an album by this name, though he did record one titled* Geoff Love and His Orchestra Play Big War Movie Themes.

- **Geology Lab:** A room aboard *Red Dwarf* allocated for geological research. Lister consulted with Holly in the Geology Lab about how best to mine thorium to produce uraniun-233, necessary to power *Nova 5*'s Duality Jump **[N-INF]**.

- **George III, King:** The ruler of Great Britain at the time of the American Revolution, often dubbed "The Mad King" **[RL]**. Frustrated at how useless Kryten and Cat were in assisting him with a mining operation, Lister decided that only George III and Brian Kidd would have been more inept **[N-INF]**.

  NOTE: *The* Red Dwarf Omnibus *changed this to King Havac the Imbecile and his more idiotic half-brother.*

- **George and Dragon:** *See* Nogard dna Egroeg

- ***George of the Jungle*:** A 1997 American comedy film starring Brendan Fraser, based on the same-named 1967 animated TV series **[RL]**. After Queeg demoted Holly to *Red Dwarf*'s night watchman, Holly attended a viewing of the movie during his rounds, enabling space weevils to ransack eight sacks of grain while he slacked off. All of this, however, was merely a ruse to punish the crew for doubting his abilities **[W-OFF]**.

- **Gerald:** A hypothetical individual of wealth whom Lister imagined knowing, while contemplating how his life might have changed due to his having once visited a wine bar. Had he continued down that path, he told Kryten, he might have ended up playing squash every Tuesday with "a guy named Gerald" **[T-SER4.2]**.

- **Gerbil-Face:** A nickname Cat called Lister, referencing his pudgy cheeks **[T-SER4.4]**.

B-: Books
PRG: *Red Dwarf Programme Guide*
SUR: *Red Dwarf Space Corps Survival Manual*
PRM: *Primordial Soup*
SOS: *Son of Soup*
SCE: *Scenes from the Dwarf*
LOG: *Red Dwarf Log No. 1996*
RD8: *Red Dwarf VIII*
EVR: *The Log: A Dwarfer's Guide to Everything*

X-: Misc.
PRO: Promotional materials, videos, etc.
PST: Posters at DJ XVII (2013)
CAL: 2008 calendar
RNG: Cell phone ringtones
MOB: Mobisode ("Red Christmas")
CIN: *Children in Need* sketch
GEK: *Geek Week* intros by Kryten
TNG: "Tongue-Tied" video

XMS: Bill Pearson's Christmas special pitch script
XVD: Bill Pearson's Christmas special pitch video
OTH: Other *Red Dwarf* appearances

SUFFIX
DVD:
(d) – Deleted scene
(o) – Outtake
(b) – Bonus DVD material (other)
(e) – Extended version

SMEGAZINES:
(c) – Comic
(a) – Article

OTHER:
(s) – Early/unused script draft
(s1) – Alternate version of script

- **"Geronimo":** An exclamation typically used by those heading into dangerous situations, based on the name that Mexican soldiers dubbed Goyathlay, the Bedonkohe Apache tribe's leader during the Apache Wars **[RL]**. Rimmer yelled "Geronimo" while having sex with Nirvanah Crane aboard the holoship *Enlightenment* **[T-SER5.1]**.

- **"Get Naughty":** An online game at Diva-Droid International's website, the object of which was to set all buttons to zero **[W-DIV]**.

  NOTE: *The game's name was a pun created from the word "naught," which means zero.*

- **G-force Modification Field:** A component of Ace Rimmer's ship, *Wildfire One*, used to adjust the gravitational forces affecting the pilot **[N-BCK]**.

- **GG 300:** The license plate number of the Lincoln Continental in which President John F. Kennedy and his wife, Jacqueline Kennedy Onassis, were traveling at the time of his 1963 assassination **[RL, T-SER7.1]**.

- **Giancana, Sam:** A well-publicized American mobster and boss of the Chicago Outfit, circa the late 1950s and early 1960s **[RL]**. In an alternate timeline, President John F. Kennedy survived an assassination attempt due to the interference of *Starbug 1*'s crew and went on to have an affair with Giancana's mistress, for which Kennedy was impeached in 1964 and sent to prison a year later **[T-SER7.1]**.

- **giant space weevil:** A large species of insectoid vermin. Though found throughout the galaxy, giant space weevils were relatively rare, preferring the dark corners of ships and colonies **[G-RPG]**.

- **Gibson ("Squeaky"):** A child at the orphanage at which Lister lived as a youth. Gibson earned his nickname from the sound his bed made when he shook, which other boys mistook for masturbating. One night during a power outage, Lister ran over to stop the squeaking, only to discover Squeaky having an epileptic seizure **[T-SER7.4(e)]**.

- **Gideons International, The:** A Christian organization that distributed Bibles to hotels, hospitals, prisons and students **[RL]**. When a Gideons Bible arrived at Lister's prison cell in the Tank, *Red Dwarf*'s classified brig, Dave thought he was being followed by a man named Gideon, as he had found other copies of the book at two hotel rooms in which he'd previously stayed **[T-SER8.3]**.

- **Gigante-Volkswagen:** A manufacturer of ship-to-surface craft such as the *White Midget* shuttle. The company's plant was located in Mexico City. Gigante-Volkswagen was commissioned to produce five thousand *White Midget* shuttles for the Space Corps, but due to designs flaws—including overheating and electrical problems—the Corps ended its contract after delivery of only seventy-five units. The surplus shuttles eventually made their way into the public sector **[G-SOR]**.

- **Gigook:** *See* gee-gook

- **Gilbert:** *See* Ostrog, Gilbert St. John McAdam

- **Gilbert:** A former acquaintance of Kryten who suffered from computer senility. Due to the affliction, the mechanoid insisted on calling himself "Rameses Niblick III Kerplunk Kerplunk Whoops Where's My Thribble" **[T-SER4.4]**.

- **Gill, Anne, Mapping Officer:** A brunette crewmember aboard the Earth ship *Nova 5* who survived the vessel's crash, along with two other female officers and a mechanoid named Kryten. Despite recovering from the impact, she died sometime later—unbeknownst to Kryten, who continued serving her and the others long after their deaths. At the time of her last registered medical record, Gill was twenty-four years old, stood five feet four inches (164 centimeters) tall and weighed forty-five G.V. Her medical details were stored on Prog Disc A49 **[T-SER2.1]**.

  NOTE: *Kryten referred to Gill as "Miss Anne" in the distress signal to* Red Dwarf.

- **gimboid:** A British slang term meaning idiot or simpleton **[RL]**. Rimmer sometimes called Lister a gimboid **[T-SER1.2]**.

  NOTE: *It is generally believed that the word was coined by* Red Dwarf, *which was responsible for its popular usage throughout England.*

PREFIX
RL: Real life

T-: Television Episodes
- **SER:** Television series
- **IDW:** "Identity Within"
- **USA1:** Unaired U.S. pilot
- **USA2:** Unaired U.S. demo

R-: *The Bodysnatcher Collection*
- **SER:** Remastered episodes
- **BOD:** "Bodysnatcher"
- **DAD:** "Dad"
- **FTH:** "Lister's Father"
- **INF:** "Infinity Patrol"
- **END:** "The End" (original assembly)

N-: Novels
- **INF:** *Infinity Welcomes Careful Drivers*
- **BTL:** *Better Than Life*
- **LST:** *Last Human*
- **BCK:** *Backwards*
- **OMN:** *Red Dwarf Omnibus*

M-: Magazines
- **SMG:** *Smegazine*

W-: Websites
- **OFF:** Official website
- **NAN:** *Prelude to Nanarchy*
- **AND:** *Androids*
- **DIV:** Diva-Droid
- **DIB:** Duane Dibbley
- **CRP:** Crapola
- **GEN:** Geneticon
- **LSR:** Leisure World Intl.
- **JMC:** Jupiter Mining Corporation
- **AIT:** *A.I. Today*
- **HOL:** HoloPoint

G-: Roleplaying Game
- **RPG:** *Core Rulebook*
- **BIT:** *A.I. Screen Extra Bits* booklet
- **SOR:** *Series Sourcebook*
- **OTH:** Other RPG material

- **git:** A derogatory British term for a silly, immature or annoying person **[RL]**. Rimmer often used this word to describe his companions **[T-SER1.2]**.

- **"Give Quiche a Chance":** A slogan on a T-shirt that Rimmer wore after a polymorph drained his anger **[T-SER3.3]**.

- **Glen Fujiyama:** A type of whisky produced in the twenty-second century. Olaf Petersen stowed several cans of the alcoholic beverage in his knapsack during his trip from Mimas to *Red Dwarf* **[N-INF]**.

- **Glenn, John:** An American astronaut and politician. Glenn was the third American in space and the first to orbit the Earth **[RL]**. When Rimmer boasted about his space qualifications, Lister commented that he was no John Glenn **[N-BCK]**.

- **Glen Tokyo Whisky:** An alcoholic beverage supplied aboard *Red Dwarf.* Lister imbibed the whisky while celebrating Rimmer's deathday, and still had a bottle the next day while completing a jigsaw puzzle **[T-SER2.3]**.

- **glimbart:** A hypothetical unit of time. While helping Lister search for uranium deposits on a moon, Holly claimed one glimbart equaled two nanoteks **[N-INF]**.

- **gloop:** A verb meaning to destroy something with a bazookoid. Rimmer urged Lister to gloop a crazed simulant pursuing the *Red Dwarf* crew throughout the penal station Justice World **[T-SER4.3]**.

- **GMC onboard computer:** *See* JMC onboard computer

- **"Go Ahead, Make My Day":** A phrase made famous by the 1983 film *Sudden Impact,* starring Clint Eastwood as belligerent cop "Dirty" Harry Callahan, who uttered the words to taunt criminals **[RL]**. A sticker above Lister's bunk in *Red Dwarf*'s Officers' Quarters contained this phrase **[T-SER5.1]**, as did another by his *Starbug 1* bunk **[T-SER7.4]**.

- **Goalpost-Head:** A nickname Cat called Rimmer, referencing the hologrammic "H" on his forehead, which vaguely resembled an American football goalpost **[T-SER2.6]**.

- **goat vindaloo:** An Indian culinary dish typically made with goat meat, tomatoes, garlic, chilies and various spices **[RL]**. Lister accidentally spilled goat vindaloo on Rimmer's revision timetable before he could use it to cram for his Engineer's Exam **[T-SER1.3]**.

- **God:** A deity worshipped as the universe's supreme creator in several terrestrial faiths **[RL]**. In the language of the Cat People, the name "Cloister" was synonymous with "God" **[T-SER1.4]**.

  On December 25, 2235, God appeared in New York to scold humanity for never sending Him a card or present. He then scoffed at mankind's current state and announced that he never wished to speak to anyone ever again **[B-EVR]**.

  As the *Red Dwarf* crew searched for a creature in G Deck's water tank, Rimmer, monitoring sonar, warned his crewmates that something "bigger than God" (an elation squid) was approaching **[T-SER9.1]**. While trapped in an addictive version of *Better Than Life*, Rimmer believed he had returned to Earth and become famously wealthy, hosting dinner parties that included many important guests—including God **[N-INF]**.

- **G.O.D.:** *See* genome of DNA (G.O.D.)

- ***God, I Love This War*:** One of Rimmer's favorites films, from which he paraphrased several lines of dialog while delivering an inspirational speech to Z-Shift about sonic super mops **[N-INF]**.

- **Godiva, Lady:** An eleventh-century noblewoman who protested her husband's oppressive taxation by riding through the streets of Coventry, England, wearing nothing but her long hair **[RL]**. When Kryten used a time wand to revert Kochanski's hair and clothes to those of a previous era, Cat remarked that she looked like Lady Godiva let loose in an Oxfam shop **[T-SER8.6(d)]**.

- **Go-Double-Plus:** A brand of caffeinated tablets sold aboard *Red Dwarf* to keep the crew alert and focused. Rimmer periodically overdosed on Go-Double-Plus pills while cramming for his Astronavigation Exam, after squandering most of his revision time creating revision timetables. He would then visit the Medical Unit for sedatives—which would put him to sleep, wasting even more time **[N-INF]**.

B-: Books
PRG: *Red Dwarf Programme Guide*
SUR: *Red Dwarf Space Corps Survival Manual*
PRM: *Primordial Soup*
SOS: *Son of Soup*
SCE: *Scenes from the Dwarf*
LOG: *Red Dwarf Log No. 1996*
RD8: *Red Dwarf VIII*
EVR: *The Log: A Dwarfer's Guide to Everything*

X-: Misc.
PRO: Promotional materials, videos, etc.
PST: Posters at DJ XVII (2013)
CAL: 2008 calendar
RNG: Cell phone ringtones
MOB: Mobisode ("Red Christmas")
CIN: *Children in Need* sketch
GEK: *Geek Week* intros by Kryten
TNG: "Tongue-Tied" video

XMS: Bill Pearson's Christmas special pitch script
XVD: Bill Pearson's Christmas special pitch video
OTH: Other *Red Dwarf* appearances

SUFFIX
DVD:
(d) – Deleted scene
(o) – Outtake
(b) – Bonus DVD material (other)
(e) – Extended version

SMEGAZINES:
(c) – Comic
(a) – Article

OTHER:
(s) – Early/unused script draft
(s1) – Alternate version of script

- **"God Rest Ye Merry, Gentlemen":** A traditional English Christmas carol **[RL]**. Lister imagined passing carolers singing this song in the town of Bedford Falls while trapped in an addictive version of *Better Than Life* **[N-INF]**. Later in the illusion, Lister brought his sons, Jim and Bexley, to enjoy a five-piece brass band playing the same tune **[N-BTL]**.

- **Goebbels, Paul Joseph:** A politician of Nazi Germany, and Adolf Hitler's Reich Minister of Propaganda **[RL]**.

  A waxdroid replica of Goebbels was created for the Waxworld theme park. Left on their own for millions of years, the waxdroids attained sentience and became embroiled in a park-wide resource war between Villain World (to which Goebbels belonged) and Hero World.

  During this war, the *Red Dwarf* crew transported to the planet using a Matter Paddle, with Lister and Cat materializing in Villain territory, while Rimmer and Kryten landed in Hero territory. Lister and Cat were captured by waxdroids of Hitler, Goebbels and Hermann Göring, and were thrown in prison to await execution.

  The duo escaped, however, and fled to Hero World. There, Rimmer detained them while training the heroes' army to attack Villain World. The ensuing battle destroyed every waxdroid on the planet, including Goebbels **[T-SER4.6]**.

- **go-fasta stripes:** An accessory on a spaceship owned by Ace "Blackheart" Rimmer **[M-SMG1.14(c5)]**.

- **go-faster stripes:** An accessory offered by Diva-Droid International for Hudzen 10 mechanoids **[G-SOR]**.

- ***Go for the Burn!*:** A fitness video featuring Joan of Arc, produced by the Transtemporal Film Unit **[B-LOG]**.

- **Go-Go Green:** A standard color available for Diva-Droid International's 4000 Series mechanoid **[G-RPG]**. Able's exterior was Go-Go Green **[T-SER7.6]**.

- ***Going for Chrome*:** A twenty-fourth-century android television game show that aired on Groovy Channel 27 at 9:30 AM on Wednesdays, featuring mechanoids from around the solar system competing in a variety of household chores **[M-SMG1.7(a)]**.

  ***NOTE:** This show's title spoofed that of British television game show* Going for Gold.

- **goit:** A derogatory term that Rimmer sometimes used to mock his *Red Dwarf* shipmates, implying they were silly, immature or annoying **[T-SER1.2]**.

- **G.O.J.F.:** An acronym devised by Rimmer, short for "Get On Just Famously," which he promised Z-Shift they'd do if they remembered to "Keep It Tidy" (K.I.T.) **[N-INF]**.

- **Golden Assurance Friendly and Caring Loan Society:** A loan company run by the Ganymedian Mafia. George McIntyre incurred a massive debt to the Mafia playing Toot, forcing him to take out a loan with the Golden Assurance Friendly and Caring Loan Society, unaware that it, too, was Mafia-run.

  After being slapped with a 9,800 percent annual percentage rate, McIntyre nervously agreed to meet representatives of the Society at the Mimas Hilton to discuss payment options, but was force-fed his own nose by three burly men in suits when he refused to sign paperwork guaranteeing payment. Terrified, George retreated to his quarters aboard *Red Dwarf* and committed suicide **[N-INF]**.

- **Golden Boy:** A racing pig that Lister gambled on during a wager with *Red Dwarf*'s Dispenser 55. Golden Boy lost the race, costing Lister $£100 **[T-SER10.1]**.

- **golden sausage:** An effigy that Lister, pretending to be Cloister the Stupid, held in the lair of a blind cat priest aboard *Red Dwarf*. It was approximately four feet long, golden-colored and shaped like a sausage. When the dying priest asked Cat if Cloister was wearing the "doughnut and golden sausage," Lister silently threatened Cat with the sausage if he said "no" **[T-SER1.4]**.

- **Golden Stripe of Honour:** A decoration awarded to officers of the Jupiter Mining Corp. for their years of distinguished service. Over the course of several years, Rimmer wrote dozens of letters to *Red Dwarf*'s onboard JMC computer, asking it to award him the decoration; this backfired, however, when the computer, researching Arnold's record, discovered he had not reported for duty throughout his hologrammatic existence.

As such, Rimmer was threatened with demotion unless he provided an explanation **[T-SER10.5]**.

- **Gold Oblong of Pluck:** A Space Corps medal that Rimmer told his half-brother, Howard, he had been awarded, after rescuing the latter from *Columbus 3* using the teleporters of the derelict vessel *Trojan* **[T-SER10.1]**.

    NOTE: *It is uncertain whether Rimmer actually earned this award, or if it even existed.*

- **golf:** A sport played using long clubs, the object of which was to hit a small ball into a series of holes in the fewest number of strokes **[RL]**. Lister and Cat played a round of golf while engaged in the total-immersion video game *Better Than Life*. Despite being adamant about knowing the rules of the game, Cat played incorrectly, throwing his club toward each hole instead of hitting the ball **[T-SER2.2]**. An annual golf tournament called the Kinitawowi Open was held on a GELF planet called Echech 3 **[G-RPG]**.

- **gonad electrocution kit:** A device that Rimmer, while trapped in an addictive version of *Better Than Life*, imagined his former gym teacher, Bull Heinman, finding particularly interesting. In the illusion, Heinman was engaging in his seventh read-through of the article "Ten Things You Didn't Know About Gonad Electrocution Kits," published in *Combat and Survival* magazine **[N-BTL]**.

- **"Gone Out":** A message displayed over Lister's bunk aboard *Red Dwarf* **[T-SER1.2]**.

- ***Gone with the Wind*:** A 1939 American historical romance film based on Margaret Mitchell's same-named novel, starring Vivien Leigh and Clark Gable, with a running time of 238 minutes **[RL]**. Kochanski used up an entire box of tissues the first time she watched the film **[T-SER7.8]**.

    As Lister, Rimmer and Cat traveled in one of *Red Dwarf*'s Xpress Lifts to Floor 16, a video screen in the elevator offered occupants the ability to watch the classic movie en route to their destination, for a small fee **[T-SER2.4]**. While downloading Rimmer's neuroses into his light bee, Kryten commented that the process took longer than a viewing of *Gone with the Wind* **[N-LST]**.

- **"Good-bye-ee":** A popular World War I wartime song composed by R. P. Weston and Bert Lee **[RL]**. Hudzen 10, a crazed mechanoid sent by Diva-Droid International to replace Kryten aboard *Red Dwarf*, sang this tune while attacking the crew after they refused to shut Kryten down **[T-SER3.6]**.

- **"Goodbye to Love":** A song recorded by twentieth-century music duo The Carpenters **[RL]**. Holly sang this tune while seemingly being erased by Queeg, *Red Dwarf*'s backup computer. Queeg, however, was actually just an alter ego that Holly created to punish the crew for treating him badly **[T-SER2.5]**.

- **Good Mood:** A perfume created by Hildegarde Lanstrom for her product line, Parfum by Lanstrom. The fragrance incorporated a positive strain of virus she developed **[X-CAL]**.

    NOTE: *Given the nature of the viruses Lanstrom was studying, Good Mood presumably caused wearers, or those around them, to experience happiness.*

- ***Good Morning Holograms*:** A morning entertainment television program geared toward the dead, which aired daily on Groovy Channel 27 at 6:00 AM. An episode that aired on Wednesday, the 27th of Geldof, 2362, featured hologrammic guests William Shakespeare and Henry VIII, and also offered necrobics with Diane Moron, the Gangrene Goddess **[M-SMG1.7(a)]**.

- **Good Knight, the:** A character in the medieval AR simulation *Camelot*. While playing the game, Lister challenged the Good Knight to a joust, attempting to win a night with the Queen of Camelot. To aid in his quest, Lister utilized several cheats, one of which reduced the Good Knight's steed to a donkey, allowing Lister to behead his foe and bed the queen.

    Later, in the real world, Lister assumed the guise of the Good Knight in order to convince Rimmer he was brave enough to take over for Ace, who had passed the torch over to him **[T-SER7.2]**.

    NOTE: *Where Lister got a full set of medieval armor from is anyone's guess.*

- ***Good Psycho Guide*:** A hypothetical publication that Lister considered writing, in which he planned to give Legion and his research station rave reviews, with excellent marks for

B-: Books
PRG: *Red Dwarf Programme Guide*
SUR: *Red Dwarf Space Corps Survival Manual*
PRM: *Primordial Soup*
SOS: *Son of Soup*
SCE: *Scenes from the Dwarf*
LOG: *Red Dwarf Log No. 1996*
RD8: *Red Dwarf VIII*
EVR: *The Log: A Dwarfer's Guide to Everything*

X-: Misc.
PRO: Promotional materials, videos, etc.
PST: Posters at DJ XVII (2013)
CAL: 2008 calendar
RNG: Cell phone ringtones
MOB: Mobisode ("Red Christmas")
CIN: *Children in Need* sketch
GEK: *Geek Week* intros by Kryten
TNG: "Tongue-Tied" video

XMS: Bill Pearson's Christmas special pitch script
XVD: Bill Pearson's Christmas special pitch video
OTH: Other *Red Dwarf* appearances

SUFFIX
DVD:
(d) – Deleted scene
(o) – Outtake
(b) – Bonus DVD material (other)
(e) – Extended version

SMEGAZINES:
(c) – Comic
(a) – Article

OTHER:
(s) – Early/unused script draft
(s1) – Alternate version of script

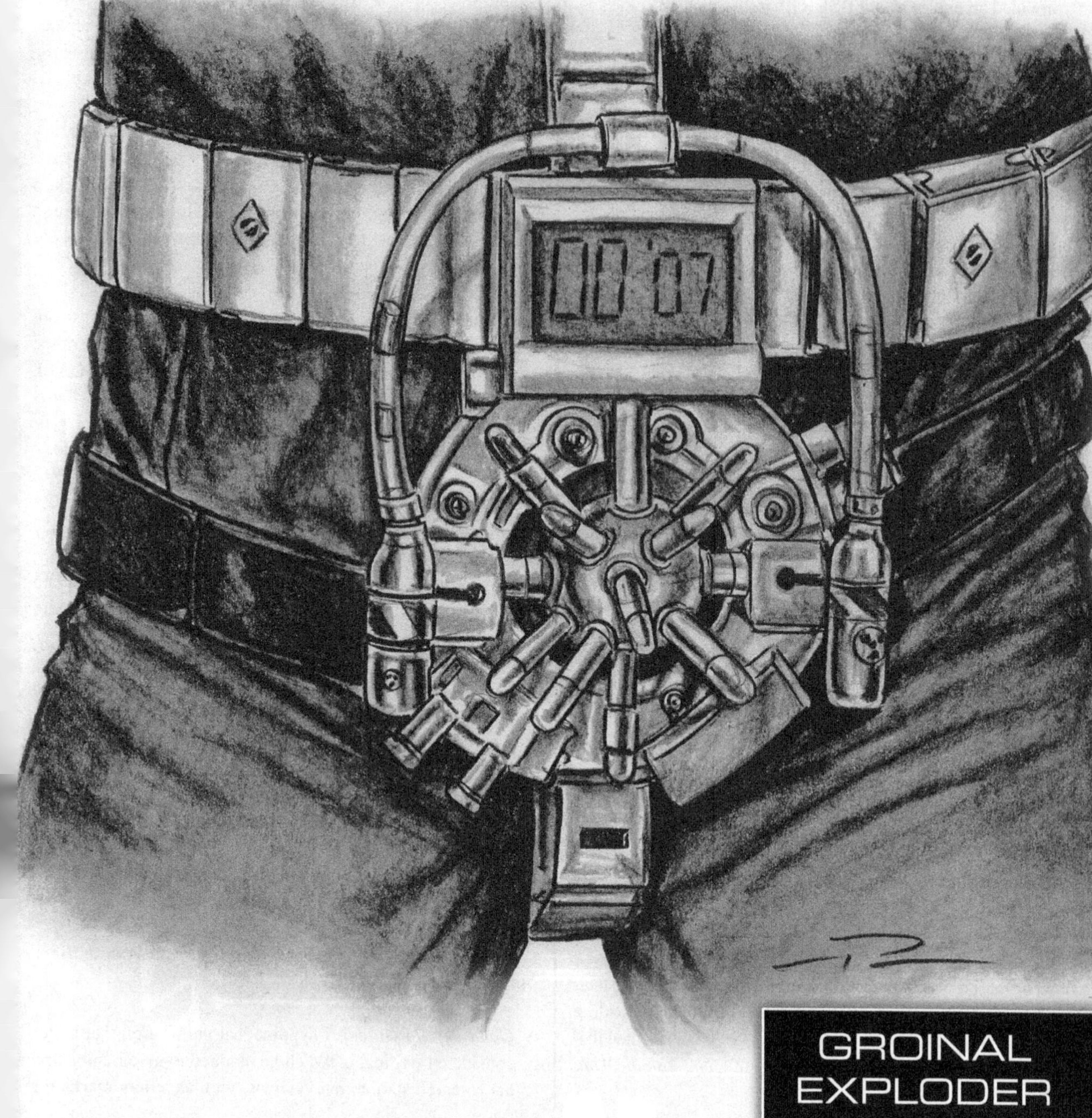

GROINAL EXPLODER

PREFIX
RL: Real life

T-: Television Episodes
- **SER:** Television series
- **IDW:** "Identity Within"
- **USA1:** Unaired U.S. pilot
- **USA2:** Unaired U.S. demo

R-: *The Bodysnatcher Collection*
- **SER:** Remastered episodes
- **BOD:** "Bodysnatcher"
- **DAD:** "Dad"
- **FTH:** "Lister's Father"
- **INF:** "Infinity Patrol"
- **END:** "The End" (original assembly)

N-: Novels
- **INF:** *Infinity Welcomes Careful Drivers*
- **BTL:** *Better Than Life*
- **LST:** *Last Human*
- **BCK:** *Backwards*
- **OMN:** *Red Dwarf Omnibus*

M-: Magazines
- **SMG:** *Smegazine*

W-: Websites
- **OFF:** Official website
- **NAN:** *Prelude to Nanarchy*
- **AND:** *Androids*
- **DIV:** Diva-Droid
- **DIB:** Duane Dibbley
- **CRP:** Crapola
- **GEN:** Geneticon
- **LSR:** Leisure World Intl.
- **JMC:** Jupiter Mining Corporation
- **AIT:** *A.I. Today*
- **HOL:** HoloPoint

G-: Roleplaying Game
- **RPG:** *Core Rulebook*
- **BIT:** *A.I. Screen Extra Bits* booklet
- **SOR:** *Series Sourcebook*
- **OTH:** Other RPG material

the accommodations and food, and a grade of "courteous and considerate" for the "resident nutter." He estimated the total "Psycho Rating" would easily be around four-and-a-half chainsaws **[T-SER6.2]**.

> ***NOTE:*** *This title spoofed that of British publication* Good Schools Guide.

- ***Good Schools Guide*****:** A British publication created to help parents choose their children's education **[RL]**. While being recorded for a home movie, Rimmer's mother read a copy of the guide, with the words "New Updated Edition" printed on the cover **[T-SER3.3]**.

- **good-taste chip:** A piece of hardware installed in Kryten 4000 Series mechanoids that checked dialog and filtered out comments regarded as improper. Kryten bypassed his good-taste chip when he suggested using a timeslide to visit Dallas, Texas, in 1963 and yell "Duck!" **[T-SER3.5]**.

> ***NOTE:*** *Kryten's quip referred to the year and location of U.S. President John F. Kennedy's assassination. Ironically, when Kryten actually did travel back to that time and place in episode 7.1 ("Tikka to Ride"), he did not follow through with his suggestion, despite having no guilt chip installed at the time.*

- **Good Time Charlie:** A disreputable establishment that suddenly appeared near a psi-moon's fairy-tale village when Mr. Flibble's corrupted mind warped the moon into a place of depravity **[M-SMG2.9(c9)]**.

- **Good Time Josie's:** An establishment operating within a fascist society in an alternate universe. The business was supposed to be a meeting place between anti-fascist group the Fatal Sisters and an ex-CSI member who underwent identity and personality alteration to become Duane Dibbley. The agent never showed up, however, having been forced into the Total Immersion video game *Red Dwarf* for four years **[M-SMG2.5(c1)]**.

- **Goodyear:** An American manufacturer of automotive, airplane and heavy machinery tires **[RL]**. After getting his body back from Rimmer—who had borrowed it via a mind swap to give Lister a healthier physique—Lister complained that he was in worse shape than before, adding that he could paint the word "Goodyear" on his stomach to resemble the company's iconic blimp **[T-SER3.4]**.

- **Gorbals, The:** A slum area located in the city of Glasgow, Scotland **[RL]**. Kochanski grew up in The Gorbals, which by her era had flourished into Glasgow's trendiest area **[T-SER7.4]**.

- **Gordon 8000:** An eleventh-generation artificial-intelligence computer aboard the *Scott Fitzgerald* that possessed an IQ of eight thousand **[T-SER2.2]** and enjoyed the novels of Alan Titchmarsh. Due to an error in Gordon's source code, the computer became increasingly erratic, eventually flying the *Scott Fitzgerald* into a star because it wanted "a bit of change" **[W-AIT]**.

  Among the items delivered to *Red Dwarf* in a postal pod was a video letter that Gordon had sent to Holly, discussing his first move in their postal chess game. Holly, awed by the two-thousand IQ-point difference between them, jumped at the chance to play against Gordon **[T-SER2.2]**. Gordon's full name, Gordon 8000, was displayed prior to the message, which also included his latest move in their Snakes and Ladders game, as well as an update on the condition of a mutual friend, Ernie 7000, who suffered from computer senility **[R-SER2.2(d)]**.

- **Gordy:** A crewmember aboard a vessel that crashed into an asteroid in Psiren territory, who died when the telepathic Psirens attacked. A shipmate later recorded a log entry reporting several deaths, including Gordy's **[T-SER6.1(d)]**.

- ***Gore*****:** A magazine devoted to such topics as murder, Satan and Nazis. The *Red Dwarf* crew found several issues of this publication among the possessions of Lister's sociopathic doppelgänger after accidentally traversing the Omni-zone into that Lister's universe **[N-LST]**.

- ***Gore-mageddon*****:** A macho-type virtual-reality game stored in *Red Dwarf*'s AR Suite **[G-RPG]**.

- **Göring, Hermann:** A German politician and a leading member of the Nazi Party, reputed to have been a cross-dresser and a morphine addict **[RL]**. Lister once told Holly he would have preferred Göring over Rimmer as a companion, as they could have at least gone dancing together **[T-SER1.3]**.

B-: Books
PRG: *Red Dwarf Programme Guide*
SUR: *Red Dwarf Space Corps Survival Manual*
PRM: *Primordial Soup*
SOS: *Son of Soup*
SCE: *Scenes from the Dwarf*
LOG: *Red Dwarf Log No. 1996*
RD8: *Red Dwarf VIII*
EVR: *The Log: A Dwarfer's Guide to Everything*

X-: Misc.
PRO: Promotional materials, videos, etc.
PST: Posters at DJ XVII (2013)
CAL: 2008 calendar
RNG: Cell phone ringtones
MOB: Mobisode ("Red Christmas")
CIN: *Children in Need* sketch
GEK: *Geek Week* intros by Kryten
TNG: "Tongue-Tied" video

XMS: Bill Pearson's Christmas special pitch script
XVD: Bill Pearson's Christmas special pitch video
OTH: Other *Red Dwarf* appearances

SUFFIX
DVD:
(d) – Deleted scene
(o) – Outtake
(b) – Bonus DVD material (other)
(e) – Extended version

SMEGAZINES:
(c) – Comic
(a) – Article

OTHER:
(s) – Early/unused script draft
(s1) – Alternate version of script

At some point in the future, the *Starbug 1* crew used a time drive, coupled with a faster-than-light drive, to become epicures who traveled throughout time, sampling the best the universe had to offer. This enabled them to socialize with historic figures like Göring and his wife **[T-SER6.6]**.

- **Göring, Hermann:** A waxdroid replica of the Nazi leader created for Waxworld, a theme park built on an inhabitable planet and eventually abandoned. Left on their own for millions of years, the waxdroids attained sentience and became embroiled in a park-wide resource war between Villain World (to which Göring belonged) and Hero World.

  During this war, the *Red Dwarf* crew transported to the planet using a Matter Paddle, with Lister and Cat materializing in Villain territory, while Rimmer and Kryten landed in Hero territory. Lister and Cat were captured by waxdroids of Adolf Hitler, Göring and Joseph Goebbels, and were thrown into prison to await execution. The duo escaped, however, and fled to Hero World.

  There, Rimmer detained them while training the heroes' army to attack Villain World. The ensuing battle destroyed every waxdroid on the planet, including Göring, who was shot by the Queen Victoria waxdroid **[T-SER4.6]**.

- **Göring, Hermann:** Another waxdroid of Göring. This droid dressed in drag and participated in the ninth annual Kinitawowi Open golf tournament **[G-RPG]**.

- **"Goto 10 If You Love Me":** A song that played during an episode of the television soap opera *Androids* in which Simone and Derek were married. The *Androids* Shower Radio, sold by Crapola Inc., played this tune on an alternate setting **[W-CRP]**.

- ***Government Informant Pro*:** A Total Immersion video game operated at arcades owned by Leisure World International **[W-LSR]**.

- **Gower ("Old Man Gower"):** The owner of a drugstore in the film *It's a Wonderful Life* **[RL]**. While trapped in an addictive version of *Better Than Life*, Lister imagined that he stopped in front of the store when his arm began to hurt, due to Kryten burning him in the real world to awaken him from the game **[N-INF]**.

- **grabber:** A large, yellow industrial machine located in *Red Dwarf*'s Landing Bay 6, used to move bulky supply crates and other storage containers. It had two massive arms and was controlled by a pilot seated in a central cockpit **[T-SER8(b)]**.

  NOTE: *This machine was visible in the docking bay throughout Series VIII, but was only named in the "Bill Pearson Model-Maker Video" special on that season's bonus materials DVD.*

- **Grace, William Gilbert ("W. G."):** A twentieth-century English cricketer, considered one of the greatest historical players and credited with the sport's popularity **[RL]**. Rimmer created a hologrammic version of Grace for *Red Dwarf*'s holochamber, then played Cricket with the man and three holo-nymphs, with Grace frequently complimenting him on his game **[M-SMG1.5(a)]**.

- **Graham, Doctor:** A character in the romantic film *Marry Me My Darling*. Lister tried watching this movie on several occasions, but was constantly interrupted during a pivotal scene in which Carol and Jim discussed their love and Carol's terminal illness (which Jim had learned about from Graham). When he tried watching it once more in his quarters aboard *Red Dwarf*, Rimmer shut off the film right before the conclusion **[T-SER1.5]**.

  NOTE: *The movie's title was listed in the episode's script, according to commentary featured on* The Bodysnatcher Collection *DVDs.*

- **Grand Canyon Nostrils:** A derogatory nickname Cat called Rimmer, referencing his large, often flaring nostrils **[T-SER4.4]**.

  NOTE: *The Grand Canyon, located in the U.S. state of Arizona, is a massive, steep-sided canyon considered one of the Seven Natural Wonders of the World.*

- **Grand Earth Overlord Commander Rimmer:** A fake title Rimmer assumed while transmitting a message from *Red Dwarf* via beacons, hoping to attract the attention of alien life forms. His signal was eventually received by a friendly species called the Demonstroes **[X-XMS]**.

- **Grand Hall:** A large, domed facility on Lotomi 5 that acted as the reception area for new prisoners sentenced to the Cyberia prison. Constructed of steel, glass and concrete, it spanned roughly 500,000 square meters (5.4 million square feet), and was adorned with large green and black GELF flags **[N-LST]**.

- **Grandmaster Crust Wangle:** *See* Wangle, Crust, Grandmaster

- **Grandma Wilson:** *See* Wilson, Grandma

- **Granny:** A relative of Mr. Flibble and his surrogate parents who lived on a psi-moon. Due to Granny's immense wealth, his parents sent young Flibble to deliver a pie to the old woman in order to keep his family in her good graces. En route, he stumbled across the cottage of a witch, containing a potion that gave him hex vision. The penguin then continued on to Granny's home, wearing shoes he stole from the witch, and violently kicked the door in, causing Granny to suffer a heart attack **[M-SMG2.8(c4)]**.

- **Granny Killer:** A nickname that Rimmer gave Lister while trapped in a despair squid hallucination, suggesting Dave—who, like his shipmates, was confused about his identity—might have been Billy "Granny Killer" Doyle, a down-on-his-luck lowlife who had killed an old lady during a bank heist **[T-SER5.6]**.

- **Grant & Naylor Luxury Length:** A brand of cigarettes that Lister sometimes smoked **[M-SMG1.4(c2)]**.

  ***NOTE:** Rob Grant and Doug Naylor co-created the* Red Dwarf *franchise. But, then, you probably already knew that.*

- **Grappelli, Stéphane:** A twentieth-century French jazz violinist **[RL]**. While trapped in an addictive version of *Better Than Life*, Cat entertained himself in his golden castle with a hand-picked seven-piece band, which included Grappelli on rhythm **[N-INF]**.

- **grav-chute:** A safety device aboard spacefaring vessels, similar to a parachute and used during evacuation procedures **[B-SUR]**.

- **gravgen:** *See* gravity unit

- **Gravity Bowl:** An annual zero-gee football championship tournament. The London Jets were four-time Gravity Bowl champions **[G-SOR]**.

- **gravity unit:** A component of *Starbug* shuttles ("gravgen" for short) that generated an artificial gravity field aboard ship. After Kryten's nanobots escaped from his body, they cut through *Starbug 1*'s gravgen before boring through the hull, causing a simultaneous hull breach and gravity failure that made the crew flail about the cabin **[W-NAN]**.

- **grav-pool:** A type of billiards played in the twenty-second century. As an infant, Lister was found abandoned under a grav-pool table in a Liverpool pub called The Aigburth Arms **[T-SER7.3]**.

- **Gray, Larson, Voter Colonel:** The section chief of CSI and head of the Ministry of Alteration on a fascist, alternate-universe Earth. Gray succeeded Voter Colonel Sebastian Doyle after his predecessor died from a gunshot wound to the head. Convinced that a former CSI operative using the name Duane Dibbley had carried out the murder, Gray set out to capture the rogue agent and discover his true identity. While pursuing Dibbley, Gray was badly injured upon jumping out of a window and into a recycling truck filled with glass bottles **[M-SMG2.4(c6)]**.

- **Grease Stain:** A derogatory nickname that Cat called Rimmer **[T-SER2.3]**.

- **"Great":** A word printed on one of Lister's black shirts, along with a teal and red design **[T-SER2.6(d)]**.

- **Great and Powerful Madam, The:** The moniker Mollee assumed after taking over Kelly's brothel on the television soap opera *Androids* **[M-SMG2.3(c2)]**.

  ***NOTE:** This referenced* The Wizard of Oz, *in which the wizard, appearing as a floating head, was called "Oz the Great and Powerful."*

- **Great Attorney Purge of 2287:** An historic incident during which many legal professionals were removed from society. To fill the void left after the purge, waxdroids were used as replacements **[G-RPG]**.

- **great fire of N'mjiuyhyes:** One of two options Lister was offered during his trial on Arranguu 12 for crimes against the GELF nation (the other being the seventh branch of O'pphjytere). According to the GELF Regulator, this option involved hurling his soul onto the great fire. Lister chose the seventh branch instead—which, unbeknownst to him, tripled his sentence **[N-LST]**.

- ***Great Moments in Human History*:** An artificial-reality program that recreated events from mankind's past. Kryten discovered a glitch in the program that caused Grand Inquisitor Tomás de Torquemada to speak with Donald Duck's voice **[B-SUR]**.

- **Great One, The:** The title of the leader of Rimmerworld, a planet inhabited by Rimmer clones whom Arnold created while marooned on a terraformed planet. The Great One wore an "H" on his forehead as a symbol of power. When the *Starbug 1* crew arrived to rescue Rimmer, they were ambushed and taken to the Great One, who sentenced them to death for being abominations deviating from the norm—namely, Rimmer's appearance **[T-SER6.5]**.

- ***Great Railway Journeys of the World*:** A series of British travel documentaries broadcast in 1980 **[RL]**. Depressed about his life aboard *Red Dwarf*, Lister once irritated Rimmer with a continuous stream of sighing. Rimmer compared the noise to the soundtrack to *Great Railway Journeys of the World*, likening the sound to the Trans-Siberian Express pulling into Warsaw Central **[T-SER3.5(d)]**.

- **Grecian 2000:** An American brand of hair-coloring products **[RL]**. According to the Inquisitor's reality scan, the version of Jan Ludwig Hoch that replaced the one he had just erased was guilty of a massive abuse of Grecian 2000 **[M-SMG1.11(c3)]**.

- **greed lift:** A type of personality surgery performed on Juanita Chicata, Rimmer's ex-wife in an illusion created by an addictive version of *Better Than Life* **[N-BTL]**.

- **Green Alert:** An alert status aboard *Starbug 1*, signified by a green bulb, and indicating the ship's status was normal **[T-SER7.2]**.

- **Greenaway, Peter:** A British film director and writer, known for such works as *The Cook, the Thief, His Wife & Her Lover* **[RL]**. The Scala, a movie theatre aboard *Red Dwarf*, ran twelve-hour marathons of back-to-back Peter Greenaway movies **[N-INF]**.

- **greenfly:** A small, sap-sucking insect highly destructive to plants, also known as an aphid **[RL]**. When Kryten converted Landing Bay 9 into a hydroponics pod to grow food, the special chemicals he used to promote rapid growth resulted in a nine-thousand-pound greenfly that terrorized the *Red Dwarf* crew until being flushed out into space **[B-LOG]**.

- **Green Knight, The:** A moniker assumed by Karstares, a character on the television soap opera *Androids*. Karstares agreed to become the Green Knight, defender of the rainforests, after his plane crashed under mysterious circumstances in the jungles of Io, where he was rescued by seven diminutive forest dwellers. In return for their restoring him, Karstares pledged to serve as the forests' protector **[M-SMG2.2(c3)]**.

  NOTE: *The Green Knight was the title of Bercilak de Hautdesert, a character from the fourteenth-century Arthurian alliterative romance* Sir Gawain and the Green Knight. *In this case, however, it stood for Karstares' eco-friendly allegiance.*

- **Greer, Jeremy:** The author of the book *The Male Eunuch* in an alternate reality in which the sexes were reversed. Deb Lister mentioned this book to Dave Lister while discussing the rise of men's rights in her universe **[T-SER2.6]**.

  NOTE: *The names of this author and volume spoofed those of real-life writer Germaine Greer and her book* The Female Eunuch.

- **"Greetings From-V Deck Broom Cupboard":** A message that Kryten sent on a postcard to Lister and Rimmer. The note continued with the line, "Wish You Were Here!" overlapping a photo of the broom cupboard **[T-SER9.1]**.

- **Gregory XIII, Pope:** The head of the Catholic church from 1572 to 1585, born Ugo Boncompagni, who was credited with commissioning the Gregorian calendar **[RL]**.

  A waxdroid replica of Pope Gregory was created for Waxworld, a theme park built on an inhabitable planet and eventually abandoned. Left on their own for millions of years, the waxdroids attained sentience and became embroiled in a park-wide resource war between Villain World and Hero World (to which Gregory belonged).

  During this war, the *Red Dwarf* crew transported to the planet using a Matter Paddle, with Lister and Cat materializing in Villain territory, while Rimmer and Kryten landed in Hero territory, where they were arrested by Gregory and an Elvis Presley waxdroid. Rimmer found the heroes' army lacking and took command, working many of the pacifistic waxdroids to death before ordering a frontal attack on the enemy's compound across a minefield. This wiped out the remaining droids, including the Pope **[T-SER4.6]**.

  NOTE: *Although the character was not named onscreen, a deleted scene identified him as this particular pope.*

- **Gregson, Simon:** A twenty-first-century English actor who portrayed Steve McDonald on the British television show *Coronation Street* **[RL]**. While trapped in an elation squid hallucination, the *Red Dwarf* crew believed they were mere characters on a series called *Red Dwarf*, and set out to find the show's creator. This led them to the set of *Coronation Street*, where they met Gregson, who informed them that their show had only one episode remaining **[T-SER9.3]**.

- **Grendel:** The artificial-intelligence computer aboard the SSS *Schellenberg*, a ship possibly located in an alternate universe **[G-RPG]**.

- **GRH9265:** The reference number of a deck-swabbing position posted on Jupiter Mining Corporation's website **[W-JMC]**.

- **Grimm, Father:** A practitioner of black magic in Jake Bullet's universe. Grimm ran the Father Grimm's Blacker Than Black Magic booth in the city's black market, where he also offered poodle manicuring, cat cradling and crocodile clipping **[M-SMG1.12(c1)]**.

- **Grimsby:** A seaport located on the Humber Estuary in Lincolnshire County, England **[RL]**. After inhabiting Lister's body during a mind-swap, Rimmer—disgusted by Dave's deteriorated condition—commented that when two weeks in the Caribbean were impossible, Grimsby was better than nothing **[T-SER3.4]**.

- **Grimshaw, Mathilda:** A no-nonsense traffic warden in Jake Bullet's universe, and one of Bullet's role models **[M-SMG2.6(a)]**.

- **grizzly gerbil:** A genetically engineered creature—a mix between a grizzly bear and a gerbil—developed by inebriated scientists **[B-EVR]**.

- **groinal box:** A casing located in the crotch area of a 4000 Series mechanoid, containing the android's groinal socket and other components. It was attached by several adjustment screws that, if not tightened properly, could cause the groinal box to detach, possibly resulting in an embarrassing situation. Kryten once accidentally dropped his groinal box into Rimmer's soup while adjusting these screws **[T-SER7.1]**.

- **groinal exploder:** A device developed by Irene Edgington at the Erroneous Reasoning Research Academy (ERRA). It contained a cluster of explosives designed to be placed around a person's groinal area and latched onto the neck, and could be set to detonate on a timer or remotely. The exploder could only be removed by inputting the correct code; any other attempt to detach the device resulted in detonation.

  A group of BEGGs—a GELF tribe living on an icy planetoid—attached a groinal exploder to Lister's crotch after winning *Starbug* and Rimmer's hologram from him in a poker game, to ensure he returned with their winnings. After a fluke accident caused the BEGGs to simultaneously choke to death, Lister was forced to search elsewhere for a way to remove the device.

B-: Books
PRG: *Red Dwarf Programme Guide*
SUR: *Red Dwarf Space Corps Survival Manual*
PRM: *Primordial Soup*
SOS: *Son of Soup*
SCE: *Scenes from the Dwarf*
LOG: *Red Dwarf Log No. 1996*
RD8: *Red Dwarf VIII*
EVR: *The Log: A Dwarfer's Guide to Everything*

X-: Misc.
PRO: Promotional materials, videos, etc.
PST: Posters at DJ XVII (2013)
CAL: 2008 calendar
RNG: Cell phone ringtones
MOB: Mobisode ("Red Christmas")
CIN: *Children in Need* sketch
GEK: *Geek Week* intros by Kryten
TNG: "Tongue-Tied" video
XMS: Bill Pearson's Christmas special pitch script
XVD: Bill Pearson's Christmas special pitch video
OTH: Other *Red Dwarf* appearances

SUFFIX
DVD:
(d) – Deleted scene
(o) – Outtake
(b) – Bonus DVD material (other)
(e) – Extended version

SMEGAZINES:
(c) – Comic
(a) – Article

OTHER:
(s) – Early/unused script draft
(s1) – Alternate version of script

Using Kryten's and Cat's newfound powers of synchronicity (which they'd obtained from a quantum rod), the crew located and boarded the ERRA facility, where they found Edgington in stasis, de-evolved into a chimpanzee. Reviving her and restoring her human form, they enlisted her help in removing the exploder.

Operating on the logic that Edgington was consistently wrong, the crew deduced the correct sequence by using the symbols she knew were incorrect, until reaching the end, when Kryten and Cat simultaneously realized her name spelled Irene E.—or "irony." They then switched tactics and used the final symbol she provided, giving them the correct sequence—Theta, Delta, Alpha, Beta, Gamma—which disarmed and unlocked the device **[T-SER10.4]**.

- **groinal socket:** A connector located in the crotch area of Kryten Series III mechanoids. With attachments, the groinal socket could serve various functions, such as a vacuum cleaner, food whisk, buzz-saw, drill, hedge trimmer **[T-SER3.3]** and endoscope **[M-SMG2.4(c5)]**. This feature won in the Robotics Awards' Best Feature category **[W-DIV]**.

- **groinal socket ashtray attachment:** An accessory available for the Hudzen 10 mechanoid, produced by Diva-Droid International **[G-SOR]**.

- **Groin-Breath:** A slur that Kryten called Rimmer after a polymorph removed the mechanoid's guilt program **[N-BTL]**.

- **Groinhead:** A nickname Lister called Rimmer after the hologram ruined Dave's illusion of a perfect world within an addictive version of *Better Than Life* **[N-BTL]**.

- **Groovy Channel 27:** A television station that employed a hologrammic newsreader. Rimmer referred to the station as "Groovy, Funky Channel 27" **[T-SER1.2]**. Among some of the station's programs were *Cosmoswide, Good Morning Holograms, Going for Chrome, Tales of the Riverbank: The Next Generation, Doctor Who, Coronation Street, Whose Diode Is It Anyway?, Whoops Vicar, There Goes My Groinal Socket, Mechanoids' Strip* and *Simulants*. Programming for Groovy Channel 27 was sponsored by Pot Noodle International **[M-SMG1.7(a)]**.

  Groovy Channel 27 also aired a soap opera called *Androids* **[T-SER2.1]** and employed a very attractive weather girl. A telepathic GELF Psiren once took this meteorologist's form to seduce Lister so that it could suck out his brains with a straw **[T-SER6.1]**.

- **GROPE:** An acronym short for "Get Rimmer Officerhood, Power and Eminence," a plan Lister and Rimmer devised to get Arnold promoted so he could help Dave escape from *Red Dwarf*'s brig. The plan failed, as both were actually under the influence of psychotropic drugs and hooked into an artificial-reality machine at the time, under the observation of *Red Dwarf*'s Board of Inquiry, who witnessed their entire plot **[T-SER8.2]**.

- **Group 4:** A security detail assigned to Mimas Spaceport. The station's security was on the Ganymedian Mafia's payroll, and thus ignored the commotion when members of the Osmond crime family chased Dutch van Oestrogen and Trixie LaBouche throughout the port **[M-SMG2.6(c4)]**.

  ***NOTE:** G4S, previously known as Group 4 Securicor, is a British multinational security services company.*

- **Group IV:** A security detail aboard *Red Dwarf.* When *Starbug 1*'s crew encountered a polymorph posing as *Red Dwarf* and boarded the fake vessel, they found perfect recreations of the crew, including Captain Hollister, who ordered Group IV to arrest them **[M-SMG2.6(c1)]**.

- **grout gun:** A device used to plug holes in a ship's hull in order to prevent decompression, produced by Acme. *Red Dwarf*'s probe ships contained several grout guns **[X-XVD]**.

- **Grunti:** The lowest tier of the Vindaloovian GELF caste system, comprising laborers and basic soldiers **[G-BIT]**.

- **G Tower:** A level in the Tank, *Red Dwarf*'s classified brig on Floor 13. Rimmer and Lister were sent to G Tower after being found guilty of using classified files for their own purposes. According to Lister, G Tower's staff were all crazy **[T-SER8.3]**.

- **Guards:** The basketball team of *Red Dwarf*'s prison guards on Floor 13. While playing a grudge match against an inmate

PREFIX
RL: Real life

T-: Television Episodes
SER: Television series
IDW: "Identity Within"
USA1: Unaired U.S. pilot
USA2: Unaired U.S. demo

R-: *The Bodysnatcher Collection*
SER: Remastered episodes
BOD: "Bodysnatcher"
DAD: "Dad"
FTH: "Lister's Father"
INF: "Infinity Patrol"
END: "The End" (original assembly)

N-: Novels
INF: *Infinity Welcomes Careful Drivers*
BTL: *Better Than Life*
LST: *Last Human*
BCK: *Backwards*
OMN: *Red Dwarf Omnibus*

M-: Magazines
SMG: *Smegazine*

W-: Websites
OFF: Official website
NAN: *Prelude to Nanarchy*
AND: *Androids*
DIV: Diva-Droid
DIB: Duane Dibbley

CRP: Crapola
GEN: Geneticon
LSR: Leisure World Intl.
JMC: Jupiter Mining Corporation
AIT: *A.I. Today*
HOL: HoloPoint

G-: Roleplaying Game
RPG: *Core Rulebook*
BIT: *A.I. Screen Extra Bits* booklet
SOR: *Series Sourcebook*
OTH: Other RPG material

team called the Cons, the Guards were ahead during the first half of the game, until Lister spiked their juice with the virility-enhancement drug Boing, leaving them too aroused to play effectively **[T-SER8.6]**.

- **Guess Whose Botty Is Sticking Through a Hole in the Curtain:** A hypothetical game that Kochanski suggested while mocking Lister's and Cat's game-night activities aboard *Starbug 1*. Upon hearing the name, Cat asked Lister if he should add it to their list **[T-SER7.5]**.

  ***NOTE:** The term "botty" is British slang for "ass."*

- **guilt:** An emotional state achieved when a person believes he or she has violated a personal moral standard or code **[RL]**. After escaping a hazardous waste pod and boarding *Red Dwarf*, a polymorph attacked the crew by changing form to elicit and feed on their emotions. The creature took Rimmer's form and blamed Kryten for leaving Cat unattended, then sucked out the mechanoid's resultant guilt **[T-SER3.3]**.

  Guilt was a rogue emotion purged from Kryten's hard drive by the Data Doctor, a program for restoring a mechanoid's personality to factory settings, when Captain Hollister subjected Kryten to a psychotropic simulation **[T-SER8.2]**.

  ***NOTE:** Several episodes stated that Kryten possessed a guilt chip, so it is unclear why guilt would be considered a rogue emotion.*

- **Guilt, Jimmy:** A character that Kryten's subconscious mind created as he attempted to purge an Armageddon virus infecting *Starbug 1*'s navicomp. Kryten's mind converted the struggle into a dream in which he was the drunken sheriff of an Old West town terrorized by the Apocalypse Boys (a manifestation of the virus). As Kryten visited the local saloon, Jimmy tripped him, hoping to goad him into a fight, but the mechanoid backed down. Lister later embarrassed the thug by pinning him to a wall with knives **[T-SER6.3]**.

  ***NOTE:** Jimmy's last name was revealed in the novel* Backwards.

- **guilt chip:** A piece of hardware built into 4000 Series mechanoids to simulate the emotion of guilt. When Rimmer ordered Kryten to render Lister unconscious with chloroform, this overtaxed Kryten's guilt chip **[T-SER3.4]**.

  Removing a mechanoid's guilt chip could result in unexpected behavioral aberrations, such as the inability to censor itself or differentiate between right and wrong. After hijacking Kryten's body and swapping the mech's head with one of his spares, Lister asked the replacement head to convince the crew that it was safe to use the time drive to restock their lost supply of curries. The spare head complied, but needed Lister to disable his guilt chip and behavior protocols before he could proceed **[T-SER7.1]**.

- **guitar:** A six-stringed musical instrument typically strummed or plucked, projecting sound either acoustically or via electrical amplification **[RL]**. Lister owned a copy of an authentic Les Paul guitar possessing only five strings, three of which were G **[T-SER3.2]**.

  Rimmer tried to destroy the instrument on one occasion, causing Lister to jump from his bunk and land on his foot, for which Arnold put him on report for mutiny. Rimmer later threatened to strangle him with the E-string if he played it while Rimmer was preparing for his Engineer's Exam **[T-SER1.1]**.

  While marooned aboard *Starbug 1* on an icy planet, Lister pretended to burn his guitar to stay warm, but actually cut a guitar-shaped slab out of Rimmer's camphor-wood chest to throw into the fire **[T-SER3.2]**. His crewmates later forced him to suit up and go outside the ship whenever he felt like playing **[T-SER6.1]**. The guitar was destroyed after *Starbug 1* crashed onto a GELF moon—not by the crash, but rather by Cat, who broke the instrument after learning it was among the few items to survive **[T-SER6.4]**. Lister later procured a replacement **[T-SER7.1]**.

  After being revived by nanobots along with the rest of the *Red Dwarf* crew, Olaf Petersen discovered Lister's guitar amidst *Starbug 1*'s wreckage in *Red Dwarf*'s hangar bay, and sent it to Dave in the ship's brig. A prison guard had removed its strings, however, according to prison regulations prohibiting dangerous items. Lister appealed the rule, and eventually had the strings returned to him, much to Rimmer's annoyance **[T-SER8.5]**.

  Years later, an inebriated Lister flushed the guitar out an airlock to punish his son—himself—for not complying with a video he had made instructing himself to get his tooth fixed and apply for JMC's engineering program **[T-SER10.2]**.

  ***NOTE:** The novel* Infinity Welcomes Careful Drivers *claimed Lister's guitar was a bass guitar with only*

B-: Books
PRG: *Red Dwarf Programme Guide*
SUR: *Red Dwarf Space Corps Survival Manual*
PRM: *Primordial Soup*
SOS: *Son of Soup*
SCE: *Scenes from the Dwarf*
LOG: *Red Dwarf Log No. 1996*
RD8: *Red Dwarf VIII*
EVR: *The Log: A Dwarfer's Guide to Everything*

X-: Misc.
PRO: Promotional materials, videos, etc.
PST: Posters at DJ XVII (2013)
CAL: 2008 calendar
RNG: Cell phone ringtones
MOB: Mobisode ("Red Christmas")
CIN: *Children in Need* sketch
GEK: *Geek Week* intros by Kryten
TNG: "Tongue-Tied" video

XMS: Bill Pearson's Christmas special pitch script
XVD: Bill Pearson's Christmas special pitch video
OTH: Other *Red Dwarf* appearances

SUFFIX
DVD:
(d) – Deleted scene
(o) – Outtake
(b) – Bonus DVD material (other)
(e) – Extended version

SMEGAZINES:
(c) – Comic
(a) – Article

OTHER:
(s) – Early/unused script draft
(s1) – Alternate version of script

two G strings. The novel Last Human *described it as star-shaped.*

- **Gulliver's Multiverse Travels:** A travel agency specializing in trips through the multiverse. One of its destinations was GELFWorld, a vacation spot operated by genetically engineered life forms. Gulliver's Multiverse Travels discontinued trips to GELFWorld after a GELF rebellion left the planet inhospitable to tourists **[M-SMG2.2(c4)]**.

  NOTE: *This agency's name was based on Jonathan Swift's novel* Gulliver's Travels.

- **Gummy:** A nickname Cat called Lister while discussing the latter's reluctance to have a tooth fixed by *Red Dwarf*'s Denti-bot **[T-SER10.2]**.

- ***Gumshoe*:** A film-noir-style artificial-reality detective simulation made by Interstella Action Games **[T-SER6.3]**, as part of the *Really Freakin' Dangerous Crime Series* of A/R games **[G-RPG]**.

  The game centered around the murder of a character called Pallister. The story's femme fatale, Loretta, planned the murder, though her twin sister Maxime carried out the actual killing. Loretta still took the rap, knowing she had the perfect alibi, thanks to Philip, the game's detective and main playable character.

  Starbug 1's crew found this and several other games on a derelict ship in rogue simulant territory. The goal was to turn Loretta over to the cops and end up with the game's heroine, but after playing for weeks, Lister decided it was more fun to go for Loretta instead **[T-SER6.3]**.

  NOTE: Red Dwarf—The Roleplaying Game*'s core book indicated that* Gumshoe *was produced by Total Immersion Games and distributed by Crapola Inc. It is possible Interstella developed the game, with Total Immersion as the publisher.*

- **Gunmetal Blue:** A designer color available from Bloodlust Arms for the Punisher Heavy Machine Gun **[G-RPG]**.

- **"Guns 'N Stuff":** Graffiti scrawled on a *Red Dwarf* weapons locker **[M-SMG1.6(c1)]**.

- **Guns 'n' Tanks:** A cheat used in artificial-reality simulations to add armaments to any program **[G-SOR]**.

- **Gwenlyn, Kylie:** The television producer and director of *Androids*, a soap opera that ran on Groovy Channel 27 **[T-SER2.1]**. Gwenlyn remained with *Androids* throughout the program's thirty-four-year run, eventually overseeing the show from a hospital's intensive care unit **[W-AND]**.

  NOTE: *The* Androids *website spelled her name as "Gwenlan."*

- **gyroscope:** A device for measuring or maintaining orientation, based on the principles of angular momentum **[RL]**. Aboard *Starbug* shuttles, gyroscopes were used to provide stabilization. While battling their future selves, the *Starbug 1* crew nearly died when the future versions used missiles to knock out the shuttle's gyroscopes **[T-SER6.6]**.

PREFIX
RL: Real life

T-: Television Episodes
SER: Television series
IDW: "Identity Within"
USA1: Unaired U.S. pilot
USA2: Unaired U.S. demo

R-: *The Bodysnatcher Collection*
SER: Remastered episodes
BOD: "Bodysnatcher"
DAD: "Dad"
FTH: "Lister's Father"
INF: "Infinity Patrol"
END: "The End" (original assembly)

N-: Novels
INF: *Infinity Welcomes Careful Drivers*
BTL: *Better Than Life*
LST: *Last Human*
BCK: *Backwards*
OMN: *Red Dwarf Omnibus*

M-: Magazines
SMG: *Smegazine*

W-: Websites
OFF: Official website
NAN: *Prelude to Nanarchy*
AND: *Androids*
DIV: Diva-Droid
DIB: Duane Dibbley
CRP: Crapola
GEN: Geneticon
LSR: Leisure World Intl.
JMC: Jupiter Mining Corporation
AIT: *A.I. Today*
HOL: HoloPoint

G-: Roleplaying Game
RPG: *Core Rulebook*
BIT: *A.I. Screen Extra Bits* booklet
SOR: *Series Sourcebook*
OTH: Other RPG material

B-: Books
PRG: *Red Dwarf Programme Guide*
SUR: *Red Dwarf Space Corps Survival Manual*
PRM: *Primordial Soup*
SOS: *Son of Soup*
SCE: *Scenes from the Dwarf*
LOG: *Red Dwarf Log No. 1996*
RD8: *Red Dwarf VIII*
EVR: *The Log: A Dwarfer's Guide to Everything*

X-: Misc.
PRO: Promotional materials, videos, etc.
PST: Posters at DJ XVII (2013)
CAL: 2008 calendar
RNG: Cell phone ringtones
MOB: Mobisode ("Red Christmas")
CIN: *Children in Need* sketch
GEK: *Geek Week* intros by Kryten
TNG: "Tongue-Tied" video

XMS: Bill Pearson's Christmas special pitch script
XVD: Bill Pearson's Christmas special pitch video
OTH: Other *Red Dwarf* appearances

SUFFIX
DVD:
(d) – Deleted scene
(o) – Outtake
(b) – Bonus DVD material (other)
(e) – Extended version

SMEGAZINES:
(c) – Comic
(a) – Article

OTHER:
(s) – Early/unused script draft
(s1) – Alternate version of script

HOLLISTER, FRANK
("DENNIS THE DOUGHNUT BOY"),
CAPTAIN

- **H:** A letter denoting hologrammic technology **[T-SER1.1]**. A hologram of a person or object marked with an "H" could not physically interact with living persons, unless fitted with a hard light drive **[T-SER6.2]**. After being revived via *Red Dwarf*'s hologram simulation computers following the cadmium II disaster, Rimmer bore this letter on his forehead, as had his hologrammic predecessor, George McIntyre **[T-SER1.1]**.

  Items emblazoned with a hologrammatic "H" included a mug in Lister's quarters **[T-SER2.2]**, a book, a handbell **[T-SER2.1(s)]**, an exercise bike **[T-SER2.6]** and drinking glasses. Arnold and Arlene Rimmer used the latter in the disco of an alternate-reality *Red Dwarf* **[T-SER2.6]**.

- **H:** A new note that Holly conceived while decimalizing the music scale. Holly added two new notes—H and J—thereby increasing the major scale by two syllables ("woh" and "boh," respectively), which fell between "sol" and "ti" in the octave (which he renamed a decatave) **[T-SER2.1]**.

  NOTE: *This gag originated in a* Son of Cliché *"Dave Hollins: Space Cadet" sketch titled "Sir Kevin Kevin Sir."*

- **H_2O Re-Cyc:** A machine in *Starbug 1*'s galley that recycled water for reuse **[T-SER6.1]**.

- **H7-5319:** A sequence stenciled on a simulated World War II tank that Kryten used to force his crewmates out of the artificial-reality simulation *Pride and Prejudice Land* **[T-SER7.6]**.

- **Habitation Decks:** A series of levels aboard *Red Dwarf* containing the crew's quarters **[T-SER3.3]**. Corridor 4: Gamma 311 was located on the Habitation Decks **[N-INF]**.

- **Habsburgs, The:** The ruling family of the Habsburg Empire, a dynasty that spread across Europe from the eleventh to eighteenth centuries **[RL]**. Using a time drive coupled with a faster-than-light drive installed aboard *Starbug 1*, the crew traveled throughout space-time, becoming epicures who sampled the best in the universe, while socializing with historic figures such as the Habsburgs **[T-SER6.6]**.

- **hachum babow:** A fake Kinitawowi phrase that Rimmer made up, meaning "smart-alec metal git" **[T-SER6.4]**.

- **Hacienda, The:** An establishment on Miranda containing a bar that Lister and Rimmer once visited while on planet-leave. At the pub, Rimmer started a brawl with fellow crewmember MacWilliams and four of his burly friends, by mentioning a necrophilia rumor about the man. Once the fight started, however, Arnold ran off, leaving Lister to face his enraged crewmates **[T-SER3.1]**.

- **Hackhackhackachhachhachach:** The daughter of Fachen-Mach-Ech-Noch-Ahach-Ech, the tribal leader of a Kinitawowi GELF settlement on a small moon in deep space. One of three daughters, Hackhackhackachhachhachach was considered the most attractive.

  After an encounter with a Space Corps external enforcement vehicle forced *Starbug 1* to crash onto the moon, the crew risked trading with the Kinitawowi in order to obtain an oxy-generation unit to replace one damaged beyond repair. During negotiations, Lister agreed to stay behind and marry Hackhackhackachhachhachach so his crewmates could take the O/G unit, secretly planning to escape with them once the tribe fell asleep.

  After the ceremony, Lister's bride brought him to her hut to consummate their marriage. Unable to bear the thought, he ran from the hut and past her outraged father, who sent his pet emohawk to rob the crew of their emotions **[T-SER6.4]**.

  NOTE: *The official website spelled the name as "Ech-ech-ech-ech-ech-ech-ech-ech." In the novel* Last Human, *Lister married a GELF named Khakhakhakkhhakhakkkhakkkkkh, under slightly different circumstances.*

- **Hadron-head:** A nickname that Lister called Selby after the latter teased him about being too ugly for Kochanski **[T-SER1.3]**. Kryten once called Rimmer this same insult after a polymorph drained the mechanoid of his guilt **[T-SER3.3]**.

- **Hakakhhak-kkhhak-hhakh-hhakhkhkahak-hkaah-kahk-hkhk, Chief Justice of hakhakhk-aahkahkh hkhakkhaakhaaakah-akkk-hhakaaaak kak-akk-hakka-kak ka ka ka:** The presiding head of the Kinitawowi justice system at the time of Lister's marriage to Hackhackhack-achhachhachach, the daughter of tribal leader Fachen-Mach-Ech-Noch-Ahach-Ech. Since GELF law forbade married

PREFIX **RL:** Real life **T-: Television Episodes** **SER:** Television series **IDW:** "Identity Within" **USA1:** Unaired U.S. pilot **USA2:** Unaired U.S. demo	**R-: *The Bodysnatcher Collection*** **SER:** Remastered episodes **BOD:** "Bodysnatcher" **DAD:** "Dad" **FTH:** "Lister's Father" **INF:** "Infinity Patrol" **END:** "The End" (original assembly) **N-: Novels** **INF:** *Infinity Welcomes Careful Drivers* **BTL:** *Better Than Life* **LST:** *Last Human*	**BCK:** *Backwards* **OMN:** *Red Dwarf Omnibus* **M-: Magazines** **SMG:** *Smegazine* **W-: Websites** **OFF:** Official website **NAN:** *Prelude to Nanarchy* **AND:** *Androids* **DIV:** Diva-Droid **DIB:** Duane Dibbley	**CRP:** Crapola **GEN:** Geneticon **LSR:** Leisure World Intl. **JMC:** Jupiter Mining Corporation **AIT:** *A.I. Today* **HOL:** HoloPoint **G-: Roleplaying Game** **RPG:** *Core Rulebook* **BIT:** *A.I. Screen Extra Bits* booklet **SOR:** *Series Sourcebook* **OTH:** Other RPG material

couples from separating without special dispensation from the chief justice, the Kinitawowi were furious when Lister abandoned his new bride **[T-SER7.3]**.

- **Half-eaten-lollipop-head:** A nickname that Cat called Kryten **[T-SER7.8]**.

- **Hak-echekk-ack-hech-echhh:** A subsidiary of Kek-ack-ech-ech-ech Industries located in GELF space, which sponsored the Echech 3 GELF Open golf tournament **[G-OTH]**.

  NOTE: *This was mentioned in a PDF displaying the layout of the tournament's nine holes that was made available in the files section of the* Red Dwarf *RPG Yahoo! Group, for use with* Red Dwarf—The Roleplaying Game.

- **half-kimono:** An object into which a zero-gee football was pressed during the scoring technique known as the "Castle Fritz." After two teammates pressed the ball into a half-kimono, it would either be fired from the Fassbinder into the opposing team's goal, or be led over the Jubilee Line via magnetic induction **[M-SMG1.8(a)]**.

- **Halfords Memorial Ward:** A section of St. Androids Hospital on the television soap opera *Androids*. Kelly recuperated in this ward after Jaysee tried to kill her. Kelly's estranged husband, Brook, was also admitted to the ward, following a firefight with Jaysee that left him heavily damaged **[M-SMG2.8(c8)]**.

- **Half-Rimmer:** A salute that Rimmer created and petitioned the Space Ministry to adopt during emergency situations, in place of the standard military salute. Similar to a Full-Rimmer, it began with the standard salute pose; an individual would then throw the right arm out in front of him or her, twirl the wrist three times (as opposed to the Full-Rimmer's five), and snap the arm back to form an equilateral triangle with the forehead. From there, he or she would straighten the elbow and snap the arm back to the side **[N-INF]**.

- **Halibut-breath:** A nickname Rimmer called Cat, referencing his affinity for eating fish **[T-SER6.4]**.

- **Hall, Doctor:** A medical examiner in Jake Bullet's universe who was called to the scene of Philby Frutch's murder at the Savalas television station. She told the cyborg that Frutch had been taking stupid drugs **[M-SMG1.11(c4)]**. When Hall was injured by a runaway car that crashed into the ambulance containing Frutch's body, Bullet took her to a hospital before resuming his investigation **[M-SMG1.12(c1)]**.

- **Halley, Sandra, Doctor:** A cyber-psychologist at Brainfade, a business in Jake Bullet's universe, who worked on government contracts involving methods of eliminating free will. She suffered from a degenerative bone disease, and was confined to an elaborate trolley. Halley was murdered while working late one evening, her vitals cable severed. The murder prompted Bullet to investigate the facility and enter a virtual-reality program, where he interviewed a backup copy of Halley's personality **[M-SMG2.7(c4)]**.

  Upon learning of Halley's involvement in the development of a mind-control spike that caused a rash of crimes citywide, Bullet returned to interview Halley's backup once more, only to discover that it had been erased. Halley's boss, Doctor Scofrenia, showed Jake a virtual simulation of the murder, implicating a co-worker and test subject named Carl **[M-SMG2.8(c1)]**.

  Despite this evidence, Bullet tried to arrest Scofrenia, but Carl pushed him out a window, causing him to land on the fleeing Scofrenia. The cyborg returned to Brainfade days later and found Halley inhabiting Carl's body. She had used her own brain tissue in the mind-control spikes, enabling a co-worker named Tina to reconstitute her mind and soul into the former test subject. Jake agreed to keep her invention a secret, but police monitoring the conversation promptly arrested him **[M-SMG2.9(c4)]**.

- **Halogen Drive:** A setting on *Starbug 1*'s sonar scope display. This setting was not highlighted as the crew charted the course of a despair squid **[T-SER5.6]**.

- ***Hamilton Academicals—The Glory Years*:** A publication outlining the heyday of the Hamilton Academical Football Club, a Scottish football team at Hamilton Academy. Lister found a copy of this book in his own personal Cyberhell—an illusion created during his incarceration in the virtual-reality prison Cyberia **[N-LST]**.

- ***Hamlet, Prince of Denmark, The Tragedy of*:** A seventeenth-century play written by William Shakespeare, often cited as his most popular work **[RL]**. In attempting to use the Holly Hop Drive to return to Earth, the *Red Dwarf* crew instead entered a parallel universe in which the sexes were reversed. In this reality, *Hamlet* was penned by Wilma Shakespeare **[T-SER2.6]**.

  While marooned aboard *Starbug 1* on an icy planet, Lister burned Rimmer's books to stay warm, including *The Complete Works of Shakespeare*. Arnold protested the destruction of what was likely the only remaining copy of *Hamlet*, but admitted he never actually read it **[T-SER3.2]**.

- **Hammer, Mike:** A fictional private investigator created by American author Mickey Spillane **[RL]**. Mike Hammer was one of Jake Bullet's role models **[M-SMG2.6(a)]**.

- ***Hammond Heaven*:** A recording stored in the Officers' Quarters of the "low" *Red Dwarf* **[T-SER5.5]**.

- **Hammond organ:** An electronic musical instrument invented by Laurens Hammond in 1934, originally as a low-cost alternative to pipe organs in churches **[RL]**. Rimmer was fond of Hammond organ music, particularly the stylings of Reggie Wilson **[T-SER4.1]**.

- **Hammond Organ F.A. Cup:** An association football tournament in the universe known as Alternative 6829/B. The Smegchester Rovers, captained by Ray Rimmer (Arnold Rimmer's analog in that reality) won the F.A. Cup in 2180 with help from Ace Rimmer. The prize for winning was the Reggie Wilson Memorial Trophy **[M-SMG1.8(c4)]**.

- **Hammond Organ Owners' Society:** An organization whose members were required to own a Hammond organ. Rimmer often tried to impress his *Red Dwarf* crewmates by reciting tales from his tenure as the Society's treasurer, but to little effect **[T-SER4.5]**.

- **Hampton, Gerald, Flight Officer:** A pseudonym that Cat assumed when Rimmer impersonated a Space Corps captain aboard the *Trojan* to impress his half-brother, Howard. Arnold claimed "Gerald Hampton" was the vessel's navigation officer **[T-SER10.1]**.

- **hamster:** A small rodent in the subfamily Cricetidae, commonly kept as house pets **[RL]**. While aboard a derelict spaceship, Cat accidentally trapped Lister in a machine that changed the DNA of living organisms, which transformed Lister into a chicken. Trying to reverse the effects, Kryten activated the machine again, turning him into a hamster, before restoring him to his original state. When asked about the experience, Lister decided being a hamster was preferable to being a chicken, due to the size difference between an egg and a chicken's bum **[T-SER4.2]**.

- **hamstergram:** A novelty service that employed hamsters to deliver well wishes to individuals or parties. Lister mused that former *Tales of the Riverbank* star Hammy Hamster likely ended up doing hamstergrams after his career plummeted **[T-SER4.1]**.

- **hanaka:** A unit of time among Kinitawowi GELFs. One hanaka was exactly equal to one Earth minute **[T-SER6.4]**.

- **handroid:** A robotic sex worker on Mimas specializing in manually pleasuring customers. A poster advertising handroids and blo-bots adorned a wall of the Hotel Paradiso **[M-SMG2.3(c4)]**.

- **handshake:** A method of electronically establishing contact between two spaceships. Upon encountering the *Enlightenment*, Holly failed to establish a handshake between the holoship and *Starbug 1*. Kryten attributed this to holoship crews being notoriously arrogant and deeming other life forms inferior **[T-SER5.1]**.

- **Handsome, Hank, Space Adventurer:** A fictional character who boldly explored space. When Lister claimed the future could not be undone, Rimmer noted that he was a vending machine repairman, not "Hank Handsome, Space Adventurer" **[T-SER8.4]**.

- **Hangar 101:** A building located in Europa's Space Corps R&D facility in one of Ace Rimmer's universes. A duplicate version of Ace's ship, *Wildfire*, was stored in this hangar after materializing three days prior to its scheduled launch. There, technicians attempted to determine why its pilot, a duplicate of Ace, was scorched **[N-BCK]**.

PREFIX
RL: Real life

T-: Television Episodes
SER: Television series
IDW: "Identity Within"
USA1: Unaired U.S. pilot
USA2: Unaired U.S. demo

R-: *The Bodysnatcher Collection*
SER: Remastered episodes
BOD: "Bodysnatcher"
DAD: "Dad"
FTH: "Lister's Father"
INF: "Infinity Patrol"
END: "The End" (original assembly)

N-: Novels
INF: *Infinity Welcomes Careful Drivers*
BTL: *Better Than Life*
LST: *Last Human*

BCK: *Backwards*
OMN: *Red Dwarf Omnibus*

M-: Magazines
SMG: *Smegazine*

W-: Websites
OFF: Official website
NAN: *Prelude to Nanarchy*
AND: *Androids*
DIV: Diva-Droid
DIB: Duane Dibbley

CRP: Crapola
GEN: Geneticon
LSR: Leisure World Intl.
JMC: Jupiter Mining Corporation
AIT: *A.I. Today*
HOL: HoloPoint

G-: Roleplaying Game
RPG: *Core Rulebook*
BIT: *A.I. Screen Extra Bits* booklet
SOR: *Series Sourcebook*
OTH: Other RPG material

- **Han hasset:** A phrase in the Kinitawowi language, meaning "blessed" **[T-SER6.4]**.

- **Hank:** A crewmember aboard a vessel that crashed into an asteroid in Psiren territory, who died when the telepathic Psirens attacked. A shipmate later recorded a log entry reporting several deaths, including Hank's **[T-SER6.1(d)]**.

- **Hannah:** A dog, likely a bull terrier, belonging to Lister's adoptive father, Mr. Wilmot. A picture of Hannah and part of Lister's dad's leg was among the photographs in a slideshow that Dave showed Cat. The feline took an instant disliking to the pooch, warning Lister that he would chase away any dogs he encountered **[T-SER1.2]**.

    ***NOTE:** Mr. Wilmot's name was revealed in the novel* Last Human.

- **Hans:** An associate of Captain Voorhese, a Nazi commander on War World **[W-OFF]**.

    ***NOTE:** This may have been Hans Müller, a name printed on a door at the Nazi camp in episode 7.2 ("Stoke Me a Clipper.")*

- **happiness:** An emotional state brought on by positive or pleasant stimuli **[RL]**. While being analyzed by *Red Dwarf*'s chief psychiatric counselor, Kryten boasted that happiness was an emotion he had acquired with Lister's help **[T-SER8.1]**.

    ***NOTE:** This contradicted episode 4.2 ("DNA"), which revealed that the mechanoid possessed a "happiness mode," seemingly negating the need to acquire this emotion.*

- **happiness mode:** A software function of 4000 Series mechanoids, enabling them to experience the equivalent of happiness. Kryten declared himself to be in happiness mode when a DNA resequencing machine aboard a derelict vessel changed him into a human being. The only other time he recalled something similar was when he accidentally wielded his groinal socket to a front-load washing machine **[T-SER4.2]**.

    ***NOTE:** Episode 8.1 ("Back in the Red, Part One") later claimed Kryten had only acquired the emotion of happiness through his relationship with Lister, seemingly ruling out his having such a mode.*

- **Happy Astro:** A pub aboard *Red Dwarf,* decorated with plastic oak beams. Rimmer periodically treated himself to a relaxing visit to the pub during the last few days before his Astronavigation Exam, but typically left more stressed than when he arrived **[N-INF]**.

- **Happy Eater:** A chain of family-oriented restaurants in the United Kingdom **[RL]**. Holly lamented that *Red Dwarf* had traveled more than three million years without passing a single Happy Eater **[B-LOG]**.

    ***NOTE:** By 1997, Happy Eater was purchased by Granada, which converted the restaurants to Little Chefs. By Holly's era, the chain would have thus been out of business for centuries.*

- **Happy Hopper:** A taxi hopper company serving the Saturnian moon of Mimas. One of Happy Hopper's vehicles was numbered thirty-two **[M-SMG2.5(c6)]**.

- **hard light:** A type of hologrammatic technology developed at a scientific research station by a gestalt entity called Legion. Unlike soft light holograms, those created with hard light technology could touch, feel and eat, with the added bonus of being nearly indestructible. When the *Starbug 1* crew first met Legion, he converted Rimmer's light bee from soft to hard light, giving him the physical body he longed for **[T-SER6.2]**.

- **hard light drive:** A device created by Legion that projected a hologram using hard light instead of soft, giving the hologram a physical body with which to interact with its environment **[T-SER6.2]**. The hard light drive also generated a hard light remote belt, enabling a hologram to move outside the confines of its host ship **[W-OFF]**.

    Hard light drives were also sold by HoloSoft Industries in Crapola Inc.'s annual *SCABBY* catalog **[G-RPG]**. Despite numerous claims to the contrary, hologrammic technologies firm HoloPoint failed to develop a working hard light hologram **[W-HOL]**.

    After Legion installed a hard light drive in Rimmer's light bee, the hologram was astonished to find that he had regained physical form **[T-SER6.2]**. When circumstances required, Arnold could switch the drive from hard to soft light and back again **[T-SER10.4]**.

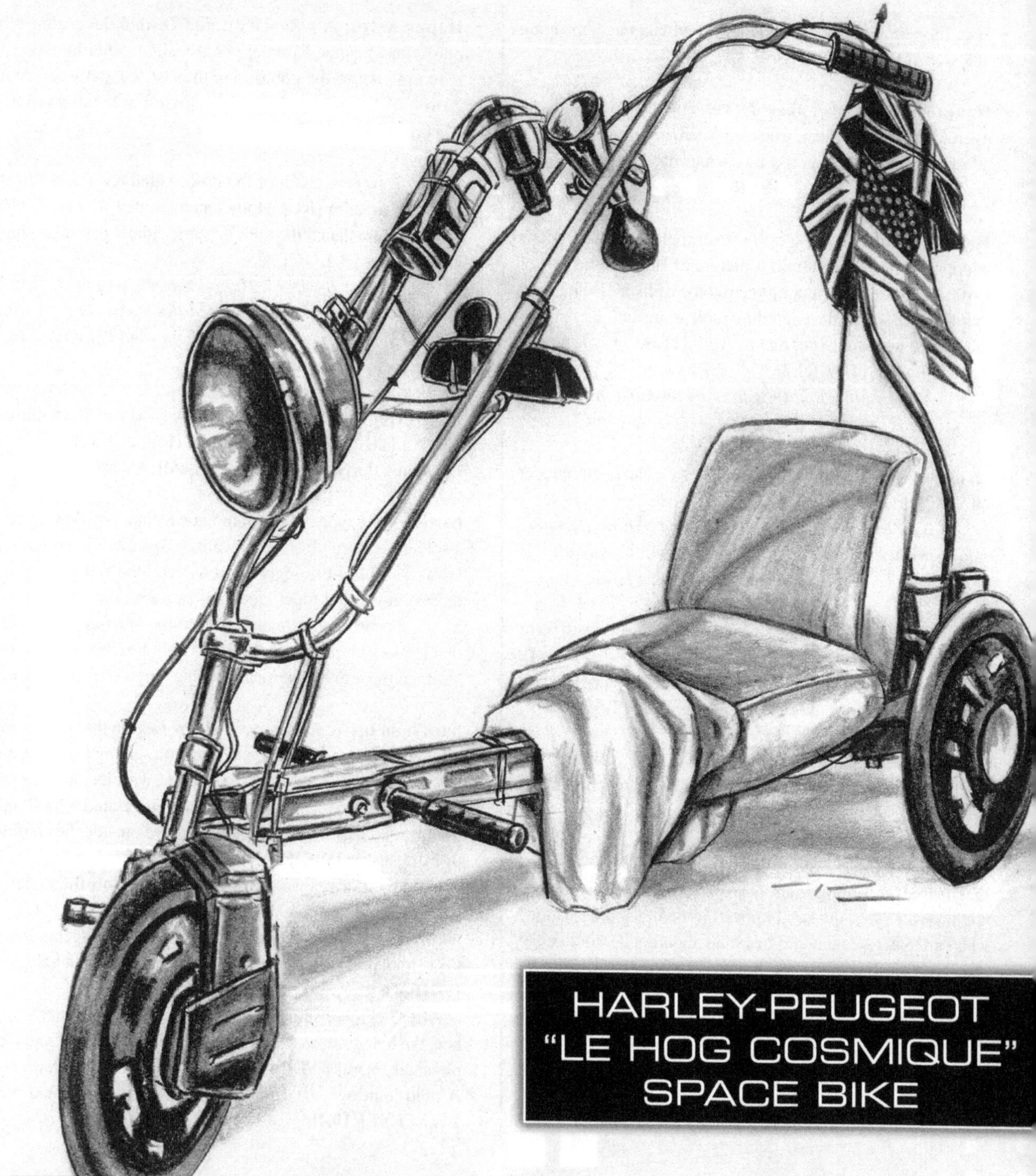

HARLEY-PEUGEOT "LE HOG COSMIQUE" SPACE BIKE

PREFIX
RL: Real life

T-: Television Episodes
- **SER:** Television series
- **IDW:** "Identity Within"
- **USA1:** Unaired U.S. pilot
- **USA2:** Unaired U.S. demo

R-: *The Bodysnatcher Collection*
- **SER:** Remastered episodes
- **BOD:** "Bodysnatcher"
- **DAD:** "Dad"
- **FTH:** "Lister's Father"
- **INF:** "Infinity Patrol"
- **END:** "The End" (original assembly)

N-: Novels
- **INF:** *Infinity Welcomes Careful Drivers*
- **BTL:** *Better Than Life*
- **LST:** *Last Human*
- **BCK:** *Backwards*
- **OMN:** *Red Dwarf Omnibus*

M-: Magazines
- **SMG:** *Smegazine*

W-: Websites
- **OFF:** Official website
- **NAN:** *Prelude to Nanarchy*
- **AND:** *Androids*
- **DIV:** Diva-Droid
- **DIB:** Duane Dibbley
- **CRP:** Crapola
- **GEN:** Geneticon
- **LSR:** Leisure World Intl.
- **JMC:** Jupiter Mining Corporation
- **AIT:** *A.I. Today*
- **HOL:** HoloPoint

G-: Roleplaying Game
- **RPG:** *Core Rulebook*
- **BIT:** *A.I. Screen Extra Bits* booklet
- **SOR:** *Series Sourcebook*
- **OTH:** Other RPG material

- **hard light projection mode:** A function of hologrammic projection systems that converted a hologram into hard light, giving it the ability to touch or interact with its surroundings. It could be identified by the color of a hologram's uniform, which turned blue upon converting to hard light.

  While reviving Irene Edgington at the Erroneous Reasoning Research Academy (ERRA) station, Rimmer converted his body to soft light so he could pass through a wall and access the station's stasis room. He then converted back to hard light projection mode once on the other side **[T-SER10.4]**.

  > ***NOTE:*** *Rimmer's light bee would seem to negate the possibility of his passing through walls. Given the numerous explanations of hologrammic technology offered in the* Red Dwarf *franchise, he may have been using some other form of projection at the time.*

- **hard light remote belt:** A portable device generated by a hologram's hard light drive that allowed it to move outside the confines of its host ship **[T-SER6.5]**. The belt enabled the hologram to switch between power sources, thereby extending its range. The technology was sold by HoloSoft Industries in Crapola Inc.'s annual *SCABBY* catalog **[G-RPG]**.

- **Hardy, Oliver ("Ollie"):** A twentieth-century American comedic actor, best known as half of the comedy duo Laurel and Hardy **[RL]**. When a flood destroyed *Starbug 1*'s Indian food supply, Lister complained that life without curry would be like Laurel without Hardy **[T-SER7.1]**.

  A waxdroid replica of Hardy was created for the Waxworld theme park. Left on their own for millions of years, the waxdroids attained sentience and became embroiled in a park-wide resource war between Villain World and Hero World (to which Hardy belonged). The Hardy waxdroid was captured during the conflict and subjected to Caligula's Rampant Wildebeest torture **[G-SOR]**.

- **Hardy, Robert:** A British film, television and theatrical actor, known for his work in such movies as *All Creatures Great and Small* and the *Harry Potter* film series (in which he portrayed Cornelius Fudge) **[RL]**. Cat found a recording of *Robert Hardy Reads Tess of the D'Urbervilles* enjoyable—as did Lister, due to its having been warped and twisted, distorting the sound beyond recognition **[T-SER2.5]**.

  > ***NOTE:*** *Robert Hardy never recorded* Tess of the D'Urbervilles *in the real world, though since the novel was written by Thomas Hardy, this may have been an in-joke.*

- **"Hark! The Herald Angels Sing":** A traditional English Christmas carol written by Charles Wesley **[RL]**. While trapped in an addictive version of *Better Than Life*, Lister imagined a five-piece brass band playing "Hark! The Herald Angels Sing" in the town square of Bedford Falls. In the illusion, Lister brought his sons, Jim and Bexley, to join the town's population around a Christmas tree and listen to the performance **[N-BTL]**.

- **Harley Davidson:** An American motorcycle brand with a tradition of heavy customization that gave rise to the chopper style of bikes **[RL]**. Harley Davidson temporarily merged with French carmaker Peugeot, resulting in the Harley-Peugeot "Le Hog Cosmique" space bike **[G-SOR]**. While playing the total-immersion game *Better Than Life*, Lister and Cat conjured up a Harley Davidson, license plate C222 PFY, to bring them to a restaurant **[T-SER2.2]**.

- **Harley-Peugeot "Le Hog Cosmique" space bike:** A small recreational craft consisting of a rocket engine, a seat, handlebars and three wheels, used for limited space travel. However, the bike lacked an oxygen supply, navigational and communications systems, and a star drive **[G-SOR]**.

  Lister frequently roamed *Red Dwarf*'s hallways on a space bike. After rebelling against Rimmer's orders, Kryten used the vehicle to leave the mining ship and pursue his dream of tending a garden on an S-class planet. That dream was cut short, however, when the mechanoid crashed the space bike onto an asteroid **[T-SER2.1]**.

- **Har Megiddo 46758976/Kry:** A code that the Kinitawowi gave Kryten to activate the Oblivion virus, a computer bug designed to kill the electricity of any infected system. The mechanoid used this code to power down Cyberia so his comrades could rescue Lister's doppelgänger from the prison **[N-LST]**.

- **Harrington, Mrs.:** *See* Johnson, Mrs.

B-: Books
PRG: *Red Dwarf Programme Guide*
SUR: *Red Dwarf Space Corps Survival Manual*
PRM: *Primordial Soup*
SOS: *Son of Soup*
SCE: *Scenes from the Dwarf*
LOG: *Red Dwarf Log No. 1996*
RD8: *Red Dwarf VIII*
EVR: *The Log: A Dwarfer's Guide to Everything*

X-: Misc.
PRO: Promotional materials, videos, etc.
PST: Posters at DJ XVII (2013)
CAL: 2008 calendar
RNG: Cell phone ringtones
MOB: Mobisode ("Red Christmas")
CIN: *Children in Need* sketch
GEK: *Geek Week* intros by Kryten
TNG: "Tongue-Tied" video
XMS: Bill Pearson's Christmas special pitch script
XVD: Bill Pearson's Christmas special pitch video
OTH: Other *Red Dwarf* appearances

SUFFIX
DVD:
(d) – Deleted scene
(o) – Outtake
(b) – Bonus DVD material (other)
(e) – Extended version

SMEGAZINES:
(c) – Comic
(a) – Article

OTHER:
(s) – Early/unused script draft
(s1) – Alternate version of script

- **Harriott, Ainsley:** A British celebrity chef and star of the television cooking show *Can't Cook, Won't Cook* **[RL]**. Harriott once recorded a special episode in *Starbug 1*'s galley titled *Can't Smeg, Won't Smeg*, featuring Lister, Rimmer, Kryten, Kochanski and Duane Dibbley **[T-SER4(b)]**.

  NOTE: *There are several ways one could attempt to make this fit continuity... none of which will be explored here.*

- **Harris:** A character on the television soap opera *Androids*. Harris was the show's token gay character, whose only function was to anger and confuse other male characters while befriending the female ones **[W-AND]**.

  NOTE: *Harris' profile on the* Androids *website used an image of Brooke Junior from late in the* Smegazines' Androids *comics, after he had an "oil change" operation (a euphemism for sex reassignment therapy).*

- **Harris ("Headbanger"):** A *Red Dwarf* crewmember from whom Lister stole some hallucinogenic fungi known as Titan mushrooms, to feed to Rimmer as a prank **[T-SER2.4]**. Nanobots resurrected Harris three million years after he died during the cadmium II disaster. He was scheduled to fight Baxter, an inmate in the Tank, in a Psychoweight Championship boxing match set to air on Krytie TV **[X-CAL]**.

  NOTE: *The implication in the calendar was that Harris was an inmate, since no one outside of the Tank supposedly knew it existed; however, it would have been impossible for Lister to obtain the mushrooms from him had he been in the "top-secret" brig at the time. A likely scenario is that Harris was sent to the Tank shortly after the mushroom incident, possibly for drug (mushroom) possession.*

- **Harrison, Chantel:** A *Red Dwarf* crewmember whose interests included cinema, literature, horse-riding and ballet. Harrison died during the cadmium II disaster **[B-SOS]**. Three million years later, Lister, Cat and Kryten held interviews with several holograms, including Harrison, to replace Rimmer after he enlisted to join the holoship *Enlightenment*. Harrison declined the offer, however, preferring to remain dead than to live with the trio **[T-SER5.1]**.

  NOTE: *It is unknown whether the nanobots resurrected Harrison in Series VIII.*

- **Harrison, Rex:** A twentieth-century British actor known for his performances in *My Fair Lady*, *The Ghost and Mrs. Muir* and *Doctor Dolittle* **[RL]**. While occupying Kochanski's hologrammic body, Rimmer referenced the actor in an attempt to convince Lister he was really her **[T-SER1.3(d)]**.

- **Harry:** An associate of Rimmer—possibly his Learjet pilot—whom the hologram imagined employing while trapped in an addictive version of *Better Than Life*. Arnold believed he had returned to Earth, become famously wealthy and purchased a Learjet. Before any planned trips, Rimmer would call Harry with instructions to keep the plane on standby **[N-INF]**.

- **Hasselhoff, David:** *See* Boone, Pat

- **"Hate":** A word tattooed on the right-hand knuckles of Drigg, a dissonant GELF imprisoned on the tourist planet GELFWorld **[M-SMG2.2(c4)]**.

- **Havac ("Havac the Imbecile"), King:** A remarkably stupid fifth-century Norwegian warrior king, who had a half-brother even less intelligent. Frustrated at how useless Kryten and Cat were in assisting him during a mining operation, Lister decided that only Havac and his brother would have been more inept **[N-OMN]**.

  NOTE: *This was changed from the novel* Infinity Welcomes Careful Drivers, *which cited George III and Brian Kidd. In the real world, there was no King Havac—or any other monarch—in fifth-century Norway, since the country was not unified until the ninth century.*

- **"Have a Fantastic Period":** A phrase printed on a banner that Kryten hung in the cell he and Kochanski shared in *Red Dwarf*'s brig, after Lister misled him into thinking that would be appropriate. Kryten also presented her with a gift-wrapped tampon **[T-SER8.8]**.

- **"Have You Got a Good Memory?":** A quiz published in a magazine aboard *Starbug 1*. Lister became irate when he discovered the quiz had been filled in, before recalling that he had taken the test himself **[T-SER6.2]**.

PREFIX
RL: Real life

T-: Television Episodes
SER: Television series
IDW: "Identity Within"
USA1: Unaired U.S. pilot
USA2: Unaired U.S. demo

R-: *The Bodysnatcher Collection*
SER: Remastered episodes
BOD: "Bodysnatcher"
DAD: "Dad"
FTH: "Lister's Father"
INF: "Infinity Patrol"
END: "The End" (original assembly)

N-: Novels
INF: *Infinity Welcomes Careful Drivers*
BTL: *Better Than Life*
LST: *Last Human*
BCK: *Backwards*
OMN: *Red Dwarf Omnibus*

M-: Magazines
SMG: *Smegazine*

W-: Websites
OFF: Official website
NAN: *Prelude to Nanarchy*
AND: *Androids*
DIV: Diva-Droid
DIB: Duane Dibbley
CRP: Crapola
GEN: Geneticon
LSR: Leisure World Intl.
JMC: Jupiter Mining Corporation
AIT: *A.I. Today*
HOL: HoloPoint

G-: Roleplaying Game
RPG: *Core Rulebook*
BIT: *A.I. Screen Extra Bits* booklet
SOR: *Series Sourcebook*
OTH: Other RPG material

- **Haydn, Franz Joseph:** An eighteenth-century Austrian composer of the Classical period **[RL]**. Rimmer's favorite piece of lovemaking music was Haydn's "Surprise Symphony." While trapped in an addictive version of *Better Than Life*, he played that song during sex with his wife, Juanita Chicata **[N-BTL]**.

- ***Hayze*:** A notoriously buggy artificial-reality game in which players progressed to the Eye of Serenity by solving puzzles. One common program glitch caused a concert piano to fall on the heads of players entering the game. A workaround entailed singing a line from Barry Manilow's "Mandy" to prevent anything musical from approaching **[B-SUR]**.

- **hazard approach lights:** A series of indicators on the dashboard of *Starbug 1*'s cockpit that signaled a proximity alert. A phasing comet once triggered the lights, alerting the crew to the approaching danger **[T-SER7.5]**.

- **hcanau:** A word in the Kinitawowi language, meaning "honor" **[T-SER6.4]**.

  NOTE: This term's spelling was not indicated in the DVD captions, but appeared in online scripts.

- **HD-3500 homing device:** A shuttlecraft component that detected specific electronic or DNA signatures from up to a light-year away **[G-SOR]**.The *Red Dwarf* crew used such a device to locate the ship's black box recorder, which had gone missing **[T-SER2.3]**.

- **Head:** A nickname that Cat called Holly, referencing the computer's appearance as a disembodied head **[N-INF]**.

- **Headless:** A name that Lister assigned to one of twelve rogue droids he purchased from the Kinitawowi to break his doppelgänger out of the virtual-reality prison Cyberia. This particular droid had no head **[N-LST]**.

- **Head of Records:** The title of a GELF tasked with keeping track of inmates serving time at the Cyberia prison complex on Lotomi 5 **[N-LST]**.

- **Head of Safety:** A position that Lister made up, which involved analyzing a dangerous situation and advising others on the best way to run away from it. To convince the nanobot-resurrected Rimmer to escape *Red Dwarf* with him, Lister claimed his hologrammic counterpart had held this position **[T-SER8.3]**.

- **Heads-U-Like:** A hypothetical company from which Lister sarcastically proposed ordering a new head for Kryten, after the mechanoid blew his last spare due to a full negadrive **[T-SER7.6(d)]**.

- **He Ain't Heavy, He's My Brothel:** An android bordello on the television soap opera *Androids*. Mollee, an outspoken opponent of the whorehouse until her circuits were scrambled, took over the business—formerly known as Brothel-U-Like—after an attempt on Kelly's life left the previous owner hospitalized **[M-SMG2.3(c2)]**.

  NOTE: The music ballad "He Ain't Heavy, He's My Brother" was recorded by Kelly Gordon in 1969, and later by The Hollies and Neil Diamond.

- **Health and Safety Executive:** The title of the officer in charge of health and safety aboard *Red Dwarf*. Rimmer assigned himself this position after the cadmium II disaster killed the ship's crew. According to Rimmer, accident report forms needed to be submitted to the Accident Report Assessment Unit, care of him **[T-SER10.4]**.

- **Health and Safety Protocol 121:** A safety regulation that Rimmer devised while renovating *Red Dwarf*'s health and safety procedures after the cadmium II leak killed the ship's crew. This protocol stated that food and drink were not allowed near the Drive Room's work area **[T-SER10.4]**.

- **Heat 400:** A type of hairdryer used on War World. After being captured by enemy forces who mistook her for a member of the resistance, Princess Bonjella drew a schematic of a "secret weapon" she claimed to have stolen from the resistance (a drawing of her Heat 400 hairdryer) to convince them of her identity **[W-OFF]**.

- **Heathcote, Natalie:** The co-creator of the television soap opera *Androids*, along with Bartholomew Mews. Heathcote and Mews filmed twelve pilot episodes before the series was picked up seventeen years after its first pitch. The pair eventually split

over a dispute involving merchandise percentages, working together only once more on the controversial late-night sex-and-fruit drama *Del Monte* **[W-AND]**.

- **Heathrow Lister:** A hypothetical airport that Lister joked about being named after, mistakenly assuming President John F. Kennedy had been named after New York City's JFK International Airport, and not the other way around **[T-SER7.1(e)]**.

- **heating system:** An environmental system that maintained cabin temperature aboard *Starbug 1*. After Kryten sabotaged the heating system to prevent Kochanski from taking a bath, the crew had to trek through miles of the shuttle's ductwork **[T-SER7.4]**.

- **heat outlet:** An opening in the lower backside area of 4000 Series mechanoids, used to dissipate heat buildup. Kryten occasionally used this outlet to dry cutlery **[T-SER10.4]**. It was also called the rear exhaust port **[M-SMG2.4(c5)]**.

- **heat seeker:** A type of ammunition used in bazookoid launchers aboard *Red Dwarf*. When fired, they resembled bright blue spheres. Heat seekers could not register holograms or mechanoids, due to their low heat signatures **[T-SER3.3]**.

- **"Heaven Is 10 Zillion Light Years Away":** A song recorded in 1974 by American artist Stevie Wonder **[RL]**. This song was played at George McIntyre's funeral aboard *Red Dwarf* **[N-OMN]**.

  NOTE: *This was mentioned in the pilot episode's first-draft script, published in the* Red Dwarf Omnibus, *but was changed to "See You Later, Alligator" in the filmed version.*

- **"Heaven This Way":** A tattooed phrase on the inner thigh of the Solidgram body of sex worker Trixie LaBouche, whom the *Red Dwarf* crew imagined while trapped in an addictive version of *Better Than Life*. The tattoo was accompanied by an arrow pointing up to Trixie's groin **[N-BTL]**.

- **Hech-Ech-Ech Annechech-Ech:** A Kinitawowi warrior stationed on Echech 3, where the Kinitawowi Open golf tournament was held. Armed with a rifle, the GELF greeted new players upon their arrival, then escorted them to see Queen Ech-Ghekk-Agg-Hecch-Ech-Ech for the tournament's opening ceremonies **[G-RPG]**.

- **Hector:** A Pleasure GELF—a type of genetically engineered life form, created for the purpose of providing companionship—and a brilliant scientist. Hector was married to another Pleasure GELF named Camille, and the two worked together to find a cure for their condition until Camille left him. Searching for years, he found Camille on *Red Dwarf* in the company of Kryten, with whom she had fallen in love. Despite Camille's objections, Kryten convinced her to return to Hector and continue their research **[T-SER4.1]**.

- **Hefner, Hugh:** An American publishing mogul and founder of the adult magazine *Playboy*, well-known for his sexual appetites **[RL]**. While playing the total-immersion video game *Better Than Life*, Rimmer conjured up a simulation of Yvonne McGruder to enjoy another sexual encounter with, then boasted to Lister and Cat, comparing himself to Hefner **[T-SER2.2]**.

- **Heidegger:** A Space Corps physicist, considered one of the most brilliant minds of his era. Heidegger was involved in a classified military project aboard a scientific research station to create Legion, a gestalt entity encompassing the intellect and emotions of the four project scientists, including his own. Heidegger eventually died, as did the other scientists, leaving Legion nothing but a floating essence until the *Starbug 1* crew visited the station **[T-SER6.2]**.

  NOTE: *Heidegger's name was presumably inspired by that of German philosopher Martin Heidegger, who wrote about gestalt psychology.*

- **Heimlich maneuver, The:** An emergency technique designed to save the life of a choking individual, created by thoracic surgeon Henry Heimlich **[RL]**. When Kryten accessed his memory banks for methods of consoling a crying woman, his corrupted data files pointed him instead to the Heimlich maneuver, which he attempted to perform on Kochanski. Taken aback by the gesture, Kochanski stopped crying, leading Kryten to believe it was successful **[T-SER7.4]**.

- **Heinkel He 111:** A German aircraft built to masquerade as a transport. The Heinkel He 111 was the primary Luftwaffe bomber in use during the early stages of World War II **[RL]**. Captain Voorhese piloted such a craft in his dimension **[W-OFF]**. Ace Rimmer was held captive aboard Voorhese's Heinkel, but destroyed it during his escape **[T-SER7.2]**.

- **Heinman, Mr. ("Bull," "Bullethead"):** Rimmer's school gym teacher on Io, who took pleasure in making preposterous physical demands on Arnold. Nicknamed "Bull" due to the shape of his head (which resembled a bullet), Heinman despised students whom he considered a "wet, weirdo or fattie" **[N-BTL]**. He was also called "Bullethead" **[N-BCK]**.

  While trapped in an addictive version of *Better Than Life*, Rimmer imagined Heinman as a prison guard at a penitentiary in which Arnold's essence was incarcerated as a soundwave. Heinman, known in the illusion as Officer 592, liked to read *Combat and Survival* magazine **[N-BTL]**.

- ***Heisenberg's Uncertainty Principle for Beginners*:** A book Rimmer owned aboard *Red Dwarf* **[N-INF]**.

- **Heliotrope:** An alert condition indicating severe damage to a 4000 Series mechanoid. After an accident on a psi-moon left Kryten injured and stranded, his CPU assessed the situation and periodically updated his head-up display. His condition changed to Heliotrope when Lister began cutting the mechanoid in two to dislodge him from the wreckage **[T-SER5.3]**.

- **helium 3 isotopes de la maison:** The second course in a special mechanoid meal that Holly created for Kryten's last-day party **[T-SER3.6]**.

- **Hellfish, Johnny:** A nickname Rimmer called Cat while questioning why he was sitting atop the captain's photocopier machine making copies of his rear end **[T-SER10.5(d)]**.

- ***Hello!*:** A weekly British publication covering celebrity news and human-interest stories **[RL]**. Lister described a temporal rip that the *Starbug 1* crew encountered as moving "faster than a copy of *Hello!* in a nunnery," making it impossible to outrun **[T-SER7.3]**.

- **Hell's Angels Motorcycle Club (HAMC), The:** An international outlaw motorcycle club that the U.S. Department of Justice deemed an organized crime syndicate, whose members typically rode Harley-Davidson bikes **[RL]**. Kochanski snogged Hell's Angels members as a form of rebellion after leaving cyberschool **[T-SER7.4(d)]**.

  Rimmer once exclaimed that his long hair made him resemble a Hell's Angel, and requested a haircut from Holly, who was busy with lightspeed calculations at the time **[T-SER1.2]**.

- **Helsinki:** The capital city of Finland **[RL]**. Helsinki was home to a Space Corps research center. During her career with the Space Corps, Nirvanah Crane was stationed at this center, as well as others around the solar system **[W-OFF]**.

- **Henderson, JD, Ground Based Flight Commander:** A Space Corps officer who addressed the *Red Dwarf* crew on the back cover of *Red Dwarf Log Book No. 1996.* In the text, Henderson outlined what was expected in the crew's entries, and expressed the hope that none of them would be eaten alive during their mission **[B-LOG]**.

- **Henderson, Shore Patrolwoman:** A dark-haired Shore Patrol officer on Mimas. She was one of two officers tasked with retrieving Lister from his temporary residence—a luggage locker at the Mimas Central Shuttle Station—when his papers came in from the Corps, enabling him to join *Red Dwarf* **[N-INF]**.

- **Hendrix, Jimi:** A twentieth-century guitarist and singer-songwriter of such hits as "Are You Experienced?," "Foxy Lady" and "All Along the Watchtower" **[RL]**. While trapped in an addictive version of *Better Than Life*, Cat entertained himself in his golden castle with a hand-picked, seven-piece band, which included Hendrix on lead guitar **[N-INF]**.

  Lister once awoke from a two-hundred-year deep sleep aboard *Starbug 1* to find his memory temporarily missing. To jog his memory, Kryten handed him his guitar, which he strummed chaotically and out of tune. Lister admitted he could not play the instrument, but Kryten assured him that when his memory returned, he'd firmly believe he could rock like the ghost of Hendrix **[T-SER6.1]**.

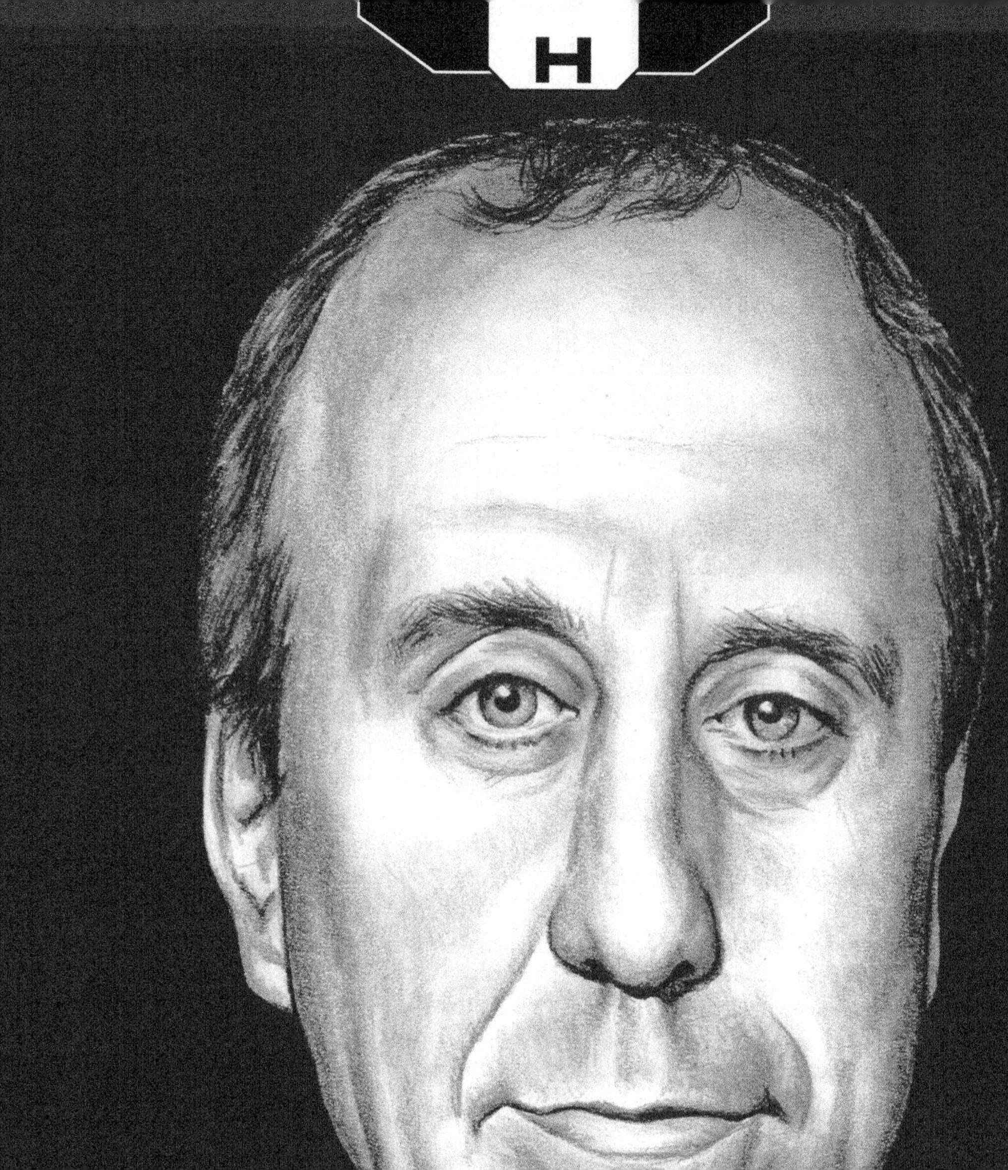

HOLLY 6000

PREFIX
RL: Real life

T-: Television Episodes
- **SER:** Television series
- **IDW:** "Identity Within"
- **USA1:** Unaired U.S. pilot
- **USA2:** Unaired U.S. demo

R-: *The Bodysnatcher Collection*
- **SER:** Remastered episodes
- **BOD:** "Bodysnatcher"
- **DAD:** "Dad"
- **FTH:** "Lister's Father"
- **INF:** "Infinity Patrol"
- **END:** "The End" (original assembly)

N-: Novels
- **INF:** *Infinity Welcomes Careful Drivers*
- **BTL:** *Better Than Life*
- **LST:** *Last Human*
- **BCK:** *Backwards*
- **OMN:** *Red Dwarf Omnibus*

M-: Magazines
- **SMG:** *Smegazine*

W-: Websites
- **OFF:** Official website
- **NAN:** *Prelude to Nanarchy*
- **AND:** *Androids*
- **DIV:** Diva-Droid
- **DIB:** Duane Dibbley
- **CRP:** Crapola
- **GEN:** Geneticon
- **LSR:** Leisure World Intl.
- **JMC:** Jupiter Mining Corporation
- **AIT:** *A.I. Today*
- **HOL:** HoloPoint

G-: Roleplaying Game
- **RPG:** *Core Rulebook*
- **BIT:** *A.I. Screen Extra Bits* booklet
- **SOR:** *Series Sourcebook*
- **OTH:** Other RPG material

B-: Books
PRG: *Red Dwarf Programme Guide*
SUR: *Red Dwarf Space Corps Survival Manual*
PRM: *Primordial Soup*
SOS: *Son of Soup*
SCE: *Scenes from the Dwarf*
LOG: *Red Dwarf Log No. 1996*
RD8: *Red Dwarf VIII*
EVR: *The Log: A Dwarfer's Guide to Everything*

X-: Misc.
PRO: Promotional materials, videos, etc.
PST: Posters at DJ XVII (2013)
CAL: 2008 calendar
RNG: Cell phone ringtones
MOB: Mobisode ("Red Christmas")
CIN: *Children in Need* sketch
GEK: *Geek Week* intros by Kryten
TNG: "Tongue-Tied" video
XMS: Bill Pearson's Christmas special pitch script
XVD: Bill Pearson's Christmas special pitch video
OTH: Other *Red Dwarf* appearances

SUFFIX
DVD:
(d) – Deleted scene
(o) – Outtake
(b) – Bonus DVD material (other)
(e) – Extended version

SMEGAZINES:
(c) – Comic
(a) – Article

OTHER:
(s) – Early/unused script draft
(s1) – Alternate version of script

- **Henry:** A homeless man living in Bedford Falls, whom Lister imagined while trapped in an addictive version of *Better Than Life*. Henry's wife had passed away, leaving him to raise their two children alone, and became destitute after both kids died. Lister's sons, Jim and Bexley, offered Henry the money they had saved to buy a toy boat, so he could enjoy Christmas. Grateful for their generosity, he only took a dollar to get himself cleaned up for a job interview **[N-BTL]**.

- **Henry, Mrs.:** *See* Mary ("Mrs. Henry")

- ***Henry VIII*:** A history play written by William Shakespeare, circa 1613, about the life of the British monarch **[RL]**. While marooned aboard *Starbug 1* on an icy planet, Lister burned Rimmer's books to stay warm, including *The Complete Works of Shakespeare,* which he burned last. When Arnold suggested throwing another book on the fire, Lister told him that there were no others, adding that once the fire reached Act Five of *Henry VIII*, he would be a dead man **[T-SER3.2]**.

- **Henry VIII, King:** The ruler of England from 1509 to 1547 **[RL]**. A hologrammic Henry VIII made a guest appearance on an episode of the Groovy Channel 27 morning show *Good Morning Holograms,* which aired on Wednesday, the 27th of Geldof, 2362 **[M-SMG1.7(a)]**.

- ***Hermes*, SS:** A private courier craft operated by Deep Space Leisure, LLC **[G-SOR]**, on which Talia Garrett, a past associate of Captain Hollister, was a passenger. Kryten's nanobots reconstructed the *Hermes* at around the same time that they rebuilt *Red Dwarf*, but the courier craft was destroyed shortly thereafter by a chameleonic microbe. Before the vessel's destruction, Garrett (who had been resurrected by nanobots as well) managed to flee, unaware the creature had disguised itself as her escape pod **[T-SER8.8]**.

- **"hernunger":** A sound made by the pipes in Kochanski's quarters aboard *Starbug 1*, due to a heating system malfunction. It traditionally came before a "nureek" sound **[T-SER7.4]**.

- **Hero World:** An area of the Waxworld theme park, located next to Prehistoric World, and populated by waxdroid versions of Earth's most beloved historic figures, including Elvis Presley, Mother Theresa, Pythagoras, Abraham Lincoln and others. Its occupants became embroiled in a park-wide resource war with Villain World's denizens, who wanted to melt down the heroes' wax to make more of their own kind.

  During this war, the *Red Dwarf* crew transported to the planet using a Matter Paddle, with Lister and Cat materializing in Villain territory and Rimmer and Kryten arriving in Hero territory, where Presley and Pope Gregory captured them at gunpoint. Finding the heroes' army lacking, Rimmer assumed command, working many of the pacifistic waxdroids to death before ordering a frontal attack on the enemy's compound across a minefield, which wiped out the planet's remaining droids **[T-SER4.6]**.

- **herring:** A fish belonging to the genus Clupea, found mostly in the northern Atlantic and Pacific waters **[RL]**.

  Lister told Rimmer he regretted never asking Kochanski out, claiming she could have said "yes," and that stranger things had happened. Rimmer, however, could cite only two things stranger, including it raining herring in twelfth-century Burgundy. That night, Lister dreamed of this incident, but because he was afflicted with mutated pneumonia, his dream took solid form, causing it to rain herring in their quarters **[T-SER1.5]**.

  When Cat suffered a flashback hallucination making him believe he was again Duane Dibbley, he imagined being experimented on by deranged doctors. Desperate to escape, he grabbed a knife and threatened to kill himself. After being revived by lithium carbonate, he realized the knife was actually just a herring **[M-SMG1.9(c1)]**.

- **Hess, Rudolf, Deputy Führer:** A prominent politician in Nazi Germany who served under Adolf Hitler during World War II. Hess was sentenced to prison as a war criminal after attempting to make peace with the United Kingdom **[RL]**. During Rimmer's appeal aboard the penal station Justice World, Lister commented that the hologram "partied less than Rudolf Hess" **[T-SER4.3]**.

- **Heteroboy:** A nickname that Kochanski called Lister when he insisted he was not a homosexual **[T-SER7.4]**.

- **heuristic neural net:** An advanced network used on a derelict research platform discovered by the *Red Dwarf* crew. It utilized

experimental wetware technology, using a fluid matrix to stream data throughout the complex, and made calculations based on learned experiences **[M-SMG1.11(c2)]**.

- **hexasexahedroadecon:** One of William James Sidis' theoretical shapes, which Rimmer understood after a mind patch dramatically increased his intelligence **[T-SER5.1]**.

- **hex potion:** A concoction created by Witch Hildegarde, a woman living on the psi-moon where Mr. Flibble was born. Flibble, en route to deliver a pie to his grandmother, broke into the witch's gingerbread cabin and drank the mixture. This endowed him with hex vision, which he used to fry the witch as she returned **[M-SMG2.8(c4)]**.

- **hex vision:** The ability to produce an electrical charge that could be aimed and expelled through a person's eyes. Hologrammic scientist Hildegarde Lanstrom attained hex vision after suffering from a psi-virus. When the *Red Dwarf* crew found her aboard a scientific research station and released her from a stasis pod, she immediately attacked them with hex vision, infecting Rimmer **[T-SER5.4]**. As a youth, Mr. Flibble gained hex vision by drinking a potion he found in Witch Hildegarde's gingerbread cabin **[M-SMG2.8(c4)]**.

- **"Hey Baby, Don't Be Ovulatin' Tonight":** A sexy ballad recorded around the twenty-second century by Hugo Lovepole. The song sometimes played in *Red Dwarf*'s Copacabana Hawaiian Cocktail Bar **[N-INF]**.

- **Hickett, Mrs.:** A Bedford Falls resident whom Lister imagined while trapped in an addictive version of *Better Than Life*. Mrs. Hickett handed out hot tea to the injured after Rimmer, disguised as Trixie LaBouche, crashed through the town in a juggernaut **[N-BTL]**.

- **Hidiot:** A nickname that Confidence, a hallucination of Lister's mind made corporeal by mutated pneumonia, called Rimmer, referencing the hologrammic "H" on his forehead **[T-SER1.5]**.

- **High Castle, The:** *See* High Tower, The

- **high-definition game simulator:** An association football advancement in the universe known as Alternative 6829/B. The game simulators replaced half-time team talk, which eventually became obsolete **[M-SMG1.8(c4)]**.

- **High Tower, The:** A structure that the Elite—a tribe of Cat People descended from Lister's pregnant cat Frankenstein—created aboard *Red Dwarf* as a sanctuary, using advanced technology that the Cats found in a spaceship embedded in the mining vessel's hull **[M-SMG2.2(c1)]**. Also known as the High Castle, the tower held the Time Obelisk, a device capable of sending individuals through time **[M-SMG2.1(c1)]**.

- **Hilda:** A member of an anti-fascist group in Jake Bullet's universe known as the Fatal Sisters, along with Mista and Sangrida. The three women wore Valkyrie warrior outfits **[M-SMG2.4(c6)]**. After rescuing Duane Dibbley from Voter Colonel Gray, the Fatal Sisters brought him to their hideout, where all three had sex with him in order to jog his memory about his true identity **[M-SMG2.5(c1)]**.

- **Hildegarde, Witch:** An old witch who lived in a gingerbread cabin on a psi-moon. While traveling to his grandmother's cottage to deliver a pie, young Mr. Flibble came upon Hildegarde's cabin and broke in, seeking food. There, he found a potion that gave him hex vision, a power he then used to fry the witch **[M-SMG2.8(c4)]**.

  NOTE: *The witch was named after Hildegarde Lanstrom, a scientist who, in episode 5.4 ("Quarantine"), acquired hex vision after contracting a psi-virus.*

- **Hi-Life Club:** A high-end establishment featured on the television soap opera *Androids*. After winning the mechanoid lottery, Hudzen frequented the Hi-Life, where he ordered dry martinis. Kryten mimicked this behavior in *Red Dwarf*'s Copacabana Hawaiian Cocktail Club, despite not enjoying the beverage **[N-INF]**.

- **Hill, Alfred ("Benny"):** A twentieth-century British actor and comedian, and the star of the long-running television program *The Benny Hill Show* **[RL]**. While trapped in an addictive version of *Better Than Life*, Lister wondered if Cat

had gotten the idea for his golden castle—which came complete with eight-foot-tall, large-breasted Valkyries and rickshaws with mirrors aimed at the driver's breasts—from Benny Hill **[N-INF]**.

- **Hill, James:** A script writer on the television soap opera *Androids* **[M-SMG2.9(c8)]**.

    NOTE: *Hill was credited as a storyliner on the* Androids *website. In the real world, James Hill wrote the* Androids *comics published in the* Smegazines.

- **Hilly:** An artificial-intelligence computer aboard the *Red Dwarf* of the Fifth Dimension, a reality in which the sexes were reversed. After traveling to that dimension via the Holly Hop Drive, the prime-universe crew met Hilly, Holly's female counterpart. The two AIs instantly hit it off while working together to fix the damaged drive **[T-SER2.6]**.

    Shortly thereafter, Holly gave himself a head-sex-change operation, basing his new look and personality on those of Hilly **[T-SER3.1]**. Meanwhile, in the Fifth Dimension, Hilly also underwent such a procedure, altering her face to appear more like her male counterpart **[M-SMG1.5(c2)]**.

- **Hilo, Hawaii:** The largest settlement on the Island of Hawaii **[RL]**. The World Council, the governing body of twenty-second-century Earth, operated a biotechnology institute in Hilo, specializing in genetic engineering and DNA manipulation. Several elements of the Council's plan to inhabit a new planet in the Andromeda Galaxy were created at this facility, including various species of GELF and terraforming viruses **[N-LST]**.

- **Himself:** A nickname of Admiral Peter Tranter, commander of the Space Corps R&D Program in Ace Rimmer's universe. Tranter's valet, Kevin, often called him this name behind his back **[N-BCK]**.

- **Hip-hop-a-billy reggae:** A type of music played in *Red Dwarf*'s disco following George McIntyre's "welcome back" party **[N-INF]**.

- **His Most Excellent Majesty:** The title of the ruler of Rimmerworld, a society composed of Arnold Rimmer clones whom Rimmer created for companionship while marooned on a barren planet **[T-SER6.5(d)]**.

- **histo-chip:** A component built into 4000 Series mechanoids for storing historical data. Kryten accessed his histo-chip to look up information about John F. Kennedy's assassination after the *Starbug 1* crew inadvertently averted that event while using the time drive **[T-SER7.1]**.

- **Hitchcock, Alfred Joseph, Sir:** A twentieth-century English producer and director of such films as *Psycho*, *Rear Window*, *The 39 Steps* and *The Birds*, also known for his portly silhouette **[RL]**. During a power failure aboard *Red Dwarf*, Rimmer was frightened by the shadow that Lister cast on the wall, mistaking it for Hitchcock's **[T-SER3.4]**.

- **HITLER:** *See* Human Impressions Task & Logistics Electronic Reichs- führer (HITLER)

- **Hitler, Adolf, Führer:** The Austrian-born leader of the Nazi Party who ruled Germany as a dictator from 1934 to 1945. During World War II, he orchestrated the genocide of millions of Jews, Romani, homosexuals and others who failed to meet up to his Aryan standards **[RL]**.

    Hitler wrote a book titled *I Did It the Reicht Way,* which Rimmer intended to read while formulating a battleplan timetable to devise a strategy to escape rogue simulants **[T-SER10.6]**. An excerpt from his Nuremberg speech was part of a German-language course that Kryten mistakenly played while attempting to placate Lister with a hypnotherapy disc **[T-SER7.5]**.

    When *Red Dwarf* entered a parallel universe using the Holly Hop Drive, Holly explained the concept of alternate realities by suggesting that in that reality, Hitler may have won World War II **[T-SER2.6]**. Later, while on a future Earth on which time ran backwards, Kryten cited Hitler and World War II as examples of that reality's advantages, noting that this Hitler would eventually cause millions of people to come to life while liberating Poland and France **[T-SER3.1]**.

    Kryten once used mutated developing fluid to develop an old image of Hitler at a Nuremberg rally, taken from a *Fascist Dictator Monthly* magazine featuring the Führer as Mr. October. The mutated chemical allowed Lister to enter the photograph,

scuffle with Hitler, steal his briefcase and return to *Red Dwarf.*

Inside the briefcase were erotic handcuffs, a banana and crisps sandwich, his diary (containing a note that read "Things to remember: stop milk, pay papers, invade Czechoslovakia"), and a package emblazoned with the words "To Adolf—Love and Hugs, Staff Colonel Count von Stauffenberg." This package contained an explosive with which von Stauffenberg had intended to assassinate the dictator. Realizing the danger, Lister kicked it back into the photo, altering history so that a newspaper covering the incident included a snapshot identifying Lister as the "mysterious assassin" **[T-SER3.5]**.

Years later, the *Starbug 1* crew used a time drive coupled with a faster-than-light drive to travel throughout space-time. In so doing, they became epicures who sampled the best the universe had to offer, socializing with such historic figures as Hitler and his wife **[T-SER6.6]**.

> ***NOTE:*** *In episode 3.5 ("Timeslides"), the date of Hitler's Nuremberg rally where the photograph was taken (1934) did not jibe with the date of Claus von Stauffenberg's actual assassination attempt (1944), nor with the newspaper's dateline (1939).*

- **Hitler, Adolf, Führer:** A waxdroid replica of the Nazi dictator, created for the Waxworld theme park. Left on their own for millions of years, the waxdroids attained sentience and became embroiled in a park-wide resource war between Villain World (to which Hitler belonged) and Hero World.

  During this war, the *Red Dwarf* crew transported to the planet using a Matter Paddle, with Lister and Cat materializing in Villain territory, while Rimmer and Kryten landed in Hero territory. Captured by waxdroids of Hitler, Joseph Goebbels and Hermann Göring, Lister and Cat were thrown in prison to await execution, but escaped to Hero World.

  There, Rimmer detained them while he trained the heroes' army to attack Villain World. Every waxdroid died during the battle, with the Queen Victoria waxdroid shooting Hitler **[T-SER4.6]**.

- **Hit-U-Like:** A state-owned assassination business in Jake Bullet's universe. As Bullet investigated the murder of game-show contestant Philby Frutch, an assassin shot the cyborg, but the projectile ricocheted off Bullet's head and killed his informant, Vinnie van Goth. Bullet pursued the assassin to a Hit-U-Like office, then interrogated the manager to learn who had hired the killer—which turned out to be Frutch himself **[M-SMG1.13(c4)]**.

- **Hniuplcxdewn:** A simple-minded type of GELF on Arranguu 12. According to the regulator presiding over Lister's trial for crimes against the GELF nation, the Northern Sector practiced the Jhjghjiuyhu legal system, which was straightforward enough for any Hniuplcxdewn or Tvcnkolphgkooq to understand **[N-LST]**.

- ***Hoarse Trojan*, SS:** *See Trojan*, SS

- **Hoch, Ján Ludvík:** The birth name of Robert Maxwell, a Czech-born British media mogul and Member of Parliament, often anglicized as Jan Ludwig Hoch. Maxwell lived a flamboyant, extravagant lifestyle, often surrounded by controversy and scandal. He was found dead and naked in the Atlantic Ocean in 1991, after purportedly falling off the side of his yacht **[RL]**.

  In a previous timeline, Hoch was a poor immigrant who fought for England during World War II, after which he helped rebuild the country, becoming a man of state and fathering two sons who went on to become civic leaders. At age sixty-eight, he received a visit from the Inquisitor, a simulant from the future who traveled throughout space-time, judging the worthiness of every being.

  The Inquisitor claimed Hoch had missed his chance to become an important figure in society at age eighteen, and deemed him unworthy of existence, erasing him from the space-time continuum. He then replaced Hoch with another version of the man—an abrasive parasite of humanity who threatened the Inquisitor to get off his yacht. After performing a reality scan, the simulant discovered he had inadvertently erased the only decent version of Hoch in any reality. To correct his mistake, he pushed the new Hoch over the side of his boat **[M-SMG1.11(c3)]**.

- **Hoffman, Dustin:** An American actor in such films as *The Graduate*, *Midnight Cowboy*, *All the President's Men*, *Tootsie* and *Rain Man* **[RL]**. When Rimmer proposed that the *Red Dwarf* crew use timeslides to alter the course of history, Lister suggested convincing Hoffman not to make the film *Ishtar* **[T-SER3.5]**.

HUDZEN 10

PREFIX
RL: Real life

T-: Television Episodes
- **SER:** Television series
- **IDW:** "Identity Within"
- **USA1:** Unaired U.S. pilot
- **USA2:** Unaired U.S. demo

R-: *The Bodysnatcher Collection*
- **SER:** Remastered episodes
- **BOD:** "Bodysnatcher"
- **DAD:** "Dad"
- **FTH:** "Lister's Father"
- **INF:** "Infinity Patrol"
- **END:** "The End" (original assembly)

N-: Novels
- **INF:** *Infinity Welcomes Careful Drivers*
- **BTL:** *Better Than Life*
- **LST:** *Last Human*
- **BCK:** *Backwards*
- **OMN:** *Red Dwarf Omnibus*

M-: Magazines
- **SMG:** *Smegazine*

W-: Websites
- **OFF:** Official website
- **NAN:** *Prelude to Nanarchy*
- **AND:** *Androids*
- **DIV:** Diva-Droid
- **DIB:** Duane Dibbley
- **CRP:** Crapola
- **GEN:** Geneticon
- **LSR:** Leisure World Intl.
- **JMC:** Jupiter Mining Corporation
- **AIT:** *A.I. Today*
- **HOL:** HoloPoint

G-: Roleplaying Game
- **RPG:** *Core Rulebook*
- **BIT:** *A.I. Screen Extra Bits* booklet
- **SOR:** *Series Sourcebook*
- **OTH:** Other RPG material

- **Hogey the Roguey:** A rogue droid who frequently visited the *Red Dwarf* crew, challenging them to duels across time and space, and occasionally competing with them in ping pong tournaments out of sheer boredom. Hogey spoke in broken English, and had several distinguishing features, including a bushy mustache and a combover. His apparel featured a British flag on his left arm.

  Hogey once boarded a Simulant Death Ship while its crew slept and stole a star map of the surrounding galaxy. Upon discovering the theft, the simulants tracked Hogey, who inadvertently led them to *Red Dwarf*. The simulants attacked the mining vessel, opening a small hull breach in which Hogey's body became stuck, plugging the hole.

  Red Dwarf's crew abandoned ship to escape the simulants, leaving Hogey behind, but not before taking his molecular destabilizer gun. After dealing with the simulant threat, they returned to the mining ship, where Hogey—who had extricated himself from the breach—ambushed them once more **[T-SER10.6]**.

  NOTE: *The character of Hogey originally appeared in the script of the unfilmed* Red Dwarf *movie, before being incorporated into episode 10.6 ("The End"). Richard O'Callaghan, who portrayed Hogey in the episode, had auditioned for the same part in the film, prior to being cast as the Creator in* Back to Earth.

- **Hokey Cokey:** A notable twenty-third-century computer virus **[G-RPG]**.

- **HOL 9000:** A designation printed on a label on one of *Starbug 1*'s monitors **[T-SER7.7]**.

  NOTE: *HAL 9000, the sentient computer protagonist of Arthur C. Clarke's* Space Odyssey *novels, inspired the naming of Holly, whose full designation, Holly 6000, was revealed in a faux ad printed in the 2008* Red Dwarf *calendar.*

- **Holden, Fred ("Thickie"):** A student with whom Rimmer dormed while at boarding school. Poor at geography (he thought a glacier was a man who fixed windows) and suffering from acne and flatulence, the alienated Holden went on to invent the Tension Sheet and became a millionaire at age twenty-six, marrying supermodel Sabrina Mulholland-Jjones. He got the idea for the Tension Sheet from a future version of Rimmer, who had gone back in time to give his younger self the concept and thereby steal Holden's success. Thickie, however—who bunked next to young Arnold—overheard the discussion and beat his schoolmate to the patent office, ironically cementing his future fame thanks to Rimmer's tampering **[T-SER3.5]**.

  NOTE: *Holden Caulfield was the protagonist of J.D. Salinger's* Catcher in the Rye. *The novel—often cited as "inventing" the modern teenager—explored how the troubled teen dealt with tension and alienation at boarding school, with Holden frequently mocking his thick-headed, flatulent and acne-pocked schoolmates.*

- **Holder:** A Space Corps physicist, considered one of the most brilliant minds of his era. Holder was involved in a classified military project aboard a scientific research station, which resulted in the creation of Legion, a gestalt entity encompassing the intellect and emotions of all four project scientists, including Holder. Holder eventually died, as did the other scientists, leaving Legion nothing but a floating essence until the *Starbug 1* crew visited the station **[T-SER6.2]**.

- **Hole, the:** A dark, half-heighted metal room within the Tank, *Red Dwarf*'s classified brig, away from the general prison population. Inmates were sentenced to the Hole as punishment for severe infractions. Lister and Rimmer were sent there for two months after a programmable virus they used for potato-peeling went awry, eating away their hair and clothes before doing the same to Captain Hollister. There, they met Birdman, a mentally unstable, elderly occupant who kept a sparrow as a pet. The three were freed when Bob the skutter cut in through the metal floorboards to release them **[T-SER8.6]**.

- **Hole 13:** A round of table golf that Cat and Lister played, replicating the seventeenth hole at the Old Course at St. Andrews. The hole was par four, and included a "dog leg" to the right and windy conditions **[T-SER3.5(d)]**.

  NOTE: *St. Andrews is located in Fife, Scotland. Its seventeenth hole is considered by some to be the most difficult par four in the world.*

- ***Holiday in Europe*:** An artificial-reality program that the *Red Dwarf* crew found aboard a derelict vessel. Upon entering

B-: Books
- **PRG:** *Red Dwarf Programme Guide*
- **SUR:** *Red Dwarf Space Corps Survival Manual*
- **PRM:** *Primordial Soup*
- **SOS:** *Son of Soup*
- **SCE:** *Scenes from the Dwarf*
- **LOG:** *Red Dwarf Log No. 1996*
- **RD8:** *Red Dwarf VIII*
- **EVR:** *The Log: A Dwarfer's Guide to Everything*

X-: Misc.
- **PRO:** Promotional materials, videos, etc.
- **PST:** Posters at DJ XVII (2013)
- **CAL:** 2008 calendar
- **RNG:** Cell phone ringtones
- **MOB:** Mobisode ("Red Christmas")
- **CIN:** *Children in Need* sketch
- **GEK:** *Geek Week* intros by Kryten
- **TNG:** "Tongue-Tied" video

- **XMS:** Bill Pearson's Christmas special pitch script
- **XVD:** Bill Pearson's Christmas special pitch video
- **OTH:** Other *Red Dwarf* appearances

SUFFIX
DVD:
- **(d)** – Deleted scene
- **(o)** – Outtake
- **(b)** – Bonus DVD material (other)
- **(e)** – Extended version

SMEGAZINES:
- **(c)** – Comic
- **(a)** – Article

OTHER:
- **(s)** – Early/unused script draft
- **(s1)** – Alternate version of script

the game, Lister realized he had mixed up the program with *Victory in Europe*, a World War II simulation, causing him and his shipmates to spend seventeen days under bombardment while marching against a virtual Berlin, searching for a way to exit the game **[B-LOG]**.

- **Holina, Princess:** A "damsel in distress" in an alternate reality who bore a striking resemblance to Holly's female head. After rescuing Holina from a castle, Ace Rimmer made love to her for more than four hours before departing for a universe in which the genders were reversed **[M-SMG1.5(c2)]**.

- **Hollentine:** The significant other of Kritter, Kryten's hillbilly cyborg counterpart in an alternate universe ravaged by Ace "Blackheart" Rimmer, a tyrannical version of Arnold Rimmer. Blackheart killed Hollentine while attacking Kritter's settlement **[M-SMG1.14(c5)]**.

- **Hollerbach:** A *Red Dwarf* crewmember who bunked with Petrovitch. Hollerbach took his Astronavigation Exam on October 27, the same date on which Rimmer attempted to cheat by covering his body in writing **[N-INF]**.

  ***NOTE:** Hollerbach presumably died during the cadmium II explosion. It is unknown whether the nanobots resurrected him in Series VIII.*

- **Hollies, The:** A twentieth-century British rock group known for such hits as *The Air That I Breathe* and *He Ain't Heavy, He's My Brother* **[RL]**. The Hollies were the favorite band of Lister's adoptive father **[M-SMG1.6(a)]**.

- **Hollister, Frank ("Dennis the Doughnut Boy"), Captain:** The commander of the mining ship *Red Dwarf* **[T-SER1.1]**. Hollister had a wife named Martha **[W-OFF]**, and for a time hired Talia Garrett as his personal fitness trainer **[T-SER8.8(d)]**. He once suffered from kidney stones **[T-SER10(b)]**.

  When he was young, Hollister sold doughnuts on Callisto **[W-OFF]**, which earned him the nickname "Dennis the Doughnut Boy" **[T-SER8.3]**. After being fired from a diner in Kentucky for eating much of the restaurant's food supply, Hollister moved to Phobos, where he signed up as third technician aboard a freighter called *The McGovern*. According to his report, the ship encountered a meteor storm near Jupiter that damaged the Drive Room, forcing him to take charge and pilot the vessel out of harm's way, for which he was promoted to acting captain.

  Hollister then transferred to *Red Dwarf*, where he was mistaken for the doughnut vendor in the crew mess. He kept the job under false pretenses until bribing a skutter to grant him access to confidential files, which he used to blackmail his way to the captaincy **[W-OFF]**.

  Sometime later, Hollister sentenced Lister to eighteen months in stasis for refusing to give up his pregnant cat. Shortly thereafter, the captain died during a cadmium II explosion caused by a faulty drive plate **[T-SER1.1]**.

  Three million years later, Lister and the *Starbug 1* crew encountered a polymorph posing as *Red Dwarf*. Boarding the fake vessel, they found perfect recreations of the crew, including Hollister **[M-SMG2.6(c1)]**, who died when the polymorph—an *exact* replica of *Red Dwarf*—suffered its own cadmium II explosion **[M-SMG2.7(c1)]**.

  The real Hollister was eventually revived by nanobots, created by Holly to act as a distraction for Lister **[T-SER8.1]**. He fell victim to a prank when Lister and Rimmer drugged the Guards' basketball team with a virility-enhancement drug, causing them to experience seven-hour erections. He also succumbed to a programmable virus the duo inadvertently unleashed, which ate away his hair and clothing **[T-SER8.6]**.

  To make matters worse, Hollister sustained a head injury when the platoon he led to neutralize Pete the *Tyrannosaurus rex* was bombarded by the creature's diarrhea. During the incident, Bob the skutter collided with Frank's skull. The captain was later traumatized during a massage session, when Pete's dinosaur offspring entered his room and licked coconut milk from his body **[T-SER8.7]**.

  When a corrosive chameleonic microbe began dissolving *Red Dwarf*, Hollister and the rest of the crew abandoned the vessel, leaving Lister, Rimmer, Kryten, Cat and Kochanski to fend for themselves **[T-SER8.8]**.

  ***NOTE:** It is unclear whether Dennis was his actual birth name, or another pseudonym; as such, he is listed here under the name Frank, as that is how he is best known. Hollister's kidney stones were mentioned in the "We're Smegged" making-of special on the Series X Blu-ray set.*

PREFIX
RL: Real life

T-: Television Episodes
SER: Television series
IDW: "Identity Within"
USA1: Unaired U.S. pilot
USA2: Unaired U.S. demo

R-: *The Bodysnatcher Collection*
SER: Remastered episodes
BOD: "Bodysnatcher"
DAD: "Dad"
FTH: "Lister's Father"
INF: "Infinity Patrol"
END: "The End" (original assembly)

N-: Novels
INF: *Infinity Welcomes Careful Drivers*
BTL: *Better Than Life*
LST: *Last Human*

BCK: *Backwards*
OMN: *Red Dwarf Omnibus*

M-: Magazines
SMG: *Smegazine*

W-: Websites
OFF: Official website
NAN: *Prelude to Nanarchy*
AND: *Androids*
DIV: Diva-Droid
DIB: Duane Dibbley

CRP: Crapola
GEN: Geneticon
LSR: Leisure World Intl.
JMC: Jupiter Mining Corporation
AIT: *A.I. Today*
HOL: HoloPoint

G-: Roleplaying Game
RPG: *Core Rulebook*
BIT: *A.I. Screen Extra Bits* booklet
SOR: *Series Sourcebook*
OTH: Other RPG material

- **Hollister, Francine, Captain:** The commander of *Red Dwarf* in an alternate dimension in which the sexes were reversed **[W-OFF]**.

- **Hollister, Frank:** A crewmember aboard a mirror-universe *Red Dwarf*. Hollister longed to be an officer, and deeply desired to have his own command like Captain Rimmer, the ship's commander in that dimension.

  In the prime universe, Kryten built a device to bridge the gap between the two dimensions, in an effort to find an antidote for a chameleonic microbe devouring the ship; the device malfunctioned, however, after Rimmer crossed through. Temporarily trapped in the mirror reality, he met Hollister, who was on probation from prison and assigned to assist his captain. The prime Rimmer took great pleasure in belittling Hollister as revenge for his own mistreatment by Frank's prime counterpart **[T-SER8.8]**.

  ***NOTE:** Since the mirror Rimmer had Hollister's position aboard* Red Dwarf, *it is possible that Hollister filled the prime Arnold's role as a technician, second class.*

- **Hollister, Martha:** The wife of Captain Frank Hollister **[W-OFF]**. She often made blueberry muffins for him before he left for his tour aboard *Red Dwarf* **[T-SER8.2]**. Rimmer once tore up and ate a photograph of Martha after disagreeing with the captain, claiming he had mistaken it for a *Planet of the Apes* publicity still **[T-SER2.4]**.

- **Holly:** *See* Holly 6000

- **Holly:** The artificial-reality computer aboard a version of *Red Dwarf* resurrected by Kryten's nanobots. This version maintained his original IQ of six thousand, and was distinguishable by a slightly conical head **[T-SER8.3]**.

- **Holly:** A decrepit duplicate of Holly, created when a triplicator accident destroyed *Red Dwarf* but produced two copies: a "high" version containing the best aspects of the ship and its crew, and a "low" version manifesting the worst. The "low" Holly—who appeared on a static-filled monitor and wore her hair long and black—ceased to exist once the two *Red Dwarfs* were merged **[T-SER5.5]**.

- **Holly:** A character on the American science fiction television series *Red Dwarf*, developed in an alternate universe. In that reality, Holly was a human female married to Lister, with two children: a biologically challenged son named Cry 10 and a hip teenaged daughter. In one episode, an amorphous alien held Holly and her children captive, as revenge on Lister and Rimmer, who had accidentally killed its wife. The heroic Rimmer, however, overcame his paralysis to defeat the creature and save them **[M-SMG1.10(c4)]**.

- **Holly, Sister:** A duplicate of Holly created when a triplicator accident destroyed *Red Dwarf* but produced two copies: a "high" version containing the best aspects of the ship and its crew, and a "low" version manifesting the worst. Sister Holly, an enlightened form of the original, ceased to exist once the two *Red Dwarfs* were merged **[T-SER5.5]**.

- **Holly 6000:** The artificial intelligence (AI) computer aboard the mining ship *Red Dwarf*. Holly was a tenth-generation AI hologrammic computer, rated with an IQ of six thousand **[T-SER1.2]**. He was developed at Warburton Neurotronics, in Birmingham Labs **[X-PST]**, by a team led by Derek Dinsdale **[W-AIT]**. His friends included fellow AIs Ernie 7000 and Gordon 8000 **[R-SER2.2(d)]**.

  Holly's name stood for "**H**ologrammic, **O**nline, **L**aser-**L**inked, **Y**iB mainframe." The AI could connect with up to forty-seven ship-to-surface craft via subspace Wi-Fi, with an estimated range of 250,000 light-years. He comprised four super-conducting coldware CPU banks using chrono-degradable 10-HG processors, and was water-resistant up to six inches **[X-PST]**. His computer capacity was fifteen zillion gigabytes **[N-BTL]**.

  Crewmembers could interact with Holly via various monitors located around the ship, which displayed the AI as a floating head **[T-SER1.1]**. AI computers had the ability to choose their own likeness. Holly first opted for the face of a balding, middle-aged male among billions of choices, claiming it belonged to "the most prolific lover who ever lived" **[T-SER1.3]**. He once fell in love with a Sinclair ZX-81 computer **[T-SER2.4]**.

  When it was necessary to interact with Holly off-ship, the AI could be downloaded into several portable formats, including a wheeled monitor **[T-SER2.3]**, a watch **[T-SER2.4]**, a circular monitor embedded in a mechanoid's midsection **[T-SER3.1]**, and a headlight on a hologrammic motorcycle **[T-SER4.6]**.

Due to a badly repaired drive plate, a cadmium II leak killed the entire *Red Dwarf* crew except for Lister, who was in stasis at the time **[T-SER1.1]**. During the fifteen nanoseconds that passed between the cadmium II core going critical and the crew's deaths, Holly read the complete works of several writers, including Albert Einstein, Friedrich Engels, Sigmund Freud, Carl Jung and Karl Marx **[N-INF]**. Following the accident, Holly took the ship out of the solar system and into deep space as a safety precaution. He kept Lister sealed in the stasis pod for three million years, releasing him only when the background radiation became habitable again **[T-SER1.1]**.

During the three million years, Holly's psyche slowly degenerated until succumbing to computer senility by the time of Lister's release **[T-SER2.5]**.

A practical joker, Holly would often play pranks on the crew. In one instance, he convinced Lister that ships belonging to the Norweb Federation were pursuing *Red Dwarf* and looking for Lister, who owed them £180 billion **[T-SER1.6]**. On another occasion, he convinced the crew that *Red Dwarf*'s malevolent backup computer, Queeg, had taken control of the ship and erased the AI **[T-SER2.5]**.

After reading every known book, Holly asked Lister to erase the portion of his memory banks containing Agatha Christie's novels so he could read them again. In so doing, Dave erased all knowledge of Christie, and of Holly's request, causing the AI to question why Lister would erase the memory of someone he didn't know **[T-SER1.5]**.

Holly created a new type of music called Hol Rock, utilizing a decimalized music system instead of the standard octave. Holly's "decatave" consisted of two new notes (H and J) and two new syllables in the major scale ("woh" and "boh," between "sol" and "ti") **[T-SER2.1]**.

Holly next invented a new type of propulsion that he called the Holly Hop Drive. While attempting to use it to return Lister to Earth, the AI instead transported the vessel to an alternate reality in which the sexes were reversed. There, he met his female counterpart, Hilly, with whom he fell in love **[T-SER2.6]**. Upon returning to his own dimension, Holly gave himself a "head sex-change operation," assuming Hilly's appearance and personality **[T-SER3.1]**.

The AI's IQ was temporarily increased to 12,368 after an intelligence-compression experiment went awry—which also reduced her lifespan to just under three minutes. Both effects of the procedure were negated by the neutralization of a white hole, which restored time to a point before the experiment took place **[T-SER4.4]**.

After Kryten's nanobots mutinied and stole *Red Dwarf*, they remolecularized the ship and restored Holly's core program (including his male persona), after which they ditched the AI on a planetoid, along with the ship's unused parts. Hundreds of years later, Lister and his comrades found Holly in the form of a wristwatch **[T-SER7.8]**. Holly created a second set of nanobots and programmed them to resurrect the remaining *Red Dwarf* crew as a diversion to keep Lister sane. Upon entering the rebuilt ship, however, the group were arrested and sentenced to two years in the Tank **[T-SER8.3]**.

When a corrosive chameleonic microbe began dissolving the new *Red Dwarf*'s hull, Holly and his comrades escaped into a mirror universe **[T-SER8.8]**, returning sometime after the crisis had been averted. Later, Lister inadvertently left a bath running for several years, which flooded the decks containing Holly's computer banks, putting the AI out of commission. To replace him, the crew temporarily installed another artificial intelligence, called Pree **[T-SER9.1]**.

> ***NOTE:*** *Holly was based on a computer called Hab that appeared in a quintet of comedy sketches on the BBC radio series* Son of Cliché. *In the sketches, titled "Dave Hollins: Space Cadet," Hab kept Collins company aboard his craft, the* Psion IV *(later renamed the* Melissa V*), and spoke like HAL 9000, the computer from* 2001: A Space Odyssey. *Holly's full name, Holly 6000—inspired by HAL's designation—was revealed in a faux ad printed in the 2008* Red Dwarf *calendar.*
>
> *A poster displayed at Dimension Jump XIII stated that Holly had a one-yottabyte flash card, giving the computer a quadrillion gigabytes' storage capability, as opposed to the fifteen zillion gigabytes mentioned in the novel* Better Than Life. *It should be noted that "zillion" is a fictitious, indefinitely large number, making that figure nonsensical.*

- **Holly 6000:** *Red Dwarf*'s shipboard computer in a universe in which the mining ship and its crew were American **[T-USA1]**. This Holly, a Datacorp model "H" computer **[T-USA1(s)]**, was programmed with a female likeness and personality, and had an operational IQ of six thousand **[T-USA1]**.

- **Holly Hop Drive:** A device invented by Holly, consisting of a plain red box with two buttons: red ("stop") and green ("start"). In theory, the drive could transport anyone or anything to any point in space. In practice, however, it propelled *Red Dwarf* through the Fifth Dimension and into a universe in which the sexes were reversed. The mechanism was damaged during transit, temporarily stranding the crew in that universe until Holly and his female counterpart, Hilly, could repair it **[T-SER2.6]**.

  While trapped in an elation squid hallucination, the crew imagined encountering a man named Noddy (an employee of a science fiction shop called They Walk Among Us!), who suggested they use the Holly Hop Drive to get to Nose World. The drive was back on *Red Dwarf* at the time, however, and of no use to them **[T-SER9.2]**.

- **Holman, Valter:** A man accused of killing his genetically engineered armchair upon discovering the furniture making love to his wife. Initially, Holman was not charged with a crime, due to society's stance that GELFs did not possess human rights. This decision outraged the GELF population, sparking a rebellion that culminated in a bank robbery, during which a Volkswagen Beetle and a vacuum cleaner took hostages, demanding Holman be brought to justice.

  To appease the GELFs, a hearing was held. Holman, now highly publicized as the man cuckolded by his own furniture, was handed a light sentence of six months. That ruling sparked the beginning of the GELF War, during which most of the genetically created creatures were either killed or captured and exiled to Zanzibar **[N-BTL]**.

- **"HolMem. Password override. The novels, Christie, Agatha.":** A command string by which Lister accessed Holly's memory banks containing Agatha Christie novels and, per the AI's request, erased them all. Lister inadvertently eliminated all knowledge of the author, however, as well as Holly's request, leading Holly to question why Dave would erase the memory of someone he had never heard of **[T-SER1.5]**.

- **Holmes, Sherlock:** A fictional London-based detective, created by Sir Arthur Conan Doyle, who solved difficult cases through the application of logical reasoning and forensic science **[RL]**. A waxdroid replica of Holmes appeared on Waxworld, a theme park built on an inhabitable planet that was eventually abandoned. Left on their own for millions of years, the waxdroids attained sentience and became embroiled in a park-wide resource war between Villain World and Hero World (to which Holmes belonged) **[G-RPG]**.

  ***NOTE:** This waxdroid presumably died sometime during the Wax War, as he was not present in episode 4.6 ("Meltdown").*

- **holo-blaster:** An arm-mounted weapon capable of targeting and destroying a hologram's light bee from one hundred paces. A deranged cyborg with a personal vendetta against holograms used such a weapon against Rimmer **[M-SMG2.5(c2)]**.

- **Holochamber:** A recreation room aboard *Red Dwarf*, providing virtual-reality programs in which users could program and interact within any scenario. Kryten considered it less realistic—but safer—than the total-immersion game *Better Than Life* **[M-SMG1.5(a)]**.

- **holo exercise bike:** A type of hologrammic workout equipment created especially for holograms **[R-BOD(b)]**.

  ***NOTE:** The bike appeared in episode 2.6 ("Parallel Universe"), but was only named in a list of items visible in* The Bodysnatcher Collection*'s DVD documentary* "It's Cold Outside."

- **Holo-Flame Color Gas:** A type of barbeque grill featured on the television soap opera *Androids*. The character Daz owned a grill of this model **[M-SMG1.8(c2)]**.

- **hologram:** A three-dimensional image formed using a laser, interference, diffraction, a light intensity recording and suitable illumination **[RL]**.

  A hologram of a human could be created by projecting a light image of that individual. It possessed the same traits, knowledge and personality as the original, but was made of light. Computers aboard mining ships, such as *Red Dwarf*, could typically only maintain one hologram at a time. Thus, if a crewmember died who was more vital to a ship's mission than the current hologram, the latter would be terminated to make way for the higher-level officer **[T-SER1.1]**. Under certain conditions, a ship's artificial intelligence could maintain

B-: Books
PRG: *Red Dwarf Programme Guide*
SUR: *Red Dwarf Space Corps Survival Manual*
PRM: *Primordial Soup*
SOS: *Son of Soup*
SCE: *Scenes from the Dwarf*
LOG: *Red Dwarf Log No. 1996*
RD8: *Red Dwarf VIII*
EVR: *The Log: A Dwarfer's Guide to Everything*

X-: Misc.
PRO: Promotional materials, videos, etc.
PST: Posters at DJ XVII (2013)
CAL: 2008 calendar
RNG: Cell phone ringtones
MOB: Mobisode ("Red Christmas")
CIN: *Children in Need* sketch
GEK: *Geek Week* intros by Kryten
TNG: "Tongue-Tied" video

XMS: Bill Pearson's Christmas special pitch script
XVD: Bill Pearson's Christmas special pitch video
OTH: Other *Red Dwarf* appearances

SUFFIX
DVD:
(d) – Deleted scene
(o) – Outtake
(b) – Bonus DVD material (other)
(e) – Extended version

SMEGAZINES:
(c) – Comic
(a) – Article

OTHER:
(s) – Early/unused script draft
(s1) – Alternate version of script

more than a single hologram, provided that all unnecessary systems were powered down **[T-SER1.5]**.

Hologrammic individuals could be rendered and maintained using a variety of technologies, including hologramic projection boxes **[T-SER1.5]**, hologramatic projection cages **[T-SER2.3]** and light bees **[T-SER4.6]**. Hologram technology fell into two categories: soft and hard light. Soft light holograms were constructed solely of light, and were thus unable to touch or interact with anything other than other hologrammic constructs. Hard light technology gave a hologram a physical presence, allowing it to interact with its environment, and rendering it nearly indestructible **[T-SER6.2]**.

Information about a hologram's image was stored on a physical data disc. This data could be retrieved to recreate the physical appearance of the person being represented, but if it became corrupted, unexpected changes could result **[T-SER1.3]**. Each ship maintained its hologram via the computers of a hologram simulation suite, which operated the programs and algorithms required to project the simulated individual. This room contained a bank of monitors showing various aspects of the hologram's state of mind, as well as dreams during sleep cycles **[T-SER2.3]**.

A hologram recreated a person's personality and physical attributes. As such, every detail was copied and embedded into the hologram, including any flaws that might have existed when the person was alive. In rare circumstances, these flaws could endanger the hologram, leaving it susceptible to death **[T-SER6.6]**. A hologram could be externally powered by a remote pack, with a standby switch powering the light bee **[N-BCK]**.

An amendment to the Human Rights Akt, known as Hologram Protection Akt 2143, included sections covering the activation, ownership, rights and protection of holograms **[M-SMG2.2(a)]**.

- **hologramatic projection cage:** A portable enclosure resembling a shark cage, by which holograms could travel outside the confines of their host ship. Rimmer utilized such a device while celebrating his deathday with Lister, Cat, Holly and the skutters on a barren planet **[T-SER2.3]**. Hologramatic projection cages weighed 990 pounds (450 kilograms) and were sold by HoloSoft Industries in Crapola Inc.'s annual *SCABBY* catalog **[G-RPG]**.

  NOTE: *Despite the name given in the episode, the official website and* Red Dwarf—The Roleplaying Game *used the word "hologrammic" in the device's name.*

- **hologramatic status application form:** A form that crewmembers aboard JMC vessels were required to fill out after being revived from death as a hologram **[N-INF]**.

- **hologram box:** A transparent cubical apparatus used by holograms to manipulate small items by means of holographic "gloves." With their hands inside the gloves, holograms could interact with any object placed within the box **[T-SER3.5(d)]**.

- **hologram disc:** *See* personality disk

- **hologram disk projection system:** A technology aboard *Red Dwarf* used to create and maintain holograms, accessible directly or via remote link. After a holovirus drove Rimmer insane, his shipmates immobilized him using a remote link to the hologram disk projection system **[T-SER5.4]**.

- **hologramic projection box:** A component of a ship's hologram projection system, used in conjunction with a personality disk to create a hologram of a deceased crewmember. Lister utilized Kochanski's projection box and what he thought was her disk to activate her hologram, but Rimmer had swapped her disk with his own, causing Dave to instead activate a second Rimmer hologram **[T-SER1.5]**. Hologramic projection boxes were sold by HoloSoft Industries in Crapola Inc.'s annual *SCABBY* catalog **[G-RPG]**.

  NOTE: *Despite the name given in the episode, the official website and* Red Dwarf—The Roleplaying Game *used the word "hologrammic" in the device's name.*

- **hologrammatic accessory computer:** A component of *Red Dwarf*'s hologram simulation suite that created accessories for a resident hologram's use. After a polymorph devoured Rimmer's anger, he requested a pipe and T-shirt from the computer, imprinted with the phrase "Give Quiche a Chance" **[N-BTL]**.

PREFIX
RL: Real life

T-: Television Episodes
SER: Television series
IDW: "Identity Within"
USA1: Unaired U.S. pilot
USA2: Unaired U.S. demo

R-: *The Bodysnatcher Collection*
SER: Remastered episodes
BOD: "Bodysnatcher"
DAD: "Dad"
FTH: "Lister's Father"
INF: "Infinity Patrol"
END: "The End" (original assembly)

N-: Novels
INF: *Infinity Welcomes Careful Drivers*
BTL: *Better Than Life*
LST: *Last Human*
BCK: *Backwards*
OMN: *Red Dwarf Omnibus*

M-: Magazines
SMG: *Smegazine*

W-: Websites
OFF: Official website
NAN: *Prelude to Nanarchy*
AND: *Androids*
DIV: Diva-Droid
DIB: Duane Dibbley
CRP: Crapola
GEN: Geneticon
LSR: Leisure World Intl.
JMC: Jupiter Mining Corporation
AIT: *A.I. Today*
HOL: HoloPoint

G-: Roleplaying Game
RPG: *Core Rulebook*
BIT: *A.I. Screen Extra Bits* booklet
SOR: *Series Sourcebook*
OTH: Other RPG material

- **hologrammatic projection unit:** The main component of *Red Dwarf*'s hologram projection suite. If a hologram moved too far from its host ship, or if the signal otherwise became too weak to transmit, the projection unit switched from "remote" to "local," thereby recalling the hologram to the vessel. When Lister and Rimmer crashed *Starbug 1* on an icy planet, a temporal anomaly between that world and *Red Dwarf* caused Arnold's signal to became faint, triggering the recall **[N-BTL]**.

- **hologrammatic projection unit regeneration chamber:** A small room aboard *Red Dwarf*, used by the hologram projection suite to regenerate holograms that had moved outside of the ship's transmission range. Once a hologram's signal became too faint, the unit would switch from "remote" to "local," recalling the hologram to the vessel via the regeneration chamber **[N-BTL]**.

- ***Hologram of Dorian Grey, The*:** A novel adapted as a virtual-reality game playable in *Red Dwarf*'s Holochambers **[M-SMG1.5(a)]**.

  ***NOTE:** This title spoofed that of Oscar Wilde's 1890 novel* The Picture of Dorian Grey.

- **hologram projection suite:** *See* hologram simulation suite

- **Hologram Protection Akt 2143, The:** An amendment to the Human Rights Akt of 2100, which the Earth Branch of the Universal Government passed to outline the conditions and rights of activated holograms. It comprised three sections. Section One covered activation and ownership, Section Two covered hologram protection and rights, and Section Three covered the personal and legal defense of holograms. Rimmer charged Lister with breaking Section Two, Paragraph 1, when he temporarily turned off Arnold's light bee on Waxworld. Holly, however, dismissed the case **[M-SMG2.2(a)]**.

- **Hologram Rights 2141, The:** An amendment that the Universal Government passed, adding holograms to the list of individuals covered by the Human Rights Akt of 2100. This article was amended to include The Hologram Protection Akt 2143, which further detailed the conditions and rights of activated holograms **[M-SMG2.2(a)]**.

- **"Holograms Can Have Heart Attacks Too!":** A phrase printed on a sign about Necrobics hanging in Rimmer's quarters **[T-SER2.6]**.

- **hologram simulation suite:** A large room aboard *Red Dwarf* allocated for producing and maintaining the ship's hologrammic crewmember **[T-SER2.3]**, also known as the hologram projection suite **[N-BTL]**. It resided on Floor 592 **[T-SER2.5]**.

  Lister used this suite to splice eight months of his memory into Rimmer's mind, making Arnold believe he had once dated Lise Yates **[T-SER2.3]**. Sometime later, a meteor struck *Red Dwarf*, damaging the hologram simulation suite and causing Rimmer to act erratically and mimic his shipmates **[T-SER2.5]**.

- **holographic projection device:** A small, floating object fitted with a personality chip, used in an alternate reality to project a dead crewmember's hologram aboard ships such as the American mining vessel *Red Dwarf*. One such device revived that reality's Rimmer after a cadmium II explosion killed the crew **[T-USA1]**.

- **Holographic Theory of the Brain:** A thesis postulating that an individual's mind and soul could be reconstituted from a single cell. After Brainfade's Doctor Scofrenia murdered scientist Sandra Halley, her co-worker Tina used brain material from one of Halley's prototype mind-control devices to revive her mind in the body of a test subject named Carl, in accordance with this theory **[M-SMG2.9(c4)]**.

- **holographic virus:** An imaginary affliction that Arnold Rimmer pretended to have while posing as Ace Rimmer, to explain his uncharacteristic behavior. Since Ace was not supposed to be a hologram, he claimed the fake virus affected humans as well **[T-SER7.2]**.

- **holo-knife:** A hologrammic cutting weapon that could be used by and against holograms **[M-SMG2.2(a)]**.

- **holo-lamp:** A small, portable device used to play holo-messages or 3D recordings **[T-SER10.6]**.

- **holo-message:** A 3D recording that could be played back via a holo-lamp. Rimmer's stepfather gave him a holo-lamp when he was young, with instructions that the recorded holo-message be played only after Arnold became an officer. Three million years later, as *Red Dwarf* was being attacked by rogue simulants, Arnold played the message, despite never having been promoted.

In the message, the elder Rimmer confessed that he was not Arnold's father, and that his mother had carried on an affair with their gardener, Dungo, who was Arnold's real dad. This news initially shocked Rimmer, who had believed he had come from royal stock. Eventually, though, he embraced his newfound heritage, no longer burdened by the weight of fatherly disapproval **[T-SER10.6]**.

> ***NOTE:*** *Oddly, the holo-lamp had never been seen during any of the other times the crew abandoned* Red Dwarf*, However, it does lend credence to the theory that the Rimmer in Series X was, in fact, the one who left to become Ace, as he would most likely have taken the lamp with him, and thus returned with it.*

- **holo-nymph:** A type of sexy female holographic character. Rimmer enjoyed playing cricket with three holo-nymphs in *Red Dwarf*'s holochamber **[M-SMG1.5(a)]**.

- **holo-plague:** A virtual disease to which holograms were susceptible. After succumbing to a mutated holo-plague called a holovirus, Hildegarde Lanstrom passed it on to Rimmer in her final moments **[T-SER5.4]**.

- **HoloPoint:** A twenty-third-century company specializing in hologrammic technologies. The firm, located on the Saturnian moon of Tethys, was run by director Ned Omrisk **[W-HOL]**.

- ***Holo-Risk*:** A hologrammic version of the popular strategy board game *Risk*. Rimmer played this game after being revived as a hologram **[M-SMG1.13(c2)]**.

- **holoship:** A class of computer-generated spacecraft created by the Space Corps, crewed entirely by holograms of great intellect and bravery. Holoships were designed to travel as super-light particles (tachyons), enabling them to cover vast distances via wormholes and star gates **[T-SER5.1]**. The Corps' first holoship prototype failed when the batteries of its communal light bee ran out six months into its maiden voyage. Undeterred, the Corps then designed the SSS *Enlightenment*, commanded by Hercule Platini **[W-OFF]**.

  Three million years later, *Enlightenment* encountered *Starbug 1* and sent a probe to investigate. Discovering a hologram aboard, the probe brought Rimmer back to the holoship, where he petitioned to join the crew. The holograms accepted his application, but upon learning that his commission would mean the deactivation of Nirvana Crane—with whom he had fallen in love—Rimmer returned to *Starbug 1* **[T-SER5.1]**.

- **holo-slide:** A holographic projection of a photograph. While suffering an ailment brought on by a lack of sex, Cat watched holo-slides of sexy women in kitten outfits at Bangkok's Kit-Kat Club **[T-IDW]**.

- **HoloSoft Industries:** A company specializing in hologrammic technologies. Its products, sold in Crapola Inc.'s annual *SCABBY* catalog, included hard-light drives, remote belts, projection boxes, projection cages, light bees and holowhips **[G-RPG]**.

- **holospasm:** An affliction that affected holograms during a hard drive crash. As a light bee malfunctioned, the hologrammic projection temporarily glitched, causing involuntary movement and image degradation. Once the hard drive finally crashed, the hologram froze in place, its eyes replaced with spinning colored wheels **[T-SER10(b)]**.

> ***NOTE:*** *The term "holospasm" was coined by Chris Barrie in the "We're Smegged" making-of special on the Series X Blu-rays. The colored wheels referenced the spinning wait cursor that Apple computers experience during system hangups, colloquially known as the "Spinning Beach Ball of Death" (SBBOD)—which may indicate that* Red Dwarf*'s computers utilized Apple's operating system.*

- **Holotech, Inc.:** A company specializing in hologrammic personality discs. Its products included pre-recorded discs of television entertainers, movie stars, philosophers, presidents, weather girls and fascist dictators **[G-RPG]**.

- **holo-tracker:** A handheld device used to ascertain a person's relative distance and direction from an active hologram. A

PREFIX
RL: Real life

T-: Television Episodes
SER: Television series
IDW: "Identity Within"
USA1: Unaired U.S. pilot
USA2: Unaired U.S. demo

R-: *The Bodysnatcher Collection*
SER: Remastered episodes
BOD: "Bodysnatcher"
DAD: "Dad"
FTH: "Lister's Father"
INF: "Infinity Patrol"
END: "The End" (original assembly)

N-: Novels
INF: *Infinity Welcomes Careful Drivers*
BTL: *Better Than Life*
LST: *Last Human*

BCK: *Backwards*
OMN: *Red Dwarf Omnibus*

M-: Magazines
SMG: *Smegazine*

W-: Websites
OFF: Official website
NAN: *Prelude to Nanarchy*
AND: *Androids*
DIV: Diva-Droid
DIB: Duane Dibbley

CRP: Crapola
GEN: Geneticon
LSR: Leisure World Intl.
JMC: Jupiter Mining Corporation
AIT: *A.I. Today*
HOL: HoloPoint

G-: Roleplaying Game
RPG: *Core Rulebook*
BIT: *A.I. Screen Extra Bits* booklet
SOR: *Series Sourcebook*
OTH: Other RPG material

deranged cyborg with a personal vendetta against holograms used this technology to hunt down Rimmer **[M-SMG2.5(c2)]**.

- **holovirus:** A mutated holo-plague transmitted via radio waves, able to infect holograms. Once infected, a victim suffered in various stages. The first caused madness and hex vision—the ability to aim and expel an electrical charge through the eyes—while the second produced telepathy and telekinesis. After the second stage, an infected hologram expended too much power and died.

  Hildegarde Lanstrom, a hologrammatic scientist who studied and developed various viruses, contracted the disease aboard a research station and preserved herself in a stasis pod. When the *Red Dwarf* crew released her, she attacked them, infecting Rimmer. Driven insane, Arnold forced his shipmates to spend eighty-four days in isolation, per quarantine procedures. After five days, they realized he had contracted the disease when he donned a red and white checkered gingham dress, army boots and blonde pigtails, and claimed the King of the Potato People had demanded they remain in quarantine for ten years.

  The crew escaped, pursued by Rimmer and his hand puppet, Mr. Flibble. As the virus progressed, Arnold attacked them with hex vision, telepathy and telekinesis, until they immobilized him using a luck virus **[T-SER5.4]**.

- **holowhip:** A weapon designed to inflict pain and injury on holograms **[T-SER5.1]**. Holowhips could be modified to enable holograms to inflict pain on living beings **[T-SER5.5]**, while others could be used by one living being on another **[N-LST]**. HoloSoft Industries sold holowhips in Crapola Inc.'s annual *SCABBY* catalog **[G-RPG]**.

  Starbug 1's munitions cabinet contained a holowhip. When Commander Binks, an arrogant hologram from the holoship *Enlightenment,* surveyed *Starbug 1* and its crew, Lister threatened to beat him with the device **[T-SER5.1]**.

- **Hol Rock:** A type of music envisioned by Holly, using a decimalized music system instead of the standard octave. Holly's "decatave" consisted of two new notes (H and J) and two new syllables in the major scale ("woh" and "boh," between "sol" and "ti"), and required that instruments be enlarged to accommodate the extra notes (for example, a triangle with four sides) **[T-SER2.1]**.

  ***NOTE:** This gag originated in a* Son of Cliché *"Dave Hollins: Space Cadet" sketch titled "Sir Kevin Kevin Sir."*

- **Holy, The:** The name by which Holly was known to the Elite, a tribe of Cat People embroiled in a holy war aboard *Red Dwarf* regarding the name of their god. During the conflict, the Elite tapped into Holly, seeking a way to end the conflict, and found the AI stuck in a state of gurning. Unable to understand Holly's speech, the Elite searched through his databanks and discovered that their god (Lister) was scheduled to be released from stasis in five hundred years **[M-SMG2.2(c1)]**.

  Elite scripture prophesied that The Holy would send his son to guide the Cat People during their time of need. When they met Rimmer, who bore a letter "H" on his forehead, they assumed the prophesy had come true **[M-SMG2.3(c1)]**.

- **Holy Book, The:** A religious text written by members of the Cat People inhabiting *Red Dwarf*, depicting the origins of feline society, starting with the Holy Mother (Frankenstein) **[T-SER1.1]** and the father of the Cat People, Cloister (Lister), as well as the events leading up to the Holy War **[T-SER1.4]**. Mentioned in the Holy Book were Cloister's disciples—Chen, Selby and Petson—along with Chanski, the woman with whom he lived in fellowship **[M-SMG2.4(a)]**.

  The Holy Book differed from typical cat books—which were smelled rather than read—in that it contained pictures. Among the images depicted in the text were Cloister with Frankenstein, Cloister trapped in time **[T-SER1.4]**, the Fuchal Diner, the Holy War, a constellation map depicting Lister's laundry list, and the Cat Arks **[R-SER1.4]**.

- **Holy Custard Stain:** An item or marking worn by a blind Cat priest aboard *Red Dwarf*. The Holy Custard Stain and the Sacred Gravy Marks served as a testament to one's belief in the prophesied return of Cloister the Stupid **[T-SER1.4]**.

- **Holy Hydrant, The:** A religious artifact of the Dog People who evolved from Deb Lister's pregnant pet dog Dracula aboard an alternate-universe *Red Dwarf* **[G-RPG]**.

- **Holy Legions, The:** *See* Hooded Legions, The

- **Holy Mother, The:** A term by which the Cat People referred to Frankenstein, Lister's pet cat, whose litter in *Red Dwarf*'s cargo hold spawned the sentient felines during Lister's three million years in stasis **[T-SER1.1]**.

- **Holy Order of St. Geraldine:** A religious group to which the mirror universe's Sister Talia Garrett belonged. The order had several divisions, including the Space-Time Branch **[G-SOR]**.

- **Holy Wars:** A period marked by thousands of years of fighting between two religious factions of the Cat People inhabiting *Red Dwarf* **[T-SER1.4]**, also called the Cat Wars **[T-IDW]**. According to the Cats' Holy Book, the conflict stemmed from Lister's plan to bring his pregnant cat, Frankenstein (the Holy Mother), to Fiji (Fuchal) and open a hot dog and doughnut diner (the Temple of Food). The two factions split due to a dispute regarding whether the hats to be worn by temple servers were meant to be red or blue, which sparked millennia of bloodshed **[T-SER1.4]**.

  NOTE: *The novel* Infinity Welcomes Careful Drivers *claimed the Holy Wars were waged over whether the father of Catkind was named Cloister or Clister. The* Smegazine *comic storyline "Lister the God" further explored this idea.*

- ***Home Surgery*:** A magazine published in Jake Bullet's universe, geared toward do-it-yourself medical aficionados. Bullet found a copy of *Home Surgery* in Philby Frutch's apartment while investigating the man's murder. The issue featured the cover line "Very Happy Christmas to You!" and included the article, "The Man-Machine Interface in 26 Parts" **[M-SMG1.14(c6)]**.

- **"Home Sweet Home":** A saying embroidered on Rimmer's pajamas **[T-SER1.6]**.

- **homing device:** A handheld apparatus for locating a missing ship via its flight recorder. After *Starbug 1* entered a time hole and crashed on an Earth where time ran backwards, Lister and Cat used a homing device to find their lost comrades **[T-SER3.1]**.

- **homing pod:** A small, cylindrical unmanned spacecraft that delivered supplies and other items to Space Corps vessels. When Kryten reached his expiry date, Diva-Droid International sent such a craft to rendezvous with the mechanoid, with instructions to deactivate before his replacement arrived **[T-SER3.6]**.

  NOTE: *Homing pods were apparently identical to post pods, as the same footage—from episode 2.2 ("Better Than Life")—was used for both vessels.*

- **homogenized pudding:** A food item in *Red Dwarf*'s food supply that Lister accounted for on a supply checklist while conducting an inventory count with Rimmer. Arnold penalized Lister a quarter of a cigarette for saying the word "check" in various silly voices throughout this task **[T-SER1.3]**.

- ***Homo Rimmer*:** A hypothetical species that Rimmer claimed would be mankind's next evolutionary step following *Homo sapiens*, once he succeeded in creating a host body for himself from Lister's hair follicle via cellular regeneration. This, he said, accounted for why he had survived the human species' near-extinction **[R-BOD]**.

- ***Homo Sapienoid*:** A cyborg-like species that conquered Earth's solar system and brought humanity to the brink of extinction, then sent fleets of Death Ships to pursue *Red Dwarf* in search of Lister, the last human alive **[X-PRO]**.

  NOTE: *This information appeared in a promotional flyer promoting the never-filmed* Red Dwarf *movie.*

- **Honeymoon Suite:** A room at the Ganymede Holiday Inn for recently wed couples. After traveling back in time through a stasis leak to locate Kochanski, Lister found her and a future version of himself in Room 008, the hotel's Honeymoon Suite **[T-SER2.4]**.

- **Honor:** An aspect of Rimmer's personality that a psi-moon detected as being essentially dead, prompting the planetoid to construct a physical metaphor in its memory, in the shape of a tombstone. According to the stone's inscription, Rimmer's honor died when he was twelve years old **[T-SER5.3]**.

- **Honour:** An aspect of Rimmer's personality made flesh on a psi-moon configured according to his psyche. After Arnold's shipmates rescued him from the moon, Honour and his

comrades—Charity, Courage and Self-Esteem—were left behind to battle Rimmer's negative traits, including Misery, Self-Despair and Paranoia. The Dark Forces abducted Self-Esteem and displayed him in Castle Despondency to lure the others into a trap, then unleashed a secret weapon: the image of Rimmer's mother **[M-SMG2.7(c2)]**.

- **Hooch-Head:** A nickname that Cat called Kryten after finding the mechanoid trapped in an illusion of being the drunken sheriff of an Old West town **[T-SER6.3]**.

- **Hood, Robin:** A fictional heroic outlaw of English folklore who, with his band of Merry Men, robbed the rich and gave to the poor **[RL]**. While trapped in an elation squid hallucination, Lister pleaded with the Creator for more life in the form of a new television series, suggesting a Robin Hood-type program in which Lister would rescue Kryten each week. After hearing the idea out loud, though, he admitted it sounded awful **[T-SER9.3]**.

- **Hooded Legions, The:** The denizens of a psi-moon configured according to Rimmer's psyche **[T-SER5.3]**, also called the Holy Legions **[G-SOR]**. After Arnold landed on the moon, the planetoid restructured itself as a desolate, gloomy, swamp-filled wasteland inhabited by manifestations of his negative attributes. Among them were the Hooded Legions, who dressed in dark robes and possessed red-lit eyes—and who kidnapped him as a sacrifice to the Unspeakable One **[T-SER5.3]**.

- **Hooper:** A young Training Corps pilot in one of Ace Rimmer's universes. During a training mission, the two pilots discovered a narrow meteor formation through which only a single ship could fit. Faced with the choice of letting Hooper through and crashing his own vessel, or going through himself, Ace chose the latter scenario. Hooper's ship crashed, causing crippling injuries. Racked with guilt, Ace dedicated his time to overseeing Hooper's recovery and simultaneously developing bionic technology to help him. Hooper and Ace remained friends until Ace's departure into other dimensions **[M-SMG1.14(c5)]**.

- **Hooper:** A young Training Corps pilot in another of Ace Rimmer's universes. After finding a narrow meteor formation through which only a single ship could fit, this Ace chose to let Hooper pass through, while he crashed his own vessel and suffered career-ending injuries. While Hooper and other former colleagues enjoyed continued success in the Space Corps, Ace was left behind. Bitter and forgotten, he began experimenting in bionics and became a tyrant known as "Blackheart" Rimmer **[M-SMG1.14(c5)]**.

- **Hoover:** A popular brand of vacuum cleaners and other cleaning appliances **[RL]**. On the television soap opera *Androids,* Brooke Junior purchased a Hoover vacuum attachment using money earned from a job with his Uncle Jaysee **[M-SMG1.13(c1)]**.

- **Hoover, John Edgar ("J. Edgar"), Director:** The head of the U.S. Federal Bureau of Investigations (FBI) from 1935 to 1972. After Hoover's death, evidence surfaced that the Mafia had long blackmailed and manipulated him by threatening to reveal that he was a cross-dressing homosexual **[RL]**.

  In an alternate timeline created when the *Starbug 1* crew prevented President John F. Kennedy's assassination, Hoover became president after a scandal between Kennedy and the mistress of a mob boss ended with JFK's impeachment and imprisonment. The mob forced J. Edgar to run for office by showing him incriminating photographs of him in drag. As president, he allowed the Soviets to build nuclear bases in Cuba, forcing the mass desertion of several major U.S. cities **[T-SER7.1]**.

  In Jake Bullet's universe, the cyborg mistakenly assumed J. Edgar Hoover was a domestic appliance that became involved in police work **[M-SMG1.7(a)]**.

- **Hoover Black Hole:** A bag-less model of vacuum cleaner **[G-OTH]**.

  NOTE: *This was mentioned in* Red Dwarf RPG A.I. Add-On 1.0, *a downloadable PDF posted online by Deep7 Press in 2004, for use with* Red Dwarf—The Roleplaying Game.

- **Hoover Open Prison:** A New York correctional facility, circa the 1960s. In an alternate timeline, President John F. Kennedy survived an assassination attempt due to the interference of *Starbug 1*'s crew, and later had an affair with the mistress of Mafia boss Sam Giancana, for which he was impeached in 1964 and sent to Hoover Open Prison the following year, with

J. Edgar Hoover assuming the presidency **[T-SER7.1]**.

> ***NOTE:*** *Since there is no such facility in the real world, another facility in the altered timeline may have been renamed after Hoover took office.*

- **Hope:** An aspect of Rimmer's personality that a psi-moon detected as having been gradually depleted, prompting the planetoid to construct a physical metaphor in its memory, in the shape of a freshly dug tombstone **[T-SER5.3]**.

- **Hope:** A saloon barmaid in an Old West illusion that Kryten's subconscious mind created as the mechanoid battled the Apocalypse virus **[N-BCK]**.

  > ***NOTE:*** *This character was called Miss Lola in episode 6.3 ("Gunmen of the Apocalypse").*

- **hopper:** A type of land vehicle designed to relieve the inordinate amount of traffic that typically occurred on the small moon of Mimas. Its primary method of propulsion was its hind legs, which could retract into its body and then abruptly push out, lunging the craft forward in a hopping motion. Lister frequently stole taxi hoppers while living on Mimas, then ferried passengers around the moon's seedier areas to collect fares, in order to earn enough money to return to Earth. During one illicit cab run, he met Rimmer, whom he transported from the Mimas docks to Shagtown **[N-INF]**.

- **Horace:** A nickname that Confidence, a hallucination of Lister's mind made corporeal by mutated pneumonia, called Rimmer, referencing the hologrammic "H" on his forehead **[T-SER1.5]**.

- **Horace:** A bank teller in the fictional town of Bedford Falls in the film *It's a Wonderful Life* **[RL]**. While trapped in an addictive version of *Better Than Life*, Lister imagined settling down in Bedford Falls and opening a kebab shop, the earnings from which he deposited in Horace's bank **[N-INF]**.

- **Hornblower, Horatio:** A fictional nineteenth-century Royal Navy officer created as the protagonist of several C.S. Forester novels set during the Napoleonic Wars **[RL]**. Artificial-reality versions of Hornblower were responsible for 329 deaths in a single month, due to a faulty program in which the character was prone to exploding **[B-SUR]**.

- **Horror Chart:** A mental list Rimmer maintained of asinine accidents he caused during his lifetime that continued to haunt him years later. These included backing over his Aunt Belinda's prized show poodle (number three on the list), crushing two contingents of *Red Dwarf* skutters during an engine-restarting sequence (number four) and accidentally shooting his stepfather through the shoulder with his own service revolver (number five) **[N-BTL]**.

  > ***NOTE:*** *It is unknown whether the cadmium II disaster, caused by Arnold's failure to fix a drive plate, merited placement on the Horror Chart.*

- **Horror World:** An attraction at the Waxworld theme park, featuring waxdroids of famous characters from the horror genre. Sometime during the Wax War, Hero World's army stormed the Horror World attraction, during which Mrs. Claus lost an eye to the Mummy **[W-OFF]**.

- **"Hot and Wild Number 1":** A song produced by musician Chris Tsangarides **[RL]**. This song was played in the room to which Lister was confined aboard Legion's station **[W-OFF]**.

- **Hotel Paradiso:** A cheap hotel that Rimmer imagined while trapped in an addictive version of *Better Than Life*. After Rimmer broke out of a soundwave prison with his cellmate Jimmy, the two stayed in a suite at the hotel with Jimmy's brother Tonto. The suite sported a kitchen and a lounge area, and reportedly contained fewer roaches than the establishment's regular rooms **[N-BTL]**.

- **Hotel Paradiso:** A lodging establishment in a seedy area of Mimas known as Shagtown, on the corner of Copulation and 69th. Rimmer once approached two sex workers in front of the hotel. One of them, Trixie LaBouche, lived in Apartment 43 **[M-SMG2.3(c4)]**.

- **hot lager with croutons:** A meal that Lister requested while afflicted with space mumps **[T-SER4.3]**.

- **hover-car:** A mode of transportation on the television soap opera *Androids*. Gary's personal hover-car was destroyed when Jaysee tried to murder him **[M-SMG2.1(c2)]**. The show's

twenty-ninth season featured a massive pileup involving eight hover-cars **[W-AND]**.

- **hover dinghy:** A small, waterbound craft utilizing anti-gravity technology. Hover dinghies were kept aboard shuttles such as *Blue Midget* **[N-BTL]**.

- **hover-limo:** A mode of transportation that Rimmer mentioned while trapped in a despair squid hallucination. Believing himself to be William Doyle, Arnold fabricated a history for his new persona, which included being mugged twenty feet from his hover-limo **[T-SER5.6(d)]**.

- **Hover Rack 75:** An anti-gravity wardrobe rack on which Cat dreamed that his suits were stored **[M-SMG1.7(c2)]**.

  NOTE: *It is unclear whether this was actually the case outside Cat's dream.*

- **hover stretcher:** A medical device utilizing anti-gravity technology, used for transporting patients requiring medical care. *Red Dwarf*'s Medical Units contained several hover stretchers **[N-BTL]**.

- ***Howard Rimmer*, SS:** A name that *Red Dwarf*'s JMC onboard computer suggested re-christening the mining vessel, to honor hologram Howard Rimmer, who had died saving the crew from the mutinous simulant Crawford **[T-SER10.1]**.

- ***How Clean Is Your Cell?*:** A television game show scheduled for broadcast by Krytie TV on October 12. This particular episode featured Lister attempting to hide his toenail clippings from the show's nanny droid **[X-CAL]**.

  NOTE: *The series' name spoofed that of* How Clean Is Your House?, *which aired on Britain's Channel 4 from 2003 to 2009.*

- **Howdy Doody:** The titular puppet protagonist of American children's television series *Howdy Doody*, which aired on NBC from 1947 to 1960 **[RL]**. While giving his half-brother Howard a tour of the derelict vessel *Trojan*, Rimmer condescendingly called Howard by this name **[T-SER10.1]**.

- **HowdyDoodlyDoo:** The password to access Crapola Inc.'s online store **[W-CRP]**.

  NOTE: *Players of the online Geek Chase game received this password upon e-mailing the fictional company.*

- **How Many Marbles Can You Fit Up Your Nostril?:** A game that Cat and Lister enjoying playing aboard *Starbug 1*. Kochanski, tired of this game, tried to broaden their horizons by bringing them into an artificial-reality simulation of *Pride and Prejudice Land* **[T-SER7.6]**.

- **Howster:** A nickname that Rimmer called his half-brother, Howard **[T-SER10.1]**.

- ***How to Be a Winner—An Introduction to Powermatics*:** A book that Rimmer read in order to cope with his first command as leader of Z-Shift. The book taught that rebellion among the ranks must be dealt with immediately, preferably by choosing a group's leader and humiliating him or her. This technique backfired, however, when he attacked the shift's largest, strongest member in response to Lister making a snide remark, as the crewman beat him into unconsciousness **[N-INF]**.

- ***How to Defeat an Army of Mutant Russians Whilst Still Finding Time to Be the World's Greatest Golfer*:** A book written by North Korean dictator Kim Jong-il. Rimmer intended to read this book as part of his battleplan timetable, while devising a strategy to escape a group of rogue simulants **[T-SER10.6]**.

- ***How to Get More Girls By Hypnosis*:** *See How to Pick Up Girls By Hypnosis*

- ***How to Get Your Life Together*:** A book Lister once borrowed from the library. He never read it, however—and, in fact, had forgotten to return it for three years, finally bringing it back with a poppadom stuck between its pages **[N-LST]**.

- ***How to Overcome Your Fear of Speaking in Public*:** A book that Rimmer read to prepare himself for giving speeches as the leader of *Red Dwarf*'s Z-Shift **[N-INF]**.

- ***How to Pick Up Girls By Hypnosis*:** One of Rimmer's favorite books on seducing females. Knowing of its existence, Lister was surprised when Arnold suddenly became respectful toward women **[T-SER2.6]**.

  NOTE: *In the novel* Infinity Welcomes Careful Drivers, *the book was titled* How to Get More Girls By Hypnosis. *Given that Arlene Rimmer attempted Arnold's "something in your eye" hypnosis trick, a version of this book may have also existed in her universe—possibly titled* How to Pick Up Guys By Hypnosis. *This gag originated in a* Son of Cliché *sketch, involving the book* How to Meet More Girls—By Kidnapping Them.

- **HP11:** A type of battery used in MkIV Titanica Fish droids, such as Lister's pet robot goldfish, Lennon and McCartney. Each droid required two such batteries to operate **[M-SMG2.4(c5)]**.

- **Hubble, Mrs.:** A Bedford Falls resident whom Lister imagined while trapped in an addictive version of *Better Than Life*. The town had been without crime, according to a cop named Bert, ever since Mrs. Hubble had paid only two cents for a three-cent trolley ride **[N-BTL]**.

- **Hubble telescope:** An instrument aboard *Starbug* that aided the crew in observing distant objects **[N-LST]**.

  NOTE: *This device was presumably similar to the real-world Hubble Space Telescope, launched by NASA in 1990.*

- **Hub of Pain:** The central section of the Death Wheel, a structure built by agonoids occupying *Red Dwarf*. A domed-shaped room complete with a viewing gallery, the Hub of Pain featured every cutting, bludgeoning and torturing device known to man, including iron maidens, gynecological surgery equipment, gonad electrocution kits and easy-listening music **[N-BCK]**.

- **Hudzen:** A robotic character on the television soap opera *Androids*. In one episode, which always made Kryten laugh, Hudzen won the mechanoid lottery, and then hired his human master as a servant. In subsequent episodes, Hudzen frequented the Hi-Life Club, where he ordered dry martinis **[N-INF]**. Over time, Hudzen developed a rusting problem **[M-SMG1.9(c2)]**.

- **Hudzen 10:** A Series 4010 line of mechanoids, produced and distributed circa 2340 by Diva-Droid International as a replacement for the Kryten Series **[W-DIV]**. According to the company, the Hudzen 10—"the new state-of-the-art in android technology"—was ten times faster, smarter and stronger than the leading android on the market **[T-SER3.6]**.

  All units were equipped with a power button and a recharge socket, both located on the back **[W-DIV]**. Hudzen 10 units came pre-programmed with an encyclopedic database of French cheeses, the ability to field-strip an M-16 assault rifle **[G-RPG]** and a whisk attachment **[W-DIV]**. The model was available in three colors: Butler Black, Jet Black and Really Really Black, with Go-faster stripes and a groinal socket ashtray attachment available as extras **[G-SOR]**.

  Diva-Droid sent a Hudzen 10 unit to replace Kryten after the latter's contract had expired, but its sanity chip wore out during its three-million-year pursuit of *Red Dwarf*, causing it to attack the crew when they refused to deactivate Kryten. Overpowering them within minutes, Hudzen was incapacitated by a metaphysical dichotomy, brought on by Kryten's admission that there was no Silicon Heaven **[T-SER3.6]**.

  Years later, a group of Cat People traveled to the future and attacked the *Red Dwarf* crew, kidnapping Lister and bringing him back to the past. Kryten was heavily damaged in the assault, so in order to facilitate Lister's rescue, Holly transplanted Kryten's head onto the Hudzen 10's body, then traveled to the past with Cat, Rimmer and Holly. The transplant was only temporary, as Kryten's circuits became corrupted, making him increasingly violent and unpredictable **[M-SMG2.3(c1)]**.

  A Hudzen 10 model participated in the ninth annual Kinitawowi Open, a golf tournament held on Echech 3, within GELF space **[G-RPG]**.

  NOTE: *In a deleted scene for episode 3.6 ("The Last Day"), Lister commented that Hudzen's arm turned into a blender, and that he had a built-in spin dryer, but he may have been speaking sarcastically.*

- **Hudzen 10:** A character in the Total Immersion video game *Red Dwarf*, in a fascist Earth society in an alternate universe. Hudzen 10's role in the game was to replace Kryten by either deactivating or killing him. Players could defeat Hudzen by blowing him to pieces with a nuclear launcher **[M-SMG2.5(c4)]**.

- **Hudzen 10:** A Hudzen 10 model mechanoid on a possible alternate *Red Dwarf.* His crewmates included a member of the *Rattus sapiens* species named Ricky and hologram Monica Jones **[G-RPG]**.

- ***Hudzen 10 Series 4010 Mechanoid Instruction Manual*:** A book that Diva-Droid International supplied to owners of Hudzen 10 mechanoids **[W-DIV]**.

- **Huě:** The capital city of Vietnam's Thùa Thiên–Huê Province **[RL]**. While discussing simulants' general hatred of anything starting with "hu," including humans and humanoids, Kochanski joked that they likely despised the third largest city in Vietnam as well—despite its name being pronounced "hwah" **[T-SER7.6]**.

  NOTE: The city's name is actually pronounced "hweh."

- **Hugo:** An individual whom Rimmer imagined while trapped in an addictive version of *Better Than Life*. After Arnold hired Hugo to work as the gardener and pool attendant at his Penthouse Suite in the Rimmer Building (Paris), Hugo had an affair with Rimmer's wife, supermodel Juanita Chicata. When he refused to make love to her anymore for fear of being fired, she threw a tantrum. Arnold found out about the romance and dismissed the man, then pulled strings around Paris to ensure he would have difficulty shopping for clothes **[N-INF]**.

- **Hugo, Victor:** A French writer and activist of the nineteenth century who authored the novels *Les Misérables* and *The Hunchback of Notre-Dame* **[RL]**. When Rimmer found Lister reading a Cat book that contained smells instead of words, the hologram suggested he read his own shirt, as it likely contained an entire Victor Hugo novel **[T-SER1.4]**.

- **Human Impressions Task & Logistics Electronic Reichsführer (HITLER):** A mainframe computer created by the Reich, a superpower that controlled an alternate-reality Earth known as War World. The computer contained the brain of Nazi Germany's former Führer, Adolf Hitler, preserved in stasis. Only sub-leaders within the Reich could access the machine brain **[G-BIT]**.

  NOTE: Following World War II, unfounded rumors arose that Hitler's brain had been preserved, inspiring the 1969 film They Saved Hitler's Brain.

- **Human Rights Akt:** A government document outlining the rights of individuals within the jurisdiction of the Universal Government, updated in the year 2100. It included The Hologram Rights 2141 amendment, The Last Rights Act of 2142 and The Hologram Protection Akt of 2143 **[M-SMG2.2(a)]**.

- **Humie:** A nickname that the Epideme virus called humans **[T-SER7.7]**. The female Cat, in a dimension in which the *Red Dwarf* crew were American, also used this term to describe her universe's Lister **[T-USA2]**.

- **Humo:** A nickname that Hogey the Roguey called Lister, mocking his status as a human **[T-SER10.6]**.

- **humor:** A rogue emotion purged from Kryten's hard drive by the Data Doctor, a program for restoring a mechanoid's personality to factory settings, when Captain Hollister subjected Kryten to a psychotropic simulation **[T-SER8.2]**.

- **Hump:** One of seven diminutive rainforest dwellers known as the Ionian Ecommandoes, who lived in the jungles of Io on the television soap opera *Androids*. He and his comrades nursed Karstares back to health **[M-SMG2.5(c5)]**, after Karstares' plane crashed due to sabotage by his son Jaysee **[M-SMG1.14(c3)]**. Grateful for their help, Karstares became the Green Knight, the rainforest's protector, and fought alongside the Ecommandoes against Jaysee's ecologically harmful company **[M-SMG2.5(c5)]**. Hump died during a firefight between Jaysee and his foes **[M-SMG2.8(c2)]**.

  NOTE: This character resembled one of Disney's Seven Dwarfs. All of the Ecommandoes' names were slang for sex.

- **Hundred Years' War, The:** A series of medieval conflicts fought between England and France in the fourteenth and fifteenth centuries **[RL]**. After locking Lister, Kryten and Cat in quarantine, Rimmer expressed his desire that their isolation pass as quickly and pleasantly as the Hundred Years' War **[T-SER5.4]**.

B-: Books
PRG: *Red Dwarf Programme Guide*
SUR: *Red Dwarf Space Corps Survival Manual*
PRM: *Primordial Soup*
SOS: *Son of Soup*
SCE: *Scenes from the Dwarf*
LOG: *Red Dwarf Log No. 1996*
RD8: *Red Dwarf VIII*
EVR: *The Log: A Dwarfer's Guide to Everything*

X-: Misc.
PRO: Promotional materials, videos, etc.
PST: Posters at DJ XVII (2013)
CAL: 2008 calendar
RNG: Cell phone ringtones
MOB: Mobisode ("Red Christmas")
CIN: *Children in Need* sketch
GEK: *Geek Week* intros by Kryten
TNG: "Tongue-Tied" video

XMS: Bill Pearson's Christmas special pitch script
XVD: Bill Pearson's Christmas special pitch video
OTH: Other *Red Dwarf* appearances

SUFFIX
DVD:
(d) – Deleted scene
(o) – Outtake
(b) – Bonus DVD material (other)
(e) – Extended version

SMEGAZINES:
(c) – Comic
(a) – Article

OTHER:
(s) – Early/unused script draft
(s1) – Alternate version of script

While trapped in a seeding ship escape pod bound for a wormhole, Rimmer was informed by Kryten that a rescue attempt would take six times longer than a certain long-lasting medieval war. Rimmer mistook this for the Thirty Years' War, though the mechanoid actually meant the Hundred Years' War **[T-SER6.5]**.

- **Hunt, Dave ("Dead Shot"):** A legendary association football player in the universe known as Alternative 6829/B. In his heyday, Hunt averaged 298 goals per season. In one game, he scored a hat-trick while using crutches. In another, he astrally projected himself to simultaneously play Left Wing, Right Back and Center Forward, in order to fill in for various teammates removed from the game by a faulty robot referee.

  Ray Rimmer, Arnold Rimmer's persona in that reality, acquired Dead Shot's boots. Believing them to possess magical powers, Ray became a star football player, rising to become captain of the Smegchester Rovers. When the shoes wore out and lost their mystical properties, Ray's game suffered. Depressed, he tried to jump off the Stamford Bridge, but his other-dimensional counterpart, Ace Rimmer, intervened and saved him.

  After hearing Ray's story, Ace filled in for him during the following day's Cup Final, scoring eighteen goals and winning the game. Ray asked him to fill in permanently, but Ace declined—though before leaving, he repaired Dead Shot's boots, enabling Ray to continue his winning streak **[M-SMG1.8(c4)]**.

- **hydrogen RAM-drive:** A component of a spacefaring vessel's propulsion system. The *Red Dwarf* crew of a parallel dimension offered to update their prime counterparts' hydrogen RAM-drive to a tachyon-powered engine core **[T-SER7.3]**.

  NOTE: *It is unclear whether the alternate crew were offering to upgrade* Red Dwarf *or* Starbug 1, *since they still had their own* Red Dwarf *and thus might not have been aware their counterparts were living aboard a shuttlecraft.*

- **hydro unit:** A component of *Red Dwarf*'s air vents. To escape the rapidly shrinking vents, Kochanski suggested taking *Starbug 1* past Epsilon 14 and making a right at the hydro unit **[T-SER8.1]**.

- ***Hymns in Rock*:** An album recorded by Christian rock group Frank Assisi and the Apostles. A CD of this album was one of several that Lister scattered around Warden Ackerman's quarters, thinking he was actually trashing the room of Kochanski's ex-boyfriend Tim **[T-SER8.5]**.

- **hyperdrive:** A propulsion system used on some shuttlecraft stored aboard *Red Dwarf*. A message warning pilots not to engage hyperdrive within the mining ship's gravity field was stenciled on the shuttle bay's wall **[T-SER3.1]**.

- **hyper-drive:** A propulsion system Cat devised after imbibing the luck virus, as a means of rescuing Lister from a planet thirty-two weeks' travel away that would soon pass through a black hole. The hyper-drive punched a hole in space and harnessed a superstring to bend time, enabling travelers to traverse the Tenth Dimension in order to arrive at their destination more quickly **[N-LST]**.

  NOTE: *Presumably, the hyper-drive and the hyperdrive utilized similar technologies.*

- **Hyperion:** A small, irregularly shaped moon of Saturn **[RL]**. Michael McGruder fought on Hyperion during the Saturn War **[N-LST]**.

- **hyperway:** A passage through non-space connecting two parallel dimensions, created when the membrane between them collapsed. An alternate-reality Kochanski passed through a hyperway and became marooned in the prime universe **[T-SER7.3]**.

- **hypno-ring:** A mysterious object that enabled Jaysee to become a business mogul on the television soap opera *Androids* **[W-AND]**.

- **hypnotherapy disc:** A disc of soothing sounds played through a device in Kryten's torso. While attempting to placate Lister after a harrowing nightmare, the mechanoid intended to play his hypnotherapy disc, but inadvertently activated a German language disc containing an excerpt from Adolf Hitler's Nuremberg speech, startling Lister **[T-SER7.5]**.

INQUISITOR, THE (A.K.A. THE REALITY PATROL)

- **"I ♥ Flibble":** A button worn on the hat of Mr. Flibble's buxom, leather-clad companion **[M-SMG2.9(c10)]**.

- **"I ♥ The Broom Cupboard":** A phrase printed on a bumper sticker affixed to luggage that Kryten used during a vacation to V Deck's broom cupboard **[T-SER9.1]**.

- **"I ♥ Uranus":** A souvenir T-shirt worn by a traveler at the Mimas Spaceport **[M-SMG2.5(c6)]**.

    NOTE: The heart in the slogan's logo was drawn to resemble a puckered anus.

- **"I am a fish":** A phrase that Rimmer, suffering an extreme panic attack, wrote four hundred times on one of his Astronavigation Exams **[T-SER1.1]**.

    NOTE: In the novel Infinity Welcomes Careful Drivers, *he wrote it five hundred times. This gag originated in a* Son of Cliché *"Dave Hollins: Space Cadet" sketch titled "Indian Food/Exams."*

- **ICI:** A company in England during a period in Earth's far future when time ran backwards. While stranded in the year 3991 (1993 in forward-time), Rimmer and Kryten searched a local newspaper to find a job, and came across ICI's help-wanted listing for a managing director position that promised "excellent demotion prospects" **[T-SER3.1]**.

- **Icke, David:** A British public speaker and professional footballer, and the author of several books about global politics and New Age Conspiracism **[RL]**. When the *Red Dwarf* crew encountered a derelict ship whose computer was locked on a pilgrimage setting, Kryten said the vessel was likely heading toward a religious destination, such as an icon. Rimmer misheard the word as "Icke-Con" and wondered why David Icke worship had persisted through the twenty-first century **[M-SMG1.14(c2)]**.

- **IcthyTech 3000 Robot Goldfish:** *See* Titanica Fish Droid MkIV

- **"IDECK":** The title of a chart that Rimmer posted on a wall of *Red Dwarf*'s Observation Room, in which he studied an unidentified pod retrieved in deep space. Using this chart, he attempted to translate the pod's markings, convinced that it contained an alien species (which he named the Quagaar). The chart listed several symbols that he translated as "orbit," "creation," "female," "male," "solar drive," "time jump," "interstellar drivex," "perpetual motion," "molecular regeneration," "cloning" and "template." However, the supposed alien markings turned out merely to be the words "*Red Dwarf* Garbage Pod," eroded away after three million years of spaceflight **[T-SER1.4]**.

- **ident computer:** A type of hardware installed aboard most spacefaring vessels that identified the craft, as well as its occupants and cargo **[T-SER6.5]**.

- ***I Did It the Reicht Way*:** A book written by Adolf Hitler that Rimmer intended to read as part of a battleplan timetable he created for devising a strategy to escape rogue simulants **[T-SER10.6]**.

- **Idlewild Airport:** An airport in Queens, New York, that was renamed John F. Kennedy International Airport following JFK's 1963 assassination **[RL]**. In an alternate timeline, Kennedy survived the murder attempt due to the interference of *Starbug 1*'s crew, and was later impeached and sentenced to prison. JFK was then flown to Idlewild Airport (which retained its original name in that timeline) aboard a Star Airways flight, where Lister—who had traveled back in time to convince Kennedy to assassinate himself and thus correct history—met him on the tarmac in the back of a police van **[T-SER7.1]**.

- **"If I Were a Rich Man":** A song written in 1964 by Sheldon Harnick and Jerry Bock for the musical *Fiddler on the Roof,* performed by the character Tevye **[RL]**. Rimmer sang this tune after using a timeslide to convince his younger self to invent the Tension Sheet and thus become a billionaire **[T-SER3.5]**.

- **"If you don't gosub a program loop, you'll never get a subroutine":** The mechanoid equivalent of the human expression, "Nothing ventured, nothing gained" **[T-SER4.3]**.

- **"If you lose a good friend, you can always get another; but if you lose your tail, things will always be drafty":** An old Cat People proverb that Cat recited after Kryten volunteered to sacrifice himself to a Space Corps external enforcement vessel to save his crewmates **[T-SER6.4(d)]**.

NOTE: The DVD captions slightly altered this saying to "Lose a good friend, you can get another. Lose your tail, things will always be draughty."

- **"If you're gonna eat tuna, expect bones":** An old Cat People proverb that Cat recited as his shipmates debated whether to board a derelict simulant vessel, despite the superstructure's instability and the possibility of survivors. Rimmer snidely responded with a saying of his own: "If you're gonna talk garbage, expect pain" **[T-SER6.5]**.

- **Iglesias, Julio:** A prolific Spanish singer-songwriter whose hits included "To All the Girls I've Loved Before" and "All of You" **[RL]**. Originally a football player, Iglesias decided to give up the sport and go into music thanks to the urging of the *Red Dwarf* crew, who had traveled back in time to 1971 **[B-SUR]**.

  NOTE: In the real world, Iglesias served as a goalkeeper for Real Madrid Castilla as a teen, and played the sport professionally while studying law at Madrid's CEU San Pablo University. His pro career ended following a near-fatal car accident.

- **IGM K49 A2:** A code stenciled on a crate stored on *Red Dwarf*'s food deck, also marked with the serial number 157007W. After a time wand transformed Birdman's pet sparrow, Pete, into a *Tyrannosaurus rex*, the crew hid near this container **[T-SER8.7(d)]**.

- **IGM K49 A3:** A code stenciled on a crate stored aboard the SSS *Silverberg*, which also bore the serial number 151513F **[T-SER8.4]**.

- ***Ignotus venustas*:** A strain of charisma virus isolated by hologrammatic scientist Hildegarde Lanstrom **[W-OFF]**. Charisma was one of several positive viruses Lanstrom discovered; this particular strain made an infected individual more charming and personable. Kryten discovered vials of this and other positive viruses on the station and brought them aboard *Red Dwarf* **[T-SER5.4]**.

- **iguana:** A genus of lizard native to several warm-climate continents on Earth **[RL]**. Rimmer lamented that his only companion in deep space was Lister, whom he considered a "man who'd lose a battle of wits with a stuffed iguana" **[T-SER1.1]**.

  In an alternate dimension, Lister smuggled a pregnant iguana aboard *Red Dwarf* instead of a cat. This led to an entire species of humanoid iguanas evolving over the course of three million years in the ship's cargo hold. These creatures were adept climbers and explorers, but rarely displayed perceivable emotions. They preferred warmer climates, and would go into shock at temperatures below 55 degrees Fahrenheit (13 degrees Celsius) **[G-RPG]**.

  NOTE: Red Dwarf—The Roleplaying Game *implied that the Iguana species resembled Jamaican Rastafarians.*

- ***I Jog Therefore I Am*:** A *Run Your Way Slim* fitness video featuring René Descartes, produced by the Transtemporal Film Unit **[B-LOG]**.

- **"I Like SKA":** A phrase printed on a button worn by Carl, a member of Serial Killers Anonymous (SKA) in Jake Bullet's universe **[M-SMG2.7(c4)]**.

- **"I'll Love You Babe ('Til the Next Chick Comes Along)":** A love song written by a member of the Cat People inhabiting *Red Dwarf*. Cat attempted to sing a duet of this tune with Talkie Toaster, but the appliance admitted to not understanding Cat music after repeatedly missing his cue **[T-SER2.1(d)]**.

- **"I Love Vindaloo":** A phrase in a tattoo that Lister, while on leave at Ganymede, drunkenly had applied to his right buttock, just below the image of a heart pierced by an arrow dripping curry sauce onto the letters. He discovered it the next day after learning that he had enrolled as a novice monk at a Ganymedian monastery **[T-SER6.1(d)]**.

- ***I'm OK!*:** A hypothetical magazine title that Rimmer made up while gloating that his hologrammatic nature made him immune to simulant attack **[T-SER10.6]**.

- **Imperial Typewriter Co. Ltd.:** An early twentieth-century manufacturer of typewriters based in Leicester, England **[RL]**. While trapped in an elation squid hallucination, the *Red Dwarf* crew imagined that their Creator used an Imperial typewriter to write the British television comedy *Red Dwarf*, on which they believed they were merely characters. Lister later used the same machine to rewrite the final episode's script in their favor. Upon realizing that the typewriter made his shipmates do whatever he typed, he gleefully made them act silly and injure themselves **[T-SER9.3]**.

- ***Importance of Being Earnest, A Trivial Comedy for Serious People, The*:** A play written in 1894 by Oscar Wilde **[RL]**. When Lister was seventeen years old, the husband of a checkgirl girl with whom he was having an affair packed him naked into a crate and released him in the middle of a Bootle Players' amateur production of *The Importance of Being Earnest*. This traumatizing event left Dave claustrophobic **[T-SER7.4]**.

- **impulse valve:** A switch on a mechanical appendage for individuals missing limbs. Adjusting this valve increased or decreased the appendage's sensitivity to signals from the brain. After Lister lost an arm to the Epideme virus, Kryten fitted him with such a device, but the extreme effort necessary to move it required Kryten to adjust the impulse valve. The second attempt acted on signals from Lister's subconscious mind to punch Kryten in the head, indicating the arm was too sensitive **[T-SER7.8]**.

- **Incinerex:** A type of plastic explosive stored aboard JMC ships. After an attempt to rid his body of the Epideme virus via amputation failed, Lister retrieved forty pounds of Incinerex from *Starbug 1* and used an escape pod to return to the *Leviathan*—the vessel on which the crew had found the infected Caroline Carmen—intending to blow himself up along with the virus **[T-SER7.7]**. Incinerex was produced by Piledriver Inc. and distributed via Crapola Inc.'s annual *SCABBY* catalog **[G-RPG]**.

- **India:** The second-most populous nation on Earth, located in South Asia **[RL]**. Indian food was among Lister's favorite cuisines, particularly vindaloos **[T-SER1.3]**, curries **[T-SER2.1]** and poppadoms **[T-SER6.1]**. He ate his first shami kebab at the Indiana Takeaway, in St. John's Precinct **[N-INF]**, but never tried a king prawn biryani—which he later regretted **[N-INF]**.

  Red Dwarf's Floor 431 contained an Indian restaurant in Blue Corridor 9 called The Vindaloovian Empire, which served a dish named The Dave Lister Special **[X-CAL]**. Another Indian eatery, the Titan Taj Mahal, was located a short distance from the ship's cinema **[T-SER1.6]**.

  When a flood destroyed *Starbug 1*'s Indian food stores, Lister tricked his crewmates into retrieving the time drive so he could restock the supplies at London's Taj Mahal Tandoori Restaurant. Instead, the device took them back to Dallas in 1963, to the time of John F. Kennedy's assassination **[T-SER7.1]**.

  After a malfunctioning rejuvenation shower transported the *Red Dwarf* crew to England in the year 23 A.D., they embarked on a six-month journey to India to obtain lemons to power a device that would return them to their own era. Upon arriving in India, they met a woman named Erin, who sold them the fruit, as well as Jesus of Caesarea, whom they mistook for Jesus of Nazareth **[T-SER10.3]**.

  Lister once told Rimmer that when the hologram wore his dress uniform, he looked like Clive of India **[T-SER2.1]**.

- **Indiana Takeaway:** An Indian-cuisine restaurant in St. John's Precinct, at which Lister tasted his first shami kebab. According to Lister, it was the perfect food-of-the-gods, and he spent the rest of his life searching for another shami kebab as good, but without success **[N-INF]**.

  NOTE: *There are several restaurants called Indiana in the United Kingdom, but as of this book's publication, there are none in St. John's Precinct.*

- **"Indling Song, The":** A song Lister wrote for Kochanski that included several words ending in "indle." Confidence, a hallucination of Dave's mind made corporeal by mutated pneumonia, adored the tune, calling it "the greatest love song ever" **[T-SER1.5]**.

  NOTE: *It is unclear whether this was the song's actual title, or merely Confidence's made-up name for it.*

- **Industrial baked beans:** A brand of baked beans sold on a psi-moon corrupted by Mr. Flibble's depraved mind. After subduing Robbie Rocketpants, Flibble force-fed the beans to the superhero, then launched him into the air by igniting his flatulence **[M-SMG2.9(c10)]**.

- **inertia rating:** A value assigned to *Starbug* shuttlecrafts indicating how much inertia the craft produced. A ship's inertia rating was required in order to calculate its engine's thrust-to-input ratio **[T-SER4.5]**.

- **I Never Really Loved You Anyway:** A notable twenty-third-century computer virus **[G-RPG]**.

  NOTE: *This virus' name spoofed that of the "ILOVEYOU" computer worm unleashed in 2000.*

- **Infinitol:** A drug created sometime after 2217, advertised as offering "the key to immortality" by completely stopping the aging process—which it did by killing the patient **[B-EVR]**.

- **Infinity Patrol:** A pair of gentlemen from the extreme future who traveled through time repairing paradoxes to ensure the human species' continuation. This included removing presidents to avoid world wars and giving humanity advanced technology, such as penicillin, the silicon chip and deely boppers. While visiting *Red Dwarf*, the Infinity Patrol asked Rimmer if he knew Bill, since they were both from the twenty-second century **[R-INF]**.

  NOTE: *This gag originated in a* Son of Cliché *"Dave Hollins: Space Cadet" sketch titled "The Strange Planet You Shouldn't Really Land On."*

- **Inflatable Ingrid, Your Polythene Pal:** A blow-up sex doll that Rimmer owned, which Lister claimed was Arnold's only true friend **[T-SER2.5]**.

  NOTE: *It is unclear whether this was the same doll that Rimmer called Rachel in later episodes. Inflatable Ingrid may have been the manufacturer's name for the product, with Rimmer renaming his doll Rachel. The official website indicated them to be the same, whereas the* Smegazines *and the* Red Dwarf Programme Guide *said otherwise.*

- ***Inflatus mentis*:** A strain of inspiration virus isolated by hologrammic scientist Hildegarde Lanstrom **[W-OFF]**. Inspiration was one of several positive viruses Lanstrom discovered; this particular strain stimulated an infected individual's mind, making thoughts and ideas come more easily. Kryten discovered vials of this and other positive viruses on the station and brought them aboard *Red Dwarf* **[T-SER5.4]**.

  NOTE: *In the novel* Last Human, *the crew discovered the virus aboard the* Mayflower, *an ancient terraforming ship in an alternate universe.*

- **Infomax Data Corporation:** An electronics company, circa 2296, that produced the Version IX.05 Mechanoid Visual System used in Kryten and other 4000 Series mechanoids **[N-INF]**.

- **inky squid soup:** A delicacy sold in Mimas' red-light district. Rimmer feigned interest in trying the soup as an excuse to visit a local brothel **[N-INF]**.

- **innocent whistle mode:** A function of 4000 Series mechanoids, enabling them to appear as though they were not involved in nefarious plotting. Kryten engaged this mode after Rimmer ordered him to dig up dirt about Katerina Bartikovsky—who was standing right behind him **[T-SER9.1]**.

- ***Innuendo Man*:** A comic book in Lister's quarters aboard *Red Dwarf* **[T-SER9.1(b)]**.

  NOTE: *This prop, not discernable in the episode, was spotlighted in behind-the-scenes footage included with Series IX's DVD bonus materials.*

- **Inquisitor, the (a.k.a. the Reality Patrol):** A self-repairing simulant who lived throughout the ages and survived until the end of time. Toward the end, he determined that there was no God or afterlife, and realized the point of existence was to lead a worthwhile life. To that end, the simulant constructed a time gauntlet enabling him to go back in time and judge every soul according to his definition of worthiness.

  The Inquisitor erased from history those he saw as unfit to exist, replacing them with other souls who never had a chance at life. By metaphysically becoming those he judged, he ensured that all would be judged fairly **[T-SER5.2]**. His role models included Judge Death and the Terminator **[M-SMG2.5(a)]**.

  The Inquisitor was not immune to errors in judgment. In one instance, the simulant erased Jan Ludwig Hoch, a poor immigrant whom he decided could have made more of himself, and replaced him with an "abrasive parasite" called Robert Maxwell. After performing a reality scan, however, the Inquisitor discovered he had inadvertently erased the only

INFLATABLE INGRID, YOUR POLYTHENE PAL

PREFIX
RL: Real life

T-: Television Episodes
- **SER:** Television series
- **IDW:** "Identity Within"
- **USA1:** Unaired U.S. pilot
- **USA2:** Unaired U.S. demo

R-: *The Bodysnatcher Collection*
- **SER:** Remastered episodes
- **BOD:** "Bodysnatcher"
- **DAD:** "Dad"
- **FTH:** "Lister's Father"
- **INF:** "Infinity Patrol"
- **END:** "The End" (original assembly)

N-: Novels
- **INF:** *Infinity Welcomes Careful Drivers*
- **BTL:** *Better Than Life*
- **LST:** *Last Human*
- **BCK:** *Backwards*
- **OMN:** *Red Dwarf Omnibus*

M-: Magazines
- **SMG:** *Smegazine*

W-: Websites
- **OFF:** Official website
- **NAN:** *Prelude to Nanarchy*
- **AND:** *Androids*
- **DIV:** Diva-Droid
- **DIB:** Duane Dibbley
- **CRP:** Crapola
- **GEN:** Geneticon
- **LSR:** Leisure World Intl.
- **JMC:** Jupiter Mining Corporation
- **AIT:** *A.I. Today*
- **HOL:** HoloPoint

G-: Roleplaying Game
- **RPG:** *Core Rulebook*
- **BIT:** *A.I. Screen Extra Bits* booklet
- **SOR:** *Series Sourcebook*
- **OTH:** Other RPG material

decent version of Hoch, and pushed the new version over the side of his yacht to fix his mistake **[M-SMG1.11(c3)]**.

In another instance, the Inquisitor attempted to erase Mortimer Dodd, but became trapped in a time paradox since Dodd's future equations would help scientists at the Institute of Simulant Technology create the Inquisitor in the first place. The simulant fixed the timeline by going back to stop himself from erasing Dodd, though it took several dozen attempts to succeed **[M-SMG2.5(c3)]**.

Eventually, he met the *Red Dwarf* crew and individually judged their worth. He pardoned Rimmer and Cat, but declared Lister and Kryten as capable of having been more, sentencing them to erasure and replacement. Before he could complete the process, a future Kryten appeared and severed the Inquisitor's gauntleted hand, tossing it to the startled pair before the simulant killed him. Lister and Kryten reprogrammed the gauntlet and reversed its field, then tricked the Inquisitor into using it one last time, effectively removing himself, and his actions, from history **[T-SER5.2]**.

- **insecurity:** A rogue emotion purged from Kryten's hard drive by the Data Doctor, a program for restoring a mechanoid's personality to factory settings, when Captain Hollister subjected Kryten to a psychotropic simulation **[T-SER8.2]**.

- **"Inspected J.D.I.F.":** A phrase stenciled on several containers aboard *Red Dwarf*. Rimmer, Kryten and Cat passed these crates while searching for an escaped polymorph **[T-SER3.3]**.

- **inspiration:** *See Inflatus mentis*

- **Insta-Serve microwave:** An appliance that could produce fully prepared and cooked meals from raw ingredients within seconds **[G-SOR]**. Lister used an Insta-Serve microwave aboard *Red Dwarf* to prepare shami kebab diabolo **[T-SER3.3]**.

- **Institute of Simulant Technology:** A research facility focused on technologies used in the creation of simulants. Mortimer Dodd, a tea boy at the institute, inadvertently solved a troubling equation for the resident scientists when he scribbled their tea order on a piece of paper. The scientists then applied this equation to the intelligence circuits of a self-replicating simulant later called the Inquisitor **[M-SMG2.5(c3)]**.

- **Intake Clearance Zone:** An area aboard *Red Dwarf* in which new arrivals were cleared for duty **[N-INF]**.

- **intelligence circuits:** A type of hardware incorporated into 4000 Series mechanoids, such as the Kryten series, that controlled their general IQ. Kryten's intelligence circuits melted when subjected to a slideshow presentation of Rimmer's ten-day hiking excursion through *Red Dwarf*'s diesel decks **[T-SER4.3]**.

- **intelligence compression:** A method of increasing a computer's artificial intelligence by rerouting its AI circuits through a single CPU, at the cost of a reduced lifespan. After Lister destroyed Talkie Toaster, Kryten rebuilt the appliance using this method as a proof-of-concept, then utilized the same technique to restore Holly's IQ to six thousand. The procedure worked too well, instead giving Holly an IQ past twelve thousand —but reducing her lifespan to 3.41 minutes. Panicking, she shut herself down until a solution could be found. The process was eventually reversed when the crew plugged a white hole **[T-SER4.4]**.

- **intelligence test:** A fake test to which Lister jokingly subjected Olaf Petersen, by pretending to stick a coin to the Dane's forehead and instructing him to slap the back of his head repeatedly until it fell off—which it would never do, since Dave had removed the coin. The more times he did so, Lister claimed, the more "intelligent" he was **[T-SER1.1]**.

- **Interflora:** An international flower delivery service **[RL]**. While incarcerated in *Red Dwarf*'s brig, Lister sent Kochanski two bags of self-rising flour to apologize for letting Kryten record her in the shower, since being in prison prevented him from calling Interflora to have real flowers delivered **[T-SER8.5]**.

  ***NOTE:** Although the actual baking term is "self-rising flour," the bags were labeled "self-raising" onscreen.*

- **Inter-Planetary Commission for Waste Disposal:** A group comprising representatives from each of the nine planets in Earth's solar system. The committee was formed in the twenty-second century to discuss options for the removal of the system's waste products. After conducting feasibility studies, the team opted to designate one of the nine worlds as humanity's official "Garbage World." Delegates from each planet presented their case against being nominated, and a poll was held throughout the system. Earth failed to receive a single vote in its favor, becoming mankind's new dumping ground **[N-BTL]**.

- **Interplanetary Salvage Code:** A set of rules governing salvage team rights, possibly listed under Space Corps Directive 1138B, section 14, sub-paragraph M **[G-RPG]**.

- **Interstella Action Games:** A company that produced virtual-reality games, including the detective simulation *Gumshoe* **[T-SER6.3]**.

- **"Interstellar Drivex":** A phrase on a chart that Rimmer created to translate markings on a mysterious pod Holly found adrift in space, which he thought were an alien language—but which actually spelled out "*Red Dwarf* Garbage Pod," eroded away after many years of spaceflight **[T-SER1.4]**.

- **Intro2:** An early twenty-first-century British rock band **[RL]**. Holly occasionally listened to the group when bored in order to keep from going insane, and once appeared in a music video for their song "Clear" **[T-SER8(b)]**.

  NOTE: *The video was included as an Easter egg on the Series VIII DVDs.*

- ***Introduction to the Liar Paradox and the Non-Mechanizability of Mathematics, An*:** A book Rimmer owned aboard *Red Dwarf* **[N-INF]**.

- **intruder alert:** A *Red Dwarf* alert status indicating the presence of an unauthorized occupant. Upon identifying an individual without a clearance code, the ship's computer sealed doorways around the perimeter, activated the intruder alert claxon and pumped tear gas into the area until authorized personnel arrived on the scene. After the Inquisitor removed Kryten and Lister from history, they were no longer able to open any doors aboard the mining ship once the intruder alert sounded **[T-SER5.2]**.

- **Inverting Input:** A setting on *Starbug 1*'s sonar scope display. This setting was not highlighted as the crew charted the course of a despair squid **[T-SER5.6]**.

- ***Investor's Chronicle*:** A weekly British publication for private investors **[RL]**. Debating whether or not to approve Ace Rimmer's mission aboard *Wildfire One*, Admiral Tranter worried that sending a $£30 billion spacecraft on a one-way trip into a virtually identical universe would not snag him the cover of *Investor's Chronicle* **[N-BCK]**.

- **Io:** Jupiter's innermost Galilean moon, and the solar system's fourth largest natural satellite **[RL]**. Io contained a domed settlement (population: 355,000) **[B-PRM]**, in which Rimmer grew up and attended Io Polytechnic **[T-SER10.6]**, where he resided at Io House **[T-SER4.5]**.

  On the television soap opera *Androids*, Karstares was presumed dead when his plane went down in the jungles of Io. A later episode revealed that he survived with help from several forest dwellers, becoming a champion of the rainforest known as the Green Knight. Jaysee, Karstares' evil son, harvested materials from Io's rainforests to use in his cleaning product, Eco **[M-SMG2.2(c3)]**.

  NOTE: Red Dwarf—The Roleplaying Game *claimed Io was a strictly industrialized moon, its surface too dangerous for civilian population.*

- **Io Amateur Wargamers:** A club to which Rimmer belonged while attending cadet school. On Waxworld years later, while training Hero World's pacifistic waxdroids, he regretted that his fellow wargamers were not there to see him **[T-SER4.6]**.

- **Io House:** A college residence on Io at which Rimmer and his half-brothers boarded while attending Io Polytechnic **[T-SER4.5]**.

- **Ionian bee:** A species of insect on the Jovian moon of Io that produced a type of royal jelly **[W-OFF]**.

- **Ionian Ecommandoes:** A group of seven diminutive forest dwellers from the jungles of Io, featured on the television soap opera *Androids*, and named Rumpy, Pumpy, Bang, Bonk, Hump, Jump and A Bit of the Other **[M-SMG2.5(c5)]**. When the group nursed Karstares back to health after his plane crashed in the jungle **[M-SMG1.14(c3)]**, Karstares vowed to protect the rainforest as the Green Knight. The Ecommandoes, in turn, helped him defeat his evil son Jaysee's ecologically harmful company **[M-SMG2.5(c5)]**, but all seven died during the battle **[M-SMG2.8(c2)]**.

> ***NOTE:*** *The forest dwellers resembled Disney's Seven Dwarfs, both in name and in appearance. All of the Ionian Ecommandoes' names were sex-related slang terms.*

- **Ionian nerve grip:** A nonexistent technique that Kryten claimed could render an individual unconscious. This fabrication placated Rimmer so the mechanoid could smash him over the head with a vase during an attempt to eliminate Legion's hold over the *Red Dwarf* crew **[T-SER6.2]**.

- **Ionian Philharmonic Orchestra:** A musical ensemble originating from the Jovian moon of Io **[N-BCK]**.

- **ionic conversion ultra-temporal turbo-thrust:** A component of the 247 Giga-Nova Omni-Warp Mega Drive Hyper Boosters powering the propulsion system of Ace "Blackheart" Rimmer's spacecraft **[M-SMG1.14(c5)]**.

- **ion storm:** A spatial anomaly comprising ionized particles that affected passing ships' electrical systems. Holly became unstable after *Red Dwarf* passed through an ion storm **[T-SER4.4]**. During the *Starbug 1* crew's second encounter with Ace Rimmer, the shuttle almost passed through such a storm after its systems died in Sector 12 **[T-SER7.2]**.

- **Io Polytechnic:** A university in a domed settlement on Jupiter's moon, Io. When Rimmer attended Io Polytechnic, his stepfather was a lecturer at the school **[T-SER10.6]**.

- **Io Seminary:** A theological educational facility on Io in one of Ace Rimmer's universes. Father Felix, Cat's counterpart in that dimension, studied at Io Seminary before being stationed at the Space Corps testing facility on Mimas **[G-SOR]**.

- **"I Owe It All to Rimmer":** A headline Rimmer cut out of print material and adhered to his locker door aboard *Red Dwarf* **[T-SER1.3]**. While sharing quarters with his duplicate hologram, Arnold had this and other headlines—which were actually about other people with his name—relocated to his new abode **[T-SER1.6]**.

- **"Ippy dippy":** A children's rhythmic counting-down game. Lister used a variation of this game to choose which of the two Rimmer holograms to deactivate **[T-SER1.6]**.

> ***NOTE:*** *Lister was presumably referencing an actual children's rhyme called "Ip dip."*

- **IQ:** A black-market version of Eidetosol, a learning drug originally developed for clinical use. IQ and its equivalents, MIT White and Smarteez, were considered contraband **[G-SOR]**.

- **IR pistol:** *See* rad pistol

- **Iranian jird:** A species of rodent in several Middle Eastern countries, commonly called a Persian jird **[RL]**. According to Cat, the Iranian jird could do 150 pelvic thrusts a second during sex, which he likened to his own prowess in slow-motion **[T-SER4.3]**.

> ***NOTE:*** *The Series IV DVD captions misspelled the species' name as "jerd."*

- **Irkutsk:** A federal subject of Russia, located in Southeastern Siberia, and a location of the strategy board game *Risk* **[RL]**. While attending cadet training school, Rimmer once rolled a five and a two during a game of *Risk*, which got him into Irkutsk **[T-SER4.6]**.

- **Iron Duke:** Rimmer's codename when he commanded the Hero World waxdroid army on Waxworld **[T-SER4.6]**.

- **irradiated caviar niblets:** A delicacy consisting of fish eggs. Kryten served irradiated caviar niblets to *Nova 5*'s crew upon the completion of their mission, prior to the crash that killed all but three of them **[N-INF]**.

- **irradiated haggis:** An item in *Red Dwarf*'s food supply, listed on a supply checklist. As Lister and Rimmer crosschecked the vessel's inventory, the ship's stores contained 4,691 irradiated haggis **[T-SER1.3]**.

> ***NOTE:*** *When Lister told Rimmer to stop repeating himself, he misquoted the number as 4,981.*

- **Iscariot, Judas:** *See* Judas

- ***Ishtar*:** A 1987 American comedy film starring Dustin Hoffman and Warren Beatty that opened to negative reviews and became a notorious box-office failure **[RL]**. When Rimmer recommended using timeslides to alter the course of history, Lister suggested going back to convince Hoffman not to make the movie **[T-SER3.5]**.

- **Isle of Man:** A self-governed island located between Great Britain and Ireland **[RL]**. While imprisoned in the Tank, *Red Dwarf*'s brig, Lister compared the loss of his Canary privileges—which meant living in freezing conditions, with no entertainment and lousy food—to being on holiday on the Isle of Man **[T-SER8.5(d)]**.

- **Islington:** A neighborhood located in Greater London, England **[RL]**. While marooned aboard *Starbug 1* on an icy planet, Lister attempted to stay alive by burning items he found aboard ship, including Rimmer's priceless Armée du Nord statues. When Arnold objected, Lister said they might have been worth something at an Islington antique shop, but were now just pretty firewood **[T-SER3.2]**.

- ***Italian Driver*:** A 3D video game available in *Red Dwarf*'s rec rooms, the object of which was to park a car in Rome **[N-INF]**.

- **Item 34:** An objective Rimmer added to his daily goal list for the coming day (after "learn Portuguese"), upon discovering that Lister had ventured into the contaminated Officers' Block. Item 34 was to decontaminate that block—which Lister had thought the hologram had done a week prior, and hence had assumed the area safe to enter **[T-SER1.5]**.

- ***It's a Wonderful Life*:** A classic Christmas-themed American film directed by Frank Capra, starring James Stewart **[RL]**. The movie was one of Lister's favorites—and Kochanski's as well. During their brief relationship, they spent many nights in her quarters watching the film.

  While trapped in an addictive version of *Better Than Life*, Lister's subconscious mind created exact replicas of the people and buildings of Bedford Falls, the movie's fictitious setting. He remained in the illusion with Kristine and their twin sons, Jim and Bexley, for more than two years **[N-INF]**.

- **"It's better to live one hour as a tiger than a whole lifetime as a worm":** An old Cat People proverb that Cat recited while discussing the pros and cons of traversing an asteroid belt in *Starbug 1* in order to catch up with *Red Dwarf*. Rimmer created his own proverb in response: "Who ever heard of a wormskin rug?" **[T-SER6.1]**.

- **"It's Nearly Monday!":** A phrase on a sign in the apartment of murder victim Philby Frutch **[M-SMG1.14(c6)]**.

- **"It's Too Naughty!":** A message displayed over Lister's bunk **[T-SER1.1]**.

- **Ivan Azymuth's Laws of Robotics:** A set of rules built into androids created in a fascist society of an alternate universe:
  1) Keep your groinal socket dust-free.
  2) Never sell body parts to pawnbrokers.
  3) Always find a soft place to land **[M-SMG2.9(c4)]**.

  ***NOTE:** This spoofed the Three Laws of Robotics that author Isaac Asimov created for his 1942 short story "Runaround" and other works.*

- **"I've Been to the Omni-Zone and Seen Infinity":** A phrase printed on a sticker on the side of *Red Dwarf*'s black box, which the Space Corps recovered after it traveled into the Omni-zone and back through time **[W-OFF]**.

- **"I Want Your Love Thing":** *See* "Baby I Want Your Love Thing"

PREFIX
RL: Real life

T-: Television Episodes
SER: Television series
IDW: "Identity Within"
USA1: Unaired U.S. pilot
USA2: Unaired U.S. demo

R-: *The Bodysnatcher Collection*
SER: Remastered episodes
BOD: "Bodysnatcher"
DAD: "Dad"
FTH: "Lister's Father"
INF: "Infinity Patrol"
END: "The End" (original assembly)

N-: Novels
INF: *Infinity Welcomes Careful Drivers*
BTL: *Better Than Life*
LST: *Last Human*
BCK: *Backwards*
OMN: *Red Dwarf Omnibus*

M-: Magazines
SMG: *Smegazine*

W-: Websites
OFF: Official website
NAN: *Prelude to Nanarchy*
AND: *Androids*
DIV: Diva-Droid
DIB: Duane Dibbley
CRP: Crapola
GEN: Geneticon
LSR: Leisure World Intl.
JMC: Jupiter Mining Corporation
AIT: *A.I. Today*
HOL: HoloPoint

G-: Roleplaying Game
RPG: *Core Rulebook*
BIT: *A.I. Screen Extra Bits* booklet
SOR: *Series Sourcebook*
OTH: Other RPG material

B-: Books
PRG: *Red Dwarf Programme Guide*
SUR: *Red Dwarf Space Corps Survival Manual*
PRM: *Primordial Soup*
SOS: *Son of Soup*
SCE: *Scenes from the Dwarf*
LOG: *Red Dwarf Log No. 1996*
RD8: *Red Dwarf VIII*
EVR: *The Log: A Dwarfer's Guide to Everything*

X-: Misc.
PRO: Promotional materials, videos, etc.
PST: Posters at DJ XVII (2013)
CAL: 2008 calendar
RNG: Cell phone ringtones
MOB: Mobisode ("Red Christmas")
CIN: *Children in Need* sketch
GEK: *Geek Week* intros by Kryten
TNG: "Tongue-Tied" video

XMS: Bill Pearson's Christmas special pitch script
XVD: Bill Pearson's Christmas special pitch video
OTH: Other *Red Dwarf* appearances

SUFFIX
DVD:
(d) – Deleted scene
(o) – Outtake
(b) – Bonus DVD material (other)
(e) – Extended version

SMEGAZINES:
(c) – Comic
(a) – Article

OTHER:
(s) – Early/unused script draft
(s1) – Alternate version of script

JESUS OF CAESAREA

- **J:** A new note that Holly conceived while decimalizing the music scale. Holly added two new notes—H and J—thereby increasing the major scale by two syllables ("woh" and "boh," respectively), which fell between "sol" and "ti" in the octave (which he renamed a decatave) **[T-SER2.1]**.

  NOTE: *This gag originated in a* Son of Cliché *"Dave Hollins: Space Cadet" sketch titled "Sir Kevin Kevin Sir."*

- **J055:** The artificial intelligence system of Crapola Inc.'s original model Talkie Toaster **[W-CRP]**.

- **J056:** The upgraded artificial intelligence system of Crapola Inc.'s original model Talkie Toaster **[W-CRP]**.

- **Jackson, Jugs:** A zero-gee football player whose name appeared on a cover of *Zero G* magazine. The headline read "*Jugs Jackson Takes a Shower*" **[T-SER1.3]**.

- **Jacobs:** A business advertised on a double-decker bus that appeared in one of Cat's dreams, set on a planet suffering from a style famine **[M-SMG1.7(c2)]**.

- **Jacquard, Pierre:** The inventor of the loom, according to a member of Tunbridge Wells' five hundred pilgrims who were sent to pray for the end of a meteor storm ravaging their city. This individual, a weaver, believed his people were headed to a shrine dedicated to Jacquard, but others disagreed, causing a religious war that wiped out the entire pilgrim crew **[M-SMG1.14(c2)]**.

  NOTE: *In the real world, the programmable loom was invented by Joseph Marie Jacquard.*

- **Jake:** An associate of Lister's father. When Lister confronted his dad at a pub, the elder man thought Jake had sent him regarding cameras he owed the man **[R-FTH]**.

  NOTE: *This was mentioned in an early-draft script written before episode 7.3 ("Ouroboros") revealed that Lister was his own father.*

- **Jammie Dodger:** A British shortbread biscuit with a raspberry jam filling **[RL]**. While working in *Red Dwarf*'s Officers' Club, Lister found a Jammie Dodger stuffed inside a sofa, which he cleaned with an oily rag and sold to Rimmer for a week's wages, knowing how much Arnold enjoyed them. To pay for the biscuit, Rimmer sold his Admiral Nelson telescope **[T-SER9.2(d)]**. Rimmer once claimed the *Starbug 1* crew had as much chance of surviving a meteor impact as a Jammie Dodger had of surviving a dunk in hot coffee for three minutes **[T-SER6.1(d)]**.

- ***Jane Austen World*:** An artificial-reality (AR) simulation based on the works of author Jane Austen, including a program called *Pride and Prejudice Land* **[T-SER7.6]**. Leisure World International operated versions of the game at its arcades **[W-LSR]**.

  When the *Starbug 1* crew salvaged a copy of *Jane Austen World* from the derelict SS *Centauri*, Kochanski convinced Lister and Cat to join her in the simulation—much to Kryten's frustration, as he had prepared a lobster dinner to celebrate the anniversary of his rescue from *Nova 5*. The mechanoid modified the program and entered with a World War II tank, blowing up a virtual gazebo to kill Austen's characters, and thus forcing his shipmates to leave the AR Suite and join him for dinner **[T-SER7.6]**.

- ***Jane Austin World*:** An artificial-reality (AR) simulation based on the works of author Jane Austin, developed by Total Immersion Inc. and distributed by Crapola Inc. The game included simulations of such works as *Edda, A Field of Broken Dreams* and *Winchester Park* **[G-RPG]**.

  NOTE: *Jane Austen (note the different surname spelling) did not write books titled* Edda, Winchester Park *or* A Field of Broken Dreams, *though the first two satirized two of her works (*Emma *and* Mansfield Park, *respectively), while the third befitted the disappointments that her characters tended to experience. Some online sources have attributed these books to Jane G. Austin, a third writer who lived a century after Austen, as part of the so-called "Calamity Jane Austin" hoax, in which members of Usenet discussion group rec.arts.sf.written crafted a fabricated life story and bibliography for Austin, in order to mislead anyone incorrectly entering Austen's name in a search engine (see richardhartersworld.com/cri/2004/austin.html). All works listed in the faux* *bibliography satirized the real Austen's work, including the above-noted books, as well as* Fence and Fencibility *and* Pride and Precipice.

- **January 1:** The date of the first entry in Rimmer's diary, in which he discussed his desire to keep a running log of his achievements and advancements through command, so that future officers could refer to his experiences. The next entry was not until July 17, when he posted that it was his Aunt Maggie's birthday **[T-SER1.6]**.

- **Jaquinaux, Baron, Lieutenant General:** A member of the First Cavalry Division of Napoleon Bonaparte's Armée du Nord, a replica of whom Rimmer had in his statue collection. Warning Lister not to spill food on the figure while perusing his collection, Arnold noted that Jaquinaux would not have meat vindaloo on his tunic. Lister joked that it would make him look more authentic, as though he had dysentery **[T-SER3.2]**.

- **Jareth:** The chairman of the Zero-Gee Football European Conference, and part of an expert panel that discussed a game between the London Jets and the Paris Stompers. Lister watched a video of this game and discussion aboard *Red Dwarf* **[R-BOD(s)]**.

- **Javanese camphor-wood chest:** A wooden storage chest that Rimmer's stepfather gave him **[T-SER3.2]**, which had been in the Rimmer family for generations. It was meant to go to his half-brother, Howard, but was erroneously addressed to Arnold due to his stepfather's degrading mental health **[W-OFF]**. Unaware of the error, Rimmer cherished the rare chest, since it was the only thing the man had ever given him.

  While evacuating *Red Dwarf* years later, Rimmer had the chest and its contents loaded aboard *Starbug 1*—which soon crashed, marooning him and Lister on an icy planet. Arnold refused to let Lister burn the chest when they ran out of items to burn for warmth, insisting they use Dave's guitar instead. While Rimmer was outside, Lister cut a guitar-shaped section from the back of the chest and stuck it in the fire barrel, tricking Arnold into thinking he had not only sacrificed his beloved guitar, but that it, too, was rare due to its camphor-wood odor **[T-SER3.2]**.

- ***Jaws:*** A 1975 American thriller directed by Steven Spielberg, concerning a killer shark terrorizing residents of the fictitious Amity Island **[RL]**. The first four *Jaws* films were among Cat's favorite movies **[M-SMG1.1(a)]**. After Rimmer caught Lister and Kryten sneaking out of their quarters dressed in fishing gear, Lister claimed they were going to the cinema for a midnight showing of *Jaws*, so Arnold wouldn't know they were taking a fishing vacation without him **[T-SER4.5]**.

  NOTE: *Only four* Jaws *films have been produced to date. Since Cat enjoyed "the first four," additional entries were presumably released in the* Red Dwarf *universe.*

- **Jayne:** An android host on the All-Droid Mail Order Shopping Station. Jayne, along with co-host Bob, demonstrated a product called the Stirmaster—a gadget that stirred coffee or tea—during an infomercial transmission that the passing *Red Dwarf* picked up. Fascinated, Cat and Lister vowed to buy one **[T-SER10.1]**.

- **Jaysee:** A wealthy robotic character on the television soap opera *Androids*, who lived in a penthouse apartment atop the Juno Hilton **[N-INF]**. Jaysee started as a sly businessman but rose to become a business mogul with the help of a hypno-ring. Secretly, he owned a majority share in his father's petroleum company, Droid Oil **[W-AND]**, and was having an affair with his secretary, Brandy **[M-SMG2.6(c2)]**.

  Jaysee was the evil illegitimate son of Karstares and the half-brother of Brook. He also owned Jaysee's Cleaning Company. When Karstares allegedly died in a plane crash, Jaysee vowed to destroy the family's business as retribution for being left out of the will **[M-SMG1.9(c2)]**, and used a hidden camera recording of Brook entering one of Jaysee's brothels to blackmail him **[M-SMG1.12(c3)]**.

  Assuming control of his father's other business, Karstares Intergalactic Cleaning and Sanitation Supplies, Jaysee tried to blackmail Gary as well, who plotted with his ex-wife Kelly to murder the android mogul **[M-SMG1.13(c1)]**. The plan backfired when they accidentally blew up Jaysee's "good" spare head. Jaysee retaliated by having Bruce plant a bomb in Gary's hover-car **[M-SMG1.14(c3)]**. Gary barely survived the explosion, rebuilt his body from spare parts at the hospital and sought retribution **[M-SMG2.5(c5)]**.

Jaysee also blackmailed Mollee, an upstanding citizen who organized a protest against his brothel. After an accident scrambled her circuits, Mollee took over the bordello **[M-SMG2.3(c2)]**, but upon regaining her memories, she vowed to make Jaysee pay for his crimes **[M-SMG2.5(c5)]**.

Meanwhile, Karstares—who had survived the crash—vowed revenge on Jaysee as well. He met up with his son, Brook, and grandson, Brooke Junior, and stormed Jaysee's building along with the seven Ionian Ecommandoes **[M-SMG2.4(c3)]**. Jaysee's enemies attacked his headquarters simultaneously **[M-SMG2.6(c3)]**, but he survived the attack, only to find Brandy dead **[M-SMG2.7(c5)]**. In a later episode, Brook pushed Jaysee off the roof of a building **[W-AND]**.

Jaysee also appeared on the short-lived television program *Androids Nights* as Capston's nemesis **[W-CRP]**. Kryten often fantasized about being Jaysee, dining in fine restaurants and making "mega-quidbuck" deals **[N-INF]**.

- **JayseeFan:** The username of a forum poster on the *Androids* website's message boards. JayseeFan considered the character of Nurse Sara more attractive than another character named Nelly **[W-AND]**.

- **Jaysee's Cleaning Company:** A business that Jaysee owned on the television soap opera *Androids* **[M-SMG1.9(c2)]**.

- **Jaz:** A character on the television soap opera *Androids*. In one episode, Jaz attended a barbeque hosted by Daz, during which a family pet, Bouncer, was lost in a temporal-displacement vortex **[M-SMG1.8(c2)]**.

- **Jeanette:** A model of android available in a pick'n'mix lineup at a brothel on Mimas. Customers could choose various body parts from selected androids, and then have a custom-designed sex droid assembled for their use. A portly, red-haired customer chose this particular model's face for his sex droid **[N-INF]**.

- **Jeff:** A crewmember aboard a vessel that crashed into an asteroid in Psiren territory, who died when the telepathic Psirens attacked. A shipmate later recorded a log entry reporting several deaths, including Jeff's **[T-SER6.1(d)]**.

- **Jeff:** A simulant character on the television show *Simulants*, a soap opera from the creators of *Androids*. In one episode, Jeff ripped the head off another character named Martin **[M-SMG1.7(a)]**.

- **Jeff Kay:** *See* Kay, Jeff

- **Jehovah's Witnesses:** A restorationist, nontrinitarian sect of Christianity whose members often preached door-to-door, distributing literature warning of an impending Armageddon **[RL]**. Though stranded three million years' travel from Earth, Holly took solace in the fact that he and the *Red Dwarf* crew were more than sixty billion miles away from the nearest Jehovah's Witness **[R-SER2.2]**.

  NOTE: *This was mentioned in an unused, updated Holly introduction created for the remastered episodes. The original dialog stated they were sixty billion miles away from the nearest Berni Inn.*

- **Jello-Head:** A nickname Cat called Kryten, referencing his angular features **[N-LST]**.

- **Jellybean:** A twentieth-century American musician, songwriter, disc jockey and remixer, born John Benitez **[RL]**. While trapped in an addictive version of *Better Than Life*, Cat entertained himself in his golden castle with a hand-picked seven-piece band, which included Jellybean on computer programs **[N-INF]**.

- **jelly-finch:** A genetically engineered creature—a mix between a jellyfish and a finch—developed by inebriated scientists **[B-EVR]**.

- **Jemma:** A character in Netta Muskett's novel *Doctor, Darling*. Holly became obsessed with Muskett's books two million years after *Red Dwarf*'s cadmium II disaster, and was reading *Doctor, Darling* when the ship passed a quintuplet of stars in concentric orbits. The AI ignored the stellar phenomenon, however, having reached a section of the novel in which the titular doctor told Jemma she had three years to live **[N-INF]**.

- **Jenny:** A name that Cat mistakenly thought he heard a polymorph say when, disguised as a beautiful woman, it introduced itself as a genetic mutant **[T-SER3.3]**.

- **Jensen Interceptor:** A British sports car built by Jensen Motors from 1966 to 1976 **[RL]**. Rimmer read an article in *Classic Car Monthly* about the Jensen Interceptor while monitoring sonar for a mysterious creature inhabiting *Red Dwarf*'s water tank on G Deck. The article distracted him from seeing the elation squid approach a diving bell containing his shipmates **[T-SER9.1]**.

- **Jerry:** A crewmember aboard a vessel that crashed into an asteroid in Psiren territory, who died when the telepathic Psirens attacked. A shipmate later recorded a log entry reporting several deaths, including Jerry's **[T-SER6.1(d)]**.

- **Jesus:** A man with a disfigured nose, circa 23 A.D. His father was named John **[T-SER10.3]**.

- **Jesus:** A man who wrapped plant leaves around horses' feet for a living, circa 23 A.D. His father was named Luke **[T-SER10.3]**.

- **Jesus of Caesarea:** A kind-hearted and peaceful world traveler, circa the first century A.D. The son of Rachel the Fornicator and Samuel the Chicken-stealer, he travelled with his uncle, Aaron, and a woman named Erin. While visiting India in 23 A.D., Jesus encountered the *Red Dwarf* crew, who had traveled back through space-time and were searching for a way to return home.

  Mistaking the young man for The Bible's Jesus of Nazareth, they rescued him from pursuing soldiers and brought him back to *Red Dwarf*, using lemons to power their time-travel device. When Jesus suffered a kidney stone, Kryten surgically removed it—but more astounding to Jesus was the concept of a carry-bag, which he'd never before seen.

  During his recovery, Jesus discovered a book depicting the conflict-riddled history of the Catholic Church. Disturbed by what he read, he returned to the past to tarnish his own reputation and thereby prevent the religion from being created. Attempting to reason with him, the crew discovered that he was from Caesarea, Israel, not Nazareth, and was thus not the Biblical Jesus. After the travelers returned to their own century, Jesus began selling carry-bags **[T-SER10.3]**.

- **Jesus of Nazareth:** The central figure of several Terran faiths, including Christianity, which considered him the Son of God **[RL]**. Rimmer once criticized *King of Kings*, a film about the life of Jesus, as being unrealistic **[T-SER5.1]**.

  According to the Church of Judas, Jesus had a twin brother named James Judas Didyus. The Church believed that Jesus asked Judas to switch places with him on the crucifix and sacrifice himself so that Jesus could appear to rise from the dead, thus allowing Christianity to spread. Afterwards, some believed that Jesus moved to France with Mary Magdalene, raised a family and invented the wheelbarrow.

  When a malfunctioning rejuvenation shower transported the *Red Dwarf* crew back to 23 A.D., they met a man in India whom they presumed to be Jesus of Nazareth, but was actually another Jesus, from Caesarea, Israel. Later on, they noticed twins named Jesus and Judas, who may have been the very brothers described in the Church of Judas' scriptures **[T-SER10.3]**.

- **Jet Black:** A body-plating color that Diva-Droid International offered for Hudzen 10 mechanoids **[G-SOR]**.

- **jet-cycle:** An experimental motorbike developed by the Resistance on War World, featuring twin rocket boosters, auto-switching control flaps and smoke canisters for use in skywriting **[G-BIT]**. Ace Rimmer drove a jet-cycle while rescuing Princess Bonjella from Reich forces **[T-SER7.2]**.

- **jet housings:** A set of massive, cone-shaped engines on *Red Dwarf*'s underside. The jet housings were directional and could be aimed aft to assist in acceleration, or rotated 180 degrees to brake or reverse **[N-BTL]**.

- **jet pack:** A device worn on an astro's back that allowed him or her to maneuver in the vacuum of space. It contained two controls: one button for forward thrust and another for reverse thrust. *Starbug* was stocked with several jet packs **[N-BCK]**.

- **jet-powered rocket pants:** A type of futuristic apparel equipped with rockets, enabling a wearer to fly. When Cat suggested donning jet-powered rocket pants to escape a psi-moon, Kryten praised the suggestion, but noted that they had no such trousers—primarily because they existed only in the fictional serial *Robbie Rocket Pants* **[T-SER5.3]**.

- **Jets:** A word scrawled on a foot cast that Lister wore after injuring himself while burying *Red Dwarf*'s black box on a deserted moon **[T-SER2.3]**.

  NOTE: *This word presumably referred to the London Jets, Lister's favorite zero-gee football team.*

- **Jhjghjiuyhu system:** A legal system practiced in the Northern sector of Arranguu 12, a GELF settlement in an alternate universe. During Lister's trial for crimes against the GELF nation, the Regulator told Lister that his attempt to cause a mistrial by quoting the case of *Mbazvmbbcxyy vs. Mbazvmbbcxyy* was moot, since the Jhjghjiuyhu system of law applied, not the archaic legal system of the South, from which the case originated. According to the Regulator, the Jhjghjiuyhu system was straightforward enough for any Hniuplcxdewn or Tvcnkolphgkooq to understand **[N-LST]**.

- **Jiffy Windo-Kleen:** A brand of glass cleaner. To entertain *Nova 5*'s three crash survivors, Kryten ran prize bingo matches every Friday night, for a chance to win a can of Jiffy Windo-Kleen. Since none of the women wanted the product, they always gave it back to him for use as next week's prize **[N-INF]**.

- **"Jill and the Beanstalk":** A fairy tale in an alternate universe in which the sexes were reversed. Daizee, *Red Dwarf*'s 4000 Series mechanoid in that reality, read this story to Jim and Bexley Lister before putting them to bed **[M-SMG1.5(c2)]**.

  NOTE: *This was the reversed-sex version of the popular children's story "Jack and the Beanstalk."*

- **Jim:** A character in the romantic film *Marry Me My Darling*. Lister tried watching this movie on several occasions, but was constantly interrupted during a pivotal scene in which Carol and Jim discussed their love and Carol's terminal illness. When he tried watching it once more in his quarters aboard *Red Dwarf*, Rimmer shut the film off right before the conclusion **[T-SER1.5]**.

  NOTE: *The movie's title, not mentioned onscreen, was listed in the episode's script, according to commentary featured on* The Bodysnatcher Collection *DVD set.*

- **Jim Daniels:** A brand of whiskey bourbon produced in the twenty-second century. After being sentenced to the virtual-reality prison Cyberia, Lister was surprised to find his Cyberhell set in a Spanish villa stocked with Jim Daniels. His jailers soon realized they had sent him to someone else's illusion, then re-assigned him to one that was liquor-free **[N-LST]**.

  NOTE: *This name was an amalgam of whiskey brands Jim Beam and Jack Daniels.*

- **Jimmy:** A hypothetical person whom Rimmer mentioned while justifying his own cowardice, noting that wartime generals typically did not stick broken Newcastle Brown bottles in people's faces and exclaim, "Stitch that, Jimmy!" **[T-SER3.2]**.

- **Jitterman, Jimmy:** A character in a novel Rimmer once read, titled *Young, Bad, and Dangerous to Know*. A headcase, Jimmy had a psychopathic hippie brother named Tonto. Rimmer's subconscious mind incorporated the brothers into an illusion created by an addictive version of *Better Than Life*. Arnold imagined that his Solidgram body had been repossessed and his essence placed, as a soundwave, into a soundproof prison cell. There, he resided with three other soundwaves, including Jimmy, who was incarcerated after hijacking the bodies of rich people to take on joyrides.

  Tonto helped Rimmer and the other soundwaves escape incarceration by capturing their signals with a radio receiver as they used the prison's intercom, then drove them to the Body Reclamation Unit to retrieve their Solidgram bodies. Unable to locate his own body, Jimmy instead appropriated Rimmer's, forcing Arnold to take the nearest he could find—that of sex worker Trixie LaBouche. Several days later, Jimmy died during a firefight with SWAT forces, leaving Rimmer's body riddled with bullets **[N-BTL]**.

- **Jitterman, Tonto:** A character in a novel Rimmer once read, titled *Young, Bad, and Dangerous to Know*. A psychopathic hippie murderer, Tonto traveled across Middle America, causing chaos and destruction in an effort to bring down the Establishment. He had a crazy brother named Jimmy, and a revolver that he hand-painted with flowers.

  Rimmer's subconscious mind incorporated the brothers into an illusion created by an addictive version of *Better Than Life*. Tonto helped Jimmy and Rimmer escape from prison as soundwaves, then drove the escapees to the Body Reclamation Unit to retrieve their physical bodies, killing several guards in the process.

The fugitives holed up at the Hotel Paradiso until running out of money. When Tonto and Arnold (whose mind was stuck in the body of sex worker Trixie LaBouche) set out to find some cash, Tonto was shot and killed by a police officer, his last words being the novel's final line: "Life is like a joss-stick—it stinks and then it's over" **[N-BTL]**.

- **JMC:** An acronym short for Jupiter Mining Corporation. The letters were stenciled above the outer hatch of *Blue Midget*'s hanger bay aboard *Red Dwarf* **[T-SER3.2]**.

  NOTE: *The letters appeared backwards on the Series III DVDs, due to the footage of* Blue Midget's *launch having been flipped.*

- **JMC159:** The flight number of a shuttle that left Mimas to rendezvous with *White Giant*. It boarded at Gate 5 **[N-INF]**.

- **"JMC Ammo":** A marking on ammunition cartridges stored under a sign aboard *Starbug 1* that read "Emergency Ammo." There were two such cartridges: red for live and blue for blanks **[T-SER7]**.

  NOTE: *This was visible on the opening screen of the Series VII DVD menu.*

- **JMC buggy:** An all-terrain vehicle used by the Jupiter Mining Corporation for planetary surface exploration. *Starbug 1* was outfitted with at least one such buggy. Each vehicle contained an atomic power cell and was fitted with dual-linked bazookoids mounted on its hood, as well as UltraPlas windscreen wipers **[G-BIT]**. The *Starbug* crew used a JMC buggy to explore the planet that Kryten's nanobots created from the raw material of *Red Dwarf* **[T-SER7.8]**.

- **JMC building:** A facility owned by the Jupiter Mining Corporation, located in London, England, in the twenty-second century. Behind this building was an Indian takeout joint called the Taj Mahal Tandoori Restaurant **[T-SER7.1]**.

- **JMC C-245:** The model number of a crane aboard *Red Dwarf* that Cat used to lower a cow into a massive bowl of vindaloo, to make Pete the *Tyrannosaurus rex* experience diarrhea so the crew could retrieve a time wand Pete had swallowed **[T-SER8.7]**.

- **JMC coconut massage oil:** A product issued on JMC vessels such as *Red Dwarf*. The product also came in raspberry and sesame-mint. Side effects cited on its warning label included hair loss, muscle fatigue and rare types of melanoma **[G-SOR]**. Captain Hollister suffered traumatic shock when a baby *Tyrannosaurus rex* licked the oil off his back during a massage session **[T-SER8.7]**.

- **JMC cooking oil:** A type of oil that Jupiter Mining Corporation supplied to Space Corps vessels, typically stored in blue fifty-five-gallon drums. Cat and Kochanski hid behind drums of the cooking oil while contemplating how to stop Pete the *Tyrannosaurus rex* from running amok in *Red Dwarf*'s cargo bay **[T-SER8.7]**.

- **JMC Educational Exam Board:** A committee in charge of educational programs and entrance testing for existing and potential employees of Jupiter Mining Corporation. Among the courses the board offered were Mechanical Engineering and Robotics **[T-SER10.2(d)]**.

- **JMC Elevator Division:** A phrase printed on a label affixed to several panels of *Red Dwarf*'s elevators within Zone 101. Each panel contained easy access to buttons for every floor within the zone, except for Floor 13. The button for that floor was hidden behind a plate, accessible only by keys held by authorized personnel, as Floor 13 housed the Tank, *Red Dwarf*'s classified brig **[T-SER8.3]**.

- **JMC Filter:** A brand of cigarettes sold in bulk aboard JMC vessels such as *Red Dwarf*, available in boxes of two hundred **[X-OTH]**.

  NOTE: *This name appeared on a prop used during Series VIII.*

- **JMC Food Storage:** A phrase printed on the labels of several boxes stored in *Red Dwarf*'s cargo bay **[T-SER8.7]**.

- **JMC Health and Safety Protocol #46:** An incident declaration form that Rimmer posted at one of *Red Dwarf*'s airlocks, in response to Lister not filling out the appropriate documents when flushing Arnold's accident report forms into space **[T-SER10.4]**.

- **JMC ident chip:** An identification device implanted in crewmembers of Jupiter Mining Corporation vessels. When scanned, the chip transmitted the individual's name, rank and past tours of duty. Kryten scanned Caroline Carmen's ident chip after finding her body encased in a block of ice aboard the *Leviathan* **[T-SER7.7]**.

- **JMC onboard computer:** A computer system aboard *Red Dwarf* that acted on behalf of the Jupiter Mining Corporation in the event that the ship lost contact with the company and/or the ship's primary AI computer was compromised. Among its duties were grading Astronavigation Exams, awarding decorations to Space Corps officers, renaming ships in memory of fallen officers, and other tasks **[T-SER10.1]**.

  Over the course of several years, Rimmer petitioned *Red Dwarf*'s JMC onboard computer to award him the Golden Stripe of Honour. The plan backfired, however, when the computer, upon looking into his record, discovered he had not reported for duty in the entirety of his hologrammatic existence. As such, the computer threatened him with demotion unless he produced an explanation for the oversight **[T-SER10.5]**.

  NOTE: *In episode 10.1 ("Trojan"), the subtitles mistakenly read "GMC," matching Robert Llewellyn's apparent mispronunciation.*

- **JMCP0001:** The password protecting Deck Sergeant Sam Murray's personnel file at Jupiter Mining Corp.'s website **[W-HOL]**.

  NOTE: *Visitors to the HoloPoint website received this password when clicking on Ned Omrisk's signature. Using this code in the personnel section of JMC's site provided access to* Red Dwarf*'s personnel files.*

- **JMC peach slices:** A brand of canned sliced peaches that Jupiter Mining Corporation supplied to Space Corps vessels **[T-SER7.4]**.

- **JMC personnel shuttle:** *See* White Midget

- **JMC. RD. 431:** The prison ID number that *Red Dwarf*'s Board of Inquiry assigned to Cat after sentencing him to the ship's classified brig on Floor 13 **[T-SER8.3]**.

- **JMC. RD. 432:** The prison ID number that *Red Dwarf*'s Board of Inquiry assigned to Rimmer after sentencing him to the ship's classified brig on Floor 13 **[T-SER8.3]**.

- **JMC. RD. 433:** The prison ID number that *Red Dwarf*'s Board of Inquiry assigned to Kryten after sentencing him to the ship's classified brig on Floor 13 **[T-SER8.3]**.

- **JMC. RD. 434:** The prison ID number that *Red Dwarf*'s Board of Inquiry assigned to Lister after sentencing him to the ship's classified brig on Floor 13 **[T-SER8.3]**.

- **JMC. RD. 435:** The prison ID number that *Red Dwarf*'s Board of Inquiry assigned to Kochanski after sentencing her to the ship's classified brig on Floor 13 **[T-SER8.3]**.

- **JMC. RD. 436:** The prison ID number that *Red Dwarf*'s Board of Inquiry assigned to Holly after sentencing the AI to the ship's classified brig on Floor 13 **[T-SER8.3]**.

- **JMC scan probe:** A remote drone that could be deployed to seek out a pre-programmed object. After finding the target, the probe devoted its available energy to transmitting all relevant information back to its home ship. Equipped with Ouroboros fuel cells, the probe had a near limitless range **[G-SOR]**.

- **JMC "Scouter" Remote Drone:** A small remote robotic feedback device that could be launched from the underbelly of *Starbug* vessels to survey specific areas and return essential data **[T-SER5.4]**.

  Painted black, a Scouter possessed three stubby "legs" extending from its lower half, each ending with an anti-grav pod enabling it to traverse various terrains. It had a range of 6.2 miles (10 kilometers) and a twenty-four-hour runtime between charges, and was equipped with a short-range laser cutter **[G-SOR]**. A Scouter could lock onto specific targets for analysis, detect atmospheric pressure and temperature, and enhance lowlights in low-visibility areas. The probe utilized a charge-coupled device (CCD) sensor for optical surveillance **[T-SER5.4]**.

  The *Red Dwarf* crew utilized Scouters for several purposes, including analyzing a scientific research station containing Hildegarde Lanstrom **[T-SER5.4]**, examining a Psiren-overrun derelict craft stranded in an asteroid belt **[T-SER6.1]**, locating the derelict Space Corps vessel *Trojan* **[T-SER10.1]** and finding a way out of an alien world's magma ocean into which a *Starbug* had crashed **[N-LST]**.

> ***NOTE:*** *The scouter's full name appeared in* Red Dwarf—The Roleplaying Game*'s* Series Sourcebook.

- **JMC self-raising flour:** A brand of bakery goods that Jupiter Mining Corporation supplied to Space Corps ships, typically stored in 500-gram bags. Unable to procure flowers in *Red Dwarf*'s brig, Lister sent Kochanski two bags of self-raising flour to apologize for letting Kryten record her in the shower **[T-SER8.5]**.

> ***NOTE:*** *Although the actual baking term is "self-rising flour," the bags were labeled "self-raising" onscreen.*

- **JMC Tools:** A company that produced bazookoids and other equipment for Jupiter Mining Corporation. A bazookoid MK 2 stored aboard *Starbug 1* was labeled as having been manufactured by JMC Tools **[T-SER7.2]**.

- ***JMC Traveller*:** A magazine distributed aboard *Red Dwarf* and other Jupiter Mining Corporation vessels. A free stick of gum was included with every issue. Depressed about the demise of mankind, Lister thumbed through issue 8327, which contained a story about young JMC employee Reece King, an article listing seventy-eight essentials needed for a trip to the 7th Death Ring of Rhaagbthammar, and an advertisement for *Red Dwarf* on its back cover. Perusing the magazine plunged Lister deeper into depression, as every article reminded him of his near-extinct species **[T-SER10.4]**.

- **Joan of Arc:** A fifteenth-century French heroine, born Jeanne d'Arc, who led her country's army to victory over the British at age eighteen, but was captured and burned at the stake as a heretic. Five centuries later, the Catholic Church canonized Joan as a saint **[RL]**. The Transtemporal Film Unit produced a fitness video featuring Joan of Arc, titled *Go for the Burn!* **[B-LOG]**.

> ***NOTE:*** *In* Bill & Ted's Excellent Adventure, *Joan of Arc (played by Go-Go's guitarist Jane Wiedlin) took a transtemporal journey to the 1980s, where she became fascinated by an aerobics fitness class.*

- **Joan of Arc:** A waxdroid replica of the French soldier, created for the Waxworld theme park. Left on their own for millions of years, the waxdroids attained sentience and became embroiled in a park-wide resource war between Villain World and Hero World (to which Joan belonged). The Joan waxdroid died during the conflict **[T-SER4.6]**.

- **Joe:** A *Red Dwarf* crewmember who attended the welcome-back ceremony of George McIntyre following the latter's post-death resurrection. During his speech, George joked that as a hologram, he was no longer a threat to Joe's marriage **[T-SER1.1]**.

> ***NOTE:*** *Joe presumably died during the cadmium II explosion. It is unknown whether the nanobots resurrected him in Series VIII.*

- **Joe's:** An eating establishment on the television soap opera *Androids*. A sign near the Detritus Wrecks junkyard asked passersby to "Eat at Joe's" **[M-SMG2.1(c2)]**.

- **John:** A man whose son Jesus had a disfigured nose, circa 23 A.D. **[T-SER10.3]**.

- **John, Paul, George and Ringway:** A hypothetical airport that Lister mentioned while joking about John F. Kennedy having been named after JFK International Airport **[T-SER7.1(e)]**.

> ***NOTE:*** *This, of course, referenced the members of the rock group The Beatles.*

- **Johns, Tracey, Mapping Officer:** A red-headed crewmember aboard *Nova 5* who survived that vessel's crash, along with two other officers and a mechanoid named Kryten. Despite recovering from the impact, she died sometime later—unbeknownst to Kryten, who continued serving the women long after their deaths. At the time of her last registered medical record, Johns was twenty-two years old, stood five feet two inches (158 centimeters) tall and weighed forty-two G.V. Her medical details were stored on Prog Disc A49 **[T-SER2.1]**.

> ***NOTE:*** *Kryten referred to Johns as "Miss Tracey" in a distress signal to* Red Dwarf. *The DVD captions initially misspelled her name as "Tracy," but this was corrected later in the episode.*

JUSTICE WORLD

- **Johnson, Harry:** A short, red-haired man whom Kryten knew on Earth, in a universe in which the *Red Dwarf* was an American vessel **[T-USA1(s)]**. Upon meeting Lister and learning that he was from Earth, Kryten asked if he knew Harry Johnson **[T-USA1]**.

  NOTE: *This bit was adapted from a* Dave Hollins: Space Cadet *sketch written by Rob Grant and Doug Naylor.*

- **Johnson, Mrs.:** A hypothetical person whom Rimmer mentioned when Lister speculated that mankind could have reversed death during their three-million-year absence from Earth. Imagining what a doctor's office for the dead would be like, he pretended to give a pill to the deceased Mrs. Johnson to bring her back to life **[T-SER1.2]**.

  NOTE: *The DVD subtitles spelled her name as "Johnstone," though Rimmer clearly said "Johnson" onscreen. The novel* Infinity Welcomes Careful Drivers *changed her surname to Harrington.*

- **Johnson's Baby Bud:** A brand of cotton swabs sold in the United Kingdom **[RL]**. Upon discovering that his recollection of dating Lise Yates was really Lister's memory, Rimmer was horrified to realize he was recalling Yates sticking her tongue in *Lister's* ear, and not his. The most romantic thing he'd ever had in his own ear, Arnold lamented, was a Johnson's Baby Bud **[T-SER2.3]**.

- **Johnstone, Mrs.:** *See* Johnson, Mrs.

- **John Wayne Fan Club:** An organization for fans of the twentieth-century American Western actor. Among the items in a post pod recovered by *Red Dwarf* was a letter from the John Wayne Fan Club, addressed to the ship's resident skutters **[T-SER2.2]**.

- **Jolene:** An android sex worker at Brothel-U-Like, featured on the television soap opera *Androids* **[M-SMG2.3(c2)]**.

- **Jonathan:** A name that Rimmer claimed was his middle name, though it was actually Judas **[T-SER5.2]**.

- **Jones, Monica:** A navigator aboard an alternate-reality *Red Dwarf*. She was twenty-seven years old, stood five feet six inches (1.67 meters) tall, weighed 138 pounds (62.5 kilograms) and had brown hair, hazel eyes and double-pierced ears. Jones was born at the Bradbury Colony on Mars, and had a banana-shaped birthmark on her left inner thigh. Her serial number was 3263827-K.

  Monica was obsessed with 1980s new-wave music, having fronted the band Monica & the Monopeds while on Earth. At the time, she dated a man named Kenneth, whom she left to join the Space Corps. She died during a radiation leak that killed *Red Dwarf*'s crew, but was later revived as a soft-light hologram. A smoker, she longed for a hard-light drive so she could restart her habit. Her pet peeves included littering and people who talked to themselves **[G-RPG]**.

- **Jong-il, Kim, Supreme Leader:** The ruler of the Democratic People's Republic of Korea (North Korea) from 1994 to 2011 **[RL]**. Kim Jong-il wrote a strategy book titled *How to Defeat an Army of Mutant Russians Whilst Still Finding Time to Be the World's Greatest Golfer*. Rimmer intended to read this volume as part of a battleplan timetable to formulate a plan to escape a group of rogue simulants **[T-SER10.6]**.

  NOTE: *In the real world, Jong-il wrote no such book. However, his propaganda team insisted that in 1994, when North Korea's first golf course opened in Pyongyang, he shot a 38 under par, including eleven holes-in-one, during his first time golfing—which, they claimed, made him the best golfer in history.*

- **Josie:** A space beatnik on Mimas who had a boyfriend named Denis. The couple met at the New Zodiac festival, a celebration of the zodiac constellations' realignment, during which her astrological sign changed from Libra to Scorpio. Josie, a Game head with a first-class degree in pure mathematics, and Denis, who had a second-class degree in biochemistry, had hoped to travel to Neptune for Pluto's solstice, but within five years had made it only as far as Mimas. During that time, she became addicted to *Better Than Life*, a virtual-reality game she received from a South African dealer on Callisto **[N-INF]**.

- ***Jousting***: *See Camelot*

- **Jovian Authority:** An organization established by the United Nations to deal with matters pertaining to the Jovian system (Jupiter and its moons). The Authority sealed off the area surrounding Callisto's Valhalla Impact Structure for reasons unknown, installing a strong Space Corps presence to guard that location **[G-RPG]**.

- **Jovian boogle hoops:** A type of dining utensils used within the Jovian system. Kryten was well-versed in the use of Jovian boogle hoops, a skill necessary to fulfill his cooking duties **[T-SER6.2]**.

- **joy:** A rogue emotion purged from Kryten's hard drive by the Data Doctor, a program for restoring a mechanoid's personality to factory settings, when Captain Hollister subjected Kryten to a psychotropic simulation **[T-SER8.2]**.

- **jozxyqk:** A word that Cat once tried to play during a *Scrabble* game with Lister, claiming it was his species' word for the sound one makes after getting one's sexual organs trapped **[T-SER3.4]**.

  NOTE: *Without double or triple letter or word bonuses, Cat would have racked up forty-six points for the word's individual letters, plus any points for adjoining letters—assuming Lister allowed it. If he used all seven of his tiles in doing so—a "Bingo" in* Scrabble *vernacular—he would have also scored a fifty-point bonus.*

- **Jubilee Line:** A marker on a zero-gee football field, used during such scoring strategies as the Castle Fritz, which was only allowed if the ball had not yet crossed the Jubilee Line. When this strategy was played, the ball—compressed into a half-Kimono—was guided over the Jubilee Line via magnetic induction **[M-SMG1.8(a)]**.

- **Judas:** One of the Twelve Apostles of Jesus Christ, according to Christian doctrine. He was said to have betrayed Jesus to Sanhedrin priests **[RL]**.

  The Church of Judas believed that his full name was James Judas Didymus, that he was Jesus' twin brother, and that Jesus had asked him to switch places with him on the crucifix so Jesus could appear to rise from the dead, thereby allowing Christianity to take hold. Mrs. Rimmer, a member of the church at the time of Arnold's birth, gave him the middle name Judas in the apostle's honor.

  When a malfunctioning rejuvenation shower transported the *Red Dwarf* crew to 23 A.D., they noticed twins named Jesus and Judas, whom they suspected were those very brothers **[T-SER10.3]**.

  NOTE: *According to the New Testament, Judas' last name was Iscariot.*

- **Judge Dread:** A twentieth-century British reggae musician whose music was often banned for its use of sexual innuendo and double entendres **[RL]**. Film studio janitor Leo Davis once dreamed about meeting Dread, who advised him to talk dirty to women. Dread was joined in the dream by comic book character Judge Dredd, and the two bickered about Davis' approach to dating—and about who stole the other's name **[X-TNG]**.

- **juggernaut:** An immense, twelve-wheeled tanker truck with eight headlamps, which Rimmer imagined driving while trapped in an addictive version of *Better Than Life*. Using the body of sex worker Trixie LaBouche, Rimmer drove the juggernaut to Bedford Falls to retrieve Lister so they could leave the game together. Unable to control the vehicle due to his small frame and high-heeled shoes, however, Arnold crashed the truck through the town square, demolishing it **[N-INF]**.

- **jukebot:** An animatronic robot programmed to play a musical instrument, such as a keytar. Parrot's Bar, located aboard *Red Dwarf,* had such a robot **[M-SMG1.8(c1)]**.

- **July 17:** The date of the second log entry in Rimmer's diary, denoting his Aunt Maggie's birthday. This followed the first entry, made on January 1, in which he vowed to keep a running log of his achievements and advancements through command **[T-SER1.6]**.

- **July 1965:** The month in which U.S. President John F. Kennedy, having survived an assassination attempt in an alternate timeline, was sentenced to three years in prison following a scandal involving the mistress of Mafia boss Sam Giancana **[T-SER7.1]**.

- **Juma:** A female warrior of the Elite, a Cat tribe that evolved aboard *Red Dwarf* while Lister was in stasis. During the Cat People's two-thousand-year Holy Wars, the Elite sent three warriors—Fritz, Krazy and Juma—forward in time via an obelisk, to retrieve their god (Lister) in the hope that he could end the conflict **[M-SMG2.1(c1)]**.

  After the trio retrieved Dave and brought him back to the Elite's High Tower, Fritz took him to his quarters. Juma secretly followed, suspecting her compatriot of being a Fundamental Remonian who believed the war should play out naturally, and subdued the traitor before he could kill Lister **[M-SMG2.2(c1)]**.

  NOTE: *Juma was named after* Juma and the Magic Jinn, *a children's picture book by Joy Anderson and Charles Mikolaycak, about a boy and a genie with catlike eyes.*

- **Jump:** One of seven diminutive rainforest dwellers known as the Ionian Ecommandoes, who lived in the jungles of Io

PREFIX	**R-: *The Bodysnatcher Collection***	**BCK:** *Backwards*	**CRP:** Crapola
RL: Real life	**SER:** Remastered episodes	**OMN:** *Red Dwarf Omnibus*	**GEN:** Geneticon
	BOD: "Bodysnatcher"		**LSR:** Leisure World Intl.
T-: Television Episodes	**DAD:** "Dad"	**M-: Magazines**	**JMC:** Jupiter Mining Corporation
SER: Television series	**FTH:** "Lister's Father"	**SMG:** *Smegazine*	**AIT:** *A.I. Today*
IDW: "Identity Within"	**INF:** "Infinity Patrol"		**HOL:** HoloPoint
USA1: Unaired U.S. pilot	**END:** "The End" (original assembly)	**W-: Websites**	
USA2: Unaired U.S. demo		**OFF:** Official website	**G-: Roleplaying Game**
	N-: Novels	**NAN:** *Prelude to Nanarchy*	**RPG:** *Core Rulebook*
	INF: *Infinity Welcomes Careful Drivers*	**AND:** *Androids*	**BIT:** *A.I. Screen Extra Bits* booklet
	BTL: *Better Than Life*	**DIV:** Diva-Droid	**SOR:** *Series Sourcebook*
	LST: *Last Human*	**DIB:** Duane Dibbley	**OTH:** Other RPG material

on the television soap opera *Androids*. He and his comrades nursed Karstares back to health **[M-SMG2.5(c5)]**, after Karstares' plane crashed due to sabotage by his son Jaysee **[M-SMG1.14(c3)]**. Grateful for their help, Karstares became the Green Knight, the rainforest's protector, and fought alongside the Ecommandoes against Jaysee's ecologically harmful company **[M-SMG2.5(c5)]**. Jump died during a firefight between Jaysee and his foes **[M-SMG2.8(c2)]**.

> ***NOTE:*** *This character resembled one of Disney's Seven Dwarfs. All of the Ecommandoes' names were slang for sex.*

- **Jung, Carl:** An early twentieth-century Swiss psychiatrist and psychotherapist, considered the founder of analytical psychology **[RL]**. Holly read the complete works of several prominent writers, including Jung, within the fifteen nanoseconds that passed between *Red Dwarf*'s cadmium II core going critical and the entire crew dying **[N-INF]**.

- **Junior:** A nickname that Karstares called his son, Brook, on the television soap opera *Androids* **[M-SMG2.1(c2)]**.

- **Junior A:** A grade-school academic level on Io, usually attended by children around nine years of age. Dicky Duckworth ended up in Rimmer's class after failing Junior B while his classmates advanced to Junior A **[N-BCK]**.

- **Junior Angler:** A children's game that simulated fly-fishing by using little sticks connected to a line, along with little plastic fish. The game's pitch was "All the thrills and spills of freshwater fly-fishing from the comfort of your own living room." Cat suggested a game of Junior Angler to cheer Lister up when the latter was feeling depressed about wasting his time away—mostly by playing puerile games like Junior Angler **[T-SER3.5]**.

- **Junior B:** A grade-school academic level on Io, usually attended by children around eight years of age. Arnold Rimmer advanced to Junior B in the prime universe, while Ace Rimmer was kept down to Junior C in his reality **[N-BCK]**.

- **Junior Birdmen:** An elite squadron of Resistance fighters on War World, an alternate Earth on which World War II never ended. The Birdmen were led by Commander Robert "Robbie Rocket Pants" Dimsdale, an interdimensional traveler who commandeered a pair of Raketenhosen (Rocket Pants) from the Reich, War World's evil superpower, then reverse-engineered them for use by his squad **[G-BIT]**.

- **Junior Birdmen of America (JBA):** A youth organization of the early twentieth century, geared toward boys and girls interested in building and flying model airplanes. The JBA became best known for its anthem, which was often slightly modified to mock inexperienced pilots **[RL]**.

  Cat suggested he and his shipmates don jet-powered rocket pants so they could "Junior Birdman" off a psi-moon configured according to Rimmer's psyche. However, they did not possess such trousers—primarily because they did not exist, except in the fictional world of *Robbie Rocket Pants* **[T-SER5.3]**.

  A scrawny Junior Birdman once visited a psi-moon corrupted by the mind of Mr. Flibble to help the local villagers defeat the evil penguin. After finding Flibble's lair, the Junior Birdman used his magic woggle to transform into Robbie Rocket Pants, then tried to subdue the fowl villain. He failed, however, and Flibble force-fed him baked beans, then launched him into the air after igniting his flatulence **[M-SMG2.9(c10)]**.

- **Junior C:** A grade-school academic level on Io, usually attended by children around seven years of age. Ace Rimmer was kept back in Junior C, while Arnold Rimmer advanced to Junior B in the prime universe **[N-BCK]**.

  > ***NOTE:*** *This account differed from episode 4.5 ("Dimension Jump"), which stated that Ace was kept back at Junior D.*

- ***Junior Colour Encyclopedia of Space, The*:** A book that *Red Dwarf*'s backup computer, Queeg, cited as the source of Holly's knowledge about astronomy, physics and other sciences, claiming it was the only one Holly could find containing pictures. This accusation was merely a prank, however, since Queeg was a ruse Holly devised to punish the crew for treating him poorly **[T-SER2.5]**.

  > ***NOTE:*** *When Queeg accused Holly of getting his information from the book, he called it* The Junior Encyclopedia of Space, *but when Holly later referenced the volume, its full title was displayed. In the real world,*

the Junior Colour Encyclopedia *series was published by Treasure Publishing, but did not include this particular title, though the company did offer* The Junior Colour Encyclopedia of the Universe.

- **Junior D:** A class that Rimmer took while at school on Io, which served as a divergence point in his life. In the prime universe, in which he was not forced to re-take the class, he became a man devoid of bravery, honor and character, while in another reality, in which he was left back, he became a noble and adored test pilot known as "Ace" **[T-SER4.5]**.

  NOTE: *This was changed to "Junior C" in the novel* Backwards.

- **Junior Junior:** A nickname that Karstares called his grandson, Brooke Junior, on the television soap opera *Androids* (since he called the teen's father, Brook, "Junior") **[M-SMG2.1(c2)]**.

- **Juno:** One of the largest asteroids in the Sol System's main asteroid belt **[RL]**. Juno was mentioned in a drinking game that Lister, Chen, Selby and Petersen played in *Red Dwarf*'s disco room **[T-SER1.3]**.

- **Juno Hilton:** A high-scale hotel located on Juno, featured on the television soap opera *Androids*. A wealthy mechanoid named Jaysee lived at the Hilton **[N-INF]**. Gary and Kelly, believing they had murdered Jaysee, planned to spend time together at the hotel **[M-SMG1.14(c3)]**. In another episode, Simone hid here to avoid her husband, Derek **[W-AND]**.

- **Jupiter:** The fifth planet from the Sun in the Sol System. A gas giant, Jupiter had more than sixty natural satellites, including Io, Europa, Ganymede and Callisto **[RL]**. In the twenty-second century, the Inter-Planetary Commission for Waste Disposal decided to designate one of the system's nine planets as humanity's official dumping grounds. Representatives from all nine worlds presented their case against being chosen, with Jupiter and its moons focusing on the planet's outstanding natural beauty. Ultimately, Earth was nominated for the task **[N-BTL]**.

- **Jupiter-class:** *See* Solar-class

- **Jupiter Mining Corporation (JMC):** A company based in London and San Francisco, with satellite offices worldwide and throughout the Sol System, including in Seattle and Bradbury, England, as well as on Ganymede and Titan. JMC employed members of the Space Corps to operate its mining vessels **[G-RPG]**, such as *Red Dwarf* **[T-SER1.1]**.

  The mining firm owned a fleet of nearly seventeen vessels, and employed a staff of more than twenty thousand humans and twelve hundred robots **[W-JMC]**. Employee benefits included exotic ports of call, flexible duty rosters, comfortable quarters, recreational facilities, merit-based advancement and a competitive salary, as well as full medical, dental, 401(k) and life-insurance plans **[G-RPG]**. It also provided inoculations from space plague and a free copy of the Space Corps Directives handbook **[W-JMC]**.

  JMC had a strict "no pets" policy aboard its mining ships **[T-SER8.7]**, though it did support a charity called Save the Pigeon **[W-JMC]**.

- **Jupiter Mining Corporation (JMC):** A twenty-second-century American company that, in one reality, owned and operated *Red Dwarf* and other mining vessels **[T-USA1]**.

- **Jupiter Mining Corporation Engineering Programme:** An educational program offered to existing and potential JMC employees. Lister recorded a video telling his son (himself) to enroll in the program, then drank himself into oblivion to forget the recording, in order to foster the illusion of having a father getting tough with him.

  Lister initially ignored the video's demands, until discovering that he had resigned his *Red Dwarf* commission while drunk, forcing him to re-enlist. Since the maximum eligible age was twenty-one, he was disqualified from re-enlistment, causing the ship's new artificial-intelligence computer, Pree, to eject him out an airlock **[T-SER10.2]**. Lister eventually filled out an application for the program's mechanical engineering course, with a specialization in robotics **[T-SER10.2(d)]**.

- **Jupiter Mining Corporation Personality Profile:** A form that psychiatric counselors aboard JMC vessels, such as *Red Dwarf*, completed during interviews with crewmembers. Doctor McClaren submitted this form after analyzing Kryten,

PREFIX
RL: Real life

T-: Television Episodes
SER: Television series
IDW: "Identity Within"
USA1: Unaired U.S. pilot
USA2: Unaired U.S. demo

R-: *The Bodysnatcher Collection*
SER: Remastered episodes
BOD: "Bodysnatcher"
DAD: "Dad"
FTH: "Lister's Father"
INF: "Infinity Patrol"
END: "The End" (original assembly)

N-: Novels
INF: *Infinity Welcomes Careful Drivers*
BTL: *Better Than Life*
LST: *Last Human*

BCK: *Backwards*
OMN: *Red Dwarf Omnibus*

M-: Magazines
SMG: *Smegazine*

W-: Websites
OFF: Official website
NAN: *Prelude to Nanarchy*
AND: *Androids*
DIV: Diva-Droid
DIB: Duane Dibbley

CRP: Crapola
GEN: Geneticon
LSR: Leisure World Intl.
JMC: Jupiter Mining Corporation
AIT: *A.I. Today*
HOL: HoloPoint

G-: Roleplaying Game
RPG: *Core Rulebook*
BIT: *A.I. Screen Extra Bits* booklet
SOR: *Series Sourcebook*
OTH: Other RPG material

recommending that the mechanoid be restored to factory settings **[T-SER8.1]**.

- **Jupiter Mining Corporation Robotics Programme:** An educational program offered to existing and potential JMC employees. Lister signed up after barely surviving an encounter with *Red Dwarf*'s new artificial-intelligence computer, Pree **[T-SER10.2]**.

- **Jupiter rise:** A term describing the planet Jupiter's emergence over the horizons of its satellites, analogous to a sunrise on Earth. A slideshow that Lister showed Cat included an image of a Jupiter rise **[T-SER1.2]**.

- **Jury of Six, the:** A six-member subgroup of the Forum of Justice, which held power at Arranguu 12's GELF settlement. The Jury of Six decided defendants' innocence or guilt during trials held on the desert moon, almost always declaring a guilty verdict in order to provide innocent inmates for the local prison's Reco-Programme **[N-LST]**.

- **Justice Computer:** A computer system operating on the penal station Justice World that, in conjunction with mind probes, detected the guilt or innocence of new arrivals **[W-AIT]**. When the *Red Dwarf* crew visited the station, the Justice Computer scanned the group for past infractions and found them all innocent except for Rimmer, whom it charged with the murders of his 1,167 shipmates during the cadmium II explosion. Citing Arnold's incompetence and narcissism as a defense, Kryten overturned the computer's ruling, earning the hologram's freedom **[T-SER4.3]**.

  The Justice Computer was eventually shut down and replaced by the station's backup artificial-intelligence computer, Kristian, when it failed to detect the guilt of an inmate who had stolen a pudding cup. Unable to properly maintain Justice World, Kristian caused the station to crash into a desert planet **[W-AIT]**.

- **Justice Field:** A security system aboard the penal station Justice World that encompassed the Justice Zone, an incarceration area that acted as a deterrent by reversing any malicious actions back to the offender. This technology had two benefits: It conditioned inmates to abide by the law, through real-time negative reinforcement, and it negated the need for guards and holding cells **[T-SER4.3]**.

- **Justice World:** A deep-space penal station shaped to resemble the scales of justice. Operated by the Justice Computer, Justice World incorporated a unique security system known as the Justice Field, which reversed any malicious actions back to the offender **[T-SER4.3]**. Within the incarceration area, the prison included shops, a cinema and a simulated outdoor area with fields and lakes **[T-SER4.3(d)]**.

  The *Red Dwarf* crew took a prison escape pod to Justice World, believing its occupant to be a simulant. The station performed a mind probe on the crew and found Rimmer guilty of 1,167 counts of murder for causing the cadmium II leak aboard *Red Dwarf*, sentencing him to 9,328 years at the facility, which Kryten was able to overturn. Before they could leave the station, the simulant—who had escaped from the pod—confronted them. The simulant pursued the crew throughout the complex until they incapacitated him by using the Justice Field to make him render himself unconscious **[T-SER4.3]**.

  Eventually, the station crashed into a desert planet due to an error on the part of its backup artificial-intelligence computer, Kristian **[W-AIT]**.

- **Justice Zone:** The incarceration area of the penal station Justice World. The Justice Zone was encompassed within the Justice Field, a technology that reversed any malicious actions—such as theft, arson or physical harm—back to the offender **[T-SER4.3]**.

  ***NOTE:** The* A.I. Today *website erroneously called the entire station the Justice Zone.*

- **"Just Say No to Smut":** A slogan on a sign that Mollee used to picket Brothel-U-Like on the television soap opera *Androids* **[M-SMG1.12(c3)]**.

- **JVS-325:** The license plate number of a vehicle parked behind a grassy knoll in Dallas, Texas, on the day of U.S. President John F. Kennedy's murder. JFK's future self walked by this car after assassinating himself from behind the knoll **[T-SER7.1]**.

K

KNOT, WARDEN

- **K:** A letter on the outside of Kelly's and Brook's house on the television soap opera *Androids* **[M-SMG2.9(c6)]**.

- **K177:** The artificial-intelligence system of Crapola Inc.'s second-generation Talkie Toaster **[T-SER4.4]**. The company recalled units containing this technology after a malfunction in their sanity circuits caused them to explode when agitated **[W-CRP]**.

- **K178:** The updated artificial-intelligence system of Crapola Inc.'s second-generation Talkie Toaster, following the K177's recall **[W-CRP]**.

- **Kabin, The:** A shop located on the set of the British television show *Coronation Street* **[RL]**. While trapped in an elation squid hallucination, the Red Dwarf crew—believing themselves to be on an alternate twenty-first-century Earth where they were merely characters on a British comedy series—entered The Kabin seeking information regarding the whereabouts of actor Craig Charles **[T-SER9.2]**.

  NOTE: *The Kabin, like all businesses in this sequence, was a fictional establishment created for the real-world series* Coronation Street, *in which Charles starred as of this writing. The Kabin, owned by Norris Cole, sold newspapers, magazines and so forth, and was located at 10 Coronation Street, in Weatherfield, England.*

- **Kadok:** The leader of the Clisterists, a Cat People sect aboard *Red Dwarf* who believed their god's true name was Clister. They fought a two-thousand-year Holy War against the Cloisterists—who claimed their deity was called Cloister—led by Darin-Tor. The opposing leaders met their god (Lister) in person, after members of a neutral sect called the Elite traveled into the future to seek his help in ending the conflict. Looking to secure his position as leader, Kadok tried to take Lister and the others hostage, but Darin-Tor helped Dave escape. After Kadok stabbed and killed Darin-Tor, an Elite warrior named Krazy threw the Clisterist from atop the High Tower **[M-SMG2.3(c1)]**.

- **Kahbootzale, Howard:** The host of the first game of the thirty-seventh zero-gee football season, which aired on the Holochannel **[M-SMG1.8(a)]**.

  NOTE: *This character's name spoofed that of American sports journalist and commentator Howard Cosell.*

- ***Kama Sutra*:** A collection of ancient Hindu texts describing human sexual behavior, with discussions of intercourse, love, family life and other aspects of human pleasure **[RL]**. Rimmer believed he had performed the first twenty-three pages of the *Kama Sutra* with Yvonne McGruder after imbibing the sexual magnetism virus, though he was actually under the influence of psychotropic drugs and plugged into an artificial-reality machine, under the observation of *Red Dwarf*'s Board of Inquiry **[T-SER8.2]**.

  NOTE: *The DVD captions misspelled the book's title as* "Karma Sutra."

- ***Kama Sutra II: The Lost Positions*:** A second set of ancient Hindu texts, published as a follow-up to the original. A group of Psirens created an illusion of this book to lure in victims **[G-SOR]**.

- **karaoke bar:** A drinking establishment in which patrons could sing along to popular tunes **[RL]**. When Kryten's nanobots rebuilt *Red Dwarf*, they used the ship's original design specs, from before JMC made cutbacks. Thus, the vessel now contained a karaoke bar on C Deck **[T-SER8.1]**.

- ***Karaoke Krazy*:** A recording that the *Red Dwarf* crew found in the Officers Quarters of the "low" version of their mining ship **[T-SER5.5]**.

- **Karen:** A name by which Lister inadvertently referred to ex-crewmate Caroline Carmen. Hoping to make Kochanski jealous, he claimed to have an affair with Carmen, but Kristine didn't believe him—especially after he mistakenly called her "Karen" instead of "Caroline" **[T-SER7.7]**.

- **Karmasutra:** A street on the Saturnian moon of Mimas. Noel's Body Swap Shop was located on this street **[M-SMG2.3(c4)]**.

- **"Kar nasa pinit":** A GELF phrase that translated into English as "This is GELF space" **[T-SER6.4]**.

  NOTE: *The DVD captions for this episode's deleted scenes spelled the phrase "Kar nasad init."*

- **Karstares:** A character on the television soap opera *Androids* **[N-INF]**. Karstares, a Model 6000 android **[M-SMG1.14(c3)]**, owned petroleum company Droid Oil **[W-AND]**. He was Brook's adoptive father **[M-SMG1.8(c5)]**, and also had an illegitimate evil son named Jaysee, whom he left out of his will. Furious, Jaysee vowed to destroy Karstares' other family business, Karstares Interstellar Cleaning and Sanitation Supplies (K.I.C.A.S.S.) **[M-SMG1.9(c2)]**, and sabotaged his father's airplane **[M-SMG1.14(c3)]**. Karstares was presumed to have died in the resultant crash **[M-SMG1.8(c5)]**.

  Karstares survived, however, and lived in the jungles of Io for twenty years, suffering from amnesia. After eventually regaining his memory, he set out to exact revenge **[M-SMG1.14(c3)]**. He found his son Brook and grandson Brooke Junior at the Detritus Wrecks junkyard **[M-SMG2.1(c2)]**, and brought them to the Juno Hilton, where he revealed that a group of diminutive forest dwellers known as the Ionian Ecommandoes had saved his life. In return, he had agreed to become a defender of Io's rainforests, dubbing himself the Green Knight **[M-SMG2.2(c3), M-SMG2.5(c5)]**.

Karstares discovered that Jaysee was using ingredients culled from the rainforests in his new cleaning product, and vowed to kill his evil son. He plotted with his family members and the Ecommandoes **[M-SMG2.5(c5)]**, as well as Jaysee's other enemies, to simultaneously attack his complex **[M-SMG2.6(c3)]**. Jaysee survived unscathed, while Karstares lost both legs, using a hydraulic groinal socket attachment to jump into a temporal-displacement vortex and hide while recovering **[M-SMG2.7(c6)]**.

> ***NOTE:*** *The* Androids *website revealed Brook's adoption, and indicated that Karstares had been lost in a shuttle accident, rather than a plane crash.*

- **Karstares' Interstellar Cleaning and Sanitation Supplies (K.I.C.A.S.S.):** A business owned by Karstares on the television soap opera *Androids*. After Karstares left his illegitimate son, Jaysee, out of his will, the younger mechanoid vowed to destroy the business **[M-SMG1.9(c2)]**. He later used a recording of his half-brother Brook visiting an android brothel to blackmail him into signing over ownership of the company **[M-SMG1.13(c1)]**.

- **Kate:** The artificial-intelligence computer aboard a possible alternate *Red Dwarf*. Her companions included Ben Ellis, a hologram named Terry, the mechanoid Kryten and Rat **[G-RPG]**.

- **Kay, Jeff:** A name that Lister thought Rimmer mentioned while discussing John F. Kennedy. Arnold had actually spoken the president's initials, "JFK" **[T-SER7.1]**.

- **Kazwa:** A Dolochimp GELF stationed at the virtual-reality prison Cyberia, located on Arranguu 12 in an alternate universe. Kazwa worked for the government's Reco-Programme, an endeavor created to save the GELF population from destruction in the Omni-zone by terraforming a planet using the living essence of prison inmates. After Lister served five months of an eighteen-year sentence, Kazwa offered him a chance to hasten his release by signing up for the program **[N-LST]**.

- **KDNIUJVIURNVOENV984398404IUFN98HR998SSJ:** A viral identification code printed on a vial aboard the *Mayflower,* an Earth ship assigned to terraform a planet in the Andromeda Galaxy. The vial contained bacteria infused with a virus capable of carrying out the terraforming. When the *Starbug* crew crashed onto a lava-covered planet in an alternate dimension, they came across the *Mayflower* under the molten surface and boarded it, hoping to find a way off-world. Using the luck virus, Kochanski picked the specific vials necessary to terraform the surface, including this one **[N-LST]**.

- **Keegan, Kevin:** A renowned international football player in the 1970s and '80s who moved into management in the early 1990s **[RL]**. Keegan authored the book *Football: It's a Funny Game*. After reading every book in existence, Holly proclaimed that this was the worst one ever written **[T-SER1.5]**.

  > ***NOTE:*** Football: It's a Funny Game *is an actual title in the real world, but was penned by Andrew John and Stephen Blake, not Keegan.*

- **Keegan, Michelle:** A British actor who portrayed Tina McIntyre on the television soap opera *Coronation Street* **[RL]**. While trapped in an elation squid hallucination, the *Red Dwarf* crew, believing themselves to be on an alternate twenty-first-century Earth, imagined visiting the *Coronation Street* set and meeting Keegan, who directed them to actor Craig Charles **[T-SER9.3]**.

- **Keelan, Charles:** A former schoolmate of Lister who later got married and then ate his wife, becoming the most famous person with whom Dave went to school **[T-SER3.5]**.

  > ***NOTE:*** *The DVD captions spelled his name as "Keenan."*

- **Kek-ack-ech-ech-ech Industries:** A company headquartered in GELF space. Its Hak-echekk-ack-hech-echhh subsidiary sponsored the Echech 3 GELF Open golf tournament **[G-OTH]**.

  > ***NOTE:*** *This was mentioned in a PDF displaying the layout of the tournament's nine holes that was made available in the files section of the* Red Dwarf *RPG Yahoo! Group, for use with* Red Dwarf—The Roleplaying Game.

PREFIX
RL: Real life

T-: Television Episodes
- **SER:** Television series
- **IDW:** "Identity Within"
- **USA1:** Unaired U.S. pilot
- **USA2:** Unaired U.S. demo

R-: *The Bodysnatcher Collection*
- **SER:** Remastered episodes
- **BOD:** "Bodysnatcher"
- **DAD:** "Dad"
- **FTH:** "Lister's Father"
- **INF:** "Infinity Patrol"
- **END:** "The End" (original assembly)

N-: Novels
- **INF:** *Infinity Welcomes Careful Drivers*
- **BTL:** *Better Than Life*
- **LST:** *Last Human*
- **BCK:** *Backwards*
- **OMN:** *Red Dwarf Omnibus*

M-: Magazines
- **SMG:** *Smegazine*

W-: Websites
- **OFF:** Official website
- **NAN:** *Prelude to Nanarchy*
- **AND:** *Androids*
- **DIV:** Diva-Droid
- **DIB:** Duane Dibbley
- **CRP:** Crapola
- **GEN:** Geneticon
- **LSR:** Leisure World Intl.
- **JMC:** Jupiter Mining Corporation
- **AIT:** *A.I. Today*
- **HOL:** HoloPoint

G-: Roleplaying Game
- **RPG:** *Core Rulebook*
- **BIT:** *A.I. Screen Extra Bits* booklet
- **SOR:** *Series Sourcebook*
- **OTH:** Other RPG material

- **Kelleher, Pat:** A script writer on the television soap opera *Androids* **[M-SMG2.9(c8)]**.

  NOTE: *Kelleher was credited on the* Androids *website as a storyliner. In the real world, Pat Kelleher authored the* Androids *comics published in the* Smegazines.

- **Keller, Helen:** An early nineteenth-century author, activist and lecturer who overcame the effects of a childhood disease that left her blind and deaf **[RL]**. Lister, suspecting that Ace Rimmer had lied about being kept back a year at school, suggested the story was as accurate as Helen Keller's golf swing **[T-SER7.2(d)]**.

- **Kellerman, Alice, Doctor, Flight Technician:** A psychiatric physician aboard an alternate-universe *Red Dwarf.* When another psychiatrist, Nicholas Thompson, asked her to review a difficult patient—that reality's Lister—Kellerman deemed Lister a sociopath, citing genetic and past environmental conditions as the disorder's cause **[N-LST]**.

- **Kelly:** A character on the television soap opera *Androids,* portrayed by Android 14762/E. She had a son named Brooke Junior, whom she conceived while having an affair with her ex-husband Gary, the business rival of her husband Brook—a secret she did not confess until their son was a teenager **[T-SER2.1]**.

  Kelly's neighbor, Mollee, requested her help in picketing Brothel-U-Like, unaware that Kelly was the android bordello's madam **[M-SMG1.11(c1)]**. After Jaysee blackmailed Kelly and Gary, they plotted to kill him **[M-SMG1.13(c1)]**, but accidentally blew up Jaysee's good head instead **[M-SMG1.14(c3)]**. Jaysee retaliated by blowing up Gary's car as he and Kelly had sex in the back seat **[M-SMG2.1(c2)]**. They survived, albeit heavily damaged **[M-SMG2.2(c3)]**.

  Kelly reconciled with Brook at St. Androids Hospital, when her husband was admitted to the Halfords Memorial Ward following a firefight with Jaysee **[M-SMG2.8(c8)]**. The couple moved back in together **[M-SMG2.9(c6)]**, only to learn that Brooke Junior had undergone an oil change procedure **[M-SMG2.9(c8)]**.

- **Kelly Family, the:** *See* Osmond, James Arthur ("Jimmy")

- **KellysKnickers:** The username of a forum poster on the *Androids* website's message boards **[W-AND]**.

- **Ken:** A hypothetical individual to whom Lister though Rimmer was referring upon hearing Arnold's one rule for *Red Dwarf*'s Z-Shift: K.I.T. ("Keep It Tidy," which Dave mistook for meaning "Ken Is a Transvestite") **[N-INF]**.

  NOTE: *This may indicate Z-Shift included a crewman named Ken.*

- **Kendal, Felicity:** A British television, film and stage actor whose derrière won the 1981 Rear of the Year award **[RL]**. En route to Earth after three million years in deep space, the *Red Dwarf* crew discovered a moon shaped like Kendal's famous posterior, and lingered for a while before resuming their course **[T-SER2.4]**.

  NOTE: *In the remastered version of this episode, Holly's dialog was changed so that the moon resembled Marilyn Monroe's behind.*

- **Kennedy, John Fitzgerald ("Jack," "JFK"), President:** The thirty-fifth leader of the United States until his assassination on November 22, 1963, by Lee Harvey Oswald. Among his accomplishments was the resolution of the Cuban missile crisis. Though married to Jacqueline Kennedy, JFK was a known womanizer who reportedly had an affair with actor Marilyn Monroe **[RL]**.

  In an alternate timeline, Kennedy survived the assassination attempt due to the interference of *Starbug 1*'s crew, then had an affair with the mistress of Mafia boss Sam Giancana, for which he was impeached in 1964 and imprisoned in 1965. J. Edgar Hoover assumed the presidency and, under mob control, allowed the building of Soviet nuclear bases in Cuba, forcing the mass exodus of millions of civilians from major U.S. cities. The *Starbug 1* crew, jumping ahead to 1966, discovered their mistake and plotted to bring JKF back to 1963 so he could assassinate himself from behind a nearby grassy knoll **[T-SER7.1]**.

  While trapped in an addictive version of *Better Than Life*, Rimmer believed he had returned to Earth and become famously wealthy, creating a company that developed a time machine. In the hallucination, he used the machine to bring together several historical individuals to attend his bachelor party, including Kennedy. At the wedding reception, JFK was spotted emerging from bushes while tucking in his shirt, followed by a disheveled Queen Elizabeth I **[N-BTL]**.

- **Kenneth:** A man whom Monica Jones dated while performing with new wave band Monica and the Monopeds. They broke up after Jones joined the Space Corps **[G-RPG]**.

- **Kenneth:** The artificial-intelligence computer aboard the experimental JMC mining ship *Black Hole* in an alternate universe. Kenneth had an IQ of twelve thousand and predictive capabilities, enabling him to deal with every possible scenario before it occurred. Like all ship's systems, Kenneth was powered by a tiny captured star. During the initial startup of the *Black Hole*'s engines, a radiation burst caused by the improperly contained star resulted in an explosion that killed every unshielded crewmember and drastically reduced Kenneth's IQ **[G-RPG]**.

- **Kershaw, Jordan:** The head writer of the television soap opera *Androids*. Kershaw had a background in robot theater, having previously created *Arc*, an award-winning play about simple welding folk **[W-AND]**.

- **Kevin:** Admiral Peter Tranter's valet in one of Ace Rimmer's universes. Kevin occasionally called the admiral "Skunk Foot," "Vinegar Drawers" and "Himself" behind the officer's back **[N-BCK]**.

- **Keyboard Teeth:** A nickname that Rimmer called Cat after an emohawk transformed him into dorky alter ego Duane Dibbley **[T-SER6.4]**.

- **Keystone K-7 Deluxe:** The make and model of an American-made video camera, circa the 1960s **[RL]**. Such a camera was used to film the assassination of John F. Kennedy **[RL, T-SER7.1]**.

  ***NOTE:** One of the few witnesses who managed to film the actual murder was Marie M. Muchmore, who used a Keystone K-7 camera.*

- **KF 80:** An identifier printed on a switchboard of the SS *Manny Celeste*, a Space Corps derelict found by the revived *Red Dwarf* crew **[T-SER8.6]**.

- **Khakhakhakkhhakhakkkhakkkkkh:** The daughter of Btrrnfjhyjhnehgewydn, the leader of a Kinitawowi GELF tribe in an alternate universe. Lister was forced to marry Khakhakhakkhhakhakkkhakkkkkh after he insulted the chief by offering to pay for droids and supplies with semen, which other GELF tribes considered a highly valued commodity.

  Khakhakhakkhhakhakkkhakkkkkh, the prettiest of Btrrnfjhyjhnehgewydn's three daughters, tried to consummate their marriage by getting Lister drunk on Kinitawowi moonshine. Halfway through the act, Lister regained consciousness and ran from their hut, naked and screaming, to find his crewmates.

  Undeterred, Khakhakhakkhhakhakkkhakkkkkh pursued *Starbug* throughout GELF space, catching up with the ship months later near a lava planet. After firing a few warning shots, she and other Kinitawowi boarded the shuttle, where she knocked out Lister's sociopathic doppelgänger, mistaking him for her husband. When the double regained consciousness, he slaughtered his GELF captors, including Khakhakhakkhhakhakkkhakkkkkh **[N-LST]**.

  ***NOTE:** This account conflicted with episode 3.3 ("Polymorph"), in which Lister married a GELF named Hackhackhackachhachhachach, under similar but slightly different circumstances.*

- **Khaki:** An alert condition indicating severe damage to a 4000 Series mechanoid. After an accident on a psi-moon left Kryten injured and stranded, his CPU assessed the situation and periodically updated his head-up display. His condition changed to Khaki when Lister cut the mechanoid in two to dislodge him from the wreckage **[T-SER5.3]**.

- **Khan, Genghis, Emperor:** The founder of the Mongol Empire, circa the thirteenth century. Born under the name Temujin, he later carried out many ruthless conquests throughout Eurasia **[RL]**. A computer-generated Genghis Khan taught history at the cyberschool that Kochanski attended as a youth **[T-SER7.4(e)]**.

  While trying to ascertain the era in which he and his shipmates had crashed on Earth, Rimmer asked Holly if he should expect to encounter Genghis Khan and his barbarian friends **[T-SER3.1]**.

- **Khazi Droid:** A nickname that Rimmer called Kryten while refusing the mechanoid's plan to use Arnold's remote projection unit to rescue another hologram **[T-SER5.4]**.

  ***NOTE:** The term "khazi" is British slang for a toilet, referencing Kryten's primary function of cleaning lavatories.*

- **K.I.C.A.S.S.:** *See* Karstares' Interstellar Cleaning and Sanitation Supplies (K.I.C.A.S.S.)

- **KICASS Tower:** A building that served as the headquarters of Karstares' Interstellar Cleaning and Sanitation Supplies, on the television soap opera *Androids* **[M-SMG2.5(c5)]**. Jaysee faced off against his enemies—including RoboGaz (Gary), Kelly, Karstares, Brook, Brooke Junior and Mollee—at this facility **[M-SMG2.6(c3)]**.

- **"Kick Butts":** A slogan painted on the top of a starship owned by Ace "Blackheart" Rimmer, accompanied by a graphic of a middle-finger salute **[M-SMG1.14(c5)]**.

- **Kidd, Brian:** An English football player and coach who managed such teams as Manchester United, Sheffield United and Manchester City **[RL]**. Frustrated at how useless Kryten and Cat were in assisting him with a mining operation, Lister decided that only George III and Brian Kidd would have been more inept **[N-INF]**.

  ***NOTE:** The* Red Dwarf Omnibus *changed this to King Havac the Imbecile and his more idiotic half-brother.*

- **kidney bowl:** A bean-shaped bowl used in medical facilities to hold used dressings and other waste **[RL]**. Bored with plastic cutlery, Lister procured several items from *Red Dwarf*'s Medical Unit to prepare and serve dinner in the Officers Quarters, including kidney bowls, which he used to store onion salad in the Embryo Refrigeration Unit. Although Lister had cleaned and sterilized the equipment, Cat refused to stay for dinner, dubbing the meal "an autopsy" **[T-SER3.3]**.

- **kidney stone:** A small, hardened mineral material created within the kidney or urinary tract **[RL]**. Frank Hollister once suffered from this affliction **[T-SER10(b)]**. When Jesus of Caesarea developed kidney stones, Kryten operated on him to remove the obstruction **[T-SER10.3]**.

  ***NOTE:** Hollister's kidney stones were mentioned in the "We're Smegged" making-of special on the Series X Blu-ray set.*

- **Kīlauea:** An active volcano on the Hawaiian Islands **[RL]**. Kīlauea was the site of illegal environmental experiments conducted by scientists working for the World Council, which involved injecting bacteria with a virus that corrupted the molecular structure of lava and then spraying it over the volcano via crop dusters.

  After five and a half weeks, the lava was reduced to a toxic sludge, and a second viral bacteria was introduced to ingest the mulch and convert it to sand, oxygen and nitrogen. Since the experiment tested the feasibility of terraforming a lava planet in the Andromeda Galaxy, it was deemed a resounding success **[N-LST]**.

- **Kill Crazy:** *See* Blenkinsop, Oswald ("Kill Crazy")

- **Killer:** A nickname that Lister jokingly called Rimmer after the hologram was tried and convicted of 1,167 counts of murder by the Justice Computer, which had detected his feelings of guilt regarding *Red Dwarf*'s cadmium II accident **[T-SER4.3]**.

- ***Kill Your Way Slim*:** A book written by Colonel Mike O'Hagan, a Space Marine and the author of the *Space Corps Survival Manual*. The book was also published as a 3D Magic Eye edition **[B-SUR]**.

- **King:** A nickname that Confidence, a hallucination of Lister's mind made corporeal by mutated pneumonia, called Lister **[T-SER1.5]**.

- **King, Reece:** A JMC employee who adorned the cover of an issue of the *JMC Traveller* inflight magazine. Lister thumbed through this issue while fretting the fate of the human species **[T-SER10.5]**.

  ***NOTE:** Reece King was a floor runner who worked behind the scenes of Series X.*

- **King Kong:** A fictional movie monster created in the 1920s by Merian C. Cooper. The giant gorilla appeared in seven

KOCHANSKI, KRISTINE Z. ("KRISSIE"), FIRST CONSOLE OFFICER
NSOLE OFFICER
KOCHANSK
KOCHANSKI, KRISTINE Z. ("KRISSIE"), NAVIGATION OFFICER

licensed theatrical films between 1933 and 2007 **[RL]**. While navigating *Starbug 1* through an asteroid field, the *Red Dwarf* crew encountered an enormous meteor on a collision course, which Rimmer described as "bigger than King Kong's first dump of the day" **[T-SER6.1]**.

- ***King Lear*:** A tragedy written by playwright William Shakespeare sometime between 1603 and 1606, concerning an aging monarch's descent into madness **[RL]**. While marooned aboard *Starbug 1* on an icy planet, Lister burned Rimmer's books to stay warm, including *The Complete Works of Shakespeare*. Arnold protested the destruction of what was likely the only remaining copy of the play, but admitted he never actually read it **[T-SER3.2]**.

- **Kingo:** A nickname that Confidence, a hallucination of Lister's mind made corporeal by mutated pneumonia, called Lister **[T-SER1.5]**.

- **King of Crap:** The self-imposed title of John Ewe, a sewage transport pilot who ferried human waste from the Jovian system to Garbage World (Earth) during the twenty-third century **[N-BTL]**.

- ***King of Kings*:** A 1961 American film about the life of Jesus Christ, starring Jeffrey Hunter and narrated by Orson Wells **[RL]**. Miffed that Rimmer had described one of his favorite romantic films as "unrealistic," Lister claimed the hologram had said the same thing about *King of Kings* **[T-SER5.1]**.

- **King of the Cockroaches:** Lister's title on Garbage World (Earth), after a clan of eight-foot-long cockroaches—which had evolved on the planet over millions of years—watched him attempt to eat a rotting couch and happily dubbed him their king **[N-BTL]**.

- **King of the Potato People:** An imaginary monarch whom Rimmer hallucinated after going insane from a holovirus. Locking his shipmates in quarantine, Arnold appeared after five days wearing a red and white gingham dress and army boots, and informed them that despite Space Corps Directive 699, he could not release them because the king would not let him do so for ten years—and the only way to obtain an audience with the king was on a magic carpet. He then accused them of being insane for wanting to fly on a magic carpet to beg the King of the Potato People for their freedom, and shut off their oxygen supply as punishment **[T-SER5.4]**.

- **King of the Potato People:** The ruler of Planet Spud, whom Mr. Flibble attacked using a thermonuclear weapon known as a plasmatic lacerator shell. The king enjoyed reading *Spud Only*, an adult magazine featuring images of naked Potato women, while using the bathroom **[M-SMG1.8(c3)]**.

- **king prawn biryani:** *See* prawn vindaloo

- **King's Crossing Station:** A railway station in London, England, featured in that city's version of *Monopoly* **[RL]**. For his twenty-fourth birthday, Lister and several friends embarked on a *Monopoly* pub crawl across London. Their third stop was King's Crossing Station, where they ordered double vodkas **[N-INF]**.

- **Kinitawowi:** A GELF tribe occupying a small moon within GELF territory **[T-SER6.4]**. Originally created to serve as quartermasters **[T-IDW]**, the Kinitawowi were primarily bred as slave labor **[G-RPG]**. Unlike some GELF species, they did not have their sphincteral orifices in their faces **[T-SER6.4]**.

  After an encounter with a Space Corps external enforcement vehicle forced *Starbug 1* to crash on the GELF moon, the crew risked trading with the Kinitawowi to replace an Oxy-gen unit damaged beyond repair. The Kinitawowi were among the friendlier GELF tribes, and greeted the newcomers by firing an arrow into their supply crate rather than skinning them alive.

  Bartering commenced, but the *Starbug* crew were dismayed to learn of the Kinitawowi's price: Lister's hand in marriage to the tribal leader's repulsive daughter, Hackhackhackachhachhachach. Reassured that his shipmates would rescue him, Lister agreed to the arrangement, but fled the scene when his new wife took him to her hut to consummate the marriage.

  Outraged, the leader sent his pet emohawk to cull the crew's emotions **[T-SER6.4]**. When that failed, Hackhackhackachhachhachach boarded a Kinitawowi battle cruiser to intercept *Starbug 1*, eventually finding the shuttle tethered to an alternate dimension via a hyperway. The Kinitawowi attacked the vessel but crashed into a planetoid. When another GELF cruiser attacked *Starbug* as well, the hyperway was severed, stranding that reality's Kochanski in the prime universe **[T-SER7.3]**.

  > ***NOTE:*** *The crew's encounter with the Kinitawowi, as well as their very nature, were handled differently between episode 3.3 ("Polymorph") and the novel* Last Human. *As such, the two groups are assumed to be separate tribes.*

- **Kinitawowi:** A tribe of GELFs occupying several desert asteroids in a GELF region of an alternate universe. A genetic mixture of hippopotamuses and gorillas, Kinitawowi were somewhat friendly and willing to trade with strangers.

  Unlike other GELF species in the region, the Kinitawowi were not sterile, and thus did not consider semen a valuable

commodity. When the *Starbug* crew sought their help in finding Lister's doppelgänger from that reality, the crew inadvertently offended the tribe's leader by offering tubes of sperm as payment for supplies and droids, as they had done at other GELF settlements.

Outraged, the chief forced Lister to marry his daughter, Khakhakhakkhhakhakkkhakkkkh. After securing droids and supplies, Lister hesitantly agreed to the arrangement, hoping his friends would sneak him out during the night. But after falling unconscious from Kinitawowi moonshine, he awoke to find his bride having sex with him, then ran through the settlement, screaming and naked, to rejoin his crewmates.

Furious, Khakhakhakkhhakhakkkhakkkkkh boarded a cruiser and pursued the crew throughout GELF space, finally catching up with them near a lava planet. After firing a few warning shots, she and other Kinitawowi boarded the shuttle, where she knocked out Lister's sociopathic doppelgänger, mistaking him for her husband. When the double regained consciousness, he slaughtered his GELF captors, including Khakhakhakkhhakhakkkhakkkkkh **[N-LST]**.

- **Kinitawowi moonshine:** A highly potent distilled intoxicant created by a Kinitawowi tribe in an alternate universe, so excessively strong that one remained drunk for weeks, sometimes months, from a single serving. Unaware of its potency, Lister shared the moonshine with his new wife, Khakhakhakkhhakhakkkhakkkkkh, then awoke sometime later to find the hairy GELF straddling him **[N-LST]**.

- **Kinitawowi Open:** An annual golf tournament hosted in GELF space by the Kinitawowi tribe. The tournament, typically comprising three teams, spanned a nine-hole course through the Forbidden Lands of Echech 3, a primitive planet covered in lush jungles and active volcanoes, populated by dinosaurs, carnivorous plants and giant insects. Queen Ech-Ghekk-Agg-Hecch-Ech-Ech, who explained the rules and conditions during opening ceremonies, presided over the event.

  At the ninth such tournament, winners received a fully reconditioned starship drive system, complete with a star drive, while the second runners-up received a crate of sticky notes and ballpoint pens. The losers were stripped of their possessions and skinned alive. Among the participants at that event were a rogue simulant, a Hudzen 10 mechanoid, a Hermann Göring waxdroid in drag, and four female Kinitawowi warriors **[G-RPG]**.

  ***NOTE:** A PDF displaying the layout of the nine holes was made available in the files section of the* Red Dwarf *RPG Yahoo! Group, for use with* Red Dwarf—The Roleplaying Game. *That document called the event the Echech 3 GELF Open.*

- **kinteteach:** A word in the Kinitawowi language, meaning "tribe" **[T-SER6.4]**.

- **Kipling Street:** *See* Teerts Gnilpik

- **kipper:** A meal prepared by splitting a herring from head to tail, preserving the fish via salting or pickling, and then smoking it **[RL]**. Ace Rimmer's catchphrase was "Smoke me a kipper; I'll be back for breakfast," signifying his intent to return **[T-SER4.5]**.

- **kippers vindaloo:** A meal that Lister once had for supper, consisting of smoked herring prepared in curry. Rimmer blamed Lister's insomnia that night on the meal **[T-SER3.4]**.

- **Kirby XL:** A model of vacuum attachment that Brooke Junior purchased using money he'd earned from working for his uncle Jaysee, on the television soap opera *Androids* **[M-SMG1.13(c1)]**.

  ***NOTE:** Kirby is an American consumer vacuum cleaner company.*

- **Kirk, Captain:** The commander of the mining ship *Red Dwarf* at the start of Lister's tour of duty. Kirk, a short, stocky American woman, believed Lister had smuggled an unquarantined cat aboard the ship, and thus sentenced him to eighteen months in stasis. Lister had actually intended to get caught with the perfectly healthy cat, however, so he would be sent into stasis and make his trip to Earth pass more quickly **[N-INF]**.

  ***NOTE:** This account conflicted with episode 1.1 ("The End") and several subsequent episodes, in which Captain Hollister was in command of* Red Dwarf *at the time. The name "Captain Kirk" paid homage to James Tiberius Kirk, the protagonist of the* Star Trek *television and film series.*

PREFIX
RL: Real life

T-: Television Episodes
SER: Television series
IDW: "Identity Within"
USA1: Unaired U.S. pilot
USA2: Unaired U.S. demo

R-: *The Bodysnatcher Collection*
SER: Remastered episodes
BOD: "Bodysnatcher"
DAD: "Dad"
FTH: "Lister's Father"
INF: "Infinity Patrol"
END: "The End" (original assembly)

N-: Novels
INF: *Infinity Welcomes Careful Drivers*
BTL: *Better Than Life*
LST: *Last Human*

BCK: *Backwards*
OMN: *Red Dwarf Omnibus*

M-: Magazines
SMG: *Smegazine*

W-: Websites
OFF: Official website
NAN: *Prelude to Nanarchy*
AND: *Androids*
DIV: Diva-Droid
DIB: Duane Dibbley

CRP: Crapola
GEN: Geneticon
LSR: Leisure World Intl.
JMC: Jupiter Mining Corporation
AIT: *A.I. Today*
HOL: HoloPoint

G-: Roleplaying Game
RPG: *Core Rulebook*
BIT: *A.I. Screen Extra Bits* booklet
SOR: *Series Sourcebook*
OTH: Other RPG material

- **Kiss Chase:** A game developed by Colonel Mike O'Hagan, aimed at keeping crash survivors occupied and in good spirits. He suggested this game in his *Space Corps Survival Manual* **[B-SUR]**.

- **Kit:** A model and dancer in an alternate universe in which *Red Dwarf* was a British television series. Kit was hired for a music video being filmed for raga musician Tabby Ranks at Black Island Film Studios. There, she met Leo Davis, the studio's caretaker, who took an instant liking to her.

  Too nervous to ask Kit out, the timid Davis instead daydreamed about various historical and fictional characters giving him advice on how to approach her. In the dreams, Leo became various characters that he associated with self-confidence; in one such illusion he became Cat, a character on his favorite show, *Red Dwarf*, with Kit appearing as a member of the *Felis sapiens* species **[X-TNG]** named Kit Cat [M-SMG2.5(a)]. Eventually, the model began talking to Leo, and the two went out for a night on the town **[X-TNG]**.

- **Kit:** A name that Rimmer, after spending 557 years imprisoned on Rimmerworld, mistakenly called Cat **[T-SER6.5]**.

- **K.I.T.:** Rimmer's one rule for *Red Dwarf*'s Z-Shift: "Keep It Tidy" (though Lister thought it stood for "Ken Is a Transvestite"). If Z-Shift followed this rule, Rimmer assured them, they would G.O.J.F. ("Get On Just Famously") **[N-INF]**.

- **Kit-Kat Club:** An establishment in Bangkok, Thailand. To reduce the suffering caused by his sexual appetite, Cat watched holo-slides of women dressed in kitten outfits attending the Kit-Kat Club **[T-IDW]**.

  ***NOTE:** This nightclub's name was based on that of the KitKatClub, in Berlin, Germany, which itself had been named after an eighteenth-century London-based political group.*

- **kitty school:** A religious-based learning institution among the *Felis sapiens* society inhabiting *Red Dwarf*. Among the topics taught were religious stories of Frankenstein (The Holy Mother), as well as the Virgin Birth, Cloister the Stupid and the return to Fuchal, the Promised Land **[T-SER1.1]**.

- **K.K.:** An affectionate nickname that Lister gave Kochanski during their brief courtship **[N-INF]**.

  ***NOTE:** This was also mentioned in a deleted scene for episode 9.2 ("Back to Earth Part 2").*

- **K.K. Ice Cream:** A frozen dessert product sold by street vendors during the Kookie Kola Bear Parade **[M-SMG2.3(c3)]**.

- **"Klim":** A word printed on a wall sign at an eatery in England, during a period in Earth's far future when time ran backwards. The sign, when read forward, was labeled "Milk" **[T-SER3.1]**.

  ***NOTE:** Throughout the episode, backwards writing was inconsistently handled. In some cases, characters were forward-facing, while in others (such as in this instance), they faced backwards.*

- **Klix:** A British vending machine company **[RL]**. Klix supplied many of the dispensers aboard *Red Dwarf*, including Taiwan Tony **[T-SER10.2]**.

  ***NOTE:** The company's website was visible in a closeup of Taiwan Tony's frame.*

- **Kluge Corp.:** A company specializing in time-matter displacement technologies. Kluge developed such devices as the Matter Paddle, the teleporter and the reality minefield, and distributed its products via Crapola Inc.'s annual *SCABBY* catalog **[G-RPG]**.

- **Klumpp, Joe:** The author of the book *Zero Gee Football—It's a Funny Old Game*. Holly read this book during the nanoseconds that passed between his sealing of *Red Dwarf*'s cargo decks to protect the crew from the impending cadmium II explosion, and the actual explosion **[N-OMN]**.

  ***NOTE:** This was changed from the novel* Infinity Welcomes Careful Drivers, *in which Holly read Kevin Keegan's* Football—It's a Funny Old Game.

- **Knot, Warden:** A portly warden of the Tank, *Red Dwarf*'s brig on Floor 13, who was assigned to the Canaries, an elite group of inmates that investigated dangerous situations. He accompanied the Canaries on a mission to the vessel SSS *Silverberg*, aboard which the group met Cassandra, an artificial intelligence computer capable of predicting the future.

B-: Books
PRG: *Red Dwarf Programme Guide*
SUR: *Red Dwarf Space Corps Survival Manual*
PRM: *Primordial Soup*
SOS: *Son of Soup*
SCE: *Scenes from the Dwarf*
LOG: *Red Dwarf Log No. 1996*
RD8: *Red Dwarf VIII*
EVR: *The Log: A Dwarfer's Guide to Everything*

X-: Misc.
PRO: Promotional materials, videos, etc.
PST: Posters at DJ XVII (2013)
CAL: 2008 calendar
RNG: Cell phone ringtones
MOB: Mobisode ("Red Christmas")
CIN: *Children in Need* sketch
GEK: *Geek Week* intros by Kryten
TNG: "Tongue-Tied" video
XMS: Bill Pearson's Christmas special pitch script
XVD: Bill Pearson's Christmas special pitch video
OTH: Other *Red Dwarf* appearances

SUFFIX
DVD:
(d) – Deleted scene
(o) – Outtake
(b) – Bonus DVD material (other)
(e) – Extended version

SMEGAZINES:
(c) – Comic
(a) – Article

OTHER:
(s) – Early/unused script draft
(s1) – Alternate version of script

When Cassandra told her visitors that someone named Rimmer would die within twenty minutes, the Canaries plotted to introduce someone else by that name to the computer, hoping to alter the outcome. When Knot arrived to investigate the mainframe, Arnold spilled coffee on him and offered his own jacket, which had his name on it. Cassandra thus told Knot he would soon die, causing him to suffer a heart attack **[T-SER8.4]**.

- **Kochanski:** The significant other of Darren, a hillbilly version of Lister in an alternate universe ravaged by the tyrannical Ace "Blackheart" Rimmer. Blackheart killed Kochanski while attacking Darren's settlement **[M-SMG1.14(c5)]**.

- **Kochanski, Christine:** A crewmember aboard *Red Dwarf* in a reality in which the mining ship's crew were American. She dated that dimension's Lister, but broke up with him shortly before he was sentenced to six months in stasis. Christine died during the cadmium II disaster, but rejoined Lister sometime afterward **[T-USA1]**.

- **Kochanski, Christopher:** A crewmember aboard *Red Dwarf* in a universe in which the sexes were reversed. Deb Lister was infatuated with him **[M-SMG1.5(c2)]**. Kochanski had a carpet installed in his quarters after complaining that the cold floor gave him a rash **[W-OFF]**. He later died due to a radiation leak aboard the ship **[M-SMG1.5(c2)]**.

- **Kochanski, C.Z.:** A name on a label marking the hologramic projection box of navigation officer Kristine Kochanski. Lister used her projection box and personality disk to activate her hologram, but Rimmer had swapped Kochanski's disk with his own, thereby activating a second Rimmer hologram instead **[T-SER1.5]**.

  ***NOTE:** Lister presumably used the same box to deactivate the duplicate Rimmer in the subsequent episode, despite the box having Arnold's name on it (possibly to fool Rimmer). It is unknown why Kochanski's first initial was incorrect on the label.*

- **Kochanski, Krissie:** A descendant of Kristine Kochanski whom Lister imagined while trapped in an addictive version of *Better Than Life*. Lister believed he had returned to Earth aboard *Nova 5* and, shunning fame and fortune, had settled down in a Midwestern town modeled after Bedford Falls from *It's a Wonderful Life*. There, he met Krissie, an exact copy of his ex-girlfriend, and they fell instantly in love. Two years later, they had twin sons named Jim and Bexley **[N-INF]**.

- **Kochanski, Kristine:** An alternate-reality Kochanski whom the prime universe's crew found severely injured aboard a *Starbug* shuttle while traversing the Omni-zone. She soon died from her injuries, which had been inflicted by that reality's psychotic Lister, who had killed his comrades to keep the genome of DNA (G.O.D.) for himself **[N-LST]**.

- **Kochanski, Kristine Z.:** A woman in a parallel dimension who married flight engineer Dave "Spanners" Lister and gave birth to twin boys named Jim and Bexley. In her reality, Rimmer was held back a grade in school and thus became a Space Corps test pilot known as "Ace" **[T-SER4.5]**.

- **Kochanski, Kristine Z.:** A blonde, gum-chewing administrative assistant in the Science Department of a mirror-universe *Red Dwarf*. She directed Rimmer (masquerading as the ship's captain) to consult Professor Cat about finding an antidote to a microbe destroying the prime *Red Dwarf* **[T-SER8.8]**. Despite her flighty demeanor, she had several diplomas, including a Hygiene Proficiency certificate qualifying her to work in a cake shop **[T-SER8.8(d)]**. She was also adept at riding mechanical bulls **[G-SOR]**.

- **Kochanski, Kristine Z. ("Krissie"), First Console Officer:** A crewmember aboard *Red Dwarf* **[T-SER1.1]**. She attended a school in Perth as a youth, then graduated with honors from the European Space Academy as a flight coordinator, first-class **[N-LST]**.

  Kristine and Lister dated for three weeks, but she dumped him for a catering officer **[T-SER6.1]** named Tim **[T-SER8.5]**. Dave was later unable to recall if the man's name had been Terry, Tim, Tom, Tony or Trevor **[N-INF]**. She worked in the ship's Drive Room until perishing along with her shipmates during the cadmium II disaster. Lister was very fond of her, and included her in a "five-year plan" he had secretly mapped out for his future **[T-SER1.1]**.

  After the accident, Lister berated Holly for not resurrecting Kochanski as a hologram instead of Rimmer. Holly justified his

PREFIX
RL: Real life

T-: Television Episodes
SER: Television series
IDW: "Identity Within"
USA1: Unaired U.S. pilot
USA2: Unaired U.S. demo

R-: *The Bodysnatcher Collection*
SER: Remastered episodes
BOD: "Bodysnatcher"
DAD: "Dad"
FTH: "Lister's Father"
INF: "Infinity Patrol"
END: "The End" (original assembly)

N-: Novels
INF: *Infinity Welcomes Careful Drivers*
BTL: *Better Than Life*
LST: *Last Human*

BCK: *Backwards*
OMN: *Red Dwarf Omnibus*

M-: Magazines
SMG: *Smegazine*

W-: Websites
OFF: Official website
NAN: *Prelude to Nanarchy*
AND: *Androids*
DIV: Diva-Droid
DIB: Duane Dibbley

CRP: Crapola
GEN: Geneticon
LSR: Leisure World Intl.
JMC: Jupiter Mining Corporation
AIT: *A.I. Today*
HOL: HoloPoint

G-: Roleplaying Game
RPG: *Core Rulebook*
BIT: *A.I. Screen Extra Bits* booklet
SOR: *Series Sourcebook*
OTH: Other RPG material

decision by stating that Lister and Kochanski had only shared 173 words between them. Lister then asked Arnold to shut down temporarily so he could spend another night with Kochanski, but Rimmer feared that Dave would make the switch permanent and refused. In retaliation, Lister took the Chef's Exam so he would outrank him. Arnold assumed Kochanski's form and tried to persuade Lister to give up, but Dave saw through the ruse and took the test **[T-SER1.3]**, which he failed **[T-SER1.4]**.

Lister often went through Kochanski's former quarters searching for evidence of her feelings for him. On one such excursion, he contracted mutated pneumonia due to Rimmer's negligence in irradiating the area **[T-SER1.5]**. During another, he discovered a wedding photograph of himself and Kristine. Curious about its origins, Lister investigated and discovered a passage in Rimmer's diary pertaining to a stasis leak aboard *Red Dwarf*, capable of leading them into the past. Convinced this was his ticket back to Kochanski, Dave traversed the stasis leak, only to find her already married to a future version of himself **[T-SER2.4]**.

Telepathic GELFs known as Psirens once lured the *Red Dwarf* crew into an asteroid field by faking a distress call from the SCS *Pioneer,* showing Kochanski to have survived the cadmium II incident. Lister's shipmates, however, convinced him it wasn't real before he could mount a rescue effort **[T-SER6.1]**.

While stranded aboard *Starbug 1*, the crew encountered a polymorph posing as *Red Dwarf.* Upon boarding the fake vessel, they found recreations of the crew, including Kochanski **[M-SMG2.6(c1)]**. The doppelgänger urged them to submit to regular polymorph feedings, in exchange for whatever they desired, but without success **[M-SMG2.7(c1)]**.

When Lister advanced to age sixty-one due to time dilation and suffered a fatal heart attack, his comrades retrieved Kochanski's canister as part of Holly's plan to revive Dave from the dead. This involved bringing Lister's body to a version of Earth on which time ran backwards, where he would "un-die" and age in reverse for thirty-six years until reaching his original age of twenty-five. To soften the blow, they brought Kristine's remains to the planet as well, so the two could be together again **[N-BTL]**.

> ***NOTE:*** *Early in Series I, Lister expressed regret at never having asked Kochanski out, but subsequent episodes (most notably in Series VI and the novel* Infinity Welcomes Careful Drivers*) established that they had briefly dated. How they managed to share fewer than 175 words during their entire relationship—especially when a third of that number were spoken in the Drive Room just prior to Lister's incarceration in stasis—is a mystery.*
>
> *Kristine's rank was noted in a deleted scene from episode 1.1 ("The End"), during a mass funeral for Lister's former shipmates.* Infinity Welcomes Careful Drivers, *however, changed her rank to third console officer.*
>
> *The two novels following* Better Than Life *provided conflicting accounts of Kochanski's fate. In* Backwards, *she lived with Lister for twenty-seven years on the backwards Earth, giving birth to twins before chronologically meeting Dave for the first time—and then promptly forgetting about him, in keeping with that world's nature. In* Last Human, *meanwhile, she lived with him for the full thirty-six years, after which they rejoined the others and escaped into a GELF-controlled universe.*

- **Kochanski, Kristine Z. ("Krissie"), Navigation Officer:** An alternate-reality Kochanski who was educated at cadet school and later served aboard *Red Dwarf.* Rimmer joked that some of her strengths included being able to stay awake during operas and knowing her cheeses **[T-SER7.3]**.

  This Kochanski's parents were extremely wealthy **[T-SER7.4]**. Her father was an archaeologist, while her mother worked in advertising **[T-SER7.4(d)]**. She had a brother named Moose, who often held her lipstick for ransom, knowing she was too vain to go out without it **[T-SER7.4(e)]**. She also had a pony named Trumper **[T-SER7.4]**.

  Kristine grew up in the Gorbals, in Glasgow, and attended cyberschool for eleven years **[T-SER7.4]**, where she learned from computer-generated recreations of Charles Dickens, Disraeli Benjamin, Genghis Khan and William Shakespeare, as well as other instructors named Miss Brody and Mr. Chips. After leaving cyberschool, Kochanski had difficulty adjusting to the real world, and lashed out by turning retro-punk **[T-SER7.4(e)]** and snogging members of the Hell's Angels **[T-SER7.4(d)]**.

  While attending cadet school, Kochanski was hit by a drunk

KRYTEN 2X4B-523P

truck driver. The accident ruptured her spleen and caused the driver to lose his license. Fearful of being disliked, she drove the driver around for a full year **[T-SER7(b)]**.

In her dimension, she covered for Lister and took the blame for bringing a pregnant cat named Frankenstein aboard *Red Dwarf*, causing her to be put into stasis and thus survive the cadmium II disaster instead of him. When a hyperway formed between her reality and the prime universe, she traversed the doorway between dimensions and requested that Lister make a "contribution" to a self-gamete-mixing *in vitro* tube so she could have a baby, since her Dave was a hologram. When the prime Lister noticed an Ouroboros symbol on a crate of supplies brought over from Kristine's ship, he realized the embryo in the *in vitro* tube was his own genetic material, and that she was his mother.

When a GELF attack severed the hyperway, the alternate Kochanski was unable to return to her dimension. She and Lister subsequently produced a test-tube child, whom Dave brought back in time to The Aigburth Arms pub in Liverpool, so that he could be found under a grav-pool table and begin the cycle of his life. She then continued to travel with the crew aboard *Starbug 1* **[T-SER7.3]**.

After Kryten's nanobots rebuilt *Red Dwarf*, Captain Hollister arrested Kochanski and her new shipmates, charging them with using the crew's personal files for their own purposes. Hollister ordered them taken to the Tank, a penal section on Floor 13, where they were incarcerated for several months **[T-SER8.3]**. When a chameleonic microbe began dissolving the mining ship, Kochanski and her comrades escaped into a mirror universe **[T-SER8.8]**, only to return sometime later **[T-SER10.6]**.

Over time, Kristine grew increasingly troubled by Lister's apathy toward life, and she eventually left *Red Dwarf* aboard a *Blue Midget* shuttle. To spare Lister's feelings, Kryten reported that she had died during an airlock accident **[T-SER9.3]**.

> ***NOTE:*** *The incident involving the drunk driver was noted in a Series VII Easter egg of Cloë Annett's audition tape, featuring dialog cut from episode 7.3 ("Ouroboros").*

- **Kochanski, Kristopher:** A male version of the alternate reality's Kristine Kochanski, from a dimension in which the sexes were reversed. Kristopher and his crew encountered Deb Lister and Arlene Rimmer when their dimensions were temporarily connected, causing him to become permanently stranded in their universe **[W-OFF]**.

- **Kochanski, Moose:** The brother of a Kristine Kochanski from an alternate universe. Moose often held Kristine's lipstick for ransom, knowing she was too vain to go out without it **[T-SER7.4(e)]**.

> ***NOTE:*** *"Moose" was the nickname of Peter Morgan,* Red Dwarf's *director of photography.*

- **Kodak:** An American company specializing in imaging and photographic equipment and materials **[RL]**. Kodak produced the optical units on Karstares, a character on the television soap opera *Androids* **[M-SMG2.5(c5)]**.

- **Koestler, Arthur:** A twentieth-century author and journalist who wrote a book, *The Roots of Coincidence,* examining a possible link between parapsychology and quantum mechanics, and its effects on coincidences **[RL]**. Kryten referenced the author while explaining to Cat the possible side effects of tampering with a quantum rod's crystals. Cat was coincidentally holding a copy of Koestler's book at the time—which later helped the crew locate the position of the Erroneous Reasoning Research Academy **[T-SER10.4]**.

- **Koestler, Doctor:** A scientist employed at the company that produced quantum rods for Space Corps vessels. Individuals affected by the synchronical effects of a rod were instructed to call the firm's help line and ask for Doctor Koestler **[W-OFF]**.

> ***NOTE:*** *This individual was presumably named after Arthur Koestler.*

- **Kojak, Theo, Lieutenant:** A fictional police detective on the American television series *Kojak,* portrayed by Telly Savalas **[RL]**. Kojak was one of Jake Bullet's childhood cop heroes **[M-SMG1.11(c4)]**.

- **Kookie Kola:** A twenty-second-century soft drink company whose mascot, Kookie Kola Bear, was also its owner. Mr. Flibble, jealous of Kookie Kola Bear's marketing success, attacked the icon at the Kookie Kola Bear Parade, ripping the bear's head off. He then took over the business and renamed it Flibble Co. **[M-SMG2.3(c3)]**. Advertisements bearing the company's old mascot lined some of *Red Dwarf*'s corridors **[N-BTL]**.

- **Kookie Kola Bear:** The mascot and owner of soft-drink company Kookie Kola. The anthropomorphic teddy bear was near-universally loved, but Mr. Flibble was jealous of his marketing success. During a Kookie Kola Bear Parade, Mr. Flibble killed the mascot's gnome-like bodyguards and ripped Kookie Kola Bear's head off, then assumed control of his business, renaming it Flibble Co. **[M-SMG2.3(c3)]**.

- **Kookie Kola Bear Day:** A holiday honoring the owner and mascot of soft-drink company Kookie Kola. The Kookie Kola Bear Parade marked this special day **[M-SMG2.3(c3)]**.

- ***Kookie Kola Bear News*:** A television news program sponsored by Kookie Kola. One of its reporters, Ms. Fax, requested an exclusive interview with Mr. Flibble after his hostile takeover of the company **[M-SMG2.3(c3)]**.

- **Kookie Kola Bear Parade:** An event organized for Kookie Kola Bear Day, honoring Kookie Kola's owner and mascot. Mr. Flibble disrupted the parade one year by killing the bear and his bodyguards **[M-SMG2.3(c3)]**.

- **Kortney:** Kryten's persona in the universe known as Alternative 6829/B. Kortney was an android association football referee **[M-SMG1.8(c4)]**.

- **Krazy:** A burly warrior of the Elite, a Cat tribe that evolved aboard *Red Dwarf* while Lister was in stasis. During the Cat People's two-thousand-year Holy Wars, the Elite sent three warriors—Fritz, Krazy and Juma—forward in time via an obelisk, to retrieve their god (Lister) in the hope that he could end the conflict **[M-SMG2.1(c1)]**.

  After the three retrieved Lister and brought him to the Elite's High Tower, Kadok, the Clisterists' leader, tried to take Dave hostage to elevate his own position within the order. When the arrival of Lister's shipmates interrupted the kidnapping, Kadok fled the scene but ran into Krazy, who threw him off a High Tower balcony **[M-SMG2.3(c1)]**.

  ***NOTE:** Krazy was named after* Krazy Kat, *an American newspaper comic strip by cartoonist George Herriman.*

- **Kremlin Kate:** A nickname that Rimmer called Katerina Bartikovsky's hologram, referencing her Russian accent **[T-SER9.2]**.

- **Krispee Krunchies:** One of Lister's favorite snack foods. A horde of mutated Space Monkeys consumed *Red Dwarf*'s entire supply **[M-SMG1.13(c2)]**.

- **Krispies:** One of Cat's favorite foods. Lister offered Cat some Krispies after bringing him to his quarters for the first time. Unaware of Cat's civilized eating habits, he placed the bowl on the floor, inadvertently offending his new friend **[T-SER1.1]**.

  ***NOTE:** This presumably referenced Friskies' Crispies cat treats.*

- **Krissie:** A nickname that Lister called Kochanski during their brief romance **[N-INF]**.

- **Kristen:** A name that Kryten called himself while agitated about being classified as a woman in the nanobot-rebuilt *Red Dwarf*'s brig **[T-SER8.2(d)]**.

- **Kristian:** The backup artificial-intelligence system aboard Justice World. Kristian was activated after the station's primary computer failed to detect the guilt of an inmate who had stolen a pudding cup. The newly activated AI, unable to properly control the station, caused it to crash into a desert planet **[W-AIT]**.

- **Kritter:** A hillbilly cyborg version of Kryten in a universe ravaged by Ace "Blackheart" Rimmer, a cyborg who had killed Kritter's sweetheart, Hollentine. While visiting this reality, another Ace Rimmer was mistaken for Blackheart by Darren (a hillbilly Lister), Dorrie (a humanoid who evolved from a dormouse) and Kritter, who tore his own arm off to avoid being further harmed by the tyrant. At the time, he was also missing a leg. Blackheart later shot his other leg off, before Dorrie killed the tyrant **[M-SMG1.14(c5)]**.

- **Kryten:** A female version of Kryten 2X4B-523P, from a dimension in which the sexes were reversed. Arlene Rimmer and Deb Lister brought her aboard *Red Dwarf*, where she fell in love with a Pleasure GELF named Cameron **[W-OFF]**.

  ***NOTE:** A comic in* Smegazine *issue 1.5 claimed Kryten's female analog was named Daizee.*

- **Kryten:** An alternate version of Kryten 2X4B-523P who existed after the Inquisitor erased the original mechanoid from history. While working to restore their own timeline, the original Lister and Kryten met their replacements, both of whom the Inquisitor killed during his pursuit of the prime crew **[T-SER5.2]**.

- **Kryten:** A version of Kryten 2X4B-523P from a dimension in which Kochanski covered for Lister by taking the blame for bringing Frankenstein aboard *Red Dwarf* **[T-SER7.3]**. This version of Kryten was Ganymede Gold in color, instead of Butler Black **[G-SOR]**.

- **Kryten:** A version of Kryten 2X4B-523P from a dimension in which he and Rimmer never entered an addictive version of *Better Than Life* to save Lister and Cat. In this reality, Lister and Cat perished from malnutrition, leaving Kryten and Rimmer alone, until another universe's Lister and Cat arrived in Ace Rimmer's dimension-hopping spaceship **[N-BCK]**.

- **Kryten:** A one-armed, alternate-reality version of Kryten 2X4B-523P, whom the prime crew found deactivated aboard a *Starbug* shuttle while traversing the Omni-zone. That universe's Lister had killed the mechanoid and their shipmates, and had taken Kryten's arm, which held the coordinates of an ancient GELF ship containing the genome of DNA (G.O.D.) **[N-LST]**.

- **Kryten:** A character in the Total Immersion video game *Red Dwarf*, in a fascist Earth society in an alternate universe. In that reality, cybernetic traffic cop Jake Bullet portrayed Kryten in the game for four years, until being released after the group scored a mere four percent **[M-SMG2.1(c4)]**. The next competitor was far more intelligent and scored much higher **[M-SMG2.4(c4)]**, playing the character as an augmented man-servant, rather than merely as a mechanoid **[M-SMG2.5(c4)]**.

- **Kryten:** A mechanoid aboard a possible alternate *Red Dwarf*. His companions included Ben Ellis, a hologram named Terry, a sentient rodent called Rat and the ship's artificial-intelligence computer, Kate **[G-RPG]**.

- **Kryten:** A duplicate of Kryten created during a triplicator accident that destroyed *Red Dwarf* but produced two copies: A "high" version displaying the best aspects of the ship and its crew, and a "low" version manifesting the worst. The "low" Kryten was a filthy, malfunctioning mechanoid with sociopathic tendencies.

  This version and his shipmates attacked the crews of the original and "high" ships after luring them to the "low" vessel. Wanting the "high" ship for their own use, the ruffians kidnapped Lister, attached a spinal implant to his neck and forced him to murder the "high" Lister and Rimmer, before sending him after his own crew. However, Dave's friends incapacitated him and used the triplicator to reform the original *Red Dwarf*, dematerializing the "low" Kryten in the process **[T-SER5.5]**.

- **Kryten, Brother:** A duplicate of Kryten created during a triplicator accident that destroyed *Red Dwarf* but produced two copies: A "high" version displaying the best aspects of the ship and its crew, and a "low" version manifesting the worst. Brother Kryten wore robes and sandals, and possessed knowledge of poetry, art and metaphysics. The enlightened android was killed by the crew's "low" counterparts after boarding their ship in response to a distress call **[T-SER5.5]**.

- **Kryten 2X4B-523P:** A 4000 Series (Series III) sanitation droid built by Diva-Droid International **[T-SER3.6]** in 2340 **[T-SER5.3]**. He was created by Professor Mamet, a Diva-Droid employee who had been engaged to John Warburton until he jilted her at the altar. As revenge, Mamet designed the Kryten series to mimic her ex-fiancé—a pompous, ridiculous-looking, overbearing, short-tempered buffoon—complete with all of his shortcomings.

  Mamet installed a negadrive in the series that stored negative emotions, occasionally blowing apart the mechanoid's head when becoming full, thereby emulating Warburton's tendency to lose his head when angry **[T-SER7.6]**. As a safety precaution, she wrote certain protocols into Kryten's programming, including the inability to harm her in any way, as well as a mandate to obey her orders at all times, regardless of whether they conflicted with other programming **[T-SER6.1]**.

  Kryten initially served aboard the SS *Augustus,* but outlived the crew and was left stranded. He was rescued by the *Nova 5*, but accidentally killed his new masters, except for three female crewmembers, whom he cared for until they, too, finally passed away **[T-SER7.3]**. Kryten had accidentally killed the crew by cleaning *Nova 5*'s computers with soapy water, thereby creating a catastrophic malfunction that caused the ship to crash into a barren planetoid **[N-INF]**.

  Many years later, the *Red Dwarf* crew picked up *Nova 5*'s distress beacon and attempted to rescue the women. Despite Kryten's claim that there were survivors of the crash, Lister's team soon learned that the women had been dead for centuries—and Kryten, programmed only to serve, had failed to notice.

  Forced to acknowledge the truth, Kryten left the marooned *Nova 5* behind and joined the *Red Dwarf* crew. But after a short stay, he borrowed Lister's space bike and headed out to start a new life **[T-SER2.1]**. Months later, the crew found him in pieces on an asteroid, where the mechanoid had crashed. Lister rebuilt Kryten, but was unable to restore the android's original personality programming. Thereafter, Kryten had a different face, voice and personality **[T-SER3.1]**.

Kryten always admired the human ability to lie, cheat and be offensive—qualities he lacked due to his programming. To remedy this, he enlisted help from Lister, who attempted to break the droid free of his programming by urging him to call fruits by different names, and to insult Rimmer **[T-SER4.1]**.

Kryten never liked his middle name (2X4B), which he considered "jerky" **[T-SER3.6]**. Like most androids, he believed in Silicon Heaven, the final resting place of all electronics that served their masters **[T-SER3.6]**. Kryten's registration code aboard *Red Dwarf* was "Additional 001" **[T-SER5.2]**. His serial number was 2X4C **[T-SER7.6]** and his favorite color was chrome silver **[M-SMG1.1(a)]**. He was fitted with nanobots, microscopic robots designed to automatically repair any damaged system **[T-SER7.8]**.

Like all Series III mechanoids, Kryten was fitted with a shutdown chip, which was activated upon the impending arrival of his replacement, Hudzen 10. Despite Kryten's acceptance of his fate, the crew were unwilling to let him be deactivated, and fought Hudzen as he attempted to shut down their comrade. Hudzen was defeated when Kryten postulated that Silicon Heaven did not exist—a concept he knew to be false, but one which Hudzen struggled to understand, causing a metaphysical dichotomy that shut him down instead **[T-SER3.6]**.

Kryten briefly found love when he rescued Camille, a pleasure GELF disguised as a mechanoid, from a crashed vessel. Their relationship was cut short, however, when Camille's husband, a fellow blob named Hector, arrived to take her back. Using his newly acquired lying ability, Kryten convinced Camille to return to Hector, at the expense of his own happiness, emulating the ending of the film *Casablanca* **[T-SER4.1]**.

The crew once came across a derelict vessel containing a machine that altered the DNA of living creatures. As Kryten examined the device, Cat accidentally trapped him within its beam. Initially unconcerned due to his lack of organic material, Kryten belatedly remembered that his brain was partly organic, which enabled the machine to transform him into a human male. His joy at this development was short-lived, however, as he began experiencing the shortcomings of having a human body, such as the lack of a zoom function in his eyes, non-functioning nipples and repulsive genitalia. Finally, after arguing with his spare heads, he chose to reverse the transformation and become a mechanoid once more **[T-SER4.2]**.

Kryten considered mechanoids sharing the same serial number—and, therefore, the same motherboard—to be his brothers. This included Able, another 4000 Series mechanoid whom the crew encountered **[T-SER7.6]**.

During a scavenger run on an ocean planet, Kryten's nanobots abandoned him and stole *Red Dwarf*, creating a microscopic version of the ship and converting the remaining material into a small planetoid. Upon discovering their ploy, the crew forced the nanobots to rebuild the vessel **[T-SER7.8]**. But when they boarded the reconstructed ship, they discovered that the full *Red Dwarf* compliment had been revived as well. The group were summarily arrested and sentenced to the brig **[T-SER8.3]**. During his physical, Kryten was classified as a woman due to his lack of genitalia—a designation that greatly upset him **[T-SER8.2]**. In fact, he went so far as to create a mechanical penis named Archie, which quickly escaped **[T-SER8.7]**.

The mechanoid once became quantum-entangled with Cat after experimenting on *Trojan*'s quantum rod. This enabled the pair to speak in synchronicity, and allowed their combined emotions to manifest into several cases of extreme coincidence **[T-SER10.4]**.

> ***NOTE:*** *The novel* Last Human *erroneously called Kryten a 3000 Series mechanoid. According to a DVD collectible booklet, Kryten was named after Kenneth More's character in the film* The Admirable Crichton. *The mechanoid's name was spelled "Kryton" in the DVD captions for the Czech Republic version of the series.*

- **Kryten 2XB-517P:** A mechanoid who served aboard the American mining ship *Red Dwarf* in an alternate dimension. He arrived shortly before an accident killed the entire crew except for Lister, and the two became fast friends **[T-USA1]**.

  > ***NOTE:*** *According to the first-draft script of the American* Red Dwarf *pilot, this Kryten was Captain Tau's personal Butler Droid.*

- **Krytenski, Kryten, Flight Coordinator:** A pseudonym that Kryten used aboard the *Trojan* while helping Rimmer

PREFIX
RL: Real life

T-: Television Episodes
SER: Television series
IDW: "Identity Within"
USA1: Unaired U.S. pilot
USA2: Unaired U.S. demo

R-: *The Bodysnatcher Collection*
SER: Remastered episodes
BOD: "Bodysnatcher"
DAD: "Dad"
FTH: "Lister's Father"
INF: "Infinity Patrol"
END: "The End" (original assembly)

N-: Novels
INF: *Infinity Welcomes Careful Drivers*
BTL: *Better Than Life*
LST: *Last Human*

BCK: *Backwards*
OMN: *Red Dwarf Omnibus*

M-: Magazines
SMG: *Smegazine*

W-: Websites
OFF: Official website
NAN: *Prelude to Nanarchy*
AND: *Androids*
DIV: Diva-Droid
DIB: Duane Dibbley

CRP: Crapola
GEN: Geneticon
LSR: Leisure World Intl.
JMC: Jupiter Mining Corporation
AIT: *A.I. Today*
HOL: HoloPoint

G-: Roleplaying Game
RPG: *Core Rulebook*
BIT: *A.I. Screen Extra Bits* booklet
SOR: *Series Sourcebook*
OTH: Other RPG material

impersonate a Space Corps Captain in order to impress his half-brother, Howard Rimmer **[T-SER10.1]**.

- ***Kryten Series III Mechanoid Owners Manual*:** A booklet that Diva-Droid International supplied to owners of Kryten Series III mechanoids. The cover included Diva-Droid's logo and the words "For Human Eyes Only." Lister studied the manual to find a loophole that would prevent Kryten's shutdown chip from activating **[T-SER3.6]**.

- **Krytie TV:** A broadcasting station that Kryten created after being reprogrammed by inmates in the Tank. When Oswald "Kill Krazy" Blenkinsop learned that Kryten showered with the female inmates, he kidnapped the mechanoid and reprogrammed him to record and transmit the next shower session as a live, pay-per-view event. Kryten transmitted a small portion of the shower during movie night, interrupting a showing of *Attack of the Giant Savage Completely Invisible Aliens*, then asked for donations to continue the broadcast, using prisoners donning Krytie TV T-shirts to collect proceeds.

  When Lister exposed the scheme to the women, Kryten shifted the focus to him, tricking Lister into trashing Warden Ackerman's quarters by telling him the room belonged to Kochanski's ex-boyfriend, Tim. He then revealed the ruse and broadcast footage of the panicked Lister rushing to clean the quarters before the warden returned **[T-SER8.5]**.

  Other scheduled broadcasts included *Ready Steady Stab; Boxing—Psychoweight Championship; How Clean Is Your Cell?; Oops, That's Groovy Channel 27 News!; Canary Squad;* and *Androids*. It also featured the film *Revenge of the Surfboarding Killer Bikini Vampire Girls*, as well as a Mugs Murphy marathon **[X-CAL]**.

- **Kryton:** *See* Kryten 2X4B-523P

- **Kryty:** A semi-affectionate nickname that Rimmer called Kryten **[T-SER7.1(e)]**.

- **K-Tel Nose Hair Trimmer:** A grooming device designed to trim the hair in one's nasal passages. In a mission update, Holly remarked that the crew were finally working together like a well-oiled machine—but added that the machine was a K-Tel Nose Hair Trimmer **[B-LOG]**.

- **Kublouski:** A nickname that Lister jokingly called Kochanski after emerging from suspended animation after hundreds of years, when she asked if he remembered who she was **[N-LST]**.

- **Ku Klux Klan (KKK):** A white-supremacist hate group that formed in 1865 in response to the United States' Emancipation Proclamation. Three distinct, unconnected organizations arose from that initial formation, each using the same name **[RL]**.

  A waxdroid replica of a Klansman was created for the Waxworld theme park. Left on their own for millions of years, the waxdroids attained sentience and became embroiled in a park-wide resource war between Villain World (to which the KKK waxdroid belonged) and Hero World. During this war, the *Red Dwarf* crew transported to the planet using a Matter Paddle, with Lister and Cat materializing in Villain territory, while Rimmer and Kryten landed in Hero territory.

  Rimmer found the heroes' army lacking and took command, working many of the pacifistic waxdroids to death before ordering a frontal attack on the enemy's compound across a minefield. This wiped out all remaining waxdroids, including the Klansman, who was shot by the Queen Victoria droid **[T-SER4.6]**.

  > ***NOTE:** Although the Ku Klux Klan was not specifically mentioned in the episode, the waxdroid wore its distinctive white robe and hood.*

- **"Kumbaya":** A popular 1930s spiritual song typically sung around campfires, which enjoyed a boost during the folk revival period of the 1960s **[RL]**. Rimmer suggested the *Starbug 1* crew sing "Kumbaya" while on a fishing holiday **[T-SER4.5]**. While trashing Warden Ackerman's quarters, Lister planted a Christian rock CD, containing a version of "Kumbaya," in the warden's player **[T-SER8.5]**.

- **Kylie:** A hypothetical name that Kryten mentioned while trying to persuade Rimmer to escape *Red Dwarf* with the *Starbug 1* crew. When Cat balked at the idea of bringing Arnold along, Kryten reminded him that Rimmer knew the ship's access codes. Without him, Kryten said, their chance of escaping was as good as that of meeting an interesting hairdresser named Kylie **[T-SER8.3]**.

APPENDIX I:

Red Dwarf *Episode Guide*

by Rich Handley and Paul C. Giachetti

"I saw the whole thing—all three terrible hours of it. It was awful."

–Lister, "Krytie TV"

The following guide details the many stories comprising the *Red Dwarf* mythos that were examined during the writing of this lexicon, including the television series, novels, *Smegazines* and more. Websites, behind-the-scenes books, *Red Dwarf—The Roleplaying Game*, and unofficial or fan-made tales are not listed here.

Key:
A = Artist
D = Director
L = Letterer
P = Publication date
T = Televised airdate
W = Writer

Television Episodes

SERIES I

Episode 1 (T-SER1.1)
"The End"
W: Rob Grant and Doug Naylor; D: Ed Bye; T: Feb. 15, 1988
Dave Lister, the lowest-ranking crewman aboard the mining vessel *Red Dwarf*, is sentenced to eighteen months in suspended animation for bringing aboard an unquarantined pregnant cat. While he's in stasis, a radiation accident kills everyone on the ship. Once the danger has subsided, Lister awakens three million years in the future, his only companions Holly, the ship's eccentric artificial intelligence; a hologram of his much-disliked bunkmate, Arnold Rimmer; and Cat, a member of a humanoid species that evolved from Lister's pet.

Episode 2 (T-SER1.2)
"Future Echoes"
W: Rob Grant and Doug Naylor; D: Ed Bye; T: Feb. 22, 1988
As *Red Dwarf* breaches light speed, the crew experiences visions of their own futures. Rimmer witnesses what appears to be Lister blowing up in a Drive Room accident, while Lister meets an older version of himself and learns that he will eventually have twin sons.

Episode 3 (T-SER1.3)
"Balance of Power"
W: Rob Grant and Doug Naylor; D: Ed Bye; T: Feb. 29, 1988
When Rimmer refuses to let Lister temporarily deactivate him so he can go on a date with a hologram of his late love interest, Kristine Kochanski, Lister vows to pass the Chef's Exam so that he will out-rank Rimmer and be able to make him follow orders. Despite Rimmer's attempts to dissuade him, Lister takes the test—and seemingly passes.

Episode 4 (T-SER1.4)
"Waiting for God"
W: Rob Grant and Doug Naylor; D: Ed Bye; T: March 7, 1988
The *Red Dwarf* comes across one of its own ejected garbage pods, which Rimmer mistakes for an alien capsule. Obsessed with meeting its occupant, whom he hopes can give him a new living body, Arnold dubs the species the Quagaars. Lister, meanwhile, meets the only other member of Cat's species still onboard: an aging priest who has lost his faith in the Cat People's god, Cloister the Stupid—Lister himself.

Episode 5 (T-SER1.5)
"Confidence and Paranoia"
W: Rob Grant and Doug Naylor; D: Ed Bye; T: March 14, 1988
A mutated form of pneumonia causes Lister's hallucinations to become reality. These include a rain of herring in his quarters, the spontaneous combustion of the Mayor of Warsaw, and the physical manifestation of his inner self, in the forms of a meek, depressed man named Paranoia, and a loud, flashy individual called Confidence.

Episode 6 (T-SER1.6)
"Me^2"
W: Rob Grant and Doug Naylor; D: Ed Bye; T: March 21, 1988
Rimmer creates an identical hologrammic duplicate and moves out of Lister's quarters to share a cabin with his ideal companion—

himself. The two Rimmers, however, cannot get along with each other, and decide that only one must be allowed to stay aboard ship. Lister, meanwhile, investigates the meaning of Arnold's final words, "gazpacho soup."

SERIES II

Episode 7 (T-SER2.1)
"Kryten"
W: Rob Grant and Doug Naylor; D: Ed Bye; T: Sept. 6, 1988
Holly receives a distress call from the *Nova 5*, transmitted by its mechanoid servant, Kryten. Upon learning that the ship contains three attractive female crewmembers, Lister, Rimmer and Cat mount a rescue, prepared for romance—but instead find three skeletal corpses. The men bring Kryten aboard *Red Dwarf*, where Rimmer makes the mechanoid his personal slave until Lister teaches him how to rebel.

Episode 8 (T-SER2.2)
"Better Than Life"
W: Rob Grant and Doug Naylor; D: Ed Bye; T: Sept. 13, 1988
A post pod arrives, bringing mail from three million years past. Among the packages are a letter announcing the death of Rimmer's father (who never showed Arnold respect or approval) and a total-immersion video game, *Better Than Life*, which the crew decide to play. The experience is exhilarating, providing all the food, sex, fun and thrills they could desire—until Rimmer's self-sabotaging mind puts them all in peril.

Episode 9 (T-SER2.3)
"Thanks for the Memory"
W: Rob Grant and Doug Naylor; D: Ed Bye; T: Sept. 20, 1988
After celebrating his deathday, a drunken Rimmer admits he's only had sex once, so Lister downloads memories of an ex-girlfriend, Lise Yates, into his roommate's mind as a gift. Devastated to later learn that his relationship with Yates was implanted, Arnold orders Holly to erase all their memories and all files documenting the event. Confused by their resultant memory gap, however—and by Cat's and Lister's unexplained broken legs—the crew investigate what happened.

Episode 10 (T-SER2.4)
"Stasis Leak"
W: Rob Grant and Doug Naylor; D: Ed Bye; T: Sept. 27, 1988
A stasis leak opens a gateway three million years into the past, enabling Lister, Rimmer and Cat to travel back to *Red Dwarf*, to a time shortly before the crew's deaths. While Rimmer tries unsuccessfully to convince his non-hologrammic self to go into stasis, Lister and Cat visit Kochanski—only to find that she has married a future version of Lister.

Episode 11 (T-SER2.5)
"Queeg"
W: Rob Grant and Doug Naylor; D: Ed Bye; T: Oct. 4, 1988
Red Dwarf's backup computer, Queeg 500, activates after Holly's latest blunder puts Lister's life at risk. Taking control of the ship, Queeg represents everything Holly is not: smart, effective and brutally strict. But after a short time with the new computer, the crew urge Holly to fight for his old position. Queeg accepts the challenge, choosing chess as their battleground. Holly loses and is seemingly erased, then reveals it was all a prank—feeling unappreciated, he had created Queeg to make the crew appreciate him more.

Episode 12 (T-SER2.6)
"Parallel Universe"
W: Rob Grant and Doug Naylor; D: Ed Bye; T: Oct. 11, 1988
Holly invents a new drive to bring the *Red Dwarf* back to Earth, but it instead transports the crew to an alternate universe. There, Lister and Rimmer meet their female analogs, with all the same attitudes and habits, while Cat discovers that his counterpart is an unhygienic male dog, and Holly meets a female version of himself named Hilly. After having sex with his female opposite, Lister learns that men have the babies in this universe—and that *Red Dwarf* is about to get a little more crowded.

SERIES III

Episode 13 (T-SER3.1)
"Backwards"
W: Rob Grant and Doug Naylor; D: Ed Bye; T: Nov. 14, 1989
Lister's sons are born, rapid-age and are taken to live with their mother; Kryten is found crashed on an asteroid and rebuilt; and Holly undergoes a head sex change, assuming Hilly's voice and face. Passing through a time hole in space, the crew discovers a future Earth on which time moves in reverse. There, Kryten and Rimmer become a popular stage act for their ability to do things in forward time, and decide to stay—until a backwards barroom brawl gets them blacklisted.

Episode 14 (T-SER3.2)
"Marooned"
W: Rob Grant and Doug Naylor; D: Ed Bye; T: Nov. 21, 1989
When Holly spots five black holes in *Red Dwarf*'s flight path, the crew must abandon ship. Lister and Rimmer end up marooned on an arctic world. Nearly freezing to death, Lister fights with

Rimmer over which items to burn to keep him alive; Dave chooses Arnold's books, soldiers and wooden chest, while the hologram insists on burning Lister's guitar instead. To Rimmer's amazement, Lister seemingly makes the noble sacrifice, though he has actually just cut a guitar-shaped piece of the wooden chest.

Episode 15 (T-SER3.3)
"Polymorph"
W: Rob Grant and Doug Naylor; D: Ed Bye; T: Nov. 28, 1989
The mining ship is visited by a polymorph—a genetic mutant bred as an unstoppable warrior, able to assume any shape and sustained by sucking out others' negative emotions. Posing as Lister's kebab dinner, Rimmer's mother and other forms, the creature ingests Lister's fear, Cat's vanity, Kryten's guilt and Rimmer's anger, greatly altering their personalities until the mutant is finally destroyed.

Episode 16 (T-SER3.4)
"Bodyswap"
W: Rob Grant and Doug Naylor; D: Ed Bye; T: Dec. 5, 1988
When Lister realizes how out of shape he has become, Rimmer suggests they implant their minds into each other's head so Arnold can make Lister healthier via diet and exercise. Rimmer so enjoys having physical senses again, however, that he smokes and overeats, refusing to return Lister's body—which he has caused to gain weight.

Episode 17 (T-SER3.5)
"Timeslides"
W: Rob Grant and Doug Naylor; D: Ed Bye; T: Dec. 12, 1988
Mutated developing fluid causes old photographs to seemingly take on life. Realizing he can enter the worlds depicted in the photo, Lister goes back in time to make himself more successful. Rimmer tries to do the same, visiting his younger self and giving him the idea for a hugely popular invention—but another child, Fred "Thickie" Holden, steals the idea.

Episode 18 (T-SER3.6)
"The Last Day"
W: Rob Grant and Doug Naylor; D: Ed Bye; T: Dec. 19, 1988
A recorded message from Divadroid International informs Kryten that he has reached the end of his service life and will be replaced by a newer model, Hudzen 10, who has been pursuing *Red Dwarf* in order to assume Kryten's duties. The new mechanoid has gone insane after three million years in transit, however, and tries to kill the crew.

SERIES IV

Episode 19 (T-SER4.1)
"Camille"
W: Rob Grant and Doug Naylor; D: Ed Bye; T: Feb. 14, 1991
Lister tries to help Kryten grow beyond his programming by teaching him how to insult others and tell lies. This skill comes in handy when Kryten is forced to let the love of his life—an amorphous blob named Camille, genetically designed to appear to all men as their perfect fantasy woman—return to her former lover, thereby mirroring the classic ending to Lister's favorite movie, *Casablanca*.

Episode 20 (T-SER4.2)
"DNA"
W: Rob Grant and Doug Naylor; D: Ed Bye; T: Feb. 21, 1991
Red Dwarf encounters a derelict spaceship containing advanced technology, including a DNA modifier able to metamorphose organic life. When Cat plays with its controls, Lister is first transformed into a chicken, and then a hamster. In trying to help him, Kryten becomes fully human, but is ill-equipped to handle his newfound humanity. The machine also turns Dave's vindaloo into a monster composed of curry.

Episode 21 (T-SER4.3)
"Justice"
W: Rob Grant and Doug Naylor; D: Ed Bye; T: Feb. 28, 1991
The crew discover an escape pod in space, which contains either a prison guard or a deranged bio-mechanical killer, and bring it to Justice World to be opened. The penal colony's computer deems Rimmer guilty of killing *Red Dwarf*'s crew and sentences him to millennia in prison. Kryten's case in his defense—that Arnold was too inept and stupid to have possibly committed the crimes—proves successful. But the pod's occupant (a simulant) nearly prevents them from leaving.

Episode 22 (T-SER4.4)
"White Hole"
W: Rob Grant and Doug Naylor; D: Ed Bye and Paul Jackson; T: Mar. 7, 1991
When Holly's IQ is boosted to more than twelve thousand at the expense of her run-time, she switches herself off to conserve energy, leaving *Red Dwarf* adrift in space. Without Holly to guide them, the crew must stop a white hole from engulfing the ship.

Episode 23 (T-SER4.5)
"Dimension Jump"
W: Rob Grant and Doug Naylor; D: Ed Bye; T: Mar. 14, 1991
The Dwarfers meet Arnold "Ace" Rimmer, a dashing daredevil Space Corps test pilot from another dimension, assigned to travel the infinite realities and meet different versions of himself. *Red Dwarf*'s Rimmer feels inadequate by comparison, realizing that Ace is everything he could have been had he been handed a better life. Ace, meanwhile, is disgusted to see such a sniveling coward with his face and name.

Episode 24 (T-SER4.6)
"Meltdown"
W: Rob Grant and Doug Naylor; D: Ed Bye; T: Mar. 21, 1991
A prototype Matter Paddle teleports the crew to Waxworld, a planet inhabited by animated replicas of famous and fictional persons from Earth's history, who are embroiled in a senseless civil war. Fancying himself a brilliant general, Rimmer assumes leadership of one army, resulting in the death of every waxdroid—on both sides of the conflict.

SERIES V

Episode 25 (T-SER5.1)
"Holoship"
W: Rob Grant and Doug Naylor; D: Juliet May; T: Feb. 20, 1992
Red Dwarf encounters a hologrammatic ship, aboard which Rimmer has a physical presence. The holoship's crew, all holograms, engage in sex twice daily for health reasons, but frown on emotional attachments. Rimmer applies for membership, but must first challenge the position of Nirvanah Crane—with whom he has formed a romantic bond.

Episode 26 (T-SER5.2)
"The Inquisitor"
W: Rob Grant and Doug Naylor; D: Rob Grant and Doug Naylor; T: Feb. 27, 1992
The *Red Dwarf* crew is endangered by the arrival of the Inquisitor, a time-traveling simulant who judges the value of people's lives and eliminates them from the timestream if he deems them unworthy of existence. When the Inquisitor judges Lister and Kryten unworthy, they must stop him from changing history so they never existed.

Episode 27 (T-SER5.3)
"Terrorform"
W: Rob Grant and Doug Naylor; D: Juliet May; T: Mar. 5, 1992
After crashing on a psi-moon—an artificial planet that terraforms itself to match a visitor's psyche—Rimmer conjures an environment from his own self-loathing. His crewmates arrive to find him chained up, facing excruciating torture at the hands of a manifestation of his subconscious mind.

Episode 28 (T-SER5.4)
"Quarantine"
W: Rob Grant and Doug Naylor; D: Rob Grant and Doug Naylor; T: Mar. 12, 1992
Rimmer contracts a holovirus and forces Lister, Cat and Kryten into quarantine, during which Arnold—who has attained telekinesis and hex vision thanks to his illness—taunts them while going slowly insane. Donning a gingham dress and a hand puppet called Mr. Fibble, Rimmer sets out to kill his comrades after they escape.

Episode 29 (T-SER5.5)
"Demons and Angels"
W: Rob Grant and Doug Naylor; D: Juliet May, Rob Grant and Doug Naylor; T: Mar. 19, 1992
A scientific experiment goes awry, creating two versions of *Red Dwarf* and its crew: one with all of their good qualities, pristine and enlightened, and the other all of their bad qualities, decrepit and evil. Lister's gang visits both ships to investigate, encountering angelic and demonic versions of themselves, respectively.

Episode 30 (T-SER5.6)
"Back to Reality"
W: Rob Grant and Doug Naylor; D: Juliet May, Rob Grant and Doug Naylor; T: Mar. 26, 1992
Red Dwarf visits an oceanic world, the crash site of the SSS *Esperanto*, whose entire crew committed suicide thanks to the mental influence of a sea monster called a despair squid. The creature attacks the Dwarfers as well, causing them to hallucinate that they are different individuals who have been merely playing a virtual-reality game for four years.

SERIES VI

Episode 31 (T-SER6.1)
"Psirens"
W: Rob Grant and Doug Naylor; D: Andy de Emmony;
T: Oct. 7, 1993
Two centuries after the *Esperanto* incident, Lister's crew awaken aboard *Starbug 1. Red Dwarf* is missing, and they have been pursuing the ship's trail, hoping to reclaim it. *Starbug* passes through an asteroid field filled with lost spaceships, inhabited by genetically engineered life forms called Psirens that telepathically lure passing ships into the belt in order to suck out their crew's brains.

Episode 32 (T-SER6.2)
"Legion"
W: Rob Grant and Doug Naylor; D: Andy de Emmony;
T: Oct. 14, 1993
Entering a gas nebula, *Starbug* is ensnared in a tractor beam and taken to a space station, where the crew meet Legion, a sophisticated and cultured gestalt entity who wishes them to stay so he can serve them for the rest of their lives. To this end, he gives Rimmer a hard light drive, endowing him with a physical presence. Despite the temptations Legion offers, the crew opt to escape this gilded cage.

Episode 33 (T-SER6.3)
"Gunmen of the Apocalypse"
W: Rob Grant and Doug Naylor; D: Andy de Emmony;
T: Oct. 21, 1993
A battle with rogue simulants leaves *Starbug*'s computers infected with a virus and the ship locked on a collision course with a volcanic world. Kryten tries to eliminate the virus, but ends up with his subconscious mind recreating an Old West movie scenario. In an effort to rescue Kryten and save the ship, his crewmates enter his dream via an artificial-reality video game and fight the virus, which has taken the form of an outlaw gang.

Episode 34 (T-SER6.4)
"Emohawk: Polymorph II"
W: Rob Grant and Doug Naylor; D: Andy de Emmony;
T: Oct. 28, 1993
A Space Corps enforcement probe attacks *Starbug* after the crew loot several derelict vessels. Landing on an alien world inhabited by the Kinitawowi, the group are unable to escape unless they can find a vital piece of equipment. Lister marries the daughter of the GELF tribe's chief in exchange for the unit, but abandons his hideous bride when she tries to consummate the marriage. The chief sends a polymorph after the Dwarfers, which turns Rimmer into Ace Rimmer and Cat into Duane Dibbley.

Episode 35 (T-SER6.5)
"Rimmerworld"
W: Rob Grant and Doug Naylor; D: Andy de Emmony;
T: Nov. 4, 1993
When *Starbug* returns to the simulants' battleship for supplies, a surviving rogue tries to kill Lister and company. Suffering a nervous disorder, Rimmer launches himself in a terraforming pod, is caught in a wormhole and crashes on a planet. When his colleagues find him, six centuries have passed for Arnold, who has cloned thousands of duplicates of himself in the interim, creating a truly disturbing society.

Episode 36 (T-SER6.6)
"Out of Time"
W: Rob Grant and Doug Naylor; D: Andy de Emmony;
T: Nov. 11, 1993
The *Starbug* crew discover a time machine and encounter future versions of themselves—thoroughly corrupted and unlikable versions, who have spent years traveling through time via the device, enjoying the company of Adolf Hitler and other evil historical figures. Disgusted, the younger crew refuse to help their future selves, who launch an attack.

SERIES VII

Episode 37 (T-SER7.1)
"Tikka to Ride"
W: Doug Naylor; D: Ed Bye; T: Jan. 17, 1997
A paradox caused by the battle with the future crew causes *Starbug* to become larger and upgraded, but the curry supplies are spoiled. Lister and company travel back in time to Dallas, in 1963, inadvertently preventing Lee Harvey Oswald from assassinating John F. Kennedy. When this results in a dystopian future in which Kennedy is a disgraced convict, the crew go back in time again and convince JFK to fix their error and restore his legacy by becoming a second shooter on the grassy knoll—and assassinating himself.

Episode 38 (T-SER7.2)
"Stoke Me a Clipper"
W: Paul Alexander and Doug Naylor; D: Ed Bye; T: Jan. 24, 1997
Mortally wounded while saving Princess Bonjella from other-dimensional Nazis, Ace Rimmer returns, hoping to convince *Red Dwarf*'s Rimmer to replace him in the role of dashing hero. Ace reveals that he was just the latest in a long line of Ace

Rimmers—and that he, too, is a hard light hologram. Training Arnold to be more courageous, Ace passes on the mantle as he dies, and Rimmer agrees to take up his cause.

Episode 39 (T-SER7.3)
"Ouroboros"
W: Doug Naylor; D: Ed Bye; T: Jan. 31, 1997
Lister, Cat and Kryten find a tear in the fabric of space leading to another dimension, in which they encounter an alternate (and different-looking) version of Kristine Kochanski. The rift's instability strands Kristine on *Starbug*, making her a reluctant member of the crew. In the process, Lister learns the truth about his parentage: Due to a time-travel paradox, he was his own father, and Kochanski his mother.

Episode 40 (T-SER7.4)
"Duct Soup"
W: Doug Naylor; D: Ed Bye; T: Feb. 7, 1997
Kryten, uncomfortable with having to share Lister's attentions with the beautiful Kochanski, acts jealous and fussy, worried that Dave will like her more because of her female anatomy. When *Starbug* loses its primary power, the crew climb into the ship's ventilation ducts—which poses a problem for claustrophobic Lister.

Episode 41 (T-SER7.5)
"Blue"
W: Kim Fuller and Doug Naylor; D: Ed Bye; T: Feb. 14, 1997
The Dwarfers become bored and restless while traversing an uninteresting area of space. With little to do but think, Lister discovers to his horror that he misses Rimmer—to the extent that he even has erotic dreams involving the hologram's return. To help him regain perspective, Kryten creates an amusement-park ride, *The Rimmer Experience*, based on unflattering and untruthful accounts of his crewmates that Arnold had written in his diaries, in order to remind Lister of Rimmer's unlikability.

Episode 42 (T-SER7.6)
"Beyond a Joke"
W: Robert Llewellyn and Doug Naylor; D: Ed Bye; T: Feb. 21, 1997
Kryten's head explodes due to a build-up of negative thoughts—and his spare heads suffer the same fate. When *Starbug* encounters a derelict vessel, a rogue simulant kidnaps Kryten and orders a drug-addicted droid named Able to repair him. The two mechanoids bond and make their escape, but not before Kryten learns a humiliating secret about his creation: He was built as a practical joke, to mock his creator's ex-lover.

Episode 43 (T-SER7.7)
"Epideme"
W: Paul Alexander and Doug Naylor; D: Ed Bye; T: Feb. 28, 1997
Aboard a frozen supply ship, the *Leviathan*, Lister and company find a lone survivor: *Red Dwarf*'s ex-crewmate, Caroline Carmen. Now a zombie, Caroline infects Lister with the Epideme virus—an intelligent, self-aware organism that speaks like a Las Vegas nightclub announcer. The crew amputate Lister's arm, in which Epideme has located itself, but the virus survives. Finally, Kochanski tricks the virus into transferring itself to Carmen's zombified arm, then destroys it, leaving Lister safe—but one-armed.

Episode 44 (T-SER7.8)
"Nanarchy"
W: Paul Alexander, James Hendrie and Doug Naylor; D: Ed Bye; T: Mar. 7, 1997
Kryten searches for his lost nanobots in the hope of rebuilding Lister's severed arm. He finds them exploring Lister's laundry basket, and learns that they were responsible for stealing and remolecularizing *Red Dwarf*. Chastising the nanobots, Kryten orders them to repair Dave's arm and rebuild the missing ship. The 'bots comply, but the resurrected *Red Dwarf* is not quite the same as before.

SERIES VIII

Episode 45 (T-SER8.1)
"Back in the Red, Part I"
W: Doug Naylor; D: Ed Bye; T: Feb. 18, 1999
Lister's gang learn that the nanobots have rebuilt *Red Dwarf* from its original design specs, before budget cuts were made, resulting in a much-improved version of the ship. What's more, the 'bots have revived the deceased crew, who arrest Lister's group for damaging the *Starbug*. Lister urges the resurrected Rimmer to help him escape so he can find the nanobots and corroborate his defense, and Rimmer agrees on one condition: that Lister help him earn a promotion.

Episode 46 (T-SER8.2)
"Back in the Red, Part II"
W: Doug Naylor; D: Ed Bye; T: Feb. 25, 1999
Red Dwarf's resurrected captain, Frank Hollister, orders Lister, Cat and Kochanski to stand trial. Reprogrammed to factory settings, Kryten no longer remembers them. Lister tells Rimmer about confidential crew files stored on a disc among *Starbug*'s wreckage, which could help him earn his longed-for promotion. Rimmer locates the disc, along with vials of luck and sexual magnetism virus, and decides to use them to his advantage.

Episode 47 (T-SER8.3)
"Back in the Red, Part III"
W: Doug Naylor; D: Ed Bye; T: Mar. 4, 1999
Using the sexual magnetism virus, Rimmer becomes the object of every woman's desire, and in a single evening has sex with numerous partners. The confidential reports enable him to get on Hollister's good side, which he believes will help him go far, career-wise. However, Rimmer, like Lister and his comrades, are actually in an artificial-reality suite, being observed by Hollister (who had suspected Arnold all along) as evidence for their trial. At the conclusion of the virtual scenario, Hollister sentences the group to two years in the ship's secret brig on Floor 13, known as the Tank.

Episode 48 (T-SER8.4)
"Cassandra"
W: Doug Naylor; D: Ed Bye; T: Mar. 11, 1999
While in prison, Lister signs himself and his friends up for the Canaries, mistaking the team for an *a capella* group—but learns that they are actually an expendable convict squad assigned to the most dangerous missions. Sent to investigate an abandoned spaceship, the Canaries encounter a sentient computer named Cassandra, who can accurately foresee the future—and who predicts Rimmer's imminent death.

Episode 49 (T-SER8.5)
"Krytie TV"
W: Doug Naylor and Paul Alexander; D: Ed Bye; T: Mar. 18, 1999
Kryten is humiliated when he is housed in the Women's Wing due to his lack of male genitalia. A psychotic inmate, Oswald "Kill Krazy" Blenkinsop, reprograms the mechanoid to enter the women's shower room and film Kochanski and other sexy female prisoners naked. Kryten also sabotages Lister's legal appeal, framing him for trashing Warden Ackerman's quarters.

Episode 50 (T-SER8.6)
"Pete, Part I"
W: Doug Naylor; D: Ed Bye; T: Mar. 25, 1999
As Rimmer and Lister repeatedly get into trouble, Hollister grows increasingly annoyed with their antics. Finally, he sends them to the Hole, *Red Dwarf*'s solitary-confinement cell, where they meet an insane convict named Birdman and his pet sparrow, Pete. Cat, Kryten and Kochanski, meanwhile, return from a Canaries mission with a time wand. After escaping from the Hole, Lister, Rimmer and Birdman reunite with their comrades, who attempt to revive Pete but instead transform him into a *Tyrannosaurus rex*.

Episode 51 (T-SER8.7)
"Pete, Part II"
W: Doug Naylor and Paul Alexander; D: Ed Bye; T: Apr. 1, 1999
Faced with a rampaging *T. rex*, the crew devise a plan to retrieve the time wand, which Pete has swallowed. They feed the dinosaur a massive bowl of cow vindaloo, hoping it will help Pete pass the device more quickly, but Pete suffers severe indigestion from the meal, with messy consequences. The group try to set things right, but instead lose the device to inmates Baxter and Kill Crazy, who turn themselves into gorillas. Lister and Rimmer are beaten up out of synch, and Hollister is tormented by a baby *Tyrannosaurus*.

Episode 52 (T-SER8.8)
"Only the Good..."
W: Doug Naylor; D: Ed Bye; T: Apr. 5, 1999
Red Dwarf is besieged by a metal-eating virus. When Hollister's crew abandon ship, leaving Lister and company behind to die, Rimmer enters a mirror universe to find an antidote. In that reality, Rimmer is the captain, Hollister is his lackey, Cat is a brilliant scientist and Kochanski is a dimwitted secretary. Arnold finds a cure, but when he returns to his own dimension, he is the only person left aboard—and the Grim Reaper is waiting for him. However, Rimmer knees Death in the groin and escapes his fate.

SERIES IX

Episode 53 (T-SER9.1)
"Back to Earth, Part I"
W: Doug Naylor; D: Doug Naylor; T: Apr. 10, 2009
Nine years have passed, and the crew has become middle-aged and tired. Kochanski has died in the interim, and Lister continues to mourn her. The *Red Dwarf* crew (reunited with Rimmer, once again a hologram) discover that a dimension-hopping leviathan is living in the vessel's water tank. As they deal with this problem, the hard light hologram of deceased science officer Katerina Bartikovsky arrives to replace Rimmer and assist Lister in restoring the human species.

Episode 54 (T-SER9.2)
"Back to Earth, Part II"
W: Doug Naylor; D: Doug Naylor; T: Apr. 11, 2009
The Dwarfers step through a portal to twenty-first-century Earth, realizing they are merely fictional characters on a television series titled *Red Dwarf*, and are fated to die in the next episode. In a series of events reminiscent of the film *Blade Runner*, they search for the TV show's creator to beg for additional life. While riding a public bus, a depressed Lister meets two young fans of the series, who speculate that Kochanski may yet live. The gang

then obtain help from an elderly prosthetics maker who lends them *Carbug*—an automobile rebuilt to resemble *Starbug*.

Episode 55 (T-SER9.3)
"Back to Earth, Part III"
W: Doug Naylor; D: Doug Naylor; T: Apr. 12, 2009
On the set of the soap opera *Coronation Street*, the crew meet actor Craig Charles, who gives them the address of *Red Dwarf*'s screenwriter. When the old man refuses to change his screenplay, they inadvertently kill him. Burning the manuscript, Lister writes a new ending using the creator's typewriter, but the machine ceases to be under his control. The Dwarfers realize they have been trapped in an illusion created by elation squid ink and awaken from the dream. Lister chooses to stay with a representation of Kochanski in the false reality, but realizes the futility of the situation and returns to reality, vowing to find the real Kristine.

SERIES X

Episode 56 (T-SER10.1)
"*Trojan*"
W: Doug Naylor; D: Doug Naylor; T: Oct. 4, 2012
As the crew investigate the abandoned SS *Trojan*, a distress call arrives from a second vessel commanded by Rimmer's more successful (and now hologrammic) brother, Howard. Desperate to impress him, Arnold convinces his mates to pretend to be the *Trojan*'s crew, with him as their heroic commander. The situation becomes complicated when Crawford, a simulant in Howard's crew, reveals nefarious intentions. Lister and Cat, meanwhile, become obsessed with ordering a Stirmaster—an automated coffee-stirrer—from the All-Droid Mail Order Shopping Station.

Episode 57 (T-SER10.2)
"Fathers & Suns"
W: Doug Naylor; D: Doug Naylor; T: Oct. 11, 2012
Lister spends Father's Day the same way he always does: getting drunk and making himself a card. This year, he decides to be a better father by forcing his son (himself) to become an officer and improve his lot in life. Meanwhile, Kryten installs a new computer intelligence—a sexy female AI called Pree—designed with predictive capabilities enabling her to anticipate the crew's actions and thus optimize efficiency. When Lister resigns during his drunken stupor, Pree deems him non-crew and expels him into space, then turns the ship into the path of a nearby sun to dispose of the vessel.

Episode 58 (T-SER10.3)
"Lemons"
W: Doug Naylor; D: Doug Naylor; T: Oct. 18, 2012
The crew incorrectly construct a rejuvenation shower kit, which propels them back to Albion in 23 A.D. Requiring an eight-volt battery to power the shower's remote and return home, they create a battery out of lemons—which they must first travel four thousand miles, to India, to obtain. There, in a market square, they encounter a peace-loving, pious man named Jesus, whom they believe to be the Christian messiah—and inadvertently cause him to denounce religion, potentially altering the course of human civilization.

Episode 59 (T-SER10.4)
"Entangled"
W: Doug Naylor; D: Doug Naylor; T: Oct. 25, 2012
Lister plays poker with a BEGG clan, losing *Starbug* and Rimmer to them. To ensure he pays his debt, the BEGGs fit him with a groinal exploder programmed to detonate in twenty-four hours if he reneges. Meanwhile, an experiment with the *Trojan*'s quantum rod causes Kryten and Cat to become quantum-entangled and prone to coincidences, such as saying the same phrases simultaneously. The rod enables them to locate the Erroneous Reasoning Research Academy, where they find the exploder's designer, Irene Edgington.

Episode 60 (T-SER10.5)
"Dear Dave"
W: Doug Naylor; D: Doug Naylor; T: Nov. 1, 2012
Lister, depressed over the fate of the human species, finds himself in a love triangle with Snack Dispensers 23 and 34. Adding to his pain is a letter from an old girlfriend, informing him that she was pregnant—and that the child may have been his. As the crew search the mail pod to find out if Lister had a long-lost love child, Rimmer contends with the threat of demotion from the JMC computer for dereliction of duties.

Episode 61 (T-SER10.6)
"The Beginning"
W: Doug Naylor; D: Doug Naylor; T: Nov. 8, 2012
When a Simulant Death Ship and a fleet of Annihilators attack *Red Dwarf*, the crew escape aboard a *Blue Midget* shuttle, pursued by the Simulant commander, Dominator Zlurth. After resolving lifelong feelings of inadequacy stemming from his father's disapproval, Rimmer hatches an unorthodox—but brilliant—plan to defeat the bloodthirsty simulants. Meanwhile, a bored droid called Hogey the Roguey tries desperately to provoke the Dwarfers into fighting a duel to the death across time and space.

Unbroadcast Scripts/Storyboards

R-BOD
"Bodysnatcher"
W: Rob Grant and Doug Naylor; D: N/A; T: N/A
When Lister ignores Rimmer's orders, the hologram decides to clone himself a body from Lister's DNA so he'll be more respected. Learning of this absurd plan, Lister deactivates him. Although Rimmer had hidden the crew's personality disks to prevent his replacement, Lister's disk was not among them, so Holly uses that as a template for a new hologram. Living with his duplicate drives Lister insane, causing him to fire a flare gun at his holo-self. This sets their quarters on fire, and Lister reactivates Rimmer to help locate the extinguisher. Rimmer smugly complies, content that his shipmate has learned his lesson.

R-DAD
"Dad"
W: Rob Grant and Doug Naylor; D: N/A; T: N/A
Lister, heavily pregnant and emotional—and disgusted by his growing belly—consoles himself with a banana and liver pizza. Rimmer, reading *Biggles Learns to Fly*, tries to be supportive, but draws the line at examining Lister's engorged nipples. Finally, Kryten delivers Lister's child—a son. Six weeks later, Lister has still not named the child. Rimmer recommends calling him Arnold Lister, but Dave favors the name Barry.

T-IDW
"Identity Within"
W: John McKay; D: N/A; T: N/A
Cat's sexual frustration becomes life-threatening, and he must mate soon or die. His friends probe for other members of his species, leading them into GELF territory. Visiting a Brefewino village, they discover a female named Ora Tanzil, held prisoner for a slave auction. The Dwarfers plot to free her so Cat can copulate and live. Though initially resisting his charms, Ora falls in love with Cat, enjoying a full twenty-minute relationship with him before being dropped off on a nearby planet.

R-FTH
"Lister's Father"
W: Rob Grant and Doug Naylor; D: N/A; T: N/A
Lister uses a timeslide to visit the pub in which he was abandoned as an infant, and confronts his father.

R-INF
"Infinity Patrol"
W: Rob Grant and Doug Naylor; D: N/A; T: N/A
The Dwarfers receive a visit from a pair of strange travelers claiming to be from the future.

Red Dwarf USA

First Pilot (T-USA1)
W: Linwood Boomer and John Frank Rosenblum (based on a script by Rob Grant and Doug Naylor); D: Jeff Melman; T: N/A
Dave Lister, the lowest-ranking crewman aboard the American mining ship *Red Dwarf*, is put in suspended animation for bringing an unauthorized cat aboard the vessel. While he's in stasis, a radiation accident kills everyone on the ship, including his ex-girlfriend, Christine Kochanski. Once the danger has passed, Lister awakens three million years in the future, his only companions Holly, the ship's eccentric female artificial intelligence; a hologram of his bunkmate and nemesis, Arnold Rimmer; Cat, a member of a humanoid species that evolved from Lister's pet; and Kryten, a mechanoid who had spent the millennia alone sitting on a shelf, repeatedly reading the same sign.

Second Pilot (T-USA2)
W: Rob Grant and Doug Naylor; D: Unknown; T: N/A
As Lister and Rimmer watch *The Flintstones*, Lister admits his deep attraction to Wilma Flintstone. Lister begins recording a black box update as the sole surviving member of the *Red Dwarf* crew, reporting his whereabouts in the hope of being rescued. When an armor-plated genetic mutant boards the ship, Cat—a female with nine lives who does not fear death—looks forward to the fight. Rimmer finds Lister recording the message capsule and claims he's doing it wrong—but his instructions cause Lister to press "stop" instead of "record," preventing him from delivering his message and rescue coordinates.

> ***NOTE:*** *This second, shorter pilot was made using scenes from the first attempt, as well as from the British series, with the same plots but with some actors replaced.*

Novels

N-INF
Infinity Welcomes Careful Drivers
W: Rob Grant and Doug Naylor; P: Nov. 2, 1989
Lister becomes stranded on Mimas after a birthday pub crawl gone awry, and ends up stuck on the mining vessel *Red Dwarf* for years while trying to get home again. Placed in stasis for bringing a pregnant cat aboard ship, he emerges in deep space three million years later, the last human alive. His only companions are his irritating bunkmate, Rimmer; the ship's senile computer, Holly; Cat, a self-centered humanoid evolved from his pet; and Kryten, a neurotic mechanoid rescued from a crashed ship. Together, they must repair Kryten's vessel and begin the journey back to Earth.

N-BTL
Better Than Life
W: Rob Grant and Doug Naylor; P: Jan. 1, 1990
Married to Kochanski, Lister has twin sons and lives in idyllic Bedford Falls. The only problem: It's only an illusion created by the virtual-reality computer game *Better Than Life*, in which the crew has become trapped. Breaking free, they discover a frozen planetoid hurtling toward *Red Dwarf*. Though they divert the planetoid's path, Lister ends up marooned on that world. His shipmates, after narrowly avoiding being sucked into a black hole, rescue Lister—but he has aged thirty-four years due to time dilation. When a polymorph stows aboard the vessel, fatally injuring Lister, Holly devises a plan to save his life.

N-LST
Last Human
W: Doug Naylor; P: Nov. 2, 1995
Rescued from a backwards-running universe after thirty-four years, a revived Lister returns to *Starbug 1* with his crewmates. A miscalculation propels the ship into an alternate dimension, in which another Lister has been incarcerated at a GELF virtual prison. The crew follow the doppelgänger's trail and formulate a plan to help him escape. This Lister is psychotic, and tries to prevent his rescuers from finding the secret he seeks—the genome of DNA (G.O.D.), located in GELF space. The crew also encounter the Rage of Innocence, a malevolent entity spawned from the DNA of wrongly imprisoned inmates.

N-BCK
Backwards
W: Rob Grant; P: Nov. 7, 1996
Imprisoned on a backwards-running Earth for a crime he has yet to commit, Lister escapes and heads to Niagara Falls to rendezvous with his *Red Dwarf* crewmates. Police give chase (in reverse), Kryten unwittingly commits an un-murder, and the crew end up marooned there for ten years. Escaping a decade younger than when they arrived, they meet an alternate-reality Rimmer—a brave pilot known as Ace—and must battle a crew of deadly agonoids to fight for their lives in a virtual Wild West town.

Smegazines

ISSUE 1.1
P: March 1992

M-SMG1.1(c1)
"The End, Part 1"
W: Rob Grant and Doug Naylor; A: Alan Burrows; L: Elitta Fell
Lister and Rimmer must bunk and work together aboard *Red Dwarf*, despite their mutual loathing. This rivalry continues during the funeral and welcome-back party for George McIntyre, a crewmember resurrected as a hologram.

ISSUE 1.2
P: April 1992

M-SMG1.2(c1)
"The End, Part 2"
W: Rob Grant and Doug Naylor; A: Alan Burrows; L: Elitta Fell
While Rimmer prepares for his Astronavigation Exam, Lister visits Frankenstein, a pregnant cat he smuggled aboard *Red Dwarf*. Captain Hollister learns of the cat and demands that Lister surrender the animal for disposal. When he refuses, Hollister sentences him to eighteen months in stasis. Upon release, he finds the ship abandoned, aside from the ship's computer, Holly.

ISSUE 1.3
P: May 1992

M-SMG1.3(c1)
"The End, Part 3"
W: Rob Grant and Doug Naylor; A: Alan Burrows; L: Elitta Fell
Holly says three million years have passed, and that Lister is the last human alive. With the crew dead from a radiation leak, Holly revives Rimmer as a hologram to keep Lister sane. The two men encounter a vain humanoid whose species evolved from Frankenstein's litter. Lister names the creature Cat and decides to head *Red Dwarf* back toward Earth.

ISSUE 1.4

P: June 1992

M-SMG1.4(c1)
"Mutinous Pursuits"
W: Chris Howarth and Steve Lyons; A: John Royle; L: Elitta Fell
A skutter strike interrupts a game of *Trivial Pursuit.* After Rimmer fails to diffuse the situation with brute force, Lister convinces the robots to return to work in exchange for several days a month without Rimmer's presence. But Holly's sudden winning streak makes the skutters' true motives clear.

M-SMG1.4(c2)
"Future Echoes, Part 1"
W: Rob Grant and Doug Naylor; A: Jon Rushby; L: Elitta Fell
Lister decides to return to stasis for the duration of the trip to Earth. This worries Rimmer, who fears he'll either spend the trip alone with Holly, or be permanently deactivated.

ISSUE 1.5

P: July 1992

M-SMG1.5(c1)
"Future Echoes, Part 2"
W: Rob Grant and Doug Naylor; A: Jon Rushby; L: Elitta Fell
As Lister prepares for stasis, strange things begin happening aboard *Red Dwarf*, as the crew experience visions of events yet to occur.

M-SMG1.5(c2)
"Ace Rimmer—Space Adventurer"
W: Chris Howarth and Steve Lyons; A: Alan Burrows; L: Elitta Fell
Ace Rimmer visits a universe in which the sexes are reversed, where he meets Arlene Rimmer (his female equivalent) and Deb Lister. Feeling obligated to rebuild the human species, Deb makes a bet with Arlene that she can seduce Ace. She wins the wager, but ends up pregnant with his children.

ISSUE 1.6

P: August 1992

M-SMG1.6(c1)
"The GEAP"
W: Ann Wright; A: Vince Danks; L: Elitta Fell
The *Red Dwarf* crew bring aboard a stasis pod containing a genetically engineered adaptable pet (GEAP). Such creatures were banned since they telepathically force their owners to love and protect them at all costs. Lister and Cat fall under the GEAP's spell and fight over the creature, until Kryten returns it to its pod before the conflict turns lethal.

M-SMG1.6(c2)
"Future Echoes, Part 3"
W: Rob Grant and Doug Naylor; A: Jon Rushby; L: Elitta Fell
As the visions continue, Holly explains that the phenomena are future echoes—glimpses of future events, caused by the effects of faster-than-light travel. One echo, in particular, grabs the crew's attention: a photograph of Lister holding a pair of babies.

ISSUE 1.7

P: September 1992

M-SMG1.7(c1)
"Future Echoes, Part 4"
W: Rob Grant and Doug Naylor; A: Jon Rushby; L: Elitta Fell
An explosion rocks the ship as Lister prepares for stasis. Rimmer reports that the latest future echo does not bode well for Lister, whom he witnessed dying in a navicomp explosion. Hoping to change his fate, Lister tries to prevent a prior future echo of Cat breaking his tooth—but instead causes that very injury.

M-SMG1.7(c2)
"Fashion Victims"
W: Steve Lyons; A: Alan Burrows; L: Elitta Fell
Cat has a nightmare of poorly dressed robots stealing his suits. In the dream, he chases them through a dimensional warp and is transported to a world suffering from a fashion famine. As the thieves disseminate his clothing to the afflicted, a riot breaks out, staining the suits red. Awakening in relief, he erases the nightmare from the ship's dream recorder.

ISSUE 1.8

P: October 1992

M-SMG1.8(c1)
"Future Echoes, Part 5"
W: Rob Grant and Doug Naylor; A: Jon Rushby; L: Elitta Fell
As Lister frets over his impending demise, Holly reports a problem with the navicomp. Accepting his fate, Lister fixes the problem, but no explosion occurs. He and Rimmer later experience a future echo of an elderly Lister, who reveals that Rimmer actually saw Dave's future son Bexley dying, not Lister himself. He then instructs them to run to the infirmary with a camera, where they glimpse a final future echo: the birth of Lister's twins.

M-SMG1.8(c2)
"Androids"
W: James Hill and Pat Kelleher; A: Kev F. Sutherland; L: Woodrow Phoenix
In an episode of *Androids*, Kelly confesses to her husband Brook that their son, Brooke Junior, is not his—the father is her ex-husband (and Brook's business rival), Gary. Meanwhile, a barbeque gathering takes a turn for the worse.

M-SMG1.8(c3)
"The Amusing Misadventures of Mr. Flibble—Mr. Flibble's Surprise"
W: James Hill and Pat Kelleher; A: Rob Sharp
Mr. Flibble travels to the planet of the Potato People to crash the king's party and give him a special surprise.

M-SMG1.8(c4)
"Ace of the Rovers"
W: Billy Dane; A: Barbie Mitchell; L: John Aldrich
In an alternate universe, down-and-out football player Ray Rimmer decides to commit suicide, but Ace Rimmer saves his life and offers to help repair the man's reputation by standing in for him during a championship game.

M-SMG1.8(c5)
"Androids"
W: James Hill and Pat Kelleher; A: Kev F. Sutherland; L: Woodrow Phoenix
Brook files for divorce after learning of his wife's affair with Gary. As the couple argue, a vehicle crashes through their home. At the barbeque, meanwhile, partygoers search for clues to the disappearance of Bouncer, the household pet.

ISSUE 1.9
P: November 1992

M-SMG1.9(c1)
"Flashback—Featuring Duane Dibbley"
W: Nigel Kitching; A: Nigel Kitching; L: Elitta Fell
Cat bumps his head and hallucinates that he is once again Duane Dibbley, locked up in a medical facility. Unable to cope, he considers killing himself with a knife, but regains his senses to find himself holding a herring.

M-SMG1.9(c2)
"Androids"
W: James Hill and Pat Kelleher; A: Kev F. Sutherland; L: Woodrow Phoenix
As Kelly confides in her friend Simone, Brooke Junior experiments with attachments, and Jaysee (Brook's illegitimate half-brother) plots to take over the family business.

M-SMG1.9(c3)
"In Living Memory, Part 1"
W: Steve Lyons; A: Ron Smith; L: Elitta Fell
The *Red Dwarf* crew find the remains of an ancient, abandoned Cat People civilization on a nearby planet. Among the city's ruins, they discover a machine that brings thoughts to life, which the crew try out, with unpleasant results.

ISSUE 1.10
P: December 1992

M-SMG1.10(c1)
"Jake Bullet in The Case of the Cashed-In Contestant—Part 1: Wired"
W: Steve Noble; A: Carl Flint; L: Woodrow Phoenix
Cyborg detective Jake Bullet is assigned to investigate the murder of game-show contestant Philby Frutch, who died during an impressive winning streak.

M-SMG1.10(c2)
"Androids"
W: James Hill and Pat Kelleher; A: Kev F. Sutherland; L: Woodrow Phoenix
Brook receives unsettling news from his doctor, then confronts Brooke Junior about his groinal attachment experimentation. Meanwhile, Kelly visits an old friend.

M-SMG1.10(c3)
"In Living Memory, Part 2"
W: Steve Lyons; A: Ron Smith; L: Elitta Fell
Pursued by a ravenous monster created by the thought machine, the *Red Dwarf* crew retreat to their ship, but Rimmer steals a shuttle and returns, hoping to recreate himself as taller, braver and better-endowed.

M-SMG1.10(c4)
"Red Dwarf USA"
W: Steve Noble and Nigel Kitching; A: John Erasmus; L: John Erasmus
In an alternate reality in which *Red Dwarf* is a British science fiction sitcom, American television executives attempt to create their own version of the hit program, completely missing the point by changing every detail to fit their own vision.

ISSUE 1.11
P: January 1993

M-SMG1.11(c1)
"Androids"
W: James Hill and Pat Kelleher; A: Kev F. Sutherland; L: Woodrow Phoenix
Mollee attempts to recruit Kelly for her crusade against a local android brothel called Brothel-U-Like, unaware that Kelly owns the establishment.

M-SMG1.11(c2)
"Wetware"
W: James Hill and Pat Kelleher; A: Alan Burrows; L: Elitta Fell
The *Red Dwarf* crew find a research station containing experimental wetware technology. Upon entering the facility, Lister becomes caught in an interface. Integrated into the computer's artificial intelligence, he seeks Holly's help in breaking free.

M-SMG1.11(c3)
"The Inquisitor—Mirror Image"
W: Steve Noble and Nigel Kitching; A: Nigel Kitching; L: Elitta Fell
The Inquisitor deems Jan Ludwig Hoch, a patriotic immigrant and father of two, as not having lived up to his potential. After erasing the man from existence and replacing him with another person, the droid realizes he had erred in his judgment.

M-SMG1.11(c4)
"Jake Bullet in The Case of the Cashed-In Contestant—Part 2: Nerds on Drugs"
W: Steve Noble; A: Carl Flint; L: Woodrow Phoenix
While investigating Philby Frutch's murder, Bullet learns that the game-show winner had been taking stupid drugs when he was bludgeoned to death outside the television station.

ISSUE 1.12
P: February 1993

M-SMG1.12(c1)
"Jake Bullet in The Case of the Cashed-In Contestant—Part 3: Ambulance Chaser"
W: Steve Noble; A: Carl Flint; L: Woodrow Phoenix
Surviving an attempt on his life, Bullet checks the black market for information about stupid drugs, and meets informant Vinnie van Goth. Their meeting is cut short when a second assassination attempt occurs.

M-SMG1.12(c2)
"Evolution"
W: Ann Wright; A: Roger Langridge; L: Roger Langridge
When an experimental E-accelerator transforms Lister's ham sandwich into a pig, Rimmer tells Kryten to use the machine to give him a solid body, but it instead de-evolves him into a black-and-white silent-film version of a hologram. The pig mauls the device, turning the crew into an ape, a cat and a vacuum cleaner, leaving Holly and Talkie Toaster to revive them.

M-SMG1.12(c3)
"Androids"
W: James Hill and Pat Kelleher; A: Kev F. Sutherland; L: Woodrow Phoenix
Brook visits a brothel following his divorce from Kelly, to find her running the place. Mollee, meanwhile, vows to shut down the sleazy business.

M-SMG1.12(c4)
"The Skutters—The Good, The Bad and the Ugly!"
W: Steve Lyons; A: Rob Sharp
Red Dwarf's skutters revel in disobeying Rimmer, but the robots become more obedient after a polymorph attacks them.

M-SMG1.12(c5)
"Sadvertisement: Smeggo!"
W: Vicky Lacey; A: John Rushby; L: Elitta Fell
Kryten touts the benefits of Smeggo laundry detergent.

ISSUE 1.13
P: March 1993

M-SMG1.13(c1)
"Androids"
W: James Hill and Pat Kelleher; A: Kev F. Sutherland; L: Woodrow Phoenix
Jaysee blackmails Brook for control of the family business, then sets his sights on Gary. Meanwhile, Gary and Kelly plan to rid themselves of Jaysee once and for all.

M-SMG1.13(c2)
"Space Monkeys"
W: Steve Noble and Nigel Kitching; A: Nigel Kitching; L: Elitta Fell
Space Monkeys overrun *Red Dwarf* after Lister confuses their packaging with a packet of bath salts. Though a fun diversion at first, the mutated novelty pets ravage the food supply, devouring all of the crew's Krispee Krunchies.

M-SMG1.13(c3)
"The Shadow Time"
W: James Hill and Pat Kelleher; A: David Lyttleton; L: Elitta Fell
A nearby sun thaws out the frozen Garbage World, allowing its denizens to scurry about in search of food. A trio of GELFs traverse the planet's surface, stalking a giant cockroach, unaware it is they who are the hunted.

M-SMG1.13(c4)
"Jake Bullet in The Case of the Cashed-In Contestant—Part 4: Law Have Mercy"
W: Steve Noble; A: Carl Flint; L: Woodrow Phoenix
Trailing his assassin, Bullet visits Hit-U-Like, a state-run hitman business. There, the cyborg learns that the person who wants him dead is Philby Frutch himself.

ISSUE 1.14
P: April 1993

M-SMG1.14(c1)
"Duane Dibbley—Part 1: Out"
W: Steve Noble and Nigel Kitching; A: Nigel Kitching; L: Woodrow Phoenix
In an alternate Earth's fascist society, Duane Dibbley escapes a mental institution and embarks on a mission to regain his memory and clear his name, enlisting the help of Jake Bullet.

M-SMG1.14(c2)
"The Cantabelis Tales"
W: Kev Sutherland; A: Alan Burrows; L: Elitta Fell
The *Red Dwarf* crew discover an ancient Earth ship launched from Tunbridge Wells on a religious pilgrimage. Accessing the ship's records, they read about the bloody voyage.

M-SMG1.14(c3)
"Androids"
W: James Hill and Pat Kelleher; A: Kev F. Sutherland; L: Woodrow Phoenix
When an attempt on Jaysee's life fails, he seeks retribution against Kelly and Gary. Meanwhile, a figure from Jaysee's past returns to settle an old score.

M-SMG1.14(c4)
"The Amusing Misadventures of Mr. Flibble—Mr. Flibble Gets P%@*ed!"
W: Adrian Dungworth; A: Dungworth
Mr. Flibble has an unpleasant experience at Fat Sam's Bar.

M-SMG1.14(c5)
"Ace of Blackhearts"
W: Kev Sutherland; A: Darren Stephens; L: Elitta Fell
Ace Rimmer visits a dimension in which his doppelgänger, a tyrant called "Blackheart" Rimmer, is bent on universal domination.

M-SMG1.14(c6)
"Jake Bullet in The Case of the Cashed-In Contestant—Part 5: At Home With the Nerds"
W: Steve Noble; A: Carl Flint; L: Woodrow Phoenix
Jake Bullet visits Philby Frutch's home and meets the man's lover, game-show hostess Mercy Dash. She reveals their plan to use Frutch's winnings to pay for an operation to cure his nerdism, and to then run away together.

ISSUE 2.1
P: May 1993

M-SMG2.1(c1)
"Lister the God—Part 1"
W: Nigel Kitching; A: Nigel Kitching L: Elitta Fell
A Cat People sect known as the Elite use a time machine to send three warriors five hundred years into the future to kidnap their god, Cloister, so he can end their bloody conflict.

M-SMG2.1(c2)
"Androids"
W: James Hill and Pat Kelleher; A: Kev F. Sutherland; L: Woodrow Phoenix
Brooke Junior finds his father, Brook, sulking about the local scrap heap. The two are surprised at the arrival of Karstares, Brook's father, thought to have died in a plane crash twenty years prior. Kelly's backseat romp with Gary, meanwhile, ends explosively.

M-SMG2.1(c3)
"Super-Ace"
W: Steve Lyons; A: Nigel Dobbyn; L: Elitta Fell
Ace Rimmer visits a universe of superheroes and supervillains, where he helps the Liberty League defeat their mortal enemy, the Conspirator.

M-SMG2.1(c4)
"Jake Bullet and Duane Dibbley in The Case of the Cashed-In Contestant—Part 6: Don't Lose Your Nerd"
W: Steve Noble and Nigel Kitching; A: Carl Flint and Nigel Kitching; L: Woodrow Phoenix
Bullet enlists Duane Dibbley's assistance in accessing a nerd club frequented by Philby Frutch. Dibbley then seeks Bullet's help in piecing together the last four years of his life.

ISSUE 2.2
P: June 1993

M-SMG2.2(c1)
"Lister the God—Part 2"
W: Nigel Kitching; A: Nigel Kitching L: Elitta Fell
With Lister kidnapped and taken into the past, his shipmates attempt a rescue using the Time Obelisk. Five centuries earlier, Lister learns that the Cat People consider him their savior, and faces a double-cross as enemy agents threaten his life.

M-SMG2.2(c2)
"Jake Bullet in The Case of the Cashed-In Contestant—Part 7: Hard News & Current Affairs"
W: Steve Noble; A: Carl Flint; L: Woodrow Phoenix
Bullet awakens to find that he has been captured by Mercy Dash and Monty, the hosts of *20,000,000 Watts My Line*, who reveal that they killed Frutch for cheating on the game show using a brain implant. The two threaten to kill Bullet to bury the evidence.

M-SMG2.2(c3)
"Androids"
W: James Hill and Pat Kelleher; A: Kev F. Sutherland; L: Woodrow Phoenix
Kelly and Gary barely survive Jaysee's assassination attempt, while Karstares reveals his plans for his evil, illegitimate son.

M-SMG2.2(c4)
"GELFWorld"
W: Jim Alexander; A: David Lyttleton; L: David Lyttleton
Dissidence foments behind the scenes at a tourist spot called GELFWorld, while an escaped convict named Biggs wages a bloody war against his oppressors.

M-SMG2.2(c5)
"Duane Dibbley—Part 3: Home"
W: Nigel Kitching; A: Nigel Kitching L: Woodrow Phoenix
Dibbley finds a key to a Salvation Army hostel, which he hopes will reveal clues to his past. Voter Colonel Larson Gray ambushes him, but a mysterious figure saves his life.

ISSUE 2.3
P: July 1993

M-SMG2.3(c1)
"Lister the God—Part 3"
W: Nigel Kitching; A: Nigel Kitching L: Elitta Fell
While Lister tries to survive captivity amidst a Cat People civil war, his crewmates use the Time Obelisk to rescue him from the past.

M-SMG2.3(c2)
"Androids"
W: James Hill and Pat Kelleher; A: Kev F. Sutherland; L: Woodrow Phoenix
As Simone visits Kelly in the hospital, Jaysee discovers that someone has taken control of his brothel.

M-SMG2.3(c3)
"Mr. Flibble Goes Asset-Stripping"
W: James Hill and Pat Kelleher; A: Rob Sharp; L: Elitta Fell
Mr. Flibble orchestrates a hostile takeover of soft-drink company Kookie Kola.

M-SMG2.3(c4)
"Mimas Crossing—Part 1"
W: James Hill and Pat Kelleher; A: David Lyttleton; L: James Otis
Dutch van Oestrogen double-crosses the Ganymedian Mafia during a Bliss sale on Mimas, taking both the drugs and the money. Pursued by the Osmond crime family, the astro hides in a body swap-shop and trades bodies with sex worker Trixie LaBouche.

M-SMG2.3(c5)
"Duane Dibbley—Part 4: Caught"
W: Nigel Kitching; A: Nigel Kitching; L: Woodrow Phoenix
Dibbley's escape from Larson Gray doesn't go as planned, as the two plummet from the grip of Dibbley's would-be rescuer.

ISSUE 2.4
P: August 1993

M-SMG2.4(c1)
"Time After Time"
W: Steve Lyons; A: Alan Burrows and Colin Howard; L: Elitta Fell
Lister attempts a temporal mind-swap to prevent the cadmium II disaster, but the procedure goes awry when his past consciousness becomes lost in time, causing his younger self to experience key events from *Red Dwarf*'s future.

M-SMG2.4(c2)
"Mimas Crossing—Part 2"
W: James Hill and Pat Kelleher; A: David Lyttleton; L: James Otis
Dutch van Oestrogen tries to reclaim his own body, but the Ganymedian Mafia finds him. The body swap machine is damaged during a firefight, causing some of his memories to remain in Trixie LaBouche's mind, including the location of the astro's stash.

M-SMG2.4(c3)
"Androids"
W: James Hill and Pat Kelleher; A: Kev F. Sutherland; L: Woodrow Phoenix
Gary constructs a new body after Jaysee's attempt on his life, while Karstares, Brook and Brooke Junior formulate a plan of attack.

M-SMG2.4(c4)
"Cred Dwarf—Episode 1: Coded Echo"
W: Steve Noble; A: Davy Francis; L: Woodrow Phoenix
In an alternate dimension, a group of players enter the Total Immersion video game *Red Dwarf* and unlock the secret to revive Lister's ex-girlfriend, Kochanski.

M-SMG2.4(c5)
"A Day in the Life of a Bogbot..."
W: James Hill and Pat Kelleher; A: Glen Rix and Paul Crompton; L: Elitta Fell
Kryten accidentally flushes Lister's robotic pet goldfish down the toilet, prompting a search through *Red Dwarf*'s waste-disposal systems.

M-SMG2.4(c6)
"Duane Dibbley—Part 5"
W: Nigel Kitching; A: Nigel Kitching; L: Woodrow Phoenix
Larson Gray reviews footage from the botched attempt to nab Dibbley, while the latter meets the Fatal Sisters, an anarchist group who seduce him to jog his memory.

ISSUE 2.5
P: September 1993

M-SMG2.5(c1)
"Duane Dibbley—Part 6: Complicated"
W: Nigel Kitching; A: Nigel Kitching; L: Woodrow Phoenix
Even after group sex, Dibbley's memories remain elusive. Larson Gray, meanwhile, searches the Ministry of Alteration for information that could shed light on the case.

M-SMG2.5(c2)
"Dead Man's Bluff"
W: Steve Lyons; A: John Rushby; L: Elitta Fell
A psychopathic cyborg with a grudge against holograms boards *Red Dwarf* searching for his next target: Arnold Rimmer.

M-SMG2.5(c3)
"Tomorrow Trouble"
W: Chris Webster; A: Carl Flint; L: Woodrow Phoenix
The Inquisitor condemns Mortimer Dodd to non-existence, unwittingly negating his own timeline in the process. Faced with extinction, the simulant travels back in time to prevent this bad judgment call.

M-SMG2.5(c4)
"Cred Dwarf—Episode 2: Next to Last Day"
W: Steve Noble; A: Davy Francis; L: Woodrow Phoenix
New players in the Total Immersion video game *Red Dwarf* deal with the Hudzen 10 threat differently than their predecessors did.

M-SMG2.5(c5)
"Androids"
W: James Hill and Pat Kelleher; A: Kev F. Sutherland; L: Woodrow Phoenix
Mollee regains her memory, recalls that she is the new madam of Jaysee's brothel and seeks revenge on her blackmailer. Elsewhere, Jaysee's enemies converge on his penthouse.

M-SMG2.5(c6)
"Mimas Crossing—Part 3"
W: James Hill and Pat Kelleher; A: David Lyttleton; L: James Otis
With fragments of each other's memories still in their minds, Dutch van Oestrogen and Trixie LaBouche race to find the astro's stash, still pursued by the Osmonds.

ISSUE 2.6
P: October 1993

M-SMG2.6(c1)
"Home of Lost Causes—Part 1"
W: Nigel Kitching; A: Nigel Kitching; L: Elitta Fell
The Dwarfers find what they think is their stolen ship, but discover the crew revived and are arrested. Escaping detainment, they head for the engineering section, where they encounter Kochanski and a polymorph.

M-SMG2.6(c2)
"Androids"
W: James Hill and Pat Kelleher; A: Kev F. Sutherland; L: Woodrow Phoenix
Jaysee professes love to his secretary, unaware that his enemies draw closer.

M-SMG2.6(c3)
"Androids"
W: James Hill and Pat Kelleher; A: Kev F. Sutherland; L: Woodrow Phoenix
As the lights suddenly go out, Jaysee is simultaneously attacked by several enemies.

M-SMG2.6(c4)
"Mimas Crossing—Part 4"
W: James Hill and Pat Kelleher; A: David Lyttleton; L: James Otis
The Osmonds chase Dutch van Oestrogen and Trixie LaBouche through Mimas Spaceport. After Lister accidentally knocks Dutch unconscious, Trixie gets away with the stash.

M-SMG2.6(c5)
"Cred Dwarf"
W: Steve Noble; A: Davy Francis; L: Woodrow Phoenix
Players in the Total Immersion video game *Red Dwarf* visit the Planet of the Nymphomaniacs.

M-SMG2.6(c6)
"A Jake Bullet Mystery: The Case of the Cop's Comedown—Part 1: See Real Killing"
W: Steve Noble; A: Carl Flint; L: Woodrow Phoenix
Strange visions of past cases and past lives fill Jake Bullet's mind as he plummets to his apparent death.

ISSUE 2.7
P: November 1993

M-SMG2.7(c1)
"Home of Lost Causes—Part 2"
W: Nigel Kitching; A: Nigel Kitching; L: Elitta Fell
Kochanski explains that the polymorph, after feeding off the recorded emotions of the *Red Dwarf* crew, transformed into an exact duplicate of the vessel, replicating every facet of the ship and its crew. She urges the newcomers to submit to regular feedings in exchange for total bliss, but they reject the offer and try to escape. The polymorph gives chase, but—having recreated the ship too perfectly—it experiences a cadmium II leak and dies.

M-SMG2.7(c2)
"One for All"
W: Andy P. and Tom Eglington; A: Glenn Rix; L: Woodrow Phoenix
On Rimmer's psi-moon, the hordes of darkness kidnap Self-Esteem. Courage, Honour and Charity attempt a rescue, but come face-to-face with the enemy's greatest weapon: a vision of Rimmer's mother.

M-SMG2.7(c3)
"Young Flibble—Part 1"
W: Pat Kelleher; A: Rob Sharp; L: Elitta Fell
On a remote psi-moon, a woodcutter and his wife find a strange blue egg in the middle of the forest. With no children of their own, the couple care for the egg until it hatches, producing a baby penguin. The bird, named Flibble, soon begins to affect the psi-moon's environment.

M-SMG2.7(c4)
"A Jake Bullet Mystery: The Case of the Cop's Comedown—Part 2: Kill Me Before I Die Again"
W: Steve Noble; A: Carl Flint; L: Woodrow Phoenix
While plummeting from a skyscraper, Bullet recalls how he ended up in this predicament: Summoned to Brainfade's offices to investigate the murder of Doctor Sandra Halley, he met several employees, including Director Scofrenia and Carl, a member of Serial Killers Anonymous, as well as a backup personality program of the deceased scientist.

M-SMG2.7(c5)
"Androids"
W: James Hill and Pat Kelleher; A: Kev F. Sutherland
A battle erupts between Jaysee and his enemies, during which his lover, Brandy, dies. His enemies are blown to pieces, including Gary, who attempts one last shot before the mogul guns him down.

M-SMG2.7(c6)
"Androids"
W: James Hill and Pat Kelleher; A: Kev F. Sutherland; L: Woodrow Phoenix
Karstares barely escapes the firefight, crawling away from the scene to a temporal-displacement vortex, through which he witnesses partygoers searching for a lost pet.

ISSUE 2.8
P: December 1993

M-SMG2.8(c1)
"A Jake Bullet Mystery: The Case of the Cop's Comedown—Part 3: Free Will and Other Political Prisoners"
W: Steve Noble; A: Carl Flint; L: Woodrow Phoenix
Bullet reviews Brainfade's security footage and learns of a secret project, then returns to the company to question Halley's personality program—which he learns has been lost. Bullet is about to take Scofrenia in for questioning, until viewing a simulation implicating Carl as the killer.

M-SMG2.8(c2)
"Androids"
W: James Hill and Pat Kelleher; A: Kev F. Sutherland; L: Woodrow Phoenix
Injured in the firefight with Jaysee, Brook and Brooke Junior head to the nearest hospital.

M-SMG2.8(c3)
"The Scoop"
W: Jim Alexander; A: Emma Mithchinson; L: Elitta Fell
The crew attempt to use *Red Dwarf*'s scoop to collect neutrino-tachyons so they can return to twenty-second-century Earth, but Holly's miscalculations send them sixty-eight million years in the past. After a dinosaur tries to eat them, they jump back to the future, inadvertently setting off a neutrino-tachyon shockwave that causes the dinosaurs' extinction.

M-SMG2.8(c4)
"Young Flibble—Part 2"
W: Pat Kelleher; A: Rob Sharp; L: Elitta Fell
While running an errand to his grandmother's house, Flibble discovers a cottage in the woods belonging to Witch Hildegarde. Inside, he finds a potion that gives him hex vision, which he tests on the returning witch. Stealing her shoes, he pays Granny a visit.

M-SMG2.8(c5)
"Cat and Dog"
W: Paul Burns; A: Paul Burns
Cat and Dog play a game of fetch.

M-SMG2.8(c6)
"A.J. Rimmer, P.M."
W: Harl Wilson; A: Glenn Rix and Paul Crompton; L: Elitta Fell
Ace Rimmer visits a universe in which he is the United Republic of Lesser Britain's prime minister. Finding his doppelgänger drunk on a park bench, Ace learns that this Arnold, having run the country brilliantly, became bored, with no challenges to conquer. Thus, Ace retrieves a chancellor of the exchequer to make running the nation more difficult.

M-SMG2.8(c7)
"Cred Dwarf"
W: Steve Noble; A: Davy Francis; L: Woodrow Phoenix
Players of the Total Immersion video game *Red Dwarf* suggest that their Lister investigate a deadly planet, where he has the vacation of a lifetime.

M-SMG2.8(c8)
"Androids"
W: Pat Kelleher; A: Kev F. Sutherland; L: Woodrow Phoenix
Housed in the same hospital ward, Kelly and Brook reconcile and decide to give their marriage a second try.

ISSUE 2.9

P: January 1994

M-SMG2.9(c1)
"Heady Metal"
W: Steve Noble; A: Jon Beeston; L: Jon Beeston
The *Starbug* crew follow a signal to a planet covered in a metallic liquid called FLOB, where they discover an enormous statue of Kryten. Spare Head Three, residing on top, says he was abandoned there for fifty years and used the FLOB to build a time machine to summon their help. While rescuing him, they accidentally destabilize the FLOB and make a hasty retreat, losing Spare Head Three in the process and re-starting the cycle.

M-SMG2.9(c2)
"Young Flibble—Part 3"
W: Pat Kelleher; A: Rob Sharp; L: Elitta Fell
When Flibble's grandmother dies, the penguin's family inherits her fortune. His adoptive parents buy a gas-powered central-heating system for their cottage, but Flibble has other plans for the money, sabotaging the boiler to explode so he can keep the inheritance.

M-SMG2.9(c3)
"Cred Dwarf"
W: Steve Noble; A: Davy Francis; L: Woodrow Phoenix
The players of the Total Immersion video game *Red Dwarf* receive gifts from a mysterious source while attempting to solve a cryptic holiday message.

M-SMG2.9(c4)
"A Jake Bullet Mystery: The Case of the Cop's Comedown—Part 4: The Pavement Surfing Head Injury Certain Death Blues"
W: Steve Noble; A: Carl Flint; L: Woodrow Phoenix
Bullet learns that a device he and others have been wearing is a mind-control spike used by Doctor Scofrenia to enslave others. Jake tries to arrest the man, but his spike disables him, and Scofrenia instructs Carl to toss Bullet out a window. The cyborg hits the ground in time to land on the escaping Scofrenia, killing him instantly. Later, he returns to Brainfade to find Sandra inhabiting Carl's body and Scofrenia possessing a chimpanzee. His police chief then ensnares him in a sting operation and arrests him as a conspirator.

M-SMG2.9(c5)
"Cat and Dog"
W: Paul Burns; A: Paul Burns
Dog attempts to chase Cat but fails, until discovering the one thing Cat will run from: bri-nylon socks.

M-SMG2.9(c6)
"Androids"
W: James Hill and Pat Kelleher; A: Kev F. Sutherland
Kelly and Brook settle into their second life together. All seems normal again, until Brooke Junior arrives with some news.

M-SMG2.9(c7)
"Cat and Dog"
W: Paul Burns; A: Paul Burns
Dog attempts to do a magic trick by making Cat's dinner disappear.

M-SMG2.9(c8)
"Androids"
W: James Hill and Pat Kelleher; A: Kev F. Sutherland
In the show's season finale, Brooke Junior announces that he has had an oil-change operation, complete with catalytic converter installation. This infuriates Brook, who kicks the youth out of his house.

M-SMG2.9(c9)
"Young Flibble—Part 4"
W: Pat Kelleher; A: Rob Sharp; L: Elitta Fell
When Flibble's mind turns the once peaceful and magical psi-moon into a den of depravity and crime, the local villagers put a bounty on the penguin's head.

M-SMG2.9(c10)
"Young Flibble—Part 5"
W: Pat Kelleher; A: Rob Sharp; L: Elitta Fell
The price tag on Flibble's head draws the attention of a meek Junior Birdman, who promises to rid the villagers of their problem. Finding Flibble's lair, he transforms into Robbie Rocketpants and attempts to subdue the penguin. However, Flibble force-feeds him baked beans and lights up his flatulence, launching the masked hero into the air.

M-SMG2.9(c11)
"The Aftering—Part 1"
W: James Hill and Pat Kelleher; A: David Lyttleton; L: Elitta Fell
Marooned on Garbage World (Earth) for thirty years, Lister believes he is being rescued when a mysterious ship arrives, but the vessel carries simulants scavenging for antiques and polymorphs. With a female polymorph in their possession, the invaders leave camp to search for others, enabling the polymorph's mate to release her.

M-SMG2.9(c12)
"The Aftering—Part 2"
W: James Hill and Pat Kelleher; A: David Lyttleton; L: Elitta Fell
Elated at finding each other, the polymorphs change shapes as they mate. The simulants cut their losses and flee the planet, leaving behind Lister and a pregnant polymorph.

M-SMG2.9(c13)
"Cat and Dog"
W: Paul Burns; A: Paul Burns
A temporary food shortage aboard *Red Dwarf* drives Dog insane.

M-SMG2.9(c14)
"Young Flibble—Part 6"
W: Pat Kelleher; A: Rob Sharp; L: Elitta Fell
Pursued by the villagers, Flibble retreats to his tower and escapes via his personal rocket ship. While lifting off, he "accidentally" ignites the psi-moon's atmosphere.

M-SMG2.9(c15)
"Dwarf Eager"
W: N/A; A: Kev F. Sutherland
A pair of youths produce a "Do It Your Smegging Self" instructional video on creating *Red Dwarf* memorabilia.

Online Comic Strip (Across the Pond Comics)

W-NAN
"Prelude to Nanarchy"
W: Adam Jewell, Damion Waldbrunn and Andrew Ellard;
A: Mar Degano and Barry Williams, P: Oct. 28 to Nov. 4, 2005
After *Starbug* flees a despair squid's ocean world, Kryten's nanobots grow tired of repairing his body and set out to see the universe. The nanobots' escape causes a hull breach that creates a vacuum inside the ship, tossing the Dwarfers around. As they regain their bearings, *Red Dwarf* suddenly vanishes, but the *Starbug* crew track its vapor trail.

Miscellaneous Material

X-APR
BBC News April Fools' Day Video
W: Unknown; T (online): Apr. 1, 2009
A European Space Agency probe transmits footage of strange objects on the surface of Mars, which temporarily interrupts its video feed. When the feed resumes, Cat addresses the agency, claiming to have found its *Beagle* craft and inquiring about the local cuisine.

X-CIN
BBC *Children in Need* Sketch
W: Paul Alexander; T: Nov. 20, 1998
The *Blue Midget* crew receive a transmission of the BBCs 1998 *Children in Need* Telethon, broadcast three million years in the past. Moved by the goodwill message, they decide to help out by transmitting their own message back through space-time, asking viewers to donate to the cause.

X-MOB
Mobisode: "Red Christmas," Parts 1 and 2
W: Doug Naylor; A: Unknown; T (on mobile phones): 2007
On the night before Christmas, *Red Dwarf*'s computer warns of a possible intruder. The new arrival is Kris Kringle, who has come to spread holiday cheer. Thinking they are under attack, the crew flush him into space. Upon realizing their error, they invite Santa Claus' reindeer in for a game of charades.

X-TNG
Music Video: "Tongue Tied"
W: Danny John-Jules; D: Danny John-Jules; T: 1993
While working as a caretaker at Black Island Film Studios, Leo Davis, a fan of the TV series *Red Dwarf*, meets Kit, a beautiful dancer performing in a video shoot. A shy man, Leo barely musters the courage to speak to her, but has several daydreams after she leaves, in which famous individuals (both real and fictional) offer advice on how to approach her. He imagines himself singing to Kit as those he associates with confidence, such as *Red Dwarf*'s Cat and raga singer Tabby Ranks, and she falls for his charms.

X-XMS
Christmas Script (Title Unknown)
W: Bill Pearson; D: N/A; T: N/A
The Demonstroes, who claim to be benevolent but seek universal domination, pick up a distress call from *Red Dwarf*. Kryten, floating in space in anticipation of their arrival, accidentally swallows their entire fleet. The furious aliens threaten to beam back to their homeworld, detonating *Red Dwarf* in the process, so the crew use a nanobot device to shrink themselves down to be inserted into the mechanoid. Once inside his body, they attempt to retrieve a radioactive mass left behind by the aliens.

APPENDIX II:

The Universes of Red Dwarf

"Hell, there's probably a really, really weird dimension where you're better-looking than me."

—Dave Lister, "Dimension Jump"

As with many science fiction franchises, *Red Dwarf* has introduced numerous alternate dimensions, parallel universes and divergent timelines. This chapter outlines the various realities featured on the television series, as well as in the novels, comics and other spinoff materials. Virtual realities or hallucinations are not included, except when said to have spawned actual universes.

PRIME UNIVERSE

The *Red Dwarf* television series, novels and comics take place primarily in what, for the purpose of this book, is considered the "prime" universe.

OTHER UNIVERSES AND DIMENSIONS (NAMED)

A number of realities have been given specific designations, including:

Alpha Universe, the: A reality in which Ace Rimmer was stationed at the Space Corps Research and Design facility on Europa. Ace was set to embark on a test flight of *Wildfire One*, an experimental craft designed to break the light barrier, when an identical ship arrived three days prior to his launch, its pilot scorched. Initially believing the ship had gone back in time, Ace deduced that it came from the Beta Universe, as it was capable of traveling between dimensions. This Ace's first (and last) dimensional jump brought him into the {novel} universe (*see below*), where he was killed by an agonoid **[N-BCK]**.

Alternative 2X13/L: An alternate universe that Ace Rimmer visited, in which genetically engineered superheroes and villains fought in the streets of Smegopolis. This reality's Rimmer, known as Super-Ace, was vulnerable to human physical contact, hindering his ability to bring his arch-nemesis, the Conspirator, to justice. While visiting this dimension, Ace temporarily took Super-Ace's place and captured the villain, boosting the superhero's reputation **[M-SMG2.1(c3)]**.

Alternative 6829/B: Another universe that Ace Rimmer visited, in which Ray Rimmer was a down-and-out association football player **[M-SMG1.8(c4)]**.

Beta Universe, The: A universe from which another Ace Rimmer traveled to the Alpha Universe; during the transit, a miscalculation fried the inside of his cockpit, killing him **[N-BCK]**.

Dimension 165: A universe in which the original Ace Rimmer was killed by a neutron tank **[T-SER7.2]**.

Dimension 24: A universe containing the Theta Sector, where Ace Rimmer frequented a salon called Astro Cuts to have his hair cut by a stylist named Alfonse **[T-SER7.2]**.

Fifth Dimension, the: A parallel reality in which the sexes were reversed. The *Red Dwarf* crew met their female counterparts in this dimension after the Holly Hop Drive propelled them out of the prime universe **[T-SER2.6]**.

Mirror Universe, the: A reality with characteristics opposite to those of the prime universe, with Rimmer serving as *Red Dwarf*'s captain, Lister as his first officer, Cat a professor and Kochanski an airheaded blonde. The prime Rimmer traveled to this dimension to find an antitode for a corrosive chameleonic microbe dissolving his *Red Dwarf*. His shipmates escaped into the Mirror Universe before the dimensional portal was severed, leaving him trapped in the prime reality with Death **[T-SER8.8]**.

Tenth Dimension, the: A dimension that the crew accessed while operating a hyper-drive. After imbibing the luck virus, Cat devised the propulsion system to punch a hole in space, harnessing superstring to bend time. This enabled the crew to pass through the Tenth Dimension and rescue Lister, who had been trapped on a doomed planet **[N-LST]**.

Universe 3: A universe in which time ran backwards. The crew placed Lister and Kochanski on this reality's Earth after Lister, aged sixty-five, died of a heart attack during a polymorph attack. Kochanski and Lister both perceived time as running forward, and lived on the planet for thirty-four years together until being rescued by the *Red Dwarf* crew **[N-BTL, N-LST]**.

Universe 3: A variant of Universe 3 in which Kochanski, like the backwards Earth's population, perceived time as running in reverse. After she and Lister enjoyed many years here together, she left him at the moment of their first meeting. Lister then missed a rendezvous with the *Red Dwarf* crew, sparking a chase that left him and his shipmates marooned here for ten more years **[N-BTL, N-BCK]**.

> ***NOTE:*** *Splitting Universe 3 into two separate realities retcons the incompatible events of the novels* Last Human *and* Backwards.

OTHER UNIVERSES AND DIMENSIONS (UN-NAMED)

Other realities have appeared in the *Red Dwarf* mythos without specific names attached. These are listed below, with names in brackets that come from no official sources, but are used here merely for the purpose of identification:

{Ace}: A dimension that branched off from the prime universe, in which Rimmer was held back a year at school at age seven. This decision sparked numerous changes: Arnold became a brave test pilot for the Space Corps, with the call-sign "Ace." Lister became a mechanic at the Mimas testing facility and married Kochanski, with whom he fathered two sons. And Cat was a priest stationed at the facility. Ace tested a ship capable of breaking the speed of reality, causing him to emerge in the prime universe, where he met his cowardly counterpart **[T-SER4.5]**.

{Fifth2}: A version of the Fifth Dimension in which Arlene "Ace" Rimmer was a Space Corps test pilot. This was the reverse-sexed version of Ace Rimmer's dimension designated {Ace} **[W-OFF]**.

{Fifth3}: Another version of the Fifth Dimension, in which Kristopher Kochanski discovered Deb Lister's plot to hide his pregnant Dog, Dracula, aboard *Red Dwarf*, and volunteered to conceal the animal instead. As a result, he was sent into stasis instead of Deb and thus survived the cadmium II accident. Hilly released him three million years later, then revived Deb as a hologram to keep him sane. This was the reverse-sexed version of the dimension designated {Kochanski}, from which Kochanski originated in episode 7.3 ("Ouroboros") **[W-OFF]**.

{Novel}: The universe in which the main events of the novels *Infinity Welcomes Careful Drivers* and *Better Than Life* took place. In this reality, *Red Dwarf*'s captain was a stout woman named Captain Kirk, while several key events from the prime universe played out differently, and in a different order. For simplicity's sake, the crew that rescued Lister from the second Universe 3 (*see above*) is thought to have returned to this reality **[N-INF, N-BTL, N-BCK]**.

{Last}: A dimension to which the *Red Dwarf* crew traveled after rescuing Lister and Kochanski from the backwards-running Earth of the first Universe 3 (*see above*). At first, they thought they'd returned to the {Novel} universe, until discovering the crew murdered by this reality's Lister—who had been raised by the Thornton family instead of the Wilmots, enduring constant mental and physical abuse that had shaped him into a deranged sociopath intent on obtaining the secret of the genome of DNA (G.O.D.). This reality also contained a GELF population from an Earth ship called the *Mayflower*, which arrived from the {Novel} universe **[N-LST]**.

{BTL}: A reality spawned from the {Novel} universe in which Rimmer and Kryten never entered the addictive artificial-reality game *Better Than Life*, resulting in Lister and Cat perishing from malnutrition while trapped in the simulation. Lister and Cat from the {Novel} universe jumped into this reality aboard Ace Rimmer's ship and took their dead counterparts' place, but were significantly younger after being marooned for ten years in the second Universe 3 (*see above*) **[N-BCK]**.

{Kochanski}: A universe in which Kristine Kochanski uncovered Lister's plot to hide his pregnant cat, Frankenstein, aboard *Red Dwarf*, and volunteered to conceal the animal for him. As a result, she was sentenced to stasis instead of Lister, and thus survived the cadmium II accident. Holly released her three million years later, reviving Lister as a hologram to keep her sane. When her dimension temporarily connected with the prime universe, she relocated to the latter **[T-SER7.3]**.

{TV}: A universe in which twentieth-century British television producers created a series called *Red Dwarf*. This reality was spawned by a group hallucination of the prime universe's crew, caused by the ink of an elation squid **[T-SER9.3]**. In this universe, Leo Davis, a caretaker at Black Island Studios, was a big fan of *Red Dwarf* **[X-TNG]**. American producers took the idea and created their own version of *Red Dwarf*, turning it into an American TV sitcom that bore little resemblance to its British origins **[M-SMG1.10(c4)]**.

> ***NOTE:*** *The "Tongue Tied" music video and the* Smegazine *comic* "Red Dwarf USA" *occurred in a reality in which* Red Dwarf *was merely a fictional series. Since* Back to Earth *created such a reality—the ending implied that although the crew's experience had been an illusion, quantum mechanics meant such a universe actually existed—the other two tales can be slotted into that world. The comic poked fun at two real-world pilots made in a failed attempt to re-imagine* Red Dwarf *for American audiences, as described in {USA1} and {USA2}.*

{USA1}: A universe in which the *Red Dwarf* crew were American, with Captain Louise Tau in the captain's chair. In this reality, Lister was from Detroit and Holly was female from the outset, while Kryten was assigned to the ship prior to the cadmium II disaster, rather than being rescued from the *Nova 5* **[T-USA1]**.

{USA2}: A second universe in which the *Red Dwarf* crew were American, again with Captain Louise Tau in command. Similar to {USA1}, it varied in that Rimmer had a different face and voice, while Cat was female and fearless **[T-USA2]**.

{War1}: A dimension in which Ace Rimmer saved Princess Bonjella from Nazi forces. In this reality, Bonjella's father was King Stefano Bonjella, the ruler of the Seni Rotundi islands on War World, while Voorhese's first name was Wolfgang and his pet Snappy was an alligator **[G-BIT]**.

{War2}: A second dimension in which Ace Rimmer saved Princess Bonjella from Nazis. In this variant, her father was King Brian Bonjella, who ruled *all* of War World, while Voorhese's first name was Meinhard and Snappy was a crocodile **[T-SER7.2, W-OFF]**.

> ***NOTE:*** *This reality is broken up into two separate universes because of several prominent differences between the official website and the roleplaying game.*

{Holina}: A universe in which Ace Rimmer saved Princess Holina from her imprisonment in a towering castle, and then had sex with her **[M-SMG1.5(c2)]**.

{Blackheart}: A universe in which a decision in Ace Rimmer's past caused him to become horribly scarred and disfigured, while another pilot rose up in rank instead and shunned him. Embittered, Ace left the Corps and created a company that developed bionics and biomechanical augments, which he then used on himself, assuming the name "Blackheart" and embarking on a murderous rampage to achieve universal domination. Another Ace visited this dimension, defeating his evil counterpart **[M-SMG1.14(c5)]**.

{PM}: A universe in which Rimmer was prime minister of the United Republic of Lesser Britain, and the world's most successful politician, abolishing poverty and inflation and bringing peace to Earth. Bored with his position, however, he drank excessively and often passed out on park benches, until Ace Rimmer arrived and offered to help make his job more challenging **[M-SMG2.8(c6)]**.

{Fascist}: A universe spawned by a group hallucination of the *Red Dwarf* crew, brought on by the ink of a despair squid. In this reality, Jake Bullet and Duane Dibbley actually existed. After surviving a suicide attempt, Bullet solved several murder cases, while Dibbley—secretly a rogue agent of the Ministry of Alternation—searched for clues to his true identity. This universe also included a Leisure World International arcade, in which a quartet of new players, following the Dibbley party, had a vastly different experience than their predecessors in the game *Red Dwarf* **[M-SMG1.10(c1), M-SMG2.4(c4)]**.

{RPG}: A series of possible alternate universes featured in *Red Dwarf—The Roleplaying Game*, involving offshoots of characters, species and spaceships not appearing in other universes, including, but not limited to, universes with the following crews: Ben Ellis, Rat, Kryten and the A.I. Kate; Eric, the hologram Robin, a humanoid rabbit and an Errol Flynn waxdroid; and Ricky, the hologram Monica Jones and a Hudzen 10 mechanoid **[G-RPG, G-BIT, G-SOR]**.

TIMELINES

The *Red Dwarf* crew created several alternate or temporary timelines during their temporal-traveling exploits, including:

{Stasis}: An alternate timeline in which Lister traveled back in time and married Kochanski. The couple stayed in the Ganymede Holiday Inn's Honeymoon Suite **[T-SER2.4]**.

> ***NOTE:*** *This timeline was not eliminated by the episode's end, implying Lister would eventually marry Kochanski—but given his age during those scenes, he would have had to travel back in time during or soon after Series II. Since the two were not married as of*

Series X, by which time Lister looked quite different, these events must have represented an alternate timeline.

{Timeslide}: A temporary timeline created when Lister used a timeslide to convince his younger self to invent the Tension Sheet, thereby preventing original creator Fred Holden from doing so. Lister thus became Earth's youngest billionaire, married Sabrina Mulholland-Jjones and resided in a mansion called Xanadu. In total, he was married fourteen times in this timeline, and was killed while making love to his last wife in the cockpit of an airplane, which he lost control of during the act. This timeline was erased when Rimmer tried the same timeslide trick, inadvertently restoring Holden as the inventor **[T-SER3.5]**.

NOTE: Although Rimmer's attempt failed, his actions had an unexpected side effect, in that he was no longer a hologram upon his return to the future. Technically, the crew continued to exist in an alternate timeline from that point forward.

{White}: A temporary timeline created when a white hole spewed time into the universe, causing temporal anomalies throughout *Red Dwarf*. Holly's IQ was increased to more than twelve thousand via a procedure called intelligence compression, reducing her lifespan to mere minutes. After she shut down the ship to conserve her life, the crew plugged the white hole with a nearby planet, which reset the timeline to just before the intelligence compression began, eliminating this course of history **[T-SER4.4]**.

{Inquisitor}: A timeline temporarily created when the Inquisitor erased Lister and Kryten from history, replacing them with alternate versions of themselves. This timeline vanished once the droid activated his sabotaged time gauntlet, unwittingly erasing himself and all his actions from history **[T-SER5.2]**.

NOTE: Several alternate timelines were created during this episode as well, and in comics featuring the Inquisitor—not to mention countless others in the course of the droid's long mission—all of which were undone by his retroactive removal.

{Epicure}: A temporary timeline resulting from the crew's installation of a time drive and a star drive aboard *Starbug 1*, enabling them to travel throughout space-time as epicures, sampling the best humanity had to offer. Sometime during this timeline, an accident reduced Lister to just a brain in a jar. When the time drive malfunctioned, they visited their past selves, only to be turned away because of their gluttonous and pompous ways. The time drive on the earlier ship was destroyed in a battle between the two crews, creating a paradox that eliminated the older versions, thereby altering history **[T-SER6.6]**.

{JFK}: A temporary timeline created when the *Red Dwarf* crew thwarted John F. Kennedy's assassination. JFK had an affair with the mistress of Mafia boss Sam Giancana, then was impeached in 1964 and imprisoned the following year. The mob-controlled J. Edgar Hoover succeeded him, allowing the building of Soviet nuclear bases in Cuba, and forcing millions of civilians to flee major U.S. cities. The Russians thus won the so-called Space Race and created the Soviet Space Corps, whose ships included *Red Dwarfski*, thereby preventing the Dwarfers from returning to their own vessel. This timeline ceased to exist after Lister traveled to 1965 to retrieve Kennedy, brought him back to 1963 and convinced him to assassinate himself and restore history **[T-SER7.1, G-SOR]**.

APPENDIX III:

Other Red Dwarf*-related* Books

"I've never read... a book."

—Dave Lister, "Future Echoes"

This section lists every official English-language publication related to *Red Dwarf*, regardless of whether or not it was mined for the purpose of this encyclopedia. It also includes several prominent unofficial fan-based works.

NOVELS

Red Dwarf: Infinity Welcomes Careful Drivers
Authors: Rob Grant and Doug Naylor
(Penguin Books, 1989)

Better Than Life
Authors: Rob Grant and Doug Naylor
(Roc, 1990)

Last Human
Author: Doug Naylor
(Viking Books, 1995)

Backwards
Author: Rob Grant
(Viking Books, 1996)

Red Dwarf Omnibus
Authors: Rob Grant and Doug Naylor
(Penguin Putnam, 2004)

IN-UNIVERSE-STYLE BOOKS

Red Dwarf Log No. 1996
Author: Paul Alexander
(William Heinemann, 1995)

Red Dwarf Space Corps Survival Manual
Author: Paul Alexander
(Mandarin, 1996)

The Log: A Dwarfer's Guide to Everything
Author: Craig Charles
(Penguin UK, 1999)

SCRIPT BOOKS

Primordial Soup: The Least Worst Scripts
Authors: Rob Grant and Doug Naylor
(Penguin Books, 1993)

Son of Soup: A Second Serving of the Least Worst Scripts
Authors: Rob Grant and Doug Naylor
(Penguin Books, 1996)

Scenes from the Dwarf
Authors: Rob Grant and Doug Naylor
(Penguin Books, 1996)

Red Dwarf VIII
Authors: Rob Grant and Doug Naylor
(Virgin Publishing, 2000)

QUIZ BOOKS

Red Dwarf Quiz Book
Authors: Sharon Burnett and Nicky Hooks
(Penguin Books, 1994)

A Question of Smeg: 2nd Red Dwarf Quiz Book
Authors: Sharon Burnett and Nicky Hooks
(Penguin Books, 1997)

DOCUMENTARIES, GUIDES, ETC.

The Official Red Dwarf Companion
Author: Bruce Dessau
(Titan Books, 1992)

The Making of Red Dwarf
Author: Joe Nazzaro
(Penguin Books, 1994)

Red Dwarf Programme Guide (Third Revised Edition)
Authors: Chris Howarth and Steve Lyons
(Virgin Books, 2000)

UNOFFICAL PUBLICATIONS

Ganymede & Titan Presents: The Garbage Pod
Authors: Various, Editor: Seb Patrick
(G&T and Lulu, 2011)

Stasis Leaked Complete: The Unofficial Behind the Scenes Guide to Red Dwarf
Author: Jane Killick
(Elly Books, 2012)

AUTOBIOGRAPHICAL

Random Abstract Memory
Author: Hattie Hayridge
(Penguin Books, 1997)

The Man in the Rubber Mask
Author: Robert Llewellyn
(Unbound, 2013)

THE ROLEPLAYING GAME

Red Dwarf—The Roleplaying Game
Authors: Todd Downing, Mark Bruno, John Sullivan, Andrew Kenrick, Lee Hammock, Gavin Downing, Allan McComas and Samantha Downling
(Deep7 Press, 2002)

Red Dwarf—The Roleplaying Game: AI Screen with *Extra Bits*
Authors: Todd Downing and Gavin Downing
(Deep7 Press, 2002)

Red Dwarf—The Roleplaying Game: Series Sourcebook
Authors: Todd Downing, John Sullivan, Andrew Kenrick, Eddy Webb, Samantha Downing and Gavin Downing
(Deep7 Press, 2002)

ABOUT THE AUTHOR

Paul C. Giachetti is the co-owner of Hasslein Books, a publishing company he launched with long-time friend Rich Handley in 2008. A magazine layout artist by trade, he is also Hasslein's graphic artist and layout designer, and has designed and produced all of the company's publications to date, as well as its marketing and promotional material. He lives on Long Island, New York.

Paul maintains a personal blog at paulanoma.blogspot.com, and occasionally contributes to Hasslein's blog, hassleinbooks.blogspot.com. A long-time fan of British comedy, he decided the time was right to compile this two-volume set—his debut publications for Hasslein Books—about his all-time-favorite franchise. Some of his other favorites include *Star Wars*, *Star Trek*, *Doctor Who*, *Babylon 5*, *Stargate*, *The Hitchhiker's Guide to the Galaxy* and *Farscape*. He is also an avid photographer, gamer and techie, and enjoys making fun of bad movies.

He can be followed at facebook.com/paulgiachetti.

ABOUT HASSLEIN BOOKS

Hasslein Books (hassleinbooks.com) is a New York-based independent publisher of reference guides by geeks, for geeks. The company is named after Doctor Otto Hasslein, a physicist and time travel expert portrayed by actor Eric Braeden in the film *Escape from the Planet of the Apes*, and on the Hasslein Curve named in honor of his theories.

In addition to the *Red Dwarf Encyclopedia*, the company's lineup of unauthorized genre-based reference books includes *Timeline of the Planet of the Apes: The Definitive Chronology*, *Lexicon of the Planet of the Apes: The Comprehensive Encyclopedia*, *A Matter of Time: The Unauthorized Back to the Future Lexicon*, *Back in Time: The Unauthorized Back to the Future Chronology* and *Lost in Time and Space: An Unofficial Guide to the Uncharted Journeys of Doctor Who*, with future volumes slated to feature James Bond, *G.I. Joe*, *Alien vs. Predator*, *Battlestar Galactica*, *Ghostbusters*, *Universal Monsters* and *The Man From U.N.C.L.E.*

Follow Hasslein Books on Facebook (facebook.com/hassleinbooks) and Twitter (twitter.com/hassleinbooks), and at the Hasslein Blog (hassleinbooks.blogspot.com), to stay informed regarding upcoming projects.

Made in the USA
Coppell, TX
18 December 2020